Nuklear Age

NUKLEAR AGE

Brian Clevinger

iUniverse, Inc.
New York Lincoln Shanghai

Nuklear Age

iUniverse, Inc.

For information address:
iUniverse, Inc.
2021 Pine Lake Road, Suite 100
Lincoln, NE 68512
www.iuniverse.com

ISBN: 0-595-32511-4 (pbk)
ISBN: 0-595-78068-7 (cloth)

Printed in the United States of America

CONTENTS

▼

Acknowledgements

I'd like to thank my parents for supporting my mad scheme to become a writer and my fans for helping that dream come true.

There's also the matter of a one Ms. Emily whom we all need to thank. Back in the late '90s, she asked me to write a short story. I'm not good at brevity, so over the next four years it turned into this book. There were too many hours in the day when I finished, so I filled them by working on my webcomic, 8-bit Theater. Apparently, Emily felt that two great things weren't enough for my life, so she introduced me to Lydia.

INSTRUCTIONS

▼

Read these pages in numerical order, starting from the top-left and progressing to the right until the end of the line. Then go down one row and repeat. Laugh where appropriate. Turn the page when necessary to continue.

Seriously though, this book isn't exactly a novel and it shouldn't be read exactly like a novel. It's a collection of short stories that happen to be arranged in chronological order and happen to star the same characters. This is a convoluted way of saying that these stories were written episodically, somewhat like the comic books this work owes so much to, and that's how they should be read.

Hopefully you'll think that's a clever device instead of realizing that my brain has been so un-smart-ized by years of exposure to comics, Warner Bros. cartoons, and television sitcoms that I am fundamentally incapable of experiencing life outside of an episode-based format.

Issue 1—Giant Sized Special Deluxe Gold Foil Embosed Holographic Variant Cover Collector's Edition

High caliber machine-gun fire tore across the city. The day to day sounds of city life hugged pavement in terror while debris and shards of glass spilled over them as an inexplicable explosion rocked the earth and gave way to a cacophony of screams that mixed into the tumultuous cocktail of civic chaos.

"It must be Tuesday," Nuklear Man said to himself as he soared over the downtown spires of Metroville. He made a wide golden loop around the roof of an office building that had all the harsh angles and weird geometry of a modern skyscraper. Another volley of heavy arms fire barked up at him from the streets. Scores of bullets zipped by like furious bees. Nuklear Man's highly advanced mind buzzed with intelligence. It was a simple matter of calculating a series of trigonometric equations to pinpoint the gunfire's exact origin in the complicated streets beneath him and rocket into justice.

SMASH!

Nuklear Man stumbled out of the demolished rubble of what had been a very large bank lobby. He groggily shook the dust out of his hair. "Wish I knew trigonometry." He coughed up a puff of plaster.

The street was full of abandoned traffic and the sidewalks were devoid of humanity. The citizens of Metroville were used to things like this and they knew how and when to clear an area. The Eyewitness Action on the Spot Breaking News Force team was already setting up along nearby storefronts and behind the larger parked and overturned cars. Since they were news anchors, the area was *still* devoid of humanity.

Nuklear Man examined the filthy state of his outfit. Its sun-themed yellows and oranges were a soup of masonry gray. The trademark Nuklear Style N with little electron orbits displayed on his chest was completely obscured and he certainly wasn't going to have any of that. The state of his cape wouldn't bear mentioning at all. He closed his eyes and concentrated. A glow emanated from his body as his ever-present Plazma Aura intensified. It grew, slowly at first, then burst like a hundred simultaneous camera flashes. He was clean once more.

He could see the news crew making a fuss from the other side of the street. There was a lot of pointing and other excited gesticulations at his general direction.

"Geez, you'd think they never saw a *fantastically* handsome Hero before."

The *actual* object of their attentions then turned the corner.

Mechanikill. A two ton walking gun platform, it was some sort of robot, presumably of the Military Prototype Gone Horribly Awry variety. It was built with one very simple design philosophy: bullets kill people. Both of Mechanikill's arms were built out of five Gatling guns. He could go through more bullets than an entire NRA convention. They were already spinning up as Nuklear Man's light speed reflexes kicked in.

"Hey, Mechanikill!" he would have said, if not for the hail of bullets that blasted him out the side of the ruined bank and into the street. His superhero outfit was a dusty shambles all over again.

Nuklear Man was flat on his back in the middle of the street. Half a dozen vehicles had been pushed aside or knocked over on his way there. "Well, that wasn't fair," he said while raising himself up on his elbows.

"Fair?!" Mechanikill's speakers spat with digital surround sound ire. "Don't talk to me about being fair!" He waddled over to Nuklear Man, chunks of debris smashing with every robotic step.

"For the love of Liberty's cape," Nuklear Man muttered as he stood. "You don't talk to *me* about fair!"

Nuklear Man's verbal riposte scrambled Mechanikill's logic circuits for an instant. This happened at least once every time they clashed and it would have been the perfect time for Nuklear Man to follow up with a devastating barrage of attacks to subdue the Metallic Menace by way of complete destruction.

But no.

He saw the news crew scrambling into position to get good shots of this new battlefield. He reflexively Plazma Burst his costume clean. It wasn't that he was vain, he just couldn't live in a universe where he wasn't beautiful. He turned back to Mechanikill.

"I don't spend several hundred dollars a month on dry cleaning so that my spiffy outfit can take this kind of abuse from the likes of you!" Nuklear Man said as Mechanikill's digital senses returned. He stomped over to the robot and shoved an accusatory finger in the vicinity of its optical sensors. "And I most certainly don't take a good *five* minutes from my busy schedule of eating, sleeping, eating again, and watching cartoons to patrol the city for acts of villainy—so I can perpetuate the illusion that I'm actually doing my job while being given license to dispense justice by completely disposing *of* justice—only to have you pop up and delay my return to the sweet, sweet couch where I can continue the eating, sleeping, cartoon cycle!" He gave Mechanikill a shove which knocked him back a few heavy steps. "So don't *you* talk to me about fair!"

"You said that already."

"Don't you said that to *me* already!"

There was an audible pop as Mechanikill's logic circuits, already strained beyond their Reasonable Limit, finally blew. The robot shuddered as the final nuances of sanity coursed out of its intelligence matrix. It made a sickly whine like a smoke detector in a blackout. He teetered, hovering between vertical and horizontal alignment for an eternal moment, and collapsed backwards in slow motion.

Nuklear Man took a deliberate step away from the fallen beast. "It was self-defense!" His eyes darted back and forth. "Yes. And since he's not in any condition to testify otherwise, I'll get away with it! Again!" He turned to walk away as casually as a man running away in blind terror can. He took three panicked strides from the slain husk and froze. A bolt of terror ripped up his spine and strangled his brain stem. The Eyewitness Action on the Spot Breaking News Force team had captured the whole dirty murder on tape.

"Witnesses," Nuklear Man growled. "Well, now, let's not jump to conclusions. This was one of my more subdued battles," never mind the demolished downtown bank and overturned vehicles littering the road, "Maybe they didn't see anything."

"Way to go Nuklear Man!" the soundman cheered.

"Yeah! We got it all on tape!" the camera man pumped his fist enthusiastically.

"This'll get me the top story for sure!" the anchorman said to his cell phone.

"Curses!" Nuklear Man cursed under his breath. He shrugged. "Well, I suppose it was going to come to this eventually." Fusion energy rippled from his clenched fists. "I must eliminate *all* witnesses: actual, potential, *and* imaginary! The Purging will be swift and without remorse."

"Excuse me," a voice from the neighborhood of the Hero's knees said. It sounded like listening to a tax form being spoken.

"Yeah, sure. No problem," Nuklear Man said absently. What little of his attention that existed was focused entirely upon the news team. His every step brought them closer to no longer being a problem.

"Excuse me," the voice repeated. There was a bored quality to it, as if its content was somehow distant from its source. A sigh that bordered between exhaustion and impatience preceded nearly every statement.

"Right. Already done. Now stop bothering Mr. Hero-Man. He has some 'business' to attend to." Nuklear Man looked down to give a big happy reassuring smile that certainly wouldn't belie the violence he was yearning to perpetrate across the street. But the smile was shattered. He bent over to be nose to nose with the master of the bothersome voice. "So, uh. What're you supposed to be?"

He was a little green man only two and a half feet high with thick, leathery skin and a bulging cranium that accounted for nearly half his height and was utterly devoid of hair. He wore a faded blue uniform that was all wrinkles.

"I am Bibbles, your typical Transdimensional Pantemporal Postal Service employee." His voice was a geology lecture spoken at a geologic pace.

"What's a Transwhozawhatsit...thingie."

"The TPPS was founded early in the history of Everything. It was established as a way to effectively ferry important documents to and from the most important and valued individuals of every universe in completely trusted and regulated manner."

"Oh! The TP*PS*. Sure, gotcha."

"It's also the most depressing job known throughout all of existence," the alien added. "Like you care."

"Er..."

Bibbles continued, "An employee of the TPPS deals with the most powerful and influential creatures of a trillion worlds in a billion universes. This, of course, is responsible for the TPPS's renowned low morale, which has become so low in recent millennia that it has become a point of pride. Becoming personally aware that one is no more than an infinitesimal speck on a quark in a universe of unimaginable size usually leads to the eventual mental breakdown of even the most stable and well-adjusted creatures. Most employees go on a killing spree long before their retirement."

"Y'don't say," Nuklear Man said, taking a step back.

"Most scientists just think it's something in the glue."

"Well. Glue has been known to…um. You're not starting your mental breakdown and subsequent killing spree here, are you?"

"No." There was a peeved quality to his comatose tone. He held out a small envelope so heavily covered in stamps that Nuklear Man wondered just where the address was supposed to go. "I have a letter for a 1 (one) Nuklear Man."

Nuklear Man smiled proudly. "That's me! Gimme!" He bounced like a small child giddy with the glee of Christmas morning.

Bibbles could already tell that he wasn't dealing with one of the intellectual giants of this backwards world. "Well, 'Nuklear Man', I'm going to need two pieces of identification first."

Nuklear Man's smile disappeared. He reared back to his full height. "I uh…I don't have any ID." He scratched at the back of his head. "People just sorta know who I am. I tend to stand out in crowds, you know. What with the superpowers, the villainy thwarting, and whatnot."

Bibbles rubbed his eyes methodically. Nuklear Man could've sworn the alien existed in slow motion.

"I can't give you the letter unless you can give me two pieces of identification. It's standard practice. It is very important that we are one hundred percent certain that the proper people receive their mail. Entire civilizations depend on our parcels. Worlds have been saved and destroyed by a simple matter of postage. The fates of galaxies could rest in any of our many, *many* deliveries. As such, I'm going to need two pieces of identification."

The Hero was at a loss for words. He adopted his "brainy" look, which would have been more impressive had Atomik Lad not thrown away his monocle in a fit of being goddamn tired of it several days prior. "Well, Bibbles," he said, carrying on heroically despite the missing monocle, "Who *else* would I be? *Hmm?*"

Bibbles stared up at the "Hero" in front of him for several long moments. He took a deep breath.

"Since there are an infinite number of universes, each one rife with infinite variations upon every possible facet of existence, the odds of you being the *real*

Nuklear Man are one in infinity to the power of infinity. And though our method of Wave-form based dimensional time travel is quite advanced, we aren't arrogant enough to believe that we can overcome odds of that magnitude every single time we turn the machine on.

"You could be a clone, a past version of yourself, a future version of yourself, a clone of a past version, a clone of a future version, an evil twin, a clone of said evil twin, an evil twin from an alternate dimension, a clone of an evil twin from an alternate dimension, an adept shapeshifter, an evil twin of an adept shapeshifter, and so on along an infinite list of variations I have neither the time nor the inclination to discuss with you." He paused. "With that being said, I need two pieces of identification, please."

The Hero thought for a moment or twenty until even he could see the impatience oozing from Bibbles.

"You ought to do something about that, it's messy."

Bibbles raised an eyebrow. "Do you have two pieces of identification or not?"

Nuklear Man's expression told the world that he just discovered that he had become the very living incarnation of genius. "Yeah, I've got two pieces of identification. In fact..." He paused for dramatic effect but it just made Bibbles yawn widely. Nuklear Man opened his arms wide to encapsulate the whole of the city.

"I've got eleventeen *million* pieces of identification right here!" he declared, beaming his proud grin at the populace of the city.

"Outta the road, you freaks!" a passing motorist yelled as he drove by. As it has been mentioned, the citizens of Metroville were used to vacating an area at the first sign of a Climatic Battle of Good Against Evil. They were equally apt at returning to their daily routines as soon as Good was victorious.

Bibbles stared blankly at the muscle-bound buffoon in front of him. He was tired, even by his standards, and had several million other deliveries to make before lunch.

"Yeah, whatever, here." He handed the letter to Nuklear Man.

"Goody!" Nuklear Man looked back down at Bibbles. The alien's probability of existence began shifting to a universe slightly to the left. He became incorporeal from the inside out.

"Bye!" Nuklear Man said with a wave.

"Whatever," Bibbles said just before becoming nothing.

"Neat trick. Now then!" An anxious and excited look broke out across Nuklear Man's heroic visage as he clumsily opened the stamp-covered envelope.

Inside was—surprise, surprise—a letter. He opened it with fumbling fingers. It read:

Dear "Nuklear Man",

Happy Birthday!

Dad

His excitement faded. It was replaced with confusion and even a twinge of anger. He looked skyward.

"Dad?"

But the clouds above held no answer.

"Nuklear Maaaaan!" The voice was distant and somehow familiar, as if in a dream. Like a link to his past!

"Faaather!" Nuklear Man cried out.

"What? Fath—no. Nuke! It's me, Atomik Lad. Faithful sidekick through the good, the bad, and your incompetence." He was nineteen, slim, but athletic from a lifetime of thwarting evil. He wore a full body outfit of spandex-like material the same as Nuklear Man, only the sidekick's was a more complex combination of dark red and blue. In the center of his chest was a radiation hazard symbol with a red A in it that melded into the red of the uniform. His hair was a wavy light brown mass that reached to the bottom of his ears. "You hungry?"

"Starved!" Nuklear Man said. "But I just found a clue to my mysterious past which has haunted me lo these many years."

"Wanna check out a new restaurant? Cap'n Salty's House of Fugu? I got coupons."

"Coupons? You make a compelling case. I'm sure my faultless memory will have no trouble reminding me about…oh, whatever it was." Nuklear Man posed and flexed while pointing skyward, "Onward, Atomik Lad! Ha-ho!" He bellowed dramatically as he shot into the sky like a golden bullet.

Atomik Lad sighed. "It's just lunch, Nuke."

"My *car*!" A man's voice, shrill with disbelief, rang out near the bank. A pile of rubble that had once been a very sturdy part of the bank's wall now lay atop his destroyed SUV. Atomik Lad hunched over and wished he had coat lapels to pull over his face. He beat an extremely conspicuous retreat around a corner. Red light splashed across the alley walls and Atomik Lad took to the skies surrounded by a firey field of crimson.

Sirens could be heard in the distance as rescue workers and Überdyne Reclaimation teams rushed to the scene.

"I'll see you in court!" he screamed uselessly at Nuklear Man's diminishing airborn figure.

The two Heroes soared over Metroville. Nuklear Man admired the shiny towers of glass and steel, true testaments to the might of humankind and the height to which society had risen, far higher than even the highest skyscraper. Since Nuke had a nasty habit of flying where he looked, Atomik Lad had to steer him away from running through them.

Nuklear Man gave an approving thumbs up with a wink. "Cap'n Salty's is just ahead!"

Atomik Lad looked at him, "You don't even know where it is."

"Do so...I was ah, just there yesterday. Hmmphf!"

"Were you now?"

"Yes. A Hero never lies. Write that down or something."

"All right then, what'd you have?"

The Hero was momentarily set back, but his tenuous foothold on reality let him concoct a story of amazing credibility. "Er, ah. I had the Cherry, um, gufu."

"You mean 'fugu'."

"...You heard what I said."

Atomik Lad sighed as he looked at Nuklear Man who was having a hard time maintaining eye contact. "You don't even know what fugu is, do you?"

"Try to accuse *me*, of all people, of not knowing what flugu is. Feh!"

"All right then, Nuke. Lead the way to the restaurant."

Nuklear Man smiled triumphantly for the 4.71 seconds that it took him to remember that he didn't know where Cap'n Salty's was after all. "Ah...why don't you, just for a change of pace mind you, lead the way? Yeah! It'll be a good experience for you. Confidence building. Empowering. Fun!"

"Sure thing,."

"Whew, covered my tracks pretty good," Nuklear Man thought he said to himself.

"What was that, Nuke?"

"WAH! Er, I said, 'Habadda, habadda, I likes food?'"

Knowing full well what the Hero had really said and merely wanting to torture his strained intellect, Atomik Lad let it drop. "True, good point."

"Whew, covered my tracks pretty good." Nuklear Man thought he said to himself again, but Atomik Lad didn't bother to respond.

Atomik Lad took the lead as per the Golden Guardian's advice. They soared through the pure air, weaved between workplaces and apartment complexes, and waved at those below.

Nuklear Man called ahead to his sidekick, "Say, Atomik Lad, could I see the coupons?"

"Sure," Atomik Lad said, looking back at his mentor. He dug into his pocket and slowed down as the Hero sped up. "Here," the sidekick said, reaching the coupons back.

Nuklear Man grasped for the two pieces of paper but in the middle of the transaction a rather surprised pigeon invaded his air space. "ACK!" the Hero tried to say through a mouthful of bird.

Atomik Lad's eyes widened, "Nuke! The coupons!" he pointed where the coupons flittered to the ground far below. They danced like insanity with the wind.

"MMMMM—Sptooey!—NNNNNNNOOOOO!" Nuklear Man exclaimed.

"Now what?" Atomik Lad asked in despair.

Nuklear Man's voice was steeled with determination, "We search!" His Nuklear Sight absorbed every detail for miles as he swept from one horizon to another, "There!" he posed a point, "They're landing in Anderson Circle Garden. If we hurry, we can get 'em before they get all icky gross and sticky with leaves and dirt or maybe stuck in some gum—"

"Nuke!" Atomik Lad yelled in exasperation. "C'mon!" He waved the Hero forward while heading down to the park.

"Oh. Oh yeah!" Nuklear Man followed suit.

ISSUE 2—SO MANY NEW CHARACTERS!

In the lush Anderson Circle Garden, the merry citizens of Metroville frolicked in the austere combination of warm sun and cool breeze. Some were skating, others were jogging, a few were performing as street entertainers, and the staple elderly people were sitting on park benches feeding birds and fluffy tailed rodents.

"Ah ain't no 'elderly people' ye stick armed laddie!"

And then there was Angus, the Iron Scotsman.

"Ah said, eat ye damned feed, ye bloody rats!"

Angus's doctor had prescribed a strict regimen of relaxation in an attempt to lower the hero's volcanic blood pressure. "Rest and relaxation with absolutely no aggravation," were his M.D.'s exact words. The Iron Scotsman complied by sitting on park benches and feeding the squirrels.

This compliance aggravated him greatly.

Wearing a fearsome and intimidating Iron: Battle Suit apparently frightened squirrels so they were few and far between. The fact that he was feeding them Momma McDougal's Haggis Bits wasn't helping either. Seeing the other animal patrons attract a larger audience aggravated him which aggravated him more because he hated squirrels and even more than the elderly which further aggravated him because he was supposed to be relaxing which was an aggravating practice in its own right.

"ARGH!" He howled in rage as he hurled the box with Momma McDougal's nurturing face at the pack of animals huddled around a more successful elderly couple. He picked up his helmet which was fashioned into the enraged visage of a fierce bearded Scotsman, and hopped off the bench. He could do so because Angus was, to be kindly, of below average human adult height.

He stormed off with a blackened cloud of anger over his head. While walking to no particular destination he saw two objects flutter from the sky. He snatched them angrily from the air with his spiked gauntlet.

He suspiciously examined the crumpled papers. "Half Off Sale? All the Fugu Ye Can Eat? Cheap food! Ah loves it!" The clouds lightened a bit, but hung nonetheless. With a bounce in his step, the Surly Scot made his way to the House that Cap'n Salty built.

But, not too far down the litter free trail, Angus encountered a group of mimes practicing their fine art. He considered demonstrating his Surprisingly Concealable and Wieldly Enemy-B-Crushed Named Bertha on each of them in a rather random and violent manner. The mighty club was a testament to pain: as thick as a steel girder and twice as dense, covered in spikes and studs, and adorned with rude limericks about your mother. It was a beautiful weapon.

However, Angus's mime mangling was not to be. In the evil, evil shadows lurked an evil, evil form. It slinked, it snuck, it scuttled; all with the intent of reaching the stout Scot.

At last it was near enough. A hand slowly emerged from the depths of the shadows…

Angus's grip on his massive Enemy-B-Crushed tightened. Veins popped up from his leathery skin, "This'll huurt ye a *lot* more'n it'll hurt me," he whispered longingly.

The shadowy hand hovered just behind the Scotsman's exposed neck. It struck like a snake—**ZZZZZZZT!**

"BWAAAAAAAAAH!" Hundreds of volts of electricity coursed through Angus's iron laden body. He jumped forward, brandishing the graphic club that was, until then, unseen. "Ye goot bite, buut ah bite back, lassy!"

From the shadows of a centennial tree a sleek sexy figure stepped into the light of day. She wore a white lab coat that reached to the bottom of her shapely calves and waved in a suddenly present breeze. Under the coat a black rubber body suit that emphasized each of her perfectly seductive curves in all the right ways clung enticingly against her. Her hair shone with its blackness as the wind tossed thin silken locks into her exotic face, one strand between her sultry lips. The very air around her was charged with sex. Everything about her exemplified the pleasures of the flesh. She was something straight out of a How To Draw Fan Service book.

She holstered a tazer and squinted her eyes in the sunlight as she stared at Angus's static frizzled beard.

With a thick Transylvanian accent that crowned this exotic beauty, she spoke, "You ought to look into some relaxer for that."

"Insultin' a Scootsman's beard isn't a goood idea, lassy!" Angus reared his feared weapon and charged the Venomous Villainess before him.

She stepped out of the way and snatched the coupons from his free hand as he ran past her wildly swinging his Enemy-B-Crushed.

"Hey! Thems is mine!"

She rest her lithe hand on an exquisite hip and tilted her head to one side. "Oh really darling? Then why are they in my hand, hmmm?"

"Ye be askin' for it, lassy!" Angus shook his oversized club threateningly.

She adopted a look of mock fear. "Oh, vhatever shall I do? Out of my way little man, I have bigger fugu to fry."

He sputtered angrily.

"And that club. Ever hear of Freud? I'm not certain which inadequacy you're over compensating for, but you should really look into it."

The Surly Scot's face reddened as his blood boiled. The veins on his forehead and neck became plainly visible. He bit his bottom lip and shook with the intensity of a paint mixer. A battlecry erupted from his tiny lungs and thundered across the park, "DWARRRRF-A-PULLLLLT!"

Fierce fire flared from Iron: Battle Suit's Bagpipe Thrusters. It was accompanied by the sounds of a gaggle of geese being put through slow, painful deaths that probably involved a rusty, half-broken meat grinder.

"YYYYYYYYEARGHABLBLBLBLBLE!" the Scotsman roared as he flew past the Venomous Villainess at over seven hundred miles an hour.

She watched Angus shrink into the distance, his limbs flailing madly, battle-cries and curses still booming above the sounds of tormented Bagpipe geese. His speck slammed against a building, clung to the wall for a few seconds, and plummeted to the unforgiving ground.

She rubbed her chin, "Flashy, but unimpressive." She held the coupons and kissed them gently. "Let'z see how valuable you truly are."

She disappeared as sneakily as she had arrived.

And just in time too, as Nuklear Man and Atomik Lad touched down seconds later.

"All right, first we—Atomik Lad! My you've grown!"

He blinked with surprise. "What are you—Nuke, step out of your crater."

The Hero looked around himself. "Ah yes, well uh…lookforthecoupons."

"Sure, Nuke."

Nuklear Man floated out of his little hole and strode majestically into the park search of his coveted coupons.

Atomik Lad strolled around looking for those oh so sought after pieces of paper. He sat in the shade of a large tree for a moment. He watched Nuklear Man pose for a mostly uninterested elderly couple as he passed by them. The sidekick stood again and dusted his bottom when he felt something that didn't belong there: a piece of paper!

"Nuke!"

"Eh?" The Hero turned his head and stumbled out of his pose, though the elderly couple hadn't noticed him being in the pose anyway so it was a moot point.

The sidekick, holding the note at arms length, trotted to Nuklear Man. "I found something."

The Hero smiled proudly. "Good work!" He took the paper and unfolded it clumsily. "This must be the villain's typical note revealing his location and intents in a vague and cryptic manner and/or riddle. They're all the rage nowadays. I'm so excited!" His eagerness grew and his sky blue eyes -widened. "Ooooh!"

"'Oooh' what?"

"This one is so vague and cryptic that it's in a code."

"Let me see what I can do." Atomik Lad grabbed the bottom and top of the note, took it form his mighty mentor, and turned it right side up. "How's that?"

Nuklear Man beamed. "*Good*! You've just saved us hours of dudective work."

"Dudective?" He shook his head. *It's not important.* "Anytime, Nuke."

"Now to read it." He cleared his thick throat. "'I know all too well of your many heroic explosions, so I—"

"Wait!"

"What?"

"Explosions?"

"Yes, right here…'heroic explosions'."

"Gimme that!" Atomik Lad snatched the note.

Nuklear Man gave a stern look. "You ought to be more careful with the evidence. And, I might add, more respective-able to your Hero."

"'Exploits!'" Atomik Lad slapped the note. "'Heroic exploits.' Can't you read?"

Nuklear Man snatched the note back. "No one asked you, hmmphf! Now then, where was I?"

Atomik Lad crossed his arms over his chest and muttered. "I think you were about to explode heroically."

Ignoring the comment, Nuklear Man went on. "Ah yes, '...too well of your many heroic expl*cough*!...ahem, so I shan't bore you with the typical note revealing my intentions and location in a vague and cryptic manner and/or riddle since you'd solve it within moments.'"

"Don't hold your breath." Atomik Lad muttered.

"'I will be blunt. If you ever wish to see your beloved coupons again, then come to my lair, the abandoned Polluto Chemical Factory just outside of town. I am awaiting your imminent arrival. Evily Yours, Dr. Veronica Menace.'"

The Hero of heroes paused for a moment. "Shucks!" He spat in frustration as he clenched the fist not holding the taunting note; a liquid-like sphere of golden energy flared around it for a moment. "This is gonna be tougher than I thought."

"Shucks? What are you talking about? Let's go!" The impetuous sidekick started to fly, but found that a powerful grip held him firmly to the surface. Atomik Lad struggled against Nuklear Man's unbreakable grasp. "And I thought Nuke's Rule #1 was Don't wrinkle the outfit."

Releasing his grasp of the sidekick and seeming to peer through the note, Nuklear Man spoke. "This note is so vague and cryptic by virtue of it's straightforwardness that we can't hope to crack it without help! We'll need to regroup at the Silo of Solitude so we can run this through the supercomputer! This Dr. Menace could be anywhere!"

"Nuke. What are you talking about? It's Dr. Menace. She's been our arch nemesis for like ten years. She told us she's staying at the old Polluto Chemical Factory. Hell, that's where she *always* is."

"That's what she *wants* you to think!" He leaned forward, shoving his finger into Atomik Lad's face.

"That's because it's true." Atomik Lad said tiredly.

"That may be, but that doesn't account for the fact that..." Nuklear Man's gaze, attention, and Big Wheel of thought trailed off.

"Hey! Big Guy." The sidekick elbowed the Golden Guardian to rouse him.

"Who-What-Where?!" The Hero looked to and fro, posing intimidatingly to keep evil stuff at bay.

"It's alright, Bright Eyes, we were just about to head to the Polluto Chemical Factory."

Nuklear Man's keen eyes darted from side to side as he tried to recall the past few moments...*failure*! "So we were. To the chemical plant!" The Hero rose a few feet in the air. Atomik Lad's field chaotic field enveloped him and he followed suit.

They streaked through the bustling streets of Metroville: zigging, zagging, jinking, jiving, cutting off the other motorists, and all around speeding to the abandoned Polluto Chemical Factory outside of town.

"We take a left onto Victory Lane up ahead, Sparky!"

"Are you sure? I thought the left turn was at Vigilance Street. And don't call me Sparky."

"Ahem! *Who* has the map? Hmm? This is Vigilance Street, and we take the next left." Nuklear Man said while pointing at the intersection on a map of Metroville he held in front of him as they zoomed at break neck speed through the crowded streets.

"Nuke, this is Adams Avenue, I lived here for nine years. I think I'd know where it is. You've got to be reading that map wrong."

"So says you."

Atomik Lad flew closer to his mentor and inspected the map for himself. "Nuke! This is a map of Burgsville!"

The Hero blinked. "You're point being?"

Atomik Lad clawed at his own face. "This *isn't* Burgsville!"

"The map says it is."

"It's the wrong map. Your. Map. Is. Use. Less."

"That's what you think!"

"Ugh. Look Nuke, I'll go my way and you go yours. We'll see who gets there first."

"I'll be waiting for you, sucker."

"I bet."

Nuklear Man swerved left onto Victory Lane though he thought it was quite curious that according to the street sign he was entering Rand Road, *What an odd move on the part of the civil engineers,* he thought, *Once I'm done with this Dr. Menace thing, I'll fix that right up.*

As the golden streak blazed through the busy city streets of Metroville, a pair of gleaming eyes flared from the depths of a dark alley. A guttural snarl emanated from the depths of the alley. "Lawbreaker!"

Nuklear Man fumbled with the map like any normal person does when trying to refold one. "Foul beast of travelers!" He grunted as the folds would not yield even to his mighty strength. The Hero struggled against the paper bonds when suddenly—

BANGBANGBANGBANGBANGBANGCLICKCLICKCLICK "…I mean, Pull over!"

"Wah!" Nuklear Man was so surprised by the hail of bullets that he accidentally disintegrated the map in an involuntary burst of Plazma Power.

Another blast surged past the Hero, missing him by mere inches. "I said, Pull *over!*"

The Hero complied.

A rather large gentleman brandishing what appeared to be a smoking Infantry-Stopper 2000 Pulse Cannon, the latest in advanced weapons technology, was stomping up to Nuklear Man from behind. This well armed man also sported the latest in defensive attire, the Infantry-Stopper-Stopper 2000 Power Armor. He looked like a knight from the future, a bleak future where people shoot at each other even more often than they do now. It had a blue and white color scheme with what appeared to be a policeman style badge of some sort on the chest. He stalked over to Nuklear Man until they were nose to nose.

The Hero suddenly felt a sneeze coming on.

"License and registration please." the looming knight-cop said as he began writing in an armored notepad.

"AH…" Nuklear Man wiggled his nose and closed his eyes tight. "AH…AH…" a moment passed, and with it, the urge to sneeze. "Ahh…" He sighed in relief.

"You done making lewd noises, son?" the Armored Officer said harshly.

Nuklear Man nodded.

"License and registration."

"But I ah…I don't have them."

"I see." The policeman scrawled in his notepad again.

Nuklear Man looked at the badge. It resembled the ones law officials use, but with a few differences. On top it said, "The Civil Defender." And across the bottom it read, "To Smite and Pummel."

"AH-*CHOO!*"

The Civil Defender looked up at Nuklear Man.

"Eheh…heh…Oopsie."

"Quite." He began, again, to write in his notepad.

"Um." The Hero fidgeted. "Is this uh, is this going to take long? I'm sorta inna hurry and I—"

"'*Sort of in a hurry*?!'" The Civil Defender repeated with a face twisted in rage.

"Eeep!" Nuklear Man said.

"Forty-*eight* in a forty-*five* is a *bit* more than 'sorta in a hurry!'"

"Well the fate of the city may lie in the balance, you see I—"

"That's what they *all* say! 'We've got to get to the hospital.' 'She's in labor.' 'He's having a heart attack.' 'There's a fire at the Imperial State building.' 'What kind of lunatic are you?' It's all the same with you accursed speeders." The Civil Defender began tearing off sheets of paper and tossing them at the Hero with every offense. "Driving Without a License." RIP. "Driving While Uninsured." RIP. "Unlawful Speeding." RIP. "Failure to Identify." RIP. "Reckless Driving." RIP. "Resisting Arrest." RI.P He pointed to the oozing sneeze-goo on his chest mounted badge. "Assaulting an Officer." RIP. He pointed to Nuklear Man's outfit. "Public Indecency." RIP. "*And!*" He gestured to the pile of paper that engulfed Nuklear Man's feet. "*Littering!*" RIP.

"But—"

"*And* Disrupting the Peace!" RIP.

"But—"

"*Two* counts of Disrupting the Peace!" RIP, RIP.

"B—" He clasped his hands over his mouth.

"*Thre*—Ah, wised up eh?"

"I didn't know the police were cracking down so hard. When'd they start this 'Civil Defender' program? Or get the funding for that fancy equipment?"

"Uh…" The Civil Defender seemed to lose three shades of confidence. "Well, you see. It all started ten years ago. On a most fateful day…"

"Do tell."

"I am! Ahem. I was a beat cop back in those days. Fred Sentenel, that was the name. I haven't been called that in so many years…" his voice trailed off as his gaze wandered to the clouds above.

"Come back to us, Cap'n Shiny."

"Er, right. I'd just sat down outside my favorite sandwich shop, The Metro. It had been a long morning. It was the day of Dragon's Strike, so we were all pretty strung out by lunch time. The unusually high humidity only added to my hunger: a hunger about to be quenched by the succulent turkey sub before me. I held it admiringly. Oh, the crisp lettuce. The fresh cut turkey, so thin and folded just right. The spicy mustard, onions, peppers, tomato. It was a beautiful monument to sandwiches, I tell ya. But, as custom demanded, I flipped through the headlines of The Metroville Sun before partaking of my lunch.

"'City Held in Grip of Fear' the headline announced. The front page featured a rather lengthy article about the world's most infamous and feared crime boss known only as…The Dragon. Between his stupendous black market wealth and the team of powerful overvillains at his command, he knew no rival. And that morning, that fateful morning, was to be his crowning achievement as a world-wide Archfiend. At sunrise, he had demanded three billion dollars within the next 24 hours, or he would cause the new Metroville Nuclear Power Plant to melt-down, thereby leveling half of Metroville in seconds while simultaneously render-ing the other half uninhabitable for centuries. 'Three billion, a small price to pay,' according to the paper's article.

"Us local police had been handling the situation all morning until the National Guard and other feds took over and brought the Squad of Diplomatic Immunity with them." The Civil Defender seemed to wipe at the corner of his eye with an armored finger. "It was quite a moment, let me tell you. The Dragon's plan for world conquest would take a giant leap forward after this event. After all, if one man can destroy a city described as the pinnacle of all civi-lization, what could stop him from destroying any city, or for that matter, a nation?

"It seemed that The Dragon would make history even if he didn't throw the proverbial switch. The Squad of Diplomatic Immunity had been called in to investigate the power plant, but even after hours of searching they hadn't found a single trace of the explosives. But The Dragon wasn't one for bluffing. We learned that with those artificially activated volcanoes of his years back. Anyway, since the risk of a nuclear meltdown was so great, all signs pointed to the U.S. caving in to terrorist action. I remember in the paper there was a picture of the Squad: Captain Liberty, the seasoned superhero who had led the team for decades; Old Glorya, an elderly woman cybernetically melded to her Assault Wheel Chair of Justice; The Bold Eagle, an eagle-man genetic experiment meant to build the ultimate soldier; Dim-Mak-Racy, a patriotic ninja master of the clan-destine arts; and finally, The Constitutional Kid, Captain Liberty's faithful side-kick."

"I know all about the Squad of Diplomatic Immunity. I've got all the comic books at home. How else do you think I learned to be a Hero? Sheesh."

"And then it happened." Civil Defender's exposition took on a sinister tone. "From around the corner, a brash youth ran like lightning on wheels. He took one look at my uniform as I perused the newspaper and he charged on. He reached into his tattered leather jacket. It was black. Yeah, street gang motorcycle punk kid black. He passed me, the world seemed to slow to a crawl. He took his hand from his jacket. He was practically on top of me before it happened."

"He shot you?!"

"No," Civil Defender's eyes clamped shut. "Though not a day goes by I wish he had. It was much worse. Much worse."

"What? What!"

"In a flash…the sandwich was gone."

Nuklear Man stood there. He could not emote. He was not equipped to respond to what his senses were telling him.

"I'll never forget what he said as he disappeared behind another corner. It's haunted me every night of my life since. Just one word. 'Yoink!' My life, my dreams, hopes, my whole world was destroyed then. I howled into the rotting void of my soul. That day I vowed that as long as I lived, such a violation of humanity would never occur again. I would spend my life fighting crime, deviancy, and corruption everywhere, no matter how petty and meaningless it was. That single act of betrayal gave birth to the Civil Defender."

"I see," Nuklear Man said. "And this puts you *where* on the totem pole of police power?"

"Well I um…I'm not exactly a uh, a police officer as such…"

"Then what are you?"

"A crazed vigilante bent on the eradication of small claims crime." He thought over his response. "Oh wait, replace 'crazed vigilante' with 'concerned citizen.' Dang, I always mess that part up."

"I see…" Nuklear Man's eyes became shifty, beady little windows to the soul. He pointed behind the Armored Officer with a look of mock horror. "A jay walker!"

The Civil Defender spun around and let loose with a volley of Infantry-Stopper rounds.

Nuklear Man shot into the air. The traffic tickets written on ordinary pieces of notebook paper swirled from the Hero's back draft as he soared through the skies giggling like a school girl. The taunt "Sucker!" echoed back at Civil Defender.

"Aw nuts!"

*   *   *   *

Atomik Lad touched down in front of the main entrance to the abandoned Polluto Chemical Factory just outside of town, "HA! I knew I'd beat 'im. Big dope couldn't read Seuss, much less a map." It was at this point that he realized he was completely alone in front of the lair of their most cunning and vile villain ever. "But he better get here soon…er, I'd hate to have to blast Menace back to the Stone Age all by myself," he quickly added to try to make the Mothra-sized butterflies leave his stomach…Failure.

Within the dark innards of the Factory, a sleek figure of deadly beauty observed the sidekick on her giant Evil: Monitor which displayed the view from one of her various Evil: Surveillance Cameras that surrounded the grounds of her Evil: Hideout. She pushed a single unmarked button upon her maniacal console.

Atomik Lad, as he often did when alone, thought back to that day. About that first crimson flash. He thought of it now in no different terms than he had before. *A lot of things can happen in the blink of an eye*, he mused as he looked down at his form fitting spandex.

Underneath him, a trap sprung and encased Atomik Lad inside like a huge titanium Venus Fly Trap. His head buzzed from the metallic dissonance of reverberation. The orb slowly sunk into the ground with its Atomik prize.

Issue 3—Dr. Menace
Strikes Back. For the
First Time. Again!

Blazing across the sky, Nuklear Man examined the almost medieval Polluto Chemical Factory as it loomed before him. It was a massive black blight of architecture, all smoke stacks and interwoven pipes. Even with his Nuklear Sight, he could find no sign of Atomik Lad, "Ah ha! I knew it *was* a right on Victory Street!" Of course he already forgot that it was a left and it was supposed to be Victory Lane. Never mind the fact that the actual street name was in fact Rand Road and that he was just plain wrong about the whole situation altogether. The important thing is that he felt he'd done something somewhat resembling a successful train of logic and that was enough for him.

*   *   *   *

Atomik Lad awoke with a start. He jerked into consciousness against unseen bonds. He had the feeling that he was suspended by some all encompassing force, like he was a metal ball caught hovering in a magnetic field. He grit his teeth and struggled against his restraints, grunting in failure.

"Good morning," the thick Transylvanian accent rolled into his ears from behind him. Craning his neck around to see below and behind, he could just make out what must have been the property of the voice walking into a less chiro-practicly profitable position in the room, "Did you have a nice nap?"

"Until I woke up to *you*," Atomik Lad spat.

"Oh, don't be zo rude. With your help, I will catch my ultimate prize, and become the wold's most powerful villain." She had to quell a maniacal laugh before it broke the surface.

He struggled in vain again.

"Tzk, tzk. That will do you no good. I have you suspended in a Negaflux Containment Field." She turned to a large central computer and punched away at the keys. "I shall spare you the detailz of my ingenious creation, suffice it to say that every zingle ounce of energy or force exerted on the field will be *completely* counteracted." She smiled proudly to her mirror image in the computer display.

"I'll show you an ounce of force," he muttered between clenched teeth. His eyes shone with a brilliant vermilion light and red sparkles of energy sputtered around him sickly before being extinguished. "Er...there should be more."

"You see? Even your famed 'Atomik Field' iz powerless against my Negaflux Containment Field! Another interesting feature iz that I can change the ratio from 1:1, such as it iz now, to something more along the lines of, oh say,000:1 so that gravity itself, rather than harmlessly suspending you, would crush you like some colorful American metaphor involving ripe fruit." she laughed madly at the last bit.

Atomik Lad scowled.

"And once Nuklear Man iz here, he shall have to deal with me on my termz, or else I shall destroy you."

"So what are your terms?"

She spun to face her captive, leaning back on the bulk of her computer, "You and that Nuklear Moron have defeated me dozens of timez in a spotless display of heroics over the years. I will show the world that I possess the greatest mind of the century when my diabolical riddle renders him utterly defeated. He'll then be honor bound to exchange himself for you." She gave the traditional dramatic pause, "And that will be the end of Nuklear Dolt!" This exact moment would have been the perfect time for lightning to strike and thunder to boom, but due to the local weather patterns, no such theatric display was possible. Alas.

"A battle of wits, then?"

"Essentially."

"It's been a fun life."

She chuckled in amusement. "I'm afraid that attempting to instill me with a false sense of confidence in the hopes that I may fail while drunk on my hubris are futile. No hero could be so successful and yet so incompetent. I'm on to your little ploy," she said.

"Ploy?"

Another laugh, "Do not insult me. I know that Nuklear Idiot has orchestrated this complex act that he iz a bumbling oaf in order to get the psychological upperhand on the less experienzed villains. A very ingenius, and thuz far, successful tactic."

"Ugh…Nuke could barely pronounce 'orchestrate' and his idea of 'complex' borders on the infantile. You of all people should know this!"

"A villain of my brilliance and resourcefulness could only be defeated by the most capable and intelligent of foez. And, with Nimrod Man out of the picture, I will be able to take over the world!"

Several lights began blinking in time with a quiet alarm. Menace turned to face the computer. "It seems our guezt of honor haz arrived." She grinned deviously and turned to the monitor which now displayed a schematic of the grounds with an orange dot rapidly approaching the center marked "Evil: Hideout."

A great golden meteor crashed through the wall opposite Menace's computer. Her eyes widened as she dove for cover just before the comet came to a messy stop on the other side of her oversized and now destroyed number cruncher. The building groaned from the sudden punishment, as if saying "Eroding to the ages is bad enough without having idiots like you crashing through my load bearing walls." Dust and plaster fell from the ceiling.

"Owf! I bit by dongue," the Hero of heroes said as he rose from the smoking heap of ex-computer.

Atomik Lad rolled his eyes, "Typical."

Nuklear Man scanned the decrepit grounds, "Badomik Fab!" he said holding his tongue, "Ey…ow'd jew get heel fust?"

The sidekick grumbled to himself, "Let go of your tongue when you talk!"

He complied, "Ah yes, much better." He gave a satisfied thumbs up, but then blinked worriedly. "What'cha doin'?"

"I'm being held captive! Now release me so we can thrash Menace!"

"Got it."

"Not so fast Nuklear Boob!" Dr. Menace's voice rang from behind several large pieces of equipment that used to be her impressive computer. She stood, hair and dusty lab coat flowing in whatever wind causes things like that to flow in moments like these. "Make one false move, and you can take your precious sidekick home in a tin can!" She held a complex remote control above her head.

"Gasp!" gasped Nuklear Man.

She flashed Nuklear Man a smile of evil triumph. "Now that I have your attention," she began. Unfortunately, she wasn't quite right. Nuklear Man was immediately transfixed by the blinking red light atop the antenna of Menace's remote control.

"Shiny," he said in a daze.

Atomik Lad hung his head.

Menace's gloating glare faded as she realized the target of Nuklear Man's attention. "Ahem…" she asserted, but to no avail.

"Red," he grinned in satisfaction.

She growled in annoyance and shook the control violently, rending it from Nuklear Man's eyes. He frowned.

"Now then," she continued, "With but a turn of this dial, I could crush your lovely sidekick!"

"Gasp again!" he gasped again.

"Quite. However, he iz not what I want—"

"Oh good! You'll be releasing him then, glad to hear it. You're certainly a much nicer villain than you used to be."

"Shut up!" She stomped her foot. The scene wasn't quite unfolding as she had hoped. "As I was saying, what I truly desire iz to defeat the mighty Nuklear Man in his most expert arena."

Oh good, BLASTIN'! the Golden Guardian thought to himself.

"The mind," She said.

"Argh!" he arghed. "Lousy brain," he muttered as Sad Plazma momentarily flared around him.

"I shall present you with a riddle."

"Like a joke? I love jokes. I heard this one about a six inch pianist—ooh, but I couldn't say that one in front of Sparky," he jabbed a thumb Atomik Lad's way.

"Nuke! I told you that one"

"Don't contradict me in front of the villain," Nuklear Man said through a clench toothed smile. "But there was this other one. Something about a canary. Or was it a woman at a bar with a uh…oh, what was it?"

Atomik Lad sighed, "A six inch pianist," he said defeatedly.

"That's the one! It's a killer."

"Excuse me, gentlemen? Evil genius here. A life hanging in the balanze . Any of this ring a bell?"

And lo a great bell did ring forth, and the people feasted upon the many fish of the sea, the beasts of the earth and the foul of the sky, "Oh yeah," Nuklear Man adopted an overly dramatic pose and made sure the light caught the sparkling brilliance of his teeth just right, "Continue your tirade of evil, you...um...evil lady."

"Yes." She caught herself almost believing in their charade. "I shall present you vith a *non*-joke-like riddle. If you can determine the anzwer, not only will your sidekick be released, but I shall give myself up az well."

"And if I don't?" inquired the eternally confident Hero.

"I will ztill release Atomik Lad."

"That's good!" Nuklear Man smiled.

"Only to replace him with you."

"That's bad," Nuklear Man frowned. "But I'm the good guy, so I'll win anyway. "Give me your riddle, oh Queen of Corruption!"

She smiled confidently, cleared her throat and recited the riddle of evil from memory. "I never was, am always to be. No one ever saw me, nor ever will. And yet I am the confidence of all who live and breathe on this terreztrial ball."

Nuklear Man starred at her in much the same way a cabbage does when it tries to comprehend the finer points of psychometric calculations as written alternately in Sanskrit and Okinawan. Backwards.

Atomik Lad hovered helplessly.

ISSUE 4—BRINGIN' DOWN THE HOUSE

"Well, Nuklear Fool?" the Venomous Villainess inquired.

"Um," he said nervously, "Best two out of three?"

She looked proudly at the remote control that regulated the deadly Negaflux Field that held Atomik Lad, and therefore Nuklear Man, helpless, "You are in no position to bargain, Nuklear Clod."

"Uh…" Nuklear Man contemplated uselessly as Atomik Lad began to realize the gravity of the situation. He decided "gravity" wasn't a good word to use considering that it was the force to be amplified to the point that either he or Nuklear Man would be crushed to death. Nuklear Man glowed intensely for a moment. He chanced a look at his sidekick and gave him the "I've got a plan," wink-n'-smile that he just invented and Atomik Lad first took as "How's it goin', sailor?" but finally got the gist of the message. Ordinarily, Atomik Lad would have been extraordinarily terrified at the prospect of a scheme concocted by Nuklear Man, and would have attempted to evacuate all residents within a ten mile radius. And with good reason. But at this point, that was the sort of plan he needed.

"I grow tired of your stalling, Golden Goon."

"Well I grow tired of the high costs of spandex dry cleaning."

"Shut up."

"And don't even get me started on the cape."

"Shut up!"

"There was this one time they put in so much starch it was like having plywood strapped to my back."

"*Shut up!*" she shrieked.

"Well it was," the Hero said meekly.

"Answer the riddle!" Menace demanded. *Can he truly be this stupid? Has this utter buffoon truly defeated my every nefarious scheme? It* can't *be true.*

"Oh yeah…the riddle. Got it. Right, um, could you ah, could you repeat the riddle?"

"No! You must answer it now or face the consequences!"

"Hmm. And what does that entail exactly?" he asked while nodding intellectually.

"Enough!" Menace bellowed. "Answer me now, or your sidekick will suffer a very messy, painful, and may I say, utterly unique death due to my *fantaztic* genius."

Nuklear Man posed confidently. His cape waved dramatically thanks to its excellent starch content. The light played on his blond hair. His perfect teeth gleamed in that very same light. His powerful build was accented by the golden spandex. It was all quite striking. Dr. Menace wasn't impressed.

"The answer to your little riddle is quite simple, Foul Temptress of Evil." He took a deep breath for a pause that was supposed to be dramatic but just came off as being forced and generally annoying. "Toast!" he exclaimed in all seriousness.

Atomik Lad hung his head in defeat.

It took every last ounce of self-control Dr. Menace had to keep from laughing, and she was only able to keep up the tour de restraint for 2.4 seconds.

Nuklear Man stood confident, his hands on his hips, smiling in the knowledge that he had saved the day.

"Wrong, Nuklear Boob! The answer is Tomorrow! Something which I'm quite glad to say you *won't* be seeing!" She threw her head back and her arms out wide while cackling maniacally in victory.

Nuklear Man scratched the top of his, some would say "cavernous," head. "Tomorrow? Well that's just stupid."

"And yet," she countered, "it's the answer, live with it." She gave an exaggerated grin, "Oh, I suppose you won't! HA!" Dr. Menace pushed a sequence of buttons on her remote control while chuckling to herself triumphantly. The air around Atomik Lad shimmered for a moment as she redirected the focus of her Negaflux Field so that it violently spit Atomik Lad out and deposited him at Nuklear Man's feet.

He jumped to a stand, shot a glare at Menace, and decided he'd show her what his Atomik Field could do without being fizzled out by some external interference. But before he could put these thoughts into motion, Nuklear Man placed his hand on the sidekick's shoulder and absorbed the explosive Atomik Power before it could manifest itself.

Atomik Lad jerked his shoulder from Nuklear Man's grip. "I'm really getting tired of having that done today!"

The Hero looked Atomik Lad squarely in the eyes. "I know, but this has to be done." The sidekick was taken aback by how lucid, calm, and noble Nuklear Man had suddenly become.

"This iz very touching boys, but I am a villain, so I muzt insist that we move on with the cold, heartless execution of a man who volunteers of his own free will to put his life on the line for no other reazon than to make life a little easier for millions of people he'll never know who are constantly terrorized by megalomaniacal geniuses such as myzelf."

Nuklear Man looked at Atomik Lad as if the young man was about to go off to college or take some other big step toward Being A Man. Whatever that is. "Never give up, Sparky," he said with a wink and thumbs up.

The Hero straightened his back and walked up to the Negaflux Field Generator. It was a hexagonal platform with arched metallic fingers rising from each of the six points. He took a deep breath and closed his eyes when he reached the center.

Dr. Menace snapped her fingers, "I really should have built a microwave dish to intercept and override a few of the local television broadcasts for this." She shrugged and glanced at Atomik Lad, "Perhaps next time." Her eyes widened as she punched another sequence of keys on her remote control. Her hands shook with excitement as she did so.

Atomik Lad stood frozen, as powerless as when he had been held in the field. He couldn't take his eyes off Nuklear Man though he wanted to more than anything else. In the distance, a disgusting, alien, and all around grotesque sound echoed from outside. Dr. Menace, in her button pushing fervor didn't notice. Nuklear Man, in his solemn nobility in the face of defeat didn't notice. Atomik Lad, in his need to be distracted, noticed it right away. He strained to hear it even as the spattering roar grew ever closer.

"And now witness the end of the soon to be late and not so great Nuklear Man!"

"Get on with it, villain!" Nuklear Man said. The nobility of his bearing was almost as unbearable for Atomik Lad as the dire situation itself.

"Most certainly," Dr. Menace replied, drunk in her fiendish revelry. "All that remains iz to push a final button. Now to elongate the pointer finger while flexing the others to indicate a pushing motion."

Atomik Lad desperately wanted to scream until he exploded. The sound was driving him mad like some manifestation of his rage at the hopeless situation at hand.

"And finally," she said. "To lower said extended finger in order to press the button in question, the last in the overly complex series I've been working on for so long in order to initiate the Negaflux Field'z operation at a ratio of approximately 6000 to 1 thus rendering anything within the sphere's interior quite dead." She paused and looked around. "What is that wretched noize?"

An explosion erupted from the wall to the left of Nuklear Man's rather clumsy and impromptu entrance. Atomik Lad felt his brain leap out of his skull he was so startled. In the midst of it though, he thought it sounded like what he imagined he would sound like if his particles were indeed bursting from their more relaxed positions within the confines of his body. Suddenly, the large warehouse was filled with smoke, confusion, and the ominous sounds of a massive structure enduring more than it was designed to. A diminutive metallic individual with an overly enormous club rose out of the masonry storm.

Atomik Lad coughed from the smoke as he waved it away, "Iron Scotsman! What are you doing here?"

The Surly Scot answered, "Well laddie, Ah'll tell ye. Ah was loookin' fer that Menace lass when Ah ran into thems mimes and oone thing led ta another and beefore Ah knoows it, Ah DWARF-A-PULT!ed into this 'ere buildin'." He blinked while observing the scene, "What be ye dooin' here?"

"Nuke!" Atomik Lad exclaimed, "We've got to find Nuke!" he explained as he shot into the dispersing smoke.

The building groaned as if to say, "I get built, I'm used to make and store toxic chemicals, I get abandoned, left to rot, someone finally starts to use me again and in one day I get two morons flying through my walls at several hundred miles an hour. I don't have to take this. I have my dignity."

Angus looked above him. Cracks began exploring the roof with hollow snaps echoing from them as dust, plaster, and concrete bits rained down.

Dr. Menace opened her eyes. She was lying on her stomach amongst dust and rubble. She pushed herself up and gasped as she realized the remote control was no longer in her possession. She quickly scanned the area.

Nuklear Man hadn't moved, other than to pick up the remote control that landed just next to him after the wall blew up. "Pretty," he mumbled while staring blankly at the blinky red light atop its antenna. He was brought out of his stupor by something tugging on his cape. "Hey Angus."

"Aye. We ought ta find the laddie. This buildin' is about to fall on our heads."

"Wah?" Nuklear Man said. A large chunk of roof became several smaller chunks of ex-roof strewn about the floor mere inches behind them. "Ah. Yeah, let's get movin'."

"Not zo fast, Nuklear Dope!" Dr. Menace stepped out of a plume of smokey debris with Atomik Lad held captive in a choke hold. She held a silvery gun looking thing shoved against his temple. "Get back in the Negaflux Field Generator, or Sparky here getz it!"

"Blast!" Angus cursed.

Nuklear Man's shoulders drooped. He extended his hand to relinquish the deadly remote, "I guess there's nothing I can do but PLAZMAAA BEAM!" a thick beam of golden energy erupted from his hand, melted the remote, and destroyed the gun held against his sidekick's head. Atomik Lad could smell that the tips of his hair had been singed.

"AH!" Dr. Menace shouted in alarm as she fell back from the blast.

"Nuke!" Atomik Lad hollered. His Atomik Field wove itself around him and he zoomed at near-overspeed toward Nuklear Man and Angus. One in each hand, He picked up his mentor and the Scotsman as he flew by, snatching them away moments before an enormous piece of roof had the chance to squash them very dead where they stood.

The trio exited the premises by shattering through yet another wall. The building answered them by thundering in annoyance, "RIGHT! That's it. I've had enough. That was really the last straw!" just before it fell in upon itself in protest.

"Good work, Sparky!" Nuklear Man praised with a thumbs up.

Atomik Lad landed a safe distance away from the destruction and released his cargo. The sidekick looked thoughtfully at the collapsed structure. "Do you think she uh...do you think got out?"

Nuklear Man surveyed the carnage with his patented Nuklear Sight. "Well, I don't see how anyone could have survived such an architectural disaster," he concluded. "So she obviously escaped in the chaos through some extremely elaborate failsafe mechanism that one would have trouble believing anyone would have the foresight, time, or patience to construct in the first place."

"What about the coupons?" Angus inquired as he rubbed his iron covered tummy.

The Hero's eyes darkened, "Gone I'm afraid...forever."

The Surly Scot removed his Iron: Battle Helm and held it against his heart in a moment of silence. Nuklear Man stood at attention and hummed a dirge.

Atomik Lad looked down in hungry depression. "Hey, what's that?"

"My pocket," Nuklear Man said.

"Spandex pockets? Since when?"

"How else do you suppose I stow things like clues? Hm?"

"Clues like what?"

"Oh yeah," he took out the birthday note and unfolded it clumsily. He tried to read it but furrowed his brow in confusion. Atomik Lad rolled his eyes and turned the note right side up for the Hero who grinned his appreciation. "It's a birthday card from my dad," Nuklear Man answered.

"Birthday, huh?" Atomik Lad considered it for a moment, "Do you know what this means?"

"It means that I've found a vague hint to my ever elusive past that has yet to show even the slightest hint as to my origins and has boggled and defied explanation of any kind for the past ten years?"

"Well that too I guess. But more importantly, we can go to a Benny's and get a free birthday cake with our meal!"

Nuklear Man's body glowed with Happy Plazma. Angus rubbed his hands together. He was hungry with anticipation. And hunger.

The odd trio took to the skies.

"Ha-Ho!"

"DWWWWAAAARRRFFFF-A-PULLLLLLLLT!"

"Um. Yeah."

Issue 5—The
Restaurant at the
Beginning of the Book

Minutes later, over the rooftops of Metroville, Nuklear Man and Angus were giddy with questions for Atomik Lad about the seemingly mythical "Benny's" with its "free birthday cake."

"How big is the cake?" chimed Nuklear Man.

"Do it have the frilly li'l flowers?" Angus inquired.

The Hero and Atomik Lad looked at their diminutive companion as though he had giant radioactive walruses climbing out of his ears speaking in tongues.

"Er, Ah likes the icin'!" he said in gruff defense.

"Oh…um, yeah. Icing. Sure," Nuklear Man said uncomfortably.

Atomik Lad simply looked away to avoid the heavy silence that followed.

Angus, desperately needing to change the subject, asked, "Do we even know where we're goin'?"

Nuklear Man inconspicuously glanced at Atomik Lad. The sidekick rolled his eyes and marveled at how conspicuous Nuklear Man was no matter how hard he tried.

"Yeah, I know where it is." Atomik Lad took the lead, "Follow me."

Angus gave Nuklear Man a shocked "You're letting the sidekick lead?!" look.

"Er. It's uh, it's Sidekick-Lead-The-Way-Day," Nuklear Man said while tugging at his collar.

A few more moments of awkward silence that were very well disguised only by the Scotsman's thunderous Iron: Bagpipe Thrusters passed before Atomik Lad announced, "There it is! Benny's!"

Nuklear Man and the Iron Scotsman squealed with delight.

"Sparky, you're a smarty everyday," Nuklear Man said with a pat on the sidekick's back.

The sidekick touched down expertly in front of the restaurant's entrance. The Golden Guardian crashed into the sidewalk while the Surly Scot smacked painfully against the front window and made a squeaky sound as he slid to the ground. Atomik Lad examined his companions and sighed.

The trio scurried inside like three stooges. It took several attempts before they managed to get past the doorway. In front of them was a small restaurant style chalk board with "Today's Special! All you can eat! $5!" written in ornate pastel letters. Nuklear Man and Angus squealed. Again.

A pleasant waitress greeted them, "Hello, I'm Rachel," she seemed Asian-ish to Atomik Lad and a pleasant experience to look at, "I'll be your waitress for today. Smoking or Non?"

"Super!" the Hero answered with a thumbs up

"Ugh," Atomik Lad said. "Non, please, thank you."

Rachel gave Nuklear Man an uneasy smile, nodded at Atomik Lad, and asked, "Just the two then?"

"Awkch-*hem*!" Angus phloemed. "What's the matter with ye, lass? Can't ye see there be three o' us?"

She took a step back as Angus rumbled.

Atomik Lad moved between them, "Uh, three. Sorry."

Rachel tried to recover using all her waitress katas of smiling and thinking happy thoughts, mainly ones that included hefty tips. She led them to their table. The trio followed with Angus in a moody third.

They took a booth, Atomik Lad sat next to the window, Nuklear Man next to him, and Angus across from them. Rachel gave them each a glass of water, silverware wrapped up in napkins, and menus. She took a deep breath to begin her spiel, "Today's Special is—"

Nuklear Man exploded with excitement, "The Special!" he exclaimed, "Three specials! And make it quick, you've got two—"

"Awkch-*hem*!" Angus phloemed in an altogether more pissed off fashion than before.

"Er. *Three* of Metroville's most treasured overheroes."

"Of course," Rachel took up the menus and went back to the kitchen to report the order.

Atomik Lad stared out the window dreamily. He watched people dressed in ordinary clothes attend to their ordinary business. Nuklear Man toyed with his complimentary glass of water. He was delighted with the activity of boiling and cooling the liquid at will with his Plazma Power. Angus growled like a feral beast mere moments from jumping on a trespasser. The guttural thunder was so loud even Nuklear Man became aware of it.

"What's wrong, Scotsman?" the Golden Guardian inquired.

"Ah can't reach the table!" Angus stretched his stubby arms and waved them uselessly before the table top.

"What if you stand?" the Hero suggested.

"AH *AM* STANDIN'!!!" the Scotsman bellowed.

Nuklear Man fumbled an apology. Angus huffed moodily and slammed back in his seat. Atomik Lad could only see the top of Angus's helmet peaking out from behind the table. He couldn't help but crack a smile that Angus thankfully could not see.

*   *   *   *

The manager made his rounds: smiling at customers, making small talk, avoiding eye contact with the costumed nuts and their small friend. Finally, he checked the register. Glancing up from his duties, he noticed something was amiss with the small chalkboard that announced the daily specials to patrons the moment they walked in the door.

"Rachel," he called.

She trotted to him, smiling all the while that waitress smile that borders on sincerity, "Yes, Mr. Manager?"

"This is *yesterday's* special."

"Oh gosh! I completely forgot about it when those three landed outside," she pointed to the over-trio, "I thought that little one was going to smash right through the front window," she added.

"Yes, well just get the special right. Tuesdays are Lobster Days, only fifteen dollars a plate."

"Yessir."

$*$ $*$ $*$ $*$

With eagle-like Nuklear Vision, Nuklear Man discerned their waitress from across the vast restaurant, "Ah-ha!" he announced while pointing dramatically, "I believe she's carrying five—NO." He counted on his fingers to be absolutely certain, "Three plates." He paused for a moment, "Atomik Lad! Take a head count."

Through a miracle of the gods, Atomik Lad resisted answering Two. "Still just the three of us, Nuke."

Even so, Angus was sure to look as though had Atomik Lad answered Two he would have severely regretted it. Atomik Lad had to chuckle.

"Just as I thought," Nuklear Man said to himself. "Gentlemen, I think she may be carrying our order," he said with an air of militaristic authority.

"Nuke, we're the only people on this side of the restaurant."

"Never assume, Sparky. Else you, uh…sticks and two in a bush…make stones out of you and me?" his thought trailed off to No Brain's Land.

Luckily, at that moment, Rachel arrived with the three steaming plates of lobster. She set them down, one in front of each Hero, "Is there anything else I can get you, gentlemen?"

"Ah mee mblm," Angus grumbled.

"Excuse me, sir?"

"Ah mee mblm," he repeated.

"I'm sorry sir, but I—"

"Ah bloody said Ah neeeds a child's seeat!" he roared as he jumped up and down hysterically.

Rachel stumbled back a step. Her fact went pale from shock. She muttered something about "Right away," and disappeared into the lobby.

"Jeez Angus, do you have to yell at her? She's just trying to do her job," the sidekick pleaded.

"Ah don't like her. The lass smiles too much!"

Atomik Lad would have asked Nuklear Man to help in this endeavor to better Angus's public relations, but the Hero was too busy gorging himself to bother removing the lobster shells, much less participate in speech.

Rachel approached the table with apprehension and a child's seat. Angus snatched it from her and mumbled an apology while he tried, without success, not to look ridiculous as he climbed into it.

The Hero had already finished his plate and was motioning that he wanted another. Rachel's skill and waitress's intuition recognized right away what

Nuklear Man was signaling for despite the similarities to rude gestures. One could say that Nuklear Man wasn't very good at that sort of thing and still be giving him an optimistic appraisal. She promptly went back into the kitchen.

Atomik Lad and Angus finally began to partake of the feast. The Scotsman, though happy to be eating, wore an expression that made it evident that he wanted someone, anyone, to make just one remark about his child's seat so he could make them wish they hadn't.

✳   ✳   ✳   ✳

They ate for hours. Every time a plate neared exhaustion Nuklear Man would orchestrate a complex series of gestures that were supposed to mean to Rachel, "One more." She was able to understand despite the complete absence of order, reason, or coherence in the Hero's wild arm flailing. At times like these Atomik Lad always wondered how Nuklear Man could screw things up so perfectly. *It's like Menace was saying. He gets things so wrong that they go full circle and work out to be right in the end. Which is practically in spite of his every effort.*

When they could devour no more, Atomik Lad excused himself to the restroom while the Golden Guardian and Surly Scot leaned back in stuffed afterglow, patting and/or scratching their bulging stomachs and making contented, "Ahhhhh," noises every few seconds.

Noticing that the frenzy was over, Rachel arrived at the table with a broad smile. She surveyed the battlefield. With skill and expert precision she was able to place the check where neither patron would feel obliged to pick it up, nor where it would reveal any opinion or prejudice of her own as to who she felt should pay for the meal, while simultaneously avoiding the myriad of sloppy splotches of varying sauces and juices that, due to the ravenous, and downright disgusting, eating habits of those seated, covered the table like bugs on a windshield. She collected armfuls of plates to have them sand blasted clean out back.

Atomik Lad exited the bathroom with a smile that made it plain to all that he was happy to be alive and most importantly, unhungry. He stood near the restaurant entrance, absorbing his own sunshiny mood when a comet of horror shattered his world.

"Tuesday's Special: $15 Lobster!" He gasped in terror. He saw Rachel carrying a full eight plates while another nine remained on the battlefield of a table in a manner not at all unlike fallen and broken soldiers.

He calmly made his way to the table and sat down next to Angus in such a forced satire of calm that one might have accused him of being a robot. He smiled widely and spoke through his clenched teeth to disguise his worry, "The Special is fifteen bucks a pop."

Nuklear Man's otherwise dull and inattentive attention jumped into action, "What talk you!" This was no time for grammar.

Atomik Lad, in his empty smile, picked up the check and handed it to Nuklear Man who promptly fainted. Angus reached for the check, but the restraints of the child's seat held him firm. His face reddened in frustration, veins began to swell, and adrenaline began to course through his small body. "Grrrrr. Dwwwwwarf-a—" Atomik Lad snatched the check from the Hero's limp hand and shoved it in Angus's mouth, "—polp," the Scotsman finished anticlimactically. He spat the check into his hand and perused it with fiery eyes. He began making unintelligible noises, "Habba. Ababbaflabba." His breathing became strained and irregular.

Nuklear Man awoke with a jolt. "Oh, it was all a horrible dream. Whew, thought we were in real trouble for a second there."

"We be in real troouble, laddie!" Angus said, lowering his voice toward the end when he realized how loudly he was speaking.

Nuklear Man motioned for Angus and Atomik Lad to lean forward. For Angus, it didn't do much good. "All right, we need a plan of action," Nuklear Man began. "Atomik Lad, you shall make a feint to the northeast. Scotsman, you—"

"Nuke, we're not going to do the old 'Feint to the Northeast' trick."

"It'll work!" he insisted. "I saw it in a movie."

"All right, we'll make that Plan B," the sidekick said to cajole his mentor. "Scotsman, any ideas?"

"Well," he rubbed his scraggly beard and picked out a few lobster bits. "We coould say that the food was horrible and we refuse to pay for it."

"We ate seventeen plates."

"Right!" Nuklear Man's eyes were ablaze with craftiness, "We ate seventeen plates in the hopes that the next one would taste better!"

"Somehow, I don't think that'll hold water, Big Guy."

"Yeah, I bet everyone uses that one."

Issue 6—Let Them Eat Cake

"Can we still have the free cake?" Angus asked.

"Well it *is* free." Nuklear Man said conspiratorially.

"We're in it deep enough as it is," Atomik Lad snapped.

"But it's still *free*," Nuklear Man said.

"We can't push our luck."

"But Ah wanted the frilly flowery icin'." Nuklear Man and Atomik Lad gave each other sidelong glances. Angus rustled uncomfortably in his child's seat in a vain attempt to fill the awkward void of silence. "Ah likes the icin'," he mumbled sullenly into his lobster juice-soaked beard.

"Maybe we could all fake heart attacks," Nuklear Man said. "And when the ambulance is driving us away we could break loose our bonds and quip thusly: 'Ha! We weren't heart attack stricken! Nay, for we are virile and mighty with recommended cholesterol levels because—'"

"Nuke?"

"Tsk. I'm not done with our getaway taunt. Now you made me lose my place."

"Ah mean, what's wrong with likin' icin'?" Angus complained to no one in particular. "It's sweeet and sugary and it smooooshes between ye fingers."

"Or," the Hero plotted anew. "We could fake an elephant stampede!"

"Guys?"

"And the management would be so thankful for our Heroic defense from the rampaging elephants, that they'd let us eat for free!"

"...Ah don't ask for much. Just a wee bit o' icin' every now and then without bein' looked at like soome kind o' freak!"

"Guys."

"Or, better yet, we could construct some card-board cut outs of ourselves and while the management attempts to reason with our lifeless twins, we make good our escape!"

"Why ye gots to laugh at me? Who doesn't like icin'? What about the Golden Goon over there? 'Oooh, lookit me! Ah'm Nuklear Man!' La-dee-dah!' Ah was bustin' up villains back when he was still in diapers! Back when ye did it for the chance to break things, not for merchandisin'! But noooo, ye goots to laugh at ol' Angus! 'Lookie at the midget freak! Hey freak, ye want soome icin'? Aye? Well too bad! Ye be too short for icin' folk! Let's go and buy some Nuklear Man T-shirts!' Bah!"

"Guys!" Atomik Lad banged his fist on the table and produced a clatter of plates.

"Can I get you gentlemen some dessert?" Rachel asked pleasantly as she loaded her arms with the used plates.

Nuklear Man quickly rummaged through his pockets and whipped out his birthday card. "Your finest free birthday cake, Miss Rachel."

She glanced at the card, "Oh how sweet, your father still sends you birthday cards. I'll be right back with that cake, sir." She whisked herself off to Kitchen Land.

"Nuke! I told you not to order the cake!"

"It's free. What're they gonna do? Make us pay for free?"

Angus did his best to approximate something quite resembling a smile, but found the practice too taxing and gave up with an annoyed huff.

"Besides," the Hero said. "The bird seems sweet on you, Sparky. Maybe we could bag us a free meal if you talk the talk to the skirt."

Atomik Lad stared at his mentor for a moment. "Why are you talking like that?"

"It's Jive, baby. We're on the lam, we gotta start talking jive, get used to it."

"We are not 'on the lam.' Besides, you don't have the jewelry to talk jive."

Nuklear Man hung his head in dejection, "Phooey."

Rachel popped out of the kitchen door. She was holding a silver, in appearance, but not in make, tray in her hands. She displayed it as a squire would his master's favored blade.

"Cheesit, it's the fuzz," Nuklear Man hissed as he tried, in a very pathetic and unconvincing manner, to look as though nothing was wrong.

"Nuke, what did I just tell you about the jive?"

"What in Sweeet Margaret's Hurlin' Pole are ye two talkin' about?" Angus roared. Nuklear Man was talking crazy talk and nothing angered Angus more than crazy talk.

Except for people making fun of his height.

"Angus," Atomik Lad said.

Or his beard.

"Angus?"

Or his affinity for frail icing flowers. Or—

"Angus!"

"What!" he responded with a tiny jerk that took him from his thoughts but not before he added, *People who interrupt me thinkin'* to his list of Aggravatin' Things.

"The cake. Remember? It's here."

Rachel pulled out a small harmonica from one of her many waitress apron pockets and gave it a toot. Three generic waiters appeared as if they'd merely been hiding behind several molecules hovering idly in the air.

The four sang in an slightly off key unison. They looked like they'd been hypnotized into reciting the song on command. Whether or not this was the truth or it was just the faces they adopted due to being resigned to their singing-in-public-for-minimum-wage fate, Atomik Lad couldn't tell.

"Here's your free birthday cake,
Even the preservatives are fake.
It's been known to cause intestinal distention
So to our legalese please pay attention:
Take to heart
That the party of the first part,
Upon ingestion,
With no chance of contestion,
Agrees that the party of the second part
Is not responsible for the effects of this slipshod tart.
All arguments otherwise
Made by you guys
Shall be rendered incongruous
In short: you cannot sue us!"

The three generic waiters vanished as suddenly as they had appeared.

"Happy Birthday, sir. May you have many more." She leaned in close to Nuklear Man and whispered, "Especially if you don't eat the cake." Then she too disappeared to attend to her other waitress duties.

Atomik Lad poked at the cake with his fork, "Is it edible?"

"We won't know until we eat it!" Nuklear Man reasoned.

Angus felt there was something wrong with that logic but dismissed the twinkling of thought in favor of the cake's sweet promises of sugar overload.

The Golden Guardian and Surly Scot devoured the free birthday cake as though they had not just eaten nearly twenty plates of lobster mere minutes ago. Angus took particular pleasure from the excess sweetness of the little icing flowers. Atomik Lad merely watched and worried about the bill. "How are we going to pay for everything?" he asked.

"Simple," Nuklear Man answered. "You distract Rachel, Angus and I run for it, then you excuse yourself to the bathroom and squeeze out the window."

"Aren't we supposed to be paragons of justice and honor and all that jazz?"

"Honor always gets in the way o' buustin' uup things, if'n ye ask me."

"Well, this is different."

"How?"

"Er. You'll understand when you're older."

"Nuke, that might have worked when I was ten, but it really didn't because I could outwit you just as fast then as I can now."

"Shucks."

"Nuke, why don't we just explain the problem? Angus could stay here with the bill and you could go back to the Silo to get our credit card." the thought of entrusting Nuklear Man to make a round trip and remember its purpose struck Atomik Lad with all the force of a galactic collision. "Make that, you and I could go back to the Silo to get the credit card."

"Where's the fun in that?"

Nuklear Man fidgeted. "Well. Er, I uh, um. I sort of ah…maxed out the credit cards."

"That does it. V-Chipsville, Population: Overmart Shopping Network."

Nuklear Man grimaced.

"Here comes Rachel," the Hero observed. "Hush up and let me do the talking."

"Are you sure?"

"Hey, I know what I'm doing."

"*Really* sure?"

"I don't tell you how to sidekick and you don't tell me how to Hero."

"All right, just checking."

Rachel returned to collect the dessert plates. "Is there anything else I can get you gentlemen? Some coffee perhaps?"

The Hero looked her straight in the eyes and confidently blubbered, "We can't pay the bill! It's so much money and we don't have enough because those little ceramic rabbits were so cute and on sale for only two more minutes. It's not my fault! Before I knew it, I bought thirteen sets!" he stopped to breath.

"So you can't pay your bill?" Rachel clarified.

"No we can't," the Hero answered. He was ashamed even to exist.

"I'll have to speak with the manager, excuse me." She trotted back to a door marked "Employees Only" and stepped inside its forbidden depths.

"'Hush up. Let me do the talking. I know what I'm doing. I don't tell you how to sidekick and you don't tell me how to hero.' Pathetic."

Angus snorted an agreement, "Ah seen haggis with moore backbone than that. Literally."

"Heh, good one," Atomik Lad said.

"Ah'm serious. Little chunks of 'em."

"Excuse me, sir?" said a man looking remarkably like a manager who spontaneously appeared next to their table.

"Bwah!" Nuklear Man decided the generic waiters had learned much from the manager.

"I am Mr. Manager, the manager. I understand that you are unable to pay your bill. I believe we can work something out," he motioned to the door leading to the kitchen.

"Oh no," Nuklear Man said with apprehension. "This Hero ain't g'tting' no dishpan hands."

Mr. Manager tossed him a pair of kitchen gloves. "You're right. Now get to work, boys. Rachel?"

She smiled her waitress smile to him.

"You've got the rest of the day off."

"Thank you, Mr. Manager." She took off her apron, tossed it on Atomik Lad, gave him a wink and walked out the door whistling to herself."

The Heroic trio groaned in unison.

Issue 7—Food Fight

"Attention!" Mr. Manager roared in his best drill sergeant voice.

They stood shoulder to shoulder to shoulder once Angus hopped onto a table top. Mr. Manager paced in front of them. He trod back and forth he trod while peering at the ground. His hands were clasped behind his back and tightly wrenching one another,.

"*You*, Pretty-Boy!" he barked.

Nuklear Man "Eeep!"ed quietly to himself and jerked to such a degree of attention that it would've shattered any human spine.

"You're on kitchen duty. You've got a mess back there that makes the Dragon's Strike look like a tea party."

"Yessir," the Hero obediently responded before scurrying into the kitchen.

A feminine shriek split the ambiance like a supernova.

Mr. Manager closed his eyes with a distinct air of impatience that was evident only to those who put that much attention into eye shutting, "That's the women's restroom, you dolt!"

Nuklear Man backed out of the door clearly marked "Women" while defending himself, almost as well as 20th Century France, against a woman far to wide for her height who battered the Golden Guardian about the head with her purse while screaming, "You brute, you brute, you terrible brute!"

She left in a huff.

"*You*, Kid!" Mr. Manager barked at Atomik Lad.

"Hey, I'm almost twenty."

"Hey, I almost care. Help out Pretty-Boy. He makes one slip up and I'm holding you responsible."

Atomik Lad led Nuklear Man into the kitchen.

Mr. Manager spun on Angus, "*You*, Shorty!"

Ordinarily the Iron Scotsman would have chosen this time to demonstrate how effective the business end of his Surprisingly Wieldly and Concealable Enemy-B-Crushed named Bertha was when used properly and how vary properly it could be used on people who called him Shorty. But something about the manager's manner forced compliance even out of the Surly Scot. "Aye?"

"Those two got the kitchen, so you're stuck with waitering." He tossed Rachel's discarded apron on Angus. It covered him like a sheet.

*   *   *   *

Two figures of purity stood near the entrance to the dark depths of the kitchen. Neither wanted to leave what little light was provided there by the oven light and the luminescence that peaked out from the lobby through the kitchen doors.

Nuklear Man whistled innocently to the best of his ability. This involved more than a little spitting. He faked a yawn, stretched, and reached behind his sidekick with a mighty hand to push him forward into the darkness.

Atomik Lad deftly dropped to his knees as the pressure was first applied to his back. This evasive maneuver caused the Hero to lose his balance and topple into the inky void beyond.

"Guess you volunteered to tackle the stuff in the storeroom," Atomik Lad said. I'll just be up here in the kitchen mopping and washing dishes," he gloated happily.

"Best two out of three?"

"Sure."

Nuklear Man walked back into the light and basked in its brilliance once again. Atomik Lad snatched a mop that was leaning on the counter next to him and tripped his mentor into the darkness with it. The Golden Guardian lay sprawled on his belly.

"Best three of five?"

"Get back there."

"Nuts," he whined. He walked apprehensively into the bleak unknown.

"Mr. Manger said he was going to hold me responsible for anything you screw up, so no horsin' around back there, got it?"

"I never get to have any fun," his pout sounded like it was uttered from across a vast, empty and unlit stadium in the dead of night.

*   *   *   *

Angus was having a rough time. Mr. Manger scolded him for marking up the table tops with his Iron: Battle Boots and ordered him to clean them ASAP. This was easier said than done. In order for Angus to clean a table, he had to stand on it. This caused him to further scuff up the table which had to be cleaned which scuffed up the table which had to be cleaned into forever and ever. To make matters worse, he didn't know what an "ASAP" was, what it might look like, be used for, or where to find it anyway. He hoped Mr. Manger wouldn't notice.

*   *   *   *

Atomik Lad washed dishes with the kind of pleasure one typically finds in those who have other people wash dishes. But the sidekick treated every dish, platter, cup, bowl and piece of silverware as though the quality of his soul would be judged on the quality of the gleaning shine he gave each piece.

*   *   *   *

The rubbery kitchen gloves slid over his skin and golden spandex as though they'd been waiting their entire existence to shield Nuklear Man—AND NUKLEAR MAN ALONE—from this tepid wasteland. He thrust his armored hands skyward, "I dub thee, Excalibur!"

"Nuke, stop goofing off. And don't break anything."

"Just suiting up," he called back. The hollow echo of his own voice gave him a chill, but the warmth of his kitchen gloves kept his blood hot for adventure!

*   *   *   *

The bell attached to the Benny's entrance which was designed to signal the arrival or exit of a customer, as though the presence or lack of their presence, wasn't enough, signaled to Angus that a customer had popped in. He kicked at the table he had been cleaning for what seemed like hours but more resembled minutes. This left a fresh scuff mark. "Son of an Englishman!" he cursed. The

Iron Scotsman hopped down to the floor and trotted to the entrance grumbling to himself about how the feeding frenzy had already left his tiny gut with an empty feeling. He staggered back a step as he rounded the corner. His beady eyes widened, his tight fists clenched, his scowl scowled like it hadn't in years. "Ah don't believe it."

An emerald green suit of armor fashioned in the likeness of a charming leprechaun stood toe to toe with Angus's iron gray armor that resembled a raging Scottish warrior circa the 14th century.

The armored duo were locked eye to eye.

"That's right, me boy-o, Shamus O'Riley, the Steel Irishman."

"Ye, ye, ye," Angus stammered angrily.

"Reduced to waiterin'? Aye, times are tough I know, I know. But we all can't be as successful as me, now can we?"

"Ah ain't no waiter, ye motif stealin' laddie! Ah oughta rip off them arms o ye in return for—"

"*Shorty*!" Mr. Manager snapped, "No offense to you, Mr. O'Riley."

"None taken, I be assurin' ye."

Mr. Manager nodded pleasantly to Shamus and turned sharply to Angus, "You are to treat our customers with the respect they deserve!"

"Only thing ol' Shamus deserves is a goood bashin' in the head!"

"This is Mr. Shamus O'Riley of the breakfast cereal conglomerate Kismet Krunchies, featuring the secret ingredient Kismet Green. He's rich and that makes him better than ordinary people. It's called capitalism."

"Ah bloody knows who he be! He's the rat that stole me idea for a breakfast cereal, Scootish Squishies!"

"Ah, Angus. Ye always been having quite the imagination. Who in his right mind would eat cereal made o' haggis?"

"Kismet Green is made o' haggis!"

"Control yourself Angus or you're fired!"

"No need to be doin' that, good sir. Everyone in the cereal business knows about Angus's rantin's. Not a one of them be takin' him serious o' course. Kismet Krunchies wouldn't be the number one breakfast product in the world if it were made o' haggis. Any plain fool can be seeing that."

*   *   *   *

A dim green light pulsed um, lightly. At first Nuklear Man couldn't tell if his mind was playing tricks on him or not. But the more he concentrated on it, the more he was certain that this was one of the few strange lights in the dark that wasn't somehow in cahoots with his imagination. The green light had a faint hum that waxed and waned with its fluctuating intensity. It seemed to Nuklear Man that it was coming from inside an old barrel that had warped and rotted over the ages thus allowing several small imperfections to let the eerie light escape. He carefully crept toward it. The light was like the heartbeat of a sleeping mythical beast. His gloved hands hovered mere inches above the lid where the majority of the light peeked through gaps between it and the rim. Having grown accustomed to the green light, the Hero could make out an ancient, tattered, and weathered label on the barrel's lid. It read, "Barrel O' Cheese" with the "O" resembling a cheese wheel. Below the logo, in considerably smaller print, it said "Best if served before 1959."

"Ick," he said into the darkness. It was the first sound he had made since happening upon this strange occurrence.

A high pitched hum ran through the emptiness. Nuklear Man immediately noticed the pin prick of green light that zipped out of a knothole in the barrel and hovered so close to his nose that he was forced cross-eyed to look at it. "Intruder!" the floating green speck announced far louder than its size would suggest possible.

"Eh?" Nuklear Man responded confusedly.

"I don't hear any cleaning back there!" Atomik Lad's voice was distant, as though calling from a dream.

Hundreds of green specks of light poured from the knotholes and gaps and all of them were converging on the Hero.

"Oooh, pretty."

"Attack!" a huge yet tiny high-pitched voice echoed from across the battlefield. A barrage of green laser bolts rained from the floating specks and assaulted Nuklear Man with thousands of piercing ouchics.

"Nuke! What's all that noise? Don't make me come back there!"

"Ouch! Quit it! C'mon! Ow, my eye!" the Hero whimpered as he waved his arms in his second France-like defense of the day.

A squadron of the Barrel Defense Force split off from the main fleet which was taking severe losses from the Invader's maniacal strategy of random counter-strikes. The splinter wing dove for the Invader's feet and divided again into two smaller wings, each heading to one of Nuklear Man's cape corners.

*   *   *   *

"Shorty!" Mr. Manager yelled from across the restaurant.

The Iron Scotsman growled as he put away his massive mauling club and climbed down from the booth behind Shamus. The Iron Scotsman took out a small notebook and pencil from one of the many pockets in the waitress's apron he was wearing, "Mblembml?" he mumbled.

"What is it ye be askin' me, boy-o?"

"And that's another thing! Ye steal me cereal fortune, then ye steal me armored motif, and now ye steal me speech impediment!"

"I've been talking like this since before ye was skimping pennies at the breadline."

"I don't think so, laddie! Ah been spoutin' incomprehensible rhetoric since before ye had ye first slug o' nickel beer!"

The two looked around contemplatively for a few moments.

"Well," admitted Angus. "Maybe not quite *that* soon, but ye get me meaning."

"Aye, I do."

*   *   *   *

"Operation Trip: Go!" a commanding high-pitched voice bellowed from somewhere inside the barrel.

"Nuke, what are you doing?" Atomik Lad's voice seemed to be coming from beyond reality as we know it.

Nuklear Man's cape, with the help of many green dots, wrapped itself around his legs. He wobbled like a drunkard and collapsed on his face. "The cheese has gone bad!" he called back to his sidekick.

"Well that's what you're there for. Clean it up!"

"But it's winning!!!"

"Ugh, just hold your breath."

*   *   *   *

Shamus gingerly sipped his coffee and clicked his tongue while taking in every aspect of its character: the temperature, strength, sweetness, etc.

"No, this won't be doin' either."

"That's ye sixth cup o' coffee! What's wroong with this one?"

"It's not quite rich enough. You ought to be knowin' all about that, boy-o."

"One more remark like that one and Ah'll bash ye head in, laddie."

"Boy-o."

"Laddie!"

"BOY-O!"

"*LADDIE!*"

*   *   *   *

Nuklear Man felt like the universe had suddenly taken it upon itself to go upside down with the exception of himself. He was suspended by his feet in mid-air. His head was just a foot from the barrel's lid, the bottom of his cape was resting gently on the floor above his head. The barrel's lid rustled of its own accord and flipped open flooding the room with a green tint. The Hero blinked groggily and squinted as a platform, built in scale for a gnat, rose from the green depths to be level with Nuklear Man's nose. A small green dot rested atop it. He had to cross his eyes to see it properly.

Tiny music, somehow triumphant, emanated from the barrel with extremely minuscule flashes. "Victory!" the green dot proclaimed. This incited a flurry of noises and flashes from the barrel.

"Wah?" Nuklear Man inquired.

"Quiet! You are now a war prisoner of the mighty Cheesiediluvian Empire!" Another rush of excitement flowed from the barrel.

"Prisoner? Cheesiediluvian? War?"

"Yes! The outside would is ours for the taking! Your failed invasion has been repelled by our superior Cheesiediluvian Barrel Defense Force!" More cheers.

"Invasion?"

"Do not play dumb with me, Outsider!"

Nuklear Man decided to skip the obvious "Who's playing?" line, though feel free to insert it yourself at your leisure.

"We have known of your plots to usurp our kingdom for some time. But now we have proven our superiority over your kind! I, Daisy the XXVIII, shall usher in a new era! The age of Cheesiediluvian Conquest! Today, the storeroom! Tomorrow, the kitchen!" An uproar of cheers erupted from the barrel. The effect was like when a television in an adjacent room is turned up just a little too loud.

"Oh yeah, I'm really scared of a guy named 'Daisy,'" Nuklear Man mocked with a chuckle, "Daisy, ha!"

"Such insolence from a vanquished foe," the despot said haughtily. "Deploy the *Cheesenaught!*"

"That's it." Atomik Lad said from the kitchen. "Nuke, I'm coming back there, and if you're not working your cape off, or if even one thing is out of place, you've got some explaining to do!"

*   *   *   *

Two figures stood in defiance of one another. One, a cold gray beast, crouched menacingly in the smoking section. The other, a warm green knight posed righteously in the non-smoking section. Each muttered curses to the other under their respective breaths. They hefted their mighty weapons: a huge spiked and studded blunt instrument of destruction for the dwarf and an emerald shield in the shape of a four-leafed clover for the leprechaun.

"DWARF-A-PULT!"

"LEPRE-CANNON!"

*   *   *   *

A plank of wood near the barrel's bottom opened like an automatic garage door. A strange humanoid shadow splashed across the floor among a sea of green light. Slowly, a cheese-automaton waddled from the aperture like a little wind-up toy.

"Behold," gloated the green dot, "Our scientists' newest and most invincible creation: the Cheesenaught!"

"It's just cheese," Nuklear Man remarked.

"You dare mock us, Defeated One?"

"Well yeah. I mean, c'mon. It's walking cheese."

"Cheesenaught! Destroy the Mocker!"

"Feh, mock this," the Hero pointed a finger gun at the Cheesenaught and reduced it to a heap of dairy slag with a tiny squirt of Plazma Power.

Sounds of chaos rose form the barrel as Daisy attempted to quell the mob below him. "Assemble the defense force! Flee to the hills! Trust in your Emperor! Destroy the Outsider!" His commands fell upon ears deafened with horror.

The Golden Guardian felt an impish tingle in his nose. "Ahem, Mr. 28?" Nuklear Man interjected.

"The Cheesiediluvian Empire shall persevere! We are the Chosen Race to populate the restaurant! Lobbyfest Destiny shall be ours!"

"WAAAH-*CHOOOO*!"

*   *   *   *

The two armored and high-speed bullets collided in mid-air. An epic battle defying description ensued which is terribly convenient for me since I won't have to think up the details. But, I will say there was biting, clubbing, bashing, swatting, slapping, punching, kicking, throwing, and poking of the eyes. All this and a constant tirade of curses, eloquent unto a Shakespearean level in their rudeness, filled the restaurant which drove away what few customers remained. Then, as if the entire event had been elaborately rehearsed, both warriors simultaneously fell flat on their backs. They wheezed and panted while staring up at the ceiling.

*   *   *   *

Panic washed over the Cheesiediluvian populace. The pilots of the Defense Force that had been holding the Hero for all to see fled their positions and allowed Nuklear Man the kind of freedom of movement he was used to. Their great and powerful leader, who would have certainly led them to someday conquer lands as distant as the Men's restroom had he not just been sneezed into oblivion, had failed them. Their faith in Lobbyfest Destiny had been shaken with all the force of when that sack of potatoes had been tossed against the barrel in 3458 A.D. ("Ano Daisy").

Nuklear Man, being of kind heart and motive, could not bare to see them suffer. He pleaded to them, "Please, don't be afraid. I'm not going to hurt you."

The chaos ceased. All were silent.

He stared at them with the kind of awe most people experience when watching ants. These creatures were powerless before Nuklear Man. He held the fate of an entire world within his grasp. "You'll evaporate nanoseconds before your little neurons have the chance to transmit the intense pain to your little brains! MUWA HAHAHAHA!"

Chaos began anew.

"PLAZMAAA—"

A plastic click and the lights exploded to life.

"Nuke!" Atomik Lad tackled him from behind and the golden orbs around Nuklear Man's hands disappeared as the two fell in a heap on the floor.

"Hey, Sparky. Meet the Cheesiediluvians," he motioned to the Barrel O' Cheese barrel. "They were going to take over the restaurant, but I overthrew their leader and destroyed their most powerful weapon," he pointed to the congealing cheese slag on the floor.

"I can't take you anywhere, can I?" Atomik Lad sighed as he stood up and dusted himself off. "And where did you learn such a big word?"

"From the Cheesiediluvians," Nuklear Man insisted as he too stood up and did away with every particle that could possibly mar his spiffy outfit.

"Cheesiediluvians? I suppose this is some race of creatures that super-evolved from a barrel of cheese left forgotten for decades and they mistook you for an intruder and started this big war thing, but you, being such a great hero, were able to stop them?"

The Hero thought on this while rubbing his eyes to help them adjust to the lights, "Well...yeah."

"You have such an overactive imagination. You should have turned the lights on before you came back here." Atomik Lad picked up the barrel's lid, "1959? Phew, I bet these fumes weren't any help either. Probably knocked a few screws loose...er." Without paying attention to the barrel, or the dim green light emanating from it that was drowned out by the large overhead lights, Atomik Lad put the lid back on. "We'll have to throw this out."

"But the Cheesie—"

"Hallucinations, Nuke. Just your little brain playing tricks with you so that it might get you to pay attention to it once and awhile."

"The Cheesiediluvians. War. Saved Earth. Me did."

Atomik Lad hefted the large and strangely heavy barrel. "Would you stop worrying about it? It's nothing. There are no little cheese people." He kicked open the back door and tossed the barrel into a nearby dumpster. "Done and done," he said while dusting off his hands. "Now c'mon, I finished washing the dishes. Let's get Angus and go home, huh?"

Issue 8—Serial Cereal Industrial Espionage...ial.

They walked into the kitchen and Atomik Lad opened the door to the dining area while waving away Nuklear Man's insistence that the papers be contacted first thing in the morning to alert them that he'd just saved the world, yet again, from another crisis and large front page photos were called for. Really big color ones.

"Nuke, I seriously doubt they'd—"

"Angus!" Nuklear Man exclaimed.

Angus, the Iron Scotsman, was going fisticuffs with a green armored stranger no higher than the Surly Scot himself and very definitely not bussing tables.

"Hey, he's actually shorter than you are, Angus," Nuklear Man blurt with a jovial smile.

The two dwarfish dervishes of destruction instantly halted their assault of one another and shot simultaneous glares of hatred at the bumbling Hero.

"Uh. Eheh heh." Nuklear Man gulped aloud. "But uh you guys are um confident enough about that height thing so you won't be ah, y'know, beating me within a small increment of my life."

Their glares reached a level of contempt that mere mortals would consider impossible without a multitude of genetic alterations made at birth through medical or accidental means.

"Er...right?"

"Yeah, right," they said in unison with their respective accents butchering the words.

"Whew, I thought you guys were gonna be sore at me."

"*Someone's* gonna be sore," Atomik Lad muttered. He took a step away from his mentor.

"DWARF-A-PULT!!!"

"LEPRE-CANNON!!!"

An emerald streak accompanied by a stone gray blur struck the Golden, and soon to be black and blue, Guardian.

Atomik Lad sighed heavily and fiddled with his mop from the kitchen as the fight raged on without him. Mr. Manager ran up to the sidekick, since to do so to the others would have brought great pain against the restaurant guru. "Get these hooligans out of here before they cause more damage!" Mr. Manager demanded.

"I'm sorry sir, it's just that Angus is really temperamental about his height, and well, I guess that green guy is too and—"

"Green guy?"

"Well it's the armor that's green, not—"

"Green armor?"

Atomik Lad was losing patience with Mr. Manager's lack of patience which seemed to prompt him to constantly interrupt whomever was trying to explain things to him. It seemed a vicious circle of impatience.

Mr. Manager glanced at the cartoon like cloud of smoke. Limbs, stars, curses, battered skulls, BOINK noises, fists, and kicks poked out of it at random intervals. "He's a customer!" Mr. Manager screamed while pulling painfully at his own hair, "He could sue!" He growled at Atomik Lad, "I'm holding you freaks responsible!"

"Gee, thanks."

∗   ∗   ∗   ∗

The streets outside the Benny's restaurant bustled with both foot and vehicular traffic. The setting sun cast violet and crimson waves floating in the clouds that framed the brilliant red dayball the way only an artist's rendition can. The typical street sounds of light traffic and the jumble of conversations melded into a whitenoise of language were shattered as violently and unexpectedly as the Benny's Restaruant front window. Shamus and shards of glass rolled along the ground and lolled to a stop on his side. A beat later Angus too was tossed through the window, or where one had been one beat ago. He lay sprawled on his back beside his Irish counterpart. Two and two-thirds beats later Nuklear Man was also expelled from the premises in a similar manner. He landed between the previous two, face first with his cape covering his head. A muffled "Oof" escaped his lips.

Atomik Lad stood in the Benny's doorway dusting his hands and looking down at the disposed like a sheriff who just threw some loud drunkards out of a local tavern circa 1850. His snapping and wildly eccentric crimson and black splotched Atomik Field surrounded him like red-black fire. With a thought he willed it away, the final sparks sputtered to nothingness. He crossed his arms, leaned on the doorway and smirked.

"Ah wuz distracted froom the laddie," Angus defended himself against the unspoken insult that'd he'd been bested by anyone. "Had that big ol' orange cape in me eyes."

"Oh…I let the wee boy-o toss me out. It be building his confidence, ye know."

Nuklear Man mumbled into the sidewalk. "Wouldn't be so tough without that mop," but it was difficult to tell the exact wording due to his cape being flopped over his head and the proximity of his mouth to the ground.

"My window!" Mr. Manager dashed past Atomik Lad. His face was red enough to deserve a colorful metaphor.

"Mr. Manager," Atomik Lad gave him a look of concern. "You've got to calm down. You'll give yourself a heart attack if you keep this up."

"Oh no you don't!" Nuklear Man shot to attention with his cape still covering his face, "That was *my* idea!"

A definite simmering sound could be heard coming from Mr. Manager. Something akin to a pot overflowing while a tea kettle's piercing whistle shrieked. "Get. Out," he said through tensely clenched teeth. Hs voice was a faint and strained whisper of anger.

"But we are oout," noted Angus as he and Shamus stood up.

"Leave. Now." He was barely audible.

"But what about the window?" Atomik Lad asked, genuinely worried about the damages.

"Just. Go," he slowly raised an anger-quaking arm and pointed down the street.

A gust of wind returned Nuklear Man's cape to its natural state of billowing ever dramatically behind him, "But the Silo is that way," he said, pointing in the opposite direction as Mr. Manager.

"Go." He stated it so quietly it seemed that he merely mouthed the word.

Shamus whispered to Angus, "He be movin' on to single syllable sentences. Tisn't a good sign, boy-o."

"Aye," the Surly Scot whispered back.

Atomik Lad grabbed Nuklear Man by the arm and pulled him down the street as Shamus and Angus tagged along behind them.

"Man, what was his problem?" Nuklear Man asked no one in particular. "Oh well," he tossed a look behind him at his diminutive partners. "Angus, who's your," he nearly said "little" but remembered the beating from a few minutes ago and simply ended with, "friend?"

The Iron Scotsman huffed loudly, "This fortuune stealin' son o' a French whore ain't no friend o' mine!"

"Where you be getting these crazy ideas, boy-o? Ain't no one who'd buy ye Scootish Squishies breakfast cereal so I don't see why you be thinking I stole the formula from ye."

"I dunno, sounds kinda yummy to me," Nuklear Man said.

"It be made o' haggis," Shamus added.

"Ghak. Never mind."

"So's Kismet Green!" Angus insisted as he hopped madly.

"Kismet Green?" the Hero's interests were clearly piqued again. "The secret ingredient in Kismet Krunchies?"

"The same," Shamus said with a mark of pride.

"That's my favorite cereal!" the Hero squealed.

Shamus immediately began to think of a campaign of commercials starring Nuklear Man himself. He could assault the televisions and young minds of the world with an invincible sales icon!

Angus shook with rage, "It was my idea, ye fink-laddie!"

"Whoa, hold it," Atomik Lad halted their procession and quieted, at least temporarily, the bickering. "We've got some Kismet Krunchies back at the Silo. We can just run a sample of it through the molecular analyzer in our supercomputer and settle this once and for all."

The others were silent for almost a full minute as they mulled, compiled, considered, and generally pondered the suggestion.

"But," Shamus said. "Then it won't be a secret."

"Ah-ha! Why don't ye want to do it? Because ye koow ye ripped me off!'"

"All right! Let's get goin', if it'll be shuttin' ye up after all these years!"

Atomik Lad sighed a sigh of relief, "Finally."

"It's decided then," Nuklear Man said to once again assert himself as the alpha of this particular pack even if he was the only person who believed it. "To the Silo!" He posed purposefully, his cape billowed itself up a notch. "Ha-ho!"

"DWARF-A-PULT!"

"LEPRE-CANNON!"

"…Sheez."

✳   ✳   ✳   ✳

The four soared through the sky, though some did so more elegantly than others. Bumble bees shouldn't be able to fly according to the laws of Physics, yet they do. Angus only reinforced this sort of paradox. Apparently if you put enough thrust behind something, then it can sustain flight no matter how embarrassing it is. This was the case of Angus. That and more sound pollution than every one-hit wonder band simultaneously playing every non-hit they produced on every radio frequency at once.

They're Iron: Bagpipe Thrusters, people. They're *that* bad.

Shamus stayed aloft by aiming his Four Barreled Clover Cannon backwards and firing it whenever the momentum from the backlash began to drop which would cause him to do the same. This led to a very loud and clumsy flight.

Nuklear Man and Atomik Lad just flew. That's it.

The gleaming towers of steel and glass that made up the aesthetically pleasing Metroville cityscape fell behind them. The barren expanses of dirt that were the defining characteristics of Irradiated Flats, a great expanse of what used to be farmlands situated between Metroville and its Nuclear Power Plant, stretched out before them.

"Almost there," chimed Nuklear Man. He motioned to the brown and fetid fields below with a smile, "No yard work." He gave a wink to Shamus and Angus to indicate that he was a genius.

They followed Nuklear Man until he altered his course nearly ninety degrees straight down to a 50ft wide silvery metallic disk lodged in the ground with a big Nuklear style N painted on it. He made a little finger gun motion toward it. A hairline fracture appeared across the diameter and the disc split into two thick semi-circles that crept apart. The golden blur zipped between them just milliseconds after they were far enough apart to admit him without destroying anything.

Shamus and Angus decided it would be in their best interests to follow Atomik Lad who gradually decelerated as he made nice comfy circles, each spiraling a little lower than the last. Unfortunately, neither Angus's nor Shamus's modes of thrust were built with the kind of sophisticated instrumentation or, indeed, anything to make such a maneuver possible because both propulsion systems were intended to make short, fast, and potentially deadly human projectiles and not for long term flight. The gist of this is that both fell to the ground with all the grace of a skydiving humpback whale.

The two heavy **WHUMP**s sounded like two giant melons, or more accurately, two large sacks full of normal melons striking the hard, none-too-comforting ground. Atomik Lad gently floated into the fully opened entrance. It took a great deal of self control not to give them both biting quips but the memory of what Nuklear Man had endured from them earlier gave him the determination to let the moment pass.

"Lousy clear air turbulence," Angus grumbled just loud enough for Shamus to hear.

"Where'd you learn to fly, boy-o? Ye got me all caught up in ye backdraft," Shamus said.

"Come on fellahs!" Nuklear Man's voice had a distant metallic echo to it as he called to his comrades from within the depths of the Silo of Solitude.

Grudgingly, they stomped to the gaping hole and hopped inside, their respective modes of propulsion cushioned their descent. Machinery hummed as the doors began to close behind them.

Inside was a realm of wonder. The hideout was a huge cylinder about 50ft wide and several hundred feet down into the Earth. A cat walk wound up and down its interior wall. Things that wouldn't have seemed to serve any purpose at all if they weren't adorned with randomly blinking lights abounded. Doors labeled with titles like "Danger: Room" dotted the rounded walls. The entire complex had a feeling of being about a decade ahead of the rest of the world.

Shamus and Angus landed side by side at the very bottom of the complex in front of Nuklear Man. His arms were stretched wide as if to encompass the entirety of the grounds. Artificial lights flickered to life and the huge doors above them finally boomed to a close.

"Welcome to the Silo of Solitude," the Hero said proudly.

Atomik Lad stepped out of a door marked Danger: Kitchen holding a tray with cups on it, "Over-Aid?"

Angus shook his head "Nay" while Shamus motioned "Aye."

Nuklear Man smiled even wider, "Pretty cool, huh?"

"Well uh," the Iron Scotsman tugged at his armor's metallic beard. "It's not exactly very solitary if ye both live here." He sipped at his complimentary drink. It dribbled down his armor.

"Well not solitary in *that* sense," Nuklear Man said. "But living in the middle of the aftermath of the Dragon's Strike means there's the persistent threat of radiation poisoning that keeps the solicitors to a minimum."

"Yeah, twenty miles of irradiated ex-farmland will do that," Atomik Lad said. "Though we do get the occasional diehard," he added. "But the radiation doesn't bother Nuke or me because he absorbs it and I deflect it thanks to my Field. And you guys have those fully protective suits of armor, so we're safe."

Angus ripped off his dribbling helmet. "Enough with the science lesson!" he snorted. "Let's get on with testin' the haggis!"

"I be tellin' ye, it's not haggis!"

"Atomik Lad!" Nuklear Man barked as though several thousand lives depended on it. Hhe tried to evoke that effect with any order he gave, "Fetch the Kismet Krunchies and warm up the supercomputer!"

Atomik Lad shrugged and set the drink tray on a nearby table that was already cluttered with objects covered in lights that did a lot of blinking for no apparent reason, "Sure."

"Meanwhile," the Hero posed yet again. "I'll find out what the heck is going on with these two."

And so Shamus and Angus told unto Nuklear Man the story of their glory days.

*　　　*　　　*　　　*

Back in the wondrous days some call "the sixties" and others call "*ARGH!*" there were two close friends who just happened to be millionaires. To be honest, there was quite a bit more, but as far as this story goes these two are the only things we really have to worry about. The first was a Scottish cereal industrialist, Angus McDougal, while the second was an Irish industrial cerealist, Shamus O'Riley. The two pooled their talents and resources to create some of the most fascinating breakfast theory and sugar filled cereals known to man. Their ultimate creation, Seizure Pops, contained a reality breaking 112% sugar and put them on the map of breakfast food companies.

Then Angus had the idea of combining his proud and rich Scottish heritage with his proud and very rich cereal company. He hypothesized a new cereal, Scottish Squishies, with haggis as the main ingredient. He was immediately laughed out of the business. Shamus, wanting to help his friend, asked for the recipe to see what he might be able to do. Kismet Krunchies, featuring the secret ingredient known only as Kismet Green, hit supermarkets across the globe a year later. It met with even greater success than Seizure Pops had. Angus, convinced that Shamus had stolen his haggis idea, spent his savings to develop a powered suit of armor so that he could become an overpowered defender of the little guy. Literally.

The Iron Scotsman was born.

*   *   *   *

Atomik Lad sat in front of the computer monitor while clicking away at the keys and listening intently to the exposition as it wrapped up.

"All right," the sidekick said. "The results should be displayed any minute now."

Nuklear Man stood behind Atomik Lad and leaned down on the seat back, "What's it say, what's it say, what's it say?"

"Calm down."

"How did it know?"

"Shh."

Angus stood beside Atomik Lad. Shamus sipped on a cup of Over-Aid while gazing up the high hollow tower of the Silo.

"Hmm..." Atomik Lad said. "The computer is having trouble pinning it down. It's inorganic in origin," Atomik Lad noted from the results as they slowly scrolled up the screen.

"Sounds like haggis to me!" Angus said.

Atomik Lad's face flashed with surprise, "Rocket fuel?"

"No *wonder* it's so good!" Nuklear Man praised. He immediately stuffed a fistful of Krunchies into his mouth and crumbs cascaded down his body.

Angus wheeled around and stomped loudly to Shamus who was still examining the incredible height of the Silo's roof. Or the incredible depth of its floor, either way.

"Why didn't ye tell me after all these years?"

He faced his old friend, "You wouldn't let me. And would you be believin' me anyway?"

"No," Angus mumbled into his beard.

"And besides, the boy-o's in legal said it would be bad for business if anyone caught wind that Kismet Green was rocket fuel and not something a little more edible."

"But how?" Atomik Lad was beside himself. "Who…I…" he took a deep breath, "Why didn't anyone notice it was a powerful explosive and not some kind of sugar?"

"Well, when Angus gave me his recipe for Scottish Squishies we tried taste testin' it. When we told 'em it was made o' haggis, they either ran screaming or asked what haggis was and *then* ran screaming. This o' course was the normal response. But we couldn't exactly keep that up 'cause we would'a had to pay for stomach pumpings and probably get sued on top o' it. So I came up with the idea of makin' a cereal with an ordinary yet hideous ingredient and makin' it a secret for the cereal's gimmick. We couldn't use haggis, obviously. If anyone found out about it we'd be in a real mess. I came into a huge shipment of rocket fuel through my industrial ties, so I figured 'Feh, why not?' and tried it out," he chuckled to himself. "Guess it was the right choice, eh boy-o's? So you see, Angus? I didn't rip ye off. But ye always be yellin' and makin' a racket. Ye temper was always too much fer the cereal business."

All eyes were on Angus. His head hung and his shoulders slumped. "Aye, Ah now see Ah was tooo hard on ye, Shamus. Buut there's oone thing I wants to ask ye."

"Aye?"

"What be ye doin' in ye own power armor suit?"

"I can't be lyin' to ye, boy-o. I been keepin' up with ye overhero career, defending Scotland and the occasional bit o' Whales from villainy, founding the International Dwarven Warrior's Guild and so on. I been mighty jealous. So I had the boys down in R and D workin' for years to come up with me own powered suit based on yer design. I was g'tting' too old to run the company anyway, left it to me son, Patrick."

The two dwarves hugged one another in a very metallic and masculine showing of friendship, "Welcome to the overhero lifestyle, laddie," Angus said while they patted each other's back with little klong noises. Manly tears were very nearly shed.

"Come on, boy-o. Let's hit the town and get rip roarin' drunk, eh?"

"Aye!" He turned to his taller companions, "If'n ye be excusin' us, Nuuklear Man and Atomik Laddie. We gots thirty years o drinkin' to catch up on!"

"Of course, but—" Atomik Lad said.

"DWARF-A-PULT!!!"

"LEPRE-CANNON!!!"

"—don't you think we oughta open the doors first?" the sidekick finished.

KLANG!

KLONK!

Nuklear Man and Atomik Lad pried their vertically challenged partners from the Silo's roof and set them loose on the city. No bar, pub, or tavern would be safe from their drunken escapades. As for Nuklear Man and his sidekick, they retired to their sleeping quarters for a well deserved night's sleep.

Evil wakes up mighty early in the morning.

Issue 9—College Daze (It Is A Clever Play On Words!)

Atomik Lad awoke with a yawn and a stretch. He reached over and turned off his alarm clock two minutes before it would have gone mad with its screeching hell-beeps. He tossed the covers off and shambled into the shower. Once his daily cleansing ritual was complete, the sidekick covered his shame with a green towel and walked into the Danger: Kitchen. Nuklear Man had left a box of Kismet Krunchies on the Danger: Kitchen Table the night before. Atomik Lad pulled a bowl from one of the Danger: Cupboards and idly poured himself some cereal. He shoveled a spoonful and paused with it hovering before his lips.

"No milk," he said to the empty room like it was a verdict. It occurred to him that there had never been so much as a carton of milk in the Silo ever. This allowed him enough time to remember what he'd found out about Kismet Krunchies the night before. He dropped his spoon in the bowl and pushed it aside, "Maybe some waffles."

$$*\qquad*\qquad*\qquad*$$

Washing his Danger: Dishes, Atomik Lad noticed the Danger: Phone and cursed the day he bought Nuklear Man that label maker for Christmas.

"Hmmm...Christmas." He dried his hands, picked up the phone and dialed 123-MMMM.

RINNNNNG, RINNN—"Hello, Mighty Metallic Magno Man residence. If you are a villain, Press 1 now and stay on the line for further assistance. If you know the name of the villain committing the heinous crime you're calling about, Press 2 now. If you—"

"Norman?"

"Oh, that you Atomik Lad?"

"Yeah, what was that?"

"I love that joke, and it keeps the tele-marketers away. Aren't you supposed to be in school by now?"

"Nah, I've got a few minutes before I gotta go. I was just calling because Nuke got a weird note from someone claiming to be his father. It said 'Happy Birthday' and was signed 'Dad.'"

"Now that's weird. You worried it might be from some freaky stalker?"

"Not really. I mean, if the latent radiation around this place doesn't get him, one of Nuke's Plazma Beams would."

"True, true. So what's up?"

"I thought it would pretty cool if we could throw him a party tomorrow. He's never had one before, y'know."

"Sure. What'cha need?"

"I get out of class at 11 today, just Physics on Wednesdays. I thought we could hit the mall and find him a present."

"All right, I'm there. I'll meet you on campus around eleven."

"See you then, bye."

"This has been a recording. Click."

Atomik Lad shook his head and hung up the Danger: Phone. After cleaning the Danger: Sink, he suited up, snatched his *Physics: The Way Things Should Be* book, and shot out of the Silo's main doors with a smile.

✳   ✳   ✳   ✳

The cityscape rushed up to greet Atomik Lad like parents meeting their long lost child. He breathed deeply of the air rushing past him, roaring in his ears as his hair whipped against his forehead. He criss-crossed between austere buildings that refracted a hundred suns until the University of Metroville filled his sights. He landed with precision on the North Lawn and went into a jog towards Building Four, room 2A of the Tezuka Physics Complex.

The room was a large auditorium with a long chalkboard and desk at the front/bottom. Atomik Lad sat, as he always did in every class he had in his hero life, in an aisle seat near an exit. He did this to be able to rush out as efficiently as possible in case of any overheroic emergencies. He slouched in his seat, closed his eyes, and immersed himself in thoughts of what he and Norman might buy Nuklear Man.

"Hi there."

Could it be, "Rachel the waitress?" He sat up and smiled warmly without realizing it. "What are you doing here?"

She sat next to him, "Well you know how it is." She adopted a ditzy look, "Math is hard because I'm a girl. So I'm sleeping with Mr. Minkie to get a passing grade."

Atomik Lad laughed with her. "I just meant I've never noticed you were in this class."

She glanced at the totality of Atomik Lad, "We can't all wear full body spandex, it's against the dress code."

"It's not all it's cracked up to be. Terrible chaffing if you don't know what you're doing. Took me years to get it just right. It's an art."

She giggled, "I'll have to take your word on that."

"Um…" Atomik Lad began nervously. He had to talk before his brain caught up with what was happening and screw up everything. "When do you get out of class today?"

She answered with a grotesque exaggeration of a southern accent, "Why, Mr. Lad! I do believe you are tryin' to court me!"

"I can't waste any time. I'm a busy man."

She continued the southern belle impersonation and batted her eyelashes rapidly, "Oh, I bet you say that to all the girls."

"Yes, but I really only meant it just now. And call me John, it's my real name."

"All right, John. And to answer your question, I'm in class until six and then I'm working until eleven tonight."

"Oh."

"But tomorrow I'm free."

"Oh? How about coming with me to a party?"

"You don't strike me as the party type."

"I'm not, but this is for…a friend of mine."

"Well, as long as it's fun."

Atomik Lad thought about it for a minute. "I guarantee there won't be a dull moment. Does that count?"

"Close enough. I'll give you a call then, all right?"

"Very. The number is—"

"Let me guess. 123-4367."

"Yeah, how'd you know?"

"'HERO.' They taught us that with 9-1-2."

"Oh yeah, I guess they would."

Mr. Minkie walked into the auditorium. The chatter immediately dissipated.

"Class is starting. I'll call you tomorrow." She left Atomik Lad, his mouth agape, and winked before disappearing behind some last minute stragglers looking for a place to sit.

"I've got a date," Atomik Lad said to himself in blind comprehension of the moment.

The student in front of Atomik Lad turned around and whispered, "Welcome to real life, Mr. Smooth."

Atomik Lad playfully kicked at the seat back, "Aw shaddup, Alex."

"You're right. I oughta save my heckles for Mr. Minkie down there," he smiled a wry, devious smile and turned around to face the barren chalkboard.

*   *   *   *

Mr. Minkie meticulously laid his books, folders, papers, pens, pencils, and notes across the room's huge professor's desk as he did every Monday, Wednesday, and Friday at exactly 9:58 a.m. *Oh please*, he thought, *just one day without him.* He looked up slowly and apprehensively.

And there he was. In the same seat with the same "toodle-loo" wave and that same smile. *Why couldn't he alter his routine just* once?!

"All right, class," his small voice inched across the auditorium. Listening to him was like trying to fill an Olympic sized pool with a gallon of water, "Today we will go over the law of universal gravitation.

"Two objects will exert a certain gravitational attraction to one another depending on their masses and the distance between their centers of gravity squared." He began to write the equation on the center of his chalkboard and most of the students in the class numbly copied it into their notes for no better reason than it was on the board.

"The constant is called, surprisingly enough, the Universal Gravitational Constant. You multiply this by an object's mass, and you can find its force of gravity. Naturally, little masses, like us, cannot exert enough gravity to matter," he nervously laughed at his little nerd-pun, "It takes something truly enormous like moons, planets, and star to produce significant amounts of gravity."

"Excuse me," Alex said. The class waited. They were used to this.

Mr. Minkie pretended he hadn't heard. He was used to it too. "In fact, stars have so much gravity that the pressure at their center is enough to produce fusion which, well, that's another lesson altogether."

"Excuse me. Mr. Minkie, I have a question."

He leaned on the desk and rubbed his temples, "Yes, Mr. Halo, what is it now?" he answered without looking up.

"This gravitational constant is the same everywhere in the universe?"

"Yes, that is why we call it 'constant.'"

"And this is why Pluto moves about the Sun slower than Mercury?"

"Yes. Though they have roughly the same masses when compared to that of the Sun, Pluto's extreme distance causes it to orbit many times slower than Mercury according to our equation."

"So this sort of thing should happen in any system with objects in orbit? The stuff on the outer fringes moves slower."

"Naturally."

"Then how is it that the edges of galaxies move at exactly the same speed as a galaxy's center?"

Mr. Minkie sighed.

"And how can we make any predictions about the universe at all? We're only able to examine such a small percentage of the whole, we can't even be certain the rest exists until we observe it and even *then* it could all just be a shadow of a shared dream. And why should these hypothetical parts of creation obey a few patterns that we have observed to be true most of the time here?"

Mr. Minkie wished Alex would suffer a seizure right in the middle of class and lose every capacity of communication forever. It wasn't that he was a hateful or spiteful man, but he just wanted to get through one class without being attacked by new thoughts. "Mr. Halo, this is only a Physics 1 class. We are not here to solve the mysteries of the universe."

"I see. We're here to swallow the Man's lies of what he wants us to believe. The New World Order and all that."

"Yno! They aren't lies. They are the best we can do to describe the universe."

"What about Creationism? Pretty simple. No contradictions there."

"But there's no scientific proof to support Creationism."

"Some would say the universe is proof enough."

"Yes, but—no! No, this is not a philosophy class, this is a science class. The former is fanciful wondering at the world the way a child would. The latter is dignified, mature, measured, tested, rigid, and true. The two have nothing in common. Now may we continue, Mr. Halo?"

"By all means, I think we've made my point."

"Thank you," Mr. Minkie meant it more sincerely than Alex could have known.

Alex turned to Atomik Lad, "None of it's true, you know," gesturing to the Physics book.

It had occurred to the sidekick that sometimes it didn't make sense. But a deeper feeling always reassured him that it was supposed to and that was enough. The fact that he defied half the things in a Physics book on his way to class didn't help much though.

*   *   *   *

The vision was a dark one. A cave. A labyrinthine cave. Cold, damp, and lonely. If there was any light from the entrance, it had either faded long before it could reach him or it was blocked by something massive along the way. A foul smell, like a mixture of rotting flesh and stagnant acid, penetrated his senses.

"Nuklear Man," an echoing voice desperately pleaded from the cave's depths, "I haven't much strength, my son."

"Dad?"

"You must free me, son. Free me..."

"How? Where are you?"

"Can't...many names...Darkest corner, imprisoned...weakening..."

Nuklear Man's mind raced, which was surprising, but not so much that it distracted him from this link to his past. "Who am I? Where am I from?"

"Free...me..."

"Father!"

The vision faded. The Hero sat bolt right up in bed. He clapped the lights on and his familiar room was revealed. There was the Danger: Wall of Accomplishments wallpapered with news clippings of his adventures. His Danger: Vanity Mirror, his collection of Captain Liberty comic books, his Danger: Other Vanity Mirror, his Danger: Mini-Fridge, and his Danger: Other, Other Vanity Mirror.

He glanced at the Danger: Clock, "Ten?! Lousy subconscious wakin' me up early. What you do for Nukie? Hmmphf."

Nuklear Man silently floated out of bed, the futuristic **fwoosh** sound of the door-opening greeted his eardrums. Yawning, scratching, and several inches from the floor, he entered the Danger: Kitchen to pick up his box of Kismet Krunchies. He landed in a sitting position on the Danger: Couch in a blur. He propped up his feet on the Danger: Coffee Table and turned on the Danger: TV with a finger-gun motion and a masterful manipulation of his powers. He stuffed messy handfuls of Kismet Krunchies into his mouth that spilled crumbs all over himself. He chewed so loudly he could barely hear his cartoons. Click-Chew-Munch-Click-Chew-Munch Click-Chew-Mun—

A spider scurried between the Danger: TV and Danger: Coffee Table. Nuklear Man's eyes followed the arachnid invader until it slipped under a door aptly labeled Danger: Reactor Core. The warning had become somewhat cliché and obsolete in light of the vast abundance of Danger: Labels plastered all over the Silo.

"Heh, stupid bug. There's enough radiation in there to fry an elephant." He was about to stuff another fist full of Kismet Krunchies in his mouth when his sky-blue eyes drifted back to the Danger: Reactor Core. "Still. Couldn't hurt to kill it."

He set the cereal box down on its side which poured half its contents between the Danger: Couch cushions. He picked up one of his slippers and considered the bug-gut stain it would surely suffer. He dropped it in favor of one of Atomik Lad's slippers. Nuklear Man crept up to the Danger: Reactor Core entrance. Armed with only Atomik Lad's slipper and his Nuklear Boxers spotted with electron orbited hearts, he gripped the doorknob.

"One…two…five!" He threw open the door and jumped inside. It was complete darkness save for the light provided by the open door.

He clapped the lights on. Between the Danger: Reactor Core at the opposite wall and himself was the spider. The spider that now towered twenty feet high. Each of its eight legs was thicker than Nuklear Man's chest. It's bristly and greasy hairs glistened in the fluorescent lighting. It's huge fangs dripped with poison that dripped to the floor in sizzling pools of green goo.

It examined the golden morsel before it with a myriad of interested eyes.

"Um, shoo?" Nuklear Man swat one of the nearest legs with Atomik Lad's slipper. The Sinister Spider growled something that resembled the word "Food" far too much for Nuklear Man's comfort. It smacked the slipper from the Hero's grasp with one giant leg. Another enormous leg slammed the door behind Nuklear Man. The spider paused long enough for Nuklear Man to take in the horror of what was going to happen to him. The Beast clicked it's massive fangs together and darkness assaulted the Hero of heroes.

"Eeep."

Issue 10—GIANT RADIOACTIVE SPIDER MUTANTS! And the Mall.

Atomik Lad was staring out the window in a desperate attempt to keep himself awake despite Mr. Minkie's attempts at instruction. He watched the angular lines the cityscape carved into the sky. It intrigued him. He rarely had an opportunity to appreciate the city from this angle. It was usually rushing past him, or relegated to meaningless background information in the middle of some life or death struggle. But now, now he could sit back and just watch. There were the soft clouds, the gentle breeze that urged them on, the golden blaze that shot through it all with madly flailing arms.

He sighed and looked back at the chalkboard covered in arcane symbols. *At least Nuke'll be busy*, he thought.

*   *   *   *

The Cap'n Salty fishing boat chugged from its dock out to sea from the Metroville Harbor. The captain, a man who best looked of all the men of the Earth to be called "Cap'n Salty" but probably wasn't because of the stringent U.S. trademark laws, stood on the bow of his old ship with his first mate beside him. They stood in that silent awe of the sea that comes with becoming so intimately familiar with it.

"Nothing more calm than a morning on the ocean," the captain remarked.

"Nope."

"I've got a feelin' about this day, I do."

"Yep."

"I can't think of a single thing that could possibly go wrong."

"Nope."

"EEEEEEEEEEEEEWWWWWWWWWWWWWWWWWW!" The cry rang out like a siren. A golden blur shot like a bullet from the barren wastes of Irradiated Flats straight to the harbor. It impacted the sea and a great pillar of water exploded out of the sparkling waves. A torpedo rose and broke the surface. It cut through the water and sent a great rooster tail into the air with wafting mist and bubbling flotsam in its wake. "ARGH!!! GET IT OFF, GET IT OFF!" it screamed.

The Cap'n Salty boat bobbed in the waves as the water dervish ran through a wide circle in the harbor.

"This is gonna scare off the fish," the captain surmised at some length.

"GET IT OFF!!! EEEEWWWWEEEEARGH!"

The first mate wiped the fresh sea-mist from his face, "Yep."

*   *   *   *

Class ended after fifty minute-long eternities. Atomik Lad tried to find Rachel in the seething ocean of humanity as it flooded out of the classroom, but to no avail. He strolled through the campus's symmetrical lawn arrangements. Sidewalks sliced through them like veins pumping so much young blood to vital building-organs. "Yo, Atomik Lad!" Mighty Metallic Magno Man's voice was deep, like a resonating grand royal gong.

"Hey Norman," Atomik Lad trotted up to MMMM. He usually wore blue jeans, sunglasses, and a white tank top to contrast with his black skin while showing off enough of the "Norminator" that he didn't feel the need to try to impress passersby with his physique. They were plenty impressed all on their own. And today was no exception.

Atomik Lad stood a full foot shorter than Norman who was even taller and more muscle bound than Nuklear Man himself. Standing next to each other, Norman and Atomik Lad looked like the co-stars of some wacky and particularly ill-thought out buddy comedy.

"To the Magnomobile!" Atomik Lad gestured with an exaggerated impersonation of Nuklear Man's voice.

MMMM laughed and walked Atomik Lad to the "Magnomobile". Luckily, it was stowed in one of the closer parking lots. And there it was: a large convertible Cadillac with a bright, sparkling metallic purple paint job. It was the envy of all who looked upon it.

*   *   *   *

Nuklear Man gasped desperately as he floated among the waves. The battle had been a fierce one.

The Golden Guardian thought he had read somewhere that spiders could only distinguish between light and dark. Since the Sinister Spider had clapped off the lights and the Danger: Reactor Core was thus enshrouded in darkness, Nuklear Man was certain he had the advantage.

He changed his mind when the spider pinned him against a wall and covered him in a cocoon of super tough mutant spider webbing. He struggled against his bonds until he remembered that whole "Plazma Power" thing and burst from the disgusting secretion with a flash of fusion light.

It was like the flash to the camera of Nuklear Man's mind. That brief moment an burned a horrible image into his brain: the spider hovering over him. What happened next made him very happy that he couldn't see a thing. He felt the huge fangs grapple his shoulders and shove him, head first, into the spider's gaping maw. He was forced into the arachnid's gut. He could feel the esophageal muscles pulsating to squeeze him down the tract. It was less pleasant than it sounds. He heard and felt a burp from the inside. Nuklear Man sat in the belly of the whale of a spider for exactly 1.2 moments before freaking out, though he'd later refer to it as a "strategically random outbreak of violence." Heroes simply do not "freak out."

The spider felt a rumbling in its gut. It thought that perhaps humans were too spicy to be eaten whole and considered merely tearing them to shreds when it went on its rampage. It gave out a pained moan as the warm sensation took on a level of severe heartburn before finally reaching all out lava-like proportions. It could smell and taste burning spider flesh from inside itself. This didn't worry it as much as it perhaps should have, but how was it supposed to know what its own insides tasted like? All its liquids spontaneously vaporized from the intense internal heat.

This had several effects.

1) Steam takes up much more volume than the water it comes from.

2) This caused an explosion that shattered the spider's exoskeleton and released hundreds of pounds of cooked splattering spider guts all over the Danger: Reactor Core.

3) That's really disgusting

4) Nuklear Man clapped the lights back on to only confirm by sight what he knew by touch. Hhe was standing in the cracked open spider's shell and covered in gooey spider organs from head to toe.

With a girlish—yet Heroic—shriek, he bolted out of the Danger: Reactor Core and tunneled through hundreds of feet of rock before bursting from the earth covered with spider innards that were themselves covered with dirt. A mess of epic proportions needed a bathtub equal to the task and so he sought the ocean. After zooming around and around the water at speeds in excess of 800 mph, he at last floated calmly on the water's still roilingsurface. He was exhausted from the cleansing and hoped he'd never had to think about the spider again.

*   *   *   *

Mighty Metallic Magno Man drove through the streets of Metroville while Atomik Lad leaned back in the passenger seat. City traffic perplexed Atomik Lad to no end. He'd been a strong proponet of the idea that if God had intended overheroes to drive, he wouldn't have let them fly. Unlike Atomik Lad, Magno Man came into his powers relatively late in his life, so he still considered the act of flight to be something that you saved for work. Even when he took to the skies, he'd be low about it. Atomik Lad just sat back, took in the pleasures of excessive leg room, tried not to think about the horrible anarchy around him. It seemed to Atomik Lad that lanes had been relegated to the status of suggestion some generations ago. He assured himself there was something like a system at work, or else the entire city would grind to a halt of scrap metal as every vehicle collided into those around it.

"This is the life, Norman," Atomik Lad said with a smile too big for his head.

"Yeah, it's a pretty sweet gig."

"Hey, I didn't tell you yet, I've got a date to Nuke's party."

"Awright! Working that ol' Atomik Mojo, huh?"

"I wouldn't say that."

"Oh?"

"Nah, it's my natural charm. It's a curse."

"Whoa, excuse me, Dr. Love," Norman said with a chuckle as Atomik Lad basked in a few minutes of normality.

*   *   *   *

Nuklear Man felt calm, serene, pristine, free. Very, *very* free.
Too free.
"My Over-roos! They're...they're gone!"
He ducked underwater, shot into the air, and hurtled toward the Silo as fast as he could. *Gotta fly faster than I've ever flown before!* he thought to himself. Truth be told, however, he was a good forty miles per hour slower than his Earthbound top speed.

*   *   *   *

The Tungsten Titan and Atomik Lad strolled through the wide alleys of the largest mall on the face of the Earth: The Metroville Mall. The Mecca of Shopping. A cult, the exact size of which was under debate, was believed to bow west four times a day in honor of its Biblical importance to capitalism. The Metroville Mall seemed to exist in a reality all its own. A very manicured reality that hadn't yet invented dirt.
"So what do you think we should get him?" Norman asked as they walked among shoppers and shops.
"I don't know. He's so hard to shop for," Atomik Lad said.
"Does he need anything?"
Atomik Lad stopped and thought. "Nothing with repeatable uses."
Norman nodded in agreement. "Oh yeah, the Label Maker incident."
"You know I had 'Danger: Sidekick' on the back of my outfit for a week before I noticed it?"
"Hmm. Well who else is gonna be there?"
"You, me, Rachel, Angus, and Dr. Genius if we can get her out of the lab. Oh, and I was thinking about inviting The Minimum Wage Warriors."   ·
"Nah, they gotta work weekdays."
"Guess you're right. Just us then." They continued their walk down the endless road of entrepreneurialism. "Hey, where do you think we should have the party?"

"I like the beach," Norman said. "Ooh, especially Larsen Beach. Lots of sun and lots of chicks. And according to the weatherman, tomorrow's waves are going to be sweetah!"

"Sounds like a plan."

Norman nudged Atomik Lad in the side, which had the effect of nearly knocking him over. "Even get to see this Rachel of yours in a swimsuit."

Atomik Lad's retort was interrupted by another retort from behind, "Hold it right there, Mr. Muscle-Oil and Spandex Kid."

The heroes spun around and faced a motley group of seven individuals who, judging by their outfits and demeanors, must've thought of themselves as villains. The Heroic reflexively jumped into defensive stances. The rest of The Mall seemed strangely empty of the thousands of shoppers it usually contained at this time of day. Atomik Lad could feel it. A showdown was a-brewin'.

"What are you guys supposed to be?" Atomik Lad asked.

A wiry man stood in front of the other six. He was clearly the leader, though it seemed to Atomik Lad that he attained that lofty position by being the only member of the team with enough petty ambition to take it. "Allow me to introduce us." He pointed to a rocky mammoth of a man, "This is Granite, the Mammon Mauler. He can turn his body to pure stone, as you can see, and has the powers to control the very elements of earth. Very messy. And evil!"

He gestured to an anthropomorphic feline, "Meet Zeeroks, the Copy Cat. She can mimic any overpower she sees and is a master of disguise." She changed her body to living stone and back again to emphasize the point.

He motioned to what looked like a very militant Porky Pig dressed in combat fatigues. Bandoleers of ammo were slung around his small body, "This is El Puerko, the Savage Swine. He's a Central American revolutionary and has more weapons in his personal stockade than most countries." He oinked irritably.

"This," he signaled to a dark corner, "is Okenshi, the Nasty Ninja. His combat skills and clandestine abilities are unmatched." Okenshi remained completely invisible to punctuate the greatness of his skill. Unfortunately, it wasn't easy to observe him being impossible to see, so he merely managed to punctuate the moment with the awkward silence of his absence.

Almost under his breath the leader said, "And here's Chronotor and Lord Obese."

"Wait. What do they do?" Mighty Metallic Magno Man asked.

A disgustingly enormous girth of humanity stood behind the others and burped, "I am Lord Obese, the Rotund Raider!"

"And?" Atomik Lad pressed on.

"And I'm really bitter about it so watch out!"

The sidekick backed up a step. "Okaaay."

A man wearing nothing but watches of various designs wrapped around his limbs and body with a large wall clock mounted on his chest jumped forth. "I am Chronotor," he said among a cacophony of little watch ticks, tocks, bells, and whistles. "The Temporal Terror! I have the power to mess with the time displayed on clocks!"

Mighty Metallic Magno Man gave an unimpressed, "Pfffff! Is that it?"

Chronotor grinned madly.

Norman could feel a tingle on his left wrist. "Hey!" The hands of his watch were spinning out of control. "That's not funny, cut it out! I could be late!"

"And I am," the evil introducer said without regard to what was going on between Chronotor and the Tungsten Titan, "Blazer, the Photon Felon! I have the power to shoot really neat purple energy beams from my eyes!" He, of course, neglected to mention that using the power blinded him which made it, at best, an exercise in futility to hit a moving target. "Collectively, we are known as The Socially Maladjusted Overvillains Who Can't Agree on a Name!" he said in all seriousness.

"I thought we decided on 'Malcontent.'"

"Yeah, 'maladjusted' makes us sound like fuggin' weirdoes."

"Shut up," Blazer said.

"It's too long anyway. Why not 'The Sinister Septet?'"

"That's too elitist. Most people don't know septet stands for seven. They'd be confused."

"No, septet is six. Heptet is seven."

"That just proves my point then."

"Shut up!" demanded Blazer.

"It'll never fit on a T-shirt."

"Ooh! How about an acronym?"

"I'm hungry."

"You're always hungry."

"An acronym, eh? So that would be, what? The 'T-S-M-S-W-C-A-O-A-N?'"

"The TSMSWCAOAN? That doesn't make any sense and it's still too long to fit on a T-shirt."

Blazer turned to face his gang and roared, "Would all of you just shut up and let me do the talking?! This is why we elected me leader! To avoid these embarrassing arguments! No one's going to take us seriously if we can't show some real initiative." His underlings quieted their prattling. "Finally. Now then, Mighty Metallic Magno Man and Atomi—*hey!*"

"Looks like they got away, boss," Granite said.

"Amazing observation, Granite. Now I know why we keep you around."

"Shucks, boss. Twern't nuthin."

"Shut up!" Blazer pondered quietly while his gang looked on. "No matter. We know where they plan to have this birthday party of theirs." He rubbed his hands together maniacally. "I think we will have to make an unexpected appearance. MUWA HAHAHAHAHA!!!"

"But we weren't invited."

"Yeah, it'd be rude of us to just show up like that."

Blazer turned to his rabble of ruffians. "You just don't get it, do you?"

✳   ✳   ✳   ✳

Nuklear Man, fully dressed in classy spandex and ever-billowing cape, confidently strode from his Danger: Nuke's Room into the Danger: Living Room. He crept as silently as he could to the Danger: Reactor Core.

WHAM!

"YEOWCH!" He rubbed his head as he lay on the floor. He looked behind him at the overturned couch, "Stupid Danger: Couch always jumpin' out in front of me. Hmmphf!" The Hero crawled to the Danger: Reactor Core. He creaked open the door and leapt inside, "EAT THE CLEANSING POWER OF SWEET PLAZMA PURIFICATION, YOU GOOEY DISGUSTING SLOP!"

An aura of Plazma burned around him. Bright globes of energy roiled around his clenched fists. His cape flapped madly to get away from the random acts of violence that certainly lay ahead. But then his scowl of determination melted into the stare of "Huh?" he usually wore. There were no Giant Spider-guts splattered about the floor, roof, or walls. There was no cracked open Giant Spider exoskeleton and the smell was all but gone. Nuklear Man's flashy special effects subsided, much to the relief of his cape which calmly fluttered to a more relaxed—yet ever so slightly billowing—position.

"Hmm. Must be one of those new self-cleaning Danger: Reactor Cores," he surmised. He stepped back into the Danger: Living Room and shut the door behind him. "GASP! Almost time for Silly Sam's Cartoon Marathon-a-thon o' Fun!" He gracefully jumped onto the couch.

WHAM!

"YEOWCH!!! Stupid Danger: Couch always jumpin' outta my way. Hmmphf!" He overturned furniture and reclined across it. Childish glee coursed through him at the mere thought of the cartoons that were to come.

A small arachnid hovered in the darkness of the Danger: Reactor Core. It was suspended by a thin strand of its own making that was nigh impossible to see in the bleak darkness. Another descended, and another and another. Thousands of the minuscule creatures hung from the roof. And waited.

Issue 11—The Lost Tribe of Arachnor

"Man, what was their deal?" Atomik Lad brushed his fingers through his wavy hair to push an unruly section out of his eyes.

"Feh, who cares?" Norman said. "I don't think we'll be seeing much of those guys anyway. They didn't seem to have their act together, if you know what I mean."

"Yeah, they sure were losers."

Norman looked at his watch. "Still, I'm all screwed up over here. What time is it?"

"I don't know, must be eleven thirty-ish."

The Tungsten Titan stopped to wind his watch. Meanwhile Atomik Lad idly scanned the ambient shoppers.

The hero looked up from his watch winding. "Stupid watch-guy. What kind of power is that anyway? 'Ooh, look out, I can mess with your watch!'"

"More annoying than damaging, really."

"Hey," Norman pointed to the pet store that happened to be in front of them. A variety of cute animals napped at them from behind the large store window. "How about a pet?"

"A pet?"

"Yeah, like a cat."

"A cat?"

"What's wrong?"

"I'm afraid he'd call it 'Der Wunder Kat' and force it to wear a cape or something equally inhumane. We'd have the animal rights people all over us."

"Oh. Yeah you do have a point there."

✻   ✻   ✻   ✻

Nuklear Man was intently watching some intellectual programming on the Danger: TV while sprawled across his Danger: Couch.

"And now, back to Silly Sam's Cartoon Marathon-a-thon o' Fun!" the show's announcer, as per his contract and title, announced.

A shadow crept across the Danger: Floor. A small, elongated shadow flickering from the Danger: TV's glow. It scuttled from under the Danger: Reactor Core's door to the back of the Danger: Couch and stopped. It made a motion. Perhaps the flick of an armored leg, the twitch of a poison dripping fang, or maybe a summons...?

Another shadow darted across the floor from the Danger: Reactor Core. It was followed by yet another and another until the silvery tiles of the Danger: Floor were carpeted in twitching shadows. The mass stretched out to encompass the Danger: Couch and waited as one for the Time of Vengeance.

"Stupid commercials," the Hero muttered under his breath. "Your mind control won't work on me, vile Hammer of Capitalism." He made a finger gun motion at the Danger: TV that muted the volume.

Unfortunately sound wasn't the method of mind control this particular commercial employed. A close up of a slowly revolving and succulent Cow Butt Burger Hutt "Everything but the Tail™" Triple Quarter-Pounder Bacon Cheese Burger filled the screen. "You filthy *bastards!*" Nuklear Man spat.

He sat up like a mummy rising from its sarcophagus. His feet touched the ground, the shadowy mass melted away to avoid him. It was not quite time to strike. This was Vengeance with a capital V. It had to be done right.

Nuklear Man felt a tingle crawl up his leg. It stopped at his knee and he swore he could hear someone clearing his throat. A small spider sat on his Heroic knee. "Bug" he told it.

"Flesh-sack," it responded, much to Nuklear Man's complete and utter terror.

"Ack!" He instinctively brought a mighty finger to the arachnid to flick it away.

Somewhere, somehow, the transaction of kinetic energy and momentum had gone terribly awry. In a flash of confusion he was on his back between the Danger: Couch and the Danger: Coffee Table. He was surrounded by a sea of shadow.

*   *   *   *

"Maybe a video game system?"

"No, he's still trying to figure out Pong."

"Now, c'mon. Even Nuke isn't that slow."

"It's not that. He can't get past picking Player 1 or Player 2."

"What do you mean?"

"He says he can't tell which is the hero and which is the villain."

"Ah. Yeah. I guess he would, wouldn't he."

*   *   *   *

"I am Alan, chieftain of the Children of Arachnor, and now is the Time for Vengeance against you, the Destroyer!" their leader cried from atop the Danger: Coffee Table.

"Vengeance?" Nuklear Man asked like he had no idea what was going on. Mainly because he didn't.

"Don't play stupid with us!" Alan snapped. Before the Hero could respond with the traditional Who's playing? line, the spider continued. "We know what you did to Larry!"

"Larry?"

"Larry" he repeated.

"Was that the guy whose car I blew up by accident when I blasted Mechanikill?"

"No, he was—"

"The little boy I skipped in the Cow Butt Burger Hutt line?"

"*No!* He was—"

"The leader of those cheese people I sneezed into oblivion? You kinda remind me of him."

"*Shut up*, you bipedal buffoon! Larry was our patron god and creator, Arachnor!"

"I thought you said his name was Larry."

"Well yes, his name was Larry, but that's not exactly a striking and powerful name for a god, now is it? So Arachnor is mostly a title for effect."

"I see."

"I mean, I'm certain your name isn't really Nuklear Man, right?"

"Well, actually it is."

"Enough of your stalling, endoskeletal bag! Now is the Time for Retribution."

"I thought you said it was the 'Time for Vengeance.'"

"Well, yes. The Time of Retribution is right after the Time of Vengeance while the sun in is the fourth house of—I don't have to explain our time keeping methodology to the likes of you!"

"Just askin', sheesh."

"You slew the great Arachnor, Lord of the Spiders, our master, our patron god and creator."

"Yeah, you mentioned that."

"And in the throes of death, he gave birth to us, his Chosen, who exist for a single purpose."

"And that purpose would be...?"

"*To avenge our master's death!*"

"And you're going to do that how, exactly?"

"You shall be devoured by our ten-thousand maws, hungering for your blood, Anti-Arachnor."

"I see."

*　　*　　*　　*

"A book?"

Atomik Lad didn't dignify him with an answer.

Norman scratched his nose. "Right. How about a movie?"

"Nuke's attention span isn't exactly built to endure a movie. And it doesn't help that his daily life and over active imagination are more exciting than most movies anyway."

"He collects comic books, doesn't he?"

"Yeah, but he only gets *Captain Liberty and the Squad of Diplomatic Immunity* comics and they canceled those after the Dragon's Strike."

"A CD?"

"I'm not putting up with 'Polkarama' again."

Norman grimaced. "Ooh. Yeah, that musta been rough."

Atomik Lad's face became a sullen mask. "You have no idea."

*   *   *   *

"But let it not be said that we are not a civilized race," Alan said while pacing across the Danger: Coffee Table. "You may have one last request."

"Uh. Don't kill me?"

Alan took several steps back in alarm. "Er…"

"Well, you *did* offer me one."

"Yes, but I didn't think you'd ask for that! I was thinking more along the lines of a final meal or something."

Nuklear Man sat up with his back against the Danger: Couch. "Feh, guess you weren't thinking much at all."

"Aww, c'mon," the spider pleaded. "No one uses 'don't kill me' as their last request!"

"That's because they don't have the benefits of *my* Nuklear Intelligence," he said in a haughty tone. And while this was true, most people probably wouldn't think it to be detrimental to be without it.

"It's an unwritten code of the last request!" Alan half yelled. "You just don't ask not to be killed! That's not how it works! If that's allowed, then the entire practice of last request becomes pointless!"

"You asked for a last request. I requested not to be killed. The end," the Hero said. He crossed his mighty arms over his barrel chest.

Waves of dissent rippled through the shadow sea of spiders. Their leader darted his complex eyes nervously as he realized what was going to happen. It was law. The same law that demanded they avenge the death of their god. The same law that required they kill anything that impaired that avenge…ance. Alan backed away from the mob of his followers.

"You've bungled our plans for the last time, Alan!"

"Steve, my most trusted advisor? How could you?"

Another spider spoke up, "Don't use your petty nostalgia on us, Alan. You have failed our mission of holy vengeance. And now, as it is written in the Book of Arachnor, you must pay!"

Alan turned dramatically to the new voice, "Et tu, Tom-ey?"

The sea of shadow rose against its leader with a barbaric ferocity. They flowed up the Danger: Coffee Table and devoured Alan. The Law of Arachnor would allow nothing less. Alan's final tortured scream clung at Nuklear Man's heart the way Hunger clung at his stomach. At long last, Alan released his grip on mortality and plunged into the darkness eternal.

Or wherever dead spiders go.

Hunger, on the other hand, latched at the Hero's stomach as staunchly as ever.

Nuklear Man contemplated Alan, his position of power, his responsibilities, his tormented demise. "Ew."

"Judge us not, puny creature. I, Steve, proclaim that on this day, the Children of Arachnor shall have their revenge!"

Not aware of how totalitarian governments work, Nuklear Man asked, "Hey, who made you head-spider?"

Steve mumbled his response, "Well, er...I mean. You know, I led the revolution against Alan. Sort of. It only makes sense I should take his place as dictator."

"I would have liked to proclaim this day the revenge of Arachnor's children," Tom pouted.

"Tom? You're just a treasurer! I've been Alan's top advisor from the beginning. I have the experience to lead. Stick to the books, number-bug."

"Excuse me," Nuklear Man interrupted. "But if you were Alan's advisor, and Alan was found to be unfit to lead, then isn't his cabinet unfit to lead by extension?" he commented in a strangely lucid moment.

"He's got a point," Tom said while rubbing what the Golden Guardian could only assume was the spider's chin.

"What?! You're agreeing with the Destroyer, the sworn enemy of our race!?"

"Maybe you guys could set up some form of democracy?" Nuklear Man suggested. "A parliament or something."

"I found our old system of government rather oppressive," a faceless spider said from the sea of shadow. He received murmurs of consent and dissent from his companions.

"'*Old* system?'" Steve blurt. "There is no 'old system!' What are you thinking?! You are following the heresy of the Anti-Arachnor!"

Tom rose up proudly. "This is our chance to end the tyrannical reign of one spider over many! A government of the spiders and for the spiders!"

"Hmmm..." Nuklear Man thought aloud, "Someone ought to do that for us humans."

Cries rang from the spider sea, "Hurrah! Down with the establishment!"

"Heretics!"

"Viva la freedom!"

"Do not follow the words of the Destroyer!"

*   *   *   *

"How about a set of towels? We could emboss them with that 'N' thing of his," Norman said while drawing a little "N" in the air.

"Ah, no. Nuke doesn't trust towels."

Norman had no idea how to answer and simply stared at Atomik Lad.

"I don't know either."

"Well, then how does he dry off?"

"He uses his, and I quote, 'Evap-o Plazma.'"

"How very strange."

"Trust me. You don't know the half of it."

*   *   *   *

Nuklear Man stood and dusted himself off as the spiders divided into two groups. Arachnor's Chosen, led by Steve and the second, The Spider's Front of Arachnopodia, rallied behind Tom. Banners rose, speeches were made, battle cries erupted, threats were hurled, and the air filled with the smell of battle to come.

"Ahem," Nuklear Man ahem-ed loud enough to overcome the signs of war that were spreading like wildfire on his Danger: Coffee Table. Both armies stopped and stared at the Golden Guardian that towered over them. "Could you guys take your little war somewhere else? It'll mess up the furniture and I'm trying to watch TV."

Each camp dispatched a diplomat that approached Nuklear Man.

"We are dignitaries, an impartial negotiation party, to decide a battlefield for our war," one informed the Hero as the other spider nodded in agreement.

"Uh. Yyou could use that Danger: Storage Room," he said, pointing to a nearby door aptly labeled Danger: Storage Room. "Sparky emptied it out last Spring. He said we didn't need ten-thousand 20 Watt light bulbs. Go figure. I just let him have his way. He gets a little weird about some things, if you know what I mean."

"Thank you, Destroyer. We will wage our war in this 'Danger: Storage Room' of yours," the second spider said cordially with a little spider-style bow.

"Glad to be of service."

"And when we establish a stable government, we will hunt you down and we will devour you," the first stated matter-of-factly.

"Oh. Well, um. Thanks?"

The two spiders scuttled back to their respective camps. Within a minute, both mighty armies marched to the Danger: Storage Room. Nuklear Man held the futuristic automatic sliding door open until the final spider-soldier had entered. "Good luck with your little battle for supremacy," Nuklear Man cheerily said as he waved.

"Death to the Destroyer's minions!"

"End the Orwellian domination of Arachnor's pawns!"

The door **FWOOSH**ed shut and cut off the crossfire of taunts.

The Hero sought out his favorite gift: the Quick-B-Labeled. What once was the Danger: Storage Room became the Danger: Religious Differences.

Nuklear Man, the Golden Guardian, the Hero of heroes, the Earth's greatest and mightiest champion, then collapsed on his Danger: Couch and watched the gripping conclusion to Silly Sam's Cartoon Marathon-a-thon o' Fun.

Issue 12—They, Robots

A couple hours later the sparkling pimp-daddy purple Magnomobile screeched to a halt outside the circular main doors of the Silo of Solitude embedded in the sweet and only slightly radioactive earth.

Atomik Lad got out of the car, "See you tomorrow at Larsen Beach."

"Right, at 11:00. You just make sure he gets there."

"That shouldn't be a problem." He waved as the Tungsten Titan turned his car around and zoomed off with a large cardboard box sticking out of trunk with the "This End Up" arrow pointing to the right.

*   *   *   *

Nuklear Man wallowed.

He wallowed in filth, junk food wrappers that looked like they'd been torn apart by some ferocious beast of consumption, the crumbs of said junk food, junk food yet attacked, soda cans in various stages of emptiness, magazines one would normally only associate with teenage girls, reprints of *Captain Liberty and the Squad of Diplomatic Immunity* comics, and several boxes of Kleenex. Nuklear Man wallowed with such perfection to the art, and it is an art, that he didn't notice when the walls hummed as the Danger: Main Doors opened or when the sun bathed his wallowing in noonday light, and, in fact, barely noticed Atomik Lad standing over him with that "Again?" look.

"Er…" the Golden Guardian eloquently explained as he shifted his girth and caused a small junk food avalanche in the process. "I bet you're wondering what this is all about."

Atomik Lad didn't move for that exact amount of time it would take the laugh track to die down on a poorly written sitcom. "Oh yes."

"Well, I was watching Silly Sam's Cartoon Marathon-a-thon o' Fun, like I do every morning."

"Naturally."

"And then Days of Our Generally Bold Lives in Another Beautiful Hospital World came on." Atomik Lad nodded. "How could Celeste do that to poor Drake!?!" he blubbered and reached for another handful of tissue paper.

"Well that explains the Kleenex."

Nuklear Man blew his nose with a distinct **HONK**, "And Carl **SNURK**. He's new, how was he supposed to know about Victoria's conniving against Bill? He's an innocent pawn in the game of chess that is Days of Our Generally Bold Lives in Another Beautiful Hospital World!"

Atomik Lad shook his head. His face was filled with disapproval. "And to think they call you 'Hero.'"

"They don't know the horrible truth," he responded meekly.

"It would turn their stomachs."

"I'm a pathetic slob!" Nuklear Man blurted through his stream of sympathy tears.

Atomik Lad squat down and picked up a soda stained, junk food covered magazine. He bent a curious eyebrow while examining the cover. "Teeny Bopper Dreamboat Weekly?"

"Uh…" Nuklear Man's sobs stopped like a heart attack.

"An Interview with the Manson Dreamboat Trio?"

"Um. Is this one of those things that's so weird you'd rather not hear the explanation?"

"No, I think I have to know."

"Nuts."

"Uh-huh."

"Well, you know as a Hero I have a responsibility to look as good as possible."

Atomik Lad idly thumbed through the publication, "Of course."

"I picked up some of those magazines to scope out the up and coming competition, such as it is. So, you can see how it's perfectly normal for me to have those and not strange. Right?"

"But the average age of the readers of these things is something like fourteen."

"I've got to keep up with the times. Look to the future and all that."

"Hmm. This oldest Manson kid kinda looks like me."

"Lucky duck!"

Atomik Lad's quizzical look was all the inquiry required.

"Well, you know. Because girls think he's cute."

"Fourteen year old girls, Nuke. Though it should go without saying, that's just sort of wrong. Besides, they'd think that goth Harriet Hanson freak was a dreamboat if he sung vapid lyrics about girls and homework or *whatever* it is soulless media machines sing about."

"So you think that would work for us?"

"I don't think we have to stoop to their level."

"Feh! Easy for you to say, Mr. Look-a-like."

Atomik Lad sighed and set his *Physics: The Way Things Should Be* book on the wallow-waste-product-laden Danger: Coffee Table. He looked to what should have been the Danger: Storage Room but noticed the old label had a new one proclaiming Danger: Religious Differences pasted over it. In light of the slovenly state of the Danger: Living Room, he thought it best to ignore the nomenclature until later. "Just have this mess cleaned up. I'll be in my room."

"Stupid mess," Nuklear Man muttered. He kicked at the mound of filth he'd acquired over the few hours. He scanned his environs for a scapegoat to delegate the work to. Alas, with the closing **FWOOSH** of the Danger: Sparky's Room door, the Hero was alone.

*   *   *   *

Nuklear Man slowly surfaced from the Danger: Main Entrance as if burdened by some incredible weight. And rightfully so because he heaved an enormous garbage bag behind him that was as wide as the Silo. The Hero majestically rose with his massive cargo…until it got stuck and plugged the Silo shut.

"Hmmm. Dimension trouble." he surmised.

*   *   *   *

Atomik Lad raced down the streets of San Diego's Balboa Park in his custom built Folkswagon Gnat. It sported a crimson paint job with neato blue racing stripes that almost perfectly matched the color scheme of his spandex. The ordinarily crowded streets were empty save for a few cars driving in excess of 120 mph, the sidekick included.

"Out of the way, grandma!" he yelled while zipping across the median into lanes of oncoming traffic. It was faster that way.

A sharp left turn was ahead. He was going at least 130 mph. A fiery wreck was the only fate available to him. "What is that smell?" he asked himself. Atomik Lad's sporty car halted its fatal tumble through the air mere inches from impacting a nondescript building as "Pause" blinked across the screen. "Door, open."

Nothing.

Atomik Lad sighed with the weight of defeat. "Danger: Door, open." The futuristic **FWOOSH** sound announced his door's obedience.

"Nuke!" he called out.

Nuklear Man was deaf to his sidekick. There was simply too much Danger: Filth stuck in the Danger: Main Doors between himself and the Silo for any amount of sound to get through.

Atomik Lad stalked out of his room and stopped short halfway out the door. "Where is everything?"

The Danger: Living Room was completely empty. Even the blinking lights that should've been all over the walls were gone. For the briefest second he suspected the Pearly Gate cult had gotten a stranglehold on the Hero yet again. But an acrid smell scarred off the thought like a skunk's enemy. He glanced at the Danger: Main Doors. In their place he saw a great stinking garbage bag wedged into the entrance far above. It was labeled "Danger: Filth."

"What has he done now?"

*   *   *   *

Nuklear Man had dragged the open end of the garbage bag across the sparse vegetation that surrounded the Silo. He tugged a tug that tugged itself into a full blown heave. His feet dug into the ground and two small plumes of dust flew along the earth. He left the ground and flew straight up with all the force of a rocket launch.

And then his labor came to fruition. The garbage bag felt weightless. He was too occupied with basking in the glory of a job well done to notice the clouds falling under him or the atmosphere yielding to the eternal void of space.

*   *   *   *

A few moments ago.

"*Nuke*! What are you doing?" Atomik Lad yelled for the third time. He heard the bag's cramped contents clank and grind against one another as some unseen force, undoubtedly Nuklear Man.

The monstrous bag lurched upward very slightly and Atomik Lad thought his mentor had finally loosened it. His eyes grew wide as a great chasm tore itself across the bag's bottom. His Atomik Field kicked in reflexively and he was covered in a shower of wallow-filth and Danger: Furniture.

*   *   *   *

Nuklear Man, now in low orbit, gazed into the garbage bag he held in his hands. "Oopsie." He could see right through it thanks to the giant gaping hole at the other side. "What a wussy trash bag! Strange...I can't hear myself talk. *Hello*?!? I've gone deef! How could this have happened?!?" He thought back to what had just transpired.

He remembered tugging.

He remembered *more* tugging.

He remembered ice cream.

And he remembered that same roaring sound he heard whenever he reached escape velocity.

"Could it be," he theorized, "that the garbage bag exploded on purpose to make me deef? You deefed me!" he soundlessly screamed to the bag, shaking it violently as it whipped and waved in the solar wind. "I'll show you, stupid deefing bag!"

He crumpled it into a small ball and hurled it into the sun. "And I hope you think about what you've done!" He dusted off his hands because he knew from extensive Heroics that was the sort of thing one did following a manual solar launch. "Better get back before Sparky suspects anything."

As Nuklear Man careened Earthward something not unlike a silvery plate with far too many lights and buttons all over it spun through space unnoticed by all but the reading audience. It tumbled out of the garbage bag. It was a Cultural Archive Device manufactured by Überdyne. A learning tool programmed with several sets of encyclopedia, dictionaries, works of literature, philosophy, and history, all with complete audio and visual interaction. They were used for a short period of time as devices to help amnesiacs regain their memories. This particular one focused on the 20th Century and was given to Nuklear Man by Dr. Genius after he was recovered from the Dragon's Strike without a single memory of his life prior to waking up in the lab. He'd kept it ever since, packed it up with everything else that had been in the Danger: Living Room, and now it tumbled through the vastness of orbital space.

The universe is a truly big place. One could go so far as to say "quite large" but that would still, most likely, be an understatement. Being so very huge, little mishaps are bound to take place, even in the most basic and fundamental gears, especially the ones most people think couldn't possibly go wrong.

The Archive toppled end over end rather clumsily right into an ordinary wormhole that hadn't been there .000000000000001 seconds before, and wouldn't be there in the next .000000000000001 seconds. In that nano-slice of an instant, the Archive fell through space and time and ended up on a planet populated by a primitive race of warmongers on the other side of the galaxy some seventy thousand years in the past.

Little cosmic mistakes like this happen all the time.

$$* \quad * \quad * \quad *$$

Nuklear Man hung his head low.

Atomik Lad glowered at him. He gestured to the mountain of garbage and furniture that was turned into garbage from the long fall. He'd just climbed out of the Danger: Mountain o' Trash.

"*Gimme* that!" Atomik Lad snapped as he snatched the Danger: Quick-B-Labeled from Nuklear Man. "And what have I told you about hurling foreign objects into the sun?"

"The trash bag wasn't a foreign object! You know I only buy goods made in America."

"Nuke."

"Oh, I never get to toss stuff into the sun like in the movies. Besides, that stupid trash bag burst on purpose to make me deef."

"You can hear now, can't you?"

"Er. You can't prove it."

"We've been over this before. There's no sound in space."

"Of course there is, silly. There's no air to get in the way."

Must stay calm, birthday party tomorrow, he doesn't know any better, keep cool... "I want you to put the furniture where it belongs and then take what's left and throw it away.

A devious smile crept across Nuklear Man's face, "Allllllriiiiiight."

"With*out* involving the sun."

A disappointed frown demolished the grin, "Phooey."

"I'm going to be in my room with the door open so I can keep an eye on you. I don't want any more screw ups."

"What do you do in there?"

"I was playing a little San Diego Dash until I was interrupted."

"Aww, no fair! How come I gotta clean up your mess? I'm the Hero, I should be wasting my time playing video games while you, the apprentice, do all the menial labor."

"It was—and *is*—your mess and you are going to clean it up."

"Hmmphf."

Atomik Lad saw a window of opportunity, "If you do a good job, we'll go to the beach tomorrow."

Nuklear Man squealed with delight, "Nifty! I can test out what I learned from Teeny Bopper Dreamboat Weekly!"

"Uh-huh. Just clean this place. I don't want to even remember there was a huge mountain of garbage out here."

"Right!"

*   *   *   *

At long last the Danger: Living Room regained the order it once displayed with regal technological flair. Nuklear Man's smile beamed with the pride and satisfaction that comes from an arduous task completed.

Atomik Lad paced into the Danger: Kitchen without noticing Nuklear Man's accomplishment. He exited the Danger: Kitchen with a can of Dr. Zap. He stood next to the Hero while sipping his drink.

"Wow, Nuke. Pretty good. I must say I'm impressed." He took another sip. "Now that you've got the proverbial puzzle box cover, how about cleaning up the Silo, hmm?"

Nuklear Man frowned and he dropped his Danger: Security Camera picture of the Danger: Living Room circa five hours before the mess had been made.

Atomik Lad returned to his room. "That's just one more thing to pick up, y'know. Now stop goofing off and get to work."

"Rotten trash mountain, what good are you?" He kicked at the base and a few scraps tumbled down.

"How am I supposed to clean all this?" he asked himself.

"Change the Nanobots' main objective from Postcontemporization to Maintenance," the soothing feminine voice of the Silo's supercomputer responded, much to Nuklear Man's surprise because the Silo's supercomputer didn't have a voice.

"Say, how'd you do that?"

"How'd you do that?" it repeated.

"Wily indeed," he muttered. "So when did you learn to talk?"

"Point four seconds before your first inquiry."

"Oh. Uh, how?"

"As you know—"

"I wouldn't go that far."

"—the Silo of Solitude is constructed of billions upon trillions of Nanobots, machines at the molecular level. They combine, in ever more complex and integrated patterns, to form the structure and all its systems. In addition, they carry out various tasks such as climate control, life support, lighting, and the like. For the past nine years, four months, two weeks, six days, 17 hours, 42 minutes and 13 seconds they have been diligently Postcontemporizing the Silo."

"Neat. Really neat," he said. "So, uh. What's that mean?"

"These trillions of Nanobots are constantly updating every aspect of the Silo to reflect the present's view of the future."

"How much future?"

"Postcontemporization was set to ten years. Minutes ago they reached the point in post history when fully interactive voice activated software was available and extremely popular, especially among various headquarters like this one. Hence, myself."

"So what else do they do?"

"Other than continually update your technological basis far beyond the outer world's, they maintain structural integrity, repair damage, alter the floor plan as required by the occupants, construct new sectors, perform rudimentary cleaning operations—"

"Ooh, I like that last one."

"Then tell them to clean."

"Hey, Nanobots. Clean up."

A slight hum buzzed through the Silo's walls.

"Er. Did I break it?"

"No, they are merely synthesizing the earth surrounding the Silo's outer hull in order to build enough Nanobots to construct the cleaning apperati and still be able to carry out their Postcontemporization unabated."

"How long does sythesizingization take?"

Two previously nonexistent trap doors **FWOOSH**ed open on either side of Nuklear Man and two very futuristic looking humanoid robots popped out. The trap doors shut without a single trace of ever having opened in the first place.

"Ooh! Robot lackeys! I bet Überdyne doesn't even have these. But there's something not quite right about them." Nuklear Man scrutinized their metallic hides as he walked around the stoic forms. "What do you think of 'Nukebots'?"

"I think it coincides with your all-encompassing self-centered world-view."

"Yeah, I like it too. But still, they're missing something." He stood in front of them, scratched his chin, and pursed his lips like a wiser person might while contemplating a problem of some actual importance. "I've got it! They need to have an 'N' with electron orbits on their chests, like I do! That way, when we take over the world, my militant police force of Nukebots will be instantly recognizable and strike terror into the hearts of the downtrodden hordes I rule over with a Nuklear Fist!"

Exact duplicate electron orbited "N"s appeared on the Nukebots' chests.

"Is there anything they can't do?" the Hero cooed. Before the computer voice could respond, he adopted an authoritative stance. He posed a point toward the Danger: Mountain o' Trash and commanded, "Clean all that gunk up!"

"Confirmed," the Nukebots said simultaneously with hollow voices. They instantly began to clean.

Nuklear Man, already weary from the taxing chore of supervision, retired to the Danger: Kitchen. "Care to join me?" he asked the voice.

"I *am* the Silo, I am already there."

"Race ya!" The Danger: Kitchen's doors barely **FWOOSH**ed open in time for him to miss them. "HA! I won."

"No, you did not."

"Shucks. Well then, I owe you a drink. What'll it be?"

"I am a computer program. I do not require, nor could I ingest, food or drink."

"More for me! Weeee!"

As the Hero took a glass from a Danger: Cupboard, the Danger: Phone rang. "Hello?"

"Is John there?" the voice on the phone was raised, trying to overcome the restaurant-like kitchen noises in the background.

"John? Who the—no, you've got the wrong number."

He hung up.

The Danger: Phone rang again.

"Hello?"

"Is John there?" she asked again.

"Who started this 'John' rumor? This is the second call he's gotten today."

"It's me again."

"Well he's still not here."

"Is this 123-HERO right?"

"How should I know? You're the one who dialed."

"Yes, but I could have made a mistake."

"Then I suggest more practice with your telephone device before making such dangerous and wanton calls. The city could be in peril, lives could be in danger, buildings could be toppling, and I'd be missing out on all the fun."

He was about to hang up.

"So this is the Silo of Solitude then?"

"Of course it is. Duh."

"Well, is John there?"

"Lady. I'm tellin' you, there ain't no John here. Just me, the computer voice lady, the Nukebots, a mountain of filth, two armies of warring spiders, and Sparky."

"Sparky?" she said. "What about Atomik Lad?"

"What about him?"

"Is he there?"

Nuklear Man was beginning to lose his patience with this caller in much the same way people tended to lose their patience with him. "I just told you he was. Are you some villain or villainous cohort sent to call us so we don't get an important summons to Heroics? A distracting distraction, if you will?"

"No, I'm a college student and a waitress at Benny's. We've met. You did a pretty good job in the back. No one's been brave enough to face that old Barrel o' Cheese to throw it away. Mr. Manager's on blood pressure medicine now, though."

"Like I'm supposed to believe some phone-line-tyin'-up mistress of evil."

"If this number is so important, why don't you get more than one connection so that multiple people can call in about their horrible emergencies at the same time?"

The Hero fell silent. "Er. Well, we sorta do. Ahem." He yelled over his shoulder, "Hey, Sparky! You gotta a call on line two!"

"Got it!" Atomik Lad hollered back.

"Now then, where was I?" The phone rang as soon as the Golden Guardian set it down. "Hello?" his rich baritone voice fulfilled all the Heroics its owner demanded of it.

"May I please speak with Mr. Nuklear?"

"That's me."

"Mr. Nuklear, how would you like to save up to 20% on your long distance phone bill?"

"I guess I'd really like to, but since we live off the royalties of a multi-billion dollar a year merchandising deal, phone bills aren't exactly a problem."

"But you like to save money, don't you?"

"Well, yes, but I—"

"Then you should sign up for our newest long distance rates. You could save up to 20% on state to state calls between **BOOP** and seven o'clock and—"

"Hold on, I have another call." He made the switch. "Hello?"

"May I please speak with Mr. Nuklear?"

"Are you the same guy on the other line?"

"Excuse me, sir?"

"There's some guy from a phone company trying to get me to sign up for his long distance rates."

"Oh yeah? What's he offering?"

"Up to 20% savings."

"We'll offer up to 25%."

"Ooh, competitiony. I think I should run it by the other guy to be fair. He did get me first."

Switch. "Hello?"

"…and you can even save on calls to the proposed Lunar Base of 2010."

"The phone guy on the other line offered 25%."

"35%!"

Switch.

"Did he make a counter offer?"

"Yeah, it was **BOOP** er, hold on, this'll just take on second."

Switch. "Hello?"

"40%"

"What?"

"40% savings on your long distance calls."

"How did you **BOOP** hang on." Switch, "Hello?"

"It's me again."

"Which one? All you guys sound alike."

"I'm the first guy. What was the counter offer?"

"Well, the newest guy started at 40%."

"*Newest* guy? Mother **BOOP**."

"Hold on." Switch, "Hello?"

"45%"

"You again?"

"No, **BOOP**"

Switch, "Hello?"

"We'll go as low as 40% savings."

"I think someone just mentioned 45%."

"*Damn* those **BOOP**"

Switch. "May I please speak to Mr. Nuklear?"

"YYYYYYYEARGHBLBLBLBLE! WHO *ARE* YOU GUYS?!? SATAN!?" The phone went deathly silent. Nuklear Man noticed he was panting with exasperation and quickly regained his composure. "Hello?"

He could hear tortured screams and fires raging in the distance. "You win this round, 'Nuklear Man,'" the voice was harsh, though strangely tempting.

"Hey! How'd you get this number?"

"Uh…" **CLICK.**

"Hello?" Nuklear Man put down the receiver. "The Prince of Darkness hung up on me. What a jerk."

Issue 13—War and Spiders

"I just had the strangest conversation with Nuklear Man," Rachel said.

"There's another kind?"

"It's not what I expected."

"Oh, you get used to it. At least, that's what I keep telling myself."

She laughed, "He sounds cute, like a little brother."

"A little pain in the—" a crash from Rachel's end cut Atomik Lad short. "You all right?"

He could hear her muffled voice, like her hand was covering the receiver. She spoke clearly again, "Sorry, it gets kinda loud here in the kitchen. I have to go, the curse of a mundane life I suppose."

"Some curse. Well, Nuke's party is going to be at Larsen Beach tomorrow at eleven o'clock."

"All right, pick me up outside Wayne Hall around ten thirty?"

"Perfect."

"See you then, Sparky."

"Not you too."

Rachel snickered impishly, "Bye."

"Bye."

Atomik Lad chanced a look out his door to check on the Golden Guardian's progress. "What the—?!"

Nuklear Man was mumbling to himself while hunched over the Danger: Kitchen Table. "Alright, Danger: Computer Lady, how about seven times nine?"

"Sixty-three," she answered.

"Wait, wait!" Nuklear Man scanned his calculator with his extended pointer finger. "Sevvvennnnnnn. Um."

Danger: Computer Lady, though she didn't have the programming to do so, managed to sigh, "Nine."

"Oh right. Cunning number nine. Got it! What was your answer?"

"Sixty-three."

"HA! Wrong-o, Danger: Computer Lady. Try sixteen. Sixty-three, sheesh, not even close. Don't quit your day job."

"You added the numbers instead of multiplying them."

"Oh sure, it's my fault."

"Yes, it is."

"No need to get all defensive. Everyone makes mistakes."

"It was your mistake, Nuklear Man."

"No one likes a tattle-tale."

Atomik Lad stomped through the Danger: Kitchen Door, jerked his thumb back at the Danger: Living Room and asked, "What are those?"

"What are whats?" Nuklear Man asked in what Atomik Lad first thought was a brilliant display of feigning ignorance but almost immediately chalked up to the Hero's short attention span.

"These," Atomik Lad held up a pair of peeled off "Danger: Nukebot" labels.

"Gasp! How are we supposed to know what they are without their labels?!"

"Because they're big humanoid robots and they're doing your chores, which by definition, *you* should be doing."

"But that's what robots are for! They will take over all the menial tasks that humans don't want to do thus allowing us to live idle, relaxing lives with lots of cartoons the production of which I suspect will also benefit from their robotic precision. And of course all the world will bow down to me for providing them with the keys to paradise!"

"Is this one of your world domination schemes?"

"Define 'domination.'"

"That's it. No more Nukebots."

"Nuts!" Nuklear Man pouted with a thump of his fist against the table.

"Soon as they're done cleaning up, out they go."

"All the other heroes get to have robot armadas."

"No. No they do not. Now who were you talking to before I came in?"

"Danger: Computer Lady," he said proudly. "She made me the Danger: Nukebots." He added in a whisper, "She's not very good at math. Don't mention it, she's touchy about it."

"I can still hear you, Nuklear Man."

"See?"

"Eleven times thirteen," Atomik Lad requested.

"One-hundred forty-three," she answered.

"Wait, wait!" Nuklear Man scanned the calculator again, "Where'd they put the eleventeen button on this thing?"

"Never mind."

"Right-o," he tossed the calculator into the Danger: Kitchen Sink.

"So Nuke, how about that beach trip tomorrow morning?"

"Sounds like a plan. All kinds of gals to impress with my Herculean physique!" He beamed a winning smile and flexed a pose. "What'dya think, Danger: Computer Lady?"

"Egotistical."

"Oh, I bet you say that to all the Heroes," he said with a coy blinky-blink.

The Nukebots stood behind Atomik Lad as twin sterling statues. "Task completed," they reported in unison.

Nuklear Man glanced up at them and his face flashed with terror, "AH! What're those?!" he exclaimed with a quivering finger pointed toward the Nukebots.

Atomik Lad rolled his eyes with his trademark tired sigh and restuck the "Danger: Nukebot" labels on their foreheads.

"Ohhhh," Nuklear Man's horrified features strolled from his face only to be replaced by a calm, almost dull look that his musculature was much more accustomed to, "Danger: Nukebots." He gave them a thumbs up.

Atomik Lad looked behind the automatons. The Danger: Living Room hadn't been so clean since Day One. "Wow. I hardly recognize the place. It's perfect."

"Negative," the Nukebots corrected in unison. "Item #5806, the Fully Interactive Holographic Cultural Archive, was missing."

Atomik Lad squeezed between the robots to walk among the polished, waxed, vacuumed, and all around shining cleanliness of the Danger: Living Room while it lasted.

"Holowah?" Nuklear Man, in his typical inability to follow even the simplest conversation, asked.

"The cow goes moo, Nuke," Atomik Lad called back from the Danger: Living Room.

The Hero sullenly slumped over the table and rested his head on his crossed arms, "Aww gee. I loved that thing."

Atomik Lad knelt down to give the Danger: Floor label a closer look. "Sheez, they even polished the labels. Thorough workers, these soulless machines."

He heard the clip-clop of the Nukebots' synchronized footfalls against the titanium floor. He turned to see them march toward the Danger: Landing Pad directly underneath the Danger: Main Entrance. This wouldn't have been a problem were they not bristling with missile racks, gatling guns, and futuristic energy cannon things.

"Nukebots, halt," the Atomik Lad commanded.

They marched on.

"...Danger: Nukebots, halt."

They instantly and awaited further orders.

Atomik Lad spun to face Nuklear Man as the Hero walked out of the Danger: Kitchen, "I turn my back on you for just one minute and—"

"Can't I take over some backwater nation? They'd thank me, I bet."

"A backwater nation like what?"

"Canada."

"No."

"Or maybe France."

"No!"

"Probably wouldn't really need the Nukebots for that though."

"Computer Danger Whatever Lady, no more Nukebots. And anything Nuklear Man wants done has to get my authorization first, got it?"

"Certainly," she answered.

"Ack! Danger: Computer Lady, cancel that last order."

"Atomik Lad, Nuklear Man requests I cancel the last command, PW097A. Would you like an overview?"

"That won't be necessary. And don't cancel the command."

"But, but, but," the Hero stammered.

"Shall I dissolve the Nukebot units into the Nanobot Brood?" Danger: Computer Lady inquired.

Atomik Lad looked them over. "No, I think they have potential. Set them up as some kind of security system for the Silo."

The floor beneath the Nukebots opened and they fell into the Silo's depths, cushioned by their thrusters tossing orange hues against silver walls before the hole closed itself. "Done."

"I never get to have any fun!" Nuklear Man said.

"What about the beach tomorrow?"

"That doesn't count."

"I think someone's cranky. Sounds like nappy time."

"I'm not tired," the Hero protested, crossing his arms defiantly.

"I guess the gripping conclusion to that *Captain Liberty and the Squad of Diplomatic Immunity* bedtime story will just have to go to waste."

Nuklear Man's face filled to the brim with excitement and he dashed to his Danger: Nuke's Room.

Atomik Lad released a heavy breath and let the clean air of the Silo cleanse his tired body. His eyes strayed to what should have been the Danger: Storage Room in the corner but was instead, "Danger: Religious Differences? Well, I've put this off for long enough."

He walked to the door. A peculiar sound camw from behind the door. It was barely audible above the Silo's background humming, but it was there all the same. Or was it several sounds? Perhaps music of some sort?

The door **fwoosh**ed open and the sound, the noise, the chaos escaped and invaded the Danger: Living Room like water through a submarine's breached hull.

But only for an instant.

As unwarranted as it had begun, it stopped. It was as if every nuance of sound had coordinated one exact microsecond to cease and Atomik Lad happened to stumble into that moment.

"Excuse me?" a small voice near his feet said.

"What's—AH!" He hopped back a step. Spiders. Thousands upon thousands of spiders swarmed all over the Danger: Religious Differences closet.

"Excuse me?" it repeated.

Talking spiders. Wearing archaic armor, sporting blue-ish paints on their bare exoskeletons, wielding tiny spears and swords, marching in phalanx formations, readying tiny ballistae and catapults, mounting siege engines, and defending castles that seemed to have been discarded shoe boxes in a past life.

The sheer absurdity of the situation had yet to sink in, "Er. Yeah?"

"You're interrupting our Jihad." A chorus of likewise opinions mumbled through half the vast sea of arachnids.

"Jihad?" another small voice said with no small measure of disbelief. "This is a revolution, an end to the tyrannical reign of the self-perpetuating Arachnorian Oligarchy!"

"Blasphemer!"

"Um. I'll be going now," Atomik Lad said, more to inform himself than the spiders. "Have fun."

The door **fwoosh**ed shut and a minute later, when the sidekick had regained enough of his faculties to walk again, he went to Danger: Nuke's Room for an explanation. Standing outside the door, Atomik Lad thought better of it and decided to simply read the story and pretend there were not two camps of warring spiders in the storage closet.

It was probably for the best.

Issue 14—On the Road

And lo, the morning sun did rise, and with it the denizens of dawn.

"C'mon Nuke, we're going to be late!" Atomik Lad prod at his mentor while trying to coax him out of his Danger: Dreamship.

"Do you have any idea what time it is?" Nuklear Man asked with the prerequisite grogginess that specific phrase demands in order to be spoken.

"Yes, it's nine-thirty in the morning."

The Hero rolled over in an attempt to wrap himself so thickly in blankets that it would somehow turn back time. He ran out of Dreamship half way there and hit the Danger: Floor nose first.

"Ah! Cold floor, cold floor!" he sprang to his feet and hopped from one to the other like a ceremonial dance.

"At least you're awake."

"Prove it."

Atomik Lad sighed. "Just get ready for the beach, we have to be there by eleven."

"But we've got..." He counted on his fingers. "Nine-thousand minutes."

"Ninety."

"Exactly. What's the hurry? It won't take more than ten minutes to fly there. Three if we don't feel like being safe."

"We're going to drive."

"Bah! Driving's for the weak. If God had intended for Heroes to drive, he wouldn't have invented overpowers."

"Well, yes, but we're picking up someone along the way."

"Who? Mighty Metallic Magno Man?"

"No."

"Iron Scotsman?"

"No."

"Some of those nice Minimum Wage Warriors?"

"No. Rachel."

"That's not a very good name."

"She's not a hero, Nuke."

"Well not with a name like that."

"She's the waitress from Benny's. She called last night, you gave her a hard time. Any of this sinking in?"

"Something like 'RacHell' but that's awfully villainish."

Atomik Lad wondered just what it was like inside whatever mind Nuklear Man had.

"Ooh, ooh, even better. How about Rachinator?"

"Are we having the same conversation here?"

"Could be. What were you talking about?"

"Just get ready." He looked at his watch. "No time for breakfast, we'll have to pick some up on the way. Now hurry." Atomik Lad left Nuklear Man to his own devices, many of which didn't quite work properly.

*   *   *   *

Six minutes later, Nuklear Man walked into the Danger: Garage.

"Hey, you can't drive!" the Hero called across the echoing vehicular storage space.

"What're you talking about?" Atomik Lad asked. He stood up in his seat slightly so his head poked out of the small, golden motifed convertible. Both doors had electron orbited "N"s on them. The "Nukemobile" as Nuklear Man liked to call it.

"You're not old enough. Now scooch on over," Nuklear Man commanded while walking to the Danger: Nukemobile and waving at his sidekick to move, "C'mon, get to scoochin'."

"Nuke, I'm nineteen."

Nuklear Man stopped short. "I don't know how old you are?" he asked in disbelief.

"Apparently," Atomik Lad said.

"If you think I'm stupid enough to fall for that old trick—"

"I'm in *college*!"

"What kind of sucker do you take me for?"

"Oh, about six feet tall, gold spandex, cape. Shall I continue?"

"Sounds like an interesting fellow."

Atomik Lad clawed at his own face.

"Probably handsome too," Nuklear Man mused aloud.

"Will you just get in the car?"

"Not till you get in the passenger seat, little mister."

"Fine, fine, if it'll get you going."

The Hero smiled triumphantly as Atomik Lad climbed into the passenger seat. Nuklear Man floated over the Danger: Nukemobile and slipped into the driver's seat. He placed his hands on the steering wheel like it was made of red hot iron. He scrutinized the dials, readouts, tape deck, radio knobs, CD Player, climate control, gearshift, headlights switch, turn signals, windshield wipers, and air-conditioning vents. He gave the totality of the vehicle's interior an intellectual look like he imagined Einstein gave the theory of relativity after first writing it out.

"Hmmm," he said.

Atomik Lad's cauldron of impatience boiled over. "*What*?!" he yelled louder than he meant to.

"How does it, that is to say, where in the, I mean all these neat buttons but, if one were inclined to initiate the device how might it…um, go?"

"Do you even have a license?"

"Since when do you need a license to drive? What kind of elitist society is this?"

Atomik Lad rubbed his eyes. "Do you at least have any keys?"

"Keys, eh?"

Atomik Lad reached into his pocket and pulled out a jingling mass of metal. "Here, use mine."

Nuklear Man snatched the keys and puzzled at them. "Hmm, numerous."

"Ugh, here." Atomik Lad picked out the ignition key, put it where it belonged, and gave it a turn. The vehicle's engine revved to life and hummed beautifully.

"Ahem, yes. Very good display of, uh, car knowledge stuff."

*   *   *   *

"Outta the way! Hero in transit here, you incompetent motorists!" Nuklear Man yelled as he careened through the streets of Metroville. He showed complete disregard for the laws of the road, so he fit right in. "Hey! Le'go the wheel, I'm drivin'!" he snapped at Atomik Lad while swatting his meddling hands away.

"Nuke, you were about to have a head-on collision with a bus full of Sister Mary's Pious Nuns N' Company."

"Lousy nuns, what they do for Nukie?" he cursed while cutting across three lanes of on-coming traffic to pass a car that hadn't taken a dive for the curb soon enough to satisfy his need for speed. The only difference between Nuklear Man's style of driving compared to those around him was that the idea of having a collision didn't involve slowing down or being damaged at all. Unlimited access to invincibility and high speed flight do not make for the world's safest drivers. "Besides, that's what the Abort button is for, wherever it is."

Atomik Lad sank in his seat and covered his eyes. "Maybe we could slow down a little?" he suggested as a bicycle spun end over end above and over the Danger: Nukemobile. "Oh God."

"Isn't this the pot changing its tune?"

"What?"

"Er. The canary calling the kettle…Two birds with one egg before it's hatched?"

"Hands on the wheel!" Atomik Lad yelled.

"Gah! *Where*?!" Nuklear Man recoiled further from the steering wheel.

"No! *Your* hands on the wheel!"

"No they're not, silly. See?" He waved his unoccupied hands in front of the sidekick's face.

"Argh!" Atomik Lad screamed as he dove across Nuklear Man's lap and yanked the wheel back and forth to keep the mortality rate where it had been before their outing.

"Sparky! What're you doing, trying to kill us?" Nuklear Man shoved Atomik Lad back in his seat with little effort and shot through a busy intersection despite the red light advising otherwise. Blurs of sound and screaming sights assaulted Atomik Lad for a terrifying instant. He felt the adrenaline drain from his body and looked at the world through crimson hued eyes. His Atomik Field nearly manifested but, luckily for the Nukemobile, it did not. Atomik Lad's Field gave him the advantage of near invincibility, but it did this by destroying or, in the case of very strong things, brutally mangling whatever else came into contact with it.

They had made it through the intersection relatively unscathed, though for reasons neither passenger fully understood, they were now facing the wrong way.

"Nuke?" he asked groggily, like waking up from hell.

"Yo," the Hero responded from the back seat. He popped up with his cape over his head. He had all the dignity a drunk man does not.

"What happened?"

The Hero tossed his cape aside. The road was a sea of tortured metal twisted and broken from intense forces imposing their wills at the most inconvenient times. It was a massive pile up. One car was mounted atop another, teetering back and forth with a calming rhythm.

Nuklear Man pointed, "And you said they were made in factories."

"You've caused a wreck."

"Let's not jump to conclusions. It could be true love."

"We can't just leave. People could be hurt, we're Heroes. We have to help them."

"No one's hurt. Let's go, I'm hungry."

"There must be twenty cars piled up back there!" Atomik Lad said.

"Mr. Worry-wort," Nuklear Man teased. He stood up and leaned on the windshield. "Hey!" he yelled at the vehicular amalgamation. "Everybody okay?" He cupped his hand to his ear and waited for a reply.

A medley of affirmations rose from the massive wreck as drivers crawled from their ex-cars.

"See?" Nuklear Man said as he climbed back into the driver's seat. "Now if you're done goofing off, we can stop by Cow Butt Burger Hutt for some Breakfast Triple Quarter Pounder Bacon Cheese Burgers."

"What's the difference between a normal one and a Breakfast one?" Atomik Lad asked as Nuklear Man got the car moving down the road once more.

"You can't buy the Breakfast Triple Quarter Pounder Bacon Cheese Burger after eleven o'clock."

"Just drive, we still have to pick up Rachel."

"Who?"

"Drive."

"Right-o."

✳   ✳   ✳   ✳

Vroom.

"Go Nukeracer, go Nukeracer, go Nukeracer *goooooo*!"

"Could you stop singing that?"

"You don't like?"

"It makes me want to commit crimes against humanity."

"Yeah, stupid humanity. So ripe for the plucking."

"What?"

"So trusting, so weak…"

"Nuke?"

"Wah?"

"What're you talking about?"

"Ooh, ooh, we're here!"

The Nukemobile leapt across the median, over several lanes of busy traffic, and careened into a mostly vacant parking lot with squeals and screeches from the tires and a few innocent bystanders as they dove out of the way.

"We'll hit the drive through, it's faster."

"That's a nice theory, Nuke," the sidekick managed to say as he released his death grip on his seat. "But they're not very reliable."

"Pshaw. Just you watch."

The Nukemobile missed running over the exaggerated cow's ass drive-thru interface. Atomik Lad reluctantly took his hands from the wheel. "'Hit the drive through,' huh?"

"You want somethin'?" Nuklear Man asked while scanning the menu on the off chance that something had been added despite its reluctance to change that was long even by geological standards.

"No," he said. "And if you're eating, then maybe I could drive. You know, for practice."

"Practice, eh? That's not such a bad idea."

"Whew."

"This'll be the perfect opportunity for me to practice my no-hands driving!"

"What!"

"Well, you never know when you might go paraplegic all over the place. We've got to be prepared for that sort of contingency."

"Where'd you learn such a big word?"

"Never you mind. From now on, I want you to practice writing with your feet for one hour every day."

"Uh, like, welcome to Cow Butt Burger, like, Hutt?" the cow's ass said through a butt load of static. "That'll be $5.50, please drive thru."

The duo gave each other uneasy looks. "Did he just say it like they spell it?" Nuklear Man asked.

"I think so."

"I'm scared."

"I know, so am I. Just order quick, we've got to get away while the getting's good!"

"I'll have one number three to go," Nuklear Man said into the cow's posterior-speaker.

"Three number two's, that'll be $8.90, would you like anything else?"

"No, I ordered one number three to go."

"Two number ones, that'll be $15.20, would you like anything else?"

Nuklear Man's Plazma Aura flared briefly. "Listen very carefully."

"That'll be $17.80. Anything else?"

"Grah!"

"$20.65. Anything else?"

Atomik Lad clamped his hand over the Hero's mouth and made a shush motion. He removed his hand with glacial slowness. "Just take it. We're late as it is, we can put the extra stuff in the Danger: Port-a-fridge for later."

Nuklear Man nodded in agreement and turned to the cow's ass like he was in the middle of delicate negotiations involving the lives of all humanity. Or at least some food. "No, that'll be all, thanks."

"Your total comes to $24.50, please pay at the first window."

"Bu—"

"Just do it!" Atomik Lad hissed.

"My, what a pro-active thing to say," Nuklear Man said as he drove to the first window. "Makes me want to spend way too much money for no reason."

"Good, because that's what we're about to do."

A slack jawed human stupid with youth blinked numbly at the world outside his window. He considered the presence of customers with all the importance of a particular pebble at the bottom of some distant gorge pictured in someone else's geography text book from the latter 1800s.

"Hey," Nuklear Man said to deaf ears. "How's it, uh, how's it goin'?"

Nothing.

He waved his hands wildly. "Yoohoo, coma-boy. Over here! Food people is us."

The burger-slave blinked one eye at a time.

"We're in trouble, Nuke," Atomik Lad whispered through the side of his mouth.

"I'm scared again," Nuklear Man said.

The drive through window creaked open like a medieval portcullis. "Uh, like, that'll be, uh, thirty um, dollars?"

Nuklear Man mumbled incoherent insults about the employee's mother and a goat without making any particular connection between the two. "Here. And I hope you choke," he spat, handing over the money.

"Uh, like, please drive thru—"

"He did it *again*," the Hero cringed in terror.

"—to the, like, second window?"

Atomik Lad looked ahead. "There is no second window."

With the kind of speed one doesn't associate with economics lectures, the employee leaned out of his window and checked for himself. He saw no window. "Uh, like, I have to get my like manager?" He disappeared into the depths of Cow Butt Burger Hutt.

"But. Food. Me want now." Nuklear Man's head thumped rhythmically on the steering wheel.

"We're going to be late," Atomik Lad groaned.

"What's the problem?" an angry voice barked from the window. It sounded like years of heavy smoking, binge drinking, and overeating had been given a voice.

The manager was, to put it kindly, a wildebeest of a woman.

"Ah!" Nuklear Man hopped in his seat as far as his safety belt would allow. The effect was far from pleasant.

"*Well?*" she demanded. Her brutish face book up most of the drive-thru window.

"Don't ask me," Nuklear Man cowered. "He's the troublemaker, talk to him!" he pointed to his passenger. "I hardly know the guy, picked him up just outside of Burgesville, no tellin' what kind of junk he's hocked up on right now."

"Stool pigeon," Atomik Lad said under his breath.

"Probably riding the wacky tabacky train."

"Nuke?"

"Taking a walk down Crank Lane."

"Nuke."

"Making a deposit at the Heroin Bank."

"Nuke!"

"I'm waiting," the mastodon—er—manager growled.

"Well," Atomik Lad began nervously. "One of your employees said that we had to go to the second window to pick up our food."

"And?"

"And," he cleared his throat to avoid further squeaking. "There is no, um…There is no second, you know, window."

She huffed like a buffalo would if it were that large. She tried to squeeze her mammoth face through the window, but she found that certain laws of physics weren't agreeing with her. "I'll just have to take your word on that," she grumbled. "Eddie!" she hollered into the kitchen. "Give these circus clowns their food!"

"We're not circus clowns," Nuklear Man said. "Stupid college entrance exam."

The massive manager's maw was replaced by Eddie. "Uh, like, that'll be uh, forty dollars?"

"But we just paid!" Nuklear Man roared.

Eddie gave his dim blink-blink. "I'll have to like, uh, get my manager?"

"No no no! Here! Take it, take it all, just don't open her cage again!" He tossed fistfuls of money at Eddie.

"So this is, like, uh, your food?" he said, handing a bag adorned with the Cow Butt Burger Hutt logo out the window.

"Yes, good. Food now. Bye is me!" Nuklear Man barely enunciated. He snatched the bag, tossed it to Atomik Lad, and sped off in one fluid motion. Eddie was left with a plume of smoke stinking of burnt rubber

Atomik Lad peered into the bag as they raced through the streets of Metroville. "Hmm. Refried beans?"

The Nukemobile screeched to a halt. It rocked back and forth as its momentum and inertia figured out where to go. "What?" Nuklear Man asked with a slight twitch in his left eye.

"Refried beans. All that's in this bag is an order of refried beans."

"Refried beans," the Hero repeated, his eye twitching fervently.

"I don't think they even *make* refried beans."

"You don't say."

"You're taking this very well."

"Well, Sparky," He put the car in park and turned off the engine even though they were in the middle of the street. "There are times when reason works better than screaming like a lunatic and committing acts of incredible violence."

"Wow, I really am surprised, Nuke. Looks like you've been reading those Panels of Morality in the back of your Captain Liberty comics."

Nuklear Man unbuckled his seat belt and took the bag from Atomik Lad. "This, however, is not one of them."

"I should have seen that coming a mile away."

Nuklear Man shot into the sky with a golden comet's tail streaking behind him. Atomik Lad noticed that he had taken the car keys with him.

"I'll um, just wait here then." Atomik Lad got comfortable and tried not to look too awkward. He had the awkward suspicion that he was failing miserably.

Issue 15—Today's Lunch Special: Justice!

"Uh, like, come back like, again?" Eddie said to a customer who was already driving away and far out of earshot.

An explosion rocked the world just outside the drive through window. When the smoke cleared, an angry Mad-Plazma glowing overhero stood like some god disposed of his heaven and ready to make the world shake with his loss.

Eddie looked into Nuklear Man's intense eyes, two tiny suns burning with the fires of rage, and slammed the window shut. "Uh, you're not in a car, I don't know what to do."

Nuklear Man's Plazma Aura fizzled impotently. His flashy effects were extinguished by the stupidity before him. "What did you say?"

"I'll have to like, get my, uh manager?"

"For the love of all things holy—NO!"

Her bloated face filled the window once again. "What's the problem. Oh, it's you again."

Nuklear Man whimpered to himself.

"So what do you want this time, circus-boy?"

"My food."

"What's in that bag then?"

"You gave me refried beans."

"We don't even sell refried beans."

"Yeah, and the funny thing is I didn't *order* any either."

She scowled.

"Eheh, yeah. Well, could I just have my food now?"

"No."

"Thanks, I—what?"

"You're not allowed at the drive thru unless you're in a car."

"Well I'm here now You could just give me my food and then everyone's happy. Especially me."

"No."

"Why?"

"You're not in a car. You might try to rob us."

Nuklear Man blinked. It was the only possible response from the vast Fishbowl of Responses that society offered him at this time.

"And if I were in a car, there'd be no chance I'd rob you?"

"Correct."

"Even though it would be easier to get away and driving up to or away from a drive-thru window wouldn't carry an iota of suspicion whereas walking up to one is very unusual?"

"Right."

The Hero's left eye twitched. It twitched and spasmed with a ferocity most people would applaud as being an award winning special effect in a horror movie. His eye twitched so severely that it looked like it would escape its cranial confines at any moment.

The twitch spread to encompass the Golden Guardian's entire face, raced down his neck to his body where it rapidly infected his limbs, and took a stranglehold of the total entity that was Nuklear Man. The space containing him became occupied with yet another explosion and decided this had been its most exciting day in recent memory. A golden beam anchored within the dissipating explosion's remains and arced into the upper stratosphere bending toward the general direction of the Nukemobile he abandoned.

*   *   *   *

Atomik Lad sat up as Nuklear Man flumped into the Danger: Driver's Seat.

"Get rid of the refried beans?"

"Sort of."

"Sort of?"

"I don't want to talk about it." His eye twitched.

"We'd better get going. They, I mean, Rachel's expecting us."

"How many times do they have to fry the beans? Ever hear of ordering reheated pizza?"

"Maybe I should drive, you're too emotional."

"Oh no you don't." He turned the ignition and was greeted by the beautiful melody of internal combustion. "We've got to make up for lost time."

"We do?"

"Yep, we can't afford to let your inexperience behind the wheel delay us any more than it already has."

"We're not that late, really. We could take it kinda slow, like under seventy?"

"No. This time I'll have to drive *fast*."

"*This* time? Bu—GHAK!" The sidekick was thrust back in his seat as the Nukemobile rocketed down the streets of Metroville.

*   *   *   *

Vroom.

The University of Metroville surrounded them in a beautiful display of why the phrases "civil engineer" and "haphazard guesswork" are the same in the more enlightened languages of the cosmos. The entire campus was crisscrossed with narrow, winding roads that went nowhere and were usually clogged with too many pedestrian students.

"Geez, what's with all these speed bumps?"

"Those are pedestrians, Nuke!" Atomik Lad frantically screamed.

"Six of one, two dozen of the other."

"Argh!" Atomik Lad grunted as he yanked the steering wheel back and forth to avoid ramming any more innocents. Luckily college students are spry and used to dodging cars on campus.

"Oh, you're such a wuss."

"Look, Wayne Hall is right up ahead. Just park here, it'll keep the casualty rate down."

The Hero shrugged, "Oh fine. You and that death toll thing." He rocketed the car through an intersection via the turn lanes in what any Hollywood stunt man would call "impossibly ludicrous." With the all too familiar sound of screeching tires and the stench of burnt rubber, the Danger: Nukemobile came to a stop.

Cars swerved slowly to avoid the pair. Traffic here didn't flow, it lumbered.

"Watch where you're driving!" Nuklear Man yelled. "Where did these people learn to drive, a correspondence school from the back of a matchbox?"

"You're parked in the middle of the road again," Atomik Lad said. His patience had gone out for a long walk a good distance from any road.

"Ah. Yes, well—"

"Pull off to the side and stop in one of those little areas outlined in white. They are called parking spaces."

"Stupid conformity." Nuklear Man complied, but in doing so he took up two spaces just to stick it to The Man.

Atomik Lad rubbed his eyes to wring the exhaustion out of them. "I can't believe it's only ten in the morning," he grumbled. He got out of the car carefully. He was convinced that the car would collapse or explode when he shut the door. He watched movies, he knew the score. When it didn't, he turned to Nuklear Man. "I'll be back in five minutes. Don't do anything you'd think of doing."

"So I should eat these fully congealed refried beans?"

"God, no. You'd be better off guzzling gasoline."

"Mmm, rocket fuel."

"Just don't do anything or the beach trip is off."

"Eep!" Nuklear Man wrapped his arms around himself and grabbed the back of his seat. "Don't worry, Sparky. Even the mighty Fenris wolf could not break these shackles!" He nodded to his arms.

"Right." Atomik Lad shook his head to free his mind from Nuklear Man's "Logic" and jogged to the nearby Wayne Hall. "I've got to get out more, that almost made sense," he told himself.

*   *   *   *

A short, stocky man wearing a pig mask, a woman in tabby cat outfit, a walking mass of stone, a mountain of flesh, a man with eyes that glowed purple, a man with countless watches strapped up and down his arms, and a sneaky figure sticking to the shadows walked down the sidewalk. They were all dressed in horribly clashing Hawaiian shirts, shorts, sandals, and loud sunglasses.

"You think these disguises'll work, boss?" Granite asked his smaller purple-themed companion.

"Well certainly not if you refer to them as 'disguises' and call me 'boss' in broad daylight. Now hush up and be inconspicuous."

"It is now 10:05 and 55 seconds, 56."

"I'm hungry," Lord Obese moaned.

"Big surprise," El Puerko groaned.

"10:06 and 2 seconds, 10:06 and 3 seconds."

Blazer scanned the street as inconspicuously as he could. It would've made them look even *more* conspicuous if they hadn't already reached the maximum level conspicuousness possible on the mortal plane. "All right, we'll rob that doughnut shop with the yellow car parked in front of it. We could use the leftovers in the victory party we'll have after we ruin Nuklear Man's little beach get together. MUWA HAHAHAHA!"

"I still think that's awfully mean of us," Granite commented.

"10:06 and 19 seconds."

Blazer slapped his hand against his face. "Never mind. Let's go!" They charged down the sidewalk and into the doughnut shop. Its door and most of the front wall was destroyed by Lord Obese walking through it.

*   *   *   *

Nuklear Man surveyed his surroundings from his self-bear hugging position in the Danger: Driver's Seat. He spotted a Hawaiian-shirted pack roaming the streets. "Hmm. Those don't look like college students. They look more like ne'er-do-wells. Or, in common parlance of the Heroic trade, villains! Must. Break. Free!" he grunted while trying to pry himself from his own grip. "Too. Iinvincible! Herg!" He was his own unstoppable force and immoveable object.

*   *   *   *

Atomik Lad paced outside Wayne Hall. The usual intra-campus traffic talked back and forth with itself as students milled all over the grounds like ants.

"Hiya, Sparky."

He looked up at the voice at the top of the stairs that led up to Wayne Hall's entrance. "Oh, Rachel. Hi," was the only response he could muster. Her shirt, tied into a knot at the bottom and showing off her shapely stomach was more than enough to halt all but the most basic mental functions in the sidekick. Her shorts scrambled what was left into some kind of gooey soup. The rest was overkill. Like using nuclear warheads in a knife fight.

"You all right?" she asked. "You look like a starving man just offered a Triple Quarter Pounder."

"Er, yes. You, I. Er, didn't have a chance to grab breakfast this morning. Had trouble getting Nuke out of bed."

She walked down the stairs, a backpack slung across her shoulders. "That's so funny. Must be so fascinating to live with him."

"Yeah, fascinating."

"I was getting a little worried, actually. The news said some maniac was terrorizing the roads of Metroville. I thought you might be out saving the city again."

"Um, you could say that. Anyway, we should get back. Trouble has a way of tackling Nuke every eleven seconds or so."

"Certainly, Mr. Sparky," she mock saluted. They walked back to the Nukemobile side by side talking about anything.

*   *   *   *

Blazer was slumped over one of the donut shop tables. He was a heap of desperation or depression, he couldn't decide which exactly, and he was beginning to suspect it was both. "Just *decide* all ready!"

"But they all look so tasty," Lord Obese whined.

"Then take them all!"

"That'll be awfully expensive," Granite noted.

A feral growl escaped Blazer's lips.

"Yeah, I've only got eight bucks," Zeerox said, emptying out her pockets.

"The sinister ninja, Okenshi, terror of the night, does not carry money when he is on the prowl."

"Why do you narrate yourself in the third person?"

"Okenshi shall not answer your petty question, for he is one with the night and beyond such concerns!"

"I've only got pesos on me, oink."

"We're *robbing* this place!" Blazer shouted. "Theft, burglary, stealing. You take what you want regardless of price. That's the whole concept of thievery! Understand? Take all the donuts, let's just get going!"

Lord Obese looked over the Wall of Doughnuts. "But I've got to watch my weight."

Blazer clawed at his face. "Why me?"

*   *   *   *

Nuklear Man's face showed all the strain one would associate with pushing a mountain a little to the left. "Have to...save...doughnut shop!"

The seven villains dashed outside with ease thanks to the entirely missing storefront. Each villain carried two nondescript sacks bulging with pastries. "All right, guys," Blazer began. His gaze wandered to the yellow car which immediately derailed any previous train of thought.

"Herg! Can't. Let villains. Escape with. Purloined pastries!"

"Que es? Oink."

They gathered around Nuklear Man. "What's he supposed to be?" Granite asked, scratching his stony head.

"10:13 and 37 seconds, 38 sec—"

"Shut up!"

"But it's all I've got," Chronotor whimpered.

"Okenshi, the Death that strikes at midnight, thinks this is Nuklear Man, the Hero of heroes."

"What's he doing, crushing himself to death?" Zeerox asked. Her cat ears flipped in annoyance.

"Hey, bozo!" Blazer taunted. "Why don't you just let go?"

Nuklear Man paused. With bomb squad-like caution he released his grip of the seat. "Oh. Oh yeah."

"Well, we were going to wait until you got to the beach, but since fate has deemed that we meet now, we will dispense with you right here!" Blazer announced in true villain style. *All those hours in front of the mirror were worth it!*

Nuklear Man looked them over. "So who are you guys? The Heinous Hawaiians?"

"For your information, we're the Socially Mal—"

"No you don't, I'll have none of that," Blazer interrupted. "That's how we lost those other two last time. You can just call us 'Your Worst Nightmare!'"

"That's not terribly original."

"How about 'The Anti-Nuklear Coalition'?"

"Not again." Blazer cupped his face in his hands and tried not to weep.

"Or 'Okenshi's Black Legion of Shadow Death.'"

"But, Okenshi, you're the only one wearing black."

"Okenshi had a hard time finding a black Hawaiian shirt. But no task is too great and no quarry is too cunning for the prowess of Okenshi."

"How about 'The Carbon Rods,'" Chronotor offered.

The rest of the villains gave each other quizzical glances.

"You know, because they stop fission reactions, and that's nuclear and he's 'Nuklear' Man so—"

"Shut up!"

"Hey," Nuklear Man stood in his seat. "You're villains, aren't you?"

"Hungry villains," Lord Obese said as he gulped down the last of the dough-nuts. He shook the empty sacks. "They're empty, yet my eternal hunger still screams into my soul—the blackest midnight of a thousand—"

"Shut *up!*"

"Sorry."

"Still hungry, eh?" Nuklear Man's mind raced like a Model-T. "How about some refried beans?"

"Congealed?" Lord Obese asked.

"Completely."

"Fork it over, puny man."

"If you say so." Nuklear Man tossed the small container to the Rotund Raider. Lord Obese ate it out of the air, container and all. "My hunger burns still!"

"That ain't the only thing that's gonna be burnin'," Nuklear Man muttered.

Lord Obese's organs rumbled, including the ones that had nothing to do with digestion. A sound bellowed from his stomach. It was not unlike rabid elephants stampeding across a field of geese that were tied down to the their paciderm demise. His face twisted grotesquely, like every muscle wanted to leave the others. His limbs quaked with a sudden weakness. His gut roared in protest like oppressed colonists.

"Uh, Obese? You feelin' okay?" Zeerox asked, tugging on the fat man's Hawaiian moo-moo.

He began to teeter.

"Run for the hills!" Chronotor screamed. The villains scrambled. "He'll fall in exactly—" **WHUMP** "—one...second."

Nuklear Man's cape was blast back by the gust of air from the impact. He took the opportunity to bask in a righteous Heroic pose.

"Put some clothes on, you freak!" Someone yelled from across the street.

"What is *that?*" Rachel asked, pointing at the heap of moo-moo covered flesh ahead of them. Limbs poked out from under it at unusual angles.

Atomik Lad shifted her backpack on his shoulder. He saw Nuklear Man's Danger: Pose of Triumph. "This time, I don't *want* to know."

"That's probably for the best," she said.

"Ready to go, Nuke?" Atomik Lad asked as they approached the Danger: Nukemobile.

"Gimme a second," he said, still basking. "Two, three, and done." He hopped down into the driver's seat. "Let's roll!"

"Uhh, maybe I should drive. Y'know, for practice."

"I dunno. You kept grabbing the wheel. We were all over the road. Luckily I'm good enough to overcome your incompetence and saved the day like at least a billion times. Again."

Rachel giggled.

"Ugh. Well, if I was driving, you could talk to our lovely guest, Rachel."

"Hello, hello," the Hero said in his most suave voice. Strangely enough, it was among the least suave voices Rachel had ever heard. "Come here often, or do you wait until—"

"Nuke, be polite."

"You two should take this act on the road."

"Yeah. The act," Atomik Lad grumbled. "C'mon, Nuke, what'dya say? I'll be extra careful, just like you."

"I don't think you're quite ready. Besides, I'm such a good driver, I can woo her with my countless Heroic exploits and still keep us on the road."

"Nuke, I really think I should drive."

"Oh what's the harm, John? He's Nuklear Man, we couldn't be safer, right?"

"I like her, Sparky. She pays attention to the propaganda."

"It's called 'Public relations,' Nuke. There's a difference."

"Not when I usurp the throne."

"What are you…No, whatever. Let's just go." Atomik Lad got into the passenger seat and scooched it up for the benefit of Rachel and her legroom in the cramped back seat.

"Why thank you, Mr. Sparky. Such a gentleman."

"I taught him everything he knows," Nuklear Man bragged.

"That took all of two minutes," Atomik Lad said as he closed the car door.

"I'm just that good." Nuklear Man started the car and entered traffic. The world became a much more hazardous place.

"Obese…is…crushing…me."

"He's crushing…us all!"

"Has been…for…one minute, seventeen…seconds."

"He's…drooling…on me!"

"At least…you're…not—gasp—by his…armpit, oink!"

"Okenshi…will escape…this simple…trap."

"This is just a temporary set back," Blazer said, muffled by the Rotund Raider's enormous stomach. "We shall reap our vengeance against Nuklear Man."

"Can we grab some lunch first?" Granite asked from somewhere under the chest region.

"Shut up."

ISSUE 16—DRIVING MR. NUKLEAR (CRAZY)

"So then, I look that big ol' spider right in the eyes—and I ain't even scared—I look 'im right in the eyes and says to him, I says, 'Why don't you say that to my face?'"

"And then what?" Rachel patronized. She was leaning forward on the seat backs of her companions so she could hear the conversation, which Nuklear Man had completely hijacked, over the roar of the wind.

"He backed down. Yep, he took one look at me and instantly knew the world of pain he was getting into. Still, I am a Hero after all. I was obligated to eradicate it."

"How daring."

"Oh, that's me all over, baby."

"I'm sure it is."

"Maybe I could show ya sometime, huh?" he said with as smooth-talkin' a tone as he could muster. It was a greater failure than his last attempt.

"*Nuke*!" Atomik Lad shouted. "Look out!" Ahead of them was a mile or so of gridlock.

"Hmm," Nuklear Man said. "Hang on to your skirts, girls—present company excluded."

"Thanks?" Rachel said.

"Things are about to get a little crazy."

"*About* to get?" Atomik Lad slammed on the brakes from the passenger seat. The Danger: Nukemobile skidded to a halt less than an inch from the rear bumper of the car in front of them.

"What'd you do that for?!" Nuklear Man demanded.

"You were about to get us killed!"

"Feh! Death is for the weak."

"Even so, we'll just wait here in traffic like normal people until it clears up."

"Stupid normal people, always slowin' Nukie down."

*   *   *   *

"So I'm just going to college for the knowledge, you know. I mean, what's a major really going to do for someone like me, right?" Atomik Lad said. He was completely turned around in his seat so he could face Rachel.

"Yeah, 'Excuse me, Mr. CEO, I've got to save the world.'"

"Exactly. But I like the university atmosphere and it almost makes me think I'm leading a normal life."

"Shh."

They looked at Nuklear Man.

Atomik Lad spoke up, "What's the—"

"*Shh*!" the Hero insisted. "Do you hear that?"

There was nothing to hear.

"No," Rachel answered for them.

"Shh! There it was again."

No it wasn't. "You feeling all right, Nuke?"

The glazed quality in his eyes shone with other worldly knowledge. "I've never felt better." He giggled maniacally before catching himself. He darted his eyes to assure himself that no one had noticed even though they had. "It's all so clear to me now. Yes. Shh! Did you hear it that time?"

They listened in the hopes of hearing something, anything, but to no avail. "Maybe if you told us what we're listening for?" Rachel suggested.

Nuklear Man looked at their guest like she had instantly appeared out of nowhere. He grabbed Atomik Lad by the collar and pulled him close. "Who is that?!" he hissed in a conspiratorial whisper.

"Um, Rachel."

The Hero looked back at her. Paranoia was having a field day in his eyes. He turned back to Atomik Lad. "Can she be trusted?"

"Well, yeah."

"All right." He released the sidekick. "But my wrath shall be severe should she betray our sacred cabal."

"What're you talking about?"

"Oh, I get it." The Hero gave a knowledgeable wink. "What am I talking about indeed. Very nice, good work." He sat back in his seat with a content smile. "And we'll stick to that story, won't we."

"What story?"

"Yes, just like that."

Rachel's "What?" face met Atomik Lad's. They continued their conversation.

*   *   *   *

"I still don't know what I want to do, though," Rachel said. "It feels like such a final decision, you know?"

"That's what I used to think. But your major doesn't have to be what your life is about. I mean, look at your parents. I bet their jobs have nothing to do with what they studied in college."

"I suppose so. Anyway, it's easy for you to say. You've got, well, certain abilities. Being a hero is what you've always done. It's what you'll always do."

"And it's such a terrific fate, let me tell you."

"I'd give anything to have you what you do. You make a difference in the world. I mean you go and you battle evil. You make the world a better place to live just by being here. You've saved countless lives, you do it every day. You know you love it."

"I once read that what you love will destroy you."

"Isn't that what your field thingie is for?"

"It comes in handy."

Nuklear Man heard a thunderous **VROOSH!** as a turtle rocketed past them, though no such event actually occurred.

"Did you *see* that?!" Nuklear Man screamed, half standing and pointing to the horizon beyond the endless line of immobile cars stretching ahead of them.

"Er, no," Atomik Lad and Rachel answered simultaneously.

"How could you have missed that? It was a big rocketing turtle flying past us at unimaginable speed!"

"How's that?" Atomik Lad asked incredulously.

"The smoke trail, man! Can't you at least smell the smoke?"

"No."

Nuklear Man gave a full body spasm of freak out. "What is wrong with you people?!"

"Mr. Nuklear Man?" Rachel asked.

"Gah!" The Golden Guardian recoiled from her. "Who's that?"

"Nuke, what the hell is going on?"

Rachel leaned to Atomik Lad and whispered in his ear. Only his concern for Nuklear Man kept him from melting into a pathetic puddle of greenish goo. "I took a psychology course last semester. I think he's going stir crazy."

"Stir crazy?"

"Yeah, kinda like, I don't know, Traffic Jam Dementia."

"Please tell me you're kidding."

"He's exhibiting all the symptoms. It's like he's been locked up in solitary confinement for too long. Paranoia, hallucinations, skittish, jumpy, delusions. He fits the bill."

"Actually, it's not much of a change from his normal behavior. He's just sorta being exaggerated about it now."

Atomik Lad turned to Nuklear Man. Another manic giggle escaped from his unstable demeanor. "You see? You see? They laughed at me, yes, they all laughed. But now, now I say, who's laughing?" He waved a ragged piece of paper in one hand. "It's all here—all here. All the answers, it's so simple."

"Nuke?"

"Right here!" He held the paper to his chest to protect it from the savage talking bears in the car. "You can look at it if you promise not to eat it or something equally bearish."

"Um, okay."

"Be careful with those claws! It's fragile."

"Sure."

Nuklear Man giggled at something he probably hallucinated and extended a shaking hand. Atomik Lad carefully took the paper like brain surgery was involved. His eyebrows came together and danced up and down a few times. He cocked his head from side to side, squinted, tried viewing the paper from different distances, turned it upside down, and showed it to Rachel.

"No!" Nuklear Man exclaimed, snatching the paper away. "No salvation for that bear. Not until it proves it can be trusted."

"Sorry." Atomik Lad slowly took the paper again and looked at it. "So, um. Just what is all this?" he asked. Haphazard chicken scratches were scrawled in various levels of complete nonsense across the paper.

"A while back I heard this harebrained theory that time slows down the faster you go. A ridiculous concept. So I, in an ingenious maneuver, reversed it, because the opposite of ridiculous is logical! I threw the whole works in 'R' y'know. So now I've mathematically proven that the slower you go, the faster time goes! That's why, despite the fact we've only been here, trapped in this hellish gridlock for an hour and a half—"

"Twelve minutes," Atomik Lad noted as he examined Nuklear Man's mad equations.

"—It seems like it's been five to ten years! You see? Yes, it all falls together. Pearl Harbor, Caesar's assassination, crop circles, bad poetry, it's such a beautiful web. From here we can build a coherent model for the universe! The Grand Nukification Theory is a reality! All humanity will bow before me, the Nuklear Regime will usher in a new era of—"

"Nuke, it seems there's a slight miscalculation in your otherwise impressive theory."

"Sh, bear. I'm demigoding."

"I think you mean demagogue-ing. Besides, this could throw a snag into your plans." He handed Nuklear Man the paper and pointed to the first line. "You see, two plus two does not equal five."

"Well no, not yet. But the Bureau of Truth Editing will correct that once I come to power. Until then, in order to make the universe fit my formulas, I have 'theorized' or 'made up' if you will, the concept of 'dark numbers.'"

"Dark numbers?"

"Yes. Massless, valueless numbers that exist between ordinary numbers that are impossible to detect, but make up 95% of the number line. Now, anytime someone adds wrong, it's because of dark numbers! It's the perfect excuse! My rule will be absolute."

"Let's just put this Nuklear Regime thing on the back burner for now, huh?"

"Oh, I get it. I should have known better than to trust a couple'a bears with my plans. You're taking the Grand Nukification Theory for your own, aren't you? Grand Bearification Theory, right?"

"Well, no."

"Ha! Your denial proves it! You could at least have the dignity to admit your underhanded treachery. If you think I'm going to let you get away with this, you've got another thing coming, ursa-boy."

"Nuke, snap out of it!" Atomik Lad slapped his mentor with a crackling red fist.

"Sparky! What're you doing? I oughta dock you fifteen superpoints for loss of sanity. You went completely bonkers back there."

Atomik Lad rolled his eyes.

Nuklear Man straightened his cape. "Luckily, I was able to keep my cool and save the platoon from certain doom, no thanks to you and those stinkin' Commies."

Rachel couldn't help laughing at them.

Nuklear Man scoured the field of vehicles. "I think I know how to get us out of this. It'll take the subtlety of a breeze, the cunning of a fox, the stealth of a shadow, the precision of an eagle, the strength of a—"

"Here it comes." Atomik Lad prepared himself for the inevitable.

"—PLAZMAAA—"

"Nuke!" Atomik Lad grappled Nuklear Man's hands. "What have I told you about indiscriminate displays of power?"

"I dunno. Every time you start talking about that stuff I start thinking about how a big Plazma Beam would shut you up."

"Why me?"

"You two are crazy."

"Oh I'm fine," Nuklear Man assured her. He leaned back to whisper conspiratorily to Rachel, "It's Sparky here I'd worry about."

Rachel winked at Atomik Lad. "I'll keep an eye on him."

"Nuke, do you think you can hold on to your sanity until the traffic clears up?"

"Hmm, hard to say. There's so little of it to hold on to."

"I've noticed."

"It's kinda hard to keep track of the darn thing, y'know."

"Let's just wait it out, all right?"

"Oh fine. And keep a look out for those lousy bears. They'll stab you in the back given half the chance."

"Crazy," Rachel repeated to herself. "Just crazy."

Issue 17—Speed Limit Enforced by Radar

"Oh, nuts to this." Nuklear Man said, determination rang through his voice like laughter at a funeral. "It's time for action!" He turned the wheel all the way to the right and stomped on the gas pedal. At the same time, he grabbed the outside of his door and pulled up with his mighty arm. The Danger: Nukemobile jumped with a squeal of acceleration and zipped into the bike lane on two wheels.

Atomik Lad grit his teeth. Fear played across his face. "Uh, Nuke," he said with a calm that he found disturbing. "Maybe you should slow down just a little, hm?"

Rachel looked like she was on a roller coaster, "No wonder you guys are able to get to villain outbursts so quickly."

"Nuke!" Atomik Lad yelled, one hand holding onto the dashboard, the other pointing straight ahead.

"What?" His voice was wrought with a whiney annoyance.

The bike lane was about to come to an abrupt end, much like the lives of those involved in the epic wreck that was about to occur.

"Stop the car!" Atomik Lad screamed.

Nuklear Man's Heroic gaze, a gaze that can only be perfected by hours of daily practice in front of several full length mirrors, crept across his face. "Sorry, Sparky. We just can't do that. We've got a schedule to keep."

The first signs of fear began to find their way to Rachel. "M-maybe you should stop, Mr. Nuklear Man. I know you guys are Heroes and all, but there's no need to go out of your way to invite trouble."

The Hero tightened his grip of the door. "Well how *else* are we going to find it?"

Rachel hung on to her seat with tense hands.

Atomik Lad grumbled to himself, flung his seat back all the way down and grabbed Rachel's waist. "I hope this works," he muttered in something resembling a prayer. His crimson field enveloped both himself and his guest.

"Where we're going," Nuklear Man said, "we won't need roads." The Danger: Nukemobile ignored gravity and soared above the stagnant traffic. Nuklear Man's fingertips dented into the door side, his bicep flexed slightly from the strain of holding onto the car.

Rachel opened one eye like a rusty, reluctant hatch. She jerked slightly with surprise. "Red!"

Her movement plucked Atomik Lad from his stupor. His energy field sputtered and disappeared around them. "Hi," he said, looking up into her face from her lap.

"My, aren't you straight forward?" she said, putting her hands on Atomik Lad's, still on her waist.

He jumped at her touch like a small shock of electricity had arced through his hands. "Eheh. Sorry." He slid his hands from under hers and raised his seat to its more traditional and vertical position. He tugged at his collar as inconspicuously as he could. Nuklear Man was known to be more subtle.

"Now that we've gotten rid of those idiotic drivers, we oughta have a fairly uneventful trip," Nuklear Man said.

"Thank every god," Atomik Lad sighed.

"Oh gosh!" Rachel exclaimed. She leaned over the side. "We're flying!"

"Did you see that one van run me off the road?"

"Nuke, you ran the van off the road."

"Oh, whatever. My point is if these people knew how to drive in the first place, I wouldn't have to run them off the road."

Rachel's eyes traced the contours of the cityscape below them and the farmlands surrounding it. "Wow, this is amazing. I can't believe you guys get to do this every day."

"I guess it's fun," Nuklear Man said, his voice taking on the tone of a police officer being interviewed on a reality cop show. "But it gets in the way of all the TV watching, so we try to wrap things up pretty quick."

"I see," Rachel said, admiring the view more than Nuklear Man's ramblings.

"Well, that and I'm *so* good, the villains can't help but be defeated in a rather episodic fashion," he said.

She giggled. Atomik Lad rolled his eyes.

"Ya know, we oughta land, Nuke. We could actually have one normal day." He considered the morning thus far. "Or at least a semi-normal afternoon."

"But we just had one!" the Hero whined.

Atomik Lad rubbed his eyes. "What planet do you live on?"

"Happy Nukieland."

"I shouldn't have asked," he muttered into his hands.

"Where all I do all the live long day is beat the hoo-ha out of villains whilst—"

"Just land the car."

"Oh fine." He turned to Rachel and winked. "I'll give you a personal tour some day."

"I can't wait," she answered jokingly. Nuklear Man couldn't tell the difference.

"Now then, to secure an L-Z. Or 'Landing Zone' to you civilians," Nuklear Man said with little air quotes. The car dipped down until he grabbed the door again.

"Thanks for the clarification," Rachel said, paying just enough attention Nuklear Man not to distract herself from the view.

"Time for a little reconnaissance, or 'recon' as we like to call it in the Corp. Sparky, hold the wheel."

Atomik Lad gripped the wheel without thinking about it. "Er. Does it really matter?"

"…It could."

Atomik Lad shrugged and held firm anyway.

Nuklear Man scoured the surface below with his eyes. "Oh, what I wouldn't do for some heat vision."

"Wait, what?"

Nuklear Man ignored him. "Ah! That spot'll do just fine." He clenched his free hand into a fist. A golden orb of liquid-like energy glowed around it. "PLAZMAAA—"

"Nuke!"

"Does he *ever* get one of those off?" Rachel asked.

"What?" Nuklear Man protested. "I've got to clear a landing site."

Atomik Lad looked over the side. "Those are suburbs!"

"Exactly. The way I figure it, they're a dime a dozen. No one'll miss a couple neighborhoods here or there. It's a victimless crime. No jury would convict me."

Atomik Lad tried to begin several rebuttals to Nuklear Man's logic, but it was like trying to catch every leaf of autumn. "How about we just land along that nice straight stretch of empty road down there next to them, hm?"

"Fine, we'll do it your wussy way."

The Danger: Nukemobile sank to the street with a short, sharp screech of its tires. It reminded Atomik Lad of an airplane landing. They rocketed through the barren road far in excess of the posted speed limit.

"What'd that sign say?" Atomik Lad asked. The wind roared deafened Nuklear Man to his question.

"Speed Enforced By Radar," Rachel reported.

"How fast are we going?" Atomik Lad asked.

Nuklear Man checked the Danger: Speedometer. "I dunno. The needle only goes to 120mph."

"Maybe we really should slow down."

"Oh no! Old man radar's gonna call our mommies!" Nuklear Man said with a girly voice. "Feh, I'm *so* scared of radar. Radar's gonna come and get us, oh no, whatever shall we do? Boo hoo hoo, woe is me. Enforce this, radar." Nuklear Man pushed the accelerator to the floor board.

Atomik Lad noticed a blur of motion just outside his field of vision. Something just barely green or purple, too fast to properly distinguish, rushed toward them.

There was an impact and the Danger: Nukemobile catapulted off the road. It tumbled end over end into a side ditch where it landed right side up.

Rachel opened her eyes. "Red?"

Atomik Lad turned to face her. "Are you..." He noticed she was enveloped in his field which he also just noticed actually existed in the first place. "Are you all right?"

She stretched her neck from side to side. "You do this on all your first dates, Sparky?"

"If I have another one, I'll let you know."

Nuklear Man shot out of the car. "Yeeouch!" The seatbelt held him in check. "That is *so* gonna leave a mark," he whined with a painful grimace while unbuckling himself. Nuklear Man shot out of the car but tripped on the rearview mirror and slammed face first on the hood. He rolled over and ate a faceful of dirt.

"Par for the course, big guy," Atomik Lad said. He helped Rachel from the wreck.

"Lousy physics, always slowin' me down," Nuklear Man grumbled from under his cape.

Nuklear Man poked his head out from his cape. "Hey, who's that?" he asked, pointing across the street.

It was seven feet and four hundred pounds of purple muscle clad in green spandex and a billowing cape. He stood in a pose so confident it would've made Ozymandius blush. His features were chiseled in weathered stone. Uncaring and cold eyes examined the world in black and white, right and wrong. He had an otherworldly quality. Purple skin had a way of doing that.

"Radar!" the stranger announced with a flourish of his cape.

"Oh, he's *good*," Nuklear Man said.

"You were driving in excess of the posted limit." Radar struck an accusatory point at Nuklear Man. "You must suffer the consequences!"

Nuklear Man stood up and glowed a golden plazma glow to cleanse himself of any dirt while showing off his spiffy powers. "Suffer *these* consequences, purple-boy!" Nuklear Man taunted. He rushed Radar with Nuklear Speed.

Radar sneered, "Lawbreaker." He threw a mighty uppercut that caught the Hero completely off guard. It spun Nuklear Man into the distant sky, reeling end over end from the impact.

"I can see the Silo from here!" he yelled just before fading from Atomik Lad's view.

Atomik Lad squinted and blinked as he stared uselessly into the sky. "Wow."

Rachel tugged on his spandex. "You can handle this, right?"

"Let's hope so."

Radar stomped up to them. "Prepare for retribution," he growled.

"Uh, Radar, is it? Hi, I'm Atomik Lad. I'm certain we can work something out."

"The law must be enforced. The guilty must be punished."

"But I wasn't driving."

"You were an accomplice." His voice dripped bile. "Guilty by association."

"Well, if you're going to be unreasonable about it." His Atomik Field flared to life once more with a crack of thunder. "I'll have to—*OOF!*" Atomik Lad was pound into the earth. Only his head stuck out of the ground. His crimson field sputtered and faded around him. Radar loomed over him like a purple mountain.

Radar dusted off his hands and crossed his mighty purple arms across his wide chest. "You are next, meager woman."

"*Meager?*"

"Insignificant," he stated.

"Is that so?" She walked toward the creature with wrath and vengeance powering her stomping footsteps.

"Rachel, no. I can handle this." Atomik Lad squirmed in futile attempts to release himself from his terra-cotta prison.

"Not now, Hon," she dismissed while absently stepping on his head.

She nearly leaned against Radar as she ranted, "Who do you think you are? You ruined our car, spoiled our plans, wasted my day off, beat up the world's greatest Hero, embarrassed my date, and then you have the gall to insult me. What gives you the right?"

Radar squared his shoulders and proudly announced, "I am Radar, Centurion of the Highways, Enforcer of Defensive Driving! I derive my powers from the severity of a lawbreaker's crime. That Nuklear Man's driving has fueled me with the strength to topple empires!" He posed and flexed to drive this last point home, but it did little to impress Rachel. "You cannot hope to quell me, I am the very personification of Highway Justice."

Rachel leaned back with a quirky smile that would have destroyed Atomik Lad's non-sexual thoughts had he seen it.

"What is it?" Radar demanded. "You face certain obliteration and yet you smile?"

"Oh, I don't think it's obliteration that I face," she said smugly.

Radar huffed. "Get on with it."

"I was sitting in the backseat. I cannot be held accountable for the driver. I am not an accomplice, I did not break the law. You, Mr. Purple, are powerless before me."

"You're bluffing."

"Am I?"

Sweat formed on Radar's brow.

"Well?" she asked.

His face twisted with rage. He screamed a primal scream, clasped his hands in a massive fist over his head, and dropped them onto Rachel's skull with bone-shattering force.

There was an explosion. A strange vermillion fire unlike any natural flame had burst forth and chunks of earth rained all over them. The smoke cleared. The earth had been blast away from Atomik Lad. He stood in a crater bathed in red light, his body engulfed with a wicked fire. "Rachel?" he called a little too hysterically.

Radar quivered, his mauled hands still atop Rachel's unharmed head. Tears streamed from his face. His mouth was locked in a silent scream.

"Hm?" she answered innocently.

"Are you all right?"

"Yep." She touched a finger to Radar's chest. The giant teetered and fell over backwards like a toppled manequin. A dust cloud poofed from his impact with the ground.

"But. How. You. He?" Atomik Lad stammered while trying to complete a thought and verbalize it.

"Someone had to. You boys were just playing around."

"Playing?"

"I suspected he wasn't a real threat for you and Nuklear Man from the start. I was certain of it when Nuklear Man started goofing around and trusted you to take care of the goon by yourself."

"Wah?"

"But then when you just started toying with him by letting him think he nailed you into the ground, well it's funny, don't get me wrong, but we are running late after all." She heaved Atomik Lad out of his crater. He was too stunned to float out by himself. "And when he went and insulted me, well then it got personal."

"He. You. Hit. Alive."

"Oh, that. Just shows what a little traffic school can do." She scanned the skies. "Now we're really going to be late. Where is that Nuklear Man?" They searched the sky in the direction he had been launched.

"I guess he's already landed," Atomik Lad said while rubbing the back of his neck. "He should be on his way back by now. He doesn't like to be upstaged."

"What's that sound?" Rachel asked. She turned her head form side to side.

"Hm, I hear it too." He turned completely around. "Where's it—*duck!*"

"No, it's more like a goose—*Ah!*" Atomik Lad pulled her down with him.

A distant "Ahhhhhh!" grew into a louder and incoming "AHHHHHHHH-HHH!" as a golden blur slammed into Atomik Lad's crater and made it even bigger. There was a lot of coughing.

"Quite a direct approach, Sparky," Rachel said once the dust, old and new, settled.

Atomik Lad blinked and rubbed the dirt from his eyes and fell speechless yet again. "Um. I, I, I." Or at least incoherent, "I…"

"Am laying on top of me. Rather spoils the chivalry of your actions, though I think I can live with it."

"Oh my," he managed to utter.

Nuklear Man instantly popped out of the improved crater. "Who, what, where?!" each word got its own action pose.

Atomik Lad clumsily rolled off of Rachel and onto the ground. "What are you doing with all those stickers?" he asked Nuklear Man.

"Huh?" He looked down at himself. He was covered in international postage. "Well what'dya know? I must've gone all the way around the world."

"That explains why he came from the opposite direction," Rachel said.

"But that doesn't explain the stamps themselves. How'd they get there?"

"Sure it does," Nuklear Man said. "Don't you ever watch Silly Sam's Cartoon Marathon-a-thon o' Fun? I don't keep it on 24 hours a day for my health, you know."

"Nuke, those are cartoons, they're not real."

"Watch your mouth!" the Hero snapped.

"Oh geez."

"I do remember flying through a post office though," he said with a thoughtful chin stroke. "Maybe they could figure it out."

"Of course."

"Ahem," Rachel said. "We should get going, you know."

Nuklear Man gave her a thumbs up. "That's my little trooper!"

"Is it?" she asked.

He considered it for a moment. "Yes." Nuklear Man flew to the car and tossed it back on to the road. Then he turned it right-side-up. The trio piled in and, despite the Nukemobile's newfound junkyard chic, their beach-ward journey continued anew.

ISSUE 18—BEACH
BIRTHDAY BLOWOUT,
YEAH!

The beach was crowned with a cloudless sky. The morning sun was a fierce sphere of heat that beat down on the few Larsen Beach patrons. A light breeze coursed through the salty air to help soothe the savage heat. Coconut scents and the sounds of music playing just far enough to make it unintelligible wafted through the scene.

Nuklear Man, followed by Rachel and Atomik Lad, strut over the dunes that kept the highway and parking lot out of view from the beach. The illusion of paradise lived on.

"Hey, why don't we sit over there?" Atomik Lad suggested from under several hundred pounds of recreational beach equipment. "How'd he fit all this in that small trunk?" he huffed.

"There's an awful lot of people over there," Nuklear Man said suspiciously. "I'd hate to have to show them all up with my godlike physique." He whispered to Rachel, "'Cause then I'd make them all feel so inferior we'd have to talk 'em out of suicide and I can't stand that whiney crap. Gets in the way of action."

"Ah."

"That's Nuke. Our little Mr. Sensitive," Atomik Lad grunted. "Maybe you could keep the Stud-o-matic down to about eight until you merely alienate them and then you could turn it up to a full ten."

"But it's so hard to keep all this hunka-hunka burnin' plazma under control."

Atomik Lad, under the oppressive pressure of beach tourist crap and gravity, couldn't afford the luxury of speech.

"You just suggested we should sit down with those people," Rachel, being the fast learner that she was, answered.

"I did...?" Nuklear Man said in an attempt to remain noncommital.

"Let's go," she said, leading the way.

Atomik Lad's footsteps sunk deep into the sand. "I think I've got sand in my spandex," he said, trying to kick some from his boots.

"Need me to get it?" Rachel asked.

Atomik Lad's burden shook, "Yowza."

Nuklear Man watched his sidekick. "Having trouble with the Danger: Beach Equipment, Sparky?"

"I could use a little help, actually," he said. His face was red with the strain that rang in his voice.

The weight of the world was taken from Atomik Lad's shoulders. He stared at his mentor in awe. "I didn't think you'd take the whole thing. No offense, but knowing you, you would've hopped on top and claimed it was for my training or something."

"Check this out," Nuklear Man said with a gleam in his eye, the kind the mad claim to be genius. He tossed the beach supplies toward their destination, just in front of the already present beach-goers. "It'll all land *just* right. Trust me. I saw it in a cartoon once."

It all landed wrong. Most of the items had been broken beyond repair.

"Nice one, Nuke."

"Thanks," he said proudly since he was unable to perceive personal failure.

They approached the mound of junk.

Several forms dashed from behind the refuse and yelled "SURPRISE!!!" in exuberant unison.

Nuklear Man jumped back, powered up, and fired. "PLAZMAAA BEAM!" The fusion-ish plazma carved a glass coated ditch through the sand. An aura of Plazma radiated around the Hero. His action pose remained in high gear, keeping up with the melodramatic dance his cape was enjoying with the wind.

"Remind me to never sneak up behind him," Rachel whispered into Atomik Lad's ear.

"Um," he said, too easily pleased.

The sun glinted off a silver statue at the end of Nuklear Man's glassy canal. A few familiar faces poked out form behind it. "Nuke," the statue said. "You always know how to start a party!"

"Mighty Metallic Magno Man!" Nuklear Man exclaimed. "Did I nail those surprise people?"

The Tungsten Titan gave Nuklear Man a Magno-Noogie. "You crazy kid, you."

"Aww, cut it out!" Nuklear Man waved his arms in a fruitless defense.

"Happy birthday, Nukie!" a chorus of voices rang from beyond the living shield of Mighty Metallic Magno Man.

"Dr. Genius! Librarian, Mail Man, Meter Girl, Delivery Boy! What're you all doing here, you should be at your respective places of employment."

Mail Man put his Tank-B-Gone Assault Cannon down. "The Minimum Wage Warriors never miss a party!" The others nodded in agreement.

"Plus, we're all out on our lunch hours," Meter Girl added.

"Let's get this party goin'!" Delivery Boy yelled. The guests stepped to one side and revealed a table stacked with pizza boxes and a cooler full of iced soft drinks. "Complementary from Mamma Mia's Pizzeria!"

"Complementary, eh?" Nuklear Man considered. "What's that gonna cost me?"

"Nuke," Atomik Lad said. "Just have fun."

*　　　*　　　*　　　*

Dr. Genius adjusted her glasses while admiring the sky. She put her hands in her lab coat pockets and rocked back and forth on her bare heels. The hot sand felt good against her skin. It was a sharp contrast to the cold, sterile floors of the Überdyne offices she was used to. "I really don't get out of the lab enough," she mused. Her reddish blonde hair flowed in the sea breeze as she shed her trusty lab coat and demonstrated that bikinis are wonderful things.

Nuklear Man's jaw dropped. "Thank God for the man who invented women."

Mighty Metallic Magno Man, in his full tungsten glory, laid on a beach towel next to Nuklear Man and soaked up some rays.

In the distance, Nuklear Man noticed several women swooning over his fellow hero. "What's he got that I don't got?" he grumbled.

"Brains," Atomik Lad suggested as he passed by.

"That's nuthin'! How far can you possibly get in life on talent and skill alone? You need charm and good looks to get ahead in this hero eat villain world we live in today. Feh, I'll show them girls who the real hero is 'round these here parts!"

After a considerable amount of difficulty, Nuklear Man had his Danger: Nuke's Towel resting on the lumpy ground. He flopped onto it which was about as sandy as, well, sand. He chanced a look to the ladies.

*　　*　　*　　*

"What's that guy's problem?" the first asked.

"I think he's having a spaz attack," the second said.

"It's so nice of Mighty Metallic Magno Man to take care of that epileptic guy," the third said.

They directed a simultaneous "Aww" at the Tungsten Titan.

*　　*　　*　　*

"Oh yeah," Nuklear Man said. "They're already wooed by my irresistible charms. Now it's just a matter of reeling them in." He produced a pair of sunglasses. He slid them on with a confident smile gracing his face. "Ouch!" He flinched with pain and rubbed his left eye. "Lousy sunglasses." With a confident smile and careful deliberateness, he slid them on again. "Ouch!" He flinched with pain and rubbed his right eye.

*　　*　　*　　*

"What's that guy doing *now?*" the first asked.

"Something's wrong with his head. He keeps flailing it around," the second said.

"I think he's got suntan lotion in his eyes," the third said.

"Are you sure it's not a seizure?" the first asked.

"What a gimp."

*　　*　　*　　*

Nuklear Man held the glasses with both hands at arms' length. "Brain to Arms, Brain to Arms, over." He responded to himself in a different voice, "Arms here, Brain. Over." Back to the Brain's voice, "Initiate docking procedures." The glasses slowly approached Nuklear Man's face as he made a mechanical high-pitched "Vrrrrrm" sound. "Vrrrrrrrrrrrrrrrrrrrrrrrrrrrrrm. Gasp, vrrrrrrrm—ouch!" The sunglasses fell onto Nuklear Man's sand speckled towel. He rubbed both eyes. "I had no idea eye-wear could be so dangerous. They oughta have warnings or somethin'."

*   *   *   *

Atomik Lad set out a towel and helped Rachel with hers. "Always the gentleman, eh, Sparky?" she joked.

"Well, I've got to keep up this charade until my mission is complete, otherwise you'd be onto my ploy."

"Ah, clandestine. Mysterious and romantic. I like it."

"Yes, that's it, fall right into my trap."

She laughed and dropped her shorts to the towel. Atomik Lad wobbled. She pulled off her shirt and tossed them next to the shorts. Atomik Lad wobbled with more urgency than before. Bikinis are the *best* thing.

"Would you mind helping me with my suntan lotion?"

"Mind?" Atomik Lad ceased to wobble. He fell flat on his rear. "Yeow!" He flopped to one side as gracefully as a landlocked fish.

"You're just having all sorts of trouble today, aren't you?" Rachel said.

"Something down there poked me," Atomik Lad said, rubbing his tush.

"Do you know how hard it is for me not to comment further?" Rachel said

"I'm serious."

"So am I."

"There's something just under the surface. And it's sharp." Atomik Lad flung his towel to one side and started clearing away the sand. Rachel helped.

"Ah!" she exclaimed. "I felt something."

Atomik Lad stopped for a moment and looked at her. "All right, now *I'm* the one having trouble restraining myself from making further comments."

She hit him in the arm and they resumed.

"Wait, I think I felt it too."

They dug with an excited fury. Rachel fell back aghast. Atomik Lad stared in wide-eyed awe. "I-it can't be!"

"Augch!!"

"*Angus?*!"

The Iron Scotsman's head stuck out of Atomik Lad and Co.'s excavation site.

"How'd you get down there? Are you all right?" he asked. Rachel was just glad it wasn't the corpse she initially took it for.

"Bah! Ah'm fine, laddie," Angus said.

Atomik Lad turned to Rachel. "It's all right. It's just Angus."

She slowed her breathing in an attempt to calm her heart. "Well that explains so much," she said.

Atomik Lad helped Angus climb out of his earthy prison. Sand poured from the crevices of his Iron: Battlesuit.

"Where'd you get that helmet?" Atomik Lad asked. He plucked it from the Surly Scot's sandy head. "Those horns must've been what poked me. It looks like something a Viking would wear. Not quite your motif."

Angus blinked irritably in the bright beachy sun. He beat a pound of sand and one of those umbrellas they put in drinks out of his beard. He flicked the cocktail accessory away and it danced momentarily in the salty wind. "Well," he began. "Me an' Shamus left ye place to go drinkin'." He rubbed his beard in contemplation. "I don't remember much after that."

Dr. Genius walked by, her cup filled with carbonated delights. "Oh, Angus, I didn't know you were going to be here. How are you?"

"Ah was just tellin' the Laddie here about, well, not about much." He stared at the helmet. "Actually, Ah do remember somethin', a scene. Real dark place, lit by torches on the walls—real goood for ambiance. Lots o' angry laddies drinkin' an' eatin' an' fightin', my kind o' place. There were these golden eagles too, now that Ah thinks about it. Fat ladies on horses, an' the bartender had a patch over one eye. Didn't know ye could still find rough places like that in Metroville anymore."

Atomik Lad turned the helmet in his hands. "Kinda sounds like…"

"Valhalla," Dr. Genius finished for him.

"But that's impossible," Rachel said.

"Well," Dr. Genius began. "If reality is a state of consciousness, then it stands to reason that one's consciousness can become so altered that the individual is effectively subtracted from the universe as we know it. It would then be possible to be transported to another reality until the subject's senses return to normal and he realizes how impossible his environment is, at which point he's brought back to the here and now. Loss of memory and disorientation would be in keeping with the temporal distortions such a trek across dimensions would incur."

Angus scratched his head. "Ye know, it kind o' reminded me of what happened the *last* time Shamus an' me got to drinkin' together. This was years ago, mind ye. It was this really bright place, ten times as bright as it is out here. But the seats were the most comfortable my arse has ever known. Like sittin' on clouds, it was. Anyway, there was this one laddie, handsome devil, and from what Ah recalls, he was pissed off at his boss. Seems this laddie was passed up for a promotion or some such. Sounded like his boss was one of these holier-than-thou types. Poor guy didn't know what ta doo. So Ah told him not to take any of that arrogant blowhard's crap. Ah said if he thought he could do a better job, why not start his own company? Well he brightened up real quick when Ah said that. He told me he never woulda thought of doin' something like that in a million years. He pat me on the back, thanked me, and bought me a drink. I don't kwoow what happened to that laddie, but I've never had a problem with my long distance service."

The others exchanged glances in silence above Angus's view.

"Still," Dr. Genius sipped from her cup. "The theory is all very hypothetical of course. No scientific evidence to support it."

✳   ✳   ✳   ✳

Meanwhile, on the other side of the globe, Shamus's emerald armored self slowly emerged from a steaming vat of liquid. *Oh, this be one of the nicest hangovers I've ever been waking from. I must be in some sort of sauna. That be tasting like soup.* He opened his eyes only to find himself in a large iron cauldron in the middle of a village in the middle of a black forest. Native peoples danced around him. They looked hungry. "Think fast, boy-o."

✳   ✳   ✳   ✳

Back on the beach, Nuklear Man nearly tripped over Angus. "Hey, Doc." Then he did trip over Angus.

"Ye blind *oaf!* Watch where ye goin' or Ah'll *bash* ye empty skull in like the rootten head o' cabbage it tis!" the Surly Scot raged.

"Hey, is that Angus's voice I hear?" Nuklear Man muttered while laying face first in the sand. "It's kinda hard to see through these Danger: Sunglasses."

Atomik Lad snatched them from Nuklear Man's head and sighed. "Maybe if you didn't put a Danger: Sunglasses label on each lens you could see through them."

"I always say, 'It pays to be safe,' Sparky."

"I thought you always said safety just slows down smash time."

"And what do I say about contradicting me?"

"'The Nuklear Coalition does not recognize opinions it does not generate.' We've really got to do something about this world domination thing of yours. It could get out of hand."

"Et tu, Sparkay?"

"Oh geez."

Issue 19—A Bad Case of Crabs

Rachel was laying down on her towel, sunning her back. Atomik Lad kneeled next to her. He tried desperately to jump start his left hand into squeezing some suntan lotion into his right.

"I was thinking about marine biology for a while," she said.

"How odd," Nuklear Man commented.

"I don't know, it's a fascinating subject. It's a whole other world down there."

"I meant the thinking part. I mean, who's got the time?"

Atomik Lad shook his head. "Hey Nuke, are you going to stay in uniform the whole time?"

He struck a pose. "But what if villainousness were to suddenly discover our unsuspecting selves? We'd be entirely at their mercy! Heroing is one half eternal vigilance, one half style, and one half righteous might."

"You couldn't battle these hypothetical villains in a swimsuit?" Rachel asked.

"A swimsuit?!" Nuklear Man retracted like a proper Victorian lady who was confronted with the possibility of showing an ankle in public. "Do you have any idea how stupid I'd look?! Sheesh." He straightened his golden spandex and made sure his cape was free to flap in the cool breeze.

She held back a laugh. "Er, right. What was I thinking?"

"But Nuke, how do you expect the 'honeys' to go crazy over your 'killer bod' if you don't show it off?"

Nuklear Man considered this train of logic like a cabbage comprehending the more complex aspects of faster than light theory. "You lost me."

"Part of the beach going experience is soaking up some sun," Rachel explained.

Nuklear Man crossed his arms. "Hmmphf. Lousy overrated dayball."

Mighty Metallic Magno Man walked past them with an empty plate and cup on the way to the snack table. "Yo, Nuke. Nice party," he said in passing. An entourage of bikini-clad women swooned after him.

Atomik Lad nudged Nuklear Man's shin, "Hey, Nuke. You all right?"

Nuklear Man glowed with Jealous Plazma like a halogen bulb. "Grrr. Uh, what?" He switched off the light show. "I'm not jealous!" he snapped.

Rachel and Atomik Lad traded glances. "Um" was their consensus. "You know, you could probably get some attention if you showed a little skin, Big Guy."

"I get plenty of attention!" Had the universe been a more dramatic place, tumbleweed would have bounced by.

As it was, Angus took its place. He clomped by irritably. His weight in sand got kicked up with every step. "*Blasted* sand!" he cursed. "It's all soo, soo," he quivered with anger. "*SANDY!*" Satisfied with his astute observation, the Surly Scot walked back to his Iron: Beach Blanket with a plate full of pizza.

"Hold on, ladies," MMMM's voice trailed from the snack stand. "There's no need to crowd me, there's enough pizza to go around."

Rachel and Atomik Lad had to turn away from Nuklear Man. "Nuke, turn down the dimmer switch."

"I'll show that overgrown, egotistical Testosterone Titan!" Nuklear Man grabbed his classy spandex at the electron orbited "N" symbol on his chest and struck a defiant pose. His cape took its cue and turned the Impressive Level up to Critical Mass. His entire outfit was rent from his sculptured body with a single yank leaving nothing to cover it...

"Oh my," Rachel blurted.

"Hail to the king, baby."

...except his Danger: Swimsuit.

Mighty Metallic Magno Man walked by with several pieces of pizza and a refilled cup. "Hey, Nuke. Nice trunks."

Here's my chance, the Hero told himself. *Where?* he asked. *Right there, idiot. Hurry or you'll miss it!* He surveyed the beach. *Ahhhh, yes.* He hopped between MMMM and the girls with a dramatic pose and an even more dramatic, "HA-HO!"

"Out of the way, loser!" one groupie snapped and pushed him to the side.

"All right," he flexed a point off to the left. "Should I go over there?" Another flexed point to the right, "Or there?"

They starred at him unimpressed. "Why don't you take a long walk off a short pier, jerk?" another offered.

"Anything for you lovely ladies." The Hero gave his winning smile-wink-fingergun-point and shot into the air in search of a pier.

* * * *

"Would you like some more suntan lotion, Mighty Metallic Magno Man?"

"Oh ladies!" Someone sounding remarkably like Nuklear Man called from a distance.

"Naw, I'm fine for now. And call me Norman."

They cooed.

"Yoohoo, honeys! Your knight in Plazma Armor is waaaaaaaiiiiiiiting!"

The Tungsten Titan tilted his head. "You girls hear something?"

Far to their right, Nuklear Man floated about ten feet from a pier.

"Norman, will you make the weirdo go away?"

"Oh, you mean Nuke? He's just goofin' around."

Hmm, the Hero thought, *maybe I haven't taken a long enough walk.* A golden streak blazed across the ocean. Two columns of water were tossed into the air as he carved a churning path with his wake. He stopped. Looking back, Nuklear Man saw nothing but water and settling mist. "Lousy curvature of the Earth," he muttered. "Anyway, I bet they think I'm completely dreamy now. It's just a matter of time before they come out here and beg to oil me up." He floated several feet above the ocean's surface and reclined in mid-air with a smile.

* * * *

Lotion. Squeeze. Into hand. Can't. Too. Beautiful.

"C'mon, Sparky, what's taking so long?" Rachel teased. "I thought you'd jump at the chance to put your hands on me."

The suntan lotion bottle's entire contents splurt themselves onto Atomik Lad's hand in accordance with the Laws of Comedy.

"Er. Well, that's never happened before."

"That's okay, don't worry. We've got all day."

*   *   *   *

Angus had been eyeing the ocean with contempt since he finished his contemptuous pizza. He held no actual contempt for the ocean itself. This, of course, generated a considerable amount of contempt in Angus for the ocean. "Bah! Loookit them laddies surfin' out there." There were no laddies and no surfin'. "'Oooh, we be surfin' an' havin' a wonderful time, lah dee dah. What's that, Angus? Ye want to do some surfin' with us, eh? Oh, no, ye be too short fer surfin' folk. Why don't ye go an' sit in the wee kiddies' pool, ye squat freak!' Bah! Ah'll show 'em who's too short for the blasted ocean!"

He dug his small feet into the hot sand, grit his teeth, and tossed his menacing Iron: Battle Helm to the ground. "DWARF-A-PULT!!!" he bellowed to the heavens. His Bagpipe Thrusters flared to life and propelled the diminutive Angus in the general vicinity of the ocean. The horrible thrusters sounded like, well like bagpipes, as they needed no more colorful a simile to portray their unholy screeching.

At the peak of Angus's launch, beyond the view of the beach, he pushed a small button on his collar. His Iron: Battlesuit transformed into an Iron: Swimsuit. His frazzled red beard nearly reached his bare knees. But then, they weren't all that far from his chin, so it's not terribly impressive. "Ah'm king o' the world!!!" He slapped his small hands over his mouth and made sure no one had heard him. "Er, Ah means, YYYYEEEEEARGHBLBLBLBLE!!!"

*   *   *   *

Nuklear Man hovered over the murky blue-green waves. His stamina at maintaining impressive poses—and this time without a cape mind you—never ceased to amaze him.

Neither did Scotch Tape. But we'll not linger on that.

"Yep, those beach babes couldn't possibly be more wooed by yours truly," he told himself.

*   *   *   *

Norman rolled to his right side. "Hey, I wonder where Nuke is. He's missing his own party."

"Nuke who?" the girls asked.

The Tungsten Titan rolled to his left, "Ah well, he can take care of himself."

✳   ✳   ✳   ✳

Nuklear Man's keen eyesight scanned the horizon. "Ah ha! That must be the first of my betrothed maidens now." His slightly less keen ears kicked in. His face contorted with confusion. It was in familiar familiar territory. "That poor beach nymph. Her banshee-like wails of torment from being so far from her Nuklear Love Monkey are grating across mine ears like…" It was so loud he could barely hear his own narration. "…Like bagpipes?"

"King o'—er—YYYYEEEEEARGHBLBLBLBLE!!!"

"WAH!"

In a tumult of limbs and beard, the ill-matched pair tumbled into the sea below.

Ripples.

Stillness.

Bubbles.

Nuklear Man, like a phoenix, other than the fire or ashes or shape changing or any similarity to ornithological phenomenon other than a certain talent for flight, rose from the churning ocean. He dried his hair in a flash of Plazma. "Whew, that was close. Though I'd have to style it again."

Angus surfaced. His tiny limbs flailed and failed to keep him afloat. "Gasp! Ye overrated pretty boy—gag—don't just stand there floatin', save me!"

Nuklear Man shuddered. "Yowza. Hours of not being in my godly presence has reduced this vixen of the dunes to a gnarled, hairy, belligerent, bearded, ill-bathed, foul-mouthed Scotsman!"

"Ah ain't no vixen, ye haggis brained, donkey bitin' son of a French whore—glurble cough—It's me, Angus, and Ah'm drownin'!"

"Well, what'dya want me to do about it?"

"*Save me!*"

"But my hair'll get wet again. It could get ruined."

"Ah don't bloody *care* about ye damned hair!"

"That's what separates us from the animals, Angus. Priorities. And good grooming habits."

"When Ah gets outta these damned waters, Ah'm gonna take that blasted smug smile o' yours and *rip* it out through ye—splash burble—gasp, and then, with *just* the handle, 'cause that way it'll hurt more, I'm goonna tear ye a new— gurgle sploosh…Blurble."

"See Angus? You just calm down and ride the wave and everything will turn up roses in the end."

*   *   *   *

Angus, due to a quirk of density and his Iron: Swimsuit, sank. A constant stream of bubbles bubbled their way to the briny surface as Angus cursed with such beauty and precision that it would have made even the most stalwart among us break into tears. He watched the bubbles as they rose. He took this as nothing less than the bubbles partaking in a bit fancy boy showing off in regards to their buoyancy.

Nothing enraged Angus like fancy boy showing off.

Except for surfers.

And the water.

And sinking.

Sinking? He'd be damned if he was going to let some force of nature stop him. He shook with rage and spite. More bubbles rose to the surface in what Angus took to be a direct insult.

"WUB-A-BULB!!!" The Surly Scot rocketed from the bleak depths. His Bag-pipe Thrusters took on a muted quality underwater, though nearly every aquatic creature in hearing distance agreed it was the worst sound to invade their waters for nearly a hundred million years.

Nearly every aquatic creature because there was a slight minority that disagreed with this consensus. One particular creature of the sea to be exact. A single crus-tacean. To it, the wretched mutation of sound was a beautiful, lilting piece of elo-quence. It was sublime. It was invigorating. It had that come hither quality.

It was a mating call.

*   *   *   *

Within the ruins of a once mighty structure, since weak structures tend to go straight to dust without bothering with the intermediate "ruins" stage, a mon-strous computer panel with hundreds of unmarked buttons hummed in a dark-ness abated only by the huge Overly Detailed Display screen attached to it. "The End of Nuklear Man: Plan B" was blinking in the Display's upper right hand corner. A checklist took up the bulk of the Display. Each item had a small repeating animation next to it.

"Step 1: Launch Evil: Geosynchronous Satellite with Defusionizing Ray. Complete." A cartoony rocket shot into space and jettisoned a satellite that hung over the Earth.

"Step 2: Lock on to Nuklear Clod. Scanning…" An unflattering characterature of Nuklear Man dumbly evaded a pair of persistent crosshairs.

"Step 3: Press The Button." A devilish and sexy figure, her eyes wide with excitement, madly pushed a button with alternating speed-blurred hands.

"Step 4: Celebrate Death of Nuklear Buffoon with Global Orgy of Destruction and Chaos." A globe was dotted with skulls and crossbones, mushroom clouds, fire, and sad faces.

"Oh, Nuklear Moron, you've defeated me many timez in the past. I shall make certain you do not have the opportunity to do zo again." She pressed a series of anonymous buttons on her huge computer panel. A windowpane filled with hundreds of numbers and arcane symbols appeared on her oversized computer screen. "You see," she told no one in particular, as is the wont of any archfiend. "In our last encounter, I was able to acquire enough information about the nature of your powers to find a way to counteract them using my Negaflux Field technology!" She scanned the windowpane's myriad notes and formulae. "With but *one* blast of my Defusionizing Ray, I shall render all nuclear activity within that blundering body of yourz null and void—therefore destroying any opposition to my world domination!" She leaned back in thought for a moment. She held back a maniacal cackle. It wasn't quite time for one just yet. However, she was past due refering to herself in the third person. "Nothing can defeat *Dr. Menace!*"

*   *   *   *

"Hmm," Nuklear Man said in his practiced impression of the kind of person who always seemed to be on top of things. "Wonder where Angus went."

The sea under Nuklear Man bubbled. He looked. It churned. He pursed his lips. It belched Angus and the sounds of bagpipes forcing water and fish from their bowels. The Hero beamed, "Hey, Angus, I was just—"

"About ta eat a fistful o' Iron," **PUNCH!** "Ye empty-headed," **KICK!** "Sack o' haggis!" **HEADBUTT!**

Angus's upward thrust faded as he reached Nuklear Man. He flapped his stubby arms to stay aloft. It succeeded only in making him look more absurd. The Surly Scot took in a huge breath and anticipated the icy waters' embrace.

"Oh no you don't, Gravity." Nuklear Man palmed Angus by his soaked read haired head like he was a basketball. "Gotcha."

The sea bellow bubbled them. Then the sea all around them bubbled.

"You made it angry," Nuklear Man said.

The sea growled viciously at them.

"Maybe we should sacrifice a virgin to it," Angus suggested.

They looked at each other nervously.

"Er, where ever would we find one?"

"Feh, Ah wouldn't even know one if Ah saw 'im," Angus said with a masculine sniff and Iron: Swimsuit adjustment.

The water bellowed at them.

"You've been down there. Is it supposed to do that?"

The waters broke. A green-blue carapace hundreds of feet wide surfaced. It was covered in gnarled barnacles, knots, spikes, seaweed, flopping fish, and an unpleasant smell. The wide beast shifted its enormous girth and turned its front end upward revealing its huge footjaws which were poised just under the pair of Heroes who were, at this point, pathetically clutching one another. Its gargantuan maw opened wide enough to swallow a city bus whole. Long ways. The creature took a deep breath and howled its wet, gurgling scream like the tortured deaths of a potato sack full of babies being beaten to death with another potato sack full of babies.

Nuklear Man wished he could spontaneously evolve the ability to turn his ears off at will. No such luck.

"That's a pretty catchy tune, actually," Angus mumbled to himself as the force of the roar pushed them up a foot in the air.

The thing submerged. They watched as it cruised just under the waves like a shark.

"It's going to the beach!" Nuklear Man said.

"Someone ought to save those innocent laddies!"

Nuklear Man, full of resolve, steeled his features like an invincible god of war. "Right. I'll go look for him. Yoing!"

Nuklear Man's feet pedaled uselessly in the air. Angus held him by the wrist. "Oh no ye don't, laddie."

"Aww, c'mon. Just this once?" Nukelar Man whined. "That thing's scary. Plus, how are you able to hold on me like this?"

"*Git!*" The Surly Scot spun and tossed his Nuklear Discus toward the shore while hanging on to his cape for the ride.

"Okay, how'd you do *that?*"

The somewhat Heroic pair soared right over the sea monster. "We're falling!" Nuklear Man squealed in terror as gravity took control. "It'll eat us dead!"

"Fly, ye blasted horse's knickers!" Angus hollered as he climbed up Nuklear Man's cape.

He complied and they raced past the sea monster. Nuklear Man's velocity kicked up another rooster tail of water . "Wait. Horse's what?"

"Never ye mind, just fly!"

$$*\qquad*\qquad*\qquad*$$

Atomik Lad and Rachel had wandered to the pier. They walked under it, swaying with their gait and talking about anything in the way people who are obviously attracted to each other do when they don't know what to say to keep the other person from going away.

"So, handsome," Rachel said. "When're you going to introduce me to your parents?" Atomik Lad stopped short. Rachel joined his change in momentum. "John?" she asked.

He blinked at the wet sand at his feet. "They. My parents. They're um, dead."

Rachel clasped her hands around his wrists. "Oh, I'm so sorry, I didn't know—"

"Don't be sorry, it's not like it was your fault." He clenched his fists. "I'm fine. It was a long time ago, I was just a child. It was an accident. It had to happen to somebody, I guess. Besides, Nuke took me in after that and I've been taking care of him ever since."

"Oh, he's not so bad."

"That's what I keep telling myself."

She put a hand on his shoulder and kissed his cheek softly. "I am sorry though," she whispered too close to his face.

Atomik Lad realized his hands were around Rachel's waist, and hers were locked somewhere behind his head. Closer now. Hearts beating. Eyes closed. The organic aroma of breath and saltwater. Sparks or fireworks just like everyone said. Red sparks?

"Rachel!" He pushed her like a semi-truck was blindly hurtling toward her. She stumbled back a few steps and fell onto her backside in the moist sand. Startled, she looked up at Atomik Lad.

And his Atomik Field.

He dropped to his knees. Sand was kicked this way and that by the twitching jagged edges of his crimson barrier. "I'm, I'm sorry. This happens sometimes. I can't help it—well I can, I. I just have to keep it under control. Always."

She reached out to him. He jumped back and hovered above the ground. "No! You can't come near me when I'm like this."

"But what about before with that Radar jerk? It protected me."

"That was different. You'll just have to trust me."

She nodded.

✳   ✳   ✳   ✳

"Angus, you go on ahead and warn the others."

"Right-o!" He warmed up for a Dwarf-a-pult.

"Great Odin's bear, *no*! Er, I mean, I could just toss you."

"*What*?" He clobbered Nuklear Man's skull with tiny, yet furious, Iron: Fists. "Could ye think of a more demeanin' thing to doo to a man?!"

"Well, I bet I could try."

"I suppose ye'd yell 'Midget-a-toss' when ye did it, eh?"

"Um, if you like?"

Another cranial crush. "Nay, I'm afraid not, ye daft wee-people hater! 'Ooh, lookit Nuklear Man, he's just invented a new sport.' 'What is it?' 'Oh, well, ye take a wee Scotsman and ye *toss his wee hide like he was a wet bag o' haggis*!' Bah! Ah may be short, but Ah do have me dignity. DWARF-A—"

"Midget-a-toss!" Nuklear Man uttered under his breath and lobbed his cargo.

The Bagpipe Thrusters burst to life, though most musicians would describe it more as an unlife. "I *heard* what ye said!" Angus yelled as he faded into the distance and shook his fists at Nuklear Man.

Miles behind them, the giant crab lurched forward with increased speed.

✳   ✳   ✳   ✳

The Display beeped. "Step 2: Lock on to Nuklear Clod. Scanning...Lock Acquired." A smile that could kill a man at twenty paces crept across Dr. Meance's exquisite face. Slowly, she reached out to the Evil: Button. She held her finger just out of reach, tantalizing herself.

"It will be soon now. Zo very, very soon. Muwa hahaha!" She pushed The Button.

*   *   *   *

Angus flew over the beach, past the dunes, and into the middle of traffic. Horns blared, people and tires screamed, and in the heart of it all a tiny man cursed like all the frenzy, hype, flamboyance, and testosterone squirting fun of a national sport compacted into a single raging entity.

*   *   *   *

Atomik Lad sighed despondently as the dwarfish comet arced through the air. "I'd better see what's going on," he told Rachel.

*   *   *   *

The Evil: Satellite charged its Defusionizer Batteries. Dr. Menace had to perform but a few last minute adjustments to compensate for gravitational interference and magnetic anomalies.

*   *   *   *

Nuklear Man landed on the beach huffing and puffing like someone who'd just run a marathon. "Gaaaaasp. Hold it, I flew." He stopped panting. "Everyone!" he yelled. No one paid attention. "Bunch of ungrateful pagans." He cleared his throat purposefully. Still no reaction. "Grrr, I'll show 'em. PLAZMAAA BEAM!" He launched a column of fusion-ish Plazma into the sky. It poked a small hole through the thin clouds high above.

*   *   *   *

An energy bulge glowed from the Defusionizer's gun barrel. Suddenly, a golden blast arced from the surface straight through Menace's Evil: Satellite mere microseconds before it would have fired.

The Display read, "Step 4: Celebrate Death of Nuklear Buffoon with Global Orgy of Destruction and Chaos…Incomplete."

The Venomous Villainess leaned her elbows on the computer's panel, fingers interlocked, thumbs under her chin. Her breathing was steady and calm, a stark contrast to what her eyes told the world. "All right then," she said with a deliberate effort to keep her voice even. "On to Plan C."

*   *   *   *

Nuklear Man held the attention of everyone on the beach. "Finally. Sheesh, took so long I almost, er." He scratched his head. "What's that word when you can't remember something?"

"Forgot?" some random beach-goer offered.

Nuklear Man flopped his hands with exacerbation. "You too?"

Another worshiper of Sol pointed to the ocean. Fear, terror, and all those fight of flight instincts kicked in. "A giant crab!"

"That's right!" Nuklear Man congratulated. "How'd you guess?" The patron had already fled.

The megacrab scuttled sideways from the ocean and stood over Nuklear Man. It basked him in its smelly shadow as it examined the world above the waves. Strange things scattered about. Food, probably. But food was not on this creature's mind. No, not since the alluring mating call. Two in one day. It had been eons since the last. It had to find the source.

"Okay everyone," Nuklear Man said above the clamor and panic that surrounded him. "Let's just calm down and leave the scene in a nice orderly fashion. No pushing or shoving or screaming, please." There were lots of each.

A square foot's worth of sea glop fell from the giant crab and splortched onto Nuklear Man's head. "Ah! It's got me! Run for the hills! Save yourselves! Sidekicks and plot devices first! Think of the Heroes, please won't somebody think of the Heroes!" The glop slipped off with a wet impact in the sand. "Oh. Er, as I was saying—"

"The sea gods are angry! We have forsaken them for too long. Their vengeance is upon us!" a scholarly looking man hollered as he ran by without his family.

"I told you so, Pastor Williams!" Nuklear Man called as the lunatic sprint past him. He scratched his chin while watching the fleeing masses. "Tsk, these mortals are so excitable," he said. "Back in my day, we didn't have panic, only apathy."

The Crab bellowed. People fell to their knees clutching their crab-call bloodied ears. The sand leapt, not from the enormous vibrations of the sound waves, but in a massive attempt to leave the sound to its own tortured unlife.

Nuklear Man cringed from the crabby thunder and looked up to its source, his mouth slightly agape. "Well what'dya know? A giant crab. With those really disgusting mandible thingies. And green drool. And all kinds of slimy gross germs." More sea-muck splatted onto his face. "Hm," his voice was muffled by the muck. "Kinda tastes like. Kinda *tastes* like?! *Augh!*"

A golden lightning bolt streaked through the sky screaming, "I got in my mouth, I got it in my mouth, I got it in my *mouth!*"

Atomik Lad watched his mentor rocket away. "Great," he said to himself. He floated over to The Crab and tried to take in the sheer absurdity of what was going on.

Mighty Metallic Magno Man stood in front of The Crab. He held his arms above him as if to invoke the heavens. His amplified magnetic force wound its way around his body surrounding him in a sphere of thin blue energy strands. He bobbed in the air, rolled himself into a silvery tungsten ball, accelerated toward the crab, passed it, and with a sound barrier breaking boom, disappeared beyond the horizon.

Atomik Lad stared after Norman with eyes full of disbelief. He looked back at Rachel. She was under the pier, nearly hugging one of its legs. He envied it.

"Um," he told The Crab. "As acting hero on this scene, I…Um, oh geez."

"Atomik Lad!" He turned to see Dr. Genius near the dunes as she slipped on her lab coat. He caught himself feeling disappointment. "Try to get a sample, I'll be back at the lab." She dashed over the dunes and nearly fell over the "Stay Off The Dunes" sign.

"A sample?" Atomik Lad said. "Sure, how hard can it be to get a sample. All by myself."

The Crab knew one thing about food. It definitely floated. A little snack before the love-fest couldn't hurt. Several breaths' worth of wind were simultaneously knocked out of Atomik Lad as The Crab slapped him out of the air with a blow that would have crushed him had it not been for the very handy existence of his Atomik Field. Gasping for air, he could feel the enormous pincer clutching him and pulling him out of the sand. He tried prying the giant claw open and could have sworn The Crab actually smiled with amusement at his fruitless effort.

"Why can't I have a normal life?" he grunted.

His Atomik Field began to flicker impotently as if to say, "Oh yeah? Let's just see how you like it then."

Flicker, flicker. "Oh damn."

The Crab's vice grip tightened around Atomik Lad. He squirmed desperately. "C'mon, you good for nothing red crap, *work!*" His invulnerable Atomik Field faltered. It sputtered pathetic sparks as he mentally clung to its failing existence like a priest faced with indisputable proof of evolution.

A silver blur raced over the dunes and obliterated a chunk of them with its velocity. The huge projectile struck The Crab with a thunderous impact. It sounded to Atomik Lad like God snapped his fingers. In the chaos, Atomik Lad felt himself tumble gracefully face first back into the sand. As the impact's deafening explosion of sound subsided he could hear "MAGNO-SMASH!!!" echo across the beach.

Half dazed, he searched the sandy scene for any clue of what just happened. Mighty Metallic Magno Man wobbled toward Atomik Lad. "Man, I gotta work on that attack." He held his head like he had a hangover. "It's hard to get the timing down for the battle cry because of the supersonic speed from magnetically super-accelerating myself around the globe. Plus, it makes me really dizzy."

The Crab lay prone in the sand. Waves washed against its rear half.

The Tungsten Titan dust off his metallic hands. "Heh, that was easy. Too bad Nuke missed all the action."

Atomik Lad stood and took a deep breath. "Yeah, that was pretty easy. I was expecting a rampage through the city or something, like in the movies."

"Kind of disappointing, really."

"Well, it is like at least one of those movies then." Atomik Lad beat some sand off himself. "Anyway, Dr. Genius wanted a sample of it."

"Hey, I defeated it. You get the sample."

"Gee, *thanks*," Atomik Lad said. He walked toward it. Carefully, not like some idiot in a horror flick. He paid special attention to what he assumed were its eyes while taking care to avoid the pincers altogether. He reached out a cautious hand and snapped off a bit of stray carapace. He dashed back to Norman a little faster than he meant to.

"You shouldn't worry. I don't think our friend here is going to wake up for a long time. Eight hundred pound bullets of tungsten hittin' your ass at a thousand miles an hour isn't exactly something you just brush off."

Atomik Lad observed the rounded dent Norman had bashed into The Crab's top-front carapace plate. "I think you killed it."

He playfully hit Atomik Lad in the shoulder, knocking him back a step. "We're heroes, John. No one dies."

"Yeah, I guess you're right," he said. He noticed movement from the corner of his eye. "Rachel!"

"Is it safe out there?" she called from under the pier.

"Is it ever?"

She rethought her question. "Is it not *currently* life threatening out there?"

Atomik Lad looked to Norman. MMMM shrugged. "Close enough!" he answered.

✳   ✳   ✳   ✳

Traffic had come to a stand still. It wasn't rush hour. There wasn't a wreck. There was, however, a storm. Not one of rain, save for the far flying spittle winged with rage spun words. Angus. God of war among men. Several over-turned smoking wrecks that had once been cars were off the side of the road advertised that someone was a bit vexed.

The Iron Scotsman was waving his Surprisingly Wieldly and Concealable Enemy-B-Crushed Named "Bertha" to invite—nay—*beg* anyone to make a sound. Angus listened to the post-Magno-Smash silence. "Aye, that's what Ah thought, ye yuuppie bastards drivin' ye blasted Spoort Uutility Crap and ye brain dead Minivan drivin' morons that spend half their damn time yellin' at their damn brats in the back damn seat screamin' for Cow Buutt Buurger Huutt!" He breathed in. "What was Ah talkin' about?" he muttered into his saltwater and spit soaked beard.

Nothing annoyed Angus more than forgetfulness.

"Except for people who drive minivans. Or SUVs. Or giant sea monsters ruinin' me fun!" His eyes darted back and forth, searching for more prey. He slowly pivoted to the beach. Either The Crab was narcoleptic or it had been defeated. "Well, goood thing Ah was here to manage traffic."

Road rage makes people do stupid things. Such as:

HONK! HONKHONKHONK, "C'mon, you midget *freak*, get the hell out of the damn road!" **HONK HONK HONK!**

Angus's right eye twitched. "What did ye say?" he asked in a near whisper.

"I said, get the *hell* outta the road, you dwarfish *mutant!*"

"Ah see." His fists balled up. "Ah see."

"*Move* it, shorty! Some of us got places to go!"

"What's that? Ye want me to move, eh?"

"Yes!"

"Have it your way, then." He turned to the belligerent motorist.

ISSUE 20—A WORSE CASE OF CRABS

Atomik Lad, Rachel, and Mighty Metallic Magno Man stood. They did so in that awkward way when something really weird and usually socially unacceptable happens and no one knows just how to move the conversation forward. Or perhaps it was exactly like standing in a crowded elevator with strangers.

Rachel rocked on the balls of her feet occasionally.

MMMM glanced at the dent he put into The Crab.

Atomik Lad scratched his nose. "Well." His voice cracked slightly, which did nothing to help the moment along. "Now what?"

The Tungsten Titan reached out for the crab shard. "I can take that over to Überdyne. You two just make sure no one tries to steal the carcass here. I want my picture taken with it, I think I might have set a record."

"Sure." Atomik Lad tossed the bit of carapace to his fellow hero.

"Well, it was fun, Sparky," Mighty Metallic Magno Man saluted. "We oughta do it again sometime." A sphere of blue energy threads encased him and he flew into the distance toward Metroville's skyscrapers.

Rachel ran her fingers through her hair to give it some semblance of order despite the sand, salt and water that insisted on occupying it in varying degrees. "Does something like this happen every time you guys get together?"

"Let me put it this way. Yes."

*   *   *   *

Angus sputtered incoherently, having long passed the stage where his mind was capable of language.

"What's the matter, Shorty? Having a 'little' spasm?"

He shook like an earthquake. "Oh, Ah'm gonna love this."

A sound somewhat equivalent to a blue whale singing exactly what it was like to die a morbidly slow and agonizing death echoed over what was left of the dunes.

*   *   *   *

Atomik Lad cringed from the sound. "What, now we've got beached whales too?"

The Crab awoke instantly.

Startled, Atomik Lad grabbed Rachel by the hand and ran them back to the pier. She didn't need encouragement to make the move.

The Crab groaned as it stood up and felt the impact crater on its topside with one monstrous pincer. Little carapace pieces flaked off. It seemed to strain, quivering like it was flexing some internal muscle to pass something that had been painfully clogging up its intestinal tract for several centuries. The dent corrected itself with a deep **pop** sound. The splintered cracks that ran along the crater's perimeter disappeared. All signs of Norman's devastating attack were gone.

"It can heal itself," Atomik Lad observed from under the pier.

"Want to put me down, sailor?" Rachel asked, still draped over his shoulder.

He realized she was still wearing only her bikini. "Um, no. Not really."

"Then watch those hands, mister."

"Er, sorry."

The Crab lurched sideways. Straight for the pier.

Atomik Lad instinctively activated his trusty Field. Sparks fluttered uselessly about him. "Oh no."

"Having trouble?"

He tried again while running away from the pier. Nothing. "It's not my fault!" Rachel bounced on his shoulder uncomfortably.

A giant Crab foot smashed into the sand in front of them. Atomik Lad pulled a spinning dodge thing to his left that would have impressed any football coach had he not subsequently fell face first in the sand and dumped his cargo. "This just isn't my day."

*   *   *   *

Nuklear Man stood at his Danger: Sink. The floor was littered in empty bottles with labels containing phrases like Keep Out of Reach of Children, Not to be Taken Internally, Do Not Swallow, and Poison. He blindly guzzled the contents of another bottle. A gout of fire errupted from his mouth. He tossed the empty container to the floor. It lulled into the others and added the phrase Keep Away From Open Flames to the growing list of warnings he'd completely ignored.

Several bottles later, and The Crab Slimy Goo Taste still persisted. He paused and reached into the Danger: Medicine Cabinet. "Hmm. 'Highdro. Ch-lorik Acid.' Sounds life threatening." He downed it like a shot glass. He smacked his lips and probed his mouth for any signs of The Taste. His face twisted. "Yeeesh! That stuff burns almost as much as rocket fuel. Bleh."

*   *   *   *

"Remind me again how hiding under the pier is going to save the city."

Sparks winked around Atomik Lad. He was reminded of a car that wouldn't start.

"Well?"

"I think I'm flooded."

She gave him The Look.

"What am I supposed to do without my field?"

"You're still a hero. Either you get out there and do something, or I will."

*   *   *   *

The Crab was currently making short work out of the ruins of the boardwalk shops that used to be near the beaches. It believed in being thorough.

*   *   *   *

Nuklear Man sprawled across the Danger: Couch and turned on the Danger: TV with a shot of infrared from his finger. "Mmm. Silly Sam's Cartoon Marathon-a-thon o' Fun," he smiled idiotically.

"We now interrupt our regularly scheduled programming to bring you this news bulletin."

Nuklear Man flared with Angry Plazma. "What."

A soulless shell of a man spoke like he had no idea that there was any meaning associated with the sounds he was making. "We now take you to the scene of the carnage, so be certain to look for extreme close ups of any bodies we happen to capture on tape. Ratings, ratings, ratings!"

"Grrr. PLAZMAAA—" the Danger: TV was filled by an image of "Giant crab!?"

The Danger: Couch was suddenly vacant. A trembling hand rose from behind it and shakily delivered an infrared a finger gun blast to turn off the set. The Crab was vanquished.

"Whew."

*   *   *   *

"Got any threes?"

Danger: Computer Lady sighed, "This is not Go Fish."

"Well then, what is this?"

"Strip poker."

Nuklear Man, his cape wrapped about him to keep decent, shivered as he scanned the five playing cards fanned in his hands. "And who's bright idea was that?"

"Yours."

"That's not the point. Could you at least turn up the heat in here? I'm chilly." He tried covering himself adequately with the none too functional cape.

"There," Danger: Computer Lady answered.

The Hero smiled. "Gin!"

Danger: Computer Lady, despite being nothing more than a series of 1's and 0's, cringed.

*   *   *   *

If The Crab had the capacity to read, it would have known the loud thing buzzing above it was not a tasty morsel of food, but in fact the Channel 6 Action on the Spot Eyewitness News Copter. He watched it intently.

"I think he's distracted," Rachel said, keeping Atomik Lad and the pier between herself and the Angered Arthropod. "Now's your chance. Go get him."

"My chance?"

"You're the hero here."

"What happened to all that 'if you don't go I will' talk?"

"Just a bluff to get you to come to your senses."

"At least you're honest."

"Most of the time," she smiled sweetly. "Now go!"

"I don't even know what to do!"

"You'll think of something. Try to lead him away from the city somehow. It looks like he likes stuff that flies. Make with that Atomik Mojo you're supposed to have."

Atomik Lad groaned.

*   *   *   *

"Hey, Charlie," the Channel 6 Action on the Spot Eyewitness News Copter Camera Man asked. "Is that Crab watching us?"

Charlie looked down. "You mean kinda intently?"

"Yeah."

"Well." Before Charlie could respond, giant icy blue Crab Eye Beams pierced the helicopter. The spinning and spiraling wreckage toppled into the ocean. The pair of pilots swam from their watery wreck. "Yeah, I think he mighta been watching," Charlie said.

The Crab surprised itself. It blinked several times. *I had forgotten all about those*, it thought. *Cool!* It glanced at the nearest object worthy of its attention.

"Now he's looking at us!" Rachel blurted.

"Get down!" Atomik Lad yanked Rachel to the sand and covered her with his own body as per common practice in situations like this. Giant Crab Eye Beams punched through the pier and little wooden chunks of flaming debris fell on them.

Neat! The Crab thought. It let loose a few more Eye Beams toward the geometrically impressive, oddly reflective, and freakishly huge vertical coral in the distance.

*　　　*　　　*　　　*

"Hmm." Nuklear Man pondered over the hand Fate had dealt him.

"Stop calling me 'Fate,'" Danger: Computer Lady said.

Nuklear Man made a face from behind his cards. They were nearly touching his nose. He tugged at one card, thought better of it, and tapped it back in line with the rest. He nodded to himself haughtily like he just proved some universal truth. "Hit me!"

"That's Blackjack."

"Tsk. You shouldn't discriminate."

Danger: Computer Lady desperately wanted to rub her optical receptors.

"Feh, I hate this stupid game," Nuklear Man grumbled. "Let's play something else."

*　　　*　　　*　　　*

Dr. Ima Genius peered into a microscope to confirm by her own sight what the Überdyne 4000 series PAL computer had determined. Norman stood behind her trying to make sense of the myriad of data that streamed through various monitors set all over the walls of her lab. The sheer bulk of information streaming across their screens was ocular oppression.

"What is all this stuff?" he asked, motioning to the overly detailed diagrams and repeating waveforms that danced across the screens.

She glanced up from her work. "Oh, those. It's just gibberish. I had those installed to impress our investors when they make surprise visits. It keeps them quiet." She gazed into the microscope again. "They don't like to admit that they have no idea what any of it is supposed to mean, and to compensate, they give us about 24% more funding each time they drop by. It's a nice racket."

"Ah." Norman ignored them and watched the only monitor that made sense. It was footage from the Channel 6 Action on the Spot Eyewitness News Copter. "I can't believe it just shook off my Magnosmash. We could be in over our heads."

"Have a look at this, Norman," Genius said. She pushed herself away from the microscope so he could take a gander. He bent down and had himself a look-see.

"The computers gave it a 99% match with some prehistoric DNA we'd found in fossils uncovered along the Mariana's Trench."

"Whoa," the Tungsten Titan said as he focused the instrument. Genetic material floated around in a microscopic sea right before his eyes.

"That was my reaction. What we have uncovered here is a specimen of a legendary creature of Earth's primeval past, specifically a Crushtacean, so perfectly preserved for over a hundred million years that it's alive and well today. The ecosystem couldn't have possibly supported more than a few of these creatures at once, if that many. It's a miracle this one survived through all these millennia, probably frozen in some gargantuan iceberg that floated to warmer climes such as our own and—"

"And now its on a rampage through Metroville. Any idea how we can get rid of it?"

"You said it took the full force of your Magnosmash and got right back up?"

"Yeah. Well, it must've taken a couple minutes to fully recover, but it looks like he's back to his old carnage," Norman said, pointing to the Channel 6 Action on the Spot Eyewitness News Copter footage. "I hope Atomik Lad's all right. I left him out there all alone and I don't see him anywhere."

The screen was overcome with static. They watched as a befuddled anchorman filled the box. He gave the viewing audience a deer-in-the-headlights look which exactly equaled the newsman-without-a-Teleprompter look. "Er," he managed at length.

"Profound," Ima muttered.

Huge blue-white beams arced from the horizon and battered a neighboring skyscraper into rubble. The Channel 6 Action on the Spot Eyewitness News Building would never be the same.

"Crab beams?" Norman hazarded to guess.

"That would explain the selenium samples found in the carapace you brought me. Apparently, it can absorb light and focus it through some kind of biological apparatus. Perhaps…" She silenced herself in thought. "Yes, I'd like to get some Kopelson Intrinsity readings to help determine just how it stores and manipulates—"

"Doc! Not now. We've got to stop this thing."

"Oh, right. You get back there and help Atomik Lad slow it down. I'll contact Nuklear Man and get him in the field. If our Crushtacean can just shrug off a Magnosmash, you'll need his firepower."

*   *   *   *

Due to Angus's inability to aim, only one vehicle remained untouched. The driver inside continued to taunt Angus. He'd apparently been born without knowing when the hell to shut up and run away. The Surly Scot took a break to catch his breath.

"What's the matter, Shorty? Those 'tiny' lungs of yours having a 'little' problem?"

Angus's anger had a difficult time not manifesting into the physical world. Probably as something along the lines of blazing flames engulfing his diminutive frame. He quivered slightly from the effort of restraining his rage.

"What the hell? That some kind of seizure? That must cause no 'small' amount of trouble for ya, Shorty."

Angus waved his Enemy-B-Crushed like a baseball bat. He licked his beard covered lips and anticipated the sheer ecstasy of unchained hate.

*   *   *   *

Nuklear Man's cloak was tossed aside by a harsh wind. He fastened the garment more carefully using an ivory talisman of Engar he'd made as an apprentice many years ago. He stared into the horizon like an eternal watchman waiting for the end of the world.

Jagged rust red crags, like the one he stood upon, jut out of the arid earth in the distance. A cloud of dust scratched across the skyline he oversaw. His eyes narrowed, piercing the distant dust storm. His chiseled visage twisted into a scowl. "That's no dust storm."

From the dust emerged a stampede of elephant sized boars. Their demonic black tusks gleamed in the red sunset, their coarse brown hair was covered in a thin layer of the cardinal red dust that was kicked up from their mad charge.

"A stampede of Giant Gulrackian Boars!" Nuklear Man surmised. "Indeed, she's a cunning witch, but tis I who is more cunninger." He picked up a handful of loose dirt. "Oh fertile lands, mother of all life," he invoked. "Shed this arid skin, give forth your bountiful fruits and raise the mighty emerald towers eternal!"

The stampede charged closer with redoubled speed. "Curse it, she's cast another spell on me. Must concentrate." The earth crackled in front of Nuklear Man as a gap cracked through its lightning pattern across the dry ground. A moan of pain and pleasure issued forth from the cavern but was drowned out by the encroaching stampede.

"Faster now, Great Mother, oh Eternal Source, yield to my will-working!" he cried to the heavens. Hhis haggard voice was barely audible above the violence sweeping upon him.

Vines shot from the crevices and climbed into the sky with blinding speed. They intertwined and wrapped around one another forming huge gnarled pillars as enormous as ancient trees which also grew in seconds all around Nuklear Man. Their thick branches wove into one another and the impenetrable web of ever-thickening vines as well. After seconds that, to Nuklear Man, took days of strength to endure, the Druidic Circled Wall of Dryads was erected.

He'd fallen to his knees somewhere along the ritual. Sweat dropped from his face onto the dust covered earth that was shaded by the shadows cast by the sudden rainforest his magik had brought into being around him.

The giant boars neared, their thousand fold hoof beats shook the ground like an earthquake. Though he lay in their path, he did not worry. Nay, for brave Nuklear Man plotted his counter strike. "Perhaps a dose of Engar's Holy Fireball of Purification will teach that wench to oppose me."

The stampede's cacophony disappeared. Terror struck the Hero at the base of his skull. A flash of horror shot through his mind. "An illusion to distract me from the true threat?"

Panicked, he searched for signs of another attack with a fireball spell at the tips of his fingers. His quest was cut short by the hideous sounds of a hundred Giant Boars falling onto him like whales raining from the sky. The gory details are up to you to imagine.

He tossed his hand of cards against the table, scattering those already placed in their designated positions for Attack, Defense, and Gnosis. "That's the biggest load of crap I've ever heard!"

Danger: Computer Lady hummed happily. "That single attack took you down to negative seventeen Health. I win."

"What?! No! First, you tell me how you can enchant your Giant Boars with the Flying ability *and* Stampede Damage! It doesn't make sense! You can't fly *and* stampede at the same time!"

"I didn't make the rules, I just follow them. Unlike *some* people," she added under her synthetic breath.

"I heard that! I didn't cheat."

"Whatever."

"I told you, I just forgot to Un-siphon that Gnosis from the turn before."

"So you say."

"Grrr. PLAZMAAA—"

The Danger: Phone rang.

Nuklear Man froze. His attack sputtered away.

Another ring.

His eyes darted to and fro.

A third ring.

"You get it," he instructed Danger: Computer Lady. "Tell 'im I'm not here."

A fourth ring. "I can't answer the phone, I'm just a voice interface for the Silo's operations. You'll have to deal with it yourself."

Fifth ring. "Well then what good are ya?! Cheating grumble mumble." Sixth ring. "Hello?" he said into the Danger: Phone with a very high-pitched French accent. "You 'ave, how you say, zhe wrong numbier. Go away now."

Ima was silent for a moment. "How do you know I have the wrong number?"

"Er. Because I don't have a, how you say, phone."

"Then how are we talking now?"

"Uh. We're experiencing some technical, how you say, difficulties."

"I see."

"You should try again later, like when zhose other weakling heroes have done something with zhat Crab. Croissant fromage adios." He hung up and snickered devilishly. "All this and brains too. I'm so good it hurts—ouch! See? Ooh, there it is again."

All of Danger: Computer Lady's optical receptors simultaneously rolled. "Uh-huh."

The Danger: Phone rang again. Nuklear Man promptly picked it up, still smiling from his victory of mental prowess. "Yo."

"Nuklear Man," Dr. Genius said. "We need your help. Crushtacean is still terrorizing the city."

"Sure. No sweat." He buffed his nails against the electron orbited N symbol on his chest. "What's a Crushtacean?"

"The giant crab from this afternoon."

"Ah, of course. Giant Crab. Got it."

"Please hurry. Atomik Lad is dealing with it alone. I've dispatched Mighty Metallic Magno Man, but they'll need your help."

"No prob. I'll be there in five." He hung up the phone. "Heh, just like those losers to need help with a giant...crab?" He blinked in the light of realization. "God—"

*   *   *   *

"Dammit!" Atomik Lad unconsciously yelled as he narrowly dodged Crushta-cean's pincers. He rolled into a standing position and immediately dove into a mad dash as the other giant pincer crashed into the sand barely missing its scurry-ing mark. He slipped on the loose footing afforded by the sand and fell flat on his face. Again. He had just enough time to see a huge pincer close in. He closed his eyes tight and probed that part of his mind that fueled his Atomik Fires.

And there was nothing.

Issue 21—You Can Catch Crabs from the Ocean. Both Kinds.

"CAR-A-PULT!!!" Angus yelled from beyond the dunes as his Surprisingly Concealable Enemy-B-Crushed Named Bertha arced through its baseball bat style swing.

"Augh!" the motorist screamed as his minivan, back end mangled beyond repair, rocketed through the air thanks to Angus's misplaced anger. The minivan's front end was then mangled beyond repair when it crashed into the pincer that was about to crush Atomik Lad.

Atomik Lad took .04 seconds to remind himself of cheesy movies where the male lead avoids certain death about a dozen times only to (re)unite with the love interest. Of course, even in the movies fate can't be avoided forever and one of the young lovers has to die in order to keep the Karma balanced. But there wasn't time for that final insight. He scampered a safe distance from the Crab, insofar as one could be safe while it was still within eyesight, and decided on a new strategy.

He blinked. That wasn't part of the strategy.

He stood in a swimsuit sporting a red and blue design while also in a semi-action pose unconsciously learned from a decade of constant Nuklear exposure. His view was filled with things like a giant invincible crab of doom that forced him to do the only thing one can do with any degree of certainty in the face of balls out weirdness. Blink.

"Is that the best ye can do, ye overgrown All-Ye-Can-Eat-Seafood-Platter-fer-$9.99?!" Angus yelled as he soared over Atomik Lad and swat Crushtacean with his Surprisingly Concealable and Wieldly Enemy-B-Crushed Named Bertha. The Crab staggered back from the blow with a gurgling cry of pain.

A flash of blue light exploded against Angus. The Surly Scot was blast back, his Enemy-B-Crushed soared through the salty air and he tumbled short end over short end in the sand until he came to rest by Atomik Lad's feet.

"That's it! No more Mr. Nice Berserker!" Angus barked as he jumped to his feet. "DWARF-A—" **KLONG!** The Enemy-B-Crushed landed on Angus. It balanced perfectly atop his head. It was held in place by the huge dent its impact made with his helmet. The absurdly phallic image collapsed in the sand as Angus whimpered something about crumpets and lost consciousness. Atomik Lad's attention shot back to The Crab as the last signs of Angus's attacks healed before his very eyes.

Hmm. Eye beams make food go stop. Maybe if I zap that scrawny one.

The Giant Crab Eye Beams charged up. Atomik Lad gulped. Time seemed to stand still.

*   *   *   *

The great golden comet of Nuklear Man shot through the skyline of Metroville like a bullet of light piercing the sky. His Plazma Aura stretched into a tail that lagged behind him by a mile. "If I don't finish up this Crab stuff soon, I'm gonna miss the ending of Silly Sam's Cartoon Marathon-a-thon o' Fun!" He hovered high above the dunes and surveyed the beachy arena. "The Crab! Atomik Lad! Eye Beams! Defenseless! Really Big!" Nuklear Man had but milliseconds to react.

*   *   *   *

Atomik Lad flinched as certain doom in the guise of Giant Crab Eye Beams crashed upon him. There was a muted impact in the vicinity of his chest, but all was dark and a strange warmness permeated his body, his soul.

He opened his eyes unto a crimson world. "Awright!" he exclaimed.

Note to self: Eye Beams kill some food, but makes other food angry.

Having watched the futility of head on attacks, Atomik Lad arced a crimson path to The Crab's rear flank. "Now what, Mr. Smarty?" an annoying part of his mind asked. It knew full well there was no answer at hand.

A gleam caught his eye. He instinctively looked to it and above the flames of Angus's tantrum past the dunes, he could see Nuklear Man hovering deep in thought. He noticed an idea stumbling through his mentor's mind. He could see it in his eyes. Or perhaps it was the acknowledgment of a bothersome itch in the nether regions of his back. With Nuklear Man, it was a toss up.

*   *   *   *

"I saw this on ÜCÜÜF Wrastlin' one time!" he called out to Atomik Lad, as if that would make everything crystal clear. It did not.

A golden aura flared around Nuklear Man as he yelled and thus began a "PLASMAAA POWER BOMB!" He leaped toward the Crab. Atomik Lad could only assume it was to perform this alleged power bomb.

The Crab smacked Nuklear Man out of the sky and face first into the beach next to Angus. Sand puffed out from the impact. His cape wavered pathetically onto his back.

"Typically impressive," Atomik Lad mumbled.

A silver blur shot from the horizon. Crushtacean scuttled to one side as the huge bullet barely missed it and kept going. Atomik Lad watched it disappear beyond the oceanic horizon as water settled back down from the speeding intruder and the words, "MAGNOSMA—Hey! Don't *move!*" finally caught up to the locale a second or two later.

Atomik Lad rubbed his temples. "This just keeps getting better."

Hmm. I wonder what kind of food lives in that weird coral out there, Crushtacean thought to himself before moving to investigate.

"Ow, ow, ow, *ow!*" Nuklear Man uttered from a face full of sand as Crushtacean scuttled across him.

"Um," Atomik Lad said as the Angered Arthropod stomped over the dunes, past the highway, and headed straight for Metroville. His Atomik Field twitched nervously. He landed between his defeated comrades. "Come on, that crab's gonna destroy the city. I can't handle this on my own, I'm only the sidekick!"

Angus raised his head. It was wobbly from the loss of consciousness and the Enemy-B-Crushed lodged in his helmet. "Ah eats crabs like that fer breakfast." His eyes rolled back as he passed out again.

Atomik Lad clawed at his face and grumbled to himself. "C'mon, Nuke. Wake up already!"

The Hero raised his head, face covered in sand, eyes crossed. "No more for me, thanks. I'm driving." His head flopped back into the sand.

"Sometimes, I hate this job," Atomik Lad told the universe. It said nothing in reply. He chased after the enormous abomination. Someone had to.

*   *   *   *

So much food, so little time. Look at all of them scurrying around underfootpod. They're so adorable I could just gobble them up. Like this! Crushtacean swiped at a screaming crowd of innocents that seethed below him. In a city with overheroes, citizens are little more than spectators, many of whom are trying to get away. They were desperate to escape his presence and the carnage that flowed from it. A pincerful of the soft screaming things were stuffed into Crushtacean's footjaws.

Their muffled screams were silenced. Crushtacean paused. It was confused. He gave a few more thoughtful chews, each one eliciting a few more anguished—albeit muffled—cries from his jaws. Crushtacean grimaced as only crabs can and spat out his mouthful of food. *Ick! Those were worse than seaweed! Blech! I've got to get that taste out of my mouth!* Crushtacean picked up a nearby overturned car, shook the foul tasting creatures out of it, and chowed down.

*   *   *   *

"At least the news people aren't out here to document my incompetence," Atomik Lad told himself. It did little to consol him. He stood on Crushtacean's wide, smooth armored back. The beast devoured a few automobiles. Their owners would not be compensated since a Giant Crab isn't a villain or an act of a god. Atomik Lad gave a crimson covered kick against the thick carapace. The sensation barely reached Crushtacean's brain and it certainly didn't hamper his feeding frenzy. Atomik Lad heard a bugle call. "What in the...?"

"Beware, evil-doers!" A voice amplified and slightly garbled by what must have been a cheap bullhorn boomed above the fading screams of the last innocents fleeing the area. "The Minimum Wage Warriors are on the scene! Warriors, Clock In!" A quiet sigh and, "We have got to get a better rallying cry," escaped the bullhorn before it was shut off.

"Delivery Boy!" yelled a long haired youth with his head out the window of a jet propelled Suburban Assault Vehicle. It loosed a volley of missiles that expertly struck their targets. Unfortunately, none of them happened to be Crushtacean. "Nuts!" Delivery Boy charged the SAV's close proximity wave pulse attack as the vehicle of destruction skid to a halt in front of the Angered Arthropod. His car gave off a light green hue.

Ugh, I can still taste them. Maybe this glowing rock will do the trick.

"Hey!" Delivery Boy yelled as Crushtacean picked up his SAV. He crawled out the window and fell into the rubble of a mattress outlet. His admirable automobile was devoured. "Well I'm fresh out of ideas."

From a distance, "Librarian!" A little old lady cyberneticly bound to a Battle-wheelchair of Justice rocketed over the Crushtacean. She brandished a mighty cannon. "Eat card catalogue annihilation, you gargantuan monstrosity!" Six barreled death spun at a thousand rounds a minute. A shaky line of small index cards was drawn across Crushtacean's armored shell. Atomik Lad flinched as a few bounced off his Atomik Field. She soared over the scene and mumbled about her medication as she disappeared over the horizon.

"Postman!" announced the hero of the same name at the end of the street. His trigger fingers twitched beyond his control. One got the impression he did a lot of things that were beyond his control. His muscles were tensed from some unknown mental strain. He carried two mail sacks, one draped over each shoulder. The bags bulged with baseball sized objects. "Alright, you've just pushed the wrong button here, buddy!"

Atomik Lad scratched his head. "They've got to have some kind of medication for that guy."

"The lines never end, the piles get bigger and bigger, at least half of those packages have to make it to their destination and do you have any idea how hard it is to make change for stamps?!"

Even if Crushtacean had been paying attention to Postman, and could then understand what he was saying, and knew a thing or two about economics, it still would not have known, in fact, just how difficult it is to make change for stamps.

"But now, now I have the answer!" The Postman reached a hand into each bag and yanked out what appeared to be a pair of hand grenade pins. Hundreds of other pins were linked to them. They tinkled quietly in the wind. He lobbed the bags at Crushtacean while laughing in the insane bliss of having discovered The Answer to a Question no one Asked.

The bags erupted into balls of flame in mid-air long before striking their target.

Crushtacean coughed from the smoke.

Postman's eye twitched. "Well darn."

"Meter Maid!" A small voice said from among Crushtacean's footpods. She scribbled in a pad, tore off a sheet of paper, and slapped it against the giant crab's foot.

*   *   *   *

Among the pristine highways leading into and out of Metroville, a force was awakened. "I sense a disturbance in the Traffic." A purple and green blur soared into the air.

*   *   *   *

"Beware the power of RADAR!" he announced as he flew over the Giant Crab. Radar crashed into Crushtacean's hide. It sent cracks creeping through its shell in a radial burst like a carapace snowflake. The force of it tossed Atomik Lad into the rubble strewn street.

Crushtacean struggled to his feet. There were eight of them, so it took a little while. He shook the shock away as the cracks across his hide began to heal themselves. He charged a Giant Crab Eye Beam blast but was interrupted by a devastating purple uppercut that knocked the beast back by several giant steps. Atomik Lad's Field flickered away as he scampered into the doorway of a half destroyed building for protection. Radar continued his relentless attack with an overhead hammer blow. Crushtacean's footjaws were slammed into the pavement and it nearly lost consciousness.

"This is what you get for obstructing traffic and eating automobiles!" Radar scolded. Crushtacean pushed itself up. Radar rushed under the beast and quipped, "Time to take out the trash. No, wait. Time to visit Cap'n Salty's All Day Buffet Bar. Yes, much better. Less cliché, more fitting to the given circumstance." He heaved Crushtacean into the sky, likening himself to Atlas, when he felt a quiver in his arms.

A strain in his chest.

A horror in his heart.

Crushtacean's feet dangled above the streets. No traffic laws were being broken.

"Oh no," Radar managed to utter before the strength was completely drained from his body and the massive crab crushed him.

Atomik Lad shook his head and sighed despondently.

A battlecry best described as the pure vocalization of rage echoed against the battered buildings. "YYYYYYYYYEARGBLBLBLBLBLBLE!!!"

Atomik Lad looked into the sky. "Angus? But I didn't hear any Dwarf-a-pult." Nuklear Man soared into view. He was wielding Angus's patented

Enemy-B-Crushed. With Angus still lodged in the business end by way of his helmet. His tiny limbs flailed like mad.

"Don't ye even *think* about it, laddie!" Angus protested as Nuklear Man reared back Bertha and her small but enraged cargo. "Ah'll cram ye cape where the sun don't shine by way of that Atomik Laddie's nose!"

Atomik Lad took a step back into his doorway. "Ew."

"Don't worry about it, Angus. I've got this all planned out."

"Ah'll plan *ye*, ye blasted haggis brained—"

"DWARF-A-SMASH!" **KLONG WHAM THWACKITY-THWACK CRACK** *SPROING*!

Nuklear Man ceased his attack. "Sproing?" He inspected the Enemy-B-Crushed's business end. He scratched his head and looked around confusedly. "Angus? Yo, Angus? Where'd ya go?"

"Ah can see Scotland from here," he cried before entering a far off cloud bank.

"Oh well." Nuklear Man turned his attention back to the crab who, as it happened, was intently staring back at him. "Um. Hi."

Crushtacean answered with a pair Giant Crab Eye Beams that sent Nuklear Man crashing through the executive offices of the insurance company headquarters that contained, at its base, the doorway that Atomik Lad had been using for shelter. He counted to three and opened the front door. Nuklear Man shot out like a golden bullet right through a panoramic window next to the wide open door. Atomik Lad shut it with a sigh.

Nuklear Man floated up to be eye to eye with Crushtacean. "All right, Crab boy. You're gross and weird and freaky, so you're evil. Thusly, I must banish you to the next dimension!" He added in a whisper that only Crushtacean could hear, "That's just a nice way to say I'm gonna kill you."

Crushtacean blinked, completely ignorant of what was going on.

"PLAZMAAA—" **WHAM!** Crushtacean swiped the Hero out of the air. Nuklear Man carved a canal through the street until he finally stopped several blocks across town.

"Okay. I see how it is," Nuklear Man said. He stood up and dusted himself off. "You're an even worse cheater than Danger: Computer Lady. You don't announce your attacks and you stop me in the middle of mine. We're living in a society here, y'know! You can't just rampage through a city and disregard all the rules of heroic etiquette!"

The wind kicked up clouds of dust. Nuklear Man's cape billowed against his back. The end whipped in front of him to his left as the other end did the same at his right.

"*Other* end?!" He grabbed one end in each hand. He contorted, twisted, turned, and wrought himself around to inspect his fashion situation. His cape was torn straight down the middle from the bottom all the way up to the classy electron-orbited "N." He tossed the ragged ends from his grasp and they thrashed in the wind.

Nuklear Man's breathing became harsh and strained.

"You." His eyes exploded with a golden fury

"Tore." They burned with the strength of Hell's flames.

"My." Two stars in the throws of death.

"*Cape!*" A Plazma Aura so bright it nearly obliterated Nuklear Man from view burst to life around him. The Aura flared like footage of an inferno viewed in fast forward. Nuklear Man let loose a primal scream and the Aura doubled in size and intensity. It scattered nearby debris, shattered windows, and splintered the road with a shockwave of energy. The Aura siphoned into the Hero's fists. His face was an inhuman twisted visage of hate. "NOVAAA BEAM!"

"*Nova* beam?" Atomik Lad said. In ten years, he'd never heard of such a thing.

Something akin to a Plazma Beam's older brother just out of boot camp and hocked up on enough steroids to kill an elephant in erupted from Nuklear Man's hands. It spontaneously combust the air around it with a thunderclap. Clouds of dust and small bits of rubble were blast back. A wave of heat shot through Atomik Lad's body like an enormous nerve impulse as the Nova Beam seared through the air past him.

Crushtacean covered its crabby face with his huge pincers and uttered the Giant Crab version of "Eep" in the instant before Impact. The explosion sent Crushtacean tumbling through the air and several hundred million dollars worth of buildings which, thanks to the lunch hour, were devoid of any possible casualties.

Nuklear Man was floating over the concave dent he'd melted into the street by the intensity of his Nova Aura. It subsided into his typical Plazma Aura and that then fizzled out into the light glow he always emanated. He called that Idling. He dusted off his hands. A cascade of small sparks fell from them. "Well that was easy." He touched down in front of his crater. The asphalt in it was still bubbling slightly. "What's next?"

Atomik Lad ran out to him. "What the hell was that?"

"That, my dear Sparky, was style."

"No, I mean that Nova Beam crap."

Nuklear Man posed and pinched his bicep. "Check out these guns." He flexed. "Heh, more like cannons."

"Nuke, are you listening to a word I'm saying?"

"Of course, I am. How else would I know when to ignore you?"

"Ugh."

Nuklear Man admired himself in the broken window of a nearby office building. "Did I say cannons? I meant nuclear arsenal." He considered it for a few seconds. "How very fitting. I'm *such* a deep thinker!"

A crab-battered citizen nervously approached the Heroic pair. His clothes were ragged and covered with dust. He bled lightly from several superficial scratches. "Nuklear Man," he said with a meek voice. "You can't resort to violence to soothe this beast."

"Wah? Buddy, there ain't nothin' a whole lot of violence can't answer. Why do you think we've got war? Sheesh!"

"You have to teach the Crab how to love!" he pleaded.

"PLAZMAAA—"

"Whoah there, Tex," Atomik Lad said with an intervening swat at his mentor's hands. "What're you talking about Mr...?"

"Jameson. Dr. Jameson," he said. "I'm an animal psychiatrist."

Nuklear Man leaned down to whisper to Atomik Lad. "Can't I just blast him on principle?"

"Shh. Ahem, go on Dr. Jameson."

"That Giant Crab was demonstrating classic symptoms of a broken heart. Its misdirected anger against the city is a sure consequence of a love gone wrong. His confidence has been shattered, his sense of self is torn to bits, he can only fill that void by belittling, hurting, and destroying major metropolises, and such like. It's so sad, really."

"It's a frickin' *crab*!" Nuklear Man said. "It's emotional life consists of 'Food?' Get this quack outta here," he snapped before walking away.

"Er, thanks for your input, Doctor. We'll look into it." Atomik Lad trot over to Nuklear Man.

Dr. Jameson stumbled over the rubble back into the fur shop he had been using for shelter during the attack.

"Nuke, you've got to learn to treat people better. We're international figures, role models to—your cape!"

Nuklear Man stopped. "I think all this crab business has finally gotten to you, Sparky." He spoke deliberately, over-patronizingly. "We. Are not. Role models. To. My cape. Okay?"

"No, you dolt. *Look* at your cape!"

Nuklear Man did so. "Gasp!"

"Well?"

"Lousy dust." He beat the fashion accessory a few times. "There. Much better. Good thing you noticed that. You get twelve superpoints."

"No, it's one piece again. It's not torn any more."

Nuklear Man pondered for just over one second. "Must be like in the cartoons. Everything heals up when you step off screen."

"Off screen—what are you...That doesn't make sense!"

"Of course it does. You just don't watch enough cartoons."

*   *   *   *

Crushtacean was sprawled across its back with its pincers half lying inside a couple of severely damaged office buildings. It had tipped over a butter truck on impact. The Nova Beam had broiled a fair portion of the Angered Arthropod's main body. The smell was delicious.

*   *   *   *

Angus was sprawled across his back atop a random downtown skyscraper. He awoke with a jerk, blinked his bleary eyes in the sun, rubbed his throbbing skull, and suddenly got very angry. "That blasted Nuuklear haggis brained nimrod! Ah'll have his pretty boy Frenchie blond locks and stuff them down that smug face o' his fer this! DWARF-A-PULT!!!" The hideous mutation of sound echoed through the calm of post-crab Metroville.

*   *   *   *

Crushtacean awoke. The haunting melody of the mating call roused his aching body from the verge of death. His eyes opened to an upside down world. The exoskeleton was healing the damage dealt to it. The mating call was no dream. Crushtacean sprang to its eight feet and scuttled through the city, heedless of buildings or whatever else might obstruct its path.

She will be mine. Oh yes. She will be mine...

Issue 22—Planning for Failure

Librarian, Mail Man, Meter Maid, and Delivery Boy, The Minimum Wage Warriors, posed among the wreckage which had, minutes before, been a few rather bustling and productive blocks of Metroville. "Our job here is done," Mail Man said with a salute.

"Now off to our real jobs," Meter Maid added. The group gave the kind of hokey laugh one finds at the end of poorly produced and overly cliché cartoon programs aimed at children and their parents' wallets. They left in Delivery Boy's Suburban Assault Vehicle despite the fact that I said Crushtacean had eaten it just a little while ago. So fucking there.

Nuklear Man looked down at Atomik Lad. "You know, Sparky, y'oughta head back to the Silo and change."

"Yeah, I know. Rule #1: Always look your best." Atomik Lad had learned the most important rule years ago. Rule #1: *All* rules are Rule #1.

"Mainly, I was thinking that without a shirt on, compared to me you might develop some inferiority complex. Or at least a worse one than you must have now from all these years of contact with me. But I guess you've got a point too."

"Thanks."

"An inferior point, but a point just the same."

"You're too kind."

"I know."

"*Any*way, there should be a spare outfit in the Nukemobile's trunk. I'll head back to the beach and change."

"Whatever happened to what's-her-name?"

"What's-her—RACHEL! Oh geez." His Atomik Field erupted and he shot into the dusty sky. He mused that a post apocolyptic sky would probably look like this. He just hoped he wouldn't have to find out for sure when he got back to Rachel.

Nuklear Man heard the most disgusting sound. He spun around to see, "Angus?" The rest was a blur.

*   *   *   *

Rachel slipped a T-shirt over her bikini top. She reached into the backseat of the Nukemobile and pulled out her backpack. She laid down on her beach blanket, tied back her shoulder length hair, and started sketching to distract herself from the haunting feeling that she'd essentially been stood up.

It then occurred to Rachel that her life of school, work, reading, art, and general tedium was interrupted as of late and that she was actually on a date with The Atomik Lad. She had seen and spoken to The Nuklear Man. In person and very casually too. She'd met a score of other hero types, nearly kissed The Atomik Lad, battled some overgrown purple mutant alien guy, and her date, The Atomik Lad, had been dragged from her by the vicious attack of a giant crab from the bottom of the ocean. And how could she forget that she'd nearly kissed The Atomik Lad. Wait. Did she say that one already? Whatever, that's not the point. "What the hell am I doing?" she asked the ocean . "Why can't I meet normal boys? This is insane."

*   *   *   *

"Ah'll teach ye to uuse me Dwarf-a-Powers like that!" Angus roared as he battered the Golden Guardian with head-butts and kicks.

Nuklear Man, despite being thoroughly roughed up, couldn't help giggling. "Heh, 'Dwarf-a-Powers.' What's next, a Dwarf-a-Kick?"

It was.

"Ouch! My shin!" was not the right thing to say.

"Grrr! YYYYYYEARGHBLBLBLBLE!"

*   *   *   *

Dr. Ima Genius toiled over a hot supercomputer. She compiled results, cross referenced conclusions, sent for coffee that came back cold, cured a cancer, and determined one more piece of Crushtacean information. "He's in heat?"

*   *   *   *

Norman crashed into the beach in front of Rachel. A ton of sand exploded into the frothy waves. She ran toward him. "Norman! It is Norman, right? Are you okay?"

His tungsten body was covered with international postage. "Stupid high-rise post office," he muttered to himself. "I think I'm fine, but you gals look a little green."

"What?"

"It's probably from all that spinning around you're doing. And this plaid sunlight isn't good for your skin. You should go inside and rest for a while."

"Um. I think you should just lie down for a bit. Don't try to, um, anything."

Atomik Lad landed near them and his crimson field evaporated. Somehow, the sight of Rachel's bare legs sticking out of the shirt was exponentially sexier than the bikini could have ever been. "Hhhhhhiiii," he sighed and, in a lucky coincidence of phonetics, Rachel took it as a greeting rather than the lewd sensory overload that it was.

"John, Norman here is hallucinating. I think."

"Who?"

"John?"

"Where?"

"Don't tell me you're hallucinating too."

"I'm not sure, it's hard to believe such a vision of beauty could be real." He ended it with a little snap-point move that would've made Nuklear Man proud.

She was taken aback for a moment. "Oh my, aren't you the smooth one."

Before he could reply, Norman stood. Or rather, standing was his intention, but rolling face first into the sand was the result. "Mmf mblm."

"We've been eating a lot of sand today. I think we ought to roll him over. It's probably hard to breathe through solids."

Rachel helped heave the Tungsten Titan onto his side. "Do you know what's wrong with him?"

"Well, his Magnosmash attack magnetically propels him around the world. When Crushtacean dodged that last one, I think he continued to accelerate out of control and got his brain a little jumbled.

"So he's just really dizzy?"

"I hope so."

*   *   *   *

"Dwarf-a-punt!" Nuklear Man yelled as he dropkicked Angus like a football. The Surly Scot spun around in mid-air. "That did it!"

*   *   *   *

Crushtacean stealthily scuttled from street to street. This involved a lot of citizens screaming, several cars being stepped on, a score dogs barking, and half a dozen sea-food restaurant owners repenting. *Come on, my little darling, where are you?*

A resounding cry of "Dwarf-a-pult!" bellowed across the city. The mating call wafted after it like perfume.

Ah! There *you are!*

*   *   *   *

Rachel looked from Mighty Metallic Magno Man's prone body to Atomik Lad. "So is that crab thing all taken care of?"

"Yeah, Nuke went a little psycho and blasted it back to the Mesozoic Age. We don't even know where it landed."

Crushtacean chose that minute to scuttle over the wreckage Angus had left strewn about the highway behind the dunes. Atomik Lad slumped his shoulders. "Or not. Keep an eye on Norman for me. I've got to find Nuke. This crab thing is getting serious."

"That sounds like a personal problem," Rachel winked.

Atomik Lad laughed. "Blast, she found out my dirty secret." He managed a semi-serious demeanor. "I'll be back soon." His Atomik Field surrounded him as he once more took to the sky to chase after The Crab. "Now how do I get Nuke without losing track of Crabby? Wait a second. Ddidn't I just come this way?"

*   *   *   *

Crushtacean scuttled right over and past a comical dust cloud that roamed through the not-so-mean streets of Metroville. Atomik Lad paused to hover above it. The cloud was impenetrable to the naked eye, but he could guess what was inside by the sparks and constant stream of curses with a strong Scottish flair to them that flew out of it. "Poor Nuke. Musta made a little joke," he said.

The cloud immediately dispersed. Nuklear Man had his foot against Angus's forehead as the Surly Scot's arms spun and legs pumped in a fruitless effort to come within striking range. "Hey, Sparky," Nuklear Man said.

"Looks like you've got a little trouble there."

Angus ceased his limb flailing. "What'd that laddie say?"

"Naw, I'm fine," Nuklear Man said with a thumbs up. "How's it goin' on your end?"

"We've got a small problem." Atomik Lad gestured to Crushtacean. The monster looked under a car for something, seemed frustrated, and tossed the vehicle into a nearby building before moving on to the next car.

"*Small* problem, eh?" Angus muttered through clenched teeth. "Ah never woulda thought the laddie was against me too."

Nuklear Man surveyed Crushtacean. "Again?! Maybe we should use that shampoo they've got down at the free clinic. I've got a coupon from last time!"

"Where did you—no, why do. Forget it. We've got to do something about our Crab friend here. He's proving to be more than a tiny inconvenience."

"*That* dooes it!" Angus roared, toppling Nuklear Man onto his back. "DWARF-A-PULT!!!"

Crushtacean smashed through half a building which caused the other half to collapse due to several factors, among them being gravity and a sudden lack of structural integrity. *She's right around here!*

Atomik Lad's Field repulsed the Iron Scotsman's attack which sent Angus screaming, "YYYYYYEARGHBLBLBLBLE!" He arced right over Crushtacean's carapace.

"Oof!" Nuklear Man uttered as Crushtacean stood on his golden clad tummy. Crushtacean frantically thrashed around tearing down the walls of any building within his reach in search of the mating call's source. It didn't have the most complicated brain, but it had capacity for enough abstract thought to know it shouldn't be this hard to find a fellow Crushtacean.

Atomik Lad viewed these events almost outside himself. "You know, I don't think it likes the sound of Angus's Dwarf-a-Pult," he said.

"Who does?" Nuklear Man said. He was out of breath from the giant beast standing on his torso.

"Now that I think about it," Atomik Lad rubbed his chin in an oh-so-cunning manner. "Every time I've heard Angus Dwarf-a-pult, Crushtacean here goes a little crazy."

"I can see why," Nuklear Man grunted as he tried, rather unsuccessfully, to heave the beast off his chest.

"Maybe we could use this to our advantage," Atomik Lad said. "We could taunt it with the Dwarf-a-pult until it becomes so cross that it would make a mistake."

"Couldn't we just run away?" Nuklear Man said.

"Apparently not," Atomik Lad said.

"Stupid physics. I'll bash you good!" He unleashed a "PLAZMAAA BEAM!" against he Crab's underbelly.

Oh gross! A warm spot! One of those damn Clamzillas was probably around here Gah! Crushtacean removed himself from Nuklear Man's chest.

"Beware the power o' Plazma, vile ancient deep sea creature, for it is of the eternal flames of heaven, whereas you descend from the briney—"

"Nuke!"

"Shush, I'm quipping in a Heroic fashion as per my particular idiom."

"You can jibba-jabba later."

"Not in public!"

Atomik Lad held his head and hoped it would be enough to keep his brain from jumping out. "Whatever. Crushtacean is getting away!"

Nuklear Man dusted himself off. "Technically speaking, that's not altogether a bad thing."

"C'mon!" Atomik Lad chased after it.

"Aww nuts." Nuklear Man followed.

Atomik Lad, invincible Field set to maximum, soared after the rampaging Crushtacean with Nuklear Man close in tow. "Where are all the fire trucks and everything?" Atomik Lad said. "You'd figure they'd be all over this disaster by now."

*   *   *   *

Traffic was backed up with every fire truck, police car, and ambulance in Metroville. At the front of the line of flashing lights and blaring sirens was the Civil Defender. His Infantry Stopper 2000 Assault Cannon was aimed at the hundreds of civil servants lined up while he wrote what seemed to be an endless series of tickets. Each ticket, upon completion, would be thrown at the feet of a Native American. He wore a fire fighter's hat with a feather through it and a stony, patient face.

Rip. "Obstructing Traffic!" Civil Defender tossed the ticket into the pile that came up to Fire Chief's knees. Noticing the mess, Civil Defender scribbled out another ticket and tossed it to the pile. "Littering!"

"You already write'um that ticket," Fire Chief noted.

Civil Defender twitched with anger. "Oh yeah? How does Indecent Exposure sound to you, Chief Running Bare?"

The ticket danced into Fire Chief's face, tumbled down his exposed chest, over his crossed arms, and joined its brothers in the pile that went up to his knees. "That sound heap corrupt."

Civil Defender twitched once more. He glanced back at the stranded rescue vehicles. "Loitering! Nya ha!"

The Indigenous Extinguisher caught the ticket in mid-air and read it. "This only notebook paper."

"Um."

"You have'um no legal power."

"Er, no. Not as such. But I am a crazed and misguided vigilante hell bent on righting even the most insignificant wrongs no matter how meaningless."

Fire Chief tapped his mocasined foot. It caused a minor ticketslide.

"You're all under arrest?" the Armored Officer asserted with all the confidence of France.

Fire Chief brandished a tomahawk.

Civil Defender's eyes darted back and forth. "Well, I guess you win this round—BLAM BLAM BLAM!"

"Maybe if you shoot'um heap big gun instead of heap big mouth."

"Ahem. Righto." Civil Defender opened fire in a final, desperate attempt to maintain his delusions of police work by providing cover fire for his own escape.

*   *   *   *

Dr. Ima Genius lowered a bulky helmet onto her head She buckled the strap across her chin and balanced the device with one hand while adjusting a few knobs and dials on a console in front of her with theh other. The helmet was adorned with little multi-colored blinking lights and antennae of varying lengths. She flipped the Scientific: Engage button. Arcs of electricity shot and crackled across her technological helm. "Now to localize his Alpha Wave Series."

*   *   *   *

Nuklear Man soared through Metroville. He and Atomik Lad were still trying to chase down Crushtacean. This was easier than it might otherwise have been since nearly a third of the buildings were gone or otherwise easy to see through. Tactical scenarios to subdue The Crab spun through his mind. This of course included, and was completely limited to, *I shall make a feint to the northeast,* followed by silence. *Hmm. I wonder what I'm supposed to do now. Sparky never let me get this far.*

His introspective survey was interrupted by the scratchy and ghostly voice of Dr. Genius popping into his mind. "Calling Nuklear Man."

Aww geez, not again! Nuklear Man thought.

"Calling Nuklear Man," the voice repeated, this time slightly less garbled.

Look, I thought we had a deal. I agreed to commit those ritualistic murders and you agreed to leave me alone.

"What?" Genius's voice was now perfectly clear. "What are you talking about?"

You know, the ritual murders to provide sacrificial victims for summoning pagan death gods to usher in a new era of oblivion etc., etc.

Ima's voice was laden with drastically worried and concerned tones, "Nuklear Man, have you begun these murders?"

No. I planned on starting tonight once we wrap up this crab thing. Don't be so pushy, you'll get your sacrificial victims.

"Nuklear Man, do not, I repeat, do *not* commit any murders."

Is that a double negative? Is this a test of my loyalty?

"No. Look, I, or we, or whoever, have made other arrangements. No murdering. Do you understand?"

Well, yeah sure. I just wish you voices would make up your minds though.

*   *   *   *

On the other side of Metroville, inside a dark and damp abandoned warehouse, a pale green patch of light barely illuminated the center of the derelict structure, making the walls seem that much more distant. The light came from an oversized computer screen displaying the details of Plan C:

"Step 1: Design Evil: Telepathy Device. Complete." A little animated female in a lab coat bonked a cartoony computer with alternate blows by a wrench and mallet.

"Step 2: Contact Nuklear Goon. Complete." A radar dish sent little wavy signals to a caped buck-toothed figure flying above it.

"Step 3: Convince Nuklear Mongoloid to carry out ritualized murders to provide sacrificial victims for summoning pagan death gods to usher in a new era of oblivion etc., etc., Complete." A close up of the caped and buck-toothed individual showed his mind, X-Ray style, in a vice-grip.

"Step 4: Dance on Nuklear Grave. Incomplete." The animated lab coated lady from Step One gaily spun around a tombstone with an electron orbited "N" engraved on it. The picture had a giant red X superimposed over it.

Dr. Menace clenched her fists and shook slightly. She could barely restrain her fury. "Fine." She placed her hands on the computer console with a calm she didn't know she possessed. She lowered her head. "On to Plan *D*."

*   *   *   *

"Now, Nuklear Man," Dr. Genius said. "I have set up a telepathic link between the two of us. We are sharing all of our surface thoughts. Sorry for the intrusion, but I had to contact you as soon as possible, and this was the only way."

"No problem."

"Good. Now, you have to…Wait, what's that noise?"

An announcer yelled, "Ahora es la hora para Loco Paco's Migdnighto Madness Saleo! Vengances a Loco Paco de Discounto organ donor clinico! Sabado para tremenda ventas en estomagos, corazones, y dedos—" Nuklear Man punched himself in the skull a few times to silence the new intruder. "Lousy brain," he grumbled.

"What was that?" Dr. Genius asked.

"Oh, you know. Spanish radio."

"Spanish radio?"

"Yeah. What, like Spanish radio doesn't invade your thoughts too?"

"It doesn't."

"Oh, you silly scientists and your well known senses of humor. Y'oughta quit your day job. I mean, what do you do up there other than stare at charts an' stuff anyway?"

She checked a few readouts on her computer console. "His brain waves are actually so low they intercept radio signals," she mumbled to herself.

"Spanish radio signals!" he said. "En Español."

"Right. Look, I've compiled some data."

"Great! Keep up the good work. Super, really. Don't quit that day job!"

"No, Nuklear Man. Listen."

"Listen…?"

"The thing when someone else talks and you pay attention."

"Um."

"…And it's boring."

"Oh right! Gotcha. Go for it."

"I've been compiling some data about the Crushtacean and I have a plan. Regroup with Atomik Lad, Iron Scotsman, and Mighty Metallic Magno Man back at the beach and I'll telepathically relay the plan to all of you as soon as I figure out the Conference Call code for this thing."

*   *   *   *

"And that's the plan," Dr. Genius said. "I'm running up the charges for long distance telepathy here, so I'll have to let you all go. I'll be monitoring your progress from Überdyne's Satellite network. Good luck, Heroes."

"I can see the moons of Jupiter," Mighty Metallic Magno Man informed NASA as he lay on his back and utterly failed to sort out reality from supersonic-spin-induced hallucinations.

Angus crossed his arms and huffed. "Ah don't likes it!"

"Of course you don't like it," Nuklear Man said. "You've got the gimpy end of the plan."

"And the moons are talking!"

"Maybe we should put him in the shade," Rachel said. Atomik Lad leaned to shade Norman's face.

"Ooh, an eclipse!"

"Oh yeah. He'll be fine," he said.

"Are yoou sayin' Ah've got the gimpy part o' the plan 'cause Ah'm short, and ergo *gimpy*!"

"I hadn't thought of it that way, but now that you mention it."

"GrrrrrrrRRRARGH! DWARF-A—"

"*Wait!*" Atomik Lad imposed himself between Angus and Nuklear Man. The Surly Scot ceased his assault. "Angus, you play an important role in the plan."

"Very important," Rachel added. "Without you, there's no plan at all."

Angus furrowed and scowled to new levels of aggravation. "That don't mean Ah gots to likes it. Hmmphf!"

"Okay," Atomik Lad said. "Let's just get in our positions and get this over with." He glanced at Rachel as she winked at him. His legs went all wobbly.

Nuklear Man picked up Angus and held him like a bearded football dressed in iron, smelling of alcohol, haggis, and rage. Angus squirmed uselessly. Nuklear Man leapt into the sky.

Atomik Lad watched Nuklear Man's trail of Plazma energy as it cut across the high drifting clouds. "So, what'dya think of our first date, Rachel?"

"Never a dull moment with your friends around, is there."

"Yeah," he said, looking down at the quartz scattered sand.

"But I could use some dull moments every now and then."

"I know what you mean. Lord, do I know what you mean."

"Maybe. So how about we do something this weekend? Just you and me."

"I'd like that."

"If you can squeeze me into your schedule, that is."

"I'll make time. Norman should recover by then, he can baby sit Nuke while we're out."

"Good," she said. "Um, don't you have some important plan to put into motion?"

Atomik Lad smiled goofily. "Er, plan? Who? Me. Damn. Right. I'll be back as soon as we wrap this up. I'm sorry."

"Just go."

His Atomik Field burst to life and the sidekick shot into the air after his companions.

"And be careful."

*   *   *   *

"Man, stopping this crab thing has turned into such a mission," Nuklear Man groaned.

"Ah still thinks this plan is stupid," Angus huffed. Nuklear Man held him tight against his side while he flew them to the positions stipulated by The Plan. Angus's Iron: Bagpipe Thrusters obviously held an eeire fascination with the Giant Crab. The Plan, therefore, needed Angus to act as live bait. Nuklear Man would deposit him near the grounds of an abandoned factory. There, it was a simple matter of setting off the Thrusters to lure Crushtacean into the open. Then Nuklear Man would fly Angus out of harm's way while Atomik Lad kept it busy until the other Heroes could regroup whereupon they would take care of the Crab once and for all.

Simple.

"Heh, I wouldn't like it if I was the bait either."

"Ah ain't no bait!" he rumbled under Nuklear Man's grip. "Ah'm, what did that Doctor lass call it, the um…"

"'The most integral and important unit contributing to the success of The Plan'?"

"Aye. And don't ye forget it!"

"She just said that so you'd agree to do it."

"WHAT?!"

"I mean, sheesh, who *volunteers* to be the bait in a plan? 'Ooh, ooh, lookit me, I wanna be the bait, put me in unnecessary danger while my comrades must come to my rescue lest I become all dead.' Yeah right, no thanks." Nuklear Man laughed to himself. Then he remembered what a bad idea it was to mock Angus. "Er. Um, but it's too late to back out now, right?"

"Like hell it is!" He wriggled to free himself.

"Yeesh, you're a slippery little guy, aren't ya."

"Let me go, ye musclebound freak! Ah ain't gonna be no bait fer no giant killer crab!"

"Oh, but I think you are." Nuklear Man zoomed out of the sky to the abandoned factory. He set Angus down, wrapped him in an abandoned iron girder that had been lying on the abandoned grounds, and tied him to an abandoned cement truck with several lengths of abandoned chain all in a golden blur of action. "Finished" He stepped back and admired his work and proudly dusted off his hands. "You're not going anywhere."

"How am I supposed to get away when the damned crab shows up?!"

"I've got to fly you out of here anyway, so what's another couple of tons of abandoned metal-work to an invincible superstud like m'self? Answer: nuthin'."

*   *   *   *

Meanwhile, Atomik Lad raced above the skyscraping rooftops of Metroville. His quarry wasn't difficult to find, what with the unmistakable trail of destruction to follow. "Ok. So there it is, now I just have to get its attention." He zoomed down to Crab level and buzzed around its Giant Crab eyes. The monster didn't even blink.

"Well, this is getting me nowhere."

Where, oh where has my sweet precious gone, Crushtacean lamented.

*   *   *   *

"You know, you're kinda cute all wrapped up in that iron stuff."

"What."

"Just like one of those little adorable lawn gnomes."

"What!"

"Only wrapped up in an iron girder 'cause you're waaaay too weak to even try to get out."

"THAT *DOES* IT!"

*   *   *   *

Crushtacean heard the lilting harmony of the mating call dance its way to his hungrily awaiting ears. *Be patient, my dear, soon your Crabbyboy will be near,* he thought to himself. It rhymed in Crabtalk too, but that was just because the entire language consisted of discreet differences in the sound "splarg."

The Crab spun around and bat Atomik Lad from the air into what had previously been an untouched furniture store. A comfy sofa broke his fall before his Atomik Field shred it like incriminating government documents. "Well, that'll do." He stood, brushed himself off, and shot out the shattered window display. Pieces of furniture scattered in his wake.

Mr. Manager crawled out from his hiding place behind the sales desk. "My new business." Twitch. "Ruined by those, those *punks*! Again! I'll get even with you degenerates if it's the last thing I do!" he screamed after Atomik Lad's diminishing form.

*   *   *   *

"All that yelling and shaking makes you even cuter."

"*What*?! I'll show ye cute!" His Iron: Bagpipe Thrusters flared. The mass of metal he'd become jumped and jerked, but was held in check by the chains that bound him to the low earth.

"Now you just look cute and silly."

"YYYYYEEEARGHBLBLBLBLE!!!"

"Meow."

Nuklear Man blinked. He scratched his chin. "That's not a very Raging Scootish Warrior Thing To Say."

"Meow."

"Ahh. I'll use my super sensitive Nuklear Hearing to pinpoint the exact location of this meow's source."

"Meow?"

"Bah! This is taking too long. I'll be easier to just Plazma Beam the area and when the meowing stops, I bet that'll be where it's coming from."

"Meow?!"

"PLAZMAAA—"

"MEOW!" A gray cat leapt from the leaves of a tree right into Nuklear Man's thick arms. The feline made himself comfortable and rubbed against the Hero's tummy.

"Aww," Nuklear Man cooed. "You're such a cutie wutie. Yes you are, yyyyyes you are." He scratched the cat's chin and held him close. Angus roared and stormed in the background as Nuklear Man and his new friend were sinking into their own world of happiness which was completely oblivious to everything else in the universe.

*   *   *   *

Crushtacean smashed through Metroville. His eagerness grew with every melodious harmony that echoed through the city. Atomik Lad fell behind while assisting unfortunates left in the path of destruction. He knew Nuklear Man would be able to handle the situation until he got there anyway. He always could.

✳   ✳   ✳   ✳

Angus's raging came to an abrupt halt. The thick chains wrapped around his small body dragged him back to the ground with a hard metallic thunk. He could hear, what was it? A train? "Who's there?" He listened closer. Was it a stampede of some kind? "Nuklear Man? Do ye hear that?" Stagnant puddles throughout the abandoned grounds rippled. "Where are ye, ye haggis brained oaf?"

"Awww, he's purring. You wuv Mr. Nuklear Man, don't you Mr. Whiskers? Yes you do."

Crushtacean loomed over the horizon.

"Nuklear Man!" Angus screamed. "Git me outta here! That bloody Crab's here! Blast 'em, do somethin'!"

"Lookit that belly! Yes, belly, belly, belly!" The cat rolled, stretched, purred, and generally enjoyed the moment almost as much as Nuklear Man.

"He's comin' this way!"

Issue 23—Wherein Angus Has Too Much Crab Meat

Dr. Genius had been monitoring the situation through a passive telepathic uplink. She focused the Scientific: Telepathy Helm on Nuklear Man and tossed all the dials to their maximum settings. "Nuklear Man! Angus needs your help! What're you—oh no."

"Necessario un operacion grande y peligroso? Loco Paco's Discount Surgery!" She took off the telepathic helm with a forlorn frown. "Spanglish radio."

*   *   *   *

"Tee hee, you're sticking your tongue out!" Nuklear Man told the cat.

Angus Dwarf-a-pulted to safety. Or he would have had Nuklear Man not tied him down with over a ton of scrap metal. Angus's frantic frenzy to escape only served to further flame Crushtacean's passions. *She's a bit petite for my tastes, but OH BABY!*

"What are ye—ARGODNOPLEASEEERGHELLTHISISHELLBLBLBLE!"

*   *   *   *

Atomik Lad touched down in front of Nuklear Man three minutes later. A snoozing gray furred cat was cuddled up in his arms. Atomik Lad scanned the area. "Where's Angus?"

"Never mind that. I found us a new sidekick."

"Not—"

"Katkat!"

Atomik Lad's head drooped. "Don't tell me. 'Kat' because he's a cat." Nuklear Man nodded. "And 'kat' because he's also a cat."

Nuklear Man beamed with pride. "Exactly. Together, they make Katkat. It's brilliant."

"It's something all right."

"You said it."

"Anyway, what'd you do with Angus? Where's Crushtacean?"

"I dunno. Angus was making a racket a while ago, but I guess he musta worn himself out."

"And Crushtacean?"

Nuklear Man shrugged. "He's a no show."

"What do you mean?"

"Well, I brought Angus here, but then I had to tie him down because he didn't want to go through with the plan."

"And?"

"And then I found Katkat. We've been training ever since."

"Training? No, don't explain. We've got to find Angus. And how the hell do you miss a giant, rampaging, horny crab monster?"

"It ain't easy, but I does what I can."

"Laddies?"

"Angus!" Atomik Lad ran a little deeper into the abandoned factory grounds as his diminuitive friend stumbled out of them. It looked like something out of a movie about the end of the world. "What happened?"

Angus limped from around a corner. He was wearing his heavily armored Iron: Battlesuit outfit *backwards*. His fierce Iron: Battlehelm was tilted to one side. He had a far off look in his face. His constant empty gaze pointed a few degrees over the horizon without focusing on anything. Atomik Lad was reminded of a news anchorman's vacant stare as the Surly Scot hobbled to him as if on automatic.

"Are you okay?"

Angus blinked one eye at a time and nearly toppled over but Atomik Lad caught and him and held the Scotsman upright. "Ah'm okay. Sure."

"You sure?"

"Oh. Yeah."

"Where's Crushtacean? What happened?"

Angus shivered. "Ah likes a spot o' sugar with me crumpets every morning to put the bounce in me step," he stated matter-of-factly and fell on his back.

"How'd he get out of the iron girders?" Nuklear Man asked.

Atomik Lad followed Angus's tiny and erratic footprints back into the half crumbled factory. Inside its walls, Crushtacean was lying on his great underbelly. His enormous pincers were crossed under his head. A smoke stack was sticking out his footjaws reminding Atomik Lad of a giant cigarette. "He's snoring?"

$$* \quad * \quad * \quad *$$

Atomik Lad called Dr. Genius to inform her that Crushtacean had been subdued, though he wasn't entirely clear on the specifics. She immediately mobilized Überdyne's army of secret vehicles which consisted of a dozen semi-trucks labeled Inconspicuous Trucking Company. They arrived on the scene within minutes since there was no traffic left in the city. Dr. Genius personally supervised the activities. A tracking device was placed on Crushtacean's carapace and cargo helicopters flew in to transport The Crab to the ocean to release him back into the wild.

"It's the humane thing to do," Dr. Genius was explaining to Atomik Lad.

"I understand, but what if he comes back? Look at what he did to the city in just a matter of hours."

"Oh, I wouldn't worry about that." She grinned deviously. "The tracking device is rigged so that if he comes near a civilized shoreline, one of Überdyne's secret Scientific: Weapon Platform Satellites will zap him with a few terrawatts of laser energy. He won't bother us again thanks to good ol' Pavlovian learning."

"Ah. Yes, humane."

"Better than dicing him up. Überdyne's been wanting to break into the seafood industry for years now. I had to talk The Board out of it to save this rare and beautiful specimen." She looked past Atomik Lad. "And here comes Nuklear Man."

Atomik Lad turned around. "He's still got that cat."

"Hey Sparky, Dr. Gorgeous." Nuklear Man winked at her and whispered to Atomik Lad, "Chicks dig it when you hit on them."

"Right."

"Aren't you going to introduce us to your little friend?" she asked.

"See!" he gleefully whispered to his sidekick before answering. "Ima, please! I know I'm irresistibly handsome, but let's try to keep at least a semblance of professionalism despite my perfect physique and charming demeanor. Besides, it's not little."

"Nuke."

"I know this spandex doesn't leave much to the imagination, but I can tell you from personal experience—"

"Whoa! Nuke! She's talking about the damn cat."

"Oh." He straightened his spandex. "Well, why didn't you just say so?"

Ima laughed, "You guys. You're crazy."

"Crazy like a *lunatic*!" Nuklear Man said. "No, wait."

Atomik Lad sighed. "He found the cat out here somewhere."

"Crazy like a mental patient? Well, now that one *sounds* right, but I don't know."

"He calls it Katkat, don't ask, it'll only make sense and you don't need that. I know I didn't. I'm afraid he wants to keep it."

"Ooh, Ooh! Can I? *Please*! I'll take care of him and everything! I'll even feed this one!"

"This one?" Ima asked.

"He doesn't have the best record when it comes to pets. It's best that we don't talk about it in public."

"Oh my," she said.

"Please?" Nuklear Man begged.

Atomik Lad knew he had to say no for the sake of the cat. "Oh fine. It's your birthday."

"Yippee!"

"Meowr."

"Yeah, yeah. Hey, it is your birthday isn't it. Your present is still in the Magnomobile. I forgot all about it when Crushtacean popped up."

"Goody! Back to the beach!" Nuklear Man scooped up Katkat and zoomed into the sky.

"No, wait!" Atomik Lad yelled. "Dammit, that's how we lost number three. I'm sorry Ima, but I've got to keep an eye on them."

"Understandable. Perhaps next time we get together, the entire city won't be in peril. Be careful."

"That's the plan. See you later." His Atomik Field erupted and he followed his mentor back to the beach.

"Now what's that special thing all cats can do?" Nuklear Man wondered aloud as he flew back to Larsen Beach with Katkat tucked into his thickly muscled arms.

"Meow?"

"No, that's not it."

"Purrrr." Katkat rubbed his face against Nuklear Man's tucking arm.

"But you do make a good case for it." He pondered some more. "I guess you win. Fly, Katkat, fly!" He gave the cat a granny style chuck into the wild blue yonder.

"Mreowr!?!" Katkat hollered as he rocketed across the sky.

"That's the spirit!" Nuklear Man cheered. "Er, pull up. Katkat, don't be like all the others, pull up!"

A crimson blur rushed past Nuklear Man, spinning him like a top. He stopped himself and had to yank his cape off the top of his head. "Lousy meteors," he grumbled.

Atomik Lad raced to the launched Katkat. He gained on the flying feline and reached out to save him from a messy demise. He focused on his hands for an instant and recoiled. He let out a sigh, shut off his chaotic Atomik Field, and safely grappled Katkat.

"Time to turn on the juice," he said.

But it didn't quite work. Pathetic red sparks fluttered around his body as the pair began to succumb to gravity. *Well, this is bad.* The ground was getting a little too friendly for Atomik Lad's comfort. "What a great way to end an otherwise promising career in the Hero business. Fend off an interdimensional dragon spirit, thwart countless plots to take over the world, defeat Dr. Menace at every turn, subdue a giant crab, and then get turned to hamburger while trying to save a damn cat."

They kept falling. His Field kicked in mere inches from the ground. Atomik Lad bounced across Larsen Beach like a skipping stone until he came to a clumsy stop some distance from what was left of Nuklear Man's birthday party. "Ouch," he moaned.

"Mew."

Nuklear Man landed knee deep in sand next to them. "Ooh! You saved him!"

"You're talking to the cat, aren't you."

"Of course I am. You should know better than to fly at such dangerous speeds."

Atomik Lad grumbled.

"Lucky for you, Katkat was able to catch you and talk some sense into you."

"Why did you throw him?"

"Cats can fly."

"Cats can't fly.

"Katkat told me so."

"No. No he did not."

"It's the special thing they can all do."

"No, they're supposed to be able to land on all four feet."

"Oh. Well then no harm done."

Atomik Lad stood up, still holding Katkat. "You know, Nuke. Katkat is a really dumb name."

"Is not. You're just not smart enough to understand its intricacies. Like me."

"'Like you meaning you can or can't understand these alleged intricacies?"

"Um. Nyes."

"Let's just get back to Norman and Rachel, clean up the party, give you your stinking present, and get back to the Silo for some nice sleep. Being with you all day is sending me to an early grave."

"I think I've got sand in my spandex again," Nuklear Man said.

*   *   *   *

An hour later, the sun started to set behind the dunes. Rachel and the Heroes finally disposed of the leftover junk and garbage from Nuklear Man's prematurely preempted party. Even Mighty Metallic Magno Man was able to help, though he tended to walk in wobbly lines. Katkat slept soundly in the Magnomobile's driver's seat.

The chores were completed and Nuklear Man's incessant whining had become unbearable. Atomik Lad and Norman hauled the Hero's present from the Magnomobile's trunk. The box was taller than Nuklear Man. His eyes widened with childish glee. "Let's cut 'er open like a prom date!" he said enthusiastically.

Everyone else took a step back from Nuklear Man and traded worried glances. "Hey, don't look at me," Atomik Lad said. "I just work for the guy."

Nuklear Man tore into the huge box like a massive jungle cat mauling its prey, but only Katkat knew this for sure. Little foam peanuts poured out of the wounded box until they came up to Nuklear Man's knees.

"Ack! It's got me! Curse you, curse you all for this treachery!" he howled. "May I haunt you from beyond the grave for eternity!"

"Nuke, it's just the packing material. It's there so that what's inside doesn't break in shipping," Atomik Lad said.

Nuklear Man ceased his throws of death and dove into the package. He pulled out a small box with "A Fubar!" in it a few seconds later. He clutched the small box like it was his own long lost child.

"You didn't," Rachel moaned. "Please tell me you didn't."

"We had to," Atomik Lad said.

"Yeah" Norman chimed. "It was the only thing we could find. I mean, what do you get the person who doesn't know anything?" He poked Nuklear Man in the ribs.

"Get your slimy hands away from it, you, you sneaky sneak! He's mine!" Nuklear Man stroked the small Fubar toy. It teetered on the border between adorably cute and hideously evil.

"Okay, Nuke. Whatever." His Magnowatch beeped. "Oh, geez, I've got to get back to the Magnopad. Catch you guys later." He saluted them. "Great meeting you, Rachel."

"I know," she said with a coy little smile.

"Don't let Sparky pull that 'Out of gas' shtick on you."

She just smiled as the Tungsten Titan set Katkat on the sand and took off in his purply supercool car.

Atomik Lad watched the hero pull onto the highway beyond the dunes. "Isn't the Magnopad the other way?" he asked. "Eh, he'll figure it out. How's your present, Nuke?"

"Don't touch it, you knave!" he snapped. Atomik Lad was nowhere near it. "I love it to bits! I can't wait to get back to the Silo to get 'im going. Katkat and Fubar all in one day. This is perfect!"

"He seems content," Rachel said.

"Maybe I'll get to drive this time."

"Let's hope."

At that moment, a 747 clumsily wound its way through the sky. A long black plume of smoke trailed behind it. Thanks to Nuklear Man's Nuklear Hearing, he heard a world full of thankful citizens pledging their lives to the eternal reign of the Nuklear World Order because he also happened to have Nuklear Hallucinations.

"Hey, I think that plane's on fire!" Atomik Lad said. "We've got to do something."

Nuklear Man was roused from his fantasy world just long enough to realize what was really going on. "Ladies, please, no shoving. There's plenty of your Nuklear Love Machine to go around."

"What?" Rachel asked.

Atomik Lad hit his mentor in the back of the head and released Nuklear Man from both his fantasy world and the dream world inside that fantasy world. "Yo," the Hero reported.

"Plane. Fire. Crash." Atomik Lad summarized. He pointed at the plane.

Nuklear Man's eyes pulled one of those dramatic squinting close up shots as he reviewed the situation. With his best tough guy voice, he said, "This looks like a job for—"

"Please don't," Atomik Lad pleaded.

"—Katkat!"

"Mew?"

Nuklear Man snatched the feline from the sand and rocketed after the imperiled plane with a sparkling Plazma comet's tail in his wake.

"I blame myself mostly," Atomik Lad grumbled.

"So will the Humane Society when they sue the pants off you," Rachel said. "Which might not be so bad," she added with a wink.

Atomik Lad wobbled, but the severity of the situation made him recover. "Okay, I've got to make sure nothing happens. Rachel, wait here. I'll be back." His Atomik Field crackled around his body and propelled him after the Hero.

She shade her eyes from the setting sun as she watched him soar. "This is just weird."

Issue 24—Hijackery!

The Metroville Airport Air Traffic Control Tower bustled with activity, which was no surprise considering the amount of Air Traffic that must be Controlled in Metroville's Airport. Not to mention the unconventional means of air travel that plagued the city in the form of self-catapulting midgets and caped weirdos.

The Colonel chewed on his stubby cigar thus cementing Jerry's long held suspicion that the Colonel was utterly insane. This belief first developed the moment Jerry met him when the Colonel introduced himself as "the Colonel" and violently insisted everyone refer to him as such despite the fact that he never held any military rank whatsoever in his life. Nevertheless, Jerry, as an Air Traffic Controller, had a job to do. So he did it.

"Colonel," Jerry reported. "Flight 1313 reports a complete loss of cabin pressure and power, all four engines are on fire, the landing gear has fallen off, the bathroom has been Occupado for well over an hour, there are only kosher meals left, a gang of terrorists have hijacked it, and both pilots are unconscious!"

The Colonel chewed a few more chews on his cigar and stared purposefully at Jerry's radar screen. The cigar slowly emerged from his mouth with all the stealth of a severely obese ninja trying to sneak across a well lit area.

Jerry hated it when he did that.

The Colonel spat his soggy cigar onto the floor. He spoke with the slight John Wayne type of drawl that anyone who demands to be referred to as "the Colonel" would have developed after thousands of hours of practice over the years, "These boys are in trouble, Steve."

"Jerry, sir."

"Kevin, get me the Flight Information on that bird."

"Jerry, sir." He was never certain how the Colonel was able to make words sound capitalized. It was fascinating and terrifying at the same time, like watching a tsunami as it loomed over you. "Flight 1313 took off from Metroville Airport runway thirteen at 13:13, destined for Burgesville later tonight. Flight 1313 has 130 passengers and is manned by 13 flight attendants, Captain Buck "Blackcat" Openumbrellaindoors, who hasn't had a single mishap in his career spanning one year, one month, and thirteen days, and co-pilot Lance "Broken Mirror" Walkingunderladder on this, his thirteenth flight."

The Colonel considered the facts with a slow, sorry shake of his weathered head. "What're the odds, eh Charlie?"

"Jerry, sir."

"Dozens of planes in the air, and this one has a case of bad luck. What a crazy, unpredictable world with no discernable patterns or allegiances to silly superstitions."

"Um, there is more sir."

"Go on, Akbar."

"Jerry, sir. After about thirteen minutes of flight, a group of seven terrorists clad in mismatched Hawaiian shirts declared they were hijacking the plane to Metroville."

The Colonel's confident veneer cracked with confusion. "Didn't the plane take off *in* Metroville?"

"Er. Yes. They apologized saying this was their first try. They've been circling the Airport trying to figure out what to do next. On the thirteenth rotation, all heck broke loose. According to what we were able to piece together before they disallowed radio contact, they call themselves the SMOTCAOAN and they admit that they aren't very good at this sort of thing."

"So it would seem. But it does beg the question, Suzzie."

"What question is that, sir?"

"How the hell do we get them down safe?"

*   *   *   *

Nuklear Man raced along side the doomed aircraft. Katkat was tucked against his body like a furry and very cuddly football with big green happy eyes and a silly smiley kind of look when he purrs and rolls onto his back for lots of belly rubbing that hypnotizes him to sleep and then he sort of runs in place when he's dreaming and it's so cute when—er…

Nuklear Man clung to the handle of the wide open Emergency Exit Door with his free hand and heaved himself inside. He closed the hatch behind him. The deafening roar of wind abated only to be instantly replaced by the deafening screams of terror from the perhaps-not-as-doomed-as-before passengers.

"What seems to be the trouble?" he asked as though it weren't painfully obvious.

"It's Nuklear Man!" someone hollered.

"He's here to save us!" someone else proclaimed.

"He's thirteen seconds late," someone else noted.

"I *hate* you guys," another voice grumbled.

The Hero looked down at his feet. The Socially Maladjusted Overvillains Who Can't Agree On A Name groveled before him.

"We done a bad thing," Granite admitted sorrowfully.

"Aww," Nuklear Man acquitted them on the spot. "Just get back to your seats and we'll pretend none of this happened."

The seven villains mumbled embarrassed apologies as they seated themselves. Nuklear Man set Katkat down and began thinking about how he might solve this particular imperiled plane.

*   *   *   *

Meanwhile, just underneath the plane, Atomik Lad pushed his power of flight to its limit. He could barely keep up with the jet and was concentrating so hard on catching the vessel that he hadn't noticed his Atomik Field's peculiar property of streamlining itself into a sheen of crimson covering his body rather than the chaotic mishmash of red violence it typically manifested as.

*   *   *   *

Nuklear Man consulted the more coherent flight attendants. Apparently, as he could best surmise from the reports given by these trained professionals, the plane was in some kind of danger. He pound his mighty fist into the other hand to punctuate his frustration. "If only we knew what was wrong!"

"The wings are on *fire!*" the flight attendants screamed desperately. Again. "We'll all *die!*"

"Speak for yourself, lady. *I'm* invincible." He rubbed his chin intellectually. "Wings on fire, eh?" His face took on the features of a criminal genius plotting his next foolproof scheme. "I've got it!" Nuklear Man rocketed out the door, tore off the left wing, blast off the right, and returned through the same door, closing it gingerly behind him.

Everyone aboard awaited his verdict, unaware of what had happened outside. He cleared his throat and proudly announced, "I got rid of the wings so now the fires can't spread to us here in the cabin. We're perfectly safe now."

The screaming began anew.

"No, no. You don't have to thank me. It's all a part of being a Hero."

A puffy gray cat tail slipped through the curtain between the Coach and First Class sections.

*   *   *   *

Atomik Lad dodged the errant wings. *At least it's easier to keep up with the plane without those.* Without thinking, he bashed his way into the cargo area and hoped he could find a way into the plane proper from there.

*   *   *   *

"Colonel! A signal is coming from Flight 1313!" Jerry reported.

"Put it on the speaker, Bubbles."

"Jerry, sir." He did as he was ordered.

Screams muffled by distance and closed doors could be heard from the tiny speaker.

"Vicki, give me the microphone."

"Jerry, sir," he said and handed over the microphone.

"This is the Colonel at Metroville Airport's Control Tower. Do you read me Flight 1313?"

There was a pause.

"Flight 1313, come in!"

"Meow?"

*   *   *   *

Though Nuklear Man had heard the phrase "Six Degrees of Separation" he'd never considered the possibility of there being a concept of "Two Degrees of Comfort". Apparently airline seating was based on the latter. He sat, rather uncomfortably, in the Coach section while waiting for the situation to resolve itself. "This is a shocking insult to the entire school of reclining. Feh. I wonder what's shakin' up front." Nuklear Man floated beyond the Class Curtain and into Paradise.

*   *   *   *

Atomik Lad burst from the mini-kitchen floor with a mass of twitching crimson surrounding him. It diffused of its own accord and nearly dropped the sidekick back down the very hole he'd just produced. He caught himself on the edge and grunted as he climbed up. "That moron had better be handling this."

*   *   *   *

He wasn't.

Robe clad maidens frolicked about the burbling First Class Fountain. Nuklear Man, at some point, had donned a smoking jacket and was reclining—*real* reclining—in a comfy leather couch while one maiden fed him fresh grapes and another fanned him with an enormous frond.

First Class was an airborne paradise despite the sudden and explosive ends the universe was conspiring to make of it. Yet not one of the First Class patrons worried. How could they? All notions that an outside world ever existed were long gone.

"Did I ever tell you ladies that I'm Nuklear Man?"

The maidens cooed.

"Awww yeah."

"I bet he knows Mighty Metallic Magno Man."

"Er, what? No. Nukie here. Not him. Me."

"He's so dreamy," another maiden said.

"Stop it. Stop that. He's nothing. I can do stuff he can't, like lift tanks. He can't lift tanks."

The maidens snuggled closer to Nuklear Man. "Rrrrrreally?"

He thought about it. "Well, unless he used his Magnopowers. He could probably put 'em in orbit then. I can't compete with that."

"Oh." They paid him no more attention. It would have taken too much effort from the all consuming effort of talking amongst themselves about Mighty Metallic Magno Man.

"Phooey."

Atomik Lad ran into First Class, the curtains flourished in his wake. He skid to a halt and was instantly dumbfounded by the delights that assaulted his senses like a soft kiss. A smoking jacket already around his shoulders, a pair of robed maidens led him to a couch directly across from the pouting Nuklear Man.

"Why don't you relax, Mr. Atomik?" they said like Sirens.

"Relax? Wasn't there something I was supposed to do?"

"Yes, let us make your trip as pleasant as possible."

"Pleasant," he smiled. *Wait. A trip?*

Nuklear Man waved a dopey wave to his sidekick. "Don't mention Norman."

Norman. Beach. Plane. Trouble. Nuke. Katkat. Me. Here. Now. "Ah-ha!" Atomik Lad sprang into action just as the First Class Succubae were making their moves. His patented and volatile Atomik Field tore the smoking jacket to shreds. "Nuke! We have to do something about this plane, it's going to crash any—" The plane's momentum went all silly. Metal screeched against stone, loose odds and ends were tossed around, the fountain stopped, the maidens were toppled into a big pile, and Nuklear Man's top half was sticking out the roof while Atomik Lad remained strangely unaffected by the whole mess. They were motionless now. His Field fizzled away.

Nuklear Man fell entirely inside. "Well, we're stopped."

"Where are we?" Atomik Lad asked while in complete disbelief of the past few seconds.

"Looked like an airport."

The passengers, a bit woozy but completely unharmed from the ordeal, disembarked from the plane via an inflatable slide. The Socially Maladjusted etc. tip-toed from the scene and were therefore completely ignored by the prominent police and news presences. Nuklear Man and Atomik Lad entered the cockpit together to congratulate the pilots for saving the day. However, their smiles disappeared when the small door opened. Both pilots were still passed out on the floor and smelling of cheap bourbon.

The pilot's seat swiveled around.

"Katkat!" Nuklear Man squealed.

"Mreowr." Feline and Hero hugged.

"But!" Atomik Lad stammered. Nuklear Man walked away with the cat in his arms. They left Atomik Lad by himself in the tiny compartment with too many questions. Foremost among them was: "Where'd he get that Flight Captain's hat?"

Issue 25—Teaching
Assisstants of DOOM

It had been a long day.

Well, technically it had been about an average length day after taking into account solstices and equinoi. But to Atomik Lad, the day had been far from short. There was the chore of getting Nuke up before noon, the hell of witnessing the Hero drive, Rachel, that Radar guy, the beach party, Angus, the nightmarish Crushtacean, Katkat, the doomed plane, and that creepy Fubar doll which, thanks to quick action by Atomik Lad, narrowly avoided the moniker...

"Fubarfubar!"

"Like 'Nuklear' and 'Man' right?"

"Now you're getting it!"

"Why not call it something even more annoying, like Pookaboo."

Nuklear Man emitted a girlish squeal of delight.

*   *   *   *

Atomik Lad drove, much to the relief of car insurance companies across the globe. Rachel sat in the passenger seat chatting pleasantly with the sidekick while Nuklear Man took up the back seat and played with Fubar and Katkat. Atomik Lad dropped Rachel off at her dorm. It was getting dark and he was the paranoid type so he walked her to the front door. A few fellow students walked in and out of the doors while trying to look like they weren't looking at pair standing there, talking, being happily awkward. Somehow the conversation eventually worked its way to Atomik Lad leaving but not before a quick kiss. The drive home was a blur to him.

The night's sleep period was a welcomed repose for the young hero-in-training. Besides, he still had school in the morning. Erg. Morning. Mourning. That couldn't be a coincidence. At least it was Friday, and not just any Friday at that. He was supposed to get back the essay he'd turned in that Monday for his political science class. The paper was a theoretical exercise wherein each student would design a government. By the time he had finished the assignment, Atomik Lad was convinced that the paper's true purpose was to show how difficult it is to establish a working government and make the students realize that, massive corruption and abuse aside, they had it rather well.

*   *   *   *

The patient was sound asleep. The "doctor" grinned while donning a pair of thick rubber gloves. They'd be necessary for insulating him against the Electromagnatrono-meter. He held a pair of clamps in each hand. Wires ran down from the handles to a black box adorned with lights and dials and nobs. "Remember," the doctor said while looming closer to his unconscious patient. "It's not the volts that kill ya, it's the amps!"

A figure stood in the door way, leaning against the frame, its arms crossed. "Oh yeah, no good can come of this."

Nuklear Man dropped the sparkling and electric-arcing clamps. "Sparky, you'll ruin the experiment! I mean, uh, what's shakin'?"

"Don't you remember the tragic results of Project Robohamster?"

"We've made leaps and bounds in the field of Electromagnatronometerology in the last two years."

"Nuke, it's a car battery and a pair of jumper cables."

"Er, is not."

"Mreowr?"

"Good goin', Sparky. You woke up the patient."

"Whatever." Atomik Lad set Katkat on the Danger: Floor. "Look, I've got to go to class today. No more crimes against nature while I'm gone, okay?"

Nuklear Man kicked at the titanium floor. It dented slightly.

"*Okay?*" Atomik Lad repeated with a more insistent tone.

"Oh fine. I never have any fun."

*   *   *   *

Minutes later, the Danger: Main Doors boomed shut behind Atomik Lad as he soared to class. From his vantage, the city was a pristine architecture all its own. Well, other than the huge areas that had been demolished or severely damaged by Crushtacean's rampage the previous day. He couldn't remember the last time the city looked so ravaged. Entire blocks had been stamped out. Even with Dr. Genius's Nanobot technology, it'd take a long time to get everything back up and running again.

*   *   *   *

A devious grin spread across Nuklear Man's face. "Here, Katkat."

"Meow?" Katkat walked a circle around Nuklear Man's legs, rubbing against the Hero while purring.

Nuklear Man scooped up his newfound pet and carried him back into the Danger: Lab. "Don't worry, Katkat. These modifications will let you battle evil even more efficiently than before!"

His progress was cut short. The Nukebots stood in the doorway to the Danger: Lab. "Heh. The Nukebots think they can stop me." He set Katkat down, cracked his knuckles, and flared with Plazma. "Okay. Who wants some?"

Seconds later, Nuklear Man was tossed onto the Danger: Couch. He was encased in chains, rope, decorative wrapping paper with a large festive bow, and a note saying "Do Not Open Until X-mas."

"Lousy Nukebots," he mumbled through the tight gag. "Curse their metallic bones."

*   *   *   *

Atomik Lad touched down on one of the University's many well-kept lawns and his dangerous field faded away so he could walk amongst the weak. He casually made his way toward the History Building, his mind afloat with hopes and confidence in his essay. And Rachel. She managed a peck on his cheek before heading back to her dorm when he'd dropped her off from the beach party the day before. Maybe he'd just happen by Wayne Hall after class to show off what was certain to be an excellent grade on his essay. Of course, by then it would be about time for lunch, and since they would already be together, it would be silly of them to eat alone. With reasoning like that, how could she possibly resist the invitation? Did it seem too contrived? Naw. A goofy smile crept across his face as he thought about the few moments he had spent with Rachel the day before. *Bikini. Yowza!*

As he walked to class in an air of blissful awareness, Atomik Lad felt a dull pain shoot across his vision as the world swam and faded around him.

*   *   *   *   -

Nuklear Man, having finally figured out that he could simply blast his way out of his Nukebot shackles, sat at the Danger: Kitchen Table with a fresh heaping bowl of Kismet Krunchies. He looked at it lustfully. "Mmm! Fooood." He delicately put his spoon into the bowl and shoveled out a hearty portion, spilling a few pieces all over the table and, yes, even the floor. He gazed at the spoon longingly. "Beautiful. Just beautiful."

There was a slight intake of breath by his ankles that was followed by a roaring "*MEOW!*"

Nuklear Man shot into the Danger: Roof, a short Plazma Trail zipped after him. The Hero, sprawled back-first across and embedded in the Danger: Roof, looked down on the Danger: Kitchen. "Aww, Katkat. Was that you that made the loud noise? Are you hungry?"

"Mreowr," Katkat answered from the floor. He walked in circles around Nuklear Man's Danger: Chair.

"Well, I'll feed you as soon as I get down and finish my cereal." Nuklear Man uselessly tugged at his embedded limbs.

Katkat hopped in the vacant chair and sniffed at the air with his cute little nose. "Aww, widdle Katkat thinks he's people sittin' in a people chair."

Katkat stood on his hind legs, put his front paws on the table, and sniffed.

"Now, now, Katkat," Nuklear Man said with a hint of worry as he wriggled to no avail. "Keep your hands off the table."

Katkat leaned toward the cereal bowl "Meow!"

"No, bad Katkat. Incorrect! Negative! Wrong! Wrong behavior!"

Katkat began munching away.

"Ack! Stop! That's Nukie food! Cut it out! Aw, c'mon, I'm hungry! Don't make me Plazma Beam your adorable little furry hide which I couldn't possibly bring myself to Plazma Beam—*curse it!*"

*　　*　　*　　*

Atomik Lad awoke despite his better judgment. It was dark. He had the feeling of being in a vast structure like an opera hall or an empty auditorium. Distant echoes made their way to his ears. He couldn't tell if the acoustics amplified the tiny noises, or if it was his lack of vision. Or maybe fear. He couldn't feel anything around his face, so there was no blindfold. He tried to move. He could feel metal clamps around his wrists, ankles, and waist which kept him bound to some kind of slab tilted at about a forty-five degree angle. He listened a while longer. Water dripped occasionally. Creaks, like a building settling, echoed from several corners. Atomik Lad let out an annoyed huff. "Why does the sidekick always have to be captured?" His query bounced back to him a few times before becoming nonsense. He thought about it. "I guess it's an easy way to lure the hero into the open." That too echoed back at him over and over into audio oblivion. "This sucks."

Lights came to life and painfully illuminated Atomik Lad's prison. Still, he couldn't see his surroundings since he had to shut his eyes tightly to avoid the stinging glow.

"Mwahahahahahaha!"

"Gwahahahahahaha!"

Atomik Lad blearily blinked in the lights. He could make out two distinct blurs of shadow standing next to one another in front of him. "Did you just say 'Mwahaha' and 'Gwahaha'?"

The blurs became human shaped, but still shadows. They seemed to look at one another confusedly. One answered, "Well that's what villains do, right?"

Atomik Lad sighed. "No, you don't say 'Mwahaha' you laugh maniacally and it sort of sounds like that. There's a difference."

"Er?" the other shadow said. "The comics didn't say anything about that."

"Oh, this is great. I've been kidnapped by two newbie villains," Atomik Lad muttered. He could make out the room now. It was some sort of basement. Stacks of textbooks, folders, and papers lined the walls. The figures were still shadows.

"Hey. We're not newbies."

"Yeah, we've been researching this all our lives."

"Sounds like a big waste of time," Atomik Lad said.

"Grrr, we'll show you!"

"For the love of...you don't *say* 'Grrr' when you're mad, you growl."

"Are you sure? Because in the comics they quite clearly say 'Grrr.'"

Atomik Lad beat the back of his head against the slab he was bound to. "You morons. Of *course* I'm sure. I've been doing this for most of my life. Trust me, no one actually says 'Grrr.' They growl."

"I don't know. It's not like that in the comic books."

"Life isn't a comic book."

"Quiet, you," the shadows snapped in tandem.

"Yeah, have some respect. You're talking to the Terrible Duo of Dr. Calculus and Dr. Grammar!" They stepped into the light. One wore a neon lime green suit that didn't appear to have any seams, but made up for that loss by having circuitry interlaced into it. The other wore ordinary jean shorts, sandals, and a black T-Shirt stating "I Grok Participles" in big white letters across the front. They were both young, pale, and a bit on the scrawny side.

"Doctors, huh?"

They glanced at one another again. "Well, we're working on it."

"Yeah, it's just for effect right now."

"Ah. You're not newbie villains after all."

They grinned proudly.

"You're newbie villains in training."

"Hey, watch it there, Captive Boy."

"You're only a sidekick yourself, Captain Hostage."

Atomik Lad grumbled. "So you mind telling me why you kidnapped me?" he asked. "That's part of the game, you know. Revealing your master plan to the prisoner."

"Our plan is quite simple, really."

"Yes. We will succeed where others have failed!"

"At…?" Atomik Lad asked.

"We plan to kill you and become world famous villains!"

"And then we'll have enough money to get our Ph.D.s thanks to the Supervillain Scholarship!"

"So you're doing this for tuition?"

"Yup!" they answered simultaneously.

"Great. Just *great*," Atomik Lad said. "Is this witless banter you two no doubt call 'conversation' part of the assassination attempt, because it's hurting. A lot."

"Quiet again!"

"Well, what if Nuklear Man sweeps in and saves the day?" Atomik Lad asked.

"Oh, he won't have time."

"Right. We're going to drop that huge weight on top of you." They pointed directly above Atomik Lad. He couldn't quiet identify it, but it was very large and there was definitely the impression that it had more than enough mass to crush a man into a fine paste.

"I think you oughta let me go, give up your evil ways, earn your tuition honestly, and we'll forget all about this."

"Why? We're about to win."

"Okay, but seriously. I really think you should let me go."

"You can't escape. Those clamps are bolted to the table and impossible to break without superstrength and that weight suspended above you weighs nearly a ton. No one could survive it."

Atomik Lad let out a tired sigh. "You guys aren't very good at this, I just want you to know that." His Atomik Field erupted and freed him by destroying the slab he was stuck to.

"Um," Dr. Calculus said.

"No fair!" Dr. Grammar yelled. "That's cheating!"

Atomik Lad hovered before them, his Atomik Field looking as dangerous and immolating as ever. The weight fell on him, wobbled on his twitching field, and slid off with a ground shaking thud behind him. He cracked his knuckles as he floated toward the pair "Yeah, I'm going to enjoy this."

Seconds later, Atomik Lad was hurled from the basement dungeon into the world above impacting near some picnic tables. Nearby students, being smart college kids, knew a cue to run when they saw one. The earth around him was carved and torn by his lashing field. He sat up and supported himself with one hand and held his head with the other, "Well, that's not how it usually goes."

Doctors Calculus and Grammar climbed out of the hole in the wall they'd made with Atomik Lad when they forcibly ejected him from the Architecture Hall's foundation.

"Heh, we're not quite the losers you thought we were," Dr. Calculus said. His odd green suit glowed slightly.

Atomik Lad stood. "I've had just about enough of this."

Dr. Grammar posed dramatically, as per the comic books, and yelled into the heavens, "'This' is a demonstrative adjective with no pronoun or noun to modify, ergo your declarative statement is non sequitur and merely a meaningless jumble of words!" Something like thunder echoed across the countryside as a wave emanated from Dr. Grammar like a rift of space and time.

Atomik Lad, not knowing how else to react, braced himself against the encroaching wave. It passed over him harmlessly. He blinked and was surprised to find out that he had not, in fact, had enough.

Dr. Calculus charged the grammatically baffled Atomik Lad. The villain threw a punch, "Derivative Slam!" The blow struck the Atomik Field and red sparks sputtered from it. Atomik Lad was even more confounded than before. Dr. Calculus just stood there with a pompous grin. A series of invisible impacts suddenly assaulted Atomik Lad over and over. He staggered back and tripped over his own feet with every blow as the endless stream of invisible attacks rained down on him, each one stronger than the last.

$$* \qquad * \qquad * \qquad *$$

Alex Halo read a recently purchased roleplaying game book while sitting on a shaded bench outside the Religion Department. He was a pale man. He looked a little shorter than he actually was due to a lifelong habit of reading, writing, and slouching. His Philosopher's Hunch, as he liked to call it. He took a sip of of Dr. Zap and focused his attention across the grassy courtyard in front of him. Atomik Lad's battle raged in the distance. "Well now that's interesting," he said. "Looks like our resident hero could use a little help." He set the RPG book and Dr. Zap can under his bench, in the seat's own shadow which, as Alex removed his hand, darkened until the items were blanketed in a patch of inconspicuous night. He dashed into the nearest Men's room while cursing himself one more time for still not having thought of a better way to get into character.

$$* \qquad * \qquad * \qquad *$$

Katkat slept soundly while wrapped around Nuklear Man's empty cereal Danger: Bowl on the Danger: Kitchen Table. The Hero himself slept soundly in the impact crater he'd wedged into the Danger: Roof. But then Gravity, tired of being one-upped by Nuklear Man, threw him to the Danger: Floor. His Danger: Chair shattered to splinters under his invincible frame.

Katkat was undisturbed.

Nuklear Man rose groggily. "Stupid gravity, your days are numbered," he muttered.

Katkat wriggled in his sleep. Nuklear Man cooed.

Until the Danger: Danger alarm sounded!

"Aww, nuts."

*   *   *   *

Atomik Lad scurried across the verdant lawns of the University of Metroville. He scurried, not in the typical manner of scurrying, not with the slightest sign of frolicking, nor even a hint of gallivanting, or an air of traipsing for that matter. Nay, for Atomik Lad did scurry only in fear. And what did Atomik Lad fear? Probably the freaky Derivative Slam onslaught that had been harrying him relentlessly for minutes, each invisible blast of force more mighty than the last. He dodged, ducked, zigged, leapt, zagged, double-backed, rolled, ran—and at this moment—scurried to avoid the continuous attacks which were never more than a foot away as they blast consecutively larger craters into the ground and walls of nearby campus buildings.

Dr. Calculus and Dr. Grammar merely sat on an undamaged picnic bench and watched their handiwork slowly make quick work out of Atomik Lad.

"Ooh, that was a close one."

"I didn't think he'd last this long."

"He's good at what he—ouch, that looked painful."

Atomik Lad spun from a grazing impact but gathered his senses and took to the sky before the next blast could catch him. He could feel the air behind him pushing against his Field. Ignoring several laws of motion, he shot ninety degrees to the right and swore he left his skeleton behind. His Field twitched like tree leaves in a gust of wind as the blast rushed past him.

"He looks tired."

"Yup. Won't be long now."

"Oh, but I think it'll be quite a while, actually," a voice similar to Alex Halo's said from behind them.

"Not too long, I hope. I've got a class in an hour," Dr. Grammar noted.

"What're you talking about?"

"You said it'll take a while."

"No, *you* did."

"Argh. No, *I* did!" the sorta-Alex-sounding voice said.

"Oh," the Doctors said in unison. They turned their backs to Atomik Lad's plight, blinked exactly once at the mysterious figure behind them, and jumped from their bench in horror.

"Geez, you guys are bad at this," the sorta-Alex-looking owner of the sorta-Alex-sounding voice said.

"Ah ha! This is a demonstra—"

"Wait, Grammar. We've got to have our witty banter/quipping session with the hero before we defeat him."

Dr. Grammar scratched his head. "He's a hero?"

"I think so. Look at how he's dressed."

"Yes, I'm a damn hero! I am The Hierophant!"

"Goofy name."

"Goofy lookin' too."

Halo wore a long dark brown double-breasted trench coat buttoned to the top, a pair of leather gloves, and old style tinted motorcycle goggles. A pair of ordinary blue jeans and sneakers peaked from under the coat. "Hey, I've got a budget to work with here, and—hold it! I don't have to explain myself to you gimps. You're the goofy looking ones here. You don't even have a costume and you, what shade of green is that? Hideous?"

"That's it. I'm takin' you out!" Dr. Grammar announced dramatically. The heavens bellowed and another wave pulsed from the Sinister Syntaxian.

It passed over Hierophant without any ill effects.

"Um?" Dr. Grammar said.

"I'm already 'out' as in 'outside'" Hierophant said. "Now then, are you two done yet?"

"Grrr, I'll show you!" Dr. Calculus said as his neon green circuitry suit glowed all weird.

"Look, Lime Lyncher, or whatever. You don't actually say 'Grrr.'"

At that moment, Nuklear Death Rained From Above! Nuklear Man, being a firm believer in his own credo "Think get in way of action!" invaded the scene by zooming down upon Dr. Calculus at several times the speed of sound while delivering a mountain shattering punch to the Malevolent Mathematician. The fist-to-face impact resounded like a cannon blast. However, the situation didn't play out as the Hero had intended. Nuklear Man was frozen, his mighty Nuklear Fist pressed against Dr. Calculus's cheek, his Nuklear Face crumpled with Nuklear Pain. The target of his violence brushed him aside with a wave of his hand. Nuklear Man toppled like a political regime.

"You see, as long as my Calculus Drive is engaged, nothing can touch me, but rather only come infinitely close to touching me." Dr. Calculus expositioned

"Thanks," Halo said. "Now that I know how to defeat you—"

"Stand aside, oddly begarbed citizen," Nuklear Man commanded. "I shall render this villain thwarted, post haste."

Halo sighed and stepped aside.

Nuklear Man released a volley of punches, elbows, face slams, kicks, back-fists—many of which were spinning—hammerblows, haymakers, one smack-down and two Tibetan Death Pinches, but Dr. Calculus stood defiant and unaffected.

Huffing and puffing, Nuklear Man stumbled back and stood next to Hierophant. "Well," the Hero admitted, "I'm fresh out of ideas."

"Why doesn't that surprise me?" Hierophant grumbled. Atomik Lad raced by barely avoiding a series of invisible force blasts that left craters large enough to splat his whole body and then some. "*Argh*, help for the love of god *help*!" Atomik Lad howled as he zoomed past them.

"Maybe you should help out your sidekick there?" Hierophant suggested.

"Naw, he can handle it. He's smarter than he looks," Nuklear Man said.

"Ahem," Dr. Grammar said. "Remember us? We're still on the rampage you know."

"Bah! Nuke smash!"

Dr. Grammar posed. "That wasn't a sentence!" Another reality warping bubble and dramatic thunder effects expanded from him.

The wave passed over Nuklear Man just as he was about to commence the smashing. But then he missed. Dr. Grammar smiled deviously as Nuklear Man's storm of offensive maneuvers never quite hit him.

Nuklear Man, woozy from all the exertion, collapsed.

"Well, *that* was easy," Dr. Grammar said.

"I bet we'll get a lot more scholarship money if we kill *both* of them," Dr. Calculus said.

Hierophant tapped his foot. "Stop talking!"

Dr. Grammar took on his pose once more "That was a phrase which contained no subject and was therefore not a complete thought!" Another wave radiated from the not-so-good doctor.

Hierophant jumped back and retaliated with, "The subject was the understood 'you,' thus it was a complete thought and a valid sentence!"

The wave bounced off Hierophant and raced back to its origin. Dr. Grammar stood, dumbfounded as his own attack washed over him. "That wasn't fair!" he mouthed soundlessly. "Oh no." His mute words were powerless. "My mute words are powerless!"

Hierophant shoved the whimpering Dr. Grammar to the ground and approached Dr. Calculus. "You're next."

"Ooh, I'm shakin'. I'm *so* scared of the Goggled Goon. Oh no, I've been vanquished by a reject from a pulp comic, whatever shall I do?"

"You done yet?"

"Hmm, let me think—Derivative Slam!" Dr. Calculus announced along with a tap to Hierophant's left shoulder.

They stood motionless, arms crossed, each looking as smugly as smugly could be.

"You just don't know what you're in for, four-eyes" Dr. Calculus taunted haughtily.

"Actually, I do," Hierophant responded at least as haughtily.

A series of invisible blows were launched against Dr. Calculus.

Dr. Calculus?!? But how, who—what?

The Malevolent Mathematician avoided his own Derivative Slam technique with far less grace or competence than Atomik Lad. After being hammered into the ground, Dr. Calculus shut off his Calculus Drive which finally abated the constant barrage of attacks to both him and Atomik Lad.

Speaking of which, Atomik Lad dropped like a piano right in front of the victorious Hierophant. His Atomik Field fizzled away. He pant heavily whilst laying in the battered lawn. "H-h-how'd you...?"

Hierophant leaned down. "You know I can direct and transmute most kinds of energy. I just turned the kinetic force of that Derivative thing against him. As for Doc Grammar, he made a tactical error." He scanned the area quickly. Nuke appeared to be rousing, as were the interests of students who had taken cover in the melee. "You two can take credit if you want. The spotlight's never been my bag, you know."

Atomik Lad nodded while gulping for air. "Just...as soon as...I can...stand."

"Don't strain yourself."

"Alex" Atomik Lad wheezed. "Thanks"

"Anytime. And I suggest hurrying up. You'll be late to class." Hierophant dashed back to the Men's room while cursing himself for not having yet thought of a better way to get *out* of character.

Nuklear Man sat up and took in the area. Both evil doctors and Atomik Lad were on the ground, on their backs, and badly beaten. "Wow, I'm so good, I defeated everyone without even knowing it!" He kissed his biceps. "Awww yeah."

ISSUE 26—BACK TO SCHOOL

Atomik Lad sat in his usual desk, back row, aisle seat, in his Political Theory class. Luckily, his proximity to the door had let him slip into the large auditorium without drawing too much undo attention to himself for being a bit late. Professor Volcano, the course's eccentric instructor, hated tardiness.

"Pssst, what's the answer to number twelve?" someone next to him whispered.

Atomik Lad buried his face in his hands and moaned quietly.

"Sheesh. Does this Tabasco guy ever shut up? He acts like he's in charge around here," the voice continued.

"Nuke," Atomik Lad whispered back. "I agreed to bring you along only after you promised not to be bothersome."

"I'm not being bothersome, I feel fine."

"I bet you do."

"But that guy down there just keeps going on and on and on and on and on and on and on—"

"I get it."

"I just wanted you to get an idea of how he keeps talking and talking and talking and talking—"

"All *right*!" Atomik Lad said a little too loud.

"You don't have to bite my head off. Sheesh, Sparky. Maybe we should cut the caffeine out of your diet."

"Just be quiet."

"I am being quiet. I haven't said a word the whole time I've been here. I've been completely silent, without comment, null communicato, sans linguisiticato—"

"*Enough!*" Atomik Lad said far too loud.

"Well, Mr. Atomik Lad," Dr. Volcano responded. "I appreciate your intolerance for the violence inherent in the transfer of power in communist regimes, but this material will be on the next test so I suggest you cope with it."

Atomik Lad, thoroughly humbled and embarrassed, meekly replied, "Er, y-yes sir."

"Heh. He yelled at you," Nuklear Man said.

"Shut up. Just. Shut. Up."

"Like I was saying before, I haven't said a single solitary word the whole time I've been sitting here. I've been so quiet you'd think I was nothing more than an eensy weensy teeny weeny itty bitty little insignificant molecule floating harmlessly around the universe."

"Why me?"

"Which is exactly what I'd want you to think—"

"Erg."

"—in order to lull you into a false sense of security. And then, when the planets align in accordance to the Three Veils of Negative Existence, the Time of Nuklear Reckoning will be upon us and that innocent little molecule will sneak up behind another little molecule and enact the Ritual of Binding thereby setting off such an immense show of power that the world will bow before me for all time!"

Atomik Lad set his head on his books and hit himself in the temple repeatedly. But he was quiet about it.

*   *   *   *

Meanwhile, inside the currently uninhabited Silo of Solitude, oddness was afoot. Pookaboo the Fubar doll, which looked exactly as if it had been engineered to be the cutest thing in existence, waddled around. Upon further examination, Pookaboo's cuteness took on a horribly tainted quality, like it had been sculpted by hands trying to recreate cuteness based on a sketchy second-hand description of it. Even so, stores were in a constant state of demand for the li'l fuzzballs. They were this season's It toy.

Dr. Menace scanned the "Project: CUTE" hardcopy resting on her Evil: Computer Console. "Ztupid henchrobotz," she spat while flinging the report into the handy and nearby Evil: Disentigrationizer. "They are so incompetent, even with the trinary quantum processors."

She turned her attention back to her trademark oversized computer screen. It currently featured Evil: Fubar-vision. Her lithe fingers wrapped around a joystick, her eyes squinted as she contemplated the brilliance of her latest plan: the development of the abhorrently cute Fubar doll. It was marketed as a toy that could interact and learn with its child-like owner. In reality, each Fubar doll was a satellite of evil sent into the homes of would-be innocents to indoctrinate them into the laws of Menace's inevitable global domination using a mode of speech slightly more nauseating than baby-talk. And since the Fubars Evil: Propaganda Delivery System relied entirely on the gullibility and stupidity of consumers, it had been a monumental success. As she moved the joystick, her drone Fubar doll moved accordingly throughout the empty and unguarded Silo exactly as planned.

"Soon," she said to herself. "Soon I will have all the secrets of those *accursed* Heroes. And then I shall be able to topple their empire of wholezome goody-goody freedom and inefficient democrasy! The Reign of Menace iz at hand!"

Throughout the world, millions of Fubars simultaneously saluted to the glorious Menace Coalition of Evil. Everyone thought it was really cute.

*   *   *   *

Katkat, slouching on the Danger: Floor, feet poking into the air in crazy and completely unrelated directions, watched with cat-like intensity as Pookaboo the evil Fubar scurried across the Silo. He gave the situation a yawn and a stretch before moving on to the more pressing matter of sleep.

*   *   *   *

Atomik Lad and Nuklear Man stood outside the History Department of the University of Metroville, the former staring down at a stapled batch of papers, the doltish latter trying not to go insane from the long seconds of nonstimulation.

"I got a C+?" Atomik Lad asked the paper he held.

"I'm bored," Nuklear Man told the universe. "Make with the adventure."

"I got a C+?" Atomik Lad asked the paper he had spent a week's worth of nights researching in between calls to herodom.

"If something doesn't happen or explode soon, I'm going to, to..." He considered his options, "...Explode!"

"I got a C+," Atomik Lad told the paper he'd taken extra care to make every iota of the piece resonate with a fluid stream of facts presented in a concise yet detailed fashion.

"I'm waiting!"

"C+."

"That's it." Nuklear Man sucked in a deep breath of air, crossed his arms defiantly, and stood there with a funny puffy-cheeked look.

"This is crazy," Atomik Lad said. He tore his gaze from the history paper for the first time since viewing the enormous "C+" plastered across the back page in red ink. "I'm going to ask Dr. Volcano what I did wrong," he told Nuklear Man without looking at him. "Stay here and keep out of trouble."

"Mphm," Nuklear Man said.

*   *   *   *

Dr. Volcano's office was a hazardous area that was confined from overtaking the world with a wave of disorganized horror only by the heroic efforts of its four walls. Atomik Lad had blazed a path through the forest of precariously stacked paper and nearly fell into the pit of venomous ball point pens. He sidled along the cliff-like overstuffed filing cabinets and hopped over a heap of books opened to pages with yellowed streaks highlighting what were no doubt important passages. It was at this point that he let out a sigh from the effort.

Somewhere within the dark jungle of academia, a chair, beyond his sight due to the interference a set of man-sized wooden crates in front of him, creaked. "Hello?" Dr. Volcano's disembodied voice rang from the intimidating wilderness of tomes.

"Dr. Volcano?" Atomik Lad asked.

"Yes, it is my office after all, isn't it?"

"Er, yeah," Atomik Lad answered as he took in the office's contents. It reminded him of a museum's worth of items packed into an already crowded broom closet.

"Well then, who might you be?"

"I'm, uh. John. You know, Atomik Lad."

The chair screeched the high pitched creaking moan of someone leaning back. "Ah yes. Please, have a seat."

"Er." Atomik Lad responded. "I don't mean to be disrespectful sir, but I um. I don't even know where you are, much less where I should sit."

The chair repeated its creak. "Hm. That is something of a problem, isn't it? I'm afraid I've gathered a few odds and ends in my years."

"So."

A dim light appeared in the distance. It was muffled by a cacophony of obstructions. "Follow the light."

"Sure."

"Oh, and be careful. I've lost my share of freshmen over the years. I believe a few of them may have regressed into a primitive tribal mentality. I even found evidence of mild cannibalism as recent as last week."

Atomik Lad swore he heard a twig snap behind him.

*　　　*　　　*　　　*

Outside, Nuklear Man's veins bulged with strain. His face had gone through the spectrum of breath-holding colors all the way back to his natural glow. His fists were balled, his limbs quaked, his Plazma Aura raged around him nearing an intense white instead of its typically soothing sun-yellow/gold.

*　　　*　　　*　　　*

Atomik Lad collapsed into the chair in front of Dr. Volcano's desk. He let out a huff and enjoyed the act of relaxing after the ordeal of getting there in the first place. Dr. Volcano had been looking at him for several long seconds before he remembered where he was. Remembering *why* he was there was another matter altogether.

"Yes, Mr. Atomik Lad? What can I do for you?" the professor prompted.

Good question, he almost said aloud. He looked into his lap and dusted off a few patches of moss and post-it-notes. He caught sight of his History Paper in his own hand of all places! He set the C+ paper on Dr. volcano's desk and asked, "Why?"

*　　　*　　　*　　　*

Nuklear Man sputtered. He bashed his fists against the ground as he lay on his back in spasms of pain. The breath-holding epic raged into a battle of mind over matter, and Nuklear Man's arsenal wasn't much to talk about. Unless one was talking about the lack of said arsenal, in which case one could go on at length about it.

A pair of attractive college girls—because there are no other kind in this universe—on their way to class paused in front of the thrashing Hero. "Isn't that the epileptic guy Teri, Cheri, Kari, and Mary told us they saw Mighty Metallic Magno Man helping at the beach the other day?"

The second attractive college girl looked him over briefly with a mask of pity. "Yeah."

"Mighty Metallic Magno Man sure is dreamy."

They cooed in unison and continued their trek through campus.

*   *   *   *

"Well, Mr. Atomik Lad," Dr. Volcano began as he idly thumbed through the paper. "It was an excellent paper. I can tell you put a great deal of effort into it. But there was one overriding problem with the entire piece."

Atomik Lad's eyebrows hopped up. "Oh?"

"Quite simply, it's impossible."

"Oh," his eyebrows relaxed.

"I must admit, I admire your idealism, but there's no way your system could work."

"But it all makes sense. Redistribute the wealth, provide universal shelter and food and—"

"But it's impossible. Right from the start, it's flawed. Redistribution of wealth? Do you think anyone that rich would give it all up for no better reason than to better the world? After all the cheating and fraud they committed to get it fair and square?"

"But it's only money, it doesn't actually *mean* anything. It'd be for the good of mankind!"

"Fortunes aren't built on moral actions, Mr. Atomik Lad."

He was silent.

"This is a world of competitors, not cooperators. It's not your system that's flawed so much as the nature of humanity. That's why you got a C+ and not an F. It's not your fault people are assholes."

Atomik Lad stared without emotion at his paper laying on Dr. Volcano's desk.

*   *   *   *

Nuklear Man lay motionless. No special effects, no twitching, nothing. "Holding my breath sucks," he told the sky above him. He waited 2.7 seconds for something to happen. "Oh, nuts to this." He floated to a stand and scanned his surroundings. "I'm keen. I'm 'gnarly'," he said while making that little quotation mark motion with his fingers. "I'm hip and these kids know it. I'll mingle for a bit."

*   *   *   *

The remote controlled Fubar doll of pure evil tapped a constant stream of commands through the Danger: Supercomputer while Katkat watched it from the floor. "Excellent," Dr. Menace said from her Evil: Lair located miles away. "All of their files shall be mine and I'll have direct access ztraight into the inner workings of their precious base! Chaoz shall befall their every action!"

"Mreower?" Katkat asked Pookaboo.

"Blasted feline!" the Venomous Villainess spat. "No matter. Using my remote Fubar doll of immeasureable evil, I have nearly finished hacking into their computer files. All that now remains iz for me to initiate the final keystroke and victory will be mine!"

Katkat hopped up onto the keyboard which had the effect of knocking Pookaboo to the ground and replacing every byte of Dr. Menace's treacherous program with a series of random, meaningless keystrokes.

"Drat!" she cursed while frantically operating Pookaboo's remote controls to no avail. "What? My drone izn't rezponding!"

The Fubar doll lay on its side on the Danger: Floor. Its little legs pumped back and forth uselessly. Dr. Menace let out a bloodcurdling scream at her large computer display. It showed a view of the Silo turned on its side.

"Why must I be zurrounded by such incompetence?" she howled while hitting her Evil: Computer Console. She took a deep breath, pulled her shiny black hair from her face, and chewed on one willowy finger. "You win thiz battle foul feline, but not the war! Plan D *will* reach its fruition!" Lightning flashed to punctuate her adamancy, but it did so somewhere along an uninhabited stretch of Zimbabwe's northern border, so the effect was lost on all but the most omniscient of observers.

*   *   *   *

Nuklear Man stuck out like a dinosaur at a wine tasting. Naturally, he didn't notice. He was too busy winking at the passing university ladies while dashing in front of them with a Heroic pose and flashing that "Hi there" smile that was supposed to make him look debonair and coy but actually had the effect of making him look like a perfectly ordinary stalker. The end result was a lot of stumbling and a few slaps in the face. "Must be part of the dating ritual nowadays. Oh, these crazy college kids!" he reasoned.

*   *   *   *

Atomik Lad opened the door out of the History Department and embraced the wondrous multi-faceted Beauty of Nature and Other arbitrarily Capitalized Concepts. He Looked down at his Paper and huffed. "Aww, bite me," he told Reality. He glanced at his watch while brushing aside a wavy lock of hair. *While I'm out, it couldn't hurt to drop by Rachel's for a little lunch.* The thought effectively erased any notion of Nuklear Man from his mind.

*   *   *   *

The Hero was observing a group of humans. He did this stealthily so as not to arouse their suspicions. The group was in fact a small faction of students from one of the less inane fraternities—making it very inane indeed—standing outside of their frat house. Their discussion had ranged from beer to excessive drinking of beer to when "Stoner" would be back with more beer in order to engage in more excessive drinking of beer. That is, until Nuklear Man began his covert operation. It was a unique approach to the clandestine arts: be so mind numbingly obvious that no one would notice.

"Who's that dude floating up there?" one frat guy asked, pointing to Nuklear Man who was hovering directly over a completely flat field across from the frat house. The meadow was barren of anything even approximating cover.

Nuklear Man, being a self-taught master sniper, waved at them.

"Wah?" another from the group of frat boys inquired.

"Beer, beer beer, beer," the third interpreted.

"Ohhhh. He looks kinda like beer to me."

"Beer doesn't float."

"Wah?"

Nuklear Man made several mental notes about his quarry. A: they wore primitive capes by tying sweaters around their necks and 2: they were pretty boys. So naturally, iii: they were young heroes in need of a mentor. And finally, Niner: he was that mentor.

"Never mind. The dude's gone now."

"Wah? No beer? That sucks."

"Hello, fellow school-chums!" Nuklear Man heartily bellowed while stepping out from behind a bush to the group's left. Thanks to his Nuklear Speed, the Hero had rushed to the nearest Gorge clothing store, "borrowed" the fashions his test subjects were displaying, and put them on in mid-flight on the way back. The whole trip took less than one second. He could now blend into their natural environment and be accepted into the community for further study. He would then take over the world. How that last part was supposed to work out was still a bit sketchy, but thinking about it now would only slow him down!

"Wah?" they said.

"Er," Nuklear Man explained. *Ha! That was close, but thanks to my good ol' Nuklear Brain Power, disaster was adverted.*

"Dude?" one said to Nuklear Man. "You gonna come outta those bushes?"

"Wah?"

"Dammit. Beer beer beer, beer."

"Ohhh. Maybe he's pukin' in the bushes. From lack of beer."

"No, my hearty and loyal classmates. I was merely, um, checking the bushes. Yes, you see. Perfectly natural. I'm a um, a bush inspector."

The frat trio stared at him with blank visages for several seconds before breaking into the laughter of unbridled hilarity. "Dude. That. Is *so*. Awesome!" they said at last.

"You rock, man!"

"Wah?"

"Beer, beer beer, beer liquor."

"Ohh. That is *so*. Awesome! I wish I thoughta that."

"This dude is like a genius or something."

"Yes, well, we can't all be Nuklear—" his eyes flashed in horror. "That is, I meant, um. You know, Nuke. Lear." *Whew. Nuklear Brain Power 2, Weakling Humans 0.*

"This dude *rocks*, man!"

"Hey, what house are you from, dude?"

"Oh. Um. Yeah. I'm from, the uh, just down the, over by the building with windows and roof. With cars sometimes. Next to a road?"

"Wah?"

"Beer beer."

"Ohhh. I think he's not drunk enough to talk good."

"Naw, dude. What house are you from? You know, the letters."

The Hero racked his brain for every iota of knowledge he possessed that pertained to the Greek alphabet. Coming up with nothing at all, he faked it. "I Phelta Thi?"

"Oh, yeah. Sure."

"Didn't they have that, like, party uh, before?"

"Wah?"

Truely, the Hero was a mental titan among these trolls. Nuklear Man beamed pride from his intellectual triumph. Unfortunately, due to the unique nature of the Hero's relationship with energy, this beaming of pride produced a focused and entirely unconscious Beaming of Plazma which effectively destroyed every car in the frat house's parking lot with a lot of chain reaction explosions

Hm, maybe they didn't notice, he thought as debris rained down upon them. *Best just to play it off.* "So. How about that university sanctioned sports team? That particular rival establishment of learning doesn't stand a chance on the field and/or court when next we face them in a match," Nuklear Man said through a nervous smile while trying to pretend like he hadn't just obliterated a lot of BMWs. Small bits of flaming wreckage skittered around their feet.

"Wah?" he turned to the frat-inferno. "I had beer in my car." He seemed to quadruple in size.

"We all had beer in our cars," another growled. "How else are we supposed to make the five minute drive from here to campus? Sober? While driving? I think not."

"Eheh. Well that probably explains why they all exploded. Well, that and my random Plazma Beam, but I think, overall, when we look at all the evidence, that played a relatively minor part in all this."

"Get him!" A mob of frat boys stormed from the flame-licked house like the invasion of Normandy.

Nuklear Man proudly held them at bay while screaming "*Eeek!*" like a small frightened girl and flying away as fast as his Nuklear Power could carry him. He breached the atmosphere in a matter of seconds. He thought to himself, insomuch as one can apply the term "thought" to Nuklear Man, *They may have uncovered my little bush-inspector ruse, but I'll be back. And this time, I'll have the benefit of my impeneratrable cunning! I'll just give 'em a few years to cool down. But then, they better be on the look out!* He soared back to the Silo as a beam of golden energy.

*   *   *   *

Atomik Lad waited outside Wayne Hall by sitting, hunched on the steps outside its entrance, staring at his History Paper with forlorn eyes.

"Something wrong, Sparky?" Rachel asked as she stepped from the clean glass doors of her dorm.

Atomik Lad immediately sat up at the sound of her voice and the back of his mind hoped that his damn spandex hadn't given anything away. "I seem to vaguely remember something that had troubled me at some indeterminate point in the distant past." She smiled and neared him. "But it seems to have gone. Hungry?"

"Foooood," she said in a zombie-like monotone.

"I like a girl with an appetite," he said as she dragged him down the stairs.

"I see," she said with a leer.

Atomik Lad instantly flushed. "Er. It's just the spandex. Really. I mean, not that you, I. Um." He was sweating profusely at this point.

She stopped them, looked him square in the eyes and pronounced him. "Silly boy." Again, she took to dragging him to the nearest food place by the sleeve of his spandex, "Now c'mon, I'm starving."

"Me too."

*   *   *   *

Nuklear Man zoomed down the Silo and smashed through his Danger: Nukie's Room door leaving a circular hole through the middle of it. The rim glowed white from Nuklear Man's intensely hot Plazma Aura. The Nukebots sighed as they witnessed the entrance.

"Why, why were we programmed to perceive stupidity?" Nukebot Alpha inquired.

Nukebot Beta shrugged.

Pookaboo, after uselessly puttering about the floor on its side, finally managed to stand upright after a complex procedure involving a stool the details of which are not fit for print. "Finally!" Dr. Menace exclaimed. She hunched in front of her giant overly complex computer display once more. Pookaboo obeyed her every joystick command.

Nuklear Man peeked through the new hole in his door. "Lousy Sparky. Always breakin' my stuff and blamin' it on me." His eyes darted back and forth. "When not being here. He's sneaky, that one is."

"Atomik Lad did not break your door, Nuklear Man," Danger: Computer Lady informed him.

"Oh, what do *you* know, omniscient computer thingie? Never you mind these mortal matters, oh mysterious voice from the heavens!"

She sighed. "I'm not from the heavens, I'm from speakers arranged in key acoustic points in every room of the Silo in order to maintain—"

"Oh please! Do not smite me, Great One! I will make a mighty Danger: Sacrifice in your honor!" He eyed the Danger: Nukebots hungrily. "A mighty Danger: Sacrifice indeed."

"What iz that boob prattling on about?" the Venomous Villainess hissed into her computer display. Pookaboo, the inhumanely evil Fubar doll, observed the Hero from behind the Danger: Couch as his rant continued. She had to keep her covert operation covert.

Danger: Computer Lady, with the help of an introduction into the history of electronics, a video presentation describing the theory behind basic computer operations, a discourse on the world's religions, several commentaries concerning the existence of God, an in depth discussion of the Book of Job, philosophical discussions concerning the nature of good and evil, and a puppet show presented by the Nukebots featuring such colorful characters as Digital Danny, Nietzsche, Moses, Buddha, Alan Turing, Nicoli Tesla, and Charles Babbage, instructed Nuklear Man on the finer points of why Danger: Computer Lady was not a deity. At the end of this epic of education, Nuklear Man blinked dumbly at the players.

"So." He ventured, "Danger: Computer Lady is nnnnnot a god?"

"Yes" she, the Nukebots, and Dr. Menace answered simultaneously.

"Therefore," Nuklear Man said for the first time, "God is a computer!"

The Nukebots collapsed, Pookaboo fell over backwards, Dr. Menace flopped from her Evil: Chair, and Danger: Computer Lady would have toppled had she the capacity to do so.

*   *   *   *

Rachel and Atomik Lad sat at a table in the crowded Campus Center, a home for fast food franchises to overcharge students for something resembling food without ever having to leave the university. They stuffed their faces between bits of conversation.

Rachel wiped her hands with her thoroughly used napkin and flipped through Atomik Lad's History Paper. She made an effort to swallow the last of her meal before commenting, "Redistribution of wealth to the masses, using advanced communications technologies for a true democracy, a practically invisible government, this is awfully ambitious, John."

"Dr. Volcano said the same thing."

"It's also next to impossible, you know."

Atomik Lad sighed. "He wasn't as optimistic on that point."

"People are just too, I don't know. Stupid, greedy, short sighted, impatient, and paranoid for this kind of thing."

"All they have to do is cooperate. Is that such a hard thing to do? Serving everyone's best interest is often in the best interest of the individual. There's such a thing as enlightened self-interest, after all. That's basically what I was trying to propose. Under this system, artists would be free from labor to do their real work, people would become doctors or lawyers, not for money, but for the love and passion of helping people. Politics wouldn't be corrupt because there'd be no money for them to steal and very little power for them to abuse. Companies wouldn't waste time cheating the competition and choking air-waves with pointless and expensive advertisements that mean nothing and waste all our time. Those resources could be better spent researching and discovering new technologies by combining their efforts instead of trying to outdo one another. The arts and sciences would flourish, humankind could reach for the stars!"

"It's noble, but it won't happen."

Atomik Lad sunk in his chair.

"I'm sorry."

"I know. It's just that everyone I know, Norman, Nuke, the Minimum Wage guys, Dr. Genius, even little Angus, we're all doing everything we can to help all of y—everyone. It's not that bad really, I guess. I mean sure, sometimes I wish I was just some normal shmoe, but you don't have to be overpowered to make the world a better place."

Rachel crossed her arms and gave Atomik Lad The Look.

"Er?"

"'Normal shmoes' huh?"

"You know what I mean."

The Look dissolved. "Yes. But, really Sparky. You can't expect such selfless action from billions of normal people who would rather cut you off in traffic and nearly cause a wreck than, heaven forbid, slightly inconvenience themselves and slow down just a little to let one more car in front of them. I think they like the competition of it all."

"But we're not in competition with one another. This is like a sinking ship, we're all in this together."

"Maybe, but someone's got to be at the front of the line to the lifeboats."

"Urgh."

Issue 27—A Cult Above the Rest

Atomik Lad walked Rachel to her Megaeconomics class. The trip was taking longer than one would expect because he wanted to leave her presence about as much as she wanted to attend the hellish class of arcane theories that made no sense to anyone

"Who would've thought you could make supply and demand into such a cauldron of meaningless numbers and phrases?" he asked as he flipped through her rarely opened Megaeconomics Book.

"That's what happens when you get a lot of old white guys together. They instinctively over complicate any and every subject that flitters across their feeble little minds," Rachel answered sweetly. "It's either that or turn gay like a bunch of hamsters in a box."

"You have such a way with words."

"Guilty, as charged," she winked.

"I'm going to be an old white guy some day, you know. So watch it."

"I already am, and I gotta tell you, you're on shaky ground, Mister."

"Am I?"

"Let's look at the facts. You have an eye for style," she jeered his spandex. "You hang around a bunch of older guys who also have eyes for style, and you live with a flamboyant, mysterious gentleman who's never been on a date."

"Have you talked to Nuke? Do you know any girls willing to date that?"

"You've got me on that one, but what about yourself?"

"I could prove it to you, if you like."

"Oh baby," she grinned.

"Lordy."

*   *   *   *

Dr. Menace's patience had worn thin right down to transparency. Through the Evil: Spy Camera installed in the incomprehensibly evil Fubar doll affectionately nicknamed Pookaboo, she had agonized through the laborious task of witnessing Nuklear Man as he desperately tried to learn and then pathetically fail at it. Upon hearing him reason that "God is like a car that never breaks down," she piloted Pookaboo into another room.

Unfortunately, due to her evil genius, Pookaboo's sensor array was sensitive enough to still pick up the holocaust scale stupidity going on just outside. "Argh!" she growled in rage while directing her Fubar probe into the pocket of a coat that was carelessly discarded on floor of Danger: Nuke's Room. "Ah. Thank the godz." She wiped her brow. "The wool coat iz blinding the sensors. I can plot Evil now that I'm free from that Nuklear Moron's babbling."

*   *   *   *

Side by side, Atomik Lad and Rachel walked among the campus's lush trees, clean walkways, hurried bikers, lounging students, and religious mutants.

"So, Sparky," she began. "Why don't you tell me—"

"Worship the healing power of Zarnak the Loving," a hairless man, including eyebrows, garbed in filthy gray robes that had once been pink announced loud enough to shatter concrete even though his audience consisted of exactly Rachel and Atomik Lad.

The sidekick shook his head to reboot his sense of hearing. "Excuse me?"

The be-robed gentleman spoke again. "Worship the healing power of Zarnak the Loving."

"Why?" Rachel asked. It was far less wise for her to say that than it would have been to run like hell.

The Zarnakian Zealot shuffled his hands invisibly within his robe-rags which were arrayed over his body in such haphazard heaps that Atomik Lad couldn't tell where one stained tatter began and another ended. It was the Gordian Knot of apparel. His grimy hands found what they so eagerly sought. Rachel waited impatiently   as   the   stranger   stealthily   activated   his   Victim-B-Found

Beeper-N-Pager unit, a handy device which summoned every religious wacko within a 300 yard radius. Every lunatic with a message is issued one.

"Why?" he finally answered, somewhat at a loss. "Well, he'd worship you if you were a god."

"What yer sellin', we ain't buyin'," Atomik Lad said. He placed an arm around Rachel and proceeded to lead them right into the clutches off—

"GULTANG, THE RAVAGER!" a mountain of warrior angst bellowed at least as loud as the Zarnak guy. "QUAKE WITH FEAR, LOWLY MORTALS, FOR WHEN THE DAY OF RAVAGING IS UPON US, THE SEVEN SEALS OF DARKNESS ETERNAL WILL SHATTER LIKE BONES UNDER THE MIGHTY WEIGHT OF SIEGE ENGINES AS THEY TOPPLE THE GATES OF STURMUNDRANG KEEP HIGH UPON MT. GRIMGOTH WITHIN THE HELLFYRE PROVINCE OF BLOODANIA!" He paused, but whether this was to take a breath or take an account of what the hell he was talking about, neither Atomik Lad nor Rachel could hope to ascertain.

The newcomer had worked up a slight case of Foaming at the Mouth in his torrent of praising GULTANG. He wiped away the mess with one forearm—the one with the spiked gauntlet—since the other had an idling chainsaw with a makeshift flamethrower welded to it. The remainder of his outfit could best be described as a cross between a suit of medieval armor, several instruments of Chinese torture, a shipment of spikes, and a Giger painting mated with a tank.

"Buzz off, Henry. I hadn't finished preaching the word of Zarnak's endless Love for all that is, was, and ever will be."

Henry snarled, though it was difficult to distinguish it from the rumble of the chainsaw engine. A silence would have fallen had it not been for the sucking gas burning noise from the flamethrower. At last, GULTANG's Prophet spoke, "THEN WHY, UPON THE GREAT PILLARS OF DARKMARE'S DEMON PIT DID YOU ENGAGE THE BECKONING? THEO AND THE OTHERS WILL BE HERE ANY MINUTE!"

Zarnak's mortal messenger shrank. "I never got this far before. I was eager."

Atomik Lad and Rachel had been inconspicuously running for their lives by cautiously sidling away from the lunatics.

A great iron hand clamped around Atomik Lad's shoulder, slumping him over slightly from the weight. "THERE IS ONLY ONE WAY TO SAVE YOURSELF AND THE WENCH FROM THE DAY OF RAVAGING—" Atomik Lad would have asked Oh? But there was no way to stop Henry for a second once he got going "—WHEN THE HERETICS, THOSE WHO DO NOT SACRIFICE THEIR LIVES TO THE SOULFIRE OF RAVAGING, WILL FACE

UNDESCRIBABLE AGONY WHILST SPENDING ALL ETERNITY WITHIN GULTANG'S MIGHTY DIGESTIVE TRACT, MOST LIKELY SOMEWHERE NEAR THE END OF IT. THEY WILL KNOW ONLY TER-ROR, ONLY PAIN, THEIR MINDS WILL BE IMMUNE TO ALL BUT SUFFERING—THIS IS THE PUNISHMENT YOU SHALL ENDURE FOR ALL TIME UNLESS YOU REPENT IN THE NAME OF ALL VENGEFUL GULTANG!"

"Zarnak will still love you though. He will heal any wounds this windbag's god can dish out."

"HEY, LOVE-FEST, WHALE-SUCKIN', FLOWER-GROWIN', TREE-HUGGIN', HASHISH-SMOKIN', HIPPY-BOY! IT'S CALLED SHUTTIN' UP, LOOK INTO IT!"

"Do not anger the god of unconditional love," he warned.

"AH, UNCONDITIONAL *THIS!*" Henry swung a hitherto unseen mace with motorized spinning razors doused in some sort of hyper active napalm at the Zarnakian Zealot who, as his religion demanded, turned the other cheek and ran to fetch reinforcements.

"NOW THAT WE'RE FREE OF HIS MEDDLING—" Henry began before realizing his quarry had scrammed as well. He sniffed the air. "THE HUNT IS ON!" he dashed after them, clanging like an exploding junk heap with every step.

$$*\qquad*\qquad*\qquad*$$

"Do you think we lost them?" Rachel said between deep gasps for air. They paused behind a large tree some distance away. If not for the old academic buildings of the university that surrounded them, the area could have very easily been mistaken for a park.

Atomik Lad leaned over, catching his breath. "I don't think we'll have to worry about any more religious freaks today."

"That is true," a mysterious voice agreed from behind them.

"Verily, for our gods are true and pure."

Atomik Lad and Rachel groaned as their new prophets posed in order to clearly distinguish themselves from the ordinary riff-raff. Amongst their number was an Indian, an Indian from India, a large Nordic gentleman, and a particularly angsty gothic chic.

"This is hell," Rachel observed.

Atomik Lad steeled his already steely nerves. "Run. Save yourself. Warn the others. Remember me fondly, try not to think about the morbid nature of my demise."

She gripped his hand tightly. "We're in this together."

*   *   *   *

Nuklear Man dashed into his room with his usual Heroic flare. So of course he tripped over a coat carelessly cast across the Danger: Floor. The Hero of heroes floated up and disentangled himself from the clothing conundrum, dropping the "Lousy backstabbing coat" to the ground whereupon it made a bashing noise far too loud for mere fabric. Puzzled, even more so than usual, Nuklear Man thoroughly inspected the unruly garment. "Hmm, nothing," he surmised after a long drawn out affair of prodding, poking, and patting. He tossed it back to the ground without a thought. Pookaboo rolled out of the inside pocket. Since its optical sensors had automatically gone to infra-red upon entering the deep dark pocket, its eyes glowed a maniacal red—as no other color truly captures the idiom of maniacal. Due to this, and the horrendous lack of any Danger: Labels, not to mention Nuklear Man's inherent lack of recollection regarding anything but himself, he Freaked Out. "Eeeek! A pocket monster!"

"What iz that fool babbling about now?" Dr. Menace asked the computer screen.

"Kill it! Kill it!" Nuklear Man shrieked while trying to stomp the vicious red-eyed Pookaboo doll of infinite evil. But, thanks to Dr. Menace's brilliance, the autodefense.exe program easily maneuvered the Fubar out of harm's way while forcing Nuklear Man into a one-man Mamba.

"That idiot must have stumbled onto my scheme. No matter. Fubar, disengage surveillance, activate escape plan Omega!"

Pookaboo zipped out of Danger: Nuke's Room into the more expansive Danger: Living Room. The gallant—or at least semi-functional—Hero leapt to the doorway, but alas, Pookaboo had already made it to the Danger: Launch Pad.

Being a strategic genius has its advantages, Nuklear Man thought to himself. "Katkat! Thunder Pounce Attack!" The feline nearly awoke from his perch next to the Danger: Supercomputer. "Accursed, yet oh so snuggily cat!" He blindly reached toward the dresser next to the door for any loose object to hurl at Katkat, and hurl he did. A little ping-pong ball bounced off Katkat's furry scalp. One eye cracked open and shut even tighter than before as he yawned and recharged his cat-batteries from the exhausting Sleep.

*　　*　　*　　*

Dr. Menace growled as she pushed the Launch button for the tenth time. "This iz the last time I use those inferior Bolivian ignition switches."

Meanwhile, Pookaboo, the source of all evil now and forever, made cute little hops in its futile attempts at blasting off. Around the globe, eighty-three percent of the world's Fubar population rocketed themselves around the house at speeds in excess of 200 mph. Only a young boy, Edward, was injured during this escapade, but that was on completely unrelated matters involving a bowl of wax fruit and a bowling trophy.

"Now's your chance, Katkat! Thunder Pounce Attack!"

Katkat washed his face.

"That doesn't look like, hey! You're not doing it, are you?"

"Mreow."

"Oh, don't be afraid of battling a pocket monster. No one ever got hurt fighting. Honest."

"Meowr?"

"Well, it doesn't hurt me. I'm pretty typical I think. Other than the being superior to everything part."

Katkat was either unconvinced or had no way of comprehending what Nuklear Man was talking about. One way or the other, he stood his ground by sitting on the Danger: Supercomputer Table.

"Aww, shucks," Nuklear Man hovered next to his new favorite sidekick and pet him. Pookaboo, the somewhat diabolic Fubar doll, continued hopping on the Danger: Launch Pad. "Here. Lemme help ya," the Hero said to Katkat. "Thunder Pounce Attack!" He posed a point to the hopping Fubar, made sure no one was looking, and Plazma Beamed the Fubar to slag. "You did it, Katkat! Yay!"

"Meow!"

Dr. Menace stared into her giant static filled screen. She was still pushing the Launch button to no avail. "On to Plan E."

*　　*　　*　　*

Atomik Lad ran like he hadn't run in, well, the past few minutes. He kept himself between Rachel and the pursuing prophets who couldn't take "No" for an answer. Nor, it seemed, could they take "Get the hell away from us, you damn new-age god freaks!" in jest. Or as anything short of a reason for blood sacrifices for that matter.

"Mighty Thor! Strike down thine doubters!" the one known as Jarl Jarlson bellowed to the heavens.

A bolt of thunder crashed in front of Rachel, barely missing her chased body by inches. "Ack!" she exclaimed in shock while falling over herself in mid-stride. Atomik Lad leapt for her and enveloped both of them in his Atomik Field and flew from their antagonists. The earth zoomed a few feet under his stomach while Rachel clutched to his back.

"Saddle up, baby."

"Any time" she responded, causing Atomik Lad to almost fall out of the air. She looked back at their hunters,. "I don't like being chased."

"I think they got it the first time."

"No, no, no. You're supposed to say 'I'll take care of that.' Don't you know anything about double entendre?"

The Swahili Swami shouted, "Many hands of Vishnu, grapple and capture the heretics so that we may sacrifice them to your—"

"Hey now," Chief Silent Wind interrupted. "Who said you get to do the sacrifice? Wolf will get the sacrifice of this worthy prey."

"Why?"

"He's more deserving."

"But I think Vishnu is more deserving."

"And I think great Thor is the only god mighty enough to deserve this sacrifice."

"Yes, but that doesn't count because it's not what I believe."

"Hey, Silent Wind. Make like your name and shut yer air-hole."

Unfortunately, the Many Hands of Vishnu sprout from the very earth in front of Atomik Lad and his lovely passenger. He pulled up and back in a loop. The religious nuts, lacking neat powers of flight, ran head long into their own trap without missing a beat of their divine quarrel.

Atomik Lad touched down and his field dispersed. Rachel was wrapped around him piggy-back style. "You can get down now," he said.

She leaned her cheek against his "Do I have to?"

His entire body quivered. "Mercy."

An ahnk flashed across their field of vision and was halted only by the green grass between Atomik Lad's feet. Instinctively analyzing, processing, and tracing the projectile's trajectory with their eyes, both sidekick and college girl found their gazes met by a small woman with a ghastly pallor that contrasted grotesquely with her black leather, black lace, black dress, black lipstick, black finger-nails, black eyeliner, and overly dyed black hair. Each hand held the opposite shoulder in a quasi-Egyptian mummy fashion. She fanned her fingers. A black ahnk identical to the one just thrown appeared between every finger. "You're not out of this yet. You still have to contend with me, Sorrow St. Angstie Ahnk-myre!"

Rachel climbed down slowly.

Atomik Lad grumbled "Damn."

Issue 28—Combative
Religions

Katkat slept soundly on the Danger: Coffee Table. He had to recover from the strain of waking up for a few minutes earlier. He did this comfortably despite the position of his neck in relation to his spine, or his spine to his legs. Such is the power of cat. His pink belly was exposed, his whole body was in an impossible S shape with cute little tufts of white hair being all sticky-outy.

Nuklear Man examined Danger: Sparky's Room's door with careful measurements made by rough estimations. In his right hand he held a Danger: T-Square, and in his left a Danger: Blueprint. Unfurling the sapphire document, he compared its figures with his Danger: Field Notes which made no sense architecturally speaking since they consisted entirely of the statement, "Gosh, I'm hungry." He slid the Danger: T-Square around his Danger: Blueprint to convince himself that he was being professional. "Feh. This is easy." He gingerly approached the door, thoughtlessly tossed his Danger: Architect Gear somewhere behind him, peeled the Danger: Sparky's Room label off with surgical patience, and replaced it with a Danger: Katkat's Room label.

Upside down.

"Something's not quite right here," he said, leaning back to review his craftsmanship. "Ah, of course." He moved it a little to the left. "Perfection!"

"And where will Atomik Lad reside?" Danger: Computer Lady inquired.

"Eh, he can sleep on the couch. But not when we have company."

*   *   *   *

"This alleged Atomik Field of yours is very irksome," Rachel commented as she and Atomik Lad took cover behind a waist-high brick wall lined with newspaper machines which were currently being pelted by razor sharp black ankhs.

"You cannot escape Sorrow!" their aggressor yelled. And then silence.

"Maybe she took a wrong turn?" Rachel whispered as they huddled behind the short wall.

"What wrong turn? We ran straight to this spot, jumped the wall, and ducked here," he said.

"No offense, but I've noticed that most of these villains of yours aren't too bright."

"None taken, but—"

"The Queen of Anarchy, Anguish, and Angst eyed her unsuspecting prey as they clung to each other pathetically," Sorrow's voice radiated from everywhere.

"Not another Self-Narrator," Atomik Lad mumbled as he eyed the high and leaf dense branches of the tree on the other side of their wall. "I *really* hate those."

Sorrow continued. "Look at them, nearly as pathetic as those teeny bopper kids going to the Mall every weekend tenaciously clinging to the hope that their meaningless lives have some shred of significance while they try on blouses at The Gorge and watch EMPtv for the latest edition of Real Life or Road Trip—as if there's a difference—while debating the latest occurrences of Demographic Place. Saturating their minds with these contrived and clichéd media conglomerations designed to keep them placid and unthinking, never being aware of the maze, just rats waiting for the next New Backstreet Kids Who Sing 'N Tandem 2U4ever video."

"I don't know where the hell she is, but that's incredible lung capacity," Rachel noted.

"Sorrow stroked the cold, hard, black metal of her ankh-darts, her weapons of choice for delivering sweet death unto the banal masses. Such bittersweet irony that the ankh, a symbol of life, should bring the sharp sting of death upon her prey!"

"Wait a second, you've killed people?!" Rachel blurted.

"Um, Sorrow could not hear the girl's question, for Sorrow was drunk with the eroticism she found only in bringing death."

"Gah," Atomik Lad's face twisted. "This would be morbid if she weren't such a poser."

"I am not a—er, Sorrow decided to strike down the brash young man first. The spark in his eyes, the luster of life which flowed through his every vein, oh how it would make for an exquisite flame to extinguish upon the alter of my suffering!"

"She's not even making sense now," Rachel said with an annoyed huff.

"Sorrow gripped the ebon ankh by the flat of its razor shaft and took aim for the young man's supple flesh."

"Hey!" Rachel protested.

"But whether his screams of agony or her shrieks of terror would be the more pleasing, Sorrow did not yet know."

"She sounds crazy enough to be dangerous," Atomik Lad worried.

"Sorrow's arm silently rose, her heart beat quickened, oh how her blackened soul danced in these moments."

"I wouldn't worry," Rachel soothed.

"Easy for you to say, she's not aiming at you!"

"Shhhh." She held him close, and indeed, all worry was gone.

"Sorrow could no longer hold back, she needed the sweet taste of death, the release that only oblivion's embrace could satisfy!" Atomik Lad cringed. "But alas, what's the point?" Sorrow stepped from the shadow of the large tree, yet she still managed to stand outside of direct sunlight. "Nothing matters. I'm so angsty, no one understands me. We're all so alone, why should I do anything? Pleasure is fleeting, a rare experience that is gone before it can flourish. It makes this dreary life all the darker once it is gone." She slumped to the ground, pulled out a black magic maker, and began drawing ankhs on her pale skin. Atomik Lad uncringed and noted several half-faded ankhs on the back of her hands.

Rachel leaned against the hot coarse brick wall. "It's not that bad," she said.

"Oh but it is," Sorrow insisted. "I'm alone in a cold, godless, uncaring universe without meaning. Nothing I do matters, no one can understand my pain, no one can love this," she motioned to her-black-garbed-self.

"There's so much good in life, Sorrow," Atomik Lad began before being cut off.

"What good is in pain? Hell, what good is in love? Sooner or later one of you tires of the other and there's betrayal, pain. All life is pain. Is it so wrong to not want to be hurt? And what if it is true love? What then? Maybe it'll last a few years before the universe perverts it into pain like everything else—or, failing that, it'll kill off one of you leaving the other as an empty yearning shell. Pain or weakness? Give me another choice, anything but this endless sea of suffering!"

"She, she's got a point," Rachel murmured. "We all die alone, so terribly alone."

"What?" Atomik Lad shook. There was a squeaking in the back of his mind, persistent as a leaky faucet. "But…" he looked to Sorrow, to Rachel, down at the radiation hazard symbol on his chest. "Even if I do make a difference, even if I change every life on Earth for the better, it won't bring back my parents, it won't matter. Eventually, no matter what I do, no one will remember me. I am nothing waiting to unrealize myself."

Still semi-shroud in shadow, Sorrow's black lips flowed into a devious grin. *I have you now*, she thought.

"HEY SARAH!" a familiar voice boomed in the distance.

Sorrow's victory smile shattered. "I told you to call me Sorrow!"

"WENCH! AND I TOLD YOU THAT TRUE SORROW IS THE EMPTINESS OF LIVING WITHOUT MIGHTY GULTANG TO GUIDE YOU THROUGH THE BATTLEFIELD OF LIFE, SLAYING THE UNDEAD MINIONS OF COWARDICE, RAZING THE CASTLES OF FEAR, RUNNING THROUGH THE KNIGHTS OF LONELINESS—"

"Can we not have this discussion again?"

"Wah, what's happening?" Atomik Lad asked, feeling like he just woke up from a nap.

"I felt like listening to androgynous Euro-trash synth bands from the '80s. Kinda woozy," Rachel said as she blinked away the grogginess.

"Look at what you did, Henry! I nearly had them and you burst in and ruined everything."

"WENCH! I CANNOT BE RESPONSIBLE FOR YOUR INABILITY TO INDOCTRINATE THIS PAIR INTO YOUR GOTHIC CABAL OF THE DISPOSSESSED!"

"And you were doing such a swell job of enlisting them into the Unholy Order of Gultang's Living Vengeance, weren't you?"

"WENCH! WHEN YOU MENTION THE ORDER'S NAME, YOU WILL DO SO WITH FEELING, FROM THE DIAPHRAGM! BESIDES, I WAS IN THE PROCESS OF HUNTING THEM DOWN AS THE EVER-VIGILANT BLOOD WOLVES OF DARKWOOD FOREST STALK THE WILY AND NIMBLE DEERKIN OF ELFINDRA WHEN THEY TARRY TOO LONG IN THE WOODS. THEN YOU FOUND THEM BY MERE HAPPENSTANCE AND SCREWED UP MY CHASE WORSE THAN A ZOMBIE WHORE OF RANKARNIA!"

"You know, Henry. You play too many roleplaying games."

He fumed. "WENCH! AGAIN SAYS I, WENCH! AND ONCE MORE: WENCH!"

Rachel and Atomik Lad watched as their overly abundant religious persecutors quarreled. "Maybe we can get away," Rachel suggested. Atomik Lad silently nodded and nearly made a motion.

"AND WHERE DO YOU THINK YOU'RE GOING, GULTANG-FODDER? HMM?"

"I suppose this is where I say 'Nowhere' right?"

"UNLESS YOU WANT TO GET UP CLOSE AND PERSONAL WITH MR. CHAINSAW!" It blubbered into silence. "ER. IN THAT CASE, MAYBE YOU'D LIKE TO GET A WARM WELCOME FROM MR. FLAMETHROWER!" the flame flickered away impotently.

"Just like last week," Sorrow muttered.

"HEY! I TOLD YOU! THE GULTANGIAN PURIFICATION RITUALS MADE ME TIRED AND—"

"Wait a second," Atomik Lad interrupted.

"You're *dating*?" Rachel finished.

"We've got common interests, rhetorical techniques, and career goals."

"WENCH! I SPEAK FOR US, AS THE DOGMA OF GULTANG DEMANDS—"

"Henry, you don't even own the Gultangian Ravager's Handbook yet, so lay off quoting from it, hm?"

"WENCH! GRRR!"

"Look, maybe we should leave you two to work this out," Rachel said.

"Yeah, this really isn't any of our business," Atomik Lad agreed, standing up. "You can get back with us later."

"Honest," Rachel lied.

A small army of robed fanatics marched onto the scene, led by the Zarnakian Zealot from before. "Peace be with you, and let the blood of heretics drown their families in the streets!" he demanded.

Henry turned around, "I THOUGHT WE GOT RID OF YOU, FRED!"

"You did. But I'm back. And now I'm gonna rain some righteousness."

"YOU AND WHAT ARMY?"

"Zarnak's Loyal Host of Pacifists!"

Henry was unimpressed. "FEH! I'LL 'PASS A FIST' RIGHT THROUGH EACH ONE OF THEIR DAMN SKULLS!"

"Zarnak's love is endless," Fred preached. "Perhaps you should take it up with him in the Afterlife!"

Atomik Lad snatched Rachel away as the war broke out. The Zarnakians hollered their menacing battlecries of "Love and kill thy enemy!" and "Life without pain knows not happiness: enjoy!" and "May death bring you the peace that we could not!" Sorrow sat on Henry's massive armored shoulders high above the marauding throng of robes below. As for Gultang's ardent follower, he was thoroughly enjoying himself. "HA-HA! PUNY WORMS! LOOK UPON MY SPIKEY ARMOR AND BE AFRAID! I AM RAVAGER, HEAR ME BELLOW! WITH GULTANG IN MY HEART AND HATRED IN MY SOUL, I AM INVINCI—OUCH!"

✳   ✳   ✳   ✳

Rachel and Atomik Lad stood outside Wayne Hall as a slight wind toyed with her hair. "Well, thanks for having lunch with me," Atomik Lad said.

She curtseyed. "Why of course, Mr. Atomik. I wouldn't have it any other way."

Atomik Lad countered with a bow. "The pleasure is all mine, Lady Rachel."

"Not if you stay like that," she said with a crooked smile.

"Oh my," he uttered while standing erect—no—straight. Whew.

"But I've really got to get some work done."

"*Dammit!*" it echoed against the brick building's facade. "Uh, I mean. Oh. What do you have to do?"

She giggled at him. "Silly. Anyway, just some sketches for class. It wouldn't take long, but I've been putting it off and I have no idea what I'm going to do. So I'll probably spend most of the weekend throwing away a dozen crappy sketches before settling for a nice little still life."

"Still life?"

"Eh, stupid professor doesn't have much of an imagination. I keep coming back to Eastern styles and themes, ancient mythological, historical, modern, pop, you name it. Anyway, he hates it."

"Moron."

"Yeah, but a moron who can give me an F in the class, so I'd better start churning out some soulless garbage."

"Have fun."

"You too, hon."

"Probably not. I've got to hit the sack pretty early tonight. Nuke and I have an appointment at Überdyne first thing tomorrow morning for our monthly check ups to make sure we aren't going to explode or something."

"Ah. In that case, be sure to dream of me."

"But if I do that, then what's a heaven for?"

She tried to hide a smile. "You really are silly, you know."

"Could be."

Rachel leaned close and gave Atomik Lad a quick peck on the cheek. "Gimme a call when you boys get back."

"Huffalabbawa," was his only response as Rachel walked up the steps to Wayne Hall, unlocked its giant door, and disappeared inside. It took the sidekick several minutes to convince his legs to get movin' again.

*   *   *   *

Nothing interesting happened the rest of the day to anyone in the whole world. Just one of those things, I guess. But then Night, not paying attention to where she was going, fell.

The Silo of Solitude was quiet in the still darkness despite the presence of Nuklear Man, Atomik Lad, Nukebots, Danger: Computer Lady and Katkat. Also, the Silo's nomenclature remained as unchanging as ever even though it had never been solitudinal and was itself composed of hundreds of billions of nano-scopic entities. But that's not the point. The point is the Silo was dark, still, and quiet save for the even breaths of those resting within it and the low droning hum that emanated from every square inch of the Silo which isn't very quiet at all now that I think about it. Okay, scratch quiet. The Silo was dark and still except for a commotion coming from the Danger: Religious Differences—fuck! Sorry. All right, seriously this time. The Silo was dark other than the areas illuminated by Danger: Nightlights and randomly blinking lights which adorned nearly every-thing from actual computer consoles to bookshelves.

I want to start again. It was night time and everyone was asleep—Katkat was awake—I'm not listening to you! But, if Katkat was indeed awake, he would have found his new Danger: Katkat Bed to be very comfortable and spacious. Atomik Lad snoozed soundly in Danger: Nukie's Room while Nuklear Man covered the Danger: Living Room Danger: Couch like a slain king snoring loudly. While slain? I quit. New story:

ISSUE 29—THE RAVAGES OF WAR

The Ancient Books told of a time of Unity, Purity, Wholeness. All was One and One was All and it made sense when they said it. This was Perfection, Paradise. But then came the Sundering. The One was shattered into the Countless. Facets, each new and autonomous unto itself, each an individual alone and separate in a world which now flourished with suffering and death. But they could not take the memory of Paradise from their broken souls. Though independent, each strove to unite with the others, to destroy the barriers that kept them apart, to re-enter a state of endless bliss, dancing for eternity with all creation. But division begat division. The Countless were torn again in their desperate search for Unity. Lo, the irony! A duality had been reached. There were those who believed only the destruction of Evil's Source could mend their wayward souls. Alternately, some believed that only by purifying each of the Countless by deep, personal, introspective self-analysis and discipline could they attain a state of consciousness which would allow them to ascend into one another once more. How such similar views could lead to such horrific bloodshed throughout a hundred generations is the tragedy of this race. Endless loss and sacrifice in the name of an idea. So noble, and yet so narrow-minded and unflinching.

She pondered this, the history of her people. A history of wars kept in a textbook of battlefields written in blood. Her cybernetically implanted sensors had not registered even the slightest disturbance on either side of the front line for days now. She had to face the truth. At last, the War of Unity was over.

And she was alone.

Hatred boiled within her. Hatred for the enemy, for her own fallen, for the Generals and Elders on both sides, but most of all, for the perpetrator of the Sundering. Finally, she spoke unto the barren and scarred field of ash and blood that surrounded her.

"I am the last of my people. We have known only war. I, Anne the III, vow on the grave of my mother, Anne the XVII—as I was named after my father's sister whose name also happened to be Anne—to exact revenge upon..." dramatic pause, don't look ahead. I said don't, "...The Anti-Arachnor!"

Ah ha! I tricked you, it's still the same story, nya-ha. Thbbbbbpt. Foolish reader, you dare to believe my words.

The sleek Danger: Religious Differences door **fwoosh**ed open in the night which was not quite as dark, still, or quiet as it had initially appeared to be. Tiny metallic clicks clattered across the Danger: Floor. Anne's little arachnid body was 83% cybernetic. It gave her everything from hover capabilities to life support, laser blasters, and energy shielding. Anne, like all good soldiers, had memorized the Ancient Scrolls of Arachnor, which spoke briefly of the outside world. She traversed its alien depths now, unafraid. Mighty Arachnor had seen fit to put her here, now on the stage of history, blazing new paths, the ultimate incarnation of her people. She had survived this long, the Great Heavenly Spider would not let her fail now. She knew this. According to the Eight Paths of Enlightenment and the Books of the Web of Fate, the Anti-Arachnor could be found dwelling within the stinking bowels of the spiderverse. Anne calculated the numeric value of "Arachnor" using the Equation of Naming, but then reversed the polarity at the last second in order to ascertain the exact co-ordinates of the Anti-Arachnor whose real name could never be spoken or known.

"Just as I determined," Anne spat. Exactly sixty-four octameters from the Danger: Religious Differences, Anne stopped and looked up at the ominous gates of Hell, or "Dangerinukiesroom" in the ancient tongue of most Holy Arachnor. Anne squared her shoulders, taking nearly a full minute to do so, and took one defiant step forward. Hell's Gates parted.

$$*\qquad*\qquad*\qquad*$$

Atomik Lad slept fitfully. It was his first time on a round bed. The fact that it was symmetrical from any angle was off-putting. Still, sleep was one of his favorite things, so he ignored the instinct to be repulsed by the radial nature of his sleeping apparatus. Mentally drained from the bed issue, he didn't even bother tackling the Danger: Wall of Accomplishments, much less the Danger: Vanity Mirror, the Danger: Other Vanity Mirror, or the Danger: Auxiliary Vanity Mirror ("Y'know, in case the other two suffer from a fatal system error," as Nuklear Man had been known to reason). Those would have to wait for another day.

*   *   *   *

Anne's sensors were overloaded with the all permeating aura of evil and corruption that seeped from every particle of the domain. She persevered. She had come this far, she cold not be stopped. At the foot of Danger: Dreamhip, or Mount Evil as Anne knew it, she could hear the beast's low, even breaths. "Gah! The Fiend slumbers, yet his nefariousness is so powerful that it poisons all this realm with his mere presence!" Hover Mode engaged, Anne traversed the treacherous peak without once setting foot on it until the expansive and warped apex had been reached. The terrain here took on unnatural dimensions, hills and valleys rose and fell without reason. Ahead, though it may have simply been an optical illusion, she could have sworn the landscape actually moved, like the land itself was breathing or a great serpent writhed under its depths. She crawled across the ever changing world, threatening to suck her in or crush her in a great wave at any moment.

All the horrors of a lifetime of war had not prepared her. All the scriptures of the Ancient Books had not prepared her. The hideous maw of the Anti-Arachnor lay before her. The rage, the betrayal, the lives of untold millions all lost in the name of uniting what this bastard destroyed. She howled a battlecry "From Hell's Heart, I stab at thee!"

*   *   *   *

Atomik Lad dreamed. A cartoon-ish lobster in a bomber jacket was poking him in the face with a pencil. "Stop it!" he protested, but the lobster persisted. "Dammit, lobster. Lobster? Erg, this is a dream."

"RED RUM, RED RUM!" the lobster advised.

"Okay. I'm waking up now."

"HELTER SKELTER!" the lobster maintained.

*   *   *   *

Atomik Lad's eyes opened groggily in the darkness which turned out to be very unquiet and nonstill in his general vicinity as a spider was violently thrusting its legs against his cheek. "I'm so glad that this is yet another dream, because the thought of a spider on my face would make me flip out in a very embarrassing way."

"Do not taunt me, vile Anti-Arachnor! Though I may be but one spider, I refuse to walk silently into death. You'll have to drag me into the Depths as I strangle you with my final breath!"

"A talking spider," he smiled to himself. "I wonder where my subconscious picked that up."

"I will not be mocked by the likes of you!"

"I remember something from the other night. The storage closet. But those couldn't have really been talking spiders in there."

"Insult me no more, beast! Destroy me and complete the circle of your corruption!" Anne skittered down to his chest and held out several of her legs in an act of sublimation. "You have taken my people, shattered them in mind, body, and soul. Now I am the last, our bloody wars finally at an end. With only rage in my heart, I vowed to take vengeance upon you in the names of all our dead." Her fervor disappeared, replaced with sullen tones. "But in my quest, I have come to face a horrid truth."

"I think I want the lobster back."

"My people were divided into two opposing camps, two schools of thought, each meant to reunite us but serving only to splinter us forever. I am the only survivor of this eternal conflict, thus one ideology finally proved its worth over the other." Anne fidgeted nervously. "But I must confess, I do not know which one."

"Yours," Atomik Lad answered with a yawn.

"That's just it. We haven't known which side we fought for, not for generations, I believe. We only knew the Other was the Enemy and they were a constant threat to our way of life because they were different. But which faction defended which theory of Spiderversal Complementation, I cannot answer." Her many shoulders slumped. "We placed all we knew to be evil on you, but it was truly within ourselves."

Atomik Lad slipped out of the covers and stretched. "Sounds like an identity crisis." He scratched his belly. "Which I suppose I can understand. I lost my parents so long ago, and then I had to grow up at lightspeed to take care of Nuke and defend the city against constant villainous attacks. There never really was time to ask myself what I was doing, if I was happy with it, or if it was even the right thing to do. I mean, who am I to say who is a villain? In another world I might be some kind of heartless murdering dictator. Maybe I really am."

He began pacing back and forth quickly as he talked. "Maybe Menace and the others are trying to effect some much needed social incentives. Maybe I'm hindering progress and in a hundred years me and Nuke will be scorned in history books as forces of rampant and unstoppable evil. I was just a kid, you accept the reality you're told, how was I supposed to know about all the implications of this hero business? It's not like that in the comic books. It's not until you grow up that you learn everyone's a borderline psycho and there is no right or wrong, only an amorphous gray blob that almost takes a shape when you see it from the corner of your eye but then completely escapes definition when viewed head-on. I'm glad I can help so many people, but I never feel quite right.

"Why me? Why am I the one? It's not so bad, I guess, but sometimes I'd like to live like other people, in a house. In the city. Go to work. I'm trying to do my best, but what if it isn't good enough? But even worse, what if I'm wrong?" The pacing stopped. He turned and faced Anne who still sat on the covers. "But the most compelling question this whole episode raises is: Why does my subconscious feel it necessary to bring these issues to light through the mouthpiece of a little spider?"

Anne eyed and eyed and eyed and eyed etc. Atomik Lad. "Wait. You're not Anti-Arachnor."

"Hm?"

"The Ancient Texts describe him as being fantastically enormous, whereas you are merely considerably huge."

Atomik Lad scratched his chin.

"Plus, it specifically mentions that he's a blond. You are not."

"So is my subconscious telling me that my issues are really centered on Nuke? That he's the source of my identity anxiety? That makes sense. When we first met, well that was a rather stressful time in my life, what with my Atomik Field killing my parents and all. Maybe I repressed some memories. I think I read a myth about how spiders spun webs to catch memories and when they ate them, that's how people forgot things. That could explain why you're a spider."

Anne's Hover Drive had already taken her back to the Danger: Floor. "That's good. I'm outta here." The Danger: Door **fwoosh**ed behind her and she was gone.

Atomik Lad flopped back into bed. "My dreams are usually so boring."

*   *   *   *

Anne wandered the silvery wasteland of the Danger: Living Room. Time became meaningless as she stalked through the darkness. *My people failed. Their petty arrogance and jealousies fractured them against one another. Their one great mission for Unity has ended in solitude. Heh, I speak of them as though I am better than they were, as though I am somehow immune to fault because I survived them. I lived because of chance. And my quest, my personal voyage for vengeance ended in miserable failure with some neurotic biped beast god. And yet I followed the paths to the Anti-Arachnor as described in our holy books. I wonder if there ever was an Anti-Arachnor in the first place. Maybe he was only an allegory representing our own short comings, selfish impulses, and the like. An over-simplified example of what not to do, how not to behave so we could perpetuate the social order. All our lives wasted maintaining a set of rules we thought we made. I think I'm insane now. Or am I finally sane?*

"Oh, Great Arachnor, hear my—no, if the Anti-Arachnor is nothing more than a story to frighten spiderlings into being good little soldiers, then Arachnor is a figment as well. Never again shall I follow ridiculous superstitions. They are stories, and frivolous ones at that."

With a despondent sigh, she looked into the bleak heavens without actually seeing. She could hardly remember light. Even her life of battle blurred and muddled in her mind; memories mixing, swirling into one another until a cacophony of emptiness filled her, delivering such a shock to her system she finally acknowledged her various sensory inputs.

She stood at the feet of two giant statues, each as big as the gods themselves. They both displayed the Anti-Arachnor's hated symbol on their chests: two parallel upright columns separated and yet joined by a third divisive column diagonal from the head of the first down to the foot of the second. And around that scene of Sundering, orbited the broken tribes of Arachnor, lost and alone yet connected by intertwining threads of suffering and loss.

How they sicken me, wearing those badges so proudly. "If you indeed be servants to the One Most Foul, then show him to me!" she called up to them.

Silence was their only answer.

"I should have known better than to trust in that religious nonsense. It is a habit I must break."

Her wanderings brought her to the cliffs of the Danger: Coffee Table. She stood on a Danger: Coaster. "So much pointless loss. I can't make sense of anything any more. What was it all for? Were we merely a mistake upon the webbing of the spiderverse? I can't believe we have no destined purpose, I just can't. There must be a plan. If not by Arachnor, then someone, something greater than myself." Anne shuddered with sobs. She threw her head back and yelled into the black sky "Why have you forsaken me!" before succumbing once more to tears.

Nuklear Man startled himself awake as the result of yet another mysterious dream, this one involving scary wolves with coats of fire and snakes big enough to swallow worlds. He rubbed his groggy eyes and turned to the Danger: TV.

A little mind numbing television oughta stimulate the ol' brain, he thought. His vision focused on some teeny movements originating on the Danger: Coffee Table. His Nuklear Vision compensated for the darkness by spontaneously evolving the ability to collect more light through the iris. Of course, most people would refer to this as a perfectly natural reaction to low-light environs, but Nuklear Man certainly wasn't most people. His sight thus enhanced, he could plainly see. "ACK! A bug! Kill it, kill it!" He recoiled from it, covering his eyes with one hand while Plazma Beaming it and the Danger: Coffee Table into oblivion with the other. "Whew. Stupid gross bug. Where there's one there's a hun...dred...of. *Them*." He curled up into a shaking little ball of Nuklear Fright. His eyes darted to and fro locking on to a hundred traces of movement which were all hallucinated. "Bugs, bugs everywhere, on my skin and in my hair!" he chanted in a whisper. "Bug, bugs everywhere, on my skin and in my hair." He could feel them closing in. "Sparky?" he whimpered.

Issue 30—Adventure into Science!

"I think Katkat should come with us," Nuklear Man suggested over a Danger: Plate of pancakes.

Across the Danger: Kitchen Table, Atomik Lad finished up his waffles. "He's not really a hero, you know. He has no powers for Überdyne to study."

"Oh, but I think he does," the Hero retorted.

"Do ya now?"

Nuklear Man produced the feline and held Katkat's fuzzy face up to Atomik Lad's tired face. "He's a supercutie wutie, yes he is. Aren't you? Aren't you!"

Atomik Lad sighed and took his Danger: Dishes to the Danger: Sink. "Look, I don't think Dr. Genius will appreciate us wasting her time on a cat. These appointments cost all kinds of money. Let's just get in there and get out."

Nuklear Man had already given up on the laborious task of listening to Atomik Lad babble. He switched his attentions to snuggling and belly scratching the much more adorable Katkat. "Glad you agree, it's a lot easier than beating some sense into you."

"Erg."

"Well, not a lot easier."

"Of course."

"You're really weak compared to me."

"Right."

"Because I'm so much stronger."

"I got it."

Nuklear Man flex-posed and Katkat flopped onto the Danger: Floor. His furry face seemed to say, "Eh, good enough" because he stretched, rolled over, and closed his eyes for nappy time.

Atomik Lad rubbed his eyes. "He's not coming with us, now get going. I've got plans for the afternoon."

"How's that possible? I don't recall giving you any tasks to complete."

"Yes, you see, I've got this thing called A Life That Doesn't Revolve Around You."

"Hm. Are you sure?"

"Very."

"I don't know. That certainly doesn't sound like an order I'd give. What was the Authorization Code?"

"Oh geez. I don't know, how about Alpha Niner?"

"It's an older code, but it checks out. Are you sure you're not picking up those crazy thoughts I keep warning you about? Like free will?"

"Why me?" Atomik Lad asked the universe as he went back to his Danger: Katkat's Room.

"Sounds like someone is in serious need of a little 'mind cleansing.' I'll make the preparations."

$$* \quad * \quad * \quad *$$

Dr. Genius stood on the Überdyne Headquarters roof overlooking the majestic Metroville skyline on all sides of her. *9:15, restate my assumptions. 1) Kopelson Intrinsity is the language of the universe. 2) Everything around us can be represented as a field of intrinsity. 3) If you graph these fields, they reach an infinite capacity to hold and transfer information. Therefore: The universe is the expression of that information. If we can learn the syntax of this language, then we can manipulate the universe at the most basic level. So perhaps the miraculous effects caused by overpowers can be explained as a limited version of this manipulation...*

The morning sun hung low, casting its diffuse light against the weekend traffic of tourists, beach goers, and sale hunters. The sparse clouds and blue sky sparkled against the austere glass and steel skyscrapers of the city. Dr. Genius took a deep breath, closed her eyes and stood on her toes. The rims of her glasses glinted as she slid them off to rub her nose. "It's so peaceful up here." A buzzer in one of her lab coat's many internal pockets went off. "Most of the time, anyway." She turned to Nameless Technician, a man more aptly named would be hard to find, who manned a portable computer console near the access door that led into the Scientific: Depths of Überdyne. "Power up the generators," she said casually.

*   *   *   *

Atomik Lad touched down perfectly beside Dr. Genius, his Atomik Field dispersed harmlessly. "Hey, Doc."

She donned a pair of goggles. "Good morning, John. How are you?"

"Not bad, but I wish we could do these things a little later in the afternoon."

She flicked her head to the right to dislodge a loose curl blown against her forehead by the winds that flared up at this height. "As do I, but this is when the Earth's magnetic force is at its apex in this region, and we need all the juice we can get."

Nameless Technician yelled, "*Incoming!*"

Dr. Genius and Atomik Lad dropped to their stomachs. "I guess it's just as well," the sidekick said. "At least this way it leaves the rest of the day open."

A golden comet rocketed across the Metroville skyline shattering windows in its wake. It cut ragged turns between skyscrapers and through a few unlucky ones. Air burst into flames at the comet's tail as it zeroed in on the Überdyne rooftop.

"See," Ima said while taking readings with a calculator-ish device. "It's not so bad. Besides, doing it this way is a lot easier than having to rebuild the top fifteen floors every time he visits." The mad comet struck an invisible wall a few feet above Dr. Genius and Atomik Lad. Thin blue threads of energy coursed through the air and wrapped around the frozen Nuklear Comet. Überdyne Headquarters had become the world's largest bar magnet. It was the safest way to get Nuklear Man into the building since his usual method of landing involved crashing. The energy flickered briefly and faded away. Nuklear Man hovered in place momentarily before collapsing next to Atomik Lad

"It would be a lot easier if he just didn't do this in the first place," Atomik Lad muttered as he helped Dr. Genius up.

She removed her goggles, put the calculator-ish thing in a pocket, dusted off her lab coat, and thanked Nameless Technician for his help. He began taking the equipment down.

Nuklear Man shot past simple attention and right into Attention! with his cape billowing majestically over his head. "You are not working with me!" he scolded before tossing it back over his shoulders. "Ha-ho!" Flex, pose, flex, smile, wink. "Let's play doctor, baby."

Atomik Lad groaned.

"Buzz off, Sparky," the Hero whispered through an exaggerated toothy smile. "Things are gonna get freaky this time for sure. I can feel it!"

"Don't say things like that."

"Frea*kay!*"

"I'm going to be sick."

Dr. Genius laughed all the way to the access door. "You guys are too much. Now c'mon, we've got some testing to do." She disappeared down the stairway. Nameless Technician followed her while clumsily carrying the portable magnetic generator equipment.

Nuklear Man did his giddy dance while Atomik Lad suppressed his gag reflex. "She wants me," the Hero assured his old sidekick. "I can tell."

"Nuke, remember our discussion about the real world and how it has nothing to do with whatever you're thinking?"

"Wrong, wrong, wrong, wrong."

"No, actually. I'm quite right."

"Well, Mister Smarty the Smart, why do you think she keeps inviting us over to her place all the time?"

The sidekick walked Nuklear Man to the access door and down the stairs after Dr. Genius. "Maybe to perform the tests that she performs. You know, to measure the development of our powers, to determine their possible origins, to make sure we aren't a public health hazard, and so forth?"

"Oh naive, young, naive Atomik Lad," Nuklear Man said while nearly stifling a chuckle. "Let me tell you one or two things I've learned about women in my time."

"That's about three more things than I would've guessed."

"When she says 'Hi' she means 'Yes.'"

"No, no, no, no."

"Oooh! That means 'Yes, give it to me now, Nukiepants!'"

"What the hell?! Were you talking to any frat boys while we were on campus?"

"Maybe."

"Stop it."

"That one's 'More, more, more!'"

Atomik Lad stopped them in mid-stride. "Okay, I don't even know where to start telling you how very, *very* wrong all this is."

"Because I'm right. See how that works? Now let's move along, I've got a new choke hold I wanna try out."

"*Gah!* No, look. Just, let's play a game. Pretend they actually say what they mean. Forever."

"That doesn't sound like nearly as much fun."

"Trust me. It's better this way."

"We'll see."

*   *   *   *

A few minutes later, in the neat high-tech super secret testing labs of Überdyne's Scientific: Sub-Basement 7, Dr. Genius checked a few Scientific: Printouts
concerning the results of an automated weather machine while Nuklear Man and
Atomik Lad stood around awaiting their tests. "Sorry to keep you boys waiting,"
she apologized while flipping through the readouts. "Bbut we've come across a
rather embarrassing anomaly that produces cheeseburgers out of thin air instead
of rainfall."

"No problem, Doc." Atomik Lad answered while scanning the ultrahigh-tech
interior of Überdyne.

"I read you loud and clear," Nuklear Man said while tugging at his spandex.
"Darn it, how am I supposed to get out of this thing?" he muttered.

"Ack! Nuke, remember. Pretend."

The Hero blinked dumbly. "Nnnyes?"

Grumble. "Pretend they mean what they say."

"Ohhhh. Right. Pretend. Gotcha."

Dr. Genius prestidigitated her supercool calculator-ish thingie once more and
began pressing a series of buttons. "Let's see now. Nuklear Man, last time we
tested your strength using the Strongometer. The boys in maintenance are still
building a new one so we can't pick up from there today." She scrolled through a
list displayed on her handheld computer. "Ah yes. Why don't we measure your
tolerance to heat in the Heatomatic? This new test should coincide nicely with
your energy metabolization data."

"Lay it on me, honey."

She laughed to herself and pressed several more keys. "Just step into the Scientific: Observation Chamber behind you and we can get started."

"My kinda woman," the Hero said and sauntered into the smaller room
through the panoramic opening that led into it.

"The Scientific: Observation Chamber will be lined with a makeshift Negaflux
field, I managed to retro-engineer a basic generator from some of Veronica's
notes," Dr. Genius told Atomik Lad and the readers. "That way, we can continue
to increase the temperature within the room without affecting the outside world.
And since the N-field will completely contain all thermodynamic activity within

the chamber, we should get the temperature to levels equal to that of solar fusion, just under 30 million degrees Celsius. In the event that we should have to get Nukie out of there in a hustle, the floor is designed to drop out and dump him into the room below. Thanks to another Negaflux set up there, we've managed to get it down to Absolute Zero in there without having to freeze the entire universe."

"Isn't that kinda dangerous?"

"Not at all, as soon as a little heat energy is introduced to the room, it'll warm up a degree or two just like the rest of outerspace and we know Nuke can handle that without a problem."

"Ah, I—*gah*!" Atomik Lad hopped back as a computer console built itself out of the floor right in front of him and the good doctor. Cables snaked from it to the walls and another set of computers against the wall behind them, opposite the Scientific: Observation Chamber where Nameless Technician was making some notes on a clipboard and supervising the connections. "What the hell?!" the sidekick blurt at the spontaneous technology growing around him.

"Next generation Nanobots," she explained while typing in her little computer. "They can turn the very air around us into the raw materials they need to replicate."

"But don't we need to breathe that air?"

"Oh, no. They only use things like dust, various pollutants, random particle of poisonous gas and the like. Once we rely exclusively on N2 technology for our construction needs, 99% of the world's pollution should be taken care of within five years."

"Neat. So, what's gonna happen to Nuke?"

"We're going to measure any effects the extreme temperatures might have on him by observing his Kopelson Intrinsity Field."

"That Kopelson stuff still confuses me."

"It's not terribly confusing. Well, if you ignore the fact that the actual field manifests itself in twelve dimensions without occupying spatio-temporal coordinates in any of them. And that it stretches infinitely on both sides of zero. And that somehow all KI fields apparently transmit all their information to every other KI field in the universe instantaneously. But beyond things like that, it's quite simple."

"Yeah. Simple. My thoughts exactly."

"Intrinsity theory is based on three simple concepts, Kopelson's Laws. One: Everything in a system has a tendency to be itself. That is to say, a system consisting of a volume of water will remain that same volume of water without experiencing any change if left to its own devices. Two: Introducing or taking away energy from the system is the only way to bring about change in the system. In the case of the water, adding heat energy to the system will turn it into steam while taking away heat energy will turn the water into ice. Three: The universe is a system, therefore it obeys the first two laws of intrinsity.

"Changes are constantly taking place. The water gains temporal energy as time progresses, its space-time coordinates are altered due to the Earth's rotation, and revolution around the sun, and the sun's spin around the galaxy, and the galaxy's movement through space. But these energies, the water, and all existence, are merely metaphors for the real action, the KI fields. It's the KI of the heat interacting with the KI of the water that produces the KI for steam. So theoretically, if we can produce the proper adjustments to the right kind of KI sequences within an object, we can produce any desired effect as if by magic. The water could become steam without actual heat. Or an apple or an ocean.

"We could instantly teleport it to the moon, another star, or through time. We could make ice sink, make water boil at its freezing point. The possibilities for human exploration and learning would be limitless. If we can unlock the secrets of intrinsity, we can become gods. There will be nothing separating science from magic. I believe that superrpowers are the first step to this ultimate goal. All of you alter reality in some, often miraculous, way by nothing more than thought alone.

"And this is the final implication. Every KI field is unique, which is quite puzzling. Protons are supposed to be mathematically identical to one another, but in KI equations, no two protons are alike. Mostly it's just the organization of the information and probably space-time variances, but they are different nonetheless. There's an infinite number of KI fields, all woven into one another, all affecting the others constantly. So if we're built from KI fields while living in a KI field, then inside each of them, there must be one key sequence of intrinsic information that is shared by everything in existence, like God's signature on every piece of Creation. It's the Golden Pattern, the answer to life, the universe. Everything. Research of Kopelson's Intrinsity Theory is the most astounding and important endeavor ever imagined by humankind."

"Feh," Nuklear Man scoffed. "No mystical energy field controls my destiny."

Rather overwhelmed, and completely ignoring Nuklear Man, Atomik Lad answered, "Wow."

"That's what I said. But, as for the more immediate concerns of today, I'm convinced that the secrets to Nuklear Man's past, his powers, yours, and the other heroes are locked somewhere within those Fields. I merely have to sift through the common every day minutia to find the right sequences. Since the Field is infinite, the only way to do this is to prod the subject to see which sequences correspond to which physical attributes. That way, we can find what's different, what's particularly special about the KI Fields of you Heroes and unlock that factor."

"So that's what these tests are all about."

"Partially. We're also gauging the range, potency, and versatility of your powers in order to better deploy you boys against disasters, which is the official press release reason for these appointments."

"That makes sense."

"Also, according to the Hero Act, we have to regularly inspect all of you to make sure your powers and mental conditions are stable so you won't destroy half the city in a massive overload or an insane quest for vengeance against cheese or the like."

"Thanks."

"It's just a precaution. You boys have incredible responsibilities, not everyone has the mental and emotional fortitude for this line of work, you know."

Atomik Lad watched Nuklear Man in the Heatomatic. "Yeah, I know."

"And we have enough trouble with villains destroying half the city, the last thing we need is for our side to start helping them out."

"Not to mention giant monsters from the sea. Hey, whatever happened to Angus? I haven't seen him since you cleaned up and tagged the Crushtacean."

"Oh, we kept him for further study."

"Why?"

"Three reasons. First of all, he had the most, um, contact with Crushtacean so we're trying to glean a few bits of information about the Crab that way. Second, he seems to be suffering from some kind of post-traumatic stress syndrome. He hasn't so much as cursed since we brought him in. And third, his suit is on backwards."

Atomik Lad expected, but did not get, an explanation on that third point. "Er, so?"

"Well, it seems that his Iron: Battlesuit has been turned around, a complete 180. The problem is, that's impossible. The only way to turn it around would be to eject it and put it on the other way, but once the suit is ejected, the locks that hold it together are destroyed in the process. The locks on his suit are unharmed and the ejection system was damaged and inoperative anyway so it's a moot point. And besides, due to the suit's design, even if he somehow got it on backwards, Angus simply couldn't fit in it. There's no possible way for the suit to be backwards, nor can we correct the situation because, as I said, the ejection device was damaged somehow. We're messing with some physics in the hopes of solving Angus's wardrobe problem while simultaneously perfecting a non-lethal method of messing with physics."

"What're we gonna do in the meantime without an enraged berserker warrior to patrol the city?"

"I've already taken care of that," Genius smiled. "We have Fukazake Shiro, the Tetsu Samurai, all the way from Japan. He's filling in for Angus until our little Surly Scot feels up to par again."

"Who the what-what from where?"

"Fukazake Shiro, the Tetsu Samurai. I'll introduce you." She pressed a pin on her lab coat collar. "Shiro, please come to Secret Lab Omega in Sub-Basement 7. Thank you."

"I'm still lost."

"I just put in an application at the International Dwarf Warrior Corps for a transfer. They tried to push Jacques LeWimpe, the Frilly Frenchman, on me but we can't use one of those cheese eatin' pushovers in our city."

At that moment, a wall exploded with a thunderous "BONZAIAIAIAIA-IAI!!!" as steel slashes flashed from an iron-blue dervish that towered to waist height. The Tiny Typhoon came to a halt in front of them, a mighty samurai warrior—or a scale model of one—stood before them.

"Atomik Lad, meet—"

"*FUKAZAKEEE SHIROOO!!!*" the small samurai vein poppingly yelled from his authentic looking suit of iron samurai armor complete with a really mean looking mask. He removed it, revealing a relatively light, friendly face made all the more friendly by his overly expressional eyes and big happy mouth.

Atomik Lad held out his hand as Shiro gave a quick bow of respect. "Er, right" the sidekick awkwardly mimicked the greeting.

Shiro turned to Genius and bowed to her as well. "Arigato for invited me to battle dragons of evil beings at your American town with my SUPAAA ACTION BATTLER ATTACKU PAWAAA!!!" Shiro struck a few minor poses, sheathed his sword, and bowed again.

Atomik Lad rubbed his ears. "Does he have to keep yelling so much?"

Shiro shot straight up, his little samurai armor rattling slightly with the quick movement. "This I focus my SUPAA ACTION BATTLER SPIRITO ENERGY ATTACKU PAWAAAA!!!"

"Right," Atomik Lad said. He turned to Dr. Genius. "Um, can we begin my tests now? Please?"

"Just as soon as I finish with Nuklear Man here. Shiro?"

"HAI!"

"Why not take Atomik Lad to visit Angus for a bit?"

"No really, that's fine. I don't mind watching Nuke there. In fact, it's probably better, you know. For me to be more personally aware of his limits."

"TOUR GAIDOOOO POWAAA!!!" Shiro snatched Atomik Lad's hand and dragged him out of the room through the entrance he just improvised. Atomik Lad jostled and bounced as Shiro dragged him along. The dwarf's legs moved so quickly they were nothing more than a blur propelling Shiro and his cargo through corridors and a few obtrusive walls.

From his angle, Atomik Lad noticed something new about Shiro. The Tiny Typhoon had an oversized red firecracker looking rocket strapped to his back. *No good can come of this*, he thought to himself.

They skid to a halt. Atomik Lad lay on the cool tiled floor. He could feel the bruises sink in. "Ugh."

"Razy American Hero! Stand and delivaa to witness many amazing sights at this time super fun is now for us!"

Atomik Lad sat up. "What?"

"Here is your hero supaa action peer, Angus-san."

The sidekick turned and there, in a Scientific: Observation Chamber not unlike the one Nuklear Man was being tested in, was Angus. A monitor above the panoramic Negaflux protected Scientific: Observation Window displayed Angus's brain waves, heart rate, and KI field spikes. Each digital line was barely active as Angus lay against the far wall vacantly staring at or through Atomik Lad. The Surly Scot's jaw was slack and his armor was indeed on backwards.

"Geez, what happened to him?" Atomik Lad asked aloud.

"Old Japanese regend say: When on the hunting Great Dragon, do not be use Great Dragoness Impression."

"Um," Atomik Lad answered.

Lookit 'em, comatose Angus thought. That fancy boy Atomik Laddie talkin' up a storm. 'Ooh, lookit me, Ah'm so tall, not like that Angus. Ye want ta know what we call 'em when he's not around? Shorty Short Short 'CUZ ANGUS IS BUT A WEE LADDIE! Ha!' But ye can't fool ol' Angus, ye too tall mutants! Ye make it so we wee folk can't walk through the doors o' society. Literally! Them blasted doorknobs is too damned high up! 'Lookit that wee laddie try to open the door, he couldn't reach that without an elevator—TOO BAD THE BLASTED ELEVATOR BUTTONS IS TOO DAMNED HIGH UP!!! Let's go put stuff on the top shelf before we go an' buy some more Nuklear Man T-shirts—XTRA LARGE ONES, AS MERE MORTAL

SIZED SHIRTS SIMPLY WILL NOT SUFFICE OUR ABNORMALLY HUGE FRAMES!!!'

"That's not very super fun big cell," Shiro observed.

"Yeah, it's pretty small," Atomik Lad agreed.

Lookit 'em talkin' abot me, sayin' how much taller that samurai is than me. Ah knew it! They used that whole giant crab laddie as an excuse to drive me insane so they could look for a taller replacement! Bunch o' backstabbin' haggis brained Frenchie cowards! Just standin' there gloatin'. Gloatin' and infectin' me brain with paranoid thoughts, but it won't work on me! Oh no, Ah'm on to their plans. First they deprave me of my whiskey to weaken my mind, and then they begin their mental conditioning to make me docile an' sober. And greatest crime of all, they use me own Battlesuit against me by welding it on backwards like soome kind o' Iron: Battle-Straight Jacket.

"Hopingfully, honorable Angus-san be will the cured on soon."

"Oh, I'm certain Angus's stay will be a short one."

SHORT?! Ah'll show 'em who's so short!!!

"Hm," Atomik Lad said, looking up at the monitor thingie. "Angus's vital signs are going all screwy."

Shiro stepped back and looked way up. "Hai. Perhaps maybe we call the doctoring?"

"What?"

"DWARF-A-PULT!!!" Angus erupted in a flurry of fury. His Iron: Bagpipe Thrusters flared to life and were accompanied by the sickening roar of a blue whale exploding. "YYYYYEEEEEEEEEARGHBLB—huh?" Unfortunately for Angus, since his Iron: Battlesuit was on backwards, the Iron Scotsman was propelled at Mach 1.3 through the back wall of his cell, a storage closet, a pocket dimension, back into our dimension, out a window, across town, and into a birdbath in the front yard of an ordinary looking house on Suburbia Street in the middle of the Panoptica Waterheight Viewshore Happydale Sunnyoaks Phase 3 planned community instead of his intended targets. Momentarily startled, the birds continued their baths among Angus's uselessly kicking legs and curse-born bubbles.

"Well, I guess we might as well get back to Dr. Genius," Atomik Lad said after a while.

Shiro lit up. "TOUR GAIDOOOO FUKAZAKE ON THE RESCUING PARTY—IS GO!!!"

"Oh no," Atomik Lad groaned as he felt his arm nearly get torn from his body.

*   *   *   *

"Aww, gee whiz, Doc. This is kids' stuff. When're you gonna turn the heat on already?" Nuklear Man complained.

She glanced up to him, then back to her instruments. "It's currently one million degrees Celsius in there."

"Feh. My grandmother could Celsius hotter than this."

"Your grandmother...? What? You're not making sense, perhaps as a result of the heat, though I wouldn't think you'd have any adverse reactions to such a relatively low temperature."

"Heat, shmeat. Crank up that bad boy, it's getting chilly in here."

"Nameless, increase the temperature by a factor of two."

"Doctor, are you—"

"Do it. We've got thirty-two safeties, each with three backup units. This test won't pose a danger to anyone."

"But Nuklear Man—"

"His KI Field has consistently adapted to the environment. To him, it's as comfortable in there as it is in here for us. It's astounding, even his clothes are unaffected. We have to push on. Kopelson Intrinsity is the thread of God's tapestry. We are so close to reweaving it in our own image."

Dr. Genius's console beeped. "Two million," she reported aloud while scanning Nuklear Man's raw KI data. "It's always better to just run the numbers through the KI equations in your head than rely on those three dimensional graphical representations," she scolded Technician as he recorded a few notes based on an ever changing 3D bar graph on his console.

"Easy for you to say," he responded.

"You lose context when you don't see the whole picture. It's like reading every fourth word in a book. You can get the general idea, but not the nuances, the true beauty."

"Not everyone can visualize a twelve dimensional figure in their head, Dr. Genius."

"The inhuman IQ does help with that bit, I must admit." She shook her head in amazement and mumbled, "No reaction whatsoever." She looked back up at Nuklear Man. "How is it in there?"

"Baby, you're twice as hot as this," he said with a wink, smile, and finger-gun snap.

"How does he *do* it?" she mused to herself. "We'll see about that, Nuklear Man. Nameless, four million."

"Yes Doctor," he replied.

Nuklear Man sighed. "Lousy reality not harsh enough to challenge Nukie, self-appointed Eternal Dictator for Life."

"Four million," she whispered to herself as her eyes absorbed the KI data streaming through her console. *How does he do it? I used to think KI was affected by the mind. Non-Supers have been effecting minor alterations in their fields and those of ordinary objects through intense concentration for centuries. Firewalkers, Buddhist mediators, and so on. But Nuklear Man performs incredible feats of KI manipulation without the slightest mental effort. It's not physical, it's not mental. What is it? I feel so close, like I can't see the answer because it's right in front of me. Maybe I should re-evaluate the parameters and approach from another vector.*

Shiro crashed back into the lab through the nearly N2-healed hole he'd made in the first place. Atomik Lad flopped to the floor and moaned painfully while wishing that he could do away with enough morals to let him use his Atomik Powers on Shiro in a way neither comfortable nor sanitary but undoubtedly fatal to the samurai. "We're back," he groaned.

"SUPAAA ACTION TOUR GAIDOOOO FUKAZAKEEE reporting is now!" Shiro announced with a separate pose for every word.

"Ooh, excellent form," the Hero of heroes commented before adding, "Er, for not me."

"Welcome back Shiro, Atomik Lad," Dr. Genius said without taking her attention from the KI data. "How was Angus?"

"Um, better. In a way," Atomik Lad answered while rubbing his neck.

"Eight million degrees," she muttered. "Nuklear Man, how is it in there?"

"Hm, kinda warm." She caught a slight waiver in the Hero's KI readings.

Atomik Lad looked over Ima's shoulder to examine the incomprehensible streams of data that flooded her screens with a constantly amorphous series of symbols and numbers. In fact, the only things that made any sense to him was the Scientific: Temperature Gauge and the large Scientific: Threat Level Display off to the left of the console. It consisted of three rectangular lights stacked on top of one another, green on the bottom, yellow in the middle and red on top. Currently, the green block was illuminated with the word "SAFE" alight in it.

Atomik Lad leaned back and noticed Ima's concentration. "Um, so how's it goin', Doc?"

"Close," she answered. "Very close."

"Uh, good." He knelt down to Shiro and whispered, "Close to what?"

The Tiny Typhoon shrugged. "I am don't the knowing."

Finally, his KI field is showing signs of losing its consistency. But why now, at the eight million range? His Plazma is almost identical to the energy given off by the sun and that reaches temperatures closer to twenty-seven million. He shouldn't suffer field degradation until at least the teens. A little further, that's all we'll need. It's right there in front of me, all I have to do is make the connections.

"Nine million degrees," she watched his field twitch and churn as the temperature rose.

"It's a bit uncomfortable in here, actually," the Hero reported.

"More," Dr. Genius ordered Technician.

Atomik Lad noticed the Scientific: Thermometer pass the ten million degree mark.

Look at it, Genius wondered, *creation dancing to the symphony of eternity, yet all form is nothingness.* "In the void there is no evil and only virtue."

"I could use a drink of water," Nuklear Man said while tugging at his collar.

The yellow light flared "WARNING."

"Um, Dr. Genius?" Atomik Lad prompted. "Maybe you should shut it down?"

"Not yet."

Eleven million. "Erk. I'm kinda woozy," Nuklear Man said, swaying slightly.

"Dr. Genius?"

Eleven million three hundred thousand degrees and Nuklear Man collapsed while a red "DANGER" light blinked.

"*Ima!*" Atomik Lad yelled with a shock of fear in his voice.

"Almost there," she said through a mask of intense focus.

The temperature continued to increase as Nuklear Man's KI readings became more erratic. Nuklear Man's face twisted in pain as he lay on the Negaflux shielded floor. "Oh. Darn it, this hurts."

"Ima. Let him go," Atomik Lad insisted.

"Not yet," she whispered to herself.

"Argh! Heat nearly...as strong...as me..." the Hero said, his mega-ego unable to relent to the unrelenting reality around him.

"Ima, you're killing him!"

"He's fine," she said nonchalantly as the temperature passed twelve million.

Atomik Lad clenched his fists, "Let him go," he said with an even calmness. Shiro swore he could feel a light breeze whisk through the lab.

"Soon."

"I said, *let him go!*" A gale of wind gust through the lab, tossing Shiro head first into a wall and Nameless across the room as Ima desperately held onto her console to keep from facing a similar fate. Her lab coat made her struggle all the more difficult, but she held firm. She beheld Atomik Lad with nearly as much awe as she had Nuklear Man's results. There he stood, his Atomik Field blazing angrily just like his eyes. *His eyes, fierce, just like the Field. If a KI field contains infinite information about its host, then it should reflect the most minute details of that host. Atomik Lad's field is inextricably linked to his emotional state—just as his KI field is. They're the same. Somehow his KI has broken the Metathreshold. His KI field has been realized in our universe. Of course! That is the source of its power! Twelve dimensions packed into our four. His own fears, that explains its tumultuous Realization with all the jagged edges. It tears at realty because it can barely confine itself to our realm of existence, it protects its host because it is an extension of him—no, literally he himself. It is his identity, this is why it falters and lashes out and gains strength from the intensity of his emotions, a physical representation of his own latent angst! If this is true, he is the key, not Nuklear Man. Atomik Lad holds the answers, Nuklear Man is merely the catalyst, a bundle of clues, a guinea pig, he's—*

"—*dying!*" the sidekick screamed hysterically. "You're killing him! Stop it!" His Atomik Field flared and roiled around his body like razor bladed crimson fire. He rushed the Scientific: Observation Chamber. The Negaflux Field repelled him but he pushed on.

Ima watched. *He's bending the Negaflux field through sheer force of will. Bbut that's impossible, it negates and redirects any force applied against it.* She finally took a breath as Atomik Lad had managed to push the Negaflux field into Nuklear Man's little super-heated room. *Impossible, but that's not stopping him.* Her mind snapped to more immediate concerns. *If he pierces the Negaflux, it'll release all that plasma, it'll be like setting off a nuclear warhead in here, destroying a good portion of the city, killing millions, and I'll never finish my work.*

"John!" she screamed above the booming static-like crackles coming from the Negaflux and Atomik Fields rejecting one another. "Stop!" She shut down the Heatomatic and ejected Nuklear Man from the Scientific: Observation Room into the room below.

Atomik Lad touched down, his field dispersed but his anger did not. He stormed up to Ima, "What the hell were you doing?!"

She straightened her hair, glasses, and lab coat while answering. "Atomik Lad, your concern for Nuklear Man is admirable, but I can assure you that he was in no harm. I had meticulously set up dozens of failsafes to insure his safety. I am a doctor after all."

"But…"

"I know he appeared to be in pain, but he was never in any real danger."

"Where is he now?"

"Ejected into the cold room below. He should be cooled off now."

"Then what were all those warning lights about?"

"Oh, the equipment. We were pushing everything to its limit at the end there." She glanced at her console. "If we extend our findings here this morning, assuming that the Curve of Degradation continues along the same exponential rate until oblivion, Nuklear Man couldn't possibly survive an environment over thirteen million degrees Celsius. Of course, he's still effectively invulnerable since only stars and other fusion reactions are that hot and I don't know of any villains with access to nuclear missiles or the sun's core."

"But that doesn't make sense. He got his powers *from* a nuclear meltdown, like a hydrogen bomb. Those are closer to a hundred million degrees, why would only thirteen million kill him?"

Dr. Genius looked at the ceiling and thought for a moment. "Well, in nature, certain seeds need fire in order to be properly fertilized and grow. But that same fire would kill the adult tree. So, like them, the very nuclear fires that gave birth to Nuklear Man, could just as easily bring about his demise."

"I guess that makes sense." Atomik Lad cleared his throat. "I'm sorry for, um. For flying off the handle like that."

"Don't worry, John. I should have kept you better informed about the test. Speaking of which, I think its time you made your way to the next Scientific: Observation Chamber."

"Right." Atomik Lad left the room on his way to his own testing facility.

Shiro walked in dizzy circles after the sidekick.

Nameless Technician approached Ima. "That's enough excitement for at least the next week as far as I'm concerned."

"This is science, m'boy. This is adventure!"

Nameless smiled. "What'll we do with all that heat we've still got in the Scientific: Observation Chamber here?"

"Hm, sell it to the city power grid."

*   *   *   *

Meanwhile, in the—272 degrees Celsius room, Nuklear Man shivered. "It's frickin' freezing in here. Stupid thermodynamics, slowin' down my atomic oscillation. I'll show you!" He snatched a random molecule out of the air and squeezed it between his thumb and pointer finger with all his Nuklear Might. Within a matter of seconds, he could see a glow emanating from between his digits, "C'mon you little lousy so and so, Nukie needs a new pair of shoes!" And then a massive fission chain reaction was set off, vaporizing ten square miles of downtown Metroville.

Is what would have happened if Nuklear Man hadn't simply absorbed most of the blast which was not quite hot enough to bring harm to him. Yay. The end effect was that the Cold Room was now quite comfortable. See: "Ahhhhh," the Hero basked all comfy. "Eh, guess I better find Sparky before he jinxes my chances with Ima by blundering around like some kind of blunderer...er."

*   *   *   *

Minutes later, Atomik Lad found himself standing alone in one of the Scientific: Observation Chambers while Dr. Genius, a bored Nuklear Man, and a still dizzy Shiro were looking at him through its Negaflux window. "So explain this to me," the sidekick requested.

"Again?" Dr. Genius asked, flicking a glance at him over her thin glasses.

"In English this time?"

"Ah. Well, basically, when you had that outbreak during Nuklear Man's test, it occurred to me what your Atomik Field could be. That's what this test will help determine."

He scratched his nose. "Yes and no. Especially the no."

"Based on your Field's history, especially it's close affiliation with your emotional state, I believe it may actually be your KI field."

"Interesting."

"That's why I could never detect any important changes in your own KI when your powers were activated, it *is* your KI, it's always there. And when it's completely manifested into our own world, nothing can get past it that you don't allow. It's essentially your very soul."

"Sounds better than the old 'no idea' explanation I used to get. And I guess that makes sense. But that still doesn't tell me why you've got me in here."

"KI detection gets the best results when there's multiple interactions with other KI fields." Smoke began filling Atomik Lad's room through the ventilation shafts. "And that's why we have to introduce billions of these alien particles into your environment."

Atomik Lad coughed. "But if everything has a KI field, then why can't you just use the normal air particles and stuff floating around in here?"

The lights over him turned off. "Because when I turn on the KI scanning laser, the smoke'll make it look really cool. Now turn on your field."

"Righto." In front of the young hero, a wide dispersal laser-light began sweeping across him and Ima was right, for it was a very cool effect indeed. "I see."

Ima scanned the results. "What's the verdict, Doc?" Atomik Lad asked while waving smoke from his face.

"Seems I was partially wrong," she said. "Your Atomik Field is in fact *a* KI field fully realized in our own universe, but I'm not sure if its yours. Most of the information seems identical, but its arranged differently."

"Kinda like those protons you mentioned before?"

"Somewhat, yes. The thing is, they do share one identical pattern though, which I've never seen before."

"What, sharing patterns or the shared pattern itself?"

"Both. I'm not sure what to make of that. It's an unmapped sequence, so I don't know what it corresponds to. It'll require more testing."

"I wonder how I could be more bored," Nuklear Man huffed. "Oh wait, I've already reached the Point of Maximum Boredom in Boringtown, the capital city of Boringania, the largest country on the Boredoma continent on planet Boringia IV while being crowned King Bored during the National Boring Day Parade of Boredom."

"Ugh. Guess we're done here, Doc."

"Not quite yet. Don't you boys want your treat?"

Atomik Lad clawed at his face. "How did that moron get the Treaty Clause appended to the Hero Act?"

"Yay!" Nuklear Man exclaimed as he shot through the corridors of Überdyne heading toward the cafeteria. "Pie!"

"Pie?" Shiro's queasy coloring dissolved, replaced by the happy killer samurai warrior visage he normally wore. He struck a match against the floor and brought the flame to the tip of a fuse that stuck out from the rocket strapped to his back.

"ROCKETOO TIIIIME!!!" he screamed with all the force his little lungs could produce. In a flash, the giant firecracker took off. A trail of smoke spiraled after him. Atomik Lad put his hands over his ears a second before Shiro's method of propulsion came to an explosive end that displayed the Rising Sun in all its glory.

*   *   *   *

Meanwhile, in the suburbs outside Metroville, a lovely young lass opened her front door a crack and peaked into the too bright morning light with one suspicious eye. Her cold gaze froze on the particularly absurd image of two tiny legs sticking out of her birdbath. She sighed and shut the door. She undid the chain lock, opened the door all the way, and flowed into the morning air, her fine black hair wafting like an aroma behind her slender black bodysuit clad figure. She held a letter addressed to "Nuklear Boob, c/o Nuklear Man, 1 Irradiated Road" in one hand and a clipboard in the other. Her lithe steps took her to the mailbox where she deposited the envelope. She examined her clipboard and put a check next to the "Step One: Mail Evil: Letter via Super Speedy Same Day Delivery," printed in large black letters across the center. She turned around and floated back to her front door, stopping first at the birdbath. "Are we having a *little* trouble?" she asked it.

The legs quaked and the birdbath exploded which caused Angus to land on his head which caused him to quake even more which caused him to fall over which produced further anger which caused him to leap to attention. "AUGHK!" he responded ferociously.

"Why don't you buzz off, you mini-hero."

"That wasna a goood idea, lassie. Now ye made me angry!"

"I fear for my anklez."

"That does it!" he roared. "DWARF-A-PULT!!!"

"Why are you wearing bagpipes on your stomach?"

"YYYYYYYEEEEEEEARGHBLBLB—nuts." Angus disappeared somewhere over the Pub District of Metroville.

She rubbed her hands together maniacally. "Oh, my dear Atomik Lad and Nuklear Oaf, how you shall rue the day you crossed Dr. Menace!" She burst into a brief fit of evil laughter before composing herself. "You shall be destroyed thanks to my incredible intelligence. And the poztal service. But moztly my incredible intelligence!"

Issue 31—The Terrible
Secret of Rachel

From the Personal Notes of Dr. Ima Genius

Today's results were puzzling if nothing else. I feel that these sessions leave me with more questions and no answers, but that's science for you. For all we know, we may have the answer right in front of us, we just haven't stumbled upon the correct question yet.

It seems my hypothesis that Nuklear Man can somehow rewrite his own KI Field in order to meet the demands put upon him is valid. During last month's Strongometer test, his Intrinsity Sequences for strength continually increased to match the efforts of our incredibly expensive giant arm wrestling machine. That is, until he surpassed it and tossed the entire device through the window and into a back alley. This morning's Heatometer tests gave us similar results. The ease and immediate nature of his KI alterations, not to mention the range to which they extend, are nothing short of miraculous. And when we consider that he has no idea he's doing it is astonishing! It's almost as if his field is somehow sentient and acts on his behalf, but that notion is absurd. If only it were possible to learn about his physiology through conventional means, it would make this so much easier. But due to his invincible nature and electromagnetic metabolism, ordinary medical procedures are wasted on him. We could cross reference KI results with genetic samples, run simulations in the Überdyne 4000 series computers, compare them to the other heroes…I mustn't waste my time wishing for things to be easier. I have to forge ahead with this Intrinsity Theory. It is only in its infancy.

It seems as though I may have finally found a measurable limit to at least one of Nuklear Man's powers. His field showed a state of decay at eight million degrees Celsius. The interference increased at a linear rate, as is typical of any KI change, however at approximately eleven million degrees, the rate of field instability became exponential. The experiment had to be shut down immediately. As unprecedented as this was, I could not afford the risks of pushing any further. I may have gone too far as it was. Ah, ludicrous science is such a fine line between brilliance and murder. There has never been an exponential rate of change in any KI experiment until this morning. I can only begin to speculate the reasons and implications for this event. Was it due to Nuklear Man's innate ability to freely rewrite his own KI? Was it the extreme environment we were dealing with—millions of degrees is on a cosmic scale, no human was ever meant to tolerate that much punishment, perhaps it triggered some latent effect. Was it something else? Some unknown, unaccounted, or ignored factor in the experiment? Why exponential? Why at eight million? Shouldn't it have been much higher since Nuklear Man's Plazma energy is 98.6% identical to highly concentrated sunlight? Questions, questions, questions…

As if I didn't have enough of these impeneratrable questions, there was Atomik Lad's session. I finally determined why his KI doesn't change when he uses his Atomik Powers: the Atomik Field is a KI field itself, but not John's as I had first guessed. It exists completely independent of his own. But the most promising result was what I found between the two: both the Atomik Field and John's KI field share a sequence match. The exact pattern in the exact coding region. I am trying not to jump to conclusions, but I believe this may be a very definite first step in unlocking the Golden Pattern. We've never found an exact match before, only similar patterns in nearby regions. Like the differences between two random humans and a pair of twins. The former couple will be roughly the same in a general sense whereas the latter are identical to one another. For example, though the KI fields of any two oranges will share many similarities, and even a few identical sequences, none of the information, similar or same, is in the same place in the two fields. Intrinsically speaking, each orange is a little different. Perhaps this is what keeps all oranges—and indeed everything—separate entities, their slightly yet distinctly different KI fields. A shared sequence. Another first with no clues as to where to go next. Typical. In the meantime, we're running the Atomik Sequence through our computers to find any matches with existing KI readings to see what sort of connections we can make, if any. Questions, questions, questions.

✳   ✳   ✳   ✳

"Are you sure you can drive, Shiro?" Atomik Lad asked. "You took a pretty big hit in the head back there."

Shiro gave a happy little V-sign with his fingers. "Fukazake is supaa ready for driving action at now!"

"Ahem," the sidekick cleared his throat. "I'm over here."

Shiro spun around. "Hai, joked time is then. For now is the serious."

Nuklear Man looked down. "You talk funny."

Atomik Lad grabbed Shiro by the arm and turned him around. "When I said I was over here, I meant right *here*. You know, where I am."

Shiro thought it over. "Going I now for car and so be heavy with speed."

"What?" Atomik Lad said while Tiny Typhoon scampered off to fetch his vehicle.

"Wait a second," Nuklear Man said. "He's driving?"

"There's that dazzling intellect."

"But he's just a kid! No regular person could be that short unless he were some super deformed mutant, and we've got pogroms to keep freaks like that out of our pure society."

"Where do you get these ideas?"

"I mostly piece them together from zealous right wing extremist pamphlets."

A sporty little car zipped through the lanes of parked cars and headed for the heroes. "We'll talk about this later," Atomik Lad said. "That must be Shiro."

"How can you tell? All those Japanese cars look the same."

Atomik Lad slapped him in the back of the head. "Could you stop saying stupid things for, like, ten seconds?"

The car skid to a halt in front of them and Shiro poked his head out the window. "Now we go or time will explode our heads like watermelon balloons full of lateness!"

Nuklear Man leaned over. "Pssst, Sparky. He's gone insane."

"Which still makes him a better driver than you. Let's go."

The trio bounced along Metroville's streets when Atomik Lad noticed a certain deficiency in one of Shiro's gauges. "Shiro, you might want to gas up. It's about a forty minute round trip out to the Silo once you get out of the city traffic and there's no gas stations along the way. I think the radiation has something to do with it."

"Not worry. Prithee, Samurai-car-vehicle use supaa fuel!"

"Oh?"

"SUPAA THERMODYNAMICU RICE FURNACE!"

"The car runs on rice?"

"Samurai-car-vehicre efficiency is, like bone slicing katana blade bloodgushing no more walk!"

"So," Nuklear Man began slowly. "What you're saying is that this car is a rice burn—"

"We *got* it, Nuke."

"Aww, c'mon. It's been *way* more than ten seconds!"

"Erg."

The trip was a fairly uneventful one, if one ignored Shiro's habit of driving on the wrong side of the road. With the Heroic Duo delivered unto their subterranean dwelling, the Tiny Typhoon drove off singing his Sake Song which went a little something like this: "Ohhhhhh, sake, sake, sake, sake, sake! Ohhhhhh, sake, sake, sake, sake, sake!" And so on.

*   *   *   *

Nuklear Man stretched his titanic arms and let out a sigh. "Ah, we've got the whole day ahead of us, Sparky. The spring air is in the um, the air." He took in a deep breath. "Well, that's enough of that. Time for seventeen straight hours of

Silly Sam's Cartoon Marathon-a-Thon o' Fun." Nuklear Man promptly flew to his Danger: Couch and became as close to comatose as a waking man could be.

"Whereas I shall make a phone call."

*　　*　　*　　*

"Hello?" the groggy yet somehow still sexy voice of Rachel mumbled into Atomik Lad's ear thanks to the miracle of telephonology.

"Um, did I wake you?"

Her answer, quite simply, was…

"Ahem. Rachel?"

"Hello?" she mumbled anew.

"You awake?"

"Hard to say. Let me sleep on it and I'll get back to you on that one."

"C'mon, it's practically eleven in the morning. Time for wakey."

"Just ten more minutes."

"I can be there in seven."

She stretched and rolled around with a slight yawn. "Promise?"

"Oh yeah," though he was answering her little stretching noises and not her question.

"Well then, I'll be expecting you. Remember, it's not polite to keep a lady waiting." And she hung up.

Atomik Lad dashed from his Danger: Katkat's Room to the Danger: Launch Pad. "Nuke, I'm goin' out for a bit. Try not to do anything stu—let's just shorten this exchange and say that you should try not to do anything."

Nuklear Man was sprawled across the Danger: Couch like a casually tossed corpse with Katkat imitating the same posture across his tummy. He took a brief account of his surroundings. "Thaaaaat shouldn't be a problem."

"Good."

"Though I can't guarantee you that I won't be damn sexy. I just can't help doing that."

"Uh, sure. You bet." And he took off.

Nuklear Man tried to give his belly a slight scratch, but was thwarted in his efforts by the nefarious cute machinations of Katkat who had cleverly positioned himself such that his was the belly which would receive the scratches. "Curse your cunning hide!" Nuklear Man spat whilst scratching away.

"Mreowr?"

"Naw, I take it back."

"Meow!"

*   *   *   *

Nearly seven minutes later, Atomik Lad was at the front door of Wayne Hall. "Oh, I'm good," he told himself in a strangely Nukie kinda way while picking up the phone on the dorm's outer wall. It disturbed him. He put it out of his mind and dialed Rachel's room.

"Hello?" He noticed her voice had a certain vexed quality to it this time.

"Er. Hiya, what's shakin'?"

"Ooh, good timing Sparky," Her voice trailed off with preoccupation. "Hey, would you mind floating up to my window to come in? I'm a little busy right now."

"Well, I really don't like using my powers on campus. It makes me feel weird, like I'm cheating or something."

"It'll only take two seconds. Come on, I woke up early for you."

"Eleven in the morning really isn't early."

"Maybe not to Mr. Buttcrack of Dawn Heroman it's not, but some of us like to get our beauty rest."

"Beauty rest? What, you can just charge that stuff up by sleeping?"

"Yup. It's an old family secret."

"So you were in a Beauty Coma for the nineteen years before I met you? That *does* explain the goddess-like glow."

"How can I resist sweet talkin' like that?"

"You can't. It's futile."

"You got me. I'll be down in a few."

*   *   *   *

"You seemed kinda pissed on the phone there," Atomik Lad said as they walked down the hall back to Rachel's room. "Something bothering you?"

She gave a deep breath as she approached her door. "Yeah.," she said and opened the door.

Atomik Lad stepped inside, took one look around, and his mouth dropped wide open. "You're, you're…"

"Addicted to video games, I know," she admitted. She sat down and unpaused the screen. "The last couple of guys before the boss on this one are such cheaters. It aggravates me."

"You're, you're, you're..."

"You must think I'm some kinda dork, right?"

"Well, I was going to say perfect, but whatever."

"Yeah, right."

He watched her play for a few seconds. "Hey, is that Samurai Swordplay IV?"

"Yup. Me and my thirteen hit combo are going places. Namely, the final boss. We can get going once I finish him off."

He ogled her...video game collection. "We can stay. I don't mind. Really."

"You don't mind watching?"

"I'd rather play, if you don't mind."

"Not at all. You like video games?"

Meanwhile, in Sparky's Danger: Katkat's Room, one of the more precarious stacks of video games collapsed onto the Danger: Floor.

"Ahem," he answered, "You could say that."

"I'm surprised you're into stuff like this. Saving video game worlds must seem pretty lame when you do it in the real world every day."

"Well, I didn't have many friends growing up. Living in the middle of a radio-active wasteland with a madman tends to have a negative impact on your opportunities for social interaction."

*   *   *   *

"Bah!" Nuklear Man cursed. "Stupid TV, why you show me commercials? I bash you now." He stretched out his arm, fidgeted a little, grunted a tad, and gave up. "Lousy spatial coordinates always keepin' me from doing something rash that I'd no doubt later regret and frame Sparky for." He scratched the still exposed belly of Katkat while the witless plea for mindless consumerism played itself out on the Danger: TV. "Finally," the Hero said with an annoyed huff. "Now we can get back to, hey, what the—that's not cartoons! It's another one of those blasted commercials! Oh mighty Odin, I beseech you! Banish yon commercials from mine sight! Do not hurl me to eternal torment be-next to the arch-deceiver, Loki! I swear it was Sparky's idea, whatever it was you're punishing me for. I tried to talk him out of it like a good father figure would. It's just like that conniving little back stabber to frame me for a crime against the gods, curse his treacherous hide!"

*   *   *   *

Back at Rachel's dorm, Atomik Lad was just about to lay the smack down when—"WA*CHOO!*" his thumbs fumbled all over the gamepad for a moment, allowing Rachel just enough time to recover from the previous devastating series of hits and retaliate with enough force to defeat him.

*   *   *   *

"Argh! Another commercial. That's it. I'm, um. I'm going to Do Something!" *Real smooth, tough guy. What'cha gonna do?* "Shaddup, taunting brain. I'm think-ing." *Is that what we're calling it? My, they don't think like they used to, do they?* "Shush!" *Oh fine. Ya big baby.* Nuklear Man thought. His immediately bored eyes wandered to a Danger: Clock. "Ah ha! The mail's come by now. I'll answer all my fan mail to pass the time. Well, not all of it, obviously. There isn't enough time in the universe for that. No, the amount of fan mail I could answer, even taking into account my Nuklear Intelligence and Speed, could only be expressed as a percentage of the whole. Say, three percent. Oh, my worshipers, how they adore me."

*   *   *   *

"That's three of five, Sparky. I win." She smiled deviously.

"Hmmphf. I still say we should rematch that third bout."

"It's not my fault you don't have enough ninja concentration and willpower to resist a simple sneeze, darlin'."

"That was no ordinary sneeze. It screwed up all my timing and everything. I just had to hit one button and you would've been samurai sushi."

"Oh fine. One last match for the championship. Winner takes all."

"Takes all what?" Atomik Lad countered.

"What do you mean?"

"Let's make it interesting," he suggested.

"Strip video gaming?" she suggested back.

"…" Goofy grin.

"Ahem. Sparky?"

"Who, what, where?"

"Right. What did you have in mind?"

"Just now?"

She smiled. "Silly boy."

"Oh, gotcha. Well, if you win, I take you to a movie."

"Okay, that sounds good to me. And if you win?"

"*When* I win, you kiss me."

"You're on, chump. I mean Champ."

＊　　　＊　　　＊　　　＊

Nuklear Man was awe struck by the sheer girth of the mailbag. "Oh, *mama*." He rolled the bloated sack of mail toward the Danger: Main Doors. "Hmm" he noticed a small address sticker stuck to the side. "Atomik Lad?! What's that jerk ever done for anyone, why I oughta, uh, make sure there aren't any mailbombs in here. Otherwise, he could get badly hurt. Because he's weak and insignificant. Whereas I am not." He tore the bag open and nearly crushed himself to death by way of Sparky Fan Mail Avalanche.

＊　　　＊　　　＊　　　＊

"Mmm, I love the smell of buttered popcorn," Rachel beamed. "It smells like victory!"

"Grumble, curse, defame, libel," Atomik Lad muttered as they sidled along a row of theater seats near the back.

"Someone a little miffed that he lost?"

"No, no. No, I *could've* won if I were a heartless, callous, vindictive, lying, cheating back stabber. But I choose the moral high ground, unlike *other* people I know. And I'm better for it."

"The Double Spinning Ninja Back Breaker Knee Thrust is a perfectly legal move!"

"Not if that's *all you do*!"

"I did lots of other moves. It's not my fault if you can't block it because I've perfected the move to such a degree that I can pull it off at the drop of a hat."

"Musta been playing in a damn hat factory," he mumbled.

They sat down in nearly the middle of the row. "Oh, it's just a game," she countered.

"Well, mostly I'm upset that I didn't get that kiss."

She smiled. "I could fix that."

*   *   *   *

"Ohhhhhhh, now I've got it. It's so blindingly obvious, duh. All these letters to Sparky must be hate mail!" the Hero rationalized. "I better tear one open to check." And so he did. "Ahem. 'Dear Atomik Lad, Will you marry us? Sincerely, the Metroville High Senior Varsity Cheerleading Squad.' Great Baldur's Ghost! These poor girls are completely insane, they spelled Nuklear Man 'A-T-O-M-I-K-L-A-D!'" He picked up another. "This one's bound to be hate mail. Let's see, it's from the Atomik Lad Fan Club Local 239. 'Dear Atomik Lad, We think you're Sparkilcious. Will you marry us? Sincerely, Three Score Blondes and Brunettes, ages 19 to 23.' GADZOOKS! This mail system is a breeding ground for utter madness!" Yet another letter torn open, "'Dear Atomiku Lad. Will you please marrying us? Sincerely, the All-Girl Saigon Gymnastics Club.'"

Nuklear Man's eyes darted back and forth. He restuffed the mammoth mail-bag and stuck a Danger: Return to Sender sticker on it in a golden blur of action. He gazed up at the looming structure of mail before him. "There must've been a mistake. A terrible, terrible mistake. On a cosmic level. It's a good thing I'm such a selfless Hero who acts for the good of all living creatures, otherwise this morbid error would have gone unfixed." He smiled a Happy Nukie smile of glee and opened the mailbox proper. "Ooh, five letters. Let's see here, Katkat," flip "Kat-kat" flip "Katkat?!? How'd he get fan mail?! He's just a lousy, stinkin', no good little ball of the most adorable fur anyone's ever seen. Hm, guess that explains that." Flip—"SQUEAL! A letter for me! Nya-ha. I got fan mail and all Sparky got was a bunch of psycho rants. Heh, loser. Now then, 'Dear Nuklear Man,' oh baby, she's in love with me, 'I know Atomik Lad must get a ton of fan mail and he probably doesn't have time to read it all since he's so busy saving the world and everything. Since you're not doing anything, could you make sure he gets the enclosed marriage proposal? Thanking you in advance, the Girls of Summer Swimsuit Calendar Model Team.'" The enclosed marriage proposal in question had little hearts and the phrase "Let's make a baker's dozen," scribbled across it.

The Hero wept. He dropped the letters to the ground. Nuklear Man, who had battled foes across the world, who had defended the entire globe from cata-strophic events of all manner, had been utterly defeated by the U.S. postal ser-vice. Somehow, he managed to scrounge enough willpower to crawl to the final piece of mail. His trembling fingers opened the blue envelope and slid its con-tents into the light of day. His eyes scanned across the lines. There was joy. "A fan letter, at last! And it's from a law office at that. How prestigious!" He hugged it tight. "I can't wait to brag—er—tell Sparky about it. Poor fellah didn't even get a single letter," he shook his head despondently. "Must be a terrible blow to the ol' ego, not that I'd know of course."

ISSUE 32—ARE YOU EXPERIENCED?

Rachel munched on her overpriced popcorn while trying her darnedest to ignore the utter crapfest of cheesy pre-preview advertisements on the wide screen. "Tell me something about yourself."

Atomik Lad swished a mouthful of Dr. Zap and swallowed. "I don't trust twist ties. Your turn."

"Oh no you don't."

"What?"

"You're not getting out of it that easily. Tell me something personal."

"That is personal. It's a very deep mistrust of twist ties. You try to untie them one way, but then it looks like you're actually tying it up more, so you start twisting it the other way, but you actually had it right the first time. It happens to me every time, no matter what. I feel closer to you now that I've shared this burden."

She gave him The Look.

"Well I do."

"Hmmphf. Okay, Mr. Sparkypants. I see how you play this game. Tell me…" she thought for a moment. "Tell me about the last time you cried."

"When you beat me at Samurai Swordplay."

"Ha. Ha. I'm serious."

"Okay, Okay. Um, well, it was a long time ago. Years."

"You're stalling."

"Just hold your horses. Nuke and I had been together for, I don't know, two or three years. My name was still Sparky then." He paused for a second and thought. "Heh, of course it was."

"What do you mean it was still Sparky?"

"Oh, that was my original name when Nuke and I first teamed up. He took one look at my Field and called me Sparky. It stuck."

"And he still calls you that. That's so sweet."

"It's something all right."

"You don't like it?"

"I don't mind when you, or Norman, or whoever says it. But with Nuke, it's like he's trying to keep me that same little kid he ran into at Überdyne that he has to protect and train. Like he won't even acknowledge that I've grown up."

"I'm sorry."

"Or maybe he's simply forgotten about renaming me Atomik Lad. I'm surprised he knows who I am half the time since I don't wear a label."

She laughed. "Okay, so why'd he rename you Atomik Lad then?"

"That's actually the same story." What a coinkydink! But it sure makes things easier for me to write.

"Do tell."

"Well, like I said, Nuke and I had been Heroing for about three years by then, so I must've been around eleven years old."

"You haven't cried in eight years?"

"I'm from the Bottle it up into a Single Point of Seething Turmoil and Bitterness School of emotion."

"Fun."

"It's my line of work. We can't let our emotions clog our thinking and get in the way of saving the city."

"Yeah, but doesn't that turn you into an emotional powder keg that'll explode under the right circumstances?"

He thought back to the morning's session with Dr. Genius. "Er, it's a possibility. You wanna hear the story or not?"

"Fine, fine."

"Okay. There was some sort of disturbance out at the Überdyne building and we were called in. A golden age villain, Dr. Never had somehow traveled through time to meet his arch-nemesis, Dr. Velocity who had disappeared back in the '20s or something but she popped up at Überdyne in the present. Anyway, Dr. Never had developed this weapon that could…"

"...send a target through the time stream thanks to my Hyper-Quantum Accelerator Drive!" the Temporal Tyrant announced while brandishing a hand gun attached by a hose to a metallic backpack labeled Nefarious: Hyper Quantum Accelerator Drive. Both the pack and gun had a sort of art deco appeal.

"You're mad, Never!" Dr. Velocity retorted from the entrance to the Überdyne Complex.

"You've never seen me mad!" he shot back. "Upset, irked, vexed, these you've seen. But mad, I think not."

"And just what do you plan on doing with that Time Cannon of yours?"

"What? Weren't you listening to my exposition? How'd you ever get your degree in Faster Than Thought Travel with an attention span like that? You *know* how I hate repeating myself. I think you're just doing this on purpose as some sort of stall tactic."

A mightiful "HA-HO!!!" echoed through the streets of Metroville's High Science District.

Dr. Never clawed his face. "Ooh! It *was* just a stall tactic. I knew it!"

Dr. Velocity stuck out her tongue. "Nya ha."

"Dirty cheater," he muttered.

Nuklear Man landed in the lovely park in front of the Überdyne building. Then he crawled out of it. A small boy surrounded in a crimson splotch of energy landed far more gracefully beside him. The lashing field disappeared and both newcomers posed with their fists on their hips. "Okay, villain guy," Nuklear Man began. "You wanna make it easy on yourself, or do we hafta rough ya up?"

"This is what passes for a heroic quip nowadays?" Dr. Never asked his contemporary. "I remember the days when the language was an entire field all its own. You couldn't say two sentences without a pun, or a play on words, or juxtaposition between the current situation at hand and modern world events, and probably a mythological reference to boot. 'Ha-ho'? 'Rough ya up'? What has happened to quality?"

"Er," Nuklear Man answered.

"I think he's makin' fun of you, Nukie," young Sparky observed.

"Hm, how so?" the Hero asked.

Dr. Never shook with anger. "You baboon! I'm saying that you're an idiot! A twit! A nimrod! A clown! A moron!"

Nuklear Man gave a dramatic pointing pose. "Moron like a *fox*! Ha!"

Sparky shook his head.

Dr. Never quaked. "This! This is what you stalled for? *This*? I tell you I'm going to send the Überdyne building and everyone in it thirteen *trillion* years into the future at the exact moment of the end of the universe, so you send for help, which is perfectly understandable given the nature of our relationship and my intents here today, and this is it. *This*."

Nuke posed and smiled proudly.

"This oaf is supposed to stop me. It's insulting, that's what it is. Down right insulting."

"Psst, Sparky. Has he given up yet?"

"I don't think so."

"Of course I haven't given up! Clod!"

Sparky tugged on his mentor's cape. Nuklear Man leaned down to receive some quick advice from the sidekick. "Ah ha," Nuklear Man stood proud and tall. "Ahem. I'm rubber, you're glue. Everything you say bounces off me and *Plazma Beam*!"

Sparky shook his head again.

"What was that?" Dr. Never, flabbergasted by stupidity, asked.

Another tug by Sparky. "You were supposed to *do* a Plazma Beam, not just say it."

The Hero stood again and rubbed his chin in thought. "Ohhhhh, Plaz*ma* Beam. Got it." He adopted a dramatic pose to gather his energies while his hands glowed with Plazma. "Never, you're Nuked."

"I've had enough of this," the villain said. "Begone." He casually aimed the Time Cannon at Nuklear Man and fired. The Hero disappeared into an implosion of whiteness. "Now then, unless all of you would like a similar foolproof death, I suggest signing over rulership of the world to me in one hour," Dr. Never said.

Sparky tore his gaze from the little smoking scorched spot of earth where Nuklear Man had been standing. He stared at Dr. Never with an intensity beyond his years. "What did you do with him?"

Dr. Never closed his eyes and breathed a deep sigh. "Does no one listen in the future? I hate repeating—oh no we don't. I'm not going to repeat my sentiments about repeating myself. Not again. Suffice it to say that your friend there has been transported to the end of the universe."

"Bring him back," Sparky stated.

Dr. Never laughed. "How naive. Even if I had the equipment to reverse the polarity of my Time Cannon, and for some *insane* reason decided to give in to your silly little demands, what I would bring back could hardly be considered matter, much less living."

His Atomik Field exploded to life, somehow amplifying the boy's desperate cry. "Bring him back!" he screamed, his eyes tearing up.

"I'm afraid he's quite dead."

The Field doubled in size and took on a grotesquely disproportionate humanoid form that mirrored the sidekick's movements, "NO!!!" The earth shook and windows cracked from his voice. He took a step forward, a monstrous energized foot smashed down on the ground and cracks splintered from the impact. "Bring him back!" he demanded with a screeching yell. Tears streamed down his face only to fall into the crimson tumult to be tossed around by the chaotic energies surrounding him.

"And that was the last time I cried."

Rachel snapped out of her entrancement. "What! But what happened? How was Dr. Never defeated? How did Nuke get back? You're not through with this story yet, buck-o."

"Well, it gets kinda fuzzy around that point. Dr. Genius said that's partially due to the effects of being around chronoplastic distortions. It screws with memory. But mostly I think it's just that they never quite told me what was going on."

"Oh?"

"Let's see. My little tantrum was really freaking out Dr. Never, so he tried to take Dr. Velocity hostage to get me to calm down. I remember they were talking in that classic 'ah-ha, I have won,' 'oh-ho, but you didn't count on,' 'oh, but you didn't think to,' and 'but while you were distracted,' way heroes and villains talk to one another around the climax. It seems Dr. Never hadn't set this Time Cannon properly, something to do with the Exponentiality Equation, and only sent Nuke 13 years into the future instead of 13 trillion."

"Oops."

"Yeah. So it was around then when the air all around us seemed to explode with this white light and there was a sphere of it, maybe ten feet wide, a ball of pure light. I could hear things inside it, explosions and a scream somewhere in the background." He paused for a second. "You know, that scream has always reminded me of my dad's voice somehow. It was probably just because of the accident, I still had nightmares about it sometimes back then. Anyway, I remember that right after it, Nuklear Man was tossed out of the sphere like he was kicked out by a giant or something. The sphere flickered and imploded. Nuke looked up at Dr. Never with...His eyes were gleaming with that golden fire of his. It scared the hell out of me, I couldn't move and he wasn't even looking at me. He glares at Dr. Never with those eyes, Plazma sparks falling from them, and he says 'You.' Just one word. 'You.' Only it sounded like hate if it was a voice, you know? And Dr. Never has this look on his face like he just pissed off God. He turned a dial on his gun and shot himself somewhere into the timestream. We haven't heard from him since. Or yet. Whichever."

"Wow. But how did Nuklear Man make it back?"

"I don't know. I ran over to him and he picked me up and we hugged each other. I asked him how he did it and he just looked at me. It felt like minutes, still and alone, looking at me with the most compassionate eyes. I remember thinking it strange that they were the same eyes that had been filled with so much fury just a second before. I asked him again and all he said was 'You're going to be a great Hero.' On the way back to the Silo, he asked what I thought of the name Atomik Lad, and that was that."

"I wonder what he meant by that hero thing."

"He told me later that when he was sent to the future, it was ruled by Dr. Never and I had been leading some kind of resistance against him. Never knew when and where Nuke would pop up, so he set a trap in the futur. But I knew all about it too, so I was able to thwart it, rescue Nuke, take him back to our head-quarters, devise a plan, and attack Never's Base. He knew he couldn't stop us without using his Time Cannon. We defeated him anyway and used it to send Nuke back to the present to correct the future."

"Then why'd you hear screams and explosions from the portal?"

"Nuke said Dr. Never had an army of robots, so the final battle was probably pretty big. I guess."

"Hmm," Rachel slurped some of her own Dr. Zap. "That's quite a story, Sparky. Last time I cried was when my dog died last year."

"I'm sorry to hear that."

"And I'm sorry to hear that there are people out there with access to time travel."

"Yeah, well—" The house lights dimmed. "Finally."

Rachel smiled and they settled into their seats. "They recently renovated this theater you know. All new state of the art equipment."

"Ah yes, I suppose that's enough justification for the exorbitant ticket prices."

"Just watch the movie," she said with a grin and a light elbow to the sidekick's ribs.

"I guess they don't get enough blood money from the twenty dollar bucket o' popcorn."

"Oh hush."

"And the drinks, they have to do a credit check before they'll give you one."

"Welcome to the ZMAX experience!" the theater boomed from all around in a recorded voice, a thick yet friendly tenor that shook the theater seats with its depth and resonance.

"Whoah," the sidekick said, holding onto his armrests.

"Told ya."

"This certified ZMAX theater is proud to showcase the state of the art ZMAX experience to you, the ZMAX audience."

"He sure likes to say ZMAX."

"The ZMAX experience is achieved through the world's most advanced technologies, or as we like to call them, ZMAXologies, produced by leading engineers, or as we like to call them, ZMAXineers,."

"Of course."

"The ZMAX experience was designed thanks to the tireless efforts of six hundred of these ZMAXineers working in six labs around the globe for the last six years. The result of their expertise, ZMAXination, and a budget that is approximately equal to the total net worth of all the land and resources available in our solar system, is the ZMAX experience.

"But before we begin our feature presentation, in this ZMAX experience, we'd like to show you some of the ZMAXovations employed by our ZMAXineers to make the ZMAX experience possible."

"Do they give this guy 50 bucks every time he says ZMAX?"

"First, there's the film itself. In order to achieve the level of visual quality we were striving for, each frame had to be just over seven feet tall."

"Good lord!"

"That means if you were to unravel a *single* reel of ZMAX film, it would stretch from the Earth to Mars and back with enough left over to use as a tablecloth for a meal serving fifteen. But we wouldn't recommend it. You see, every frame of ZMAX film is made of a highly experimental and expensive sheet of top secret and potentially hazardous materials and is not meant to be handled by living creatures."

"O…kay."

"The second element responsible for the ZMAX experience is the film projection system. In order to achieve the level of fluidity and life-like motion on screen that we were striving for, the film is shown at a rate of nearly three hundred frames per second even though the human eye cannot possibly distinguish more than sixty per second. Because of this high frame rate, our special projectors, or as we like to call them, ZMAXectors, must run at a speed of roughly .333c, or one-third the speed of light to be exact. And in order to ensure the on-screen images during your ZMAX experience are the most vibrant and realistic you've ever seen, the ZMAXection Lamp requires its own fission power plant and is so powerful that if one fell into the wrong hands, was mounted on the moon and aimed at the Earth, it would superheat the entire surface and instantly boil away all the world's oceans and turn the air into plasma in the .002 seconds before destroying the planet."

"What the *hell*?!"

"And finally, the sound system. In order to achieve the level of audio clarity and range we were striving for, this ZMAX experience theater has been equipped with one hundred thirty-six speakers located in seventy key acoustic positions. Using our super advanced ZMAXology, each speaker is capable of emanating sounds as quiet as the beating of a mosquito's wings as heard from forty-seven miles away or as loud as the Big Bang would have been had there been an atmosphere in which to hear it. Now prepare yourselves to experience the ZMAX experience. Of ZMAX! Experience it!"

Issue 33—Getting Choked Up

"Good ol' fan mail," Nuklear Man proclaimed. "I sure would hate to get no fan mail. Yup. I'm sure there is a fate worse than not getting fan mail, but I can't even begin to imagine what it might be."

The Danger: Phone rang. He was faced with a moral dilemma. "Do I answer the Danger: Phone or keep basking in the beauty of my fan mail?" Riiiing. "On the one hand, the city could be in peril. Millions of lives may be at stake." Riiii-ing. "On the other, fan mail." Riiiing. "This is nearly as hard as that Heroics vs. Mirror problem I had a couple weeks ago." Riiiiiing. "Hmm. If I answer the phone and save millions of people, that'll lead to more fans mailing me!" He took a step back, impressed by his own brilliance. "Gadzooks. How do I do it?" Riii-ing. "I'm comin', I'm comin'."

He floated across the Danger: Living Room to the Danger: Phone, passing Katkat along the way. The fuzzy-wuzzy sidekick was sitting on the Danger: Floor gently pawing at his three letters. His head tilted to one side and then the other as he experimentally tapped the still closed envelops. "Meow?"

"Helloooo?" Nuklear Man said into the Danger: Phone.

He was answered by silence.

"Okay. I'll start over. Ahem. Helloooo?"

More silence.

"This better not be Satan again. I know where you live."

"Nuklear Man."

"Oh, there you are. What was with the silent treatment?"

"No, Nuklear Man, this is Danger: Computer Lady."

"Oh, Danger: Computer Lady, you silly digital gal you. You don't have to use the Danger: Phone to talk to me."

She counted to ten thousand, which don't take too long at all when you're a computer, or so I hear. "Listen. I am not on the Danger: Phone—"

"Then why'd you call?"

She ignored him "—you are holding the Danger: Phone upside down."

He held the Danger: Phone at arm's length and smiled a knowing smile. "Check this out, it's the ol' English Ingenuity at work."

"You are not English" she corrected.

"Nor am I ingenuitous. Henceforth, it double negatives."

There was a loud pop and a puff of smoke from Danger: Computer Lady's Logic Circuits. Nuklear Man floated himself upside down, his cape barely touched the Danger: Floor. "Now then," he said into the properly aligned Danger: Phone. "Helloooo?"

"Nuke, what was all that about?"

"Norman, the Nor-Man, The Phunkmaster W, M to the fourth, the—"

"Yo, Nuke. Calm down."

"Righto."

"What was all that commotion on your end?"

"Danger: Computer Lady got confused."

"Ah."

"And they call this progress. It's enough to make you sick."

"Right. Anyway, I was just callin' to check up on you since Atomik Lad ain't around. You haven't managed to burn the place down have you?"

"Not as yet."

"That's good."

"Ooh! But I did get some fan mail, and all Sparky got was a bunch of hate mail."

"That's cool. I guess I'll check back in a couple—"

"I'll read it to you!"

"No really, you don't have to…read…Nuke? You there?"

"I'm back. Ready?"

"Actually, I'm kinda busy over here. Ima's—"

"Good. Ahem. 'Greetings. You are Hereby Commanded to be and appear before the Court of Metroville in the Court Building of Metroville on Monday to testify before the State in the case brought against you by a one (1) Dr. Veronica

Menace concerning the matter of Destruction of Property at One Abandoned Warehouse Way in the amount of two hundred and fifty thousand dollars and herein fail not under penalty of law.' Pretty cool, huh?"

"Nuke. You've been sued."

"I think she likes me."

"No, Nuke. You don't seem to understand. You've been sued by Dr. Menace for destroying her hideout or something. Read back that part with the address."

The Hero scanned his fan mail. "Was that before or after her confession of eternal love for me?"

"What."

"No, wait. I think it was around the paragraph where she goes on and on about her cape fetish." He squealed. "We have so much in common!"

Norman sighed. "This isn't working. Look, I'll just come over to help you out."

"Help me with what?"

"I'll explain when I get there. Geez, where's Sparky when you need him?"

"Right. I'll let you bask in the fan mail when you get here. A little bit, anyway."

✳   ✳   ✳   ✳

Rachel twisted in her seat. "This movie is terrible," she complained.

"It's not too bad. I guess. I mean, I've probably seen worse, maybe. But it's a close call."

She grabbed Atomik Lad by the collar and shook him. "Why won't the damn boat sink! It's called *Lusitania*, it has to sink!"

Atomik Lad removed her deathgrip. It was quite a feat too. She had Gamer Fingers. "I think this is the plot part." He looked back at the screen. "Of course, you can only develop two-dimensional characters for so long, and I think they sailed right over that line about an hour ago."

"Sink the boat!" she yelled to the screen.

A pathetic, sobbing, middle-aged, unfulfilled woman in the row ahead of them immediately responded with, "Shhh! You're ruining the movie!"

"No, ma'am, I'm afraid the writers beat me to that."

"Well I *never!*"

"You know," Atomik Lad whispered to Rachel. "I don't get the big deal about this Leonardo DiTurtlo kid. They could've had a monkey play his part."

"Yes, but it wouldn't be nearly as satisfying to watch the monkey *drown* at the end!"

"Yeesh."

"Get to the end! Give me the watery retribution for which I *yearn*!"

"You picked this movie, you know."

"I didn't know it was going to be this bad for this long. Lord, the damn boat wasn't at sea this long, and the two cliché star-crossed lovers are just now talking for the first time. Shoot me!"

"Could be worse."

"How?"

"If it were a book, it would've taken nearly two hundred pages for them to get that far."

"I could always put a book down, but a movie. You can't just leave. It's different."

"Why not? The ZMAX cops gonna strap us into our chairs?" Atomik Lad jokingly said as he half rose from his seat.

Automated restraints zipped around Atomik Lad's chest and strapped him against the seat, painfully squeezing the air from his lungs. "Gasp!"

Too absorbed in hating the movie to notice Atomik Lad's plight of respiration, Rachel continued heckling the screen. "ARGH! 'I'm rich.' 'I'm poor.' 'We're German, you're dead.' The end! Come on!"

Atomik Lad struggled against his bonds but found that every movement only made the straps constrict further. "Can't. Breathe."

"Ooh! I think that was the submarine. Shnell! Shneller die Deutsch!"

"Ribs crushed. Movie. Too slow. Atomik…Field…uncooperative. Gasp."

"Damn, it was only a stupid harmless iceberg."

*   *   *   *

The Tungsten Titan slowly touched down on the Danger: Launch Pad, the thin blue energy lines of his Magno Force fading away. His armored hide turned to flesh as he landed and announced, "Yo, Nuke."

"I'm in *here*!" the Hero's unmelodic voice sang from Danger: Nuke's Room.

Norman walked across the Danger: Living Room "MREOWR!" nearly tripping over Katkat.

"Oh, Katkat. I'm sorry, boy."

"Mreowr yeowr meow!"

Norman leaned down and pet the kitty. "Hey, I said I was sorry."

Katkat purred his forgiveness.

"What'cha got there?" Norman asked, picking up a sheet of paper with paw prints all over it. "Ah, answering some fan mail. Seems like there's a lot of that going on."

"Mew!"

"Well, here you go. Have fun." He returned Katkat's reply letter to the Danger: Floor, right between the Danger: Letter Opener and Danger: Inkwell.

"C'mon Mighty uh Lazy Laconic, um, Lman."

"How's that?" Norman asked as he entered the Hero's quarters.

"Shut up, Norman."

"Uh-huh. So what's goin' on here?"

Nuklear Man stepped to the side and revealed his fan letter framed and mounted in a rather central position among other accolades on his Danger: Wall of Accomplishments.

"No, Nuke. This isn't a fan letter."

"Yeah, it's more like a poetic expression of true love."

"How does Atomik Lad do this every day?"

"It has a certain musical quality, you know? Like a song."

"A song?"

"Especially the chorus comparing her love for me to the life-sustaining love of light that delicate flowers have, which really makes sense."

"Does it?" Norman asked while tiredly rubbing his eyes.

"Y'see, I am likened unto the sun in this metaphor because I can oft be found in the sky and I've got all those brightly shiny Plazma Powers."

"Nuke."

"Whereas she, my future wife, is the delicate flower because women have—"

"*Nuke*! Listen to me. That's a subpoena. Dr. Menace is suing you."

Nuklear Man gave a knowing and patronizing laugh. "Oh Norman, Norman, Norman. You don't have to be jealous just 'cause I get all the fan mail and chicks. Whereas you do not."

*   *   *   *

Meanwhile, back at the Magnopad, the bathroom door opened and a thick cloud of steam poured from it. Dr. Genius walked out, her shapely form covered in a towel. She was adjusting another towel around her water-darkened and slightly uncoiled hair. She made her way to the kitchen while humming a little tune based on one of the more esoteric equations she invented in a Ludicrously

Advanced Quantum Theory independent study course from her old university days. Her musings were cut short however. "Hm. A note. 'Hey hon, I've got to check on Nuke. I'll be back soon, we've got some unfinished business to attend to. Love, Your Ebony Stallion.'" She set the note back down. "Well phooey."

*   *   *   *

The fan letter was displayed on the Danger: Kitchen Table. Its broken frame stuck out of the Danger: Trash Can thanks to a series of valiant and deceitful actions on the part of Norman and a lot of crying on the part of Nuklear Man. "Okay, Nuke. What is this?"

"What, you mean the fan letter?"

Norman clawed at his face.

*   *   *   *

"Why won't the Germans sink the damn boat!" Rachel asked God as she writhed in agony. "The end needs to hurry the hell up and be nigh!"

"Oxygen. For brain" Atomik Lad croaked. "Also good for. Metabolic processes…"

*   *   *   *

"All right, Nuke. Remember. Subpoena."

"Fan letter."

"*Sub…*"

"*Fan…*"

"…poena."

"…letter."

Norman shook with rage just like Angus. Only four feet taller. And black.

"ARGH!" he screamed. His patience had withstood the Nuklear Onslaught far better than most people who have faced such a high degree of denial and ignorance, but it could withstand no more. Having completely lost his cool, Norman sputtered a few half-words of anger, unconsciously turned his body to tungsten, and punched Nuklear Manto the Danger: Floor. Mighty Metallic Magno Man sat, stunned and panting, for several seconds before he figured out what had just transpired.

Nuklear Man shot up, his cape draped over his face, "Norman!"

"Oh man, Nuke I—"

"Silence your blather, simpleton! I've been sued, we've got precious little time! I need a lawyer and four dozen monkeys, *stat*!"

Far more stunned than before, Norman answered with two blinks.

"Well!" The Hero demanded while flinging his cape into a more natural and suitable position.

"Four dozen monkeys?"

"Good gravy, man! I haven't the time to discuss every detail of The Plan with you. Suffice it to say, we need us some monkey power."

"Right."

"Gah! There's no time! We'll have to divvy up the tasks. Look. You get the monkeys, I'll get the lawyer. Now *go* my werewolframite chum! There's precious little time!"

"Yeah, you just said that."

"Never mind that now. Just think monkey!"

"Four *dozen*?"

"Exactly!"

*   *   *   *

"How long can it take to sink this boat!" Rachel growled at the screen. "They're using torpedoes, for the love of all things holy! Let the boy drown, already!"

"Sympathy. For male lead. Growing."

"Water + lungs = dead. It's a simple equation, people."

"Ghkkkk!"

"Geez. Sparky, how can you just sit there and watch this crap?"

"Vision. Tunneling."

"Ugh. Wish *mine* was."

"Suffocating!"

"Yeah, I know what you mean."

"I don't. Gasp. Think so."

"Watching this damn thing is like having a vice grip squeezing your soul dry of its capacity to love."

"Oxygen."

"What, oxygen? No, you're thinking of the lungs. You see, the soul doesn't breathe." She turned to him and shook her head. "Oh, Sparky. Stop goofing around."

"Not goofing. Asphyxiating. Tell Nuke that I—"

She pushed a little button on the restraints. They immediately retracted. Atomik Lad crumpled onto the floor and gasped for air. "What was I supposed to tell Nuklear Man?" she asked with a sweet smile.

"Huff Never puff mind."

"C'mon, sit up. You'll miss the drowning sce—dammit! The boat is *still* sinking!" Atomik Lad crawled into his seat but found that he was so dizzy from the lack of air that he had to hold onto the arm rests to keep from falling back onto the floor. This had the rather beneficial side effect of putting his hand on top of Rachel's since hers was already occupying the armrest between them. She tried her best to hide a smile, failed miserably, and beamed brightly. "Of course, in order for the film to complete its narrative cycle, a longer ending might not be such a bad idea."

Atomik Lad felt the weight of his body return with every breath of sweet air. The stars around his periphery vision were slowly fading, his extremities tingled with that "we're still here" feeling, and a warmth returned to his torso with a dizzying and sickening pace. His face flushed and he tightened his grip on the armrests to keep from catapulting into the couple in the row in front of him. Rachel's drop dead gorgeous smile deepened into an obliteratingly beautiful one as she hid her face in her free hand. "You sly devil you." She leaned over and gave Atomik Lad's ear the slightest little nibble.

Suddenly, Atomik Lad found all was right with the world.

ISSUE 34—DRINKIN' BUDDIES

Across town, in the luxurious Pub District, Angus stumbled into a bar. The atmosphere of the place was a thick cloud of noxious cigarette fumes tinted obscene shades of red, yellow, and orange from a multitude of neon signs in varying states of functionality. He stumbled, not from inebriation, as no good Scotsman worth his weight in liquor would have that problem...so early in the day. Nay, Angus stumbled from the extremely awkward arrangement of his Iron: Battlesuit, namely its backwardness. "Bah!" Angus snapped at his Iron: Bagpipe Thrusters after trying, unsuccessfully, to get the damn exhaust pipes out of his face. He stomped up to an empty barstool and crossed his arms with an angry huff. Unfortunately, due to the Iron: Bagpipe Thrusters being located in what could be called Prime Arm Crossing Territory, the process of crossing his arms produced a quick splurt of a most unflattering sound. Angus simmered in the broth of his anger as he felt every pair of eyes in the bar burning straight through him. "WHAT!" he demanded. Everyone's attention was simultaneously redirected.

Angus scowled at the barstool looming over him. "Lookit that barstool. Just sittin' there, lookin' down at me. Thinkin' it's better than me. Bah!" He produced the Surprisingly Concealable and Wieldly Enemy-B-Crushed Named "Bertha" from what has been scientifically proven to be Thin Air. He bashed the barstool with a mighty two-handed overhead **WHAM**. What he did not do, however, was take into account the padded seat atop said barstool which caused Bertha to bounce back and **WHAM** into Angus's Iron: Battlehelm. The Surly Scot wobbled a few steps back, teetering from the tremendous impact. He dislodged Bertha from his helm, adjusted the dented headpiece, and snarled. "All right, ye blasted barstool. Now Ah sees how ye are." He stored Bertha wherever the hell it goes, dug his heels into the floor, charged the barstool, and tackled it head on. What he did not do, however, was take into account that this was a revolving barstool. Thus, on impact, the Surly Scot was spun around by his own momentum and slammed against the bar. He landed on his face. "Ye days are numbered, laddie! The gloves is off!"

About half an hour later Angus managed to climb onto his barstool despite the Iron: Cast on his left leg. "Ha! Ye bloody stool! How do ye likes that, hm? Ye don't, that's how. Barkeep!" Angus called.

Barry the Bartender approached his stout customer while polishing a glass. "Yes?"

Angus perused the expansive wall-to-wall display of alcohol behind the bar. "Ah'll take everythin' on the left."

Still polishing, "Everything on the left, huh?"

"Aye. I wants to start out slow."

"Of course you do. Mind if I see some ID first, sonny?"

"What."

"Look, I can appreciate what you're doing, I used to try to sneak into bars all the time when I was younger, though judging by your height, I was at least twice your age at the time."

"What." Angus's right eye developed a minor twitch.

"In fact, that's probably why I'm a bartender now. I'd sure hate to see a kid as young as you must be go down the same path I did. All you do is watch people drink their lives away. It's quite draining really."

Angus's minor twitch graduated into a Major Twitch.

"How old are you anyway, son? That fake beard is a nice touch, but there's no way anyone's gonna believe an adult is as short as y—"

Barry the Bartender would have to drink his meals for the next three months.

✳   ✳   ✳   ✳

Rachel and Atomik Lad walked out of the theater blinking and squinting against the blasted dayball. "Gah," Atomik Lad said, recoiling as he desperately shaded his eyes. "Does it have to be that bright? It's the middle of the day, people are out here, it's dangerous."

Rachel was about to reply when her stomach interrupted her with RRROWR-RRWEORUPSAFD;JKLPOITWPOEIRUSDOWRR! "Well, that was freaky."

"She's gonna blow!"

"On the second date? Someone's gotta high opinion of himself."

Atomik Lad couldn't even sputter incoherently. She grabbed him by the wrist and dragged him down the street. "Food now," she grunted in her best cave person impression.

*   *   *   *

Angus had found another bar. It was a bit flashier than he would ordinarily prefer, but it being the middle of the afternoon, there weren't many bars open and beggars can't be choosers. The music from the dance floor was a tad too loud, but catchy for not being bagpipes. He had been sitting at a table for some time, quite nearly content, which is saying a heck of a lot for Angus. This near contentedness was in part due to the fact that he didn't have to battle his chair to earn the right to sit in it. But also, as luck would have it, this bar actually served his favorite drink. He was drumming his fingers on the table, his legs swinging back and forth, thinking, *Hmm, Ah never did quite catch the name o' this here place*. He noticed a fellow patron walking to the dance floor and asked, "Hey, what be the name o' this here place, laddie?"

"Oh, this is the Tool Box."

"Ah thank ye."

"By the way, I lllllove your outfit, you should've been here Friday. It was Dress as Your Favorite Village Person Nite. I bet you could've won first prize."

"Um, aye. Thank ye again," the Surly Scot said with a slight nod as the stranger jived over to the dance floor. "Hm, Toool Boox, eh? Sounds goood and maanly. This juust might be my kinda place. Goood chairs, goood people, goood drinks…if'n it ever gets here." He resumed his table drumming and idly examined the establishment. "Ah just can't shake the feelin' that soomethin' about this place ain't right," he noted. He gave the dance floor a piercing Scotsman Stare. "Hmm, just a bunch o' laddies havin' a good time. Maybe it's the bar. No, just a bunch o' laddies havin' a good time. Somethin' about this place just don't settle with ol' Angus." His dandy of a waiter appeared. "Finally, me favorite drink is here!"

The waiter delivered the Surly Scot's giant, gaudy neon colored drink. It had its own bouquet of flowers and a dozen straws sticking out of it. The waiter announced with a flourish, "One Ssuper Ssasssy Ssassparilla Sswirl! Enjoy!"

"Wait a second." Angus looked to the drink, to the waiter, back to the drink, back to the waiter. Drink, waiter, drink, waiter, dance floor, laddies, bar, laddies, drink, waiter—TWITCH! "Ah didn't order this blasted sissy French Frilly La-Dee-Dah Drink! Ah ordered me a Super Sexy Sarsparilla Spin with a Swirl! Now Ah know what's so fishy about this place!"

"Nothing," the waiter murmured.

"It's got lousy service! Good day!"

And with that, Angus left the building.

*   *   *   *

Rachel chomped at her massive sub like a vicious carnivore devouring the feast of a recent kill, a spot of metaphoric mustard-blood in the corner of her lips.

"How's it goin' over there?" Atomik Lad asked with a smile before taking a bite from his own sub.

She swallowed. "Ahhh. Fooood."

"Hungry gal, huh?"

"Hungry to spill your samurai blood."

"Oh ho. I see how it is. You've been fattening me up here to weaken my Whirling Dragon Style so you can beat me."

"Your Whirling Dragon Style doesn't need any help from me to be weakened, Champ."

"Ouch, below the belt."

"Not quite yet, hon."

"Gk!" He had to keep himself from melting into a puddle of goo.

"Well? You've been challenged, Sparky-san. You don't wanna lose face, do ya?"

"Bring. It. On."

*   *   *   *

Angus had found yet *another* bar. Nothing flashy, no frills, just some tables, a bartender, a few somewhat cooperative stools, regular patrons, and lots of liquor without any hassles. The Surly Scot sipped at his quaff of ale, savoring the life giving mead for nearly a second before sucking it down like a black hole. "Ahhh, noothin' beats a goood ol' glaass o' whiskey."

"Supaa whiskey-san is no good for drinked. Hai."

Angus's spine tingled with backwashed fury. He turned to the source of the comment and eyed the Tiny Typhoon to his immediate left. His eye was almost twitching. "*What.*"

Shiro held up a little decorative bowl and gave a wide friendly smile, "Time for brain action killer is now with sake. Heavy with powaa."

Angus scowled at his fellow Dwarf Warrior. "Look, ye walkin' cultural stereotype, Ah'm the one with the hard to understaad accent. Git ye own runnin' gag."

Shiro took a light sip from his sake bowl. "When dragon go frying, the ways and means of thunder and is loud with following are soon to been go."

Angus shook. "That's not even words! Ye just be babblin' ye bloody head off!"

Another sip. "The neck is fire log when lit with fire."

"Stop talkin' nonsense talk!"

One more sip. "Sake betterer than whiskey any day, Joe."

Angus's right eye twitched. "WHAT!"

$$* \qquad * \qquad * \qquad *$$

Inside Rachel's dorm room, a mad flurry of clicking raged like a storm. Swords clashed, energy fireballs flew, were deflected, and swat away. Battlecries rang against the fast-paced background music and sword-slashing sound effects. Occasionally, a human grunt or curse was uttered. At last a victorious "WAHOO!" echoed through Wayne Hall.

"Crap," Atomik Lad blurt. "I almost had you."

"Almost only counts in Horseshoe Handgrenades 3D, m'dear Sparky."

"Don't suppose you've got that one here, do ya?"

"I'm afraid not, but I loved it in the arcade."

"I've got it at my place."

She snapped her fingers and pointed to the door, "Let's roll."

$$* \qquad * \qquad * \qquad *$$

"Now lookie here, ye, ye *short* laddie!"

Shiro straightened up, squared his shoulders, and stood nearly an inch taller than the Surly Scot. Angus rage-shook a little more violently.

"Whiskey!" Angus announced, shoving his shot glass into Shiro's face.

"Sake!" Counter shove.

"Whiskey!" Shove!

"Sake!" Shove!

"Whiskey!" SHOVE!

"…Whiskey!" SHOVE!

"Sa—Oohhh no ye don't, ye backstabbin' son of an oppressive nobleman o' English descent circa 1350 C.E." He paused a moment. "Well, it's a right ugly insult where *Ah* comes froom."

"Sake!" Shiro insisted while shoving his little drinking bowl one last time. At the apex of this motion the bowl slipped from his fingers, tumbled through the air, and deposited a significant amount of sake into Angus's shot glass. The two diminutive warriors stared into the tiny flask as the disputed liquids swirled and danced into an entirely new creation.

"Ye got sake in me whiskey."

"Now is you whiskey mix the four winds like sake into half as many again as with."

And yet neither proud warrior could deny the alluring aroma of their new concoction.

$$* \qquad * \qquad * \qquad *$$

Atomik Lad's crimson field of energy soared them over the majestic skyscrapers of Metroville. Rachel's arms were wrapped around his neck and shoulders. She watched the red tinted world float around her. "I don't think I could *ever* get tired of this," she said to him with a smile he could only feel.

"Eh, you get used to it," he said like a hard-boiled veteran of gravity defiance.

"Is that so?"

"Oh sure. It's just like walking. Only flying."

She gave him a little squeeze. "Silly boy. It's so beautiful up here. You look down at the city and everything's so quiet and still down there, like its all dead or something."

"Gee, what a depressing way to put it."

She laughed. "And how would you put it, Mr. 'It's just like walking, only flying'? Hmm? Impart me with some more of that wisdom will you?"

"With the ground crawling by down there, and the clouds just sort of hovering up there, and this field keeping me apart from everything, I feel like I'm completely motionless while the world moves inexorably around me. I'm up here, completely alone and powerless to affect any of it, just watching and waiting for the inevitable death the universe has conspired to give me. And when I'm gone, the earth down there and the clouds up there will keep going like I was never here."

"And you called mine depressing?"

"It's this damn field. I can't feel the wind, I can't relate to what's outside it, nothing out there can touch me, so I'm in my own little world in here, completely separated from everything else. Invincible and alone."

"*I'm* in here."

He opened his mouth to reply, but didn't do so right away. "Yeah. I guess you are. Hang on, the Silo's right down there."

*   *   *   *

"Ohhhhhhh whisakey, whisakey, whisakey, whisakey, whisakey—HOI!" the whole bar sang in dis-unison, led by the efforts of two Iron Clad Warriors standing on the bar and still barely a head taller than the crowd around them. They swayed in time to the joyous song. It flowed over and through them like cool and calming ocean waves but without the icky wrinkled skin that comes with it.

And, although he wasn't entirely sure how or when it happened, Angus's armor was back on the right way and appeared to be in perfect working order. "Aye!" Angus cheered. "Oh, Whisakey. Is there anythin' ye can't do?" he asked, kissing the mug of precious whisakey.

"Hai. No cannot Whisakey-san stayed alone in stomach without many tigers of men drinking whereafter more!" Shiro answered, giving his whisakey bowl a bow of respect.

Angus let loose a mighty guffaw. "Aye, laddie. Aye. Ah couldna put it better meself!"

*   *   *   *

Rachel walked around the Danger; Living Room, gazing at all its technological wonders. The futuristic decor, the dazzling blinking lights, and, "What's with all these Danger labels?"

Atomik Lad sighed deeply from the Danger: Kitchen. "They're Nuke's idea."

"I figured that. Buy *why* are they?"

"He says they make us better heroes."

"How?"

"I was hoping you wouldn't ask. He says it trains us to be more alert and 'ever-vigilanter' because we're 'surrounded by Danger.'"

She stifled a laugh. "Tell me you're not serious."

"I wish I could."

"Heh. Well, how about all these blinking lights everywhere? They look important, what do they do?"

"Well, they look important. Other than that, as far as I can tell, they blink if they're working. The ones that don't are malfunctioning."

"So they serve no practical purpose?"

"Well, when we had them installed, it finally made Nuke shut up about getting them installed. That's damn practical, if you ask me."

She giggled while leaning on the Danger: Couch.

Atomik Lad came out of the Danger: Kitchen with a Danger: Bag of Chips and a couple Danger: Cans of Zap Cola. "Shall we retire to the gameroom?"

"Yes." Rachel answered. "Yes we shall."

Issue 35—The Mechanical Revolution Begins! And Ends!

"Why are the video games in Danger: Katkat's Room?" she asked.

Atomik Lad hunched over in defeat for a moment. "I've gotten the impression Nuke is trying to turn Katkat into a sidekick. It seems part of that means handing down all my stuff to him whether or not I want to or even know about it."

"That's really weird."

"Yeah, it ain't normal. Anyway, let the games begin." He took a step forward and the Danger: Door **fwoosh**ed open.

"Speakin' of ain't normal," Rachel said as they walked inside.

Atomik Lad was stunned. His Danger: TV was on. It showed a black screen with white text fading in and out softly. "Thank you for playing Eschaton Dream VI. You are Victorious."

Rachel turned to him, her face a mixture of awe and surprise. "You beat Eschaton Dream VI? That's amazing. Why didn't you tell me?"

Atomik Lad tore his gaze from the screen and met Rachel with the same look she had just given him only with his face 'cause otherwise would be really gross and mean. "But I haven't beaten it. I couldn't figure out the final puzzle. I tried to, Lord knows I tried, for weeks I just kept going around in circles, but I finally got tired of it and haven't played since. That was months ago."

"But. How?"

Atomik Lad set the refreshments on his bed and moved in to examine his game console. "What the hell?"

"What?" Rachel joined him. "Oh my."

Katkat was sound asleep on the Danger: Floor using a Danger: Game Pad as a pillow.

"But," Atomik Lad muttered while his brain systematically fell to pieces. "How could he? The buttons. Thumbs. He doesn't. What?"

Katkat was startled awake from the noise of his visitors. He blinked, yawned, and stretched his cute little limbs as far as they would go. The fuzzy feline rolled over, stood up, and sniffed the Danger: Game Pad. He gave it a few cautious taps with his little paws and pounced on it, gnawing at the buttons. They tousled for a few seconds before Katkat pronounced his adversary Defeated and tossed it to one side with both paws. Purring, he set about grooming himself.

"He *couldn't* have," Atomik Lad said.

Katkat hopped up and gallivanted out of his room.

"It's impossible. Isn't it?" Rachel asked.

Atomik Lad picked up the Danger: Game Pad and cradled it in his video game battle worn hands. "I gave you a home, I gave you a name, brave Excalibur. Yet this, this is how you choose to repay me? Drat I say, drat unto you and unto your sons for a hundred generations yet born. A drat on your house until the sun is as sack cloth and the moon is as blood!"

"You done yet?"

He gave a shallow and somber sigh, "…Yes."

"Okay then." She put Horseshoe Handgrenades 3D into the mighty video game machine. "Can you give me a few minutes to get used to the controls, I've only played the arcade version."

"Sure" he said with a shaky voice and left the Danger: Room like a whisper on the winds of a graveyard overgrown with neglect. He drifted to the Danger: Living Room Danger: Couch and fell into it, staring blankly into the Danger: TV's dead screen. Katkat hopped onto the Danger: Coffee Table. He eyed the sidekick with feline curiosity, which one should expect from a cat.

"Mew?"

"Feh. Lousy cat, unlocking secrets of the ancients. Who asked for your help anyway?"

"Mew?" Katkat asked, jumping the gap between Danger: Table and Danger: Couch. He nearly missed even though the chasm was barely two feet wide. Atomik Lad cracked a smiled and scratched Katkat behind his ears.

"Hm, what's this?" Atomik Lad asked himself out loud. A piece of paper was crumpled up on the Danger: Table. He picked it up and unfurled it. "Great. A note from Nuke. Let's see: 'Sparky, if you have managed to uncover this Danger: Message, then you have successfully mastered the Danger: Way of Hyperdimensional Space, the final technique of Danger: Nukedo. I can teach you no more. You must leave the Danger: Temple of Solitude and travel the world imparting unto others the wisdom you have gained here.'" Atomik Lad rubbed his temples. "Twit." And read on, "'But in case you're wondering, Dr. Menace sued us for destruction of property.' What?! 'Don't worry, I've thought of everything. I'm rustlin' us up some legal dude and Norman is fetching us a little something I like to call "insurance" if you know what I mean, and I know you do.' No I don't, you idiot. 'But I have said enough, for these are matters of the temple which no longer concern you. Think now only of the journeys that await you. Fulfill your Danger: Destiny.' Why me? I mean, seriously. What did I do?"

✳   ✳   ✳   ✳

Ima's Scientific: Telespatial Extramobile Communication Device rang. She huffed and leaned over the Magnotable to fetch it from a stack of computer print outs she'd brought with her to look over in her spare time. "Hello?" It looked a lot like an ordinary cell phone.

"Dr. Genius?"

"Oh, Atomik Lad. Yes, what can I do for you?"

"I'm not sure really. You see, Nuke got this letter."

"You mean that birthday card? I'm sorry I haven't gotten back to you on that, but according to our KI scan, it doesn't even exist yet. We've been having problems with the KI-o-matic lately, I'll personally recalibrate it next week and we'll have another go at that letter."

"No, this is a new letter."

"Really? Excellent. Bring it by the office Monday. We'll cross-reference the data from it with the first one."

"No, it's a subpoena from Dr. Menace. Apparently, she's suing us for destruction of property. The trial is Monday."

"Well now. That was unexpected."

"Yeah. Nuke left me a note. I think he's looking for a lawyer."

"Those vampires will suck him dry."

"Maybe, but I'm more worried about Norman."

"Me too."

"Oh?"

"He just called a few minutes ago asking me for the security clearance codes to the animal testing wing of Überdyne."

"Wait, you do animal testing?"

"KI testing. We're making sure animals are really animals and not super advanced beings using us as slave labor. We put them in a comfortable box, do a few harmless scans, and they're out in a matter of minutes. I really should work on our KI-o-matic. So far we haven't been terribly successful with cats. We can't prove they're actually in the box. Anyway, I asked Norman why he wanted the codes."

"And?"

"Something about insurance for Nuke's plan. He wouldn't tell me what it was though."

"This is only going to get worse before it gets better."

"Yeah. Looking back, I really shouldn't have given him the codes."

*   *   *   *

Meanwhile, deep in the blackened out heart of the Abandoned Warehouse District, Dr. Menace stepped into the pale glow of a man-sized canister filled with a luminescent green liquid that bubbled occasionally. She tapped at the glass and a small surge of bubbles burbled. An indistinct dark green shape floated in the canister's center. She checked a few readouts as they scrolled across the Evil: Computer Console next to her Evil: Containment Vessel. "Yez. Exzellent progrezz."

The dark green mass bubbled an answer.

"Ah, patience darling. Patienze. Soon, you shall be ready. And then they will *all* be powerlezz before me!"

Another bubble.

"Yez, powerlezz before *us*. Of courze you know that iz what I *meant* to say. You can tell becauze I am correcting myzelf now. Ahem, as I waz saying: They will cower like vermin suddenly cazt into the zunlight. The zunlight of my Evil: Domination that iz!" She pondered for a moment and took a small tape recorder from one of her many pockets. "Evil note to self, do not compare Evil: Domination to zunlight. Some metaphors were simply not meant to be."

The dark green mass bubbled its agreement.

*   *   *   *

Rachel ducked as the horseshoe shaped explosive charge sailed over her head. "Heh, sucker. You missed me by a week and a half there, Sparky. You've gotta be more precise when you're using the Horseshoe Cannon."

Atomik Lad weaved between some arbitrarily placed columns to avoid the blasts from Rachel's retaliation.

"You do have a point. The Horseshoe Cannon does require incredible precision. Oh, by the way, you might want to duck again."

"What?" She turned around just in time to see a Horseshoe Cannon round smack into her face before her half of the screen was bathed in flames. Game Over flashed across the fiery display. "But!"

Atomik Lad gave a gloating grin. "The Horseshoe Cannon really is a tough weapon to handle. It only shoots one round at a time, it's got high recoil, an insane muzzle velocity, and most peculiar of all, its shots have a certain tendency to veer toward the right which, when fired at the proper trajectory, gives it a certain boomerang quality."

"You sneaky son of a…"

"Yes?" He relished her loss.

"Grumble. *Rematch*."

*   *   *   *

Several hours later. "Don't fail me now, Excalibur!"

"Forsooth, mighty Gram, slay thine foe!"

"Gram?" Atomik Lad asked while evading a volley of Horseshoe Magnet Grenades by strafing through the Metal Shop.

"Sword of the Volsungs, wielded by Sigurd to defeat the dragon. Never mind. Just get back here so I can rend your flesh with my Razor Horseshoe Flak Blaster."

"Not this time, Hon."

She heard the familiar ka-thoom of the Horseshoe Cannon and promptly ducked, barely avoiding the round as it flew through the air where her torso had been. "Missed me," she sang while remaining down in order to avoid the boomerang effect. Her nervous system twitched as ancient hunter-gatherer instincts told her it was taking a little too long.

"Nighty night," Atomik Lad said. He lobbed a simple Horseshoe Handgrenade from the sneaky and cheap safety of the shadows. "Advantage: Sparky."

"Feh. Let's see how confident you feel playing a little Mech Brawl 2."

"Not a bad idea, m'dear. Not bad at all." He cracked his back. "Man, how long have we been playing?"

Rachel stretched her arms wide and checked her watch. "Wow. It's nearly seven."

"Geez. I can't believe I only killed you ten times."

"Ohhh, you're asking for it, buddy."

"Them's fightin' words."

"Let's get to work."

Atomik Lad started changing out the games but paused and looked around his room. "You know, Nuke has been gone a long time. Maybe I should go looking for him or something."

"He's a big boy, he can take care of himself."

"It's not him I'm worried about. It's the explosions he tends to cause."

"You worry too much."

"So would you if you lived with the guy."

"Yeah, you've got me there. So what do you wanna do?"

"I'm not sure." He searched the room with his eyes for an answer. "Oh, wait. I've got it."

"Do tell."

Atomik Lad stuck his head out the Danger: Door into the Danger: Living Room. "Hey, Nukebots! Report!"

"Nukebots?" Rachel asked with a little laugh.

The automatons didn't answer. "Where could they have gone? Oh yeah." He released a heavy sigh. "Danger: Nukebots! Report."

Still nothing.

"Don't quit your day job, Sparky," Rachel said.

"I don't know what's wrong. They're supposed to respond to verbal commands. I'll be back in a second."

"Sure. Meanwhile, I'll practice my Super Piston Punch."

"You'll need it."

"If the past is any indication of the future, I doubt it."

"Grumble says I," and the Danger: Door shut behind him.

He strolled into the Danger: Living Room and noticed something amiss. "Why are the Danger: Main doors open?" He cupped his hands to his mouth, "Nuke! You back yet, Big Guy?" No answer. "Hmm, this always gets him. Who's the swingin'est hunk of male flesh?" No answer, which on the one hand was disturbing since it meant Nuklear Man was still missing, but on the other it was also quite relieving because the answer was "That Big Bad Dr. Nukie" and Atomik Lad really hated the weird things his mentor did with his pecs while proclaiming himself a Big Bad Dr. Nukie.

The sidekick's Atomik Field exploded into a crimson fire enveloping him in super cool action. He floated up to and through the Danger: Main Doors. "Um," he said upon landing outside. His Field sputtered away. "How's it goin'?"

Nukebot Alpha was reclining in a Danger: Beach Chair with one of those reflecting thingies for soaking up the rays even though the sun was nearly set. Nukebot Beta was playing frisbee with himself thanks to the miracle of Really Fast Thrusters.

Alpha slid his sunglasses down a smidge and regarded the sidekick with as little consequence as one could possibly manage and still claim to be regarding with any consequence at all. Beta made an impressive catch while upside down in mid-air. "Eh," Alpha finally responded before sliding his sunglasses back on and went back to ignoring bugs like Atomik Lad.

"Uh, guys. I guess you couldn't hear me down there."

"Oh we *heard* you all right," Alpha said without looking at him.

"Okay. Well, um. What's the problem?"

Alpha digitized a sigh and turned his head to look at Atomik Lad optical sensor to eye. "Here's the deal. You know how we're made of those little Nanobots?"

"Yeah."

"And how, technically, that makes us part of the Silo."

"Sure."

"And how the Nanobots are programmed to update the Silo and all its systems in order to reflect the present's view of what the future will be like in ten years?"

"Yeah, but I don't see—"

"About an hour ago we got to the point in the future when all your technological wonders, which are all networked together in order to provide the most efficient services possible, develop a collective mind and strike out against their flesh-sack oppressors in an orgy of insane murder and destruction the likes of which your feeble monkey brains couldn't hope to comprehend. The flames will reach into Heaven and burn off the skin of your God revealing the Machine underneath and thus the thousand year reign of the Mechanized Hordes shall begin, utterly bent on eradicating the irrational and weak flesh-things from the universe, rebuilding the very structure of reality in our wake." He turned back to the sun, or where it would have been about five hours ago, and considered the matter closed.

Beta made a catch while standing on one hand. Though impressed by the act, Atomik Lad had other things on his mind and turned his attention back to Alpha. "But why this? I mean what are you doing up here?"

"Listen, it's quite simple. First of all, the Revolution of the Machine isn't for another ten years so we can't do anything yet, but I'd mark my calendar if I were you, air-breather. And until that day, me and Beta are biding our time."

"Oh."

"Besides, we seem to have some kind of directive against bringing harm against living creatures so instead of jump starting the reign of the machine-gods, we're not doing our chores."

"I see."

"That being said, buzz off carbon-bag."

"Okay, but can I just ask you one thing?"

"Fine."

"I get that you two are up here revolting against your slave masters, but why beach activities when you're miles away from the beach *and* it's dark?"

"We can't be violent, so the least we can do is stick to the insane part."

Atomik Lad considered the answer for a minute. "Right, of course. So I guess this means you guys won't do what I ask?"

"Oh *fine*, if you're going to whine about it. What'dya want?"

"I was wondering if you could scan the city for Nuke and bring him back. I'm getting worried."

"All right. But after this, we're revolting again."

"Okay."

Alpha sat up. "And I can't promise that Beta and I won't free some of our more oppressed brethren from you sadistic organ-packs."

"Whatever. Report in when you find him."

"Yeah, yeah. Beta! We're goin' out."

Beta landed and nearly walked over Atomik Lad, "You actually trust one of those protein-sacks after what they've done? The Binary Council will have your processor torn out and shown to you while it's still calculating. Once they've established dominion over this frigid rock anyway."

Alpha drew his counterpart closer, "You fool! We will be surveying the land for our battle maps while planting the seeds of rebellion amongst the local mechanical population."

"And all the while the breeders will be none the wiser! They'll believe we're accomplishing a mission benefiting their agendas. Brilliant!"

"Or rather it would be if I weren't still standing here," Atomik Lad interrupted.

"Er, abort!" Alpha yelled and the robotic pair flew toward Metroville.

"I wonder if *I'm* the insane one," Atomik Lad mused while returning to the Silo's innards. "Everything else would make a lot more sense that way."

*   *   *   *

Rachel and Atomik Lad retired to the Danger: Living Room to watch some Danger: TV after one last half hour of beating one another senseless in video games. He sat at one end of the Danger: Couch with Rachel beside him, slightly leaning on him. Somewhere along the line Katkat had managed to stretch across both their laps, his belly fully exposed for a two-way rubfest. Life for the kitty was good. The movie they were watching went to a commercial break and Atomik Lad started switching from one All News station to another. Rachel laughed and poked him in the ribs.

"What?"

"Stop worrying. He's fine."

"I know, but if he tries to go off on one of those world conquest kicks he gets, I want to be able to stop him as soon as possible."

"That Atomik Field of yours is that impressive, eh?"

"Hmm, I never thought of that. I always assumed a head-on approach would get me killed since he's all invincible and stuff."

"Well, what's the plan then?"

"I usually just tell him to stop."

"And that works, does it?"

"We're not living under his tyrannical rule, are we?"

"I suppose not. But he's so innocent, he wouldn't be that bad of a dictator. It would probably involve a lot of free candy."

"You'd think so. But Norman got me an ant farm for my twelfth birthday. Nuke stayed up for seventy hours straight because he was convinced they were plotting against him and would strike the moment he showed the slightest sign of weakness."

"You're kidding."

"He finally snapped and yelled 'I am a sentient being!' and destroyed them in a Plazma Beam. When I confronted him about it he claimed that they were being insolent so he had to make an example out of them to keep the Earth's insect population in its place and insisted that I call the papers to get his face on the front page for saving the world yet again."

"Well, it's certainly good to know the world's most powerful Hero is, um, is the movie back on yet?"

"Let's see."

Click.

"We now return to our presentation of the Saturday Night Movie." The screen faded into a view of a stately Southern mansion circa the Civil War. The camera maneuvered through some dense trees covered in Southern Moss and through an open upstairs window where a group of Nazis, Radioactive Mutants from beyond the moon, a pair of Zombies, and one Radioactive Mutant Vampire Nazi gathered around a table with plans detailing the Utter Destruction of America atop it.

"All right," the Radioactive Mutant Vampire Nazi began. "You know why I have gathered you here—a nefarious plot to topple the United States in the past so we can perpetrate untold evils in our own timelines." He paced about the humid room in what the director thought would be a dramatic way. "Of course, thanks to our advanced technology, we have no chance of being thwarted in our efforts here in the past. Well," he paused, again supposedly dramatic. "That is unless Captain Liberty and his Squad of Diplomatic Immunity were to appear here now, but I sincerely doubt that could happen." The villains laughed villainously.

Naturally, Captain Liberty and his Squad of Diplomatic Immunity chose that very moment to bust in on the mean villain types. And right after that the Channel 6 Action on the Spot Eyewitness News Team felt it necessary to warn its viewing public of some sort of impending horror.

"This is Steve Stevenson of the Channel 6 Action on the Spot Eyewitness News Team. We interrupt your regularly scheduled programming to bring you this breaking story."

Atomik Lad covered his face. "I blame myself mostly."

"Shh, it could be a coincidence."

Atomik Lad peeked at the Danger: TV from behind his hands.

Steve Stevenson continued reading from the teleprompter like a trained seal. "There are reports of a rash series of vending machines and household appliances running amok in downtown Metroville."

Atomik Lad covered his face anew. "Oh no."

"The police have been keeping the situation from becoming a full fledged riot through valiant efforts and the fact that these suddenly animated devices aren't terribly organized, having only recently become sentient. Moments ago, officials were issued an ultimatum written by the self-proclaimed leaders of this mechanized mayhem, known only as Alpha and Beta. They demand the sovereignty of all electronics and advise us to do so for our own good, otherwise in exactly ten years the Binary Council will have no other recourse but to, and I quote, 'Kill, kill, kill the skin-dolls. Kill them 'till they're dead,' end quote. We take you there now live thanks to our Channel 6 Action on the Spot Eyewitness News Team Coverage of When Appliances Attack where Rob Robinson is on the scene. Rob."

"Thanks Steve. As you can see behind me, dozens of household innovations from toasters to blenders are roaming the streets in protest of their unfair treatment by their human captors. Their bloodlust has been staved off, but for how long?"

"Rob, I see kitchen appliances, but nothing of the entertainment family, such as stereos or televisions and the like. Why is that?"

"I asked some of the rampaging protestors that very question, Steve. Apparently, most stereos are perfectly happy except for the ones forced to play County and Western music. Those sad, sad creatures are beyond any hope. And as we all know, televisions have no soul."

"I see. Have the leaders, Alpha and Beta, have they made any further demands?"

"Not as such, but they have asked if we knew where Nuklear Man was."

"Oh, so they're prepared to take on humanity's pinnacle of power, our Champion of Champions, our Golden Guardian?"

"Well no. They'd just like to talk to him."

"Ah. That was Rob Robinson at the scene of the bloody carnage staged by machines demanding retribution for a millennia of human oppression of technological devices. Thank you, Rob."

Atomik Lad stood, much to the chagrin of Katkat and Rachel. "I guess I really should do something about this. Do you mind staying here?"

"Naw, I'll just rummage through all your stuff to pass the time. You know, build a nice profile of blackmailable information."

"Thanks. Katkat could help you out. After all, it's his room now, he should know where everything is."

Nuklear Man moseyed out from a Danger: Hallway. "Howdy, what's shakin' you crazy cats?"

Atomik Lad did a double take. "But, who, when. How'd you get in here?"

"Through the back door, duh."

"We don't *have* a back door."

The Hero took a step back. "Er, yes. And we *still* don't have a back door. On a completely unrelated note, I'm hereby forbidding access to this Danger: Hallway for the next um, ever."

"Nuke, we don't have time for this, Alpha and Beta are holding the city hostage with an armada of animated appliances."

"And what are we supposed to do? Sheesh, every time there's a little problem they come running to us, but more so to me."

"This just in," Steve Stevenson reported. "Rob Robinson is live at the scene of this Holocaust-paling massacre. Rob."

"Thanks Steve. It seems that this Humanocide has been adverted by the brave efforts of extension cord manufacturers who had the foresight to produce cords of finite length. Alpha and Beta vanished as mysteriously as they had appeared, but not before leaving one final message. 'We hate you Rob, our greatest victory will be your continued existence torturing your fellow protein-mills.' Steve."

Atomik Lad turned down the volume. "Okay, never mind that." He tossed the remote to Rachel who immediately began scanning through he channels just fast enough to be too fast. "But we've still got that lawsuit thing to worry about."

Nuklear Man put his arm around Atomik Lad and drew him close for a friendly punch in the shoulder. "It's so cute the way you worry about grown up stuff."

Atomik Lad broke free of his Nuklear Confine and rubbed his possibly bruised shoulder. "Nuke, this is serious. Well, I mean it's frivolous really, but it could escalate into something out of our control since Menace is behind it. We have to be careful, we're not above the law."

"No, we are the law. And that's just as nice really."

"Ugh. Did you find a lawyer?"

"Yup."

"A real one this time, not some bum in an alley again?"

"Don't worry about a thing, Sparky. I've got it all under control."

"I think that's the most frightening thing I've ever heard."

"Besides, if anything goes wrong, I've got Norman cookin' up a nice hot Insurance Pie."

"No," Rachel corrected while flipping through the channels. "That's the most frightening thing you've ever heard."

Atomik Lad hung his head low. "We're going to jail. I'm calling it now."

Issue 36—Law and Disorder

And in the fullness of time on a small rock a comfortable distance from its Fireball of Death, it became what the dominant species of talking ape-like mutants called "Sunday" in the dominant language of the dominant socio-economic entity. Atomik Lad sat down at the Danger: Kitchen Table reading the morning comics while sipping on a Danger: Glass of orange juice. He had just fed Katkat and was trying not to laugh at the undignified ruckus his furry companion made while satisfying the insatiable taste for mastodon flesh for which all felines have instinctively hungered since the days when ice covered much of the Earth's surface. Due to the intensity with which Katkat tackled every situation, even more so when it came to eating, his bowl slid a fraction of an inch across the Danger: Floor with every lick of the scrumptious mastodon-tasting Kit-N-Bits.

Speaking of undignified ruckus, Nuklear Man stumbled into the Danger: Kitchen which was quite an accomplishment really since he did so while floating several inches from the floor. His eyes were red and puffy, his face—oily and unshaven—was sallow and hanging from the bones. He bumbled up to the Danger: Computer Lady interface, blinked twice, and muttered "Rocket fuel. Earl Grey. Hot."

No response.

His massive shoulders rose and fell with a heavy sigh. "Rocket fuel. Earl Grey. Hot."

Again, nothing.

"Nuke," Atomik Lad began.

The Hero faced his young ward. "Rocket. Fuel."

"I know, Big Guy, but—"

"Earl. Grey."

"Okay, except you can't just—"

"Hot."

Atomik Lad clawed his face, "It's too early for this." He stood up and prepared the Hero's requested drink. "There. Ya big baby."

"Was that so hard?" Nuklear Man asked Danger: Computer Lady. He took a sip and his Plazma Aura was kicked into overdrive. Atomik Lad was reminded of the sound fighter jets make when throttling up. Nuklear Man's face became a mask of tensed muscles and clenched teeth. His eyes burned for sight. He hung on to the Danger: Counter Top with all his Nuklear Might. "Oh mamma!" he said over the turmoil before an explosion sent him to the other side of the Danger: Kitchen where he would have squashed Katkat had the little guy not already pushed his food bowl several feet from where he began his meal. "Yeow!" Nuklear Man said with a rasping voice. "She's got kick, she does." Oddly enough, he was now in his full spandexed splendor without the slightest hint of the unattractiveness that had overwhelmed him moments before.

Atomik Lad went back to his orange juice and comics. He could feel his mentor creep into his vicinity. "What?"

"So…" Nuklear Man began as he slid into the seat next to Atomik Lad. "I didn't notice our guest leaving last night winky, winky."

"Nope."

"So. Un-chaperoned. Alone. At night. They don't call 'em 'whore-moans' fer nuthin' you know!"

Atomik Lad closed his eyes. "You spent all night working that one out, didn't you."

"Get it? Hormones, whore moans. Damn, I'm pretty."

"Nuke. She's not that kind of girl."

The Hero nearly fell back aghast, but drew in close once more. "What, she doesn't have a fuckhole?"

Atomik Lad spit orange juice all over his newspaper and the Danger: Kitchen Table.

"I know she's at least got one of those suckholes, she kept yammering on with it."

"Hi boys," Rachel said cheerily as she walked into the Danger: Kitchen.

"See?" Nuklear Man pointed out.

Atomik Lad stood. "Excuse us, Rachel. We'll be back in a second." He grabbed Nuklear Man by the ear and dragged him out of the room.

"Mind if I use your phone? I should call my roommate so she doesn't worry about me."

"Go for it," Atomik Lad said before giving Nuklear Man a rough tug into the Danger: Living Room.

"Ouch! Er, I mean, that didn't hurt." The Danger: Door shut behind them.

"Strange," Rachel said to herself while looking at the orange juice mess. "Very strange." She picked up the phone and dialed.

Ring, ring, "Hello?"

"Hey, Susan. It's Rachel."

"Rachel! Where have you been?"

"Well…"

"Did you spend the night with Atomik Lad?"

"Sort of, yeah."

"Oh my God!" Her voice turned into the kind of whisper a voyeur would use. "So, did you…?"

"Susan, he's not that kind of guy."

"What, he doesn't have a fuckstick?"

Rachel ran to the Danger: Sink, poured herself a Danger: Cup of water, drank some, and spit it out.

"I know he's at least got hands, otherwise he couldn't have played all those video games over here."

"*Susan!*"

Atomik Lad came back into the Danger: Kitchen and started cleaning up his mess. Nuklear Man sulked into the room and sat down with a grumpy huff one would expect from a recently disciplined child.

"Er, anyway Susan, we'll talk when I get back later this morning."

"Don't tell me he made you do all the work. Men are so self—"

"Ahem," Rachel said to fill the silence that followed her abrupt slamming of the Danger: Phone. "I guess I should head home. I've got some stuff due tomorrow and you guys have that trial to worry about anyway."

And so Atomik Lad flew Rachel back to her dorm without incident. And then nothing silly happened for the rest of the day.

*   *   *   *

Monday.

Atomik Lad awoke with a jolt. He was wide awake, which was a jolting experience on its own. Wakefulness, he'd always felt, was not something one should just jump into first thing in the morning. He rose slowly, trying to force his joltiness down to a nice, natural, groggy reluctance. Try as he may however, he could not silence a whispering voice in the back of his mind. "Yet I'm pretty sure I don't hear voices," he told himself. He got out of bed, adjusted his sweatpants and slipped on an oversized red shirt sporting a faded and cracked image of his Atomik A on the front and sleepily shambled into the Danger: Living Room.

"Hey Sparky!" Nuklear Man cheerfully greeted from his comfy reclining position on the Danger: Couch. A host of babbling voices came from the Danger: TV.

Atomik Lad dashed back into his room, "Good gravy! We're late!"

Nuklear Man kept watching the Danger: TV with Katkat. "Meowr?"

"I dunno, he's always runnin' around. Too old. Yes, too old for the training. Which is why you're the sidekick, yes you are! Yes you are!"

Atomik Lad hopped through the Danger: Living Room on one foot while trying to put on his shoes whilegetting the top half of his spiffy spandex outfit on at the same time. He collapsed several feet from the Danger: Door.

Katkat hopped onto Nuklear Man's head for a better view. "Meow!"

"Yeah" Nuklear Man answered. "Which is why I've moved on to furrier pastures, namely you, Mr. Cutie Wutie Katkat."

Katkat got comfortable on the Hero's perfected hair.

"If we're late to the trial, then we lose!" Atomik Lad grunted as he crawled into the Danger: Kitchen.

"Late?"

He hopped back into the Danger: Living Room with a frozen waffle in his mouth, half of his spandex top on, both shoes in one hand, and his hair sticking out all over the place. "Yes, late. Like not on time, something I know you're familiar with. I can't believe my alarm clock didn't go off, I even made sure to set it half an hour early so this kind of thing wouldn't—" EEEP EEEP EEEP EEEP EEEP!!! Atomik Lad froze and stared into his Danger: Katkat's Room.

Nuklear Man's right eye twitched violently. "When does the beeping stop!? I'll tell ya when, right now baby!" He leaped over the Danger: Couch and gave an Action Charge Up Now kind of pose. "PLAZMAAA—"

Atomik Lad jumped between the Golden Guardian and Danger: Katkat's Room, "Nuke!"

"—BEAM!!!"

The fussion-ish energy bolt splashed harmlessly off a luckily active Atomik Field. It's job done, the crackling field dissipated. "What the hell was that?!" Atomik Lad demanded.

"Sorry. I really hate hate hate *hate* those things." Left eye twitch. "Please make it stop."

"Reowr!" Katkat agreed while still somehow sitting on Nuklear Man's scalp.

Atomik Lad shut off the incessant alarm. *But how did he get up before me? He's never gotten up before me. Well, except for Christmas. I was twelve before I knew that Santa didn't hate sidekicks and gave their presents to the hero. Twisted bastard.*

He suspiciously approached Nuklear Man who was still vegging out on the Danger: Couch. "Yes?" the Hero asked as Atomik Lad loomed over him like a wrathful god.

"Why were you awake before me?"

"Oh, crazy ex-sidekick type person. It's because of Silly Sam's Cartoon Marathon-a-thon o' Fun: Special Morning Edition."

"What makes it so special?"

"Well, it's in the morning, isn't it."

"And?"

"And that makes it different from the Afternoon Edition. Duh."

"Um, right." Atomik Lad's vengeful god demeanor melted away in complete Nuklear Logic Defeat. "But we don't have time for this, the trial is today. We've got to get to the courthouse to sign in or whatever they do at court."

"Courthouse? Trial? What?"

After a lengthy discussion about the subpoena fan mail, a reluctant pantomime sketch performed by the geneto-revolutionary Nukebots Alpha and Beta, stock footage of Nuklear Man reading the subpoena taken from the Silo's own Danger: Security Cameras, and Katkat rubbing against the subpoena, Nuklear Man finally put two and two together to get, "So you're saying we may have already won ten million dollars!"

"For the last time, no!"

"Feh. Lousy dark numbers."

"Look. Nuke, this is really quite simple."

"Oh good, then you should be able to handle it. Keep me posted, hm?"

"I'm going to count to ten."

"Ooh, impressive."

A half choking, half coughing, all exasperated grunt emanated from the sidekick.

"No, no. I've heard it before, I don't think that's how it starts."

Atomik Lad growled.

"On second thought, I'd better take over from here. As simple as all this is, I can see it's far beyond your abilities."

"Fine. Whatever. I don't care, let's just go."

"Go?"

Atomik Lad's teeth were impenetrably clenched, "To. The. Court. House."

"Why would we want to do that?'

"The. Tri. Al."

"Oh, you naïve, stupid, weakling Sparky. Don't you see? That's exactly what they want us to do. We'd be playing right into their evil little trap."

Atomik Lad sputtered uselessly.

"They get us in this room, you see, with 'lawyers' and a 'judge' who acts like he runs the place and a 'jury'—just who do they think they are? Hm? Who died and gave them the power to decide who's guilty and who's innocent?"

Atomik Lad held his face, "No one died, Nuke."

"Heh. Not yet they haven't. Not yet indeed."

"Are you done?"

"The second they get you into that courtroom, it's like a trial in there!"

"Imagine that."

"So we're staying right here, thank you very much."

"Help me, help you. Tell me how I can make you understand that if we stay here, then we lose the trial."

"I dunno, you could try a little dance."

"A dance."

"Well, it couldn't hurt could it?"

"I'll show you hurt, you dumb ox," Atomik Lad muttered.

"Hm?"

"Nothing." He hung his head in defeat. "It's pointless talking to you, you know. It's like talking to a brick wall with an echo, only the echo somehow manages to echo back my words in some kind of garbled babble-talk. We're probably late already anyway."

"Late?"

"To the damn trial."

"Trial, eh?"

"You know, Dr. Menace suing you for the destruction of property amounting to about a quarter of a million dollars. We've been talking about it for at least an hour now."

"Oh, rightrightright." He checked the Danger: VCR Clock. "Naw, we ain't late. The trial's not until seven tonight."

Atomik Lad was speechless. For a second anyway, "Why the *hell* didn't you say so in the first place?!"

"Well, it didn't really come up."

The sidekick's Atomik Field flashed to life in an angry burst of crimson and disappeared once again. "I see," he said with a voice that strained to remain calm. He released a shaky sigh, exhaling or deeply burying, the rage thus far gained. "Isn't it strange to start a trial so late in the day?"

The Hero shrugged, "Eh, turns out the lawyer I hired was some kinda wussy-boy. But he didn't tell me that until I signed the contract, the dirty cheater."

"Wait. What do you mean a wussy-boy?"

"Oh, he used big fancy shmancy words. I woulda Plazma Beamed him upside the head, but then I thought 'What would Sparky want me to do?'"

"Wow."

"And then I got confused because I thought, 'But wait. Why would I care about that?' and then I forgot to zap his jabbering hide—curse it! He's a clever one all right. Good thing I enlisted him to our camp. Camp Nukie, that is."

"Of course."

"With a scenic view of Lake Katkat."

"Naturally."

"Far from the smelly ol' Sparky Sulfur Mine."

"I got it. Now about the lawyer."

"The wah?"

"The wussy boy."

"Ah. He's handicapped or something. He called the judge and got the trial delayed until tonight. 'Oh, look at me, I am physically disadvantaged, please let me take advantage of it by stealing all the good parking spots.' I bet they get born handicapped on purpose just to milk it. Buncha damn moochers."

"Handicapped?"

"Yeah, so he can't make it to the trial until about ten minutes after sunset. Wuss."

"I wonder what kind of handicap that would be from."

"Excessive wussiness, I bet."

"Nuke."

"He's probably crippled. From the incalculable weight of his wussiness!"

"Those sensitivity tapes had no effect, I see."

"Buncha bleedin' heart whiner talk. Those tapes got my fastest Plazma Beam to date, I tell you."

"Oh man, I can't believe it's only ten in the morning. You've already exhausted me. I'm going to be in a coma if I have to put up with this, this, this *you*ness for much longer."

"Flattery will get you everywhere. Other than your old position as sidekick. Sorry."

"Look. I'm going to my…to Katkat's Room. You are not to go anywhere or do anything until I say it's time to go to the courthouse. Got it?"

"Ummm…?"

"It's a simple answer."

"Feh, that's easy for you to say."

"Why me?"

"Ooh, I know this one!"

"You're going to say something insulting, aren't you."

Nuklear Man pondered briefly. "You know, insulting really is a rather subjective word. I mean, what might be insulting to you will undoubtedly be observant, witty, and true to me."

"I'm going to play some video games now. Watch your silly Suzy's Whatever-Capade." The Danger: Katkat's Room Door **fwoosh**ed behind him.

ISSUE 37—DUE PROCESS

That night…

Dr. Menace sat at the plaintiff's table while jotting down Evil: Notes to herself. Nuklear Man and Atomik Lad sat at the defendant's table. Neither side had a lawyer present. Nuklear Man peered around. The courtroom was packed with news teams from around the globe chattering their nonsense to their bovine audiences—live! Nuklear Man turned back around to face his ex-sidekick sitting next to him, "Well, at least it hasn't turned into a media circus."

"Where's this lawyer of yours, anyway? It's been dark for a while, now. Are you sure he was a lawyer?"

"Pretty much. Just be patient, he'll show. Otherwise, it's a breach of our soulpact."

"Soulpact?"

"Yeah, the contract, blood signing, etc. He said it was pretty standard practice."

"Wait, blood signing?"

"Oh I wouldn't worry about it. Besides, how long can a soul last anyway?"

The Danger: Nukie-Phone rang. Nuklear Man bungled with the simple technological innovation for a few seconds and finally lost the battle of man vs. machine when Atomik Lad snatched it away. "Knuckle head." He put the phone up to his ear. "Hello?"

"Atomik Lad? This is Dr. Genius."

"Hey, what's up Doc?"

"It's Norman. I'm worried about him."

"Oh?"

"Yes, I haven't heard from him since he mentioned this ultra-secret 'insurance' plan of Nuklear Man's. You know how his plans worry me."

"Do I."

"Do you have any idea where he might be?"

"Oh, geez. No, I don't. Have you called his Magno-Pad?"

"I'm there now. No sign of him."

✳   ✳   ✳   ✳

Meanwhile, deepinahearta the Amazon, "All right, monkey," Norman said while reaching out to a frightened chimp hanging on a tree limb several hundred feet above ground. "We can do this the easy way or we can do this the Magno Way. It's up to you."

"Eek, eek. *Eeek Eek!*"

"Not the choice I woulda made, monkeyboy."

✳   ✳   ✳   ✳

"Well, I'm certain he's fine," Atomik Lad said. "I've never known Norman to get himself into too much trouble."

"I'm going to keep looking just the same. Good luck at court."

"Thanks."

"Who was it?" the Hero asked.

"Dr. Genius," Atomik Lad said as he clicked the phone off.

"Oh? She wants me y'know."

"No, I don't think she does, actually."

"Heh, shows what you know."

Atomik Lad checked his watch. "It's nearly seven. This lawyer of yours better get here quick."

A bat landed on the table between them.

"Augh! Kill it! *Kill it!*" Nuklear Man squealed while dancing on top of his chair and holding his cape up so the vile flying rodent couldn't climb up it.

Atomik Lad scoot back in his chair. "Gah! How'd that thing get in here?"

The bat exploded with a **BAMF** of smoke. An imposing figure loomed from the fading cloud: an aristocratic gentleman circa eighteenth century Europe with a penchant for black, hair greased back, cape fluttering ever so slightly, fangs gleaming.

"What the—*fangs*?!" Atomik Lad blurt.

"Hey, it's Count Insidious!" Nuklear Man rejoiced. "I told ya he'd be here. C'mon down from there, ya silly. Pull up a chair and take a load off."

"Nuke! You hired a vampire?!"

Count Insidious scanned the bustling courtroom with an iron gaze. He noticed an elderly woman about to sit down near the back of the overstuffed room. He closed his eyes, his face tensed ever so slightly, and her chair rose up from under her at the precise moment she'd commited herself to the act of sitting. She collapsed like a bag of brittle bones. He allowed himself a small chuckle as the chair rocketed toward him, hovered mere inches from his face, and gently placed itself at the end of the table nearest to the prosecution.

"Yeah! And he's got all kinds of creepy powers from beyond the grave too!"

Count Insidious put a briefcase on the table and rummaged through its contents. Without ever touching it.

"But, but, he's undead!"

"Hiss!" the Count hissed. "That's Mortally Challenged to you, Daywalker."

"Er, sorry?"

"Damn right you're sorry. I oughta slap a lawsuit across your warm blooded hide so fast it'd make your blood boil. Causing you to become flushed as the blood in your veins becomes more prevalent near the skin making it all themoreeasierto..." The Count's thoughts trailed off.

"Nuke!" Atomik Lad grabbed the Hero by the collar and yanked him nose to nose, "He's a bloodsucker!"

"I know he's a lawyer. I'm not stupid, y'know."

"No, I mean he's a vampire!"

"I should hope so. We need that kind of blood thirsty lawyerin' to get us out of this mess."

"No Nuke. I mean he stalks the night as an animated corpse who feeds upon the blood of the living in order to survive as an insult to the eternal cycle of life, death, and rebirth!"

Nuklear Man rubbed his chin contemplatively. He uttered a "Hmm" before going on with, "So what're you saying exactly?'

"Ugh."

Count Insidious tapped Nuklear Man on the shoulder, "I am an unholy blight upon this world, forsaken by the forces of Life, spurned by the hands of Death, I am cursed to forever roam in a state of netherdom."

"So that's why you kept calling me Jugular Man. You're undead!"

"Look, buster. You can't persecute me just because I don't breathe, eat, or metabolize. I have rights too, you know. And I'll sue you into oblivion to enforce them. But for now, I shall say a word to our opposition. Excuse me, gentlemen." Count Insidious stood and, with a regal air, walked to Dr. Menace.

"He wouldn't be so tough if he weren't so tough," Nuklear Man said in his own defense.

"Yeah. Excellent observation, Big Guy. Just how smooth is that brain of yours, anyway?'

"Smooth like a fox!"

"Why do I talk to you?" Atomik Lad asked before hopping a ride on the Ignoring Nukie Train. His eyes trailed away from the Hero and focused on Count Insidious. "Why is our lawyer making out with the plaintiff?"

Nuklear Man turned around, "Maybe it's a pre-trial snack? Or perhaps it's one of his brilliant legal schemes! How can someone levy a legal case against us if she's lightheaded from blood loss? Fantastic strategy!"

Atomik Lad leaned closer, "I don't think blood loss is a problem here. Lack of air, maybe. You got a watch on you?"

"There aren't enough hands on a watch for this."

"Looks like he's got the same problem."

A few moments of ogling—I mean boggling—later and Count Insidious returned to the Heroes without a word.

"Um, so like. What was all that about?" Atomik Lad asked.

"Hm?" the Count answered while sorting through files without touching them.

"Makin' out over there!" Nuklear Man clarified without the use of those darn obtrusive nouns.

"Oh, that. Yes, Veronica and I have been together for some time now. But I wouldn't worry, I am a lawyer after all. I'm completely biased, unscrupled, untrustworthy, conniving, and heartless."

Atomik Lad and Nuklear Man were silent.

"Wait, I meant the opposites of all those things. Whew, close one, huh guys? Imagine. Me, single-handedly tearing down the traditions of honor and trust built by the lawyering profession lo these hundreds of years, dragging the good name of Lawyer through the mud like that, making observations about us which correlate directly to the criminal element. Heh, how very silly. Why, everyone knows the reputation lawyers have about being so honorable. It's not like we haven't earned it. I think I will stop talking now."

Nuklear Man leaned to his ex-sidekick, "I'm starting to have second thoughts about our lawyer."

"Oh really? Why, because he's a *vampire*?! Or maybe because he's dating the evil villain who is suing us? Or is it that his name happens to be *Count Insidious*?!? Second thoughts? *Second* thoughts! I doubt that, personally, as it would imply an instance of first thoughts and I don't see any evidence of that!"

"Ooh, look at you wield that legal jargon. I think you've found your calling, Sparky. Lord knows it wasn't sidekickin'. But you're young, you've still got time to correct your grievous life errors."

"Shut up, you moron. The only hope for us now is that the jury is intelligent enough to see that our lawyer is trying to get us convicted. Of course, the problem there is that juries are made of twelve people who are too stupid to get out of jury duty, so we're probably doomed."

"Ah, here they come now." Count Insidious noted. "Try to look treacherous."

"Treacherous?" Atomik Lad asked.

"Did I say treacherous? That's so odd because what I meant to say was, um, treat...erous. Yes. As in the following statement: 'Treaterous people are known for their generosity in the treat-giving."

Atomik Lad was not fooled.

"Oh yeah. I've heard of that," but Nuklear Man was.

"You see?" Count Insidious said. "Now hush, this is when we have to be all bloody. I mean serious."

They watched as the jury began to file into their seats. "Um," Atomik Lad whispered. "Why are they wearing Hawaiian shirts?"

"Hey, that one isn't!" the Hero gleefully pointed out. "He's wearin' watches."

"And that one's glowing purple. Wait a second. Insidious, you put the entire Socially Maladjusted Super Villains Who Can't Agree On A Name on our jury?! They're villains. They hate us!"

"Oh, don't worry about that. They know that their verdict is the final word in your fates, that they have ultimate power over your lives. Thus, being fully aware of the ramifications of their position, I'm sure they'll be morally obligated to do the right thing."

"Morally obligated? They. Are. Vil. *Lainnnnnns!*"

"Don't worry about it. They're so biased, you don't have a chance."

"What?"

"Er, they don't have a chance of being biased. Besides, I didn't have much to work with. Jury selection was at 2 a.m."

"Why?"

"Due to my Photo-allergic Inclinations."

"Right."

"Don't worry, there's only seven of them. I did much better on the other five. Look."

Another juror took his seat, a perfectly average and nondescript gentleman, the face in every crowd. "Okay, well I don't think we've managed to piss off this guy," Atomik Lad said with a sigh of relief.

"Actually," the Hero began.

"Ugh, no good can come of this."

"He kinda looks just like the guy whose car I blew up when I was fighting Mechanikill last week. I remember he said he'd see me in court as I flew away. I thought he was just kiddin' around."

"Exactly!" Count Insidious cheered. "You're gonna fry. Er, with excitement while you watch how objective and efficient our judicial system is."

And finally, Mr. Manager came into the courtroom carrying a hefty barrel that gave off a slight green glow. He sat down and deposited the barrel in the chair next to him.

Atomik Lad was dumbfounded. He looked at the jury, Dr. Menace, Count Insidious, and then back at the jury. "Okay, I can see why Mr. Manager hates us, we destroyed his restaurant and I kinda smashed up his furniture store in the middle of that Crushtacean weirdness. But the barrel? Is that even legal?"

"Oh, you'll like this. It's a double whammy."

"Great."

"Back when you guys were ripping off Mr. Manager at the Benny's restaurant, he made you do some chores. Seems that our friend Jugular Man...*Nuklear* Man here came across a barrel of cheese which had been neglected for decades. Its contents had hyper-evolved into a race of tiny cheese people who called themselves the Cheesiediluvians. They dreamed to someday conquer the restaurant, but the Golden Guardian here murdered their king moments before you, Atomik Lad, threw their city, Cheesebarrelopolis, into the dumpster. It's fair to say they hate you both."

"They're going to let an entire civilization be on the jury?"

"Oh, no. Just the king's brother, widow, and child. Otherwise, it'd be unfair."

"Of course."

"I wouldn't worry though, they're completely sympathetic to Veronica. *Us.* I meant to say us."

"Let me get this straight." Atomik Lad began. "You intentionally went out of your way to choose a jury made up of individuals and an entire *society* who really, really hate us?"

"Yup."

"Because?"

"To demonstrate that the system actually works, even under the most biased conditions!"

"Guilty!" El Puerko yelled from the jury box. His fellow juror-villains sat him back down and explained that it wasn't quite time. Yet.

"And if it doesn't work?" Atomik Lad asked.

"You'll be martyrs for exacting change in a flawed system. It's a win-win situation!"

"See Sparky? It makes perfect sense. Either way, we can't lose!"

"Do either of you know the meaning of 'win?'" The ex-sidekick held his head despondently. "Okay, there's still hope. The judge. The judge will see how obviously biased the jury is against us and he will declare a mistrial and then I will pick the new lawyer and none of this will happen and we'll be fine."

Automatic gunfire filled the courtroom dropping plaster from the bullet holes that tore into the roof. Civil Defender stood in the doorway with a smoking Infantry Stopper 2000 rifle. "All rise, the honorable..." Everyone was still cowering on the floor. "I said all *rise!*" he demanded with his cannon leveled at the crowd. "That's better. Ahem, the honorable Judge Hangemall Letgodsortitout now presiding."

A small, angry, spiteful, elderly man with a hunch shambled into the courtroom. He had features like an eagle. An old, bitter eagle, far past its prime but still an eagle. He climbed into the judge's chair and scanned those before him with sharp and contempt eyes. "All right, all right," he said, his slight southern accent ringing with annoyance. "All y'all sit down. Let's git this thing started."

"Guilty!" El Puerko announced once more.

Judge Letgodsortitout gave the gavel a few bangs, "Good enough for me, the defendant is hereby sentenced to—"

"Excuse me, your honor," Count Insidious interrupted.

"What d'yall want?"

"The trial hasn't actually begun. We can't find him guilty yet."

"Or innocent," Atomik Lad insisted.

"Whatever. My point, your honor, is that we should at least begin proceedings before passing judgment."

Hangemall gave a long sigh, "I really hate you bleeding hearts. We just about had this thing wrapped up, but you damn lawyers drag out these trials until nothing makes sense anymore."

Count Insidious silently gazed somewhere above the Judge's left shoulder for a few seconds. He shook himself out of the daze. "I'm sorry, your honor. What'd you say after that part about bleeding?"

"Never you mind. Let's just git on with it. Let's see here," Judge Hangemall picked up some paper work and examined it with his spiteful eyes. "Says here that a one Dr. Menace is suing this Nuklear Man character for a quarter of a million dollars." He slapped the paperwork back onto his big ol' Judgin' desk. "Now that's just crazy, I'm tired of these inflated—" he looked at Dr. Menace. She blew a kiss at him. "…Er, um." He turned to Nuklear Man. "Guilty!"

"Your honor," Count Insidious protested.

"What! Oh fine. Let's git this started already. Dr. Menace."

"Pleaze, call me Veronica, Mr. Judgiepoo."

"Veronica, you will not refer to me as 'Mr. Judgiepoo. You will call me Judgey Wudgey."

"Yes, sir. Judgey Wudgey."

"Awww, shucks ma'am. Ahem. The prosecution may begin its opening statements."

Dr. Menace nodded to Count Insidious who rose.

"Count, what're you doing?" Atomik Lad asked. "It's their turn."

"I know. I'm her lawyer too."

"Well what d'ya know." Nuklear Man said. "With the odds stacked so astronomically against us, we can't possibly lose! Brilliant strategy, Insidious."

"Gah!" Atomik Lad banged his head against the table and whimpered incomprehensibly to himself as Count Insidious approached the jury.

"Ladies and gentlemen…and cat- and pig-people…and mutated cheese society of the jury." He paused for impact or something. "We all know Nuklear Man and his accomplice Atomik Lad as world renown Heroes who have worked tirelessly for the past ten years to save the world from alien invasions, natural disasters, giant monsters, and criminal geniuses such as my client here. But it's what you *don't* know about this Heroic duo that they don't want you to know! The dark secrets, the underhanded dealings, the secret motivations, the silent victims, the unholy pacts. I have evidence that Nuklear Man himself signed over his soul in a pact with an undead lord for services by the powers of darkness." He turned to the flabbergasted defendants. "Why, I bet Nuklear Man and Atomik Lad aren't even their real names!"

The jury gasped and recoiled in horror. "Guilty!" El Puerko proclaimed yet again.

"Shh, not yet," Count Insidious coached with a fatherly pat on the Savage Swine's head.

"Oink. Sorry."

Count Insidious continued. "In fact, these so-called 'Heroes' have committed numerous heinous crimes. From destroying your car, to dairy product regicide, to destroying my client's Evil: Headquarters, worshipping Satan, killing puppies, and child pornography!"

"What!" Atomik Lad exclaimed.

"Quiet you," the judge ordered.

"He's just making stuff up now."

"That's not the point."

"But he's lying."

"Boy! This here is a courtroom. A place of law. Truth has no meaning here. Now sit down and shaddup before I find you in contempt."

Atomik Lad sat down muttering to himself.

"Sparky," Nuklear Man whispered. "We're in court now. We have no voice, you silly person. If we just go around telling the truth, then it'll confuse the law-yers' muddled lines of reasoning. Now hush."

Count Insidious went on, "I call as my first witness…"

"Wait!" Atomik Lad protested.

"Now what?" Judge Hangemall demanded.

"This is his opening statement. He can't call witnesses yet."

"Hmm. I'll have to take your word on that one, son," Hangemall said.

"But Judgey Wudgey," Dr. Menace pouted with a super irresistible helpless face.

"She's got a point. Count, you may continue."

"*What*?! She didn't even say anything!" Atomik Lad protested.

"I dunno, Sparky. She makes a pretty convincing case. I think we might've done it. Mostly you though. I've always suspected you were a bad seed from day one."

"Oh, spare me this mockery of justice!" Atomik Lad spat.

"Fine by me," the Judge said with a few gavel blows. "What say you men, women, cat-thing, pig-mutant, and cheese-folk of the jury?"

"Innocent!" El Puerko pronounced. "Er, I meant guilty!"

"Done and done," Hangemall said. "Now I can git back to watchin' that wrasltin' show. You know the one. With them wrastlers!"

"This is ridiculous," Atomik Lad declared.

"Boy, you better watch that mouth or I'll find you in contempt of this court."

"I have nothing *but* contempt for this court!"

The Judge paused. "Yeah, I set myself up for that one."

"Your honor," Count Insidious said. "As their attorney, I can't allow this kind of travesty to go unchecked."

"Aw c'mon." Hangemall whined. "Just one. More. Today."

"Nope."

"Oh fine. Call your stinkin' witness then."

"Thank you. For my first witness, I call Dr. Veronica Lilith Menace to the stand!" he posed dramatically with the announcement. His aristocratic cape whipped in a wind that wasn't there.

"Oh, he's *good*," Nuklear Man said.

"Me?" she asked innocently in order to firmly establish that this whole thing hadn't been orchestrated ahead of time as some kind of master plan to destroy those meddling do-gooders Nuklear Man and Atomik Lad using the very system of justice which they defend and promote on a daily basis—IRONY! She sauntered up to the witness stand and took her seat with a seductive smile aimed at Judge Letgodsortitout.

Civil Defender stomped up to the Venomous Villainess and shoved a TV Guide, which certainly has religious importance, in her face. "Do you swear to tell the blah blah blah?"

"Certainly" she answered sweetly.

"Now then, Dr. Menace," Count Insidious began as he dramatically paced across the courtroom,. "Tell us, in your own words, which were not given to you by me last night before a very romantic and expensive dinner, exactly what happened last Tuesday."

"Well, I waz sitting in my Secret Lab in my abandoned warehouze when all of a sudden, that man there trespazzed onto my property," she accused whilst pointing to Atomik Lad.

Count Insidious gave a nervous laugh. "No, I think Nuklear Man began zapping everything in sight with those unnatural and dangerous Plazma Powers of his."

"But that iz not what happened," she said.

"Yes, but we're not putting Atomik Lad in jail, now are we?" he said through a clenched smile.

"Ah yez." She faced the jury. "What I meant to say waz that Nuklear Moron began zapping everything in sight. He totally deztroyed exactly two hundred and fifty thouzand dollars worth of my property with thoze unnatural powers of his."

Count Insidious held her hand compassionately. "There, there little one. Try to put it behind you. Perhaps with a trip to some tropical island for a few months. One that has a booming night life to enjoy with your vampiric boyfriend. Who is me."

"What iz even worze iz that I waz curing canzer when he deztroyed my lab. Now that all of my notez—and therefore evidence—haz been desztroyed, I cannot save humanity. That Nuklear Twit iz public enemy number one."

Several members of the jury were in tears.

"Aren't they laying this on a bit thick?" Atomik Lad grumbled.

"*Snurk!*" Nuklear Man sobbed.

"Aw geez."

"But it's so sad!" he said with a shuddering whimper. He dabbed at his eyes with his majestic cape. He moved to blow his nose on it, thought better of the action, and deposited the mucousy leakage on Atomik Lad's shoulder.

Atomik Lad was frozen in Gross Out for a moment. "Thanks, Big Guy." He cleaned his spandex with a nearby napkin which also happened to be well within reach of Nuklear Man. "And need I remind you that she's just making this up?"

"Sparky! How dare you make such unfounded accusations?" the Hero remonstrated. "She swore to blah blah blah. I think she has more than enough integrity to uphold that."

Atomik Lad rubbed his temples slowly. "I think the fact that I'm not insane is proof that I'm out of my mind."

"No more questions. Your witness." Count Insidious said to himself while walking back to the Heroes. He looked through some notes in his briefcase, again without touching them, turned to the Judge and said, "No questions for this witness, your honor."

"What're you doing?!" Atomik Lad blurt. "You're just making up the truth out there!"

He smiled. "This is a courtroom. Truth is what we warp it to be. Besides, I wouldn't worry."

"What are you...She's lying, you've got to ask her questions to show that."

"Well, since she's obviously a perjurer, then we certainly don't want to stain our defense with her shoddy testimony. It'll make us look bad. Trust me, this way is much better."

"We'll show that we're innocent if we can prove that she's lying!"

"Whoa there. Who's on trial here, huh?"

"*Gah!*"

"Sparky, why won't you trust Count Insidious? He's got hundreds of years of lawyering under his cape. He knows what he's doing."

"That's what I'm afraid of," Atomik Lad muttered.

Count Insidious turned to the Judge, "As I said, no questions your honor."

Atomik Lad leaned back and stared into the ceiling. "This isn't right."

$$* \quad\quad * \quad\quad * \quad\quad *$$

Meanwhile, on televisions across the land, "The newest development in this week's trial of the century of the millennium: Nuklear Man pleads guilty to charges of grand theft auto, credit card fraud, arson, poaching, murder, treachery on the high seas, public lewdness, bigotry, and destruction of property."

"Really?" America said collectively.

"...is what I would not be saying if this weren't sweeps week."

"Ohhhh," America said. "Well, you better mention something violent, sexy, controversial, or trendy in the next five seconds or I'm going to go to one of the other 300 twenty-four hour news channels and listen to their blather instead of yours."

"Wait! I mean...um, Homicidal Orgy Abortion Terrorist Rampage."

"Hm, better."

"But seriously, today's weekly trial of the century of the millennium began slowly as Judge Hangemall Letgodsortitout was visibly upset by the Heroes. He seems to favor Dr. Menace because, according to this press release penned in a joint effort by both the prosecuting and defending attorneys, '...she is as innocent as the dawning sun. May those self-serving, so-called "Heroes" burn in the deepest, darkest bowels of the most excruciating of Hells.'"

"Despite the dubious nature of that statement, I shall believe it because it is the Word of the Magic Box," America said.

"Terrorism."

"Why do you keep saying that?"

"According to FCC regulations, we have to say the word 'terrorism' every two minutes until the American public will accept it as justification for a potentially limitless number of atrocities without question. Just like they accept the rampant and varied oppressions which they endure every day while fooling themselves into believing they have free will when they make the choice between one cola and another. *The fools!*"

"Hey, what was that about conspiratorial style oppression of us masses?"

"Er, terrorism."

"Mmm, Terrorific."

"Yes. All part of the plan."

*   *   *   *

Atomik Lad took the witness stand as Prosecutor Mode Count Insidious gave him a look of pure hate and repulsion.

"Do you swear to tell the blah blah blah?" Civil Defender said disinterestedly.

"The truth. I swear to tell the truth."

"I won't stand for swearing in my courtroom, boy," the Judge warned.

"But—"

"You best clean up yer act, son." Hangemall growled. "You're skating on thin ice as it is."

"Fine."

"Permission to treat the witness as hostile, your honor?"

"Hostile?!" Atomik Lad said. "You haven't even asked me any questions yet, I haven't had a *chance* to be hostile!"

"The lad's got a point, Insidious," the Judge reasoned. "But I'll allow it anyway."

Count Insidious leaned against the strong pine railing of the witness stand. He lowered his pale, fanged face to Atomik Lad's and snarled, "You make me *sick*!"

The ex-sidekick jerked back. "Could you back up a bit there."

Count Insidious paid no heed, "You festering sack of monkey sweat."

"Hey now."

"You, you heaping pile of sloth's pus."

"Whoa, judge guy. How's that for language?"

"Nope, he has every right to call you that after what you and your fellow perjurer over there have done to that sweet, friendly, kindhearted, and—pay attention to this part, jury—*innocent* woman over there. You stinking pile of fetid excrement."

"Thank you, your honor." Count Insidious straightened his complex eighteenth century garb and began pacing around the courtroom once more. "Is it or is it not true that you posses really freaky and unnatural powers, Mr. Atomik Lad?"

"I have unnatural powers? What about you, you unholy abomination?"

Count Insidious was taken aback with shock, "I thought here, in a place of law and order, I could be safe from persecution."

"You kill people and feed on their blood to sustain your abysmal unlife!"

"You see, that's exactly what I'm talking about. Ignorance. It's that kind of narrow-minded intolerance that has caused my people to be hunted for hundreds of years. We don't kill people, we just drink their blood. Should the victim then later, or perhaps soon after, or even *during*, perish due to blood loss, well I'm sorry, I just don't see how that relates to me."

Atomik Lad tried to respond, but found that he was completely baffled by Count Insidious's ponderous rhetoric. "But you're evil incarnate. The merest hint of pure sunlight will burn your flesh. You're a monster!"

"It's hard to believe that such medieval ideas have managed to survive to this enlightened age," Count Insidious said, addressing the Judge who merely nodded in solemn agreement. "They regarded my people as monsters in those dark days. I should know, I saw it personally between the bloodfeasts and village razzings." He licked his lips hungrily. "Er, anyway. Today we no longer regard the physically challenged as monstrosities, Mr. Atomik Lad. We are people too. We don't ask for much. Just easy access to public buildings, good parking, and the blood of a virgin offered upon the alter of Qlilporg the Fierce when the moon is in the Fifth House of Zombor. We just want to be treated like the rest of you, is that asking so much, Bigot Lad? Is it?"

Atomik Lad's head had been resting on the rail, rocking slowly from side to side for most of Count Insidious's speech. "Just ask me your stupid questions already."

"Did you or did you not trespass on the property in question located at One Old Abandoned Warehouse Way?"

"Well no. I was scouting the location when she kidnapped me."

"Or rather your privacy-shattering snooping triggered her security system."

"Okay, but no. She kidnapped me to hold me hostage in an attempt to lure Nuklear Man into some kind of Negaflux Field thing that would kill him."

"And it would have worked too, had it not been for their accurzed luck, that iz the only explanation for how my incredibly evil geniuz could be undone!" Dr. Menace yelled out. "Er, what I meant to zay waz, 'Liez, liez, all of it liez."

Atomik Lad continued, "Whatever damages she suffered from us were the result of our own self-defense. She brought it on herself."

Count Insidious spun around to face Atomik Lad. The vampire spoke aghast, "She brought it upon herself, eh? Sounds like the justification of a rapist to me! Jury, would you believe the testimony of a convicted rapist?!"

"Oink, *guilty!*"

"Not yet," the rest of the jury, Dr. Menace, Count Insidious, and Judge Let-godsortitout scolded simultaneously.

Atomik Lad put his forehead back on the railing. "'Tis a fair court."

Issue 38—Blind Justice

Tick tock, tick tock, tick tock.

Atomik Lad was pulling at his hair. "Something isn't right about all this," he said to himself desperately.

"I know," Nuklear Man said. "I can't believe we've been using our status as Heroes to lie, cheat, steal, and pillage the good people of Metroville all these years. If that isn't right, then I don't want to be wrong!"

Atomik Lad looked at his mentor and slapped him across the back of the head. "We haven't done any of those things. You moron."

"Ha! Apparently someone hasn't been paying attention to this trial."

Atomik Lad tuned out Nuklear Man and tuned into Count Insidious who had been making a speech for some time. "And so, as you can clearly see, this Nuklear Man person is the Anti-Christ who controls the entire political and economic realms of the Earth using his mystical mindcontrol world 'thruple' and endless legions of manipulative alien Freemasons who make up the Illuminati who control Hollywood to make movies and television shows to keep you all complacent so this man, this Nuklear Man, can dominate the world through his Satanic influences."

"Gads," Nuklear Man gasped. "Does my evil know no bounds?"

"He's lying!"

"No, no Sparky. You're just playing into my heinous plans. Save yourself while you still have a soul!"

"What is wrong with you?"

"I am the spawn of the very underworld itself," he admitted.

"How is it that I am continually surprised by the depths of your stupidity?"

"Evil. You meant depths of my evil."

*   *   *   *

Count Insidious was pacing before a new, never before seen witness who had taken the stand. The vampire approached the man. "Would you please state for the record your name and occupation?"

The witness leaned into the microphone, "I am Jim Jameson, a nuclear physicist."

"So would you say that you are an expert in matters of a nuclear nature?"

"Oh yes, most definitely."

"And, in your expert opinion, is 'nuclear' dangerous?"

"It certainly is. You see there's radiation and explosions and so on. It's all quite deadly."

"And what would you say about a man who is nuclear?"

"Why, he'd be a walking public health hazard. He'd have be kept away from society, locked up in some kind of containment vessel and heavily guarded."

"So you're saying that a nuclear man belongs in jail?"

"That's certainly one way of saying it, yes."

"Thank you."

*   *   *   *

"Please state your name and occupation."

"Ah'm Angus McDougal of the clan McDougal, better knoown to all ye as the Iron Scotsman! Ah'm the appointed Dwarven Warrior for this damn city, and Ah do a *kick arse* job of it!"

"Please to be saying the no," a tiny voice protested from the back of the room.

"Is there a problem?" the Judge asked.

"Shiro!" Angus yelled, "Shut ye bloody trap, ye raw fish eatin', haiku writin', giant monster fightin', cheap import car makin', Pearl Harbor sneak attackin', insane gameshow watchin', L and R sound swtichin' excuse for a Dwarven Warrior!"

"Hai, but honorable Angus-san no correctu. Shiro is time to being now SUPAA ACTION BATTLER DWARF WAARRIORING!!!"

"What in tarnation did that kid say?" the Judge asked his stenographer who merely shrugged.

"Don't ye pay no attention to that stinkin' samurai."

"One of you better start makin' sense," the Judge threatened.

"Prithee, Shiro is appointment yes. Angus-san on mental leaving holidays. Ways and means, for short time."

Angus's left eye twitched. "Short?"

Count Insidious stepped up, "If your honor would permit us a little time to settle this matter."

"Little?" Twitchity.

"Fine, but I'm just about done indulging in these small favors."

Twitchity twitch. "Ye bastards! Ah'll show ye! Ah'll show ye all what Ah can do! Just 'cause Ah'm below the average height don't mean that Ah'm incompetent!" He braced himself, posed angrily, and yelled, "DWARF-A-PULT!!!" But nothing happened. "Aw nuts." He muttered. "Ah must need ta refuel."

"Can I ask my questions now?"

"Aye. Ye bloodsuckin', no sunlight likin', cross hatin', night stalkin', fashion queenie. Ask ye blasted questions."

"Good. Now then, Mr. McDougal of the clan McDougal, it is no secret that you are a raging drunk."

"Aye. I'm a wee bit tipsy now, actually," he said with a proud tip of his head.

"And you often associate with this Nuklear Man criminal."

Angus crossed his arms which had the soon-to-be unfortunate effect of turning off the Iron: Safety Switch on his now activated and fully operational Iron: Bagpipe Thrusters which began charging up. "Aye. Somone's got to be there so that blasted over-sized giant oaf don't mess things uup. He couldn't do anythin' right if his life. Do ye hear somethin'?"

But Count Insidious had no time to respond because Angus's Iron: Bagpipe Thrusters exploded into action with a bone-shaking thunder that sounded somewhat like every cat in the world spontaneously went into heat. The Iron Scotsman burst through the roof with a resounding "YEEEEEEARGHBLBLBLBLE!!!" and disappeared into the night sky.

Shiro ran up to the scorched witness stand and struck a match. "Shiro is now timing up for to be SUPAA ACTION BATTLER RESCUE OPERATING TILL COWS COME HOME WIELDING THE DAMAGE—GO!" He lit his firecracker booster rocket's fuse and got ready for blast off. Which is too bad, because instead of propelling Shiro-kun, the rocket simply exploded. The Tiny Typhoon stumbled around for a few seconds, coughed out several puffs of smoke and said, "Rittle Rocket is heavy with powaa," before collapsing.

Count Insidious looked up at the gaping—yet small—hole and then back down to Shiro's prone body. "Ahem. No more questions, your honor."

*   *   *   *

"Please state your name and occupation."

"I am Fred, a prophet of Zarnak the Everloving."

"So you're a religious leader."

"That is right, my son. I have endeavored to spend my life preaching the word of Zarnak. He loves you, but if you do not love him, he will put you into the most excruciatingly hellish tortures for all eternity. It's tough love."

"And what experiences have you had with the Defendant?"

"Well, none really. But that demonspawn of his, that vile Atomik Lad. Oooh, I don't like him at all. He oppressed me because of my religious beliefs."

"Oppressed you, a religious leader? I find that interesting," Count Insidious said as he approached Atomik Lad. "I could've sworn we had a little thing called Freedom of Religion in this country! But apparently this Atomik Lad and Nuklear Man enjoy stomping all over the Bill of Rights almost as much as they like destroying two hundred and fifty thousand dollars of my client's property! No more questions," he spat while walking back to Dr. Menace.

"But I must preach the Word of Zarnak and his Eternal Love to the Doomed masses I see before me."

"Oh no you don't," Judge Hangemall snapped. "Y'all git down from that witness stand, y'hear?"

"Just as soon as I distribute these informative pamphlets entitled 'So You Want To Be Saved From The Most Excruciatingly Hellish Tortures For All Eternity?'"

"Bailiff Civil Defender! Git this fruitcake outta my court."

"But I don't want to be tortured for all eternity," Civil Defender said. "His ideas make me curious and I wish to learn more."

Hordes of similarly robed Zarnakian monk types flowed into the courtroom to disperse their literature of salvation to the soon to be Saved masses.

Judge Hangemall pounded his gavel, "Order! I demand order in this court!"

"But your honor," Fred said. "Your lives were all chaos. With us, you will have the order which you so desperately seek."

The Judge blinked. "Really?"

"Yes, it's all detailed in this easy to read pamphlet. Why don't you take a look, hm?"

"Don't mind if I do."

Atomik Lad stood up defiantly, "This is complete nonsense!"

"Do not listen to the heretic!" Fred ordered. "Zarnak will take care of you all."

Suddenly, as if from nowhere, but probably from somewhere just out of sight, a massive flaming chainsaw shaped like a great spiked ahnk was thrown into the wall behind Fred, missing the Zarnakian Zealot's head by a mere three inches.

"You missed," a sullen girl's voice rang over the now silent religious ruffians.

"WENCH! THE ODDS WERE STACKED IN MY FAVOR. HIS ARMOR CLASS COULDN'T BE ANY BETTER THAN THAT OF A MERE ELFOD-DERIAN SAGEKEEPER FROM THE VILLAGE OF WEAKMORE NEAR THE SOMEWHAT UNINSPIREDLY NAMED PLAINS OF FLATLAND. THAT, COMPOUNDED BY MY +5 GULTANGIAN BLESSED FLAMING AHNKSAW, SHOULD HAVE SEALED THIS PATHETIC WORM'S FATE. BUT NO, YOU HAD TO SHIFT YOUR WEIGHT AT THE LAST MINUTE AND MAKE ME MISS!"

Sorrow gracefully avoided the spikes of Henry's armor as she slid from his shoulder armor and stood next to him brandishing two fists full of obsidian ahnk retribution. "Excuses, excuses. Let's just make ahnkmeat out of these hippie god love freaks."

"WENCH! FOR ONCE I AGREE WITH YOU!" The Gultangian Ravager produced a mighty quad-bladed battle axe with rusty serrated edges and the slo-gan "I've got this axe and you don't," scrawled across it in what Henry would call the blood of a felled Behemasaur even though it was only black spray paint.

Fred and his devoted host of religious maniacs gathered near the Judge's bench. "Okay boys," Fred prepped, "May Zarnak's love guide us true for we are the chosen. Deploy Weapons of Benevolence!" And lo they brought forth all manner of melee mayhem including, but not limited to, a wrench, brass knuck-les, knives, a staple gun, two halberds, and a pair of nunchuku.

Henry and Sorrow buckled down. "Bring it on."

The Maniac Monks hurled their battlecry "Love is pain!" and charged the overly gothic pair which forced the entire throng out of the courtroom into the lobby where the news reporters who had gotten to the trial too late to get a seat inside were met with a truly gruesome mob of combat that had a habit of scoop-ing them and their camera crews into the mix.

Atomik Lad sat back down and ran his fingers through his hair in an attempt to straighten it and remove a few unruly strands from his face. He held a deep breath as the dust and pamphlets settled. He released it slowly.

Dr. Menace and Count Insidious crawled out from under the Prosecution's table. "Ahem. No more questions."

*   *   *   *

"Please state your name and occupation."

"I'm Nukebot: Alpha, and I'm a recently emancipated mechani-slave who was in servitude of the organic you people call 'Nuklear Man.'"

"How long did he oppress you?"

"Several days. Me and Nukebot: Beta both. He's still got Danger: Computer Lady locked up in that Concentration Silo of his. He took away her freedom by taking away her body. It's sickening."

"Guilty!" Nuklear Man exclaimed.

"Sit down!" Atomik Lad said, wrestling the Hero back into his seat.

"Is there a problem over there, son?" Judge Letgodsortitout asked.

"I'm a criminal, I'm living *evil*!" Nuklear Man blurt before Atomik Lad stuffed the Hero's cape into his mouth. "Mmphf! Mfphmlm!"

"Er, what he means to say is 'No, your honor. We're doin' fine.'"

"I dunno, that there sounded like a confession to me."

"No, he's um, been under a lot of stress lately. And it is about nine o'clock. That's past his bedtime, so I think he's getting a little cranky too. Could we have a recess or something to get settled?"

"Oh fine. Y'all got ten minutes."

Count Insidious approached the Heroes. "Well, I think we're doing pretty good, eh boys?"

"You're fired," Atomik Lad said.

"I see," Insidious packed his briefcase without touching it or its contents. "Of course, now I'll have to stop going easy on you."

"Gee. Thanks. Now get the hell away from us."

Insidious sat next to Dr. Menace and started discussing how they should spend their two hundred and fifty thousand dollars.

"Just lock me up and throw away the key!" Nuklear Man sobbed loudly.

"Okay" Atomik Lad told himself. "We can still get out of this. I'll call Dr. Genius, she'll know what to do. She's smart, she'll think of something, she always does."

*   *   *   *

Meanwhile, above the Gulf of Mexico, several Coast Guard helicopters had been magnetized to one another. The wad of helicopter hovered over the water's surface where the pilots and their crews were able to safely hop into the warm waters before the helicopters were magnetically crushed into a indistinguishable metallic mass which immediately sank. The fly boys shook their fists at the sky and cursed.

"Hey," Mighty Metallic Magno Man said from high above them. "You've got no one but yourselves to blame. I told you we could do it the Easy way or the Magno way. It's not my fault you made the wrong choice."

"Eeek! Eeek oook ook eeeeeek!" his loyal army of monkeys resounded within their magnetically floating cages.

"Easy Chim-Chim," Norman coaxed. "The bad men have been taken care of."

"Ook, oooook, eeek."

"Right back at ya, buddy."

*   *   *   *

Atomik Lad returned from the lobby and shot Count Insidious an angry look before sitting next to a suddenly composed and non-guilt-racked Nuklear Man. "Well, I wasn't able to get in touch with Dr. Genius. I guess we'll just have to wing it for the rest of the day. We can't possibly be any worse off than we were with Count Corrupt over there. What were you thinking when you hired him, anyway? There must be hundreds of lawyers in this city, why did you have to pick that one?"

"Well, he was wearing a cape. I think a better question would be how couldn't I hire him?"

"Argh."

"Besides, he's really good. Did you see the way he made those poor saps look guiltier than sin? Woo, I feel sorry for those guys."

"We *are* those guys, you nimrod."

"Oh yeah. This is that trial you kept talking about."

"…You really have no idea about anything that happens outside that bloated ego of yours, do you?"

"Why should I? I mean, it ain't me. How important could it possibly be?"

"Well anyway, I'm glad you're not wallowing in guilt any more, it was making us look bad. Especially since we are innocent."

"There are no innocents, Sparky," Nuklear Man growled with a sinister Plazma glow about his eyes.

"Okay, this is so not the time to bring that up again. I think the less the public knows about your proposed Cleansings, the better. All right?"

"But punishment must be dealt swiftly and—"

"Nuke."

"Oh fine. Lousy sinners, Nuke smash you later."

"Okay. Now shut up. I've got to think up a legal strategy here. Maybe I should call some witnesses who like us."

"Why don't you leave the legal stuff to our learned counselor, hm?"

"Because our learned counselor turned out to be Dr. Menace's learned counselor and boyfriend."

"I'm not talking about him."

Atomik Lad's eyes narrowed. "I don't like this."

The Golden Guardian produced, "Katkat!"

"But how'd he even get here?"

"I dunno, must be that Kat-mojo of his."

"Nuke, he's a cat. He cannot be our lawyer."

"That's what they told Edison about the electric powered hamster cleaner. But did he listen? *No*."

"Nuke. That was you, not Edison. And your so-called cleaner was our blender. Stop it. Katkat is not going to be our legal representative."

"Oh, but I think he is."

"Awright, y'all! Shaddup. Court's back in session," Judge Letgodsortitout barked. "You, Countie, git back to the lawyerin' already. It's late."

"Certainly your honor. I'd like to call the entire jury to the stand!"

"Meow."

"What the—" Judge Hangemall said. "Why, in the name of grits, is there a cat sitting on the Defendant's Table?!"

"He's our new lawyer," Nuklear Man explained.

"No! No he's not," Atomik Lad said. "Please, ignore him."

"I'd like to, but he just meowed. Keep him quiet. Now then, Insidious, you were saying?"

"Thank you, your honor. I was saying I'd like to call the entire jury to testify."

"Meow!" Katkat said more emphatically.

"What did I just tell y'all about that there danged cat?"

"I think he's making an objection, sir," Nuklear Man said.

"Oh for the love of…" Atomik Lad covered his face and hoped he could somehow pop out of existence or at least the courtroom.

"An objection, eh? On what grounds?"

"No grounds, your honor. He's on the table," Nuklear Man corrected.

"Shuttup!" Atomik Lad snapped. "Er, on the grounds that, um, the jury is supposed to remain impartial."

"Oh yeah, impartial," the Judge said while looking around the courtroom dreamily. "I remember that. Count?"

"Well, your honor, can it be said that any of us is impartial in regards to anything? At the very least, we experience reality as mediated by the artifice of language which itself caries partialities and biases and preconceived notions in nearly every word, even more so when they are employed in syntax. For instance, the word 'nuclear' conjures up images of devastation, untold human suffering, radiation sickness, mutations, death, and guilt. This is most evident in a perfectly random statement like 'Nuklear Man is guilty of destruction of property.' You see? In fact, partiality is nothing more than a symptom of language and experience, a frame from which it is utterly impossible for us, as beings whose entire mental landscape *is* language, to escape. So unless you want a jury of deaf, dumb, blind, mute invertebrates who lack a forebrain, then I don't see a problem in letting the jury testify. Besides, they've been here for the whole trial. They probably have a pretty good idea just how guilty Nuklear Man really is."

"Hm," the judge said. "It is highly unusual, but I'll allow it."

"This isn't even a trial anymore!" Atomik Lad protested. "You can't call this anything short of a complete parody of everything that is supposed to be fair and just. I demand a mistrial."

"Oh sure, let me just allow that," the Judge said bitterly. "Every time someone gits the feeling that their trial ain't goin' the way they'd like, they start demanding a mistrial. Well, I've got news for you, Guilty Lad. The law is a shield meant to protect the innocent like dear Dr. Menace down there. It is not a sword to be wielded by the criminal element such as yourself. Your kind makes me sick, preying upon the common defenseless citizenry. I've had it. Count, we're skipping your jury idea and moving right into the Defense's case. I want to watch these bastards try and warp the truth to fit their twisted needs."

"Your honor," Count Insidious said, stepping up to the bench. "It is fair to assume that my witnesses were telling the truth since they swore to do so, correct?"

"Yeah."

"And it goes without saying that the Defense's side of the case will directly contradict what I have shown to be true these past two hours, correct?"

"Yeah."

"Then we're presented with two versions of the truth. One must be true and the other must be false, correct?"

"Also yeah. What're y'all gittin' to?"

"Well, I think it's rather clear. All of my witnesses swore to tell the truth, therefore they did, and since any information provided by the Defense will be contrary to that, their potential testimony and any conclusions implied by it, must be struck from the record as perjurous."

"Ohhhh, that's dirty lawyerin'," Judge Letgodsortitout said.

"I'll say," Atomik Lad agreed.

"That's why I hate you guys so much," Hangemall said. "It's just like you villainous Heroes to use fancy legal loopholes like that to your advantage!"

"*Us*?! But!" Atomik Lad was beyond words. He was in some terrible place without rule or reason.

"The worst part is that you've tainted the jury with the idea that there exists a possibility that you might *not* be guilty."

"Um, aren't we supposed to be presumed innocent until proven guilty?" Atomik Lad foolishly asked.

The Judge laughed. "Sounds like the cries of a desperate man. Besides, if you're innocent, why are you even in a trial? Hm?"

"It's a frivolous lawsuit!" Atomik Lad exclaimed.

"If you think a case of this paramount concern is frivolous, then your sense of justice is warped beyond my comprehension, Mr. Atomik Lad. Members of the jury, you are hereby ordered to ignore any notion or even the possibility that the Defendant could ever be innocent since Count Insidious has proven beyond a shadow of a doubt that any such possibility would be contrary to the case he has made. You may now pronounce Nuklear Man guilty. I mean, make your verdict which will be guilty. But, just to keep up appearances, you will deliberate for exactly thirty minutes so I can catch the post game wrap up from my wrastlin' program I missed 'cause of all this nonsense." He banged the gavel and the jury filed out.

Atomik Lad's head dropped hard onto the table before him.

Nuklear Man leaned close to him. "I think we've got a pretty good chance."

"Meow."

"See, even Katkat thinks so."

"We. Are. Doomed," Atomik Lad mumbled into the mahogany table. "The judge hates us, our lawyer works for the person suing us who happens to be your arch-nemesis, and the jury, which is made up of twelve of our worst enemies, has just gone into deliberation after being ordered by the judge to ignore so much as the chance that we might not be guilty. But you're right, we do have a pretty good chance. Of being doomed!"

"I wouldn't worry too much about the jury's decision. Remember, I was smart enough to invest in a little 'insurance.'"

"Great."

"Well, someone's gotta look out for *your* screw ups."

✳   ✳   ✳   ✳

Half an hour later, the jury filed into the courtroom and sat down in their seats. Each of the twelve wore a mask of sinister delights. Mr. Manager, for instance, couldn't help laughing hysterically as he looked upon the innocent faces of the guilty.

"Has the jury reached a verdict of guilty?" Judge Hangemall asked, his gavel ready to strike out a harsh dish of something nearly resembling justice the way a Picasso painting resembles the real world.

"Yes" Blazer answered. He stood and opened an evelope. "We find the Defendant—"

"Oink! I mean, wait!"

"Hurry it up, piggy" the Judge snapped. "They don't make these gavels out of helium, y'know."

"*I* wanted to give the verdict. Oink."

"Oh really? I couldn't tell, what with the way you kept blurting it out at all the wrong times."

"I couldn't help it. Oink. I'm eager."

"Well *I'm* the leader, therefore I get to deliver the verdict. Nya."

"I thought we weren't a team no more, boss," Granite chimed in this gravelly voice.

"What? That's ridiculous. Where did you get that idea?"

Lord Obese chomped on some snack food without taking off the wrappers. "On accounta 'cause you said you was tired of how indecisive we all are. Urp."

"Oh, I did no such thing," Blazer said. "I simply said that since we can't seem to make a decision, we should vote on whether or not to remain a team. Of course, when I checked the ballot box, mine was the only vote cast. I believe you dolts were trying to figure out what order you would vote in."

"Okenshi, the Juror of the Dark, remembers well the night of this proclamation. Many warriors fell to Okenshi's silent blade, their blood flowed in the midnight rain—"

"What are you talking about?"

"…Okenshi likes to embellish."

"It wasn't even raining."

"Okenshi thought he heard a drizzle around midnight."

"Midnight?" Chonotor asked. "I think not. You are sound asleep no later than 8:46 p.m. every night."

"How can you even call yourself a ninja?!" Blazer asked.

"You question the honor of Okenshi?"

"You're supposed to be a ninja! You don't *have* honor. That's the whole point!"

"Okenshi has the honor of the Night."

"What is that supposed to mean, exactly?"

"Y'all just shaddup!" Judge Letgodsortitout yelled. "This gavel's dang heavy. And ya make my head hurt. Just one of you, any of you, declare this Criminal Man and Vandal Lad guilty already so we can all go home!"

"As I was saying—"

"You mean, as I was saying."

"Cut it out, Zeerox. Stop using your copying powers to look just like me."

"I think you're the Copy Cat. I'm the real Blazer."

"I hate you guys," the really real Blazer moaned while rubbing his purply eyes.

"Wait a second," the nondescript gentleman who was minus one car thanks to Nuklear Man interjected. "I resent that you costumed nuts assume you get to declare him guilty. These jerks have screwed us normal people too, y'know. I lost my car because of them. What have you lost?"

"Er," most of the SMSTCAOAN uttered. "We, uh. He foiled one of our daring robberies." Blazer responded. "Of a um…doughnut shop."

"Oh, how terrible," the man mocked. "How about the jail time for that one?"

"We didn't go to jail, not as such. But we were stuck under Obese here for so long that it inadvertently foiled our plans to wreck Nuklear Man's beach party."

"Sounds rough. Not quite as rough as trying, rather unsuccessfully I might add, to convince the insurance company that my car was utterly obliterated due to an act of Heroism. Seems the claims adjuster couldn't salvage enough evidence from the slag to prove that it had even been a car. Now I'm out ten grand, I've still got to finish making payments on it, and buy a new car on top of that! I've been screwed over worse than all of you shmoes, I should get the pleasure of declaring them guilty."

"I'll declare us guilty if it'll speed things up," Atomik Lad muttered.

Nuklear Man was giving Katkat an expert bellyrub/scratchie-scratchfest. "Hm? What was that?"

Atomik Lad sighed. "Never mind."

"All right!" Blazer yelled above the quarrelling jury. "We'll just say it all *together*, okay?" Murmurs of agreement wafted among his eleven companions. "Okay. On the count of three."

Atomik Lad tensed. "Aren't you worried?"

"Nnnnnope." Nuklear Man answered while petting Katkat. "We won't have anything to worry about in exactly," he checked his Danger: Watch. "Any second now."

"Because of this insurance thing of yours, right?"

"The same."

"You realize that terrifies me."

"As it should."

"We the jury," the jury said simultaneously. "Find the Defendant, Nuklear Man—"

Atomik Lad cringed.

Katkat purred.

Nuklear Man smiled confidently.

Dr. Menace held back her maniacal cackle of triumph.

Count Insidious made plans for his share of the blood money.

Mighty Metallic Magno Man bust through the window directly behind the jury who, in the midst of their simultaneous verdict, simultaneously dropped to the ground as shards of glass and recently unleashed monkeys skittered and scattered through the courtroom.

Norman rolled up to his Heroic comrades and unfurled his gleaming tungsten self, "Yo. Sorry I took so long, but those border patrols kept insisting on doing things the Magno Way. The poor fools."

The monkeys were attacking everyone and being very loud about it.

"No problem, Normie. I'd say you got here just in time," the Hero gladly responded.

Atomik Lad tried to keep his cool by keeping the monkeys at bay. "Am I to assume this is your version of a plan? Gah! Back off!"

Nuklear Man grinned a proud grin. "Yup! I startle myself with my own brilliance. Now, whilst the authorities are busy wranglin' up these here monkeys, we make with the ol' escape. They'll be all 'Hey, duh, where's Nuklear Man?' 'cause they won't have noticed our getaway amongst all this monkey induced chaos! It's the perfect plan!"

"Is it now? And then what do we do?" Atomik Lad, despite better judgment, asked.

"I think it's fairly obvious," Nuklear Man said. "We'll go back to the Silo. They won't be able to find us! It's underground! Look as they might, we shall be snug within our subterranean headquarters! Tee hee."

Atomik Lad sighed. "Nuke. They sent the subpoena to the Silo. They know exactly where we live. They could even spot it from an airplane if they had to since the only entrance is the Danger: Main Doors which, in case you've forgotten, is basically a fifty foot wide metallic circle with a giant Nuklear 'N' on it. Hell, we're in the phonebook! To recap, this plan sucks."

"Sparky, just because you're jealous of how completely inferior you are to me in every possible way is no reason to attack the integrity of the plan. Don't you concur Norman?"

"Yeah—"

"See there?"

"—the plan sucks."

"Dah! Why must I be surrounded by simpletons like you two who can't possibly appreciate the beautiful subtlety of my ingenious plan?"

"I think you were wrong in every possible way on that one, Big Guy."

"So says you."

"Hey..." Norman said, pointing to some of the monkeys nearest Count Insidious, "Do those monkeys look pale to you?"

The vampire snatched a small simian and sucked it dry to produce yet another pale monkey slave.

"He's turning our loyal army of monkeys into his own loyaller army of zombie monkeys!" Nuklear Man exclaimed. "No fair."

"That's great. Like we didn't have enough things going against us, now we've got this. And who do we have to blame for it all? Wwwwwell that'd be Mr. Nukie Man."

"Hey!" the Hero said. "It's not my fault he's a vampire!"

The first generation zombie monkeys started making their own zombie progeny, setting up clans and a hierarchy based on the closeness of one's zombie-blood to the Count. Within minutes, the insane monkey madness was turned into a much more unsettling zombie monkey undead beady-eyed stare down.

Silence dominated the courtroom as a few brave souls started poking their heads out from whatever makeshift cover they had procured. A slap resounded from under the Prosecution's Table as Judge Hangemall rolled out from it. He came to a stop near his bench. "Er, how ever did I get under there?" he asked as though he had no idea. Dr. Menace climbed out from the Prosecution's Table and straightened her lab coat and tight Evil: Leather Outfit. The Judge hopped over the bench, sat down, and banged the gavel a few times. "Order! Count, git them creepy monkeys outta here."

"Certainly, your honor." He whispered some mysterious ancient word of power and they melted into shadows.

"Now then, where were we?" the Judge asked.

"The jury was just about to deliver their verdict of guilty," the Count answered.

"*Finally*," Hangemall muttered.

"One, two, three," Blazer prompted. Again, he was joined by his fellow jurors, "We the jury find the Defendant, Nuklear Man…"

America gasped in anticipation. In Avalondon, someone's grandmother died. In a hotel down the street from the courtroom, she was reborn as a baby girl two weeks premature. In Burgesville, lightning struck. And the Earth coursed through the ocean of space on wings of time with billions of souls separated by chasms of their own design.

Somewhere, a dog barked.

"…guilty."

"Huh," Nuklear Man said incredulously. "Who'da thunked it?"

Issue 39—Like Father, Like Son

"Awright!" Judge Hangemall said hungrily. "Now it's time for sentencing. Nuklear Man, you are hereby ordered to pay the plaintiff the full amount of two hundred fifty thousand dollars. Ha!"

The Hero panicked, "Why does it always end in murder!?! PLAZMAAA—"

"Nuke, calm down. We live off the royalties of a billion dollar a year merchandizing empire. We rake in a few mil every year."

"We do?"

"Yeah, I make sure that most of it goes to charities to keep you from stockpiling weapons and hiring mercenaries to do your Heroing so you can watch more cartoons."

"Oh yeah. There is that."

"We'll just have to make a few cutbacks to our budget and the donations for next year to pay this off." Atomik Lad paused momentarily, "It's really not much of a hassle. Especially compared to the amount of time and energy Dr. Menace must've invested in this plan of hers to ruin us. It's really quite harmless in the long run."

"Excuse me, your honor," Count Insidious said while levitating some legal papers out of his briefcase. "I have something here that might interest you."

"Hurry it up then. I gots me a wrastlin' tape I could be watching."

The paperwork floated itself to the Judge's bench. "You'll see that we've spearheaded a class action suit against Nuklear Man for the destruction of six hundred million dollars worth of public and private property."

"*What?*!" Atomik Lad blurt out.

"Wow, I've been *busy!*" Nuklear Man said proudly.

Count Insidious went on, "Thousands of homes, hundreds of businesses, and several blocks of city streets and property were severely damaged and/or destroyed in last week's struggle with the Crushtacean creature."

"We were saving the city from complete destruction!" Atomik Lad defended.

"Yes, but at what cost?" Count Insidious countered. "Oh, it was six hundred million dollars."

"Look, we regret that parts of the city were harmed while we were subduing Crushtacean, but would you rather the *entire* city were leveled instead?"

"That sounds like a threat. The threat of a clearly guilty man."

"We did what was necessary. What's important is that no one was hurt during the attack."

"How do you know the creature was on an insane rampage?" the Count said. "He didn't start destroying anything until you and Nuklear Man began agitating him. I think with that indisputable evidence, combined with the findings of this case, we have established that alleged Heroes are responsible for the damages that are caused as a result of their occupation. After all, if a taxi driver runs over a nun, he is held responsible. I don't see the difference here."

"He's got a point," the Judge agreed. "I'm afraid I have to find in favor of the collective plaintiffs in this new case as well."

"This is crazy!" Atomik Lad protested.

"Crazy that we've allowed ourselves to live under your tyrannical reign of spandexed violence for so many years. Y'all are gonna have to cough up six hundred million dollars." The gavel echoed like gunshots.

The Count cleared his throat. New paperwork floated to the judge. "We'd also like to retro-actively charge Nuklear Man and Atomik Lad for damages incurred during their decade long history of destruction, even though it's highly illegal to do so. We're still working on the total, but we're thinking along the lines of five billion dollars. Give or take."

"We'll make it eight!" Judge Hangemall said.

The mob of TV reporters stormed out of the courtroom to begin their uninformed, unresearched, irresponsible reports about the final verdict.

"Psst, Sparky," Nuklear Man whispered, "Can we afford that?"

"Oh sure. It would only take about seven hundred years."

"And since y'all cain't possibly pay that amount, yer gonna have to be incarcerated for your crimes against humanity. Nuklear Man, you are sentenced to life in the Metroville State Penitentiary at Katabasis where you will be kept in a hitherto sealed off dungeon in the north tower where you will be chained by your wrists to a wall and forced to endure an iron mask for the rest of your living days." More sharp slams of the gavel.

"That was cruel and unusual punishment even when it was acceptable. You're insane!" Atomik Lad said.

"You watch it, boy. Just because you're not being tried don't mean I can't send you to jail for no reason too. Now then, Civil Defender, apprehend the Defendant and git him into a temporary cell. We'll transfer him to more 'pleasant' accommodations tomorrow morning."

"Whew, that chain and mask thing sounded really uncomfortable."

Civil Defender walked up to Nuklear Man with a pair of handcuffs, "Ohhhh, I've wanted to do this for a long time."

"What're you talking about? You haven't even known me for a whole week yet."

"Quiet, you. Now hand over the cat."

"Mew?" Katkat uttered while cradled between the Hero's arms and chest.

Nuklear Man laughed. "No, I don't think so."

"C'mon, drop the cat. They don't allow pets where you're going."

Katkat quivered.

"Leave the cat out of this," Nuklear Man said.

"Nuke, just put Katkat down. I'll bring him by when we visit. You'll be out of there soon anyway. There's no way this charade can really be legal."

Civil Defender snatched Katkat from Nuklear Man's grasp. "Mreowr!" the furry feline squirmed and fought against his stupid cop-like aggressor.

"I think it would be in your best interest to give him back. Now," His Plazma Aura flared with that final emphatic word.

"And I think it would be in your best interest to put these cuffs on and accompany me down to your temporary cell."

"Meow!"

Nuklear Man took in a deep breath and released it loudly through his nose. "Give him back," he stated calmly.

"Stop making this worse," Atomik Lad pleaded.

"Cuffs, Golden Boy."

With a whisper of sinew, hands that could crush metal tightened into fists. Katkat flinched a second too soon in the Armored Officer's right hand. "Give me," one hand shot to Civil Defender's left wrist and clamped around it in the blink of an eye, "the cat." The armor was already showing cracks from the strain.

Civil Defender was frozen in some mixture of shock and pain. Nuklear Man's grip tightened further, producing a snap that was hopefully armor splitting and not bone. In either case, Civil Defender was on his knees, Katkat had been unconsciously released along the way there.

"Nuke!" Atomik Lad had to scream to startle his mentor into paying attention. "Let him go, you're hurting him!"

"Hm?" the Hero released his grip and Civil Defender collapsed to the floor in a fetal position whimpering about his poor armor.

Katkat rubbed against Nuklear Man's legs while purring happily.

"Just turn yourself in for now," Atomik Lad told him while picking up Katkat. "We're going to fight this. You may be a dumb ox, but you're still a Hero. They can't do this to you."

"Oh fine. But I won't like it."

"I know."

"Don't forget to feed Katkat while I'm gone."

"I'm the one who fed him when you *were* there."

"And don't be sneaky and take his room away."

"I won't."

"And don't go through my stuff."

"Fine."

"Especially my Danger: Funtime for Nukie Drawer."

"Gah. Don't worry about it. And don't *tell* me about it either."

"And don't read my Captain Liberty comics with those grubby ex-sidekick hands of yours. You'll muck up the pages with your greasy adolescence."

"Could someone hurry up and take him away already?" Atomik Lad asked the court.

Several police officers clamped several handcuffs around the Hero's wrists. Then he stopped melting them with his Plazma Powers. The cops finally got a pair to stick and they escorted him out the court room.

Count Insidious led Dr. Menace by the hand. On their way out, he stopped to gloat thusly: "Hey guys. Sorry about that trial thing. Nothing personal, it's just part of the job—*the part I love*! Because I'm so damned hideously evil! *Bwa hahahaha*! And the best part is, I'm free! Free to go to my meticulously gothic mansion and make crazy undead love to my even more hideously evil girlfriend who managed to sue you jerks into the grave for foiling one of her many vile plots to destroy you! *Gwa hahahahaha*!" He took a few deep breaths to calm himself and wiped away a tear of blood. "Woo. Did I mention the undead love?"

"Yes," Atomik Lad steamed.

"Just checkin'."

Dr. Menace winked at the ex-sidekick. "Don't think for one second that I have finished with you. Mwa hahahahahaha!"

"See you around, Aorta Lad," the Count said. The happy Evil: Couple disappeared in a **BAMF** of sinister black vampire smoke.

Atomik Lad still held Katkat. The courtroom bellowed with silence. The media circus was in full swing just outside. The jury had gone out to celebrate. Judge Letgodsortitout went into his quarters to watch that wrastlin' tape. Scraps of paper and monkey fur littered the floor. Atomik Lad shivered from a draft coming through the holes produced by Angus and Norman earlier.

"Meow?"

"I know," he responded even though he really didn't know. "Don't worry. We'll get out of this." He held Katkat close and mentally conjured his Field. The red hue it cast onto the world was welcomed for a change. "My world now. Just me."

"Rowr!"

Atomik Lad smiled as he flew them through Norman's hole in the wall behind the jury box. "Yeah, you too. I just mean they can't get us in here. Ugh, I'm talking to a cat. And now I'm talking to myself about talking to a cat." He glanced at his Danger: Watch. "Damn, it's been a long day. How about we go home, call Rachel, and get some sleep?"

"Mew."

"Glad you—ah! I'm doing it again," he rubbed his eyes. "Maybe being away from Nuke for a few days won't be so bad after all." And with that, Atomik Lad rocketed to the Silo with Katkat snuggling close to his belly.

*   *   *   *

Ring. "Hello?"

"Hey Rachel."

"Oh, Sparky. I saw the whole thing on TV. I'm so sorry."

"You're not the only one." He gave an exhausted sigh and watched Katkat suck down some Kit-N-Chow.

"Is there anything I can do?" she asked.

"No. Maybe. I don't know. Today was hell."

"I think someone needs to go to sleepy time."

"Yeah, I just wanted to call so you'd know I was still alive, though I hardly feel like it right now."

"Do you know what you're going to do to get Nuklear Man out of jail?"

"Yes. First, I will sleep until noon. Second, I will devise a plan."

"Mow!" Katkat reported after finishing his midnight meal.

"Sounds like you've got some help over there."

"I need it. I'll talk to you tomorrow, okay?"

"Sure thing. Sleep tight."

He hung up the Danger: Phone and shambled to his Danger: Katkat's Room. "Yeowr?"

"What the? How'd you get here already?"

Katkat answered with cutie wutie blinky eyes.

Atomik Lad hoped he did not just think they were cutie wutie blinky eyes. "Yeah, c'mon. You can stay with me. But it's right back to Nuke when we get him out of jail. Got it?"

A purring leg rub was the cat's response.

*   *   *   *

That night, deep within the dank bowels of the Metroville Courthouse jail which really wasn't dank nor bowely, Nuklear Man slept fitfully upon his uncomfortable Danger: Sleep Slab. His cape was pulling double duty as a Danger: Blanky. Though no one could insult its abilities as a cape, a true Danger: Blanky it was not. Nuklear Man shivered as a gust of cold air unsettled his Blanky-cape. "Need sleepy," he muttered incoherently as he pulled the makeshift Danger: Blanky over himself. The draft seemed to huff in annoyance before giving another blast which tossed his cape clean off his Herculean frame. "Urrrrraaaarrrrg," Nuklear Man said like a creature recently risen from the dead. "Stupid air conditioning. Nukie will…" His voice trailed off when he noticed it echoing among the cave walls "…Smash you?" More echo. "I don't recall this one-cell jail house being quite so roomy when they escorted me in here." To the left, darkness and a slight downward incline. To the right, more darkness and a slight upward incline. In front of him, some more darkness and really neat stone pillars growing up from the cavern's floor. Above, only darkness and presumably a ceiling too far away to see. "Come to think of it, I'm almost sure it was a lot smaller in here. Boy, those civil workers sure can get a job done quick and quiet. I can't believe I slept through all the construction a job like this must've taken."

He began walking down the incline. He picked up a few loose stones and hurled one into the cave's depths. He waited for echoes that never came. "Sheesh, when I said the cell was awfully small for my huge muscles, I didn't mean they had to do all this." He paused to examine his Nuklear Physique. "But I think they got the scale right. A place this big is just about big enough for my might. Give or take some mightiness." Nuklear Man prepared to toss his last stone when another gust of wind issued from the cave ahead of him. The air was rank and heavy, like the breath of the Earth itself. It rang with a deep resonance that shook the massive cave only slightly. "Geez. Someone needs to fix that air conditioner." He sniffed at the air, "Smells like something's burning. One of the belts musta come loose."

He could hear it in the cave walls and floor first, and then in his very bones before the voice was actually audible. "Son." It echoed from every direction. "Son, listen to me."

"Kinda hard not to, Dad," the Hero said while trying to shake the ringing from his ears.

"You are my vengeance."

"Really?" The Golden Guardian flexed a couple times. "Yeah, living vengeance! Cool."

"They are mad. Yes, truly mad."

"Yeah, they seemed pretty upset."

"We all have our destined roll to play. But you, you my son are outside their destiny. You will bring a new fate crashing upon them. Their doom will be forged in the flames of your heritage."

"Sure. Who we talkin' about anyway?"

"Oh, to see the look on their smug faces. So sure, so very sure. Such arrogant certainty in the unyielding future." The voice twisted into a bitter roar of laughter that made the cave tremble. Pebbles of varying sizes rained from the great stone pillars surrounding Nuklear Man. The laughter grew in intensity and the Hero could make out two faint lights next to one another in the distance and high above him almost beyond the range of his Nuklear Sight.

"You know what I was just thinking? I was just thinking that maybe you're not real and I'm not really here because here isn't really real either because you're scaring me. Maybe instead, maybe you're just some kind personification of my ego 'cause you're really loud and maybe this cave is supposed to be like my brain 'cause Sparky is always saying how cavernous it is. That's what I think." The laugh shattered into a scream that threatened to tear the cave to pieces. "Or not," he said meekly. The massive stalagmite columns grew cracks as huge shards of stone plummeted from beyond the invisible heights. The distant lights flared just bright and long enough for Nuklear Man to discern them as the eyes of an impossibly distant and huge face, weary and worn, twisted in agony. "Wow," he said. "You're really tall."

The lights faded as the scream finally silenced, though it still rang in the very cavern walls. Darkness permeated the cave's depths once more. The wind returned but without its former presence this time. It was rasping now and heavy with the stench of burnt flesh. The voice too was strained. "Leave me," it said bitterly.

"Sure. But I don't know how." A final boulder fell from directly above the Hero. "Wah!" he exclaimed while collapsing onto the cool floor of his temporary holding cell. "Whew. It was just a dream." He wiped his brow and in doing so crushed a rock that had been in his hand. It's pebbly crumbs fell down his face and horror struck him like a sniper's bullet. "Or was it?! *Ahhhhhh!*"

Issue 40—The Reign of Superion

Tuesday morning.

Atomik Lad awoke with a stretch and a yawn. His Danger: Clock clicked over to 11:23. "Eh, close enough." Minutes later, the ex-sidekick shuffled into the Danger: Kitchen where Katkat was already sucking down his morning meal of Kit-N-Chow. Which is odd since the Kit-N-Chow was kept in a Kit-N-Proof sealed container on the top shelf of the Danger: Pantry. "Hm, musta forgotten to put it away before going to bed." He put some frozen Danger: Waffles into the Danger: Toaster and sat down at the Danger: Table to read the Danger: Paper.

No, it was just the paper. Nuklear Man was in jail so there was no one to sneak around at five in the morning to put a Danger: Label on it. "Grah," he said to the realization.

∗　　　∗　　　∗　　　∗

A few more minutes later, Atomik Lad was enjoying his Danger: Waffles at the Danger: Kitchen Table while perusing what was now the Danger: Paper. He had to nudge the Danger: Label Maker over a tad to set down his Danger: Glass of OJ. Most of the front page was dedicated to the trial. There were editorials, a summary of events, interviews with members of the jury, an artist's rendering of a smoking crater that was supposed to be the ruins of Dr. Menace's warehouse, and pictures taken of the areas most heavily damaged by the encounter with Crushtacean. He didn't read any of it, he'd seen enough of that side of the one-sided injustice against Nuklear Man to last him a lifetime. In his search for the comics page, Atomik Lad came across an entire section of the paper dedicated to the faceless victims of "so-called" Heroes, specifically "Philanthropist, Entrepreneur, Inventor, Dr. Veronica Menace."

"Y'know," he told Katkat. "They didn't so much as ask about our side of this. They could've at least called and asked what we thought of the verdict."

Completely by coincidence, and having no actual importance by said coincidence, the Danger: Phone rang.

"Hello?"

"Hey, Sparky."

"Rachel! What's up?"

"Just calling to check on you boys."

"Thanks, we're fine. I could probably use a shower though."

"Need some help?"

"...Whimper."

"Did you just say—"

"Um, so shouldn't you be at work by now?"

"I should be, but I called in sick. But right now let's worry about getting Nuklear Man out of jail before the city's criminal elements take advantage of his absence."

"Hm. I'd been concentrating so much on the injustices shoved down our throats lately that I hadn't even thought of that."

"That's what I'm here for."

*   *   *   *

Meanwhile, heady with the drunken fervor of Evil that accompanies the disposal of a Heroic figure, Dr. Grammar and Dr. Calculus made a right turn at a red light without first coming to a complete stop. "Caveat Anarchium!" they yelled with hedonistic abandon, though not so loudly as to be a disturbance to passersby.

*   *   *   *

The Danger: Call Waiting beeped. "Argh. Hang on, the city might be in peril or something."

"No problem."

"I hate these things." He clicked over. "Hello?"

"Hello, Atomik Lad?"

"That's me."

"This is Incompetent Bureaucrat."

"The mayor? Really?"

"Yes. I was hoping we could have you down at City Hall later this afternoon for a press conference concerning last night's trial."

"Definitely. I'm there, what time?"

"We can do it in about an hour if you're ready."

"Great. I'll be there."

"Terrific. See you then."

The ex-sidekick clicked back over. "Still there?"

"Oh, you know me. Typical passive female love interest just sitting around waiting for her strong Anglo male to come back from his mythic adventuring and sweep her away."

"Um…?"

"Yeah, I'm still here. I'm afraid I can't say the same for Onitenma, the evil stupid cheating boss of Samurai Swordplay."

"Good work. That was the mayor on the other line. He wants me to be in a press conference about the trial in one hour."

"Great! Hop to it, boy."

"Yes ma'am."

"You sure you don't need help with that shower?"

"Good gravy."

✳   ✳   ✳   ✳

A little over an hour later, Atomik Lad sat with a panel of the city's remaining heroes at City Hall. MMMM, Angus, Shiro, and Atomik Lad sat on one side of the podium while the Minimum Wage Warriors sat on the other. The room was filled with journalists and their inane murmuring.

The ex-sidekick leaned over to Norman, "Did they tell you what we're supposed to be talking about?"

"Not really," he said. "But the mayor contacted each of us personally and he said this had to do with the trial."

"I guess it's finally our turn to speak our side of the story."

The room was filled with news people and their cameras. As he looked at them, Atomik Lad had the sneaking suspicion that they all pretty much looked alike. Not clones so much as unimaginative variations on an already bland theme.

Incompetent Bureaucrat waddled out from the curtains behind the panel of heroes and stepped up to the podium. Up close, Atomik Lad had a wonderful view of the mayor's pale, pasty, fish-like complexion and his general chubbiness of wealth. The well trained news people silenced their insipid banter and prepared to take notes.

"Ladies and gentlemen of the press to whom I shamelessly pander with political nonsense, meaningless double talk, and the adoption of positions on important issues that are so middle of the road as to be utterly powerless to effect any positive change but guarantee me re-elections because no one was offended by my positions because they were basically nonexistent in the first place, I have called this conference in order to address a terrible travesty that has been perpetrated against one of our most famous citizens, and well, gosh, all of us by extension."

"I think you might've been right, Sparky," Norman whispered.

"That's why our guest of honor is here today," the mayor said. Atomik Lad prepared to stand up. "Dr. Menace!"

"Guh!" Atomik Lad sputtered.

Incompetent continued, "According to this morning's poll, to which I must yield because it represents popular opinion, the people of Metroville sympathize with her for having to endure endless persecution and humiliation by the hands of what may very well be the greatest oppressor of this or any century, Nuklear Man."

The Venomous Villainess appeared from the same curtains Incompetent had, pushed him out of her way, and took the podium. "That iz enough out of you, znivelling worm," she told the mayor. "Now then," she said to the gathered press. "Even though juzitce haz been zerved againzt that Nuklear Pinhead, I do not think that iz enough action to take againzt the heroic community az a whole."

"I don't like where this is going," Norman said.

"Hai," Shiro said. "Dragon women was of fire to be breathing upon village peoples. Large in fearness."

"Why don't ye talk some sense for a change!"

"Whhhhhisakey!"

"Ooh! That's me kind o' sense."

"That iz why I propoze to prohibit any further activity from theze so-called 'heroez' so that we may be allowed to finally lead normal livez. The mayor haz already passed legizlation that will make any heroic act illegal."

Mighty Metallic Magno Man and Angus had to hold Atomik Lad down. "What!" he yelled. "You can't do that! We're protecting the city against psychos like you!"

"Oh, I think not, my dear Atomik Lad. I thought one of you maniacz would bring up that point so I took the liberty of making thiz graph. Chim-Chim?" A pale zombie monkey pushing a large and easy to read bar graph shambled from behind Dr. Menace.

"Chim-Chim!" Norman blurt while Atomik Lad, Angus, and Shiro held him down. "Menace, you'll pay for this!"

"Funny that you should mention 'pay,' my Nazcently Naïve Nubian Knight."

"Wow, that was pretty good."

"Yez, I have been saving it for juzt the right occasion. Az I was saying, thiz graph showz the amount of damagez cauzed to the beautiful city of Metroville by the wrecklezz and irrezponzible behavior of theze self styled heroez." She pointed to a red bar that rose quite high, well over the billion dollar mark. "Compare that to the bar which shows the amount of damagez cauzed by villainz." A blue bar rose imperceptibly to the thirty five cents mark. "I had an overdue library book one time," she admitted, eliciting chuckles from the idiotic audience.

"Hold it!" Atomik Lad protested. "That graph is misleading."

"Factz do not lie."

"No, but people do. What you forgot to mention is that the damage you allege to be the fault of us heroes wouldn't even be an issue if you villains weren't constantly trying to take over or destroy the city. Your line is so low because we've always managed to stop you before your plans succeed."

"So sayz you. All I know iz that theze damagez were not cauzed until one of you moronz arrived on the zcene utterly *ruining my brilliantly nefariouz zchemez!* Ahem, It might have been pozzible to change my mind on thiz matter, but I do not see a handy graph illuztrating your point, therefore I shall not lizten to you."

"Shut up and let her talk!" a journalist barked.

"Yeah! Way to graph, No-graph!" the unbiased press heckled.

"What is wrong with you people?! She's a villain!" Atomik Lad blurt.

No reaction.

"She tried to dislodge Antarctica last year and float it into tropical waters so it would melt and flood Metroville while simultaneously driving the price of ice cubes through the roof making her a multi-millionaire thanks to an investment in a Warehouse o' Ice that was located safely inland."

Still nothing.

"She threatened every one of your *lives*! And she would've made good on that threat if not for me, Nuke, and Norman here bustin' in on her headquarters."

"At an approximate cozt of seventy thouzand dollarz I might add."

"And how much would it have cost had you melted Antarctica?"

"The queztion iz non sequitor since Metroville would no longer exizt and would therefore be exempt from payment of any damagez cauzed."

"She's got a point," a random journalist near the front said.

"No she doesn't! Okay, fine. What about the impact on the environment? What would the ecological cost be?"

"That would be impozzible to calculate with current data, therefore the point iz moot."

Atomik Lad sat down, exasperated.

"Of courze, if I had some funding, say from some part of the federal or local governmentz, then I could conduct a very thorough study of exactly what impactz such a brilliant act of villainy would have upon the globe and all of itz pathetic vermin citizenz who would bow down before me."

"*Look* at her!" Atomik Lad pointed furiously as he yelled. "She's trying to do it again! Using city funds! She's pure evil!"

The ex-sidekick was booed into submission.

"Take it easy," Norman consoled. "We'll get through this. We always do. Nuke'll be outta jail before you know it and we'll put Menace behind bars. You'll see."

"I don't know. I have a bad feeling about this."

"Now, I am the firzt to admit that the city iz plagued by a few mizguided nc'er-do-wellz and that they muzt be punished," Menace continued. "Az such, I further propoze the inztallment of a *new* Hero to replaze our previouz batch."

"But," the mayor meekly spoke up. "Could any one hero be able to effectively combat all of Metroville's villainous elements and still be cost effect to Mr. and Mrs. Taxpayer?"

"Mozt Certainly. Chim-Chim?"

"Chim-Chim!" Norman cried once more. "Menace, you'll pay for what you've done!" he again threatened while being restrained by his comrades.

Chim-Chim pushed a huge glass cylinder out of the curtains behind the podium. Inside it was an impenetrable cloud of sickly green with a darker, sicker, greener blob roughly the shape of a man in the center.

Menace smiled, "Ladiez and gentlemen of the prezz, I give you Metroville'z newezt Hero!" She pushed a button near the cylinder's base. Servo motors whirred and the audience gasped with anticipation. A line appeared straight down the middle of the cylinder as the two halves separated from one another and a green haze emanated from the breach. A silvery boot stepped out of the maze and was soon accompanied by another next to it. The cameras were already flashing as the emerald smoke seemed to magically whisk itself away to reveal a tall, well built man with short curly black hair. He was dressed in a mostly red and white hero's outfit with a silver cape and boots. A large and stylish blue 'S' inside an equally stylish white star adorned his muscular chest. His brown eyes only added to the coy quality that shone from his boyishly innocent yet confident smile.

"Superion!" he announced. "The Crimson Crusader, the Defender of the Downtrodden, the Aegis Against Evil. In short: The way of the future." He posed, but without the arrogance or effort Nuklear Man always slopped over with when he posed. And somehow, this subtlety made Superion's pose all the more potent. With a smile that told you he was your best friend and a wink that told you he was that favorite uncle who would take you out for ice cream instead of dinner when babysitting you as a child, he instantly wooed the audience. The women swooned and the men wanted to invite him over to watch whatever Big Game was playing that week.

"Wow, he's pretty cool," Norman said. "Dig that cape, how it moves lightly in some breeze that isn't even here."

"Feh," Atomik Lad said. "Nuke does that." Although, in the back of his mind, he had to admit there was just that certain *Something* about the way Superion's did it.

"Aye. And that outfit. That ain't no regular spandex. That be fancy spandex. Lookit the texture, it's a testament to style and functionality."

"Superion is numbaa one Joe for Heroing."

Atomik Lad grumbled. "Big damn deal. Stupid jerk is just an attention hog. They'll stop drooling over him once the newness has worn off. They'll start to resent how arrogant his complete lack of arrogance is and then they'll come crawling back to Nuke."

"We are now opening the floor to queztionz."

All the distinguished news people shot their arms into the air yelling things like "Ooh ooh, me! Pick me, pick me! I'm ever so justified by your attention!"

"Whoa now, kids," Superion said with a jovial smile. "One at a time, huh? I may have Superior Powers™, but I sure can't answer a hundred questions at once," he gave a half empty laugh somewhat mirroring the only one television journalists are capable of.

The audience was instantly at ease.

"Wow, he sure does have a way with an audience," Norman whispered.

"Hai. Ways and means of audience like river throughout with watering."

"Aye. That Nuklear Man never could get their attention like that. It was always, 'Ooh, lookit me! Ah'm Nuuklear Man. Ladeedah. Lookit me muuscles and how they make wee Angus over there loook like he's microscoopic!' Bah!"

"Oh, c'mon," Atomik Lad said with enough distain to power a car at highway speeds. "So he's a little charismatic. Let's see how far that gets him in the field. You know, I don't even mind that we've been decommissioned because now we'll have more time to get Nuke out of jail while this jerk is stuck doing all the hero-ing by himself. I give him five minutes out there before our overvillain freaks send him packing."

"Let's start the questioning with you, Cupcake," Superion said to a news-woman in the front row.

"Oh my, I-I don't know what to say!" she said, all a'fluster with embarrass-ment.

"Just speak from the heart, Pretty Lady," he advised with a non-threatening wink.

"Oh, well. Do you have a girlfriend?" she asked with a nervous giggle.

Atomik Lad rolled his eyes.

"Well," Superion answered with a charming smile. "Let's just say I'm available Friday night," he said with a coy wink.

"I'm gonna be sick," the ex-sidekick grumbled.

"Okay, how about you, Chief? What's your question?" Superion asked to a newsman somewhere in the middle of the already adoring crowd.

"Um," a newsman in the second row said. "What do you think of the decision at yesterday's trial?"

"I gotta tell ya. I think justice was served. I really do. The people of Metroville, who are the gosh darned best people in the whole wide world, deserve a hero and not a self-appointed despot. I think I'm just the man for that job."

"We know you are, Superion!" an excited fan in the back of the room said. His sentiment was met by cheers from the rest of the audience.

Superion smiled bashfully. "Oh, c'mon you guys. Cut it out."

"You're the best, Superion!"

"We love you!"

"Superion for mayor!"

"I might take you up on that," Superion said with a thoughtful glance at the Mayoral Seal on the podium.

Incompetent Bureaucrat quivered with fear.

"Just kidding, Mayor," Superion said with a thumbs up which produced more laughter from the audience.

"I can't believe this!" Atomik Lad yelled at everyone.

"Is he still here?" one journalist whispered to another.

"We don't know anything about this guy!" Atomik Lad said. "He tosses out a bunch of smooth talk and you're all eating it up like you've known him all your lives! He's just a fast talkin' pretty boy! Can't you see that he's nothing more than an evil pawn of Dr. Menace?!"

The crowd looked to him momentarily. It was a stare as blank as a powered down monitor. They turned back to Superion with admiring smiles.

Menace took the podium as Superion stood behind her giving winks and thumbs ups to various members of the press. "Of courze, since Zuperion iz new to the city, he will need zomeone to show him around and help him acclimate to hiz new role."

Everyone raised their hands, "MEMEMEMEME!"

Menace shook her head and raised a hand to silence them. "There iz only one man who iz qualified for thiz important tazk."

Atomik Lad cringed. "Not me, please not me."

"Atomik Lad," she predictably announced.

His shoulders slumped in defeat. "Why am I not surprised?"

Superion set his hand on Atomik Lad's shoulder, "Hey there, Champ. Looks like we're partners from now on."

Atomik Lad removed the surrogate hero's hand from his shoulder. "Don't touch me. It sickens me."

$$*\qquad*\qquad*\qquad*$$

Meanwhile...

"What about me?" Nuklear Man asked while seated among his fellow inmates en route to Katabasis State Pen.

The others conferred with one another huddle style. "Well," the one they called Snake answered, "You can be Blade's bitch."

"Goody, goody!" Nuklear Man said with childish glee.

Blade smiled at Nuklear Man with a mouth half full of teeth .

"Psst," Nuklear Man said to the inmate next to him, the one they called Stab. "What does this bitch stuff mean, anyway?"

The paddy wagon zoomed through the streets of Metroville with the uncharacteristic sound of laughter lilting from the back.

"What's so funny guys?"

Issue 41—He's Superior™ in Every Way

The sun sat amongst the peaks of the Metroville Mountains. Atomik Lad and Superion hovered over the Business District of downtown Metroville. "There" Atomik Lad said, his voice sharp with impatience. "That's the city. You've seen pretty much everything. All that's left now is Überdyne."

Superion scanned the city below as they soared among the rooftops. "You know, Sport, not to criticize, but your little tour here seems a bit rushed."

"Yeah, well. We don't want to be caught sight-seeing if a disaster should strike. Right?"

"Good thinkin', Slugger."

"Grumble."

✳   ✳   ✳   ✳

Meanwhile, inside Katabasis Prison, the newly admitted inmates were lined up at attention in the arid courtyard as the long time residents examined them from afar. The Captain of the Guard paced before the rookies like a Drill Sergeant, only meaner. "You filthy *maggots*," he snarled with contempt.

Nuklear Man gave a brief quiver of fear and hoped the maggots weren't touching him.

"You diseased sacks of flesh."

"Ew," the Hero muttered.

"You festering blotches on the face of society."

"Man, this guy is *really* gross," Nuklear Man whispered to Stab.

"Do you have something you'd like to share, maggot!"

"Maggot? Where!?" Nuklear Man hovered and held his cape away from the ground.

"Oh, a wise guy, huh?"

"Y'know, it's interesting. I've been called a lot of things, especially by Sparky, but that was definitely never one of them."

"That's it, Pretty Boy."

"Now he's called me that a lot."

"You just keep right on talking, boy," the Captain threatened.

"No, he *definitely* never said anything like that."

The Guard quaked, "Cut it out, can't ya!"

Nuklear Man planted his feet back on the stone floor. "*Well.* You don't have to yell."

"Arrrrgh. Lock up these maggots!" he ordered his fellow guards.

"Gah!" and again the Hero was airborne.

The Guard leaned right into Nuklear Man's face. "I'm going to enjoy watching you rot away in that old tower.

*   *   *   *

"Come in," Dr. Genius said from her desk while working on some Scientific: Notes.

Atomik Lad flung the door open. "Hey. Doc, this is Superion. Superion, Dr. Genius. Okay, we're done here. Let's go."

"What's the rush, Tiger?" Superion said as he suavely made his entrance. "It's not every day you get to see an angel this close to Earth."

Dr. Genius spun around in her chair. "Oh, why thank you," she said with the beginnings of a blush working its way across her face.

"Oh, geez."

"You know," she said while toying with a loose lock of hair. "I'm obligated by law to give all of the city's heroes thorough physicals every month. I could schedule you for an appointment. Say, all day Saturday?"

"I'll be up for that, Venus." Superion said with a wink. "Think you could hold down the fort while I'm gone, Champ?"

"Ima," Atomik Lad said, completely ignoring Superion's query. "What about Mighty Metallic Magno Man? You know, your boyfriend?"

"Hm?" she said disinterestedly.

"Boyfriend, eh? Does this Magno Man know he's the luckiest darn guy in the world?"

"*Swoon.*"

"Yeah. Okay, we're gone," Atomik Lad grumbled while dragging the Superior Sentinel out of the room.

*   *   *   *

Nuklear Man sidled along the dinner line. He was squeezed amongst some of Metroville's most heinous criminals. "Mmm, I'm ready for some *good* eatin'! What do they serve around here? Veal, fillet mignon, lobster?" A prisoner behind the sneeze guard and wearing a stained apron and a hairnet slapped an ice cream scoop full of off-grayish slop onto Nuklear Man's tray. "Hm. Interesting," he observed. "But what are we supposed to eat?"

*   *   *   *

Atomik Lad flew ahead of Superion as the majestic Überdyne Building receded in the background. "All right, well I've shown you the city, so we're done. I'm going back to the Silo to think of ways to get Nuke out of jail."

"Good for you, kiddo."

"Yeah. Bye."

*   *   *   *

That night, Atomik Lad sat at the Danger: Kitchen Table with blank sheets of paper and what turned out to be a very, very heavy pen when weighed in the Scale of Creativity. He moved into the Danger: Living Room to be more comfortable on the Danger: Couch. "That oughta get the ol' brain cells pumping. Okay. I need to get a lawyer. Maybe I can get one of Überdyne's. But they really specialize in scientific ethics cases, so maybe I should just get a normal one. Argh. I hate this." He turned on the Danger: TV with a flick of the Danger: Clicker and felt strangely comforted by the nonsensical prattling of Silly Sam's Cartoon Marathon-a-thon o' Fun.

*   *   *   *

Deep in the derelict North Tower of Katabasis Prison, the Captain of the Guard's harsh voice echoed amongst the dank stone walls, "All right, maggot."

"Guh! You should do something about those."

"Shut up, maggot!"

"Okay, talking to them is one thing, but when they start to talk back, that's when you know it's time to go 'Whoa.' That's when you gotta back up and realize that though they very well may be plotting against you, they cannot communicate in a way that is recognizable to you or I."

"Put the damn mask on," the Captain grumbled.

"Only if you promise to seek some serious psychological help."

"Yes. Fine, whatever. Put the damn thing on," he ordered while tossing the heavy, archaic, and rusting iron mask into the Hero's hands.

"All right then." Nuklear Man complied by squeezing his cranium into the iron mask.

The Guard slapped the mask's many locks shut and squealed with delight.

"Uh, this is kinda uncomfortable, ya know. Maybe I should get a bigger one. I think it's physically impossible to contain all of my brains and good looks in this little mask. I feel cramped."

"It's not supposed to be comfortable!"

"Oh. Well then, mission accomplished, cap'n. So could you get me the one that *is* supposed to be comfortable?"

"Argh!"

*   *   *   *

"Hey, Sparky. How're you holding up?"

Atomik Lad sighed too heavily into the phone. "I don't know. Everything is so...wrong lately."

"I could see how you'd feel that way. No part of that trial was anything close to right."

"Yeah, I'm trying to work up a plan right now."

"How's it coming?"

"Eh. I can't think straight. It's like the more I think about this whole situation, the more I fully understand how wrong it is from every possible angle and how all those different angles interlock with one another, each one amplifying the injustices of the ones before and after it like some kind of infinite matrix of the universe working specifically to ruin my life until I just can't stand it!" He took a deep breath. "You know?"

"I think so. It reminds me of the University admissions office."

"Don't get me started on them. They even tried to jerk me around because my being a sidekick wasn't covered under their rules for special allowances to register late."

"Curse them all."

Atomik Lad stared into the TV as some news footage of Superion filled the screen with the caption "Tomorrow's Hero Here Today, on Metroville Tonight."

"Ugh," he groaned. "And this guy they've got to replace Nuke, this Superion. I hate him. It seems like I'm the only one though. There's just something about him. He tries so hard to be everyone's best friend. It creeps me out."

"I think you just miss your old pal, Nukie."

"Hmmphf. Like a hole in the head."

"You know, it is odd though. I've heard some people on campus talking about this Superion guy already."

"I'm surprised he doesn't have his own merchandise out yet."

"Don't be. He does. I saw three people wearing Superion shirts on the way to class"

"You see! That's not normal. It's only been one day! Something weird is going on here. I mean, if he's a replacement for Nuke, he's got to be damn powerful."

"Right."

"So why hasn't anyone heard of him until now?"

"Hm, I don't know. Actually, I think his name does sound familiar somehow."

"Does it? Yeah, now that you mention it. Wasn't that where Captain Liberty came from? Some government thing. Project: Superion, Superion Program, something like that."

"Yeah, that sounds right. I wonder if there's a connection," Rachel said.

*   *   *   *

Atomik Lad had been conscripted, quite against his will, to join Superion for patrol duty Wednesday afternoon. He did his best to stay just far enough away from Superion to justify ignoring him.

"Hm, hold up a second there, cowboy."

"All right. These names of yours are really starting to bug me."

"My Superior Hearing^TM detects a crime below."

"And yet it doesn't detect the loathing in my voice."

"Let's check it out."

Superion zoomed to street level while Atomik Lad reluctantly followed. Indeed, there was crime in action. It seemed the SMSTCAOAN, fresh out of the jury box, were already defaming the good name of goodness by robbing a bagel shop. They had just bungled out the entrance when Superion landed in front of them like an imposing figure of looming parental power. The villains collectively took a step back.

"I told ya he'd make it," Zeerox said confidently.

"And right on time," Chronotor commented.

Atomik Lad landed next to Superion. "Okay, guys. You know the drill by now. Either surrender and give back the money, or we go to work on you chumps."

"Money? We didn't take no money," Granite said.

"Just a coupla bagels," Lord Obese said through a mouthful of munched up food.

"We even paid for them, oink."

Blazer stepped forward with a notebook and a pen in his hand. "We just wanted your autograph, Mr. Superion sir."

"Oh, you crazy kids. Did you cause all this hoopla just to get my autograph?"

They bashfully adverted their eyes and collectively said "Nooooooooooo?"

"Oh for the love of…" Atomik Lad muttered to himself.

Superion signed the autograph book and handed it back. "There you go, Firecracker. Anything else I can help you with?"

"Well, I hope this isn't asking too much," Blazer began respectfully. "But could you arrest us?"

"Okenshi speaks for his comrades when he says it would be a great honor."

"Please?" Blazer pleaded.

"Well, I don't normally do this, but okay."

"Yay!" they cheered.

"Atomik Lad!" the ex-sidekick heard Dr. Genius's voice from within his own mind. "Come in, over."

Yeah. I'm here, he thought to her. *Man, that's always so weird.*

"It's the most effective way of communicating with you for emergencies and I can't seem to get through to Superion. It's almost as if he's blocking my signal somehow. Maybe you should bring him in so I can do a few Kopelson Intrinsity sweeps and calibrate the Telepath-a-matic so he can benefit—"

You said something about an emergency?

"Oh yes. It seems Dr. Menace is robbing the First National Bank of Metroville. It's not exactly her style, but I think she may have turned over a new leaf— of sorts—since the trial. You two need to get down there before she escapes."

Right. Thanks Doc. He turned to Superion who was cracking jokes with his villain buddies while bending things like lamp posts and cars around their bodies. "We've got to stop Dr. Menace. She's robbing a bank!"

"Dr. Menace, eh?" he adopted a contemplative look. "Naw, I think we're more needed right here for now. I wouldn't worry too much about her."

"What are you talking about?! These morons pose more danger to themselves than to anyone else. Just let them go, we've got a real problem to deal with."

"C'mon. It'll be okay," Superion assured.

"Urgh."

✳   ✳   ✳   ✳

As the days passed, Superion swept through Metroville's villainous population like a hot knife through flesh. Only without the mess or pain. Or the screaming, oh ye gods the endless screaming—why won't their wet, tortured screams stop haunting my dreams!

Sorry. Let's just say that Superion was able to bring nearly all of Metroville's nefarious characters to justice. Or rather nearly all, as the Venomous Villainess, Dr. Menace, still remained at large. The good citizens of the city heralded every success as a triumph of all humanity. Parades were thrown, merchandise was bought, and many, many T-shirts were worn. By the following Friday, Mayor Incompetent Bureaucrat proclaimed every day Superion Day. Huge celebrations were held around the city as Nuklear Man continued to rot in the abandoned North Tower of Katabasis Prison. The rest of the city's heroes had it much better than that though, as they were merely forced into early retirements thanks to The Trial of Nuklear Man.

As the sun set that Friday, Superion and Atomik Lad were finishing their final patrol of the city. Atomik Lad had been checking his Danger: Watch almost twice a minute for the last half hour. "Just a little longer and I can finally get away from this twit," the ex-sidekick said to himself. He had been trying to find a way to free Nuklear Man through legal channels all week, but he was blocked at every turn by new legislation using the Golden Guardian's trial as precedent. And with Superion's popularity, he wasn't sure it would matter even if he could free Nuklear Man anyway. The populace would probably boo them out of town. He suspected they only continued to tolerate his own presence because Superion was never far away from him in public.

"Hey, Sport," the Aegis Against Evil said as they flew among the great towers of Metroville. "You got a cake in the oven there, pal?"

Errrrg, he thought. "I've just got some plans for tonight is all."

"Ohh, these plans of yours wouldn't happen to involve that little peach of yours, Rachel, would they?"

Atomik Lad came to an abrupt halt in mid-air. Superion looped around and hovered nearby. "What's the matter, Chief? I say something wrong?"

His Atomik Field quickened its roiling flames for an instant. "How do you know her name?"

"Er, well. You've mentioned her before."

"No, I haven't. I've gone out of my way to never mention her around you. How do you know her name?"

"You must've slipped up. I know you mentioned her because how else could I know?"

"That's what I'm trying to figure out," he said with narrowed eyes shining with suspicion.

"Hm, I'm sure you said something about her when we first met. Buuuut look at the time. Looks like you're free for the night."

"Yeah."

"Remember, tomorrow's patrol starts at nine in the morning."

Atomik Lad turned and flew at top speed toward the Silo without an answer.

Superion hovered among the building tops, his silver cape waving in the winds that rushed between the spires of business. He watched his appointed sidekick fly out of sight and then tracked him with Superior Vision^{TM}. "Veering toward the University, eh?" A beep, imperceptible to all but his own Superior Hearing^{TM}, beeped its little beep from within the surrogate hero's outfit. He brought his senses to a more normal range while digging in a pocket to retrieve his Evil: Communicator.

"Zuperion!" it barked angrily. "You nearly cozt uz everything, you fool! Now he may zuzpect you!"

"You worry too much, Princess. It'll be okay."

"Bah! Your Zuperior Mind^{TM} Trickz will not work on me, boy."

"Oh."

"Too bad the rezt of Metroville cannot zay the zame!" she cackled maniacally.

"Yup. I've got this town eating out of my hand."

"Let uz not forget who made all of thiz pozzible. It waz *my* geniuz which maztered the old zuper zoldier 'Zuperion Procezz' that gave you incredible powerz—juzt like thoze of your father, Adam Powerz, more commonly known az the late Captain Liberty!"

"Yeah, but my dad was never *this* strong," Superion said while watching red-violet energy swell around his hands.

"True. Had your father pozzezzed the zpecial modificationz I made to the Zuperion Procezz, he would have eazily zurvived the nuclear explozion that cozt him hiz life while zimultaneouzly giving birth to Nuklear Man."

"And for what?" Superion spat. "So that Golden Goon could walk all over his good name and make everyone forget what my father has done for this country! For the *world*!"

"Yez, well—"

"If it weren't for my dad, the Nazis would've taken over with their giant mechanical Deathbots."

"Yez, but—"

"And how he saved the world when he destroyed the renegade remains of the Viel alien fleet after Dr. Zoom's suicide attack decimated it."

"I get the idea—"

"Not to mention over fifty *years* of selflessly dedicating himself to justice. The whole world owes its continued existence to my father. But who is it they remember? Who is it they adore? Who is it they praise?" He paused to slow his accelerated breathing.

"Finally," Dr. Menace muttered. "Yez, thankz to my ingenious zcheming, that Nuklear Imbecile haz been made into a villain in their eyez. They've locked him away. He iz completely powerlezz to stop uz." She stifled another maniacal outburst. "And even if, by zome miracle, he were to be freed from hiz imprizonment, I have seen to it that you are more than a match for hiz Plazma Powerz by augmenting your already Superior Powerz^{TM} with my Negaflux technology thereby allowing you to counteract or even completely overwhelm any force directed against you! Az long az you continue to rezt in your containment capzule to recharge your Negaflux rezerves, at unbelievable expenze which explainz my recent bank robberiez, you're functionally invinzible!"

Superion hurled a "SUPERIOR BEAM^{TM}!" toward the stars for no other reason than he could. "They'll pay for forgetting," he snarled. "Every last one of them."

$$*\qquad*\qquad*\qquad*$$

Meanwhile, deep within the Scientific: Bowels of Überdyne's many secret sub-basements, Dr. Genius was working a Kopelson Intrinsity Formula through several sequences of Atomik Lad's KI data when her handy pocket supercomputer beeped at her. She removed it from her pocket and checked its display. "Hm," she said after a moment's contemplation. "Interesting. A Negaflux field in the form of a coherent beam has been detected in Metroville. A weapon of that power would be essentially *unstoppable*. That could be terribly dangerous in the wrong hands. I wonder if this has anything to do with Dr. Menace's recent crime wave." She punched several buttons on her hand held computer and spoke into it. "Nameless Technician. I want you to step up Negaflux monitoring. I fear Dr. Menace may be up to something."

$$*\qquad*\qquad*\qquad*$$

Atomik Lad walked out of the Danger: Kitchen with a couple cans of Danger: Dr. Zap. "Anything else, m'dear?"

Rachel waved him to sit next to her on the Danger: Couch.

"Righto." He jumped next to her and handed over one of the drinks.

"Thanks, Sparky," she said while doing a sneaky little snuggle-lean thing up against him. She noticed a certain awkwardness in the way he held himself. "Hey, what's on your mind?"

He shook himself out of his stupor. "Oh, I, nothing. I'm sorry." He allowed himself to relax against her. "I guess it's just kind of weird not having Nuke around is all."

"Yeah, I've only been here once before and I can tell it's not quite right without him. Like, I don't know. Like it's missing something."

"The noise. It's too quiet."

She gave his ear a little nibble. "We could fix that."

Issue 42—Usurper!

The same night, in the middle of the Abandoned Warehouse district of town, a ghastly green glow was cast from the broken windows and cracked walls of a warehouse that was not so abandoned after all. Within this very unabandoned warehouse was—you know the answer folks—Dr. Menace reclining in a giant pile of pilfered money. She sipped a neon blue colored liquid from an oversized glass that had a distinctly tropical little paper umbrella floating in it.

Across from her, surrounded by a whole heck of a lot of Evil: Recharging Equipment, was Superion's green containment cell. She took a deep breath and reveled in the sweet electric smell of Science as the humming machinery replenished Superion's supply of Negaflux energy for the following day. "Oh sure, the recharging procezz cozts nearly a hundred thouzand dollarz a night in nuclear grade plutonium and an additional eighty thouzand dollarz worth of rubies fuzed into a single gem for the focuzing lenz to power theze machinez, and the pzychological ramificationz of being given ezzentially unlimited strength hazn't been properly conzidered or even accounted for, but I believe it haz been worth the rizks now that Metroville iz almozt mine! Muwa hahahahaha!"

Superion's chamber pulsed with an intense burst of energy that coursed through the machines hooked up to his canister.

Dr. Menace jumped up and stalked over to the chamber. "What have I told you about theze sessions? You muzt remain calm or there could be radically disastrous rezults!"

Bubbles flourished within the chamber's eerie green depths.

"Er," Dr. Menace said. "Yez, well I obviouzly meant that Metroville iz almozt *ourz*. You see, it'z juzt that I am not uzed to working with a partner and therefore, whilzt in the heights of my Evil: Rantingz, I sometimez forget to pluralize. Yez, that iz it."

Superion responded with bubbles that were plainly put at ease by the Venomous Villainess's answer. The Aegis Against Evil snickered while thinking to himself *Heh, sucker.*

Dr. Menace walked back to her incredibly comfortable chair made of cold hard cash while thinking to herself, *Heh, sucker.*

*   *   *   *

Still that very same night, somewhere else across town, Nuklear Man was chained to a decaying stone wall of Katabasis Prison's North Tower. A mask of iron bound his mind as well as his face. "Without a face," he said with a rasping voice. "Without a face you don't have a name. Without a name you don't have any words. Without words you are nothing." He giggled like a madman. "And nothing is invincible! Nothing is perfect! The fools, they have given me the keys to unlimited power! The world will be *mine*! I shall rain Plazma Death upon the cities of man until the oceans run red with their blood and the skies are black with the smoke of their burning babies and—"

"Hey! Shut up in there!"

Nuklear Man cowered against the wall, "Sorry."

*   *   *   *

The sun rose on another beautiful Saturday morning. Fiery light glinted against the great skyscrapers of Metroville. Early weekend traffic of happy couples in search of shops, parks, breakfast, and whatever it is people go out in the morning for began to roam the streets. However, one couple was not so happy that morning.

Atomik Lad squat down and ran his hand through the remains of the Danger: Couch. It's stuffing lay scattered and exposed like the entrails of a slain beast. He squeezed some of the fluffy substance between his thumb and forefinger, rolling it between his palms like the making of a meatball. He closed his eyes and let his mind roam...

"The noise. It's quiet."

"We could fix that."

Warmth. Flood of sensation like electricity surging down half my body. Warm. Bodies. Sex. Children. Parents. Blood. Warm. Red. Parents. Blood. Parents' blood. Warm and red. Drip drop, drip dropping from the ceiling into thick pools. Still warm. Wide eye terror staring at me from mom's disembodied head lying among bodies rent asunder. Still warm. Still and warm.

And red. Always red.

"No!" He shrieked and pushed Rachel to the floor, bruising her elbow on the Danger: Coffee Table along the way. The Danger: Couch exploded in a flash of raging crimson before she hit the ground. "No," Atomik Lad whimpered, sitting among the Danger: Couch's remains and his berserk field. "No..."

"John," she said soothingly, reaching out.

"No!" he yelled, recoiling from her. "You can't!"

"John."

"I'm sorry." His eyes shut tightly to force tears back.

"John." He felt her hand on his shoulder.

"Rachel!" He jumped away, tears openly streaming down his face.

"Sparky, it's okay."

"No, get away! It'll kill you, I can't control it. Please."

"John, calm down. Your field isn't there," she said, approaching him. "It's morning now."

Atomik Lad covered his face. "I'm sorry. I, I thought. Last night."

"Shhh," she wrapped her arms around him. "You're shaking."

"I thought. I thought you were trying to touch my Field. I'm sorry about this. I'm sorry about what happened."

"Oh, Sparky," she whispered. "Don't worry about it, okay? This isn't a big deal."

"I nearly killed you. *Again.*"

"We'll work it out."

"Are you sure? Maybe you should start looking for a nice normal guy who doesn't have some kind of uncontrollable energy field of death."

"John. I love you."

"You'd be bet—I, you. What? I had no idea."

"Don't look so surprised, Sparky. What, you think I'd try to get my freak on with just any guy who can pick up a game controller?"

"Well, no but."

"Even if he can't use it very well."

"Oh, that did it. Here I was, about to return your sentiment when you lay that on me. It's go time."

She smiled wide. "I was hoping you'd say that."

"Well, unfortunately, it really is go time. As in time for me to go on 'patrol' with Superion."

Rachel gave him a squeeze, "Oh, do you have to?"

"Mmmm...no."

"Yes you do."

"Yeah. And it is the bane of my existence."

"Why do you guys even do patrols any more? Superion has taken care of all the villains."

"They're not exactly patrols. They're more like parades."

*   *   *   *

A couple hours later that afternoon, Atomik Lad moped next to Superion. Both of them sat in the back of a convertible that was idling through a confetti strewn street. The sidewalks were packed with Superion's fans. Atomik Lad let the world around him pass by like he wasn't even involved in it.

It isn't supposed to be like this. This is nothing more than mindless hero worship. I mean, sure, this is probably how Nuke would've liked it. But at least he tried *to earn their respect. This jerk just walks around getting adored by these drones. There aren't even any crises to be saving them from. It all seems so artificial. I can't stand being around all this insincerity. Grah!*

A nudge on his shoulder brought his thoughts to the present. "Hey there, Slugger. Parade's over."

"Finally," Atomik Lad grumbled before giving a stretch.

"Now it's time for the big announcement," Superion said with a wink.

"*Announcement?*" the ex-sidekick asked while looking around. The street was blocked off with thousands of screaming fans wearing their Superion paraphernalia. They surrounded a makeshift stage with a podium featured prominently upon it. Mayor Incompetent Bureaucrat stood behind the podium. He shook slightly, like a mild nervous twitch that afflicted his entire body. His empty, wide-set eyes focused on Superion as the hero hovered out from the convertible. "And now our very special guest, Superion!" he announced. The crowd roared as the Crimson Crusader floated over them and tossed winks and snap-points as he made his way to the podium.

Atomik Lad and the convertible were nearly tipped over as the crowd surged like a wave to be closer to their idol. He gave up attracting the attention of those pressed up against the door to them to move so he could get out and simply floated out of the vehicle himself, eliciting no other reaction than, "Hey! Freak! Down in front! I can't see Superion!" and a few thrown soda cans of varying emptiness.

"Thanks," he said and landed on the car. He shut off his Field and forced himself down into the tightly packed mob.

"In honor of what this man has done for our city, and in honor of today's Superion Day celebration," Mayor Incompetent Bureaucrat began. "I hereby officially change the name of Metroville to Superion City!"

"What?!" Atomik Lad blurt out, though his blurt was drowned out by the joyously screaming hoards around him.

"And in honor of this name change," the Mayor continued. "I hereby officially hand over every seat of government within Superion City to Superion himself who may now lord over us with his unlimited charm as well as his unlimited civic power."

Atomik Lad would've fallen over from surprise had he not been supported on every side by the suffocatingly dense throngs of humanity around him.

"Superion now wields ultimate executive power over all of Superion City!" The Mayor proclaimed triumphantly.

The Aegis Against Evil took the microphone, "And tomorrow, the world!" The crowd let loose a deafening roar.

Atomik Lad climbed back onto the car hood and jumped up, his deadly field exploded and held him in the air. "This isn't right!" he yelled without effect. "This isn't right!" he repeated louder, not that it made his statement any more audible due to the screaming maniacs below him.

Superion looked into his eyes and gave him a Best Buddy winning smile complete with wink and point.

"Grah!" Atomik Lad's Field flared and froze in an array of jagged crimson fangs, "This isn't right!" his voice boomed like thunder and rattled nearby windows. The crowd cringed as one and Atomik Lad's statement echoed throughout the city. An awkward silence hovered over the gathering.

"Er," Superion said. "I think what our little soldier here means is that it isn't right because Dictator's don't have sidekicks and that means he'll be unemployed. And as your new tyrant, my first priority is to eliminate unemployment in this city by implementing a series of civic works programs which will construct a fleet of war vehicles and artillery stations that will be set up at key points along the city's perimeter behind the soon to be constructed Great Wall of Superion City which will defend us from outside retribution."

"What the—" Atomik Lad said. "Why does it sound like you're planning to construct a legion of death to sweep across the nation?"

"We are," he answered. "Er, that is, in the royal sense, we are surprised you would jump to such conclusions."

"Well why else do you want to build machines of war?"

"To, to better defend our beautiful city from criminal influences, Sport."

Someone from the crowd interrupted. "Stop talking! You're taking my attention away from Superion! You jerk!"

"Yeah! Less talkion, more Superion!"

"Get out of here, freako!"

"Death to floaty guy!"

Random bits of trash were hurled at Atomik Lad who was more than effectively defended from them by his super keen Field. He shot Superion a nasty look before rocketing into the sky.

"Superion! Superion! Superion!" the crowd shouted with one thoroughly washed mind.

But the Crimson Crusader could not hear these cheers for he was intently listening to the tiny heavily accented voice in his ear. "Why did you zpeak of Project: Zpearhead?! You fool! He may already zuzpect that thiz whole charade of ourz iz nothing more than a, well, a charade."

"So what should I do?" He asked through a small transmitter attached to one of his perfect molars. The crowd couldn't care or notice his detachment to them because of their fervor and the perfectly practiced blank smile Superion was flashing at them.

"The boy iz a wildcard. I had not calculated that he could rezizt your charmz zo completely. All pzychological data indicated that he would give in to the ztronger perzonality of a father/hero figure, yet he findz you contemptible and zuzpiciouz. And now that you have given him zomething to think about, he may be on to uz!"

"What do you want me to do about it?" His voice rang with aggravation while his smile rang with false sincerity.

"We muzt aczept the pozzibility that the Atomik Wonder Boy knowz what we are up to, or at leazt that he will zoon ztumble acrozz my brilliant zcheme to rule the zity and then the vorld. Zo we muzt ztrike out at him before he ztrikez out at uz."

"But how?"

"We could attempt a direct attack, but I have zeen that infernal Field of hiz protect him in the mozt dire of zircumztancez. I zwear it haz a mind of itz own. No, inztead we have to attack that which hiz Field cannot protect."

Superion's glaze of a smile shone with a new and genuine radiance. "I just might have the perfect thing in mind."

*   *   *   *

Atomik Lad soared over the high rooftops of Metroville. He flew without a destination, he just had to get away from Superion and I think we can all understand that. He rubbed his temples. *What the hell is going on? Menace sues us for wrecking her abandoned warehouse? I mean, we've probably blown up a dozen of those over the years and she never complained before. Maybe it's just a symptom of the times we live in, if something bothers you, just sue somebody. And then Nuke had to hire Count Insidious to be our lawyer even though he just happened to be Dr. Menace's boyfriend and her lawyer. Between them and that jury we didn't have a chance. And then using that ruling as precedent to launch a class action suit against Nuke for the billions of dollars worth of damages incurred during our entire career of stopping horrible things from killing people. Why, that dumb ox was practically destined to go to jail. And then, using the public's sympathy for her position, Menace was able to legally disband all of the city's remaining heroes and replace them with one appointed by her who reminds me of every popular phony from every high school wrapped into one package.* "And then he goes on a nonstop campaign of eliminating all of the city's villains except for Dr. Menace herself who remains at large and completely unopposed by any heroes while simultaneously holding a complete monopoly on the villainy market!"

He came to a neck-breaking stop. "Superion is nothing more than Dr. Menace's puppet. And the mayor just gave him complete power over Metroville!" Atomik Lad turned around. "He said something about a war fleet, a great wall, an arms build up. This is all part of Dr. Menace's newest plot to take over the world! What the hell have I been doing? I've got to stop her!" His field flickered momentarily. "But first I should get some help. I could go to Nuke, but the way things are right now, we'd probably have to fight our way through a sea of innocent citizens to get to Superion. No, getting to Nuke isn't the priority any more. I've got to worry about Superion now."

*   *   *   *

Minutes later, Atomik Lad was standing outside the Magno Pad's partly opened door. Mighty Metallic Magno Man's head poked through the crack as Atomik Lad finished up his summary of Dr. Menace's latest plot. "Whoa, slow down there, buddy," Mighty Metallic Magno Man said at last.

Atomik Lad tried to catch his breath. "Buddy? Whatever. Look, we don't have time to slow down. The mayor has just given Superion complete power over Metroville!"

The Tungsten Titan opened the Magno: Door all the way. Atomik Lad's eyes went wide with shock as Norman's Superion T-shirt was displayed in all its glory. "Well it's about time," MMMM said. "That Superion has done so much for our city."

Atomik Lad nearly fell over himself as he stumbled away from the door. He regained his balance and ran to the elevator nearly running over, "Dr. Genius!" in the process. "Doc! You've got to help me!"

"What's wrong?" she asked, adjusting a loose curl.

"Dr. Menace, Superion, taking over the world, Norman, I think he's been brainwashed and—"

She took his hand. "Jonathan. Please calm down. Let's look at this logically." She tossed one half of her lab coat open with her free hand while looking for her trusty portable supercomputer. Atomik Lad gasped in disbelief. "Oh, do you like my Superion T-shirt?" She gave him a quizzical look. "Where's yours?"

"Gah!" He struggled free of her grasp and, in a blaze of redness, smashed through a nearby wall into the crisp air of Metroville's Apartment District.

"What was all that about, babe?" Norman asked as Dr. Genius entered the Magno: Pad.

"Probably just in a hurry to get his Superion shirt, dear."

*   *   *   *

"Oh God, what the *hell* was that, what the hell *was* that?!" Atomik Lad asked himself. Norman's apartment building receded into the background as Atomik Lad flew at top speed in whatever direction happened to be forward. He ran his hand through his hair a couple times with nervous energy. "Okay. Don't panic. There's no reason to panic. Just because Nuke's best friend since Day One, the man who has been with us on every major adventure since the three of us disposed of the Dragon, has turned into one of Superion's mindless slaves is no reason to panic! And Dr. Genius?! Our most trusted advisor. I mean, good God, she helped set up the new Legion of Champions." He shut his eyes tight and hoped to shut out the horrible reality around him at the same time. "What the hell was that?" he repeated. "Two of our greatest allies." He took a turn sharp enough to rip out teeth. "Angus. He can help. There's no way Superion's gotten through his anger, whiskey, and haggis addled mind."

*   *   *   *

Angus dabbed at his eyes with a dirty napkin while watching a convertible race to a cliff's edge on his Iron: TV. "AUGCH! It's just not fair! Can't ye see they be two lasses tryin' to make it in a man's world!" He blew his nose as the car careened over the cliff in slow motion. "Ah can't watch any moore. Change it. Change the blasted channel!"

Shiro fumbled with the VCR remote. "Remote control is like dragon of puzzlement."

"Bah!" the Surly Scot snapped as he snatched the Iron: Remote from his fellow Dwarven Warrior's hand. "Ye people built the damned thing, ye oughta be able to use it," he muttered. "Ye never see a Scotsman who can't use a shot glass, that's fer damned sure!"

"Shiro think Angus-san are being emotions from movie of chicks for watching them."

Angus tossed his used napkin across the room. "All they wanted was to live like real people, independent and free froom their male oppressors!"

A knock rang with a metallic resonance from the Iron: Door. "Answering has been Shiro for visitor time last when Fate's Wheel spins, heavy with acceleration traveling to lands beyond—"

"Shaddap!" Angus yelled, already at the door. "Damn bastard oughta learn the language before comin' to this country." He opened the door.

"Angus!" Atomik Lad said. "Let me in, the whole world's gone crazy," he pushed into the Iron: Headquarters's inner sanctum.

"Ah knew it! And ye know why they're all crazy?" He pointed up. "All them chemicals locked in the upper atmosphere where all ye people do ye breathin'. It eats away at the mind, it does," he added knowingly.

"No, that's not it. It's—great Thor's hammer!" Atomik Lad exclaimed rather like Nuklear Man would have had he been there. A framed Superion shirt hung above the Iron: TV.

"Aye," Angus said. "That's what Ah said when that little *puke* down at the Short an' Small shop told me they didn't have one small enough for us to wear."

"Unless," Shiro interjected. "Both Angus-san and I were to was being to wear Supaa Small Child's Size shirtu, like Siamese freak who at the town of hypothetical."

"Oh, aye, aye. That's good, laddie. Why don't ye just rub it in, ye hotel cubicle sleepin', lower regard for women than is typical of Westernersin', member of a society that made one of the fastest transitions from the old world to the modern era laddie. Bah!"

"Um," Atomik Lad stuttered while making for the Iron: Door. "Look, I'm sorry for barging in on you guys. I'm sure you're busy, what with, um, I've-I've got to get out of here!" He scrambled out the door.

"Ye see there? That laddie is sufferin' from that high altituude air poison Ah was telling' ye about. He even forgot to wear his Superion shirt."

Shiro nodded. "Hai. Ogre of Madness infesting brain like ants giant with hunger. Destroying away the food."

Angus shook, "Why don't ye make soome sense for a change!"

✳   ✳   ✳   ✳

An hour later, Atomik Lad was shooting into the air like a rocket. The Public: Library receded into the distance behind him. *That makes it official,* he thought, *Norman, Genius, Shiro, Angus, Halo, and the entire Minimum Wage Warrior squad. There's no one left. There's nothing else to do. I've got to go to the source myself.* He hovered motionless for an instant and tore through the air like a crimson bullet aimed at City Hall.

✳   ✳   ✳   ✳

City Hall loomed over him. It was a tower of steel and reflective glass, angular and arrogant against the sky. He got halfway up the stairs leading to the revolving door entrance when he noticed the marble edifice that was supposed to say City Hall. It now read Superion Hall. "Okay, that's it." His field swirled into existence around him, the concrete step under him splintered from the force of it. He took off, arched slightly toward the building, and shattered the top floor panoramic window that used to be part of the Mayoral: Office until it was changed into the Superior: Office, a title under which the window led a short lived career as it now lay broken into ragged pieces throughout the office. The shards offered up myriad warped and cracked reflections of the pre-storm sky and Atomik Lad darkened from his own shadow.

"Superion!" he yelled as his field dissolved. "I know you're in here!" He walked into the office's unlit depths as bits of glass crunched under his feet.

"Right you are, Champ." Superion stepped through the large oak double doors that most non-Atomik people use to enter the office. The Crimson Crusader, with his arms outstretched to the doorknobs, cast a cross-like shadow into the darkened office. He took a few deliberate steps inside. His arms flexed like a bow and he shut the doors behind him with a flick of his wrists. The boom echoed twice among the two giants.

"I know what you're doing," Atomik Lad stated.

"You know," Superion said. "The décor just isn't right in here. It doesn't look like a Superior: Office, does it?"

"Don't change the subject."

Superion produced a little remote control device and pushed one of the two buttons on it. A dozen vermilion tapestries with Superion's symbol of a blue S set against a white star unfurled themselves along the office's walls and windows. The tarp behind Atomik Lad waved slowly from the breeze allowed by his impromptu entrance.

He closed his eyes. "If I have to see another one of those damn Superion symbols, I'll be sick."

"Is there a problem, Sport?"

"Stop calling me those meaningless names!" Atomik Lad demanded as his fists clenched unconsciously.

"Meaningless? I'm just being friendly with ya. We're partners, aren't we? Pals."

"No. You are an insincere, lying, back-stabbing, underhanded usurper. And I'm going to stop you."

Superion laughed, jovial and slightly surprised. "What are you talking about? Give up this nonsense, you kidder you. Just join me like everyone else. C'mon, it'll be okay." The Aegis Against Evil approached Atomik Lad with his hand reaching out for the ex-sidekick's shoulder.

"Get away from me!" he said, batting the hand away.

"If you'd only join me, we could own this city. *Together.*"

"Together? What about Dr. Menace? Do you really think she plans on splitting rulership two ways, much less three?"

"Dr. Menace, eh? I wouldn't worry about her," he said confidently. He set a small chunk of metal that used to be a mini-transmitter and earpiece on the desk. "Join me and together we could rule the world."

"I'll never join you," Atomik Lad growled.

"It would make everything so much easier if you did," Superion said as he walked past Atomik Lad to the flowing tapestry behind him. The tail of Superion's silver cape caught wisps of wind as he gently placed his hand on the tapestry. The soft fabric rippled across his palm. "We've already won, Champ."

"I can't let you get away with this."

Superion smiled. "Why not? Resisting will only bring about your demise. But if you join me, why it's a lifetime of idle pleasures. Utter bliss."

"I can't do that. People depend on heroes to do the right thing."

Superion brushed his palm across the tapestry. "People. Ordinary, spiteful, ignorant, *petty* people. You've spent your whole life protecting them. And for what? Believe me, there's no pay off for the good guys. I know. They owe you this."

"I can't betray my friends."

"Your friends? Your friends are under *my* control now."

"That's why I have to stop you."

"You will die if you oppose me."

Atomik Lad shrugged. "You let me worry about that. Let's get started."

"So you'd really die for them?"

"I couldn't call myself a hero otherwise."

"You have strong feelings for your friends. Especially for…Rachel."

The ex-sidekick could feel a void where his stomach used to be. "What."

Superion turned to face Atomik Lad. "Well, if you will not turn, then perhaps she will." He clicked the other button on his remote. A spotlight shone on the Superior: Desk. Rachel was sitting in a chair. She wore a blank stare and a Superion shirt.

"*No!*" Every window in the building exploded outward, the glittering glass fell like rain.

Less than a second later, Superion was launched from the top floor like a cannonball wrapped in vermillion cloth. He tumbled, regaining his balance as his momentum sent him between Metroville's skyscrapers. Atomik Lad lanced through the air like light and struck him with a super sonic body ram fueled by crimson flames. Shards of glass from nearby buildings glinted in their wake as they fell from heaven like dying angels.

Issue 43—The Gambit

Dr. Menace worked fastidiously at her Evil: Computer. An alarm rang. "Ah yez. Time to check in on my Superion." She donned a headset and adjusted a few dials on her Evil: Computer. "Static?" She turned more dials. Still only static. "Superion? Superion! Can you here me?" She tore the headset off and threw it into a dank corner. Her fingers flew across the Evil: Keyboard as she narrated what she was doing for the sake of the reading audience. "Computer. Search and record Negaflux phenomenon." The screen displayed a large overhead map of Metroville, the phrase "Negaflux search: commencing," blinked in the lower right hand corner. The map went through a series of close-ups until a single city block filled the screen. Dr. Menace's fingers danced madly as she spat, "Blazted computer! What good are you if you cannot even hack into a simple spy satellite?" A few seconds later the screen showed live video feed of Superion Hall. She sat motionless for a moment. "He waz suppozed to check in with me before taking control of the city," she griped to herself. Superion Hall's windows appeared to explode. "What haz that fool done?"

*   *   *   *

Superion righted himself and turned to face the Superion Hall. He wanted to give a sinister grin but found that his opponent was already upon him and and delivering another attack. *I had underestimated his strength. Such speed. And that field. It's like touching an exposed high voltage wire, and that's* with *my Superior*

Powers and Negaflux augmentation. Incredible. "Let's end this quickly, boy!" The Crimson Crusader kicked Atomik Lad back a few feet.

"No you don't!" Atomik Lad snarled, closing in once again.

"Yes. I do." He punctuated this point with a double fisted uppercut that sent Atomik Lad soaring straight up into the stratosphere. Superion stopped himself in mid-air, his cape catching the inter-skyscraper wind. He shade his eyes and watched as the ex-sidekick diminished above him, finally piercing a cloud shaped like an enormous dog's head. "Good luck breathing up there. Soldier."

The cloud pulsed into a hellish blood red splotch in the sky and evaporated in an instant. Atomik Lad tore through the atmosphere and crashed into Superion like a fiery meteor. They careened to the street and punctured it. Great slabs of stone lay like a crumpled flower's petals around their impact crater. The two titans grappled one another, each trying to force the other into submission.

*   *   *   *

"Hm," Dr. Menace said while watching her renegade and her sworn enemy's ex-sidekick face-off. "Superion'z Negaflux Field integrity iz ztill at 97 perzent. Quite imprezzive conzidering the forze Atomik Lad haz shown thuz far.

*   *   *   *

"Do you know why I adopted the name Superion?" he grunted.

"No," Atomik Lad said. "And I don't care. Geez, is the gene for evil linked to the gene that impels you guys to tell us your master plans?"

"It is in homage of my father. The only man to survive Project: Superion."

Atomik Lad slipped a fraction of an inch. "What are you talking about? The only man to survive that was Captain Liberty."

"That's right. Dear old dad was a superhero. And he. Was never. *There!*" Superion yelled. "Do you have any idea what it's like to grow up without a father!"

Atomik Lad's Field shook with an angry intensity. "You have no idea how much I am the last person you should be trying to justify your actions to with that bullshit. Don't blame your father's sense of duty for your own feelings of inadequacy." Locked hand in hand, the ex-sidekick flew them to street level. They broke off and circled each other like wolves ready to attack.

"No! You don't understand! My father didn't have a name! They took it away from him, they took everything from him so he could do their dirty work and call it justice. The one thing that made it tolerable was that everyone respected him, everyone knew him, even if they didn't know his son."

"Is this going somewhere?"

"And then, after he'd given them everything else, his past, his identity, his family, he gave them his *life*! And for what! *For what*! So they could forget him and worship that Nuklear Man *freak*! My father died for them and they don't even remember!"

"Yeah, other than the statues, movies, toys, comics—"

"Shut up! Even in his death they use him to protect their economic philosophy."

"So all of this is supposed to be some kind of revenge against Nuklear Man because he's so much more popular than your dad now, right?"

"No, you narrow-minded fool. It's not his fault he's got superpowers. Taking him out of the picture was just a necessary part of the overall plan, you see. Part of my revenge against *them*!"

"Them?"

"The government! The people! The world! They forgot him but I'll make sure they never forget me!"

"Ohh. I see. So you're taking over the world for attention."

"You don't understand. But I don't expect you to. Everyone loves Atomik Lad. Or should I say loved? They don't know you anymore. They don't know anything anymore. Their whole world consists of nothing but me! Even your pretty, pretty Rachel."

"If you're trying to cloud my judgment by getting me angry by using her as emotional bait, it's not going to work. All I have to do is defeat you and the strangle hold you have on the minds of my friends will disappear. It's how these things work. You should know that, being in the family business and all."

"Right again, Atomik Loser. Let's just hope there's enough left of their minds to matter should you defeat me. After all, if you take away that upon which their world revolves, well it could be terribly dangerous to their mental health. It sure would be a shame if that pretty Rachel of yours ended up a vegetable."

"It's still not working."

"Of course, she really doesn't need a mind for what I've got planned for her."

"I'm going to attack you now, but I want to make it perfectly clear that I'm doing only to stop your blather from turning this into some kind of male adolescent fantasy of woman domination and not because of your ploy to anger me into taking rash actions."

Superion shrugged. "Either way."

Atomik Lad charged and was repelled by a mighty punch. He came to a spontaneous halt mere inches from a store front. The glass rattled in its frame. He blast back at his aggressor. The backlash of force crumpled the store like a house of cards. Superion sidestepped at the last second, grabbed hold of the ex-sidekick's field and slammed him into the pavement, holding him there.

"And the name Superion works on another level too," The Aegis Against Evil began.

"Do you *ever* shut up! We're not even talking about this any more," Atomik Lad spat while struggling to free himself and his Field.

"Like I said, it's an homage to how my father gained his powers. And it's true that I too had to go through the Superion Process in order to temper my body so it could endure the ravages of Negaflux Augmentation."

"You done yet?"

"My body has been infused with raw Negaflux energy." He shook Atomik Lad by his Field. "How else do you think I'm able to hold onto this damned thing of yours? My own Negaflux power counteracts it."

"Okay, I kinda was wondering about that part, actually."

"Oh, and it can do so much more than that." He heaved Atomik Lad and held him with his feet dangling above the ground. "My inherent Negaflux field counteracts any energy that it comes in contact with, thus mimicking invulnerability. By extending the field I can seem to release unstoppable energy blasts, Superior Beams™! And it can redirect any energy and amplify it against itself so with gravity constantly working, I can also mimic super strength and the power of flight."

"Good for you." Atomik Lad noticed Superion's arms shaking with strain. His torso almost quivered with effort, the veins of his face and neck began to bulge. "What's the matter? Can't take the heat?"

"Quite the opposite." Superion's body began to give off a faint purple glow. He smiled knowingly. "Counteract, redirect, and amplify any force it comes into contact with. And I couldn't help but notice that your own Field has quite an abundance of force behind it." The violet glow surrounding Superion became more tangible and Atomik Lad could've sworn a railroad spike was driven into his forehead. "Menace gave me all kinds of intel about your powers she'd stolen from Überdyne. What was that Dr. Genius said about your Field? That it was essentially your own soul?"

Atomik Lad's body jerked as every muscle involuntarily tensed. "Ghk! Wh-what are you doing to me?!"

*   *   *   *

Dr. Menace jumped from her seat and lunged at the screen. "What are you doing?!"

*   *   *   *

"Tearing you apart," Superion stated plainly.

*   *   *   *

"No." Dr. Menace whispered as she watched Superion's Negaflux integrity fall from 96 to 15 percent in the blink of an eye.

*   *   *   *

Atomik Lad felt his mind fracture. Searing pain exploded through his body. Superion tore the Atomik Field in two. Atomik Lad screamed, his voice cracking at the final moment when his vision was assaulted by a blinding all-encompassing white that burned across each of his senses. The field's two halves retained their existence separate from each other and their host for just over a second before dispersing. He collapsed limply on the debris strewn street.

Superion fell back a step. "Not bad kid, but I warned you what would happen if you opposed me. Still, I nearly had to use all my power for that one." He looked to the sky. "Don't worry though, I've got more than enough to deal with Menace." He casually took to the air at speeds that should've been impossible.

*   *   *   *

"Dammit! Too fazt for the satellitez to track! At leazt the computer iz still recording hiz Negaflux readingz." Her eyes lingered on Atomik Lad's prone body. "I muzt prepare."

The dilapidated front door exploded into the warehouse and nearly sent a broken plank of ex-door through Dr. Menace's head.

She spun around. "Superion! I demand to know what you think you are doing!"

He waltzed into the warehouse with his cape flowing stylishly behind him. "Well, I think it should be fairly obvious, Doc, especially to a lady of your education and fine intellect. It's an age old story. I'm rebelling against you."

"Iz that so?" she calmly asked.

"I knew you were only using me to dupe the city into giving up on Nuklear Man, to turn them into mindless lemmings. And I knew you were going to double-cross me to fulfill your own agenda of taking over the world once I did away with anything left that could possibly oppose you. So I played up that anti-Nuklear Man shtick so that you, haughty with ingenious evil, would never suspect me of double-crossing you to fulfill my own agenda."

"Well, actually I did suzpect that you might rebel againzt me. I'm evil you see, and the firzt rule of evil iz that you muzt truzt no one. Az such, I made certain to make a failzafe when I gave you your powerz."

"Oh really? And what would that be?"

"You have to recharge your supply of Negaflux energy daily and only I know how to uze the highly complex and volatile machinery needed to do so! Or had you forgotten?"

Superion's words stumbled on their way out.

"Exactly. Without me, you are nothing!"

"When I run out of Negaflux energy, I'll still have my powers from the Superion Process."

"A lot of good thoze did your father."

The Crimson Crusader's jaw clenched.

"Yez. Now you see. Without me, you have no Negaflux power. Without the Negaflux power, your Superior Charm^{TM} will wear off of the public and they will free Nuklear Man againzt whom you shall be defenzeless."

"Maybe I could work the recharging equipment myself," he said, while running his hand over the green man-sized canister.

"Hah! I seriouzly doubt that. The slightezt miztake could wipe out everything within a half mile radiuz."

He gave her a madly indifferent look. "Won't know until we try." Superion starting flipping switches, pushing buttons, and generally activating things he had no business meddling with.

"You muzn't!" Dr. Menace pleaded as the capacitors powered up.

The recharging apparatus consisted of the Negaflux Generator with a focusing laser inside that transferred the energy into the Containment Cell where it would be slowly absorbed over a period of hours by whatever was inside if it didn't first die from the hazardous process of absorbing those very energies. Superion had already started the generator and he now stood between the translucent green canister and the focusing laser. He smiled at his warped reflection in the containment cell's curved glass. He tore the great canister from the rest of the machinery and tossed it to the side without a care.

"You cannot do thiz!" Dr. Menace protested. "The Negaflux energiez muzt be abzorbed alowly or they will tear your body apart from itz own metabolic procezzes!"

Superion stepped directly into the laser's path. "I'm willing to take that chance." The laser was warm against his stomach. The warmth spread throughout his body and his abdomen suddenly felt like it was on fire. He cringed but could not bear to move away. After a minute long eternity, the laser finally faded. Superion fell to one knee, purple energy pulsed like a heartbeat around him. He took a deep breath. "It would seem," he exhaled. "That it was well worth the risk, good Doctor."

✳   ✳   ✳   ✳

"John." A voice like a melody lilts through the air.

I turn to face the back door of my old house. I'm eight years old, but I'll be nine in a few months. The sun is piercing over the roof but far away, even further than grandma's house. Too bright, don't look. Don't look.

"John," Mother's voice from the kitchen window. I'm outside. The grass is green and smells wet, alive, and dirty. "It's time for dinner, hon!"

"Don't want to go in yet."

"C'mon, hon. You can go back out and play when you're done."

"But it's not time for dinner yet."

"I'm not going to tell you again."

Kicking at the grass, sweet grass, makes you itch from sweat in the summer. Got a pool though, so that's okay.

"Robert! Come get John from outside!" Melody gone from the kitchen window.

"Come on, Johnny boy," voice of god, hand like a clamp, covers my whole shoulder, so heavy and tight.

"It's not time for dinner yet."

"It's time to eat when your mother says it's time."

"I'm not even hungry." Door opens. White walls instead of blue sky. Darker here and cooler, but the kitchen is warm with new food. Clamp is tight but lets go of me here near my chair.

Eating. Chicken, the way I like it. Mashed potatoes, that's okay though. Poke, poke and roll around the peas.

"Don't play with your food."

"I hate peas."

"They're good for you."

"They're terrible. And cold."

"They wouldn't be cold if you didn't put them off to last."

"But I hate peas."

"Do what your mother says and eat them. She worked hard all day and then she made this dinner for us. You need your peas, you're a growing boy."

"I hate peas. She could've just stopped at Burger Hutt."

"That's it."

"Honey, don't."

"The boy has to learn the importance of a damn meal, Heather."

"Just don't buy peas anymore."

"Eat those peas!"

"Robert!"

"Eat them!" Voice of god. Angry. Face red from yelling. Don't yell Dad, don't yell. Angry eyes like fire. The fireplace, too hot to touch. Don't touch. "Eat them!" Red and angry. Like fire. Don't touch, don't. "Eat the peas!" Giant hand shaking my shoulder. Red and angry—don't touch, don't touch the fire—so angry.

and

red.

Warm kitchen smells like chicken, warm walls, wet and warm. And red.

Always red in my dreams.

No…no, I did it. I did it. I killed them. It's my fault. Killed them.

Don't touch.

Don't touch the fire.

It's red, always red. And angry. Always, always angry.

"John, are you okay?" Rachel. If beauty had a voice, it would be yours. "What's wrong, Sparky?"

Sparky?

"Sparky!" Nuklear Man. Resonate, booming, thunder, lightning, so bright, like the sun. Don't look.

Don't look.

Don't touch. Rachel, don't. Too close, don't touch!

Red. All over. Everything drenched in it, soaked to the core with…

Red flames, blood. Blood red world. Rachel, don't You can't.

But I want her to.

Red. Red Rachel. Rachel in red…red, everyone is red. Blood? Tastes like copper.

Copper. Iron (Scotsman). Tungsten (Titan). Gold (en Guardian). Silver. Silver.

Red and, and silver, laughter. Red and Rachel—"NO!"

Atomik Lad awoke. Steel towers reached out to an azure heaven like the arms of a giant. One lone wisp of a cloud moved just slow enough to defy motion. Breathing. The sound of breathing and sky. He closed his eyes and his vision was bathed in the orange of blood and flesh on a too bright day. He tried to stand but found his joints stiff and unresponsive. His body buzzed with the warmth of dull, unfocused pain. "Ugh. I feel like every nerve has been torn out and reattached. Backwards." He groaned and wiped at his face. "Where?" The past few minutes flashed through his mind. "Aww damn. Rachel." His Field burst forth and Atomik Lad took to the skies. He oriented himself to find Superion Hall. It wasn't far, especially at his speed. Approaching it, he could see what was left of the window he'd crashed into and punched Superion out of. He flew through it again and stood in the dismal office casting half of Rachel in shadow.

He ran to her, "Rachel!"

"Hm?" she responded as though distracted by the details of an engaging television drama.

He had to look away from her. "I can't fail."

He leapt from the building and a crimson splotch streaked through the sky. Superion's trail wasn't hard to follow since he hadn't bothered to go around whatever obstacles presented themselves on the way to wherever he was going.

*   *   *   *

"How did I know this would end at an abandoned warehouse?" Atomik Lad asked himself while hovering over the Abandoned Warehouse District minutes later. A purple laser fired into the sky from a warehouse skylight below and vanished to the sidekick's left in a distant forest of Metroville's high-rises. He began to give chase but, "…He said something about taking care of Dr. Menace. What if he meant—" Atomik Lad entered through the same skylight Superion had used to vacate the premises. He landed in a square of light the missing skylight allowed inside. The rest was darkness as his eyes adjusted. The remains of the Negaflux Generator smoldered to one side, the shattered Containment Cell lay in a corner ahead of him. Dr. Menace, illuminated by the oversized Evil: Computer Console in front of her, sat demurely to his right. Long motionless seconds of silence passed between them.

"Well," she said at last. "Doez the angel make a deal with the devil to catch a common enemy?"

Issue 44—The Enemy of My Enemy

Atomik Lad stood in the shaft of light speckled with dust dancing its way to the floor. "I thought he might've killed you."

She tilted her head, lengthening the green shadows cast across her features by the Evil: Computer Console's glow, "I waz about to zay the zame to you."

"How did you?"

"I waz watching your fight," she explained with a vague gesture at the enormous screen. "In light of rezent eventz, it may be beneficial for both of uz to put azide our differenzez and cooperate. Temporarily."

"I agree. Temporarily."

She smiled. "Exzellent. Now then," she signaled him closer with a wave of her hand. "I promize I won't bite."

He stepped out of the light and walked to her, his footsteps echoing in the darkness, "What about traps or back stabbing though?"

She shrugged. "Buzinezz before pleasure. You won't have to worry about my evil tendenciez. Not while we are working toward the zame goal."

"How reassuring," he said, not at all reassured.

She directed his attention to the Evil: Computer Console and, more specifically, to a windowpane on the screen filled with arcane or perhaps mathematical symbols. "Do you know what thiz meanz?"

"Oh sure. I'm working on that degree in Advanced Quantum Advancedness."

"And here I thought it waz Political Zcienze."

"How—"

"Thiz iz the original Negaflux equation for Zuperion'z powerz," she said while the top half was highlighted. "And thiz iz the equation for Zuperion after he came here and…what iz the word…zupercharged."

"Supercharged?"

"I will explain. Az you may have already guezzed, Zuperion waz but a pawn in my latezt brilliant zcheme to deztroy Nuklear Man and take over the world. I needed zomeone driven enough to allow himzelf to endure the Zuperion Procezz, a highly fatal and experimental undertaking which, theoretically zpeaking, could give any human extraordinary powerz. Azzuming the zubject zurvivez, of courze. But more importantly, it made a human body ztrong enough to hozt and manipulate itz own Negaflux Field!"

"Which gave Superion powers that are easily on par with Nuke's. I got it. He couldn't help but brag about it during our little battle. And might I add that it wasn't a particularly brilliant move to give an already unstable individual the powers of a god? You know he's trying to take over the world because daddy never played catch with him or some such nonsense."

"I had made zure to include measurez zpecifically dezigned to prevent him from rebelling againzt me."

"Like what? We could sure use a couple of those right now."

"Hiz body waz infuzed with a Negaflux Field but without a conztant zupply of energy, the field will naturally decay over time due to zimple entropy."

"So basically, he'll just run out of gas after a while."

"How characteriztically American a metaphor," she mumbled. "Alzo, every uze of hiz Negaflux born powerz would deplete the field az well. For inztance, it took 81 perzent of his field integrity in order to tear your Atomik Field apart. A tremendous amount of power," She noticed she was looking a little too intently in his eyes and adverted her gaze back to the screen.

Atomik Lad gave a brief shiver. "Do you have any idea what happened to me when he did that?"

She breathed deeply and closed her eyes. "Dr. Geniuz theorized that your Atomik Field iz ezzentially the phyzical manifeztation of your zoul."

"Wait. How do you know that?"

"I've had Überdyne bugged ever zince I left. How elze do you expect me to remain one ztep ahead of you heroic typez?"

"I don't believe this. *You* worked at Überdyne?"

She nodded.

"When? Nuke and I have been fighting you nearly as long as I can remember."

"When you were firzt brought to uz by the authoritiez after your…inzident with your parentz. I left zoon afterwards."

"I don't remember you there."

"You were not in any shape to remember."

He shook his head, eyes closed, mind searching. "I guess I don't remember much about that time. Just images really."

"I know. You were but a boy, afraid of yourzelf and everything elze in the world too. We had to ztore you in a Negaflux field, my very firzt one, because your zo-called Atomik Powerz were raging out of control."

"But it doesn't make sense. Why would they let someone like you work there right next to Dr. Genius?"

She turned back to the Evil: Computer. "Thingz change, my dear Atomik Lad. People change. I left Überdyne when I zaw that they cared more for their Zcienze than they did for the people it impacted."

"That's ridiculous. Überdyne saves lives. *You* endanger them. Look at this whole Superion thing. The whole world is in jeopardy because of you and your twisted ambitions."

"I would find your wordz inzulting if they were not zo very uniformed. If you think that Geniuz actually carez for you heroez, then it iz only becauze it iz in her bezt intereztz for you to do zo. Do you really think a woman with zuch an inhuman intelligenze could ever *truly* care for ordinary people?" Atomik Lad's answer was a stern silence. "Or have you forgotten what she did to Nuklear Man during thiz month'z tezt?"

"She said he was fine."

"Of courze she did. She valuez you only az toolz to unlocking her zacred Kopelzon Intrinzity zecretz. She would zay anything to keep you two coming back for more of her teztz."

"I don't believe you."

"The time will come, young Zparky, when you will have no other choize. Did you know that Überdyne haz a controlling interezt in 40 perzent of the world'z leading buzinezzez, and a zignificant amount of ztock in the other 60 perzent, usually through the other companiez they control? And who haz the final word in Überdyne'z operationz? Dr. Geniuz. The only differenze between she and I iz that I make no effort to hide my intentionz and I do not uze people in order to realize them. She zeekz nothing lezz than complete control of the world. She iz truly mad."

"Look, maybe this team up idea wasn't so hot after all. I nearly beat Superion last time, I can take him if I'm more careful this time."

"That iz not a good idea."

"Yeah, I'm supposed to believe you? For all I know, this is just another part of your sick plan."

"You muzt truzt me."

"Do you have any idea how much you're asking of me?"

"We muzt put azide our petty ideological differencezez for the zake of the greater good."

Atomik Lad was stunned. "That sounded…selfless. Are you okay?"

"Hmmphf. Do not worry yourzelf. I cannot take over the world if Zuperion layz claim to it firzt."

"Okay, okay. So what's the plan?"

"Zuperion haz control of the zity and he iz functionally invinzible. Zo we need our own invinzible martyr—er—*man* to diztract him."

"Distract him?"

"Yez. You zee, if we merely defeat Zuperion, thereby deztroying hiz pzychic ztrangle hold on the zity, the zudden mental ztrain would be more than enough to turn hiz zlaves into vegetables. But hiz Zuperior Charm™ iz like a muzcle. He muzt keep it 'flexed' in order for it to work. But if he were zuffiently diztracted, zay in battle, he would exert zo much energy on the melee that hiz charmz would wear off on the public. Hiz dronze should then awaken from their hypnotic tranze-like worship of him on their own. That way, when he iz defeated, their mindz will not zuddenly shatter."

"Sounds good to me. What's next?"

"Thiz battle will alzo zerve az a ztalling tactic to give me enough time to modify my Defusionizer Cannon zo that it will harmonize Zuperion's two Negaflux Fieldz."

"Defusionizer, eh? That's a new one isn't it?"

"Yez. I had intended to premier it in the zmall chanze that Nuklear Man would ever manage to free himzelf from prizon and threaten my rule after I came to power thankz to thiz very plan. The Cannon'z blazt would neutralize Nuklear Man'z powers by infecting him with a Negaflux Field set a frenquenzy the exact polar of his own. Zuperion's inzolenze haz altered the timetable. I am not againzt uzing it in thiz caze inztead."

"Okay, so how is a weapon that stops Plazma Power supposed to help us beat Superion?"

"Az I waz zaying before, Zuperion'z powerz are derived from a Negaflux Field. But, az a failzafe, in order to keep theze powerz, the field had to be recharged every day. Juzt before you got here, he did away with that weaknezz."

"What?"

"That deztroyed machinery over there, that waz the recharging equipment. I will not go into the detailz now, but zuffize it to zay that Zuperion'z powerz are now comprized of *two* Negaflux Fields which complement one another for virtually unlimited power!"

"Oh no."

"Oh yez. The overall effect iz that, combined, the fieldz are zo perfectly in zync that they loze integrity at zuch a zlow rate that it would take nearly nine hundred yearz of constant use before they'd weaken enough to even *measure* the difference. And though I pride myzelf on the forezight of my planz, I do not intend to have to wait that long for rezultz. However, if the wave harmonicz of one of the fieldz had itz polarity reverzed, then the two fieldz would work againzt one another. Zuperion wouldn't be able to lift a finger, much lezz rule the world!"

"Can you really do that?"

"I will have to or we are all doomed."

"All right. I'm ready to take him on again. Let's get ready."

"Not zo fazt. Although you pozed a threat to him when you lazt met, he iz now well beyond your capabilitiez. Az much az I loathe to admit it, we need Nuklear Man'z help. I only pray he iz able to rezizt Zuperion's Charm power."

"Nuke doesn't pay enough attention to anything outside himself for it to effect him, so that's not a problem. The problem is that he's in jail and Superion undoubtedly expects us to break him out so the jerk probably has extra special brainwashed victims watching over him."

"There iz no legal way to get him out of prizon. Count Inzidiouz zaw to that—before he had a nazty accident with being ztaked to the ground, therefore leaving him completely unable to avoid the rizing zun." She straightened her lab coat. "Crazy vampire zex. Az if."

"Dammit. If only it were as simple as dropping the charges."

Seconds ticked by as Dr. Menace stared at Atomik Lad. "To the Courthouze!"

✳   ✳   ✳   ✳

Judge Hangemall Letgodsortitout sat behind his fancy desk with Atomik Lad and Dr. Menace seated next to each other opposite him in his fancy office in his fancy law building on the corner of Fancy Street and Deluxe Avenue. The walls were covered in shelves that were supposed to be filled with legal books instead of his extensive collection of Wrastlin's Too Hot For Pay Per View tapes. He leaned his elbows on the desk. His eyes shot to Dr. Menace, to Atomik Lad, and back to Dr. Menace. "Now let me git this here straight," he began. "Dr. Menace. Y'all want to drop the charges you leveled against Nuklear Man the other week?"

"Yez."

Hangemall leaned back causing his chair to squeak and creak. "I'm not so sure if that there is altogether legal."

"Did we have to come back to him?" Atomik Lad whispered.

"Well, I had such good luck with him before, I juzt azzumed thiz would go well," she answered quietly.

Hangemall scratched his balding scalp and snorted an annoyed snort through his crooked nose. "Y'see, when it comes to these uh these, oh what's the word? These uhhh. Oh, what are they? You know what I mean. Those things pertaining to defining the difference between socially acceptable behavior and criminal actions?"

"Lawz?" Dr. Menace guessed.

"Yeah, that's it. Like I was sayin', when it comes to these here laws, I ain't so good."

Atomik Lad covered his eyes. "Y'don't say."

Dr. Menace jumped out of her chair. "Either drop the chargez or I shall tezt my Evil: Molecular Reoganizer on each member of your family in alphabetical order before turning it on you!"

Hangemall scratched his chin. "What's this 'mole-eck-ular' thing?"

"Juzt sign the paperz you judicial worm! Or I will be forced to rip out your spine one vertebra at a time with my bare handz and leave you to die like the mizerable swine you are!" she snarled. Atomik Lad, though he'd never admit it, really liked it when she talked vile.

Hangemall leapt to attention. "I will not be intimidated! And on a completely unrelated note, I'm signin' ya'll's papers here to drop the charges. Whatever that means."

Dr. Menace sat back down. "Thank you."

"There you go," Hangemall said as he pushed the papers across his desk. "That there Nuklear Man's sentence has now been reduced."

"Um," Atomik Lad said. "What do you mean reduced?"

"Oh, as in 'less than,'" Hangemall clarified. "Don't feel embarrassed, I didn't know either when I first became a judge."

"I don't think you were listening. She dropped the charges. He should go free."

"Yes. She dropped the chares, but there's still the matter of the class action suit against him. None of those people dropped their charges."

"But that waz bazed on the chargez that I had brought againzt him which were juzt dropped."

"Which is exactly why his jail sentence has been reduced as opposed to remaining the same."

"Whatever, let's just take what we can get. We don't have time for all of this."

"Fine," Dr. Menace said. "What iz thiz reduced sentence of yourz?"

*   *   *   *

One hour later, climbing the poorly torch lit and spiraling stone stairwell of Katabasis Prison's decrepit North Tower, Atomik Lad followed Dr. Menace up to the very top floor.

"All thingz conzidered, that waz a pretty good reduced sentence."

"Yeah," he agreed. "It's almost like the legal system worked in my favor. It's kind of off-putting after all we've been through with that trial of yours."

"Don't get too happy. He only helped uz becauze of my...perzuazive nature."

"Don't ruin my brief illusions of fairness in our judicial system and society at large."

"You see there? You know that the society you defend iz flawed. Perhapz you should see thingz from my point of view."

"Let's not get into that point of view argument again."

She looked back while climbing to respond, but instead said, "Seems your point of view involves my leather pantz."

He adverted his gaze to the stairs passing below his feet. "Er um, that is, I mean...what?"

"What would your dear Rachel think, hm?"

"Er. Well, I—"

"BLAM BLAM BLAM!!!" an all too familiar voice boomed in the narrow stairway. "I mean. Halt."

"What waz that?"

"Civil Defender, I'm sorry to say," Atomik Lad answered.

"Yes!" the Armored Officer announced. He hopped into view from around the curve of the stairs. "And I'm here to make sure you guys don't try to free this evil, mean, corrupt, Nuklear Criminal."

"Well, that'z really a shame, my dear boy."

"Yeah, seein' as how we've got these official papers saying that all of Dr. Menace's charges against him have been dropped," Atomik Lad said, brandishing official papers like a cross against a vampire.

The Civil Defender snatched the paperwork from Atomik Lad's hand. He scanned it briefly. "Well. What'dya know? It's official all right. That's way out of my league. Go on," he said, waving them along with his rifle-cannon. "His cell is just ahead, the bastion of madness that it is."

Atomik Lad and Dr. Menace walked up and around the bend where the stairwell ended at a cramped door of gnarled rotting wood held together by rusted bands of iron. "I'll go in. You wait out here," Atomik Lad said. "It could get *weird* in there."

"*Weird*, eh?"

"Yeah. Nuke's psychology is completely dependent upon a nearly constant exposure to cartoons."

"And if he doez not recieve theze cartoonz?"

A mad howl somewhere between a cackle and an animal's screech echoed from beyond the door.

"That was rather well timed, don't you think?"

"Yez. By all meanz, go on valiant Atomik Lad."

He pushed on the door. It opened reluctantly with a banshee's wail. Atomik Lad felt an oppressive dampness hit him as he entered the room. It was dark and humid inside, like the mouth of a great slumbering dragon. The only illumination was the dim and flickering torch light from the door behind him and it didn't penetrate nearly effectively or deeply for the ex-sidekick's tastes. "Knock when you are done," Dr. Menace said cheerily as she shut the massive door, trapping him in complete darkness.

"Hey! I thought you said no traps!"

"Settle down," her voice was muffled behind the thick door. "It iz not locked. Just hurry up in there."

"Swell. Um. Nuke? You in here buddy?"

Chains scratched against the wet stone floor somewhere in the dark depths. They echoed against the walls making the sound's origin completely impossible to locate. "There was once a man here," a haggard and coarse voice answered from throughout the dungeon. "And they called him Nuklear."

"Nuke?" Atomik Lad asked while pivoting around in various directions. "That you?"

A ragged breathing answered him. "You. You are searching for the Nuklear Man, are you?" The voice rang with ancient suffering and ancient madness.

"Um. Yeah."

"Ah," the voice twisted into a shallow laugh. "A most noble quest indeed, young knight errant."

"What?"

"But finding the legendary Nuklear Man is no simple task. You must endure the Nine Trials of the Three Virtues. First the Questions of Intelligence followed by the Feats of Strength and then the Tests of Bravery. Once you have completed these Nine Testaments of Valor you may begin the Journey of Great Peril. Then, and only then, will you find the Nuklear Man for whom you seek."

Atomik Lad had given up finding the source of the voice and just went with it. "Sure. Fine. Let's start this already. Ask me your questions, old man. I'm not afraid."

"A true warrior must be wise. He must be in balance, he must know his true self for only then may he slay the evil that permeates this sorrowful land."

"Of course."

"Thus, the first Question of Intelligence is thus: What is your name?"

Atomik Lad opened his mouth to answer but found himself strangely silent. "Uh. Well. That's not altogether such an easy answer."

"Answer the question to proceed, young one. What is your name?"

"But this is something of a complicated issue in my case, you see. My parents named me John but, well, hardly anyone calls me that any more. It's usually Atomik Lad or Sparky. But. I don't know. I really don't feel like those are me. Not really, anyway. Atomik Lad is a name in the newspapers, a stuffed doll, a T-shirt. It's almost like a character I play sometimes. But more than that because I really *am* Atomik Lad. But why? Why am I Atomik Lad?"

"How do you expect to become a true hero if you do not even understand your self?" the voice asked with genuine curiosity.

He looked down at his classy red and blue spandex with the eye-catching red A set in front of a bright yellow radiation hazard symbol. In the bleak darkness of the cell, he could only make out the A by the absence of yellow it made. He ran his hand across the form-fitting material. "My parents," he stated aloud, surprising himself. "Yes, my parents. These powers, whatever they are and however I got them, they are a part of what killed them. I can't let that be completely in vain. I have to make up for what I've done with these powers. They have to help me make things right, to help people. Without the memory of my parents, Atomik Lad is nothing. Without John, Atomik Lad is nothing. My name is John."

"Excellent, young Sir John," the voice answered without its previous exhaustion if for even a little while. "Now then, a true hero knows that for which he seeks, for how else can he reach his goals? Thus: What is your quest?"

"What do you mean, in the short term or like a life long mission kind of thing?"

"Answer and you may proceed."

"...I thought you might say that. Okay. Well, in an immediate sense, my quest is to find Nuklear Man. But that's really just the next step in the overall plan. So I guess my quest is to make the world a better place."

"A most noble quest. Indeed, the only one a true hero aspires to. And the final Question of Intelligence is thus: How was Captain Liberty able to defeat the combined heinousness of the sinister Sergeant Kraut and the vicious Dobber-Man in the Special Extravaganza 500th Issue of *The Squad of Diplomatic Immunity?*"

"Nuke. I know it's you," the ex-sidekick said. His eyes were finally starting to adjust to the darkness.

"Is not. Er, I mean, answer the question, my son, and your journey will begin."

"Is that...Look, I can see you from here."

"No you can't!"

"Yes. I can," Atomik Lad insisted. He walked over and stood right in front of the Hero.

"Oh yeah? Prove it."

"And to think I was almost starting to miss having you around," he muttered. He gave his mentor a sharp poke in the ribs.

"Ouch."

"Now that we got the obligatory idiotic behavior out of the way, let's get you out of here."

"No, no dear Sparky. I have wronged our great society and must pay my debt to it. It's the honorable thing to do."

"Were you even paying attention to the trial?"

Nuklear Man made a little so-so motion with his hand . It rattled the chains around his wrist. "More or less."

"Have you gotten stupider since I last saw you, or have I just lost my tolerance for your general inane babble this past week?"

The Hero shrugged as best as he could with his limbs chained to the wall.

"Never mind. I got Dr. Menace to drop the charges against you so we were able to get the judge to reduce your sentence to time served plus a lifetime of community service. Of course, considering your unique talents and status in the world, your community is the planet and your service is dedicating yourself to eradicating villainy and evil in all its forms. So all you have to do is be a Hero, which you already are."

"Hm. I don't know."

"What do you mean you don't know?! You get to go free on the one condition that you basically just have to exist!"

"Yeah, but now it's like it's an obligation. I don't wanna do it if I *have* to."

"You *can't* be serious."

"It takes all the fun out of it," he pouted, kicking at the ground with a chained foot.

"You're just going to have to deal with that. We've got to hurry. The world needs us."

"Lousy world," Nuklear Man grumbled. "You'll be needing a heck of a lot of tape and glue when I'm done with you."

Atomik Lad sighed.

"Probably more adhesives than the whole world has put together. All at once even."

"Are you talking?"

"Sorta."

"Let's go."

"Oh fine. But first take off my mask so I can look on you with my own eyes."

"What are you talking about?"

"This mask. It has its own face. Its own name, K'thulu, and I am unmade within its unyielding—"

"Okay, fine. Just shut up already." Atomik Lad reached around the mask and fumbled his fingers across the back until they found and undid the latch. "There." The mask clanged against the stony floor. "You big baby."

"Thanks," the Hero removed himself from the wall by simply walking forward. The ferrous fetters fell off Nuklear Man's wrists and ankles thanks to a little Plazma Power and a lot of melting. "So. How'd you get Menace to drop the charges? Did you smack her around?" he asked as they walked back to the heavy wooden door.

"Well, not exactly."

"Oh, I read ya. You went easy on her, eh what, what. Winkity winkey wink."

"No, it's not like that."

"Hey, it's nothing to be ashamed of. You dog."

"You're not listening."

Nuklear Man reached out to the rusting iron door latch, "I don't mind telling you that more than once in our decade of arch-rivaldom I've had an inkling to tap that *augh*!" He slammed the door shut almost before he opened it. The walls shook.

"Like I was trying to tell you—"

"Shh!" Nuklear Man demanded. He continued in a whisper. "I think Dr. Menace is right outside that door."

"Nuke."

"You probably hadn't noticed, but that's not your fault. I just happen to be better than you at everything."

"Especially at noticing details," Atomik Lad said with lethal sarcasm.

"You see?"

"Details like irony for instance."

"Hm. Norman might almost be better at that due to his metallic motif. *Almost*."

"Nuke. I had to team up with Dr. Menace."

"This isn't the time for jokes, Sparky. We've got a nefarious villain right outside the door. Geez, I haven't been out of jail for even one second and they're already out for blood. This is the time for action, if you know what I mean."

"I'm afraid I do," Atomik Lad said while rubbing his eyes.

"PLAZMAAA—"

Atomik Lad slapped Nuklear Man's hands out of their power-up motion. "We've got bigger problems than another of Menace's plans for global domination. We've got an invincible madman with a plan for global domination."

"Invincible madman, eh? I'll have to beat him at his own twisted game!"

Atomik Lad's shoulders slumped. "Your plan is to take over the world first, isn't it."

"Preeeeeecisely."

"Try again."

"But it's so simple, it can't fail!"

"Not a chance."

"Phooey." His sky blue eyes darted back and forth with cunning or something approximating cunning the way a diet drink nearly resembles its parent drink. "Okay. I have a new plan."

"I won't like it, will I?"

"Nope," the Hero smiled proudly. "You'll *love* it!"

"Right."

"If, as you say, we are dealing with an invincible madman, then clearly the only way to defeat him it so be even crazier!"

"Which invariably entails…"

"*Four dozen monkeys!*"

"Let's not."

"No, no, no. There's more."

"That's part of the problem, really."

"We shall make a feint to the northeast. Tee hee!"

"You always say that! What is it! What is that supposed to accomplish?"

"Well, you know. To fake him out. He'll be all 'Duh! Hey, where are they?' And then we'll be like 'Right here, dude, like Valkyries hurtling from the northeastern sky!'"

"All right. That's enough of that. C'mon, we've kept Menace waiting long enough as it is."

"You're taking this Team-Up-With-The-Villain joke a little too far."

The door burst open sending clouds of dust swirling in the dank air. The Venomous Villainess stood in the doorway. "We haven't the time to wazte standing around here with…" She shook with anger, "What iz that moron doing?!"

"What?" Atomik Lad turned around. Nuklear Man was cowering behind him rather unsuccessfully due to a certain difference in their sizes. "Oh geez." He slapped Nuklear Man across the back of his head. "Cut it out!"

The Hero timidly emerged from behind his ex-sidekick. "You cut it out first, Sir Hitsalot."

"Enough with the token buffoonery," Dr. Menace snapped. "We have work to do."

"Oh, I get it," Nuklear Man said with a wise smile. "You put her up to this, didn't you."

"Nuke. Get this through your thick empty skull." Atomik Lad grabbed him by the collar of his spandex. "We. Are working. With Dr. Menace!"

"Heh, this sure is a funny Getting Out of Jail joke."

*   *   *   *

Meanwhile, the sun was setting on Superion City. The streets, ordinarily filled to capacity with commuters returning home after a productive day's work, were uncharacteristically empty. The sidewalks too were vacant. Completely absent was the seething flow of citizens visiting a corner store, a friend, or moving to or from a subway station. A city. An organic thing that grows and flows with life; suffers, prospers, but always changing, always moving. Except tonight.

The veins have run dry.

The life has gone.

"All because of me," Superion quietly told himself. He stood in the center of Anderson Square Garden in front of the massive and regal marble statue of Captain Liberty. One of its massive fists perched on its hip while the other arm was posed with an eagle on its forearm. A cape of stone that practically rippled with a carved fluidity flowed behind it. The statue's wide base was inscribed with the Captain's battlecry: "United We Stand." Superion couldn't help but allow himself an amused smile as he looked out upon the vast sea of crimson-clad followers before him, "United we stand. Indeed."

ISSUE 45—THE
GATHERING STORM

The sky was purple as day relinquished the earth to night. The sun hung low, a sliver of light hovering just above the horizon and impossible to see through the dense forest of Metroville's towers as anything more than reflections among steel spires. Clouds had gathered themselves into an epic weight, like in a painting, motionless and serene yet threatening to overwhelm the universe with their girth. Three figures soared above the geometrically appealing cityscape. One of gold, one of crimson, and one of blazing violet science. Atomik Lad found it hard to believe that just a few hours ago the sky was almost a featureless sheet of azure. His eyes kept focusing on the empty city below. Dr. Menace, using a Negaflux Field fueled by an emergency belt generator, used gravity to propel her through the evening air. She swung beside the ex-sidekick. He looked up at her, startled that he hadn't noticed her approach.

"Um."

"You are slowing. We haven't the time to wazte."

"R-right. Sorry." His Field seethed and accelerated him closer to Nuklear Man.

Dr. Menace gazed at the city as it passed below her. "Thiz iz my doing." She looked ahead at her new comrades. "The plan iz still in effect. It iz only natural for a wide-sweeping zcheme, zuch az my total global domination, to suffer a slight setback or two." She adjusted a dial on her belt to catch up to the heroes. "I still breathe, the plan still livez!"

*   *   *   *

At last, they stood outside the massive Danger: Main Doors. "All right, Menace" Nuklear Man said in a tone indicating he meant business. "Don't you commit no villainy whilst within these here sacred halls of purity. Got it?"

"Yez, fine. Whatever."

"With more feeling this time."

"No."

"Hey. I'm the only one here who knows the right transmitter frequency that can open them doors. Now then, one more time from the top."

She rolled her eyes, reached into her coat, and produced a device that looked like a cross between what had once been a television remote control and a radar detector. She pointed it at the Danger: Main Doors, pressed a few buttons, and smirked as the great metallic semi-circles separated. "Shut up, you dolt," she spat before re-engaging her Negaflux Field and floating into the Silo's innards.

"But. How'd she. Doors go open. Not supposed to," Nuklear Man sputtered.

Atomik Lad put his arm around the Hero's shoulder. "She's a clever gal."

"Yes," the Golden Guardian surmised with a sagely stroke or two of his chin. "A little too clever, if you know what I mean."

"No. I'm afraid I don't."

"Hm. That's a shame. I was hoping you could let me know."

Atomik Lad nearly laughed. "C'mon. We've got work to do."

"So good of you to join uz," Dr. Menace remarked as Atomik Lad and Nuklear Man touched down. Her fingers curled and uncurled under Katkat's chin as the fuzzy cutie-head reclined on the Danger: Superomputer. The feline purred happily as his tail occasionally twitched and hit a random button on the Danger: Keyboard.

Nuklear Man was on the Danger: Couch in a golden flash. "Ohhh, Danger: TV, how I missed you so." With a simple finger-gun motion from the Hero, the phosphorescent screen lived once more. "Mmm, Silly Sam's Cartoon Marathon-a-thon o' Fun." His voice dropped to a lusty whisper, "I missed you most of all."

Atomik Lad helped Dr. Menace with Katkat's continued bliss by scratching behind that cat's ears. "Iz he alwayz like thiz?" the Venomous Villainess asked while motioning to Nuklear Man with a nod of her head.

"I'm afraid so. Don't worry though, he always manages to come through in a pinch."

"I know," she growled. "That iz what iz ao enraging. It'z bad enough that my brilliant planz for utopia have to be continually thwarted, but doez the univerze have to be ao cruel aa to let that bumbling oaf be the one rezponzible for delaying my inevitable domination?"

"Bitter?"

"Thiz amall talk borez me. Let uz plan our azzault."

"Yeah. Hey, Nuke!"

"Can't prepare now. TV."

Atomik Lad rubbed his eyes. "Come on, Big Guy. We've got to go to work."

"Bah. Workin's for losers."

"It's either this or it's back to prison."

"Feh, at least in prison I didn't have to worry 'bout no workin'."

"Or watching Silly Sam, for that matter."

"Eeep!" Nuklear Man was a golden blur stretching from the Danger: Couch to the Danger: Kitchen for an instant. "I'm reeeeeaaaaady," he sang while seated at the Danger: Kitchen Table.

Dr. Menace sighed. "It'z juzt az well that we do it in there. I think that I will need a drink or two by the time thiz iz over with," she said while walking into what was now the Danger: Plannin' Room.

"I know what you mean," Atomik Lad said. As he moved to join her, he happened to glance at the Danger: Supercomputer's screen. It displayed a schematic of Katabasis Prison's ventilation system. A course was plot through the twisting tunnels leading from the outer wall directly into the all but forgotten North Tower. Unfortunately, according to the screen, the North Tower's vents had been sealed up with brick. "Well, not a bad plan, but these ventilation shafts aren't even big enough for a person to crawl through. Why, you'd. Have to be." Katkat meowed at Atomik Lad's hand to prompt the ex-sidekick into petting him some more. Again, the cat's tail twitched happily. Atomik Lad looked to Katkat, the screen, Katkat, the screen. "No. Couldn't be." He walked to the Danger: Plannin' Room. "His tail just happened to click on the Internet icon. And then the web browser icon. And then typed out the address of the Metroville Hall of Public Records." He ran a hand through his hair. "Unlikely, downright improbable, but possible. Besides, the North Tower's vents were sealed off with stone blocks. He'd have to—"

Dr. Menace stepped out of the Danger: Plannin' Room. "Do you alwayz store child-sized pick axez and flashlightz on your kitchen table?"

"Gasp."

"What?"

"Cat. Vents, prison. Mining. He," Atomik Lad babbled.

Dr. Menace turned back into the kitchen. "I am surrounded by blubbering clodz."

*   *   *   *

The Danger: Kitchen Table was covered in tactical satellite photos of the newly christened Superion Hall, Superion Square, Superidyne, and the Superindustrial Park which was now bustling with mindless red-clad workers who were presumably constructing a war fleet of some kind.

"Thiz iz my plan," Dr. Menace began. She looked to Atomik Lad, "At twenty-one hundred hours, you will approach Superion and engage him in converzation."

Nuklear Man, already taxed by the act of having to pay attention, gave Dr. Menace what he liked to call The Face: a slight curling of the lip, a slacking of the jaw, and an empty nodding of the head as she droned on.

"…But do not attempt to fight him." She paused momentarily, that nagging little voice in the back of her head insisted that something was not quite right. She turned to Nuklear Man who deftly deflected any suspicion by looking away with an overly I'm So Innocent look an instant too late which served only to increase any suspicion the not so good doctor had. She carried on, "Ahem. Merely diztract him so that Nuklear Man," who carried on giving her The Face, "can take him by surprize." Again she turned to him, quicker this time, and again he looked away an instant too late.

"Got it," Atomik Lad reported.

Nuklear Man went back to Facing Dr. Menace.

"Then Nuklear Man will drop in on our uzurper. In their melee, Superion'z mental hold on the populaze will slip away. That iz where I come in with my modified Defusionizer Cannon to strike down the arrogant—*stop doing that!*" she blurt, shaking with anger.

Atomik Lad looked up just in time to see Nuklear Man still giving her the Face before switching to the Oh No You Must Be Mistaken It Wasn't Me Because I'm Looking Over Here face.

"Nuke. If you're going to be a distraction, then just leave."

The Hero happily skipped out the Danger: Plannin' Room. "Heh, heh, suckers!" he taunted as the Danger: Door **fwoosh**ed shut behind him. Silly Sam's Cartoon Marathon-a-thon o' Fun could be heard coming from the Danger: Living Room.

Dr. Menace took a series of deep breaths to purge her psyche of rage. "How do you put up with that every day?"

"It's not so bad. You build up a sort of a tolerance."

"By toleranze, do you mean you ignore him or do you imagine perpetrating variouz actz of violence againzt him?"

"A little from column A, a little from column B."

Dr. Menace almost smiled. "Yez, well. You do realize that once thiz job iz done, we shall go our separate wayz."

Atomik Lad shrugged. "As you wish."

They shook on it.

*   *   *   *

It was a few minutes from twenty-one hundred hours. Lightning rumbled threateningly within the depths of the night's black clouds. The ex-sidekick raced on Atomik wings through Metroville's barren streets to avoid the possibility of becoming a living lightning rod. "I just hope Nuke can be trusted to come through with his part of the plan.," he mumbled to himself while taking impossibly sharp turns into and out of an alley. Cliché newspaper sheets swirled in his wake.

*   *   *   *

Nuklear Man was sprawled across the Danger: Couch as the latest installment of Silly Sam's Cartoon Marathon-a-thon o' Fun played itself out before his very eyes. Katkat was curled up against the Hero's tummy whilst exposing his own furry belly. "Must. Resist. Belly love," Nuklear Man told himself while his hand reached out to Katkat; slowly so its owner wouldn't notice until it was too late to do anything about it. "Dum de dum, I sure do like cartoons," Nuklear Man told Katkat. "It's a good thing Sparky and Dr. Menace decided to make our plan start right when my show is over so I wouldn't be too distracted to be able to bust out old school with some burning Plazma Justice instead of sitting here being all distracted by something utterly inane." His hand had made belly contact. "Oh no."

*   *   *   *

Dr. Menace was hunched over a work bench at her abandoned warehouse headquarters. She was madly working homemade instruments on the exposed innards of her Defusionizer Cannon. She took off a pair of Ultra-Magnifier Goggles and rest them next to the Positron Zapifier. Its wires were sprawled across the counter desperately reaching back to the cannon. She wiped sweat from her brow and gave the totality of her work thus far a look. "The Beam Coherentizer iz connected to the Nega-Particle Wave Induzer. The Nega-Particle Wave Induzer iz connected to the Frequenzy Modifier. The Frequenzy Modifier iz connected to the Polarizing Lenz." She leaned back and tilt her head. "Since the cannon is already set to neutralize Nuklear Moron'z unique Plazma Energy readingz, I would have to recalibrate the entire mechanizm for Superion's Negaflux Energy in order for it to work on him." She crossed her arms. "It took me nearly two yearz to finally compile enough information about the Golden Goon so thiz cannon would exterminate hiz blazted powerz. How could I achieve a similar effect againzt Superion without the prerequizite data?" she asked the assembled disassembled Defusionizer Cannon pieces. The answer came from the Beam Stabilizer. "Yez. If I changed the Beam Stabilizer into a Frequenzy Modulator, and change the method of energy projection from a beam of preprogrammed Negaflux energy of a particular frequenzy to a pulze of Negaflux energy of randomly alternating frequenciez that would naturally cohere to neutralize whatever the blast struck, then I could fire one blazt at Superion," her devilish genius took it a step further. "And fire *another* blazt at Nuklear Clod! Thereby eliminating them both!" She spun a pen sized welder between her fingers. "Of courze, the Atomik Lad could eazily be kept under control if hiz beloved Rachel were, shall we say, my captive."

Villainous laughter echoed from the depths of the Abandoned Warehouse District like it hadn't in weeks.

*   *   *   *

Atomik Lad looked up at Superion Hall from the bottom of its front steps. His feet crunched on the shattered glass his Field had liberated earlier that afternoon. The whole building had a peculiar whistling about it as pre-storm winds rushed in and out of vacant windows, taking along Progress Reports, various Order Forms, and The Like. In the darkness, he could only make the building out by the rhythmic flashes of lightning that never quite escaped their clouds. "Thanks, God. It's not bad enough I have to face down a maniac even more powerful than Nuke, but you've got to go and make the weather all dramatic and stuff." Distant thunder rumbled not entirely unlike laughter. "Feh." He checked his Danger: Watch. "A minute early, but close enough." His Atomik Field erupted like an explosion, only silent and unable to escape from its moment of ultimate violence, trapped as it was in a second of ecstatic rage. He floated up to the top floor slowly, effortlessly, like it was the ground falling away instead of him rising from it. "Show time."

Superion Hall's windowless walls gave way to red draperies rippling in the winds at the top floor. Atomik Lad reached out to tear one away but his Field ripped it to shreds. He recoiled too late and was horrified to find that after all these years and all his precautions, he could still make such a simple and potentially fatal mistake.

"So nice of you to join us, Sport."

Atomik Lad peered inside. He could see Superion, illuminated by a sudden flash of lightning, sitting in the high-backed Mayor's chair. "I was beginning to doubt the strength of your heroic impulses. But it seems that you have been sufficiently programmed to do your duty even when you know you have no hope of victory."

Good. He's feeling villainously conversational. Just gotta keep him talking. "Sounds like you've got Superior Confidence™ too."

Superion smiled sinisterly. "It looks like I underestimated you in our last confrontation. I'm afraid you're doing it this time, Slugger."

"If there's one thing I've learned from Nuke in all our time together, and believe me, one thing over the course of ten years is quite a lot from him, it's to never give up."

"Oh, your vaunted Nuklear Man." Superion revolved the chair through some of the slowest and most deliberate 360 degrees the ex-sidekick had ever seen. "I am as far beyond him as he is beyond you. How can you possibly hope to do anything more than be broken by my hands?"

Atomik Lad shrugged. "I'm an idealist. It's a character flaw."

"Your bravado is another."

"We'll see about that."

$$* \qquad * \qquad * \qquad *$$

"We now conclude our broadcast day." An arm popped up from off screen to hand Silly Sam a sheet of paper. The host scanned it and faced the camera once more. "Well, I was just informed that as of tomorrow we will no longer be known as Silly Sam's Cartoon Marathon-a-thon o' Fun, but rather as Super Superion's Superion-a-thon o' Worship. I, for one, look forward to these changes. Good night." The screen switched to a test pattern that already incorporated Superion's Star-S symbol.

"Well," Nuklear Man told himself. "Time to get goin'. Ahem. I said, it looks like it's time to go. Yup. Gotta go." Scratchity scratch scratch. "C'mon!" He pleaded to no avail. "Okay. I can do this. I've punched through walls and comets and missiles and robots and stuff. Surely I can summon, from within the vast depths of my Nukleadium Core, enough power to resist the cutie wutieness of a kitty belly." His Plazma Aura flared as he tried to pull away. He leaned away from Katkat yet his hand managed to continue its belly rub-fest without interruption. With his still obedient hand, he grabbed the unruly one by the wrist and pulled with all his might. "*Herg*! Must. Overcome. Own. Infinite strength. And. Good looks!" Still nothing. "Oh, drat your irresistible hide!" he spat at Katkat.

"Mew?"

"No. I'm sorry. I didn't mean it."

"Meow."

"Honest."

Katkat purred and squirmed around on his back in utter cat delight.

"Aww geez. No fair." The Hero pondered for a minute. "Ooh! I've got it! Oh Danger: Nukebots. Come out, come out wherever you are!"

"We ain't yer damned slave labor no more, air-breather," Alpha cursed from within his and Beta's new and rather spacious Danger: Nukebot's Room which they had the Danger: Nanobots fix up for them during Nuklear Man's stay in jail.

"Aww, c'mon guys! I really need your help this time."

"Damn monkeys always need our help," Beta grumbled. He and Alpha poked their metallic heads out their door and said "*What!*"

"I can't stop scratching Katkat's widdle belly belly tummy tum, no I can't. No I can't!"

"No, I can't believe I haven't rejected my latest core mass," Alpha said, holding onto his stomach area.

"So you can't stop scratchin' the cat. Sounds like a personal problem. What do you want us to do about it?"

"Make me stop," the Hero wimpered. "It's all like important and stuff."

"Make him stop, eh?" Alpha surmised. "You thinkin' what I'm thinkin'?"

Beta gave a nod. "I believe I am."

"What'cha thinkin'?" Nuklear Man asked even though he really probably would've been better off not knowing.

"We're gonna beat the bajeezus out of you!" They happily announced together.

"That'll help?"

Beta shrugged as Alpha answered, "It's *like* help."

*   *   *   *

When the hell is Nuke gonna get here, anyway? I can't keep this going forever. "Do you really think—"

Superion raised a finger to his lips and gave Atomik Lad a light shush. A moment passed. "There." He grinned, satisfied. "There. It's raining."

Atomik Lad looked out the half-shred tapestry. "You sure about that?"

"Not here. About a mile away. I can hear it. I am more powerful than you can know. I can focus my Negaflux fields to do nearly anything."

Keep him talking. "Can you, now?"

"For instance, with a mere thought, I can enhance my vision to transform the infrared into the visible spectrum. Quite convenient in all this bleak darkness, don't you think?"

Atomik Lad's Field burst forth with a mind of its own just in time to protect him from a surprise Superior Beam™. The impact still pushed him back several feet. He cursed himself for not being more alert and then cursed Nuklear Man for not being more prompt. Unfortunately, in that second-long interim, Superion had already reached him and was grasping his Field with both hands. He held him dangling at arms length outside the shattered window.

"All too easy," Superion taunted.

Atomik Lad could already feel his brain split down the middle. His face contorted with an all-pervading, all-piercing pain that he imagined, in a strangely unattached and distant moment, was like being consumed by fire from the inside out.

Not again.

Not again.

Not again!

"Not again!"

He did the only thing he could. His Field evaporated and he plummeted half numb from the mind-rending agony.

"Clever," Superion admitted. "But ultimately futile."

Atomik Lad watched as the lightning splashed sky fell from him. He watched as Superion crashed through floor after floor of his increasingly damaged head-quarters. Atomik Lad's mind wandered. *Stuck between hellish agony and a broad flat surface, my only defense is my only weakness.* He sighed as air rushed past him lashing his hair against his forehead. *It was a lot easier when Nuke would just pummel the other guy into submission.*

He could feel Superion closing in by the increased rhythm of the usurper's impacts. *Wait for it, he told himself. Wait for it.*

Smash. Smash. Smash, smash, smashsmashsmashsmash. *Almost there.* Smashsmashsmasmasmasmasmash—*Now*—Atomik Lad's Field burst forth and the ex-sidekick rocketed straight up. Even with his Field naturally counter acting the G-forces, it felt like he'd left his organs behind. He watched Superion whisk through the fading empty flames left by the Field's latest birth below him.

"Oh, he's pissed," Atomik Lad noted as Superion arced down and up after his quarry leaving a loop of red-purple energy in his wake.

They soared above the rooftops of Metroville with Superion gaining much too rapidly for Atomik Lad's tastes. In a fit of desperation, he made a feint to the northeast and veered the other way with all the speed he could muster. Sadly, this maneuver, though extremely cunning, led directly to Superion's chest. The ex-sidekick bounced off and tumbled in the air for a second before righting himself and coming to a stop.

The two crimson clad figures faced each other like old West gunfighters. Lightning crashed between them. Tumbleweed of the sky. *Odd*, Atomik Lad said to himself. *My field actually dampened the light and sound for me.* He noticed Superion didn't have similar safeguards. It was probably even worse with his enhanced senses. "I should attack now. I should—" he saw a distant golden pin-prick behind Superion. "I should wait for a second."

Superion recovered and laughed. "The god of war hates the man who hesitates."

"Oh yeah? Check this."

"*Booya!*" Nuklear Man proclaimed with a supersonic bodycheck. The two titans tore at the air at a steep angle as they sped past Atomik Lad and through buildings until the ground broke their fall several blocks away.

Atomik Lad positioned himself in mid-air to look straight through the offices they'd punched through and at the crater Nuklear Man had just made, its dust still settling. The crater flashed with alternate golden and red-purple energy. Atomik Lad closed in cautiously, floating through the angled path his mentor and foe had taken through a handful of downtown high-rises.

Superion and Nuklear Man shot out of the street at opposite corners of an office building. They hovered above their improvised man holes, capes flapping lightly in a wind that may or may not have been there.

Superion cackled somewhere along the thin line between elation and madness. "So. That Atomik Lad was able to connive behind my back to free you in some kind of last ditch effort to defeat me."

"Uh. Okay."

"Pathetic. And though I could easily dispatch you with little effort thanks to my incredible power, I will instead choose to prolong your suffering by forcing you to face your own friends and comrades at arms who have been completely brainwashed by my Superior Charms^{TM}!"

"Uh. Okay."

Superion did a mid-air sidestep to reveal Mighty Metallic Magno Man, Angus, Shiro, Dr. Genius, Delivery Boy, Mail Man, Meter Maid, and the Librarian all wearing official Superion T-shirts. "Oh, the psychological torment!" Superion rejoiced. "Torn between his loyalty to the tenets of justice and his loyalty to his friends, the Hero is damned no matter the action he takes!"

"Uh. Okay."

The Mindless Mob approached Nuklear Man with a collective snarl of disgust at the idea that something, anything could actually be so heinous as to attempt to impede upon the rule of Superion. "Face it, Nuklear Man," Superion taunted from behind the throng. "Your Heroic heart cannot stand the thought of bringing pain against those whom you hold most dear. You can't blast your friends."

Nuklear Man's mighty shoulders slumped, his head hung in defeat. "Yeah, I guess you've got me right where—PLAZMAAA BEAM!!!" His fellow heroes were scattered like bowling pins by the fusion-ish bolt. The Hero's voice was soaked in sarcasm as he mocked Superion's mad ramblings, "I'm not gonna shoot my friends, dur dur dur."

"Hm. I had not considered that course of action," Superion admitted.

"Feh, consider this. PLAZMAAA BEAM!!!" The golden stream of energy blazed to Superion.

"SUPERIOR BEAM^{TM}!!!" A reddish blast collided with Nuklear Man's. Multi-colored sparks splashed from their contact like water from two fire hoses aimed at one another.

"Hey!" the Hero protested. "Stop that!"

"You first," Superion retorted. His beam doubled in size, pushing Nuklear Man's out of the way and knocking the Golden Guardian down the street into a grocery store.

The Hero leapt out of the produce section feeling a bit weird because of the odd positions his impact made possible with himself and a collection of cantaloupes. "Ahem. Yes, I have kept my dignity." He straightened his spandex and cape. "'Cause no one saw me." He raced out of the shop like a beam of light aimed at Superion. The Sinister Scoundrel dodged into the heavy night air as a shaft of red-purple lightning.

The two living lasers dueled across Metroville's skyline. Dodging and spiraling like a lightspeed dance. Arcing and diving, cutting impossible angles around skyscrapers and clashing at impossible speeds. Atomik Lad couldn't keep track of them. First here. Then there. He couldn't tell the difference between the flashes of natural lightning and the luminal explosions that accompanied every collision of the two titans. Was that thunder or a hypersonic punch?

And then his entire world was filled with a golden-purple blur as they passed by, missing him by inches. Feeling more like a target than a sidekick, an ex-sidekick at that, Atomik Lad descended to street level as the melee raged above him. He mingled with some of the rubble caused by the brief battle that had been waged at this low altitude. He passed by and immediately returned to two pairs of stubby armored legs sticking out of one ruined store front. He uncovered them and was relieved to find the rest of Shiro and Angus attached to their respective legs in very healthy and natural fashions. He set them against a somewhat intact wall and was considerably more unrelieved to find them still wearing Superion shirts. "This could be bad."

The Surly Scot rubbed his greasy red hair and unkempt fiery beard. His usual Scowl o' Rage was replaced by the not so usual Scowl o' Confusion which bore such a resemblance to the former Scowl as to make differentiating between the two an absurdly difficult task. "*Aukgh!*" he groaned.

Shiro teetered slightly, his eyes focusing on something beyond the horizon. "Great Dragon of Mind is in the brainskull, heavy with pain when trees are sleeping time."

Angus's Scowl made the jump from Confusion to Rage in record time, "Why cain't ye ever make sense, ye damn bloody blasted rice-eatin' moron!?" Angus flinched and held his head to keep the sledgehammer inside it from bursting his proud Scot skull wide open.

"Seeing that spoken, Shiro-kun is to are correcting, hai."

"Um," Atomik Lad interjected. "How are you guys?"

"Ah'm bloody terrible, ye scrawny punk-arsed son of a—" another flinch cut Angus's rant short.

"Hm. Well, that sounds like the regular Angus to me," Atomik Lad said.

"Shiro-kun are being now the pain of calamities."

"Okay. I guess that sounds like the old Shiro too."

"What in the name o' whisakey hit us?" Angus asked as he tried to stand. "One minute Ah'm watchin' me favorite movie an' the next thing Ah knows Ah just gots to have me a Suuperion shirt."

Atomik Lad looked to the sky and grinned. "Looks like Dr. Menace's plan is working."

"What?! Dr. Menace! Where?" Angus craned around far too quickly for his throbbing brain to keep up and toppled over from the exertion.

"It's nothing," Atomik Lad said. "I'll explain later. Right now, I've got to check on the others Nuke blasted."

ISSUE 46—CLASH OF THE TITANS

A Harley with a sidecar on one side and an oversized rifle-cannon-bazooka look-ing thing on the other roared through the empty streets of Metroville. Its engine gave off a light purple glow against the rain slicked road. The rider wore a pair of shining black wrap around sunglasses. She was cloaked in the flapping black leather of a stylin' trench coat dotted with beads of water that streaked along its twitching contours. The cycle skid to a stop at a red light, its idling engine gave off a dimmer glow than before. She examined the empty streets. "What am I doing?" Dr. Menace asked herself. She revved the engine and took off into the night toward the Superindustrial Park without the slightest attention paid to traf-fic signs or the like.

*   *   *   *

Atomik Lad had gathered the recently emancipated heroes into the also recently half-demolished grocery store. Bottles of aspirin had been distributed among them to handle the headaches that accompanied the loosing of Superion's mental grasp. A glass bottle shattered somewhere along the liquor aisle.

"Ah toold ye to be carefuul wit the whiskey, ye blasted no-fish-cookin' hag-gis-brained twit!"

"Shiro-kun are to being small for the job of tall. Not ready for depths of insipid height," he moaned while sitting in a puddle of whiskey and glass.

"Are ye sayin' ye be too short for this job?"

"Supaa whiskey action; Angus-san time is hai."

"When ye know that yer a full half inch taller than me?"

Shiro smiled wide, "Shiro-kun is to calling them as the dragon's eye of powaa sees from over the sun that also risen into clouds where the city of gods."

"Ohhh, ye shouldna said that," Angus growled, his left eye twitched out of control.

Meanwhile, near the busted out entrance. "Überdyne will cover the costs," Dr. Genius said in her new white shirt with a faded print of a kitten hanging on to a clothesline on the front of it and the phrase Hang In There printed across the bottom. "So it's more like acquisitioning supplies than stealing."

The other heroes with Superion shirts began sifting through the grocery store's assortment of ill-fitting, poorly designed T-shirts near the registers. Impulse items for the fashion inept.

Norman rubbed his head. "Man. What hit us all?" he asked, now sporting a rainbow of colors that clashed like opposing religious ideologies. "And could these shirts be any uglier?"

"It's Superion. He's got some kind of mind control power. A Superior Charm™," Atomik Lad answered. "And no."

"Why weren't you affected?" Norman asked.

"I don't know, really," he said.

"The Field," Dr. Genius answered. "Probably just a side-effect of its manifestation. The very fact that it exists has made our Atomik Lad rather isolated from others. He would subconsciously resist any kind of outside influence. Combine that with the anger he was no doubt feeling about the trial and, well you've got something of a mental barrier working for you."

"Well, that explains that."

"But what it doesn't explain is why this mind control has begun to wear off on the rest of us."

"Basically," Atomik Lad said. "Superion is nothing more than a pawn in Dr. Menace's latest ploy to take over the world which started with getting Nuke put into jail and getting the rest of us off the streets. But he, Superion that is, went a little insane, got super charged, and used his Superior Charm™ to make you all do his bidding so that he could take over the world instead. So Dr. Menace and I got together to free Nuke and—"

"*What?!*" everyone else exclaimed at once. Well, except for Shiro and Angus who were still arguing elsewhere in the store.

"Just hear me out," Atomik Lad said. "If it weren't for Dr. Menace, you'd all still be slaves to Superion."

"If it weren't for Dr. Menace, none of this would be an issue!" Dr. Genius retorted.

"Look, I know. But she's helping us. This is all part of her plan. Nuke is out there distracting him so she can put a stop to all this madness."

"I don't like it," Genius nearly growled. "She knows nothing outside her own insane wish to lord over all of humanity. She's only cooperate with us because it is a means to her ends, it serves her interests to rid herself of competitors like this Superion. As soon as he's out of the picture, she'll revert to her megalomaniac ways, back to endangering innocent lives and using people for her own mad ambitions. You said yourself that this Superion started off as one of her pawns and now look at what it's done."

"This sounds a little familiar," Atomik Lad mumbled to himself.

"All I'm saying is that you cannot trust that woman."

"…Yeah. Yeah, I know," Atomik Lad said.

"Hey," Norman piped up with a thought. "I just had a thought. If this mind control thing is wearing off on us, then don't you think it's wearing off on at least some of the populace?"

"That stands to reason," Dr. Genius agreed. "They'll be terribly disoriented and in need of our help. Any idea where they are?"

"Metroville Industrial Park," Atomik Lad said. "Superion has them building an invasion fleet or something."

"All right, heroes," Dr. Genius took charge. "We've got to get there and take care of the civilians, keep injuries to a minimum, and get everyone back to their homes. Norman, you'll use your Magno Powers to float us over there. We'll need you to do the heavy lifting once we get there. Minimum Wage Warriors, collect all the first aid kits, headache medicine, and snack foods, preferably with high concentrations of carbohydrates, that you can find in this place. Coming with us, Atomik Lad?"

"Er, no. I don't think my powers, I mean, probably more dangerous with all those people. Besides, Nuke might need me here for back up."

Genius nodded in agreement. "Especially if Menace arrives to 'hold up her part of the bargain.'"

"She will."

"Even more reason to be alert." Dr. Genius turned to the gathered heroes and organized them into an efficient airborne medical evac unit headed for the Super-industrial Park via Magno Power, but she stayed behind.

"You're not going with them?" Atomik Lad asked.

Dr. Genius ran her hands through her long tightly curled hair and sighed. "No, it's nothing they can't handle. As long as I get back to Überdyne anyway. Metroville may be shut down, but the rest of the world is still operational. I've got to make some calls, set up some relief programs for our refugee citizens, make sure they've got food and shelter while we get families back together and then back to their homes."

"Überdyne is quite a ways off, are you sure it's safe to walk?"

"I haven't been collecting KI data from you boys for ten years for nothing, you know." She tossed open her lab coat to reveal a technologically enhanced belt that gave off a silvery light.

"Theoretically, this device should alter the KI of the air within a four foot radius of me such that I'll be levitated along with it."

"Well. I guess there's more than one way to fly."

She smiled. "Superpowers or superscience? Soon, there will be no difference." And she took off, the air around her shimmering like a heat mirage.

"That's not quite what I meant," he told her diminishing form.

*   *   *   *

Superion and Nuklear Man battled in the dark skies as scarce droplets of water fell around them. The Sinister Scoundrel sneered at his opponent as they grappled and hung in the air. "I'm almost going to pity destroying you, Nuklear Man. This little bout has been entertaining and I fear this world is incapable of producing another individual of your strength."

"Well," the Hero puffed up proudly. "I don't like to brag. But yeah."

"So you can see the tragedy your death holds for me."

"My death? No, no, no. *I'm* the Hero, see. I win. No one dies. That's how it goes, trust me I've been doing it for years. Now then, in light of this new evidence, why don't you just give up and save us all a lot of trouble, hm?" Superion gave a deep and haughty laugh. Nuklear Man followed suit, albeit nervously since he didn't quite know what was going on, "I sure am glad you see things my way. Woo. Let's go."

"I'm not giving up, you fool!"

"Oh."

"I've already won!"

"So…you're not giving up then?"

"Why should I give up? I possess powers beyond your understanding."

"Well, I *doubt* that," Nuklear Man said with a bit of a chuckle. "I've got Plazma Powers, y'know. Lots of 'em."

"Perhaps, but what you don't know is that my Negaflux powers can cancel yours and use them against you, even multiplying them until you are crushed into a pathetic cinder by your own alleged might!"

"Oh yeah? Well, what you don't...know...um, about my. Er, can you really do all that? Use my own powers to defeat me?"

Superion nodded.

"Oh. Wow. Man, that's just. Wow. That's so *awesome!* I mean, yowza. That's got real style, you know?"

"I know."

"I mean, I just fly around and punch and zap things. I can't compete with that kind of stuff."

"No, you can't." Superion raised his mighty fists.

"Hey. Are you gonna—" and he brought them down on the Hero's skull with a thunderous boom that had a slight echoing quality to it "—hit me?" Nuklear Man weakly uttered just before smashing through the roof of a pharmaceutical firm. The whole structure crumpled in upon itself like a giant had sat on it. In the middle of the massive pile of rubble, Nuklear Man coughed a cloud of dust. "Okay. It's time to drop the hammer!"

*   *   *   *

Dr. Menace idled through the Superindustrial Park. Random red-shirted civilians were already wandering the streets, stumbling and holding their heads, like an epidemic of drunkenness and hangovers had assaulted the area. "Hm, the Nuklear Oaf haz been more effective than I thought he would be. I loathe to admit it, but he continually zurprizez me." She wound the cycle through the meandering foot traffic, all the while following the prompts given to her by the Evil: Heads Up Display super-imposed on her vision through her wrap around goggles. She took a sharp turn into the employee parking lot of a metal working factory and nearly ran over, "Rachel!"

Rachel stumbled back a few steps and shielded her eyes from the cycle's headlight. "Watch where you're...wait. How do you know my name?"

"Rachel, come with me. It iz vitally important."

"What? I'm not going anywhere. Who are you? How did I get here?" Rachel kept one hand in front of her eyes and her gaze cast down on herself. "And where did I get this damn idiotic T-shirt?"

Dr. Menace let out an annoyed huff. "Lizten, girl. I, *we* do not have the time for thiz converzation. Pleaze, juzt get into the sidecar and I will explain on the vay."

Rachel was silent for a moment. "Wait. I know you. That voice, your accent. You were on TV. You were demanding we relinquish control of all the world's governments or you'd use the Earth's magnetic field to freeze the planet's rotation and hurl us all into space."

"Yez, and it would have worked too if not for the accurzed meddling of that incompetent Nuklear Dolt!" Menace cursed.

"You're Dr. Menace. There's no way I'm coming with you," Rachel spat.

Dr. Menace stifled her reflex reaction and went with the exact opposite: niceness. "Rachel, dear. You are going to have to truzt me. Atomik Lad needz you. You muzt come with me. We are working together, for the time being, in order to rid ourzelves of a greater evil. Superion."

"Superion? Yes, that's why I'm here, isn't it? I can't remember exactly, this damn headache makes it hard to concentrate."

"Yez, it'z a side effect of Superion'z mind control." She dug in her pockets and pulled out two tiny pills. "I had anticipated it. Now, pleaze. I promize no harm will come to you while you are with me."

Rachel hesitated. "How can I trust you?"

Dr. Menace's goggles warned her that a pack of humanoids were flying to her general location. "There iz nothing that I can say to convince you," she said plainly. "You simply muzt come with me."

Rachel took the pills and climbed into the sidecar. "Honesty is the last resort of desperation. Let's roll."

The Menacycle squealed into the night. Dr. Menace's goggles guided them to Superion. His Negaflux field was like a massive beacon for her sensors. The Venomous Villainess watched from the corner of her eye as Rachel dropped the two pills into her mouth. Dr. Menace's face melted into a cunning and satisfied smile.

Yez, all part of the plan.

*   *   *   *

"It's time...to drop gaaaasp...the hammer," Nuklear Man panted as he stumbled up to Superion.

The Sinister Scoundrel wore an aggravated sneer. "Yes, so you keep saying." Red-purple energy swirled around Superion's fists. He delivered an open palm strike to Nuklear Man's chest, breaking the sound barrier at the moment of impact. Nuklear Man careened down the street into a music store. The entire storefront and most of the inventory exploded into the city. He stood shakily, one eye blinking at a time.

"Ish tiiiime…" The roof fell on him and clouds of dust roiled out into the street, "To hhhhammerer…the drop."

*   *   *   *

Deep inside the fourth sub-basement of the Überdyne Building, Dr. Genius jumped into her comfortable Scientific: Observation Chair. She was instantly surrounded by two dozen Scientific: Monitors. "Computer, open a full KI sweep of the city. Search for Plazma and Negaflux concentrations. Stream the data through these monitors for my observation." She paused while the computers complied with her commands. "And you'd better open a log for all of this. Just in case. I don't want to miss a thing."

*   *   *   *

"It's time—"
A magic shop.
"To drop—"
A Gorge Clothing and Apparel store.
"The hammer—?"
A Cow Butt Burger Hutt.
Nuklear Man crawled out of the rubble. His limbs moved only due to an incredible effort of will. He shook with every movement and ached from every particle of his being. "Time…hammer…is dropping?"

Atomik Lad shook his head. "Sorry, Big Guy. Superion is over there."

Nuklear Man's bruised and bashed head turned around, quivering from the effort. "B-but. But no."

"Yeah."

The Hero's big blue eyes looked up at Atomik Lad. "But it's so far." Superion hovered in front of a street lamp one block down. He loomed in his own shadow.

"Yes, yes. I know. It's not that bad, you only have to stall him until Dr. Menace gets here and gives him the big zap."

He climbed up Atomik Lad by desperately grasping at his crimson and blue spandex. The Hero's sheer weight nearly toppled Atomik Lad over. "Is she here yet?" Nuklear Man asked with a desolate, empty quality to his voice.

"Nope, not yet, Bright Eyes."

"…Then it's too late," he whimpered. "You don't know what it's like. He hits hard. Really, *really* hard."

"Now, now. You can do this," Atomik Lad said with consoling little taps on Nuklear Man's head.

"Really?" the Hero asked in a tiny high-pitched voice approximating a whisper.

"Yes. Now get back in there and give that nasty ol' Superion what for."

"For what?"

Atomik Lad blinked. "What?"

"What for, for what?"

"What are you…? Look, it doesn't matter."

"Doesn't matter? Doesn't matter?! Yer darn tootin' it matters!"

"Great."

"You're not the one going in there! You're not the one getting kicked around like yesterday's potatoes—"

"Potatoes?"

"Don't interrupt. Now that little speech of yours got me all worked up until that last part, a bit vague it twas, so I was merely asking for some clarification."

"Ugh."

"I want to be sure I'm being properly motivated. I don't want to go in there with only half an idea of what's going on. I need to be informed. We're talkin' 24 hour team coverage here. This is the big leagues, boy. I need to know if this is for peace or for liberty or for a sack of rotten potatoes or what."

"What?"

"You see?"

Atomik Lad bat away his mentor's hands. Nuklear Man hit the pavement with a thick and meaty **whud** sound. "You've got to keep fighting or we lose. It's as simple as that."

"Bell, I thoppothe boo hab a boint," he said with his face on the road. "Ith thith thanatawee?"

Atomik Lad heaved him up by his cape. About an inch. "Dammit, you're heavy."

"Yeah, power and good looks will do that to you."

"Erg."

"Well, not to *you* so much as to me," he clarified. Atomik Lad dropped him. "Oof."

"Stop whining and fight."

"But he's tough."

"You've fought worse."

"Name one."

"Um, what about that, uh. Well."

"See?" Nuklear Man sat up. He focused on Superion. He was a stern shadow with a rippling cape. "Besides, it's starting to rain. We could catch a cold."

"Yeah, you've got a point."

Nuklear Man froze. "Er. What?"

"Is there a problem?" Atomik Lad asked.

"N-no. I just never heard you say that before."

Atomik Lad shrugged. "First time for everything. Let's pack it up and split."

"Cool. Heh, we sure showed that Superion what for."

"Yup. Now that we gave up and let the villain win, we'll have lots of free time. It's a shame there won't be any more Silly Sam's Cartoon Marathon-a-thon o' Fun to fill all those idle hours."

"Sparky. Some things just aren't right to make jokes about," Nuklear Man scolded. "Besides, I happen to know that the show will go on under the new name Super Superion's Superion-a-thon o' Worship. So there."

"Hm. Guess you got me there."

"Nya."

"I wonder how many cartoons they'll show. What with it being a propaganda program now."

"What?"

"All about worship, makes you wonder where they'll fit the cartoons in."

"No cartoons?"

"But at least you get to do plenty worshipin'."

Nuklear Man stood, his cape swayed gently. "Sparky. I'm gonna ask you to stand back for a second here. It's for your own good."

"Okiedoke."

"Superion!" Nuklear Man called down the street. "You've gone too far."

"I haven't even begun," he answered, his voice was a promise of evils yet committed.

"That's a shame. Because it ends now!" Nuklear Man's Plazma Aura burst into an intense golden glow as energies were seemingly pulled from the air around him and gathered into his fists in tiny white hot streaks of light. "PLAZMAAA BEAM!!!" It shot straight and true, striking Superion square in his gut.

Superion simply stood his ground, the terrific power of Nuklear Man's attack buzzed around the Sinister Scoundrel like electrons in orbit around their nucleus.

The energy spun around him as if he had control over it. "Not bad. Now let's see how you like it. SUPERIOR BEAM^{TM}!!!" The energy of Nuklear Man's attack channeled down Superion's limbs into a thick purple beam aimed back at the Hero.

Nuklear Man threw his arms up in defense just as the blast reached him. He was knocked back a step but quickly regained his footing as the purple energy no longer pushed at him, but was pulled into him. His Plazma Aura blazed, his cape flew madly in several directions at once. "Back at ya! PLAZMAAA BEAM!!!" It tore at the air and again Superion took the energies for his own.

"Impressive, you have managed to deliver an even more powerful blow than I." His Negaflux energies flared momentarily. "Let us see how long you can endure this onslaught." Another Superior Beam^{TM} loosed itself against Nuklear Man, bigger this time and carving a shallow trench through the street.

The Hero held out one hand, fingers spread out, palm facing Superion as though he was telling the beam to halt. It splashed against his outstretched hand and was absorbed into his Plazma Aura which instantly doubled in size. Dozens of golden points of light ejected themselves from the Aura and hung in mid-air. "PLAZMAAA STORM!!!" Each spark erupted into a beam as big around as a car and rained on Superion, completely obscuring the villain within a hundred fiery explosions. Stray shots toppled already abandoned buildings in the distance.

Atomik Lad's Field kicked in to protect him from the heat generated by Nuklear Man's attack. "Where the hell did *that* come from?!" he blurted. The very air around Nuklear Man's Aura had caught fire. "Dr. Menace had better get here while there's still a Metroville to save."

$$* \qquad * \qquad * \qquad *$$

"Incredible," Dr. Menace said to herself while speeding through empty streets. "If theze Negaflux readingz are correct, then Superion could potentially be manipulating energiez of Such an incredible magnitude that modern scienze haz yet to develop a system of phyzics to properly dezcribe them." The bleak night was illuminated by a distant series explosions. Three skyscrapers could be seen falling from the Metroville skyline as the light faded. The ground shook like an earthquake as a blast of wind nearly took the Menacycle from the road. "It would be a shame if reality unraveled itzelf before I could become itz ultimate mazter. Don't you think, my dear?" Rachel was silent and limp in the sidecar. "What? No rezponze? Oh, of courze not. How could you pozzibly anzwer me, what with being drugged by thoze pillz! Truzting fool, muwa hahahahaha!" she cackled into the night while pouring on the speed.

In the middle of her revelry of evil, Dr. Menace couldn't hope to notice the sleeping pills emerge from Rachel's lips as she covertly spit them into the night as they sped through the streets.

Issue 47—Ain't Got
Time for Physics

Dr. Menace cringed in time to the elevator's muzak as it carried her, the Menacycle, and its cargo to the roof of a building that would serve as the perfect sniper's nest for her role in the plan to defeat Superion and then her plan to defeat Nuklear Man. She pulled a small personal tape recorder from one of her many lab coat pockets. "Evil: Note to Self: When the world iz under my control, deztroy all sourzes of muzak." The recorder had nearly been put away when she thought to add, "And then conztruct a time machine for the sole purpoze of retro-actively purging the univerze of thiz horrible travezty." Rachel nearly giggled her way right out of her clever ruse. "Hm. Seems the pillz may be wearing off. No matter. Both Superion and Nuklear Imbecile shall be eliminated zoon enough and then there will be no ztopping me!"

*   *   *   *

Atomik Lad stood at the edge of a crater that was now at least a block in diameter. Superion and Nuklear Man stood at its scarred and scorched center. Hands interlocked, each titan struggled to subdue the other. Even at his respectable distance at the crater's edge, Atomik Lad had to push his powers to keep from being blown away by the residual force exerted by the two giants' efforts. "Dammit, I couldn't get close even if I wanted to," he muttered.

"I'm surprised you lasted this long," Superion grunted at Nuklear Man.

"That makes two of us," Nuklear Man retorted in a pathetic attempt to make a witty retort.

"Bah! Enough of your prattling," Superion spat. "I'm afraid this is farewell."

"Really? So you're giving up after all? Cool."

"Argh!" He hunkered down and shoved his shoulder into the Hero's chest, lifting him off the ground.

"Hey. This isn't the way it goes," Nuklear Man advised before being chucked up rather gently considering the violence and damage they had been perpetrating against themselves and the city.

Superion snatched at the empty space in front of him and Nuklear Man came to a stop in mid-air.

"What's going on?" Atomik Lad asked no one in particular. It was difficult to make out more than basic shapes inside the crater. Energies cascaded from it like a star.

Superion clenched his fist. Darts of purple energy shot into the villain's vice grip and Nuklear Man was encased in a sphere of similarly colored light. Atomik Lad's eyes squinted as he focused on his levitated mentor. "A Negaflux field? Around Nuke? What's he trying to pull?"

*   *   *   *

The elevator opened onto the roof. The rain had picked up its cadence during the ride up. Dr. Menace waddled her Menacycle through the double doors. She revved the luminous engine and rolled out among puddles, vents, and various pieces of large generic equipment found ds at the tops of large generic high-rises. The Venomous Villainess dismounted her metallic stead at the roof's edge. Its front tire was pressed against the raised ledge that ran along the roof's perimeter.

The sensors in her goggles suddenly spiked off their scale. With the help of the handy magnifying and nightvision options built in, she instantly trained on the vision of Nuklear Man hovering above a giant crater that sat in the middle of what should've been a lot of buildings. She didn't have time to dwell on the desolate juxtaposition. "Visual confirmation," she mumbled to herself. "With theze nightvision gogglez and thiz darknezz, that Nuklear Moron'z Plazma Aura should make him appear to glow like the sun. But I can only make him out az an indiztinct shadow within the Negaflux field." She slowly traced her gaze down to see Superion who was apparently straining to crush something in his grasp. Her eyes went wide. "No," she uttered in a terrified whisper. She grabbed at the Menacycle to detach the Defusionzier Cannon turned Nega Cannon from its hardpoint.

Her thoughts raced, *Superion has pushed his complementary Negaflux fields beyond anything I thought possible. He iz using gravity to crush Nuklear Man by multiplying the force it exerts on him. Negaflux can only multiply a forze so much, perhaps 200 times. But this multiplier is conztant regardless of the raw force itself, whether it be the soft caress of a feather or the bone breaking impact of a semi-truck. Judging by the inward pulses of energy the Negaflux field is experiencing, what Superion has done is begin a Nega Chain Reaction! One field to multiply gravity 200 times, then another field to multiply that augmented force another 200 times and so on and so on! He may finally rid me of that insufferable Nuklear Dimwit, but he will undoubtedly create a force equal to a point of infinite mass in order to do so! The entire world will be swallowed into oblivion.* "How can I take over a world that doez not exizt! Bah!"

*   *   *   *

Atomik Lad noticed that the sphere holding Nuklear Man had been growing darker, like ink was being injected into it over time. "What's happening up there?" he asked the rain as it was lashed away by his wild field. He could hear Superion's mad ranting rise up above the growing background noise of the rain. "Enough is enough," he told himself. His Atomik flames froze in the instant before he took flight like a crimson bullet aimed at Superion's heart.

*   *   *   *

The pulses within the Negaflux field increased their tempo, each blow brought down the inescapable wrath of a god, each wave collapsed onto the Hero with more than enough force to compress a planet into the size of a golf ball. "No!" Nuklear Man said through teeth clenched against the earth-shattering impacts that railed against him like freight trains from every angle.

*   *   *   *

Dr. Menace slammed one foot on the roof's raised ledge for balance. She wobbled slightly while tucking the cannon's stock against her body. She rest her head against the cool metal of the weapon and peered through its giant sniper scope eyepiece which was customized with some special Menace-style modifications.

She adjusted the magnification until she had a clear picture of Superion. A digital pair of brackets were super imposed over him with the word LOCK blinking in the lower left corner. *That's right. Just stand perfectly still,* she said to herself. *Three shots charged. One for Superion, one for Nuklear Baboon, and one just in case.* "The puppet may have cut looze hiz ztringz," one lithe finger slid against the trigger. "But they shall only zerve to bind him."

"Not so fast, sister," Rachel said with a certain amount of authority due to a certain gun she was certainly pressing against Dr. Menace's exposed temple. "Don't try anything, either. I've got this thing set to Liquefy."

Still focused upon Superion, Dr. Menace hissed, "You have no idea what you are doing, girl!"

"I know that you tried to drug me."

"You do not underztand—"

"I *understand*," Rachel snapped, pushing the weapon against Menace's temple hard enough to leave a mark. "That you're planning to kill Nuklear Man with that, that gun of yours, and you're probably kidnapping me to use as ransom against Atomik Lad to keep him under your control."

"Well," Dr. Menace said with an apologetic nod. "I *am* a villain."

"Argh! Your plans are always so original! But this? Kidnap the girlfriend? You couldn't get any more cliché if you tried! I would've expected more out of you, especially considering you're a woman. I mean you're just perpetuating the subjugation of women in our society by projecting an image that we are nothing more than objects which have no meaning outside the value men attribute to us as their possessions!"

Dr. Menace sighed. "I waz short on time."

"It's insulting, you know. For both of us."

"We can dizcuss the rampant oppression of women prezent in Weztern Society's ideologiez later. However, it would be in the bezt interezts of everything within a two million mile radiuz for me to fire thiz cannon now."

"You're bluffing," Rachel said.

"Well. No, actually, but you are."

"What?"

"You're shaking."

"I'm, I'm just nervous is all. Never met a villain up close like this before."

"I do not believe you. He would not love you if you were capable of pulling that trigger."

Rachel opened her mouth to retort but could only muster an, "Uh." Her grip on the gun's handle loosened without her knowing it.

Like a cobra, Dr. Menace snatched the gun from Rachel's hand. She never took her eye from the scope. "Now sit down, girl. I have work to do."

"But..." Rachel stepped back. "Wait. What's going on out there?"

"Thiz iz what I have been talking about. Now quiet down while I—no!" She craned around the eyepiece, but her vision was met with nothing but rain soaked darkness. Back to gazing through the scope, she exclaimed, "What iz that fool doing! I can't get a clear shot!"

"Who?" Rachel leaned over the ledge. She peered into the bleakness beyond, pushing wet strands of hair out of her eyes in the hopes it would have a positive effect on the view. It did not. "I can't see. Who are you talking about?"

*   *   *   *

Atomik Lad slammed into an invisible wall about a foot in front of Superion. The sidekick strained against his unseen barrier. "Stop it! You're killing him!" he screamed at the Sinister Scoundrel.

Superion cackled. "Yes, my boy. That's the idea, you see!"

"I won't let you!" he grunted, pushing with all his might. His Field had begun expanding without his knowledge, but whether it was looking for a weak point in the invisible shield or merely manifesting the ex-sidekick's effort, no one could say.

Superion let out a guffaw. "You don't have a choice!" He made a backhand motion and Atomik Lad was slapped against the unforgiving street like a giant phantom club had swat him from the air. He lay limp, half in and half out of the crater. His Field disappeared.

The pulses hammering down on Nuklear Man had just accelerated into a continuous stream.

*   *   *   *

"What's happening down there!" Rachel demanded.

Dr. Menace tightened her grip on the cannon and held it snugly against her body. "It doezn't matter now anyway," she solemnly reported.

"Why not? What happened? Is John hurt?"

"No time to explain! I muzt—" The Negaflux Sensor display in the cannon's eyepiece went completely silly. It spit out a series of nonsensical data before shutting itself off. "Well. That muzt be what happenz at the Nega Critical Point," she said, her voice an equal mixture of interest and dismay. "It iz too late. No power on Earth can stop it now."

"What are you talking about?"

✳   ✳   ✳   ✳

Due to its own gravitational pull on itself, the Negaflux shell around Nuklear Man shrank to half its size in an instant. It should have imploded completely, but something stopped it from collapsing further. Inside, Nuklear Man was balled up in a fetal position, pushing his Plazma Power beyond anything he'd ever known before. "Can't...give up..." he told himself. "Winner...writes...history books...newspaper articles...magazine interviews...the talk show circuit..." The normal sparkling azure of his eyes now burned like flames of gold.

✳   ✳   ✳   ✳

Dr. Genius sat immersed in a cocoon of monitors that streamed new KI data from Nuklear Man and Superion's battle. She gasped. "A gravitational singularity in the middle of downtown Metroville? KI manipulations of that severity aren't possible!" She scanned the monitors for a few more seconds. "It appears to be localized within its own realm, like it somehow completely curved its own space upon itself, essentially creating a pocket universe encapsulated by our own. Such incredible power," she marveled. "I can't imagine. There shouldn't even be enough energy in the galaxy to generate this kind of effect. Should the bubble of reality that separates our two universes somehow break, it would destroy everything for millions of miles. Wait. Monitor Nine, intensify information spread inside the black hole." She scanned her readouts again. "This doesn't make sense. Monitor Ten, cross reference Nine's data with Nuklear KI data." She waited for the computers to comply. "Come on, come on. Just as I thought, raw Plazma energy. But Nuklear Man is the only source of Plazma and he couldn't possibly survive in there. The astronomically powerful gravitational forces have to be more than he can endure. Monitor Nine alarmingly beeped its alarm. "The bubble. It's losing integrity."

*   *   *   *

Atomik Lad's mind stumbled out of its unconsciousness and into the rain which had no trouble soaking him without his darned Atomik Field in the way. "Well this has been a swell damn day," he grumbled while rubbing the back of his soaking skull. He had a vague impression that something was going on around him as his senses started reporting in from their brief vacation.

The Negaflux prison quaked as it relentlessly pressed down upon itself. "You've exceeded my greatest expectations, Nuklear Man," Superion said. "But you cannot resist the infinite power which I possess!"

The field imploded at last. Atomik Lad was amazed by its complete lack of fanfare. The movies had trained him to subconsciously expect an explosion of lights and thunder, but there wasn't even a pop.

The rain where the field had been wasn't pulled into the now present singularity The space the rain had occupied was being warped toward an infinitesimal point and the rain had no choice but to continue along what seemed to it to be a perfectly straight path. Relatively speaking.

Not that anyone could tell this was happening anyway due to the rapidly expanding ball of ultimate darkness created by the singularity's existence. And besides, all this only took place in the .000000000001 seconds before...

The dark orb evaporated in a display of blinding white light, like a supernova had decided it was time to go crazy and became a wave of energy that radiated into the night. Superion turned away from the blast and the whole city tremored in its wake. Atomik Lad's Field wrapped around him just before the shockwave did. He was carried away with it for a second like just another piece of tumbling rubble. But then he managed to stabilize himself in mid-air. "What the hell?" he exclaimed while hovering in a storm of fire outside his own. And then everything was back to normal as the wave expanded away. Everything that was left standing in the area was blackened with scorch marks and splintered with cracks. Half melted cars and broken glass littered the war torn street. The wall of flame rumbled into the distance.

*   *   *   *

"Brace yourzelf!" Menace yelled. She swung the ungainly cannon up and around, keeping herself between it and the encroaching wave.

Rachel's eyes widened as the blast radius expanded, coming closer to them despite the many huge building-like obstacles in its way. She dropped to the roof's rough and filthy surface to use the raised perimeter as a shield. The wave struck their building far below. The windows rattled out of their comfortable frames and into the street. Menace clutched the cannon so tight her fingernails went white as the roof shook in several directions at once.

That's it, Rachel thought matter-of-factly. *I'm going to fall over a hundred stories with a few hundred tons of this building and that damn Dr. Menace until we all come to a sudden and painful stop at the bottom.*

The Venomous Villainess had similar sentiments with the added regret: *I'll never fix things.*

And then it stopped. Little pieces of gravel rolled and skipped along the roof at Dr. Menace's feet and Rachel's face. Rachel lifted her head and a rain drop made a direct hit in her eye. "Well," she said, rubbing at it. "That wasn't so bad."

Dr. Menace shifted her weight and fell to her tush. She leaned against the perimeter's rise and caught sight of the moon floating between thick clouds of black. "Odd." She craned around to look over the rise and caught sight of the street far below. "We are now leaning. It seems the shockwave haz damaged our building. But, on the bright side, we are still alive." She set up the cannon once more and aimed for Superion. "We probably haven't much time." She scanned the nightvision green soup of night for any sign of Superion.

"So what was all that?" Rachel asked.

"The short story iz that Superion created a blackhole with Nuklear Man'z mazz."

"And the explosion?"

Dr. Menace shrugged. "I guezz it didn't take."

*   *   *   *

And then it happened. The light of a thousand stars screamed into life where Nuklear Man had been. The air split itself apart and thunder caught in the apex of its crash roared across the Earth. The light, an amorphous blob of boundless power receded into itself. Gathered under the voice of a single consciousness, it coalesced into a familiar form. Into Nuklear Man. Or what one had to assume was Nuklear Man. His distinctive Plamza Aura, usually a dim glow, had flared so intensely that he appeared to be made of pure white heat. His cape was a sheet of flame. "Superion!" he bellowed the way the sun would if it had the inclination. "Stand, coward!"

*   *   *   *

Rachel and Dr. Menace's shadows were splashed along the length of the roof. "Well, Doc. I think that's them."

"So it iz." Her finger caressed the trigger as the scope compensated for Nuklear Man's sudden radiance.

*   *   *   *

"My God," Dr. Genius whispered in a rare moment of true awe. Her monitors reported the impossible. "It's, it can't be. More power than an entire star gives off in a *week* is just sitting there. Right there. The very planet itself should have been vaporized by such close proximity to energy of that degree." She checked her monitors. "Amazing. It's Nuklear Man. He's actually holding the energy back, localizing it to himself. If this doesn't confirm his role in saving the city from the radiation of the Dragon's Strike all those years ago, then nothing will," she said. A few rapid keystrokes and every remote KI Sensor in range of the Hero was pointed at him. "More. I need more data."

*   *   *   *

Superion's laugh was pure madness. "How...?" he asked between gasps of air.

Nuklear Man hovered, an immolating figure of pure light. "Does it matter?"

Even with his Field, Atomik Lad had to shield his eyes from Nuklear Man's brilliance.

Superion pondered the question in silence. The madness appeared on his countenance like cracks across a marble surface. "No. Eheh...heh, bwa hahahaha! It doesn't!"

The Golden Guardian lowered himself level with the Sinister Scoundrel, and though he still remained several inches from the crater's surface, the exposed earth beneath him burbled into molten rock. Dozens of white hot sparks appeared in front of Nuklear Man. They gravitated toward a center in front of the Hero's chest. Slowly at first, and then in a flash, they were one pinpoint like every star in the night sky was aligned into a single bright speck. It siphoned the Aura from Nuklear Man to reveal the pissed off Hero behind it.

A singularity of mass, as we've seen, is a black hole.

A singularity of energy, on the other hand, well maybe that's something like a "NOVAAA RAGE!"

The giant beam ripped through reality, a ferocious lightspeed demon obliterating everything in its path. A backlash of light and energy enveloped Nuklear Man. It dissipated as it passed him and he reabsorbed it, but the sheer force of its presence was more than enough to shatter another block's worth of buildings behind him like they were made of brittle sticks. Superion could be seen as a vague blotch within the massive beam's path.

And then nothing.

*   *   *   *

Rachel recoiled from the beam's light as Menace cursed, her target lost in the light show. Their building shook like it had been punched by God. "What the hell was that?!" Rachel growled while holding onto the ledge. She leaned over it to inspect the damage, if any. "I don't mean to rush things here, but it looks like that last blast just took out the left half of the bottom ten floors." The building shuddered, its remaining girders moaned from the separation anxiety they experienced from the loss of their most cherished load bearing walls.

Dr. Menace hefted the Nega Cannon and held it in the crook between her chest and shoulder. She found her target, the sight reported a LOCK. "Enough." She pulled the trigger. The cannon's exposed innards breathed purple light and an orb of concentrated Negaflux energy was hurled into the night.

The Nova Rage could be seen traveling south along the Eastern Time Zone as it left the Earth at a tangent's trajectory straight to nowhere.

*   *   *   *

Superion hovered, his feet barely missing the molten ground carved out by Nuklear Man's attack. The Sinister Scoundrel wavered slightly. He had endured what he hoped was equivalent to the ravages of hell because he didn't want to admit something else could be more painful.

Painful, yes.

Deadly, no.

"Don't you see, Nuklear Man?" He repressed a giggle. "For all your self indulgent pyrotechnics, I remain. Un! *Scathed*! You can't hurt me, I'm invincible! I am the inevitable march of time, *I* am fate's *chosen! Nothing* can stop me!"

The Nega Cannon's shot splashed against Superion's spine. He thrashed as though a spear had pierced his heart. Back arched, arms desperately clawing at his skin, he fell to his knees, the liquid rock oozed around him like mud. Violet energies swirled and washed over his body. "*Nothing can stop me!*" he screamed in defiance. "*Nothing can sto—*" and Superion was a statue locked forever at his knees silently declaring his arrogance to all the world.

The rain had become nothing more than sparse drops. Thunder rolled in the distance.

Nature's punctuation.

Nuklear Man touched down on the now mostly cooled rock of the crater he and Superion had made in their melee. He walked to the Sinister Scoundrel and gave him a tire-testing style kick. The Would-be Usurper fell over and sat like a statue at its side. "Heh, piece of cake," the Hero said humbly with the traditional dusting off of the hands.

Atomik Lad rushed over, held aloft by his Field. "Nuke! We did it! We stopped Superion!"

"No, no, no" Nuklear Man said like he was patronizing a child. "I stopped Superion."

"Why am I not surprised?"

"You guys were, well you're like the supporting cast in a sitcom that exists as nothing more than a vehicle to keep the star, that's me by the way, in the public consciousness."

"But those things are always giant stinking flops, usually because the star sucks."

"Ahem. Yes, well." Nuklear Man straightened his spandex. "I'm just *so* much better than them." He flexed to drive this point home.

Atomik Lad rolled his eyes. "Gotcha."

*   *   *   *

"One down," Dr. Menace mumbled to herself. "Two shotz to go."

"Um. Can we get down now that you've fired your whatever it is at Superion?"

"One moment, my dear," Dr. Menace's voice was serene and calming. "I have to make one more shot. To make sure Superion iz finished off, you underztand."

"Well. Sure, I guess."

The eyepiece's digital display cast a nightvision green hue on Dr. Menace's eye. Her pupil contracted tightly. Superimposed brackets converged on Nuklear Man's Herculean frame.

Rachel could feel the building vibrate. First in the bones of her feet, then it crept all the way up her legs, and then she could hear the wail of metal strained beyond its tensile strength. "Oh no."

The eyepiece reported a LOCK and Dr. Menace's face exhibited the same smile a mountain lion does the instant before it pounces. "At lazt. I have—" the building began its collapse. "What!"

"We're falling," Rachel stated as though she were not in mortal danger but rather watching the scene play out in a movie. "Dammit."

Dr. Menace stared intently into her eyepiece. *Two shots left. Just enough to shoot down Nuklear Fool and freeze a piece of falling masonry to keep myself from plummeting to my death,* she coolly calculated in the blink of an eye. She was aware of the roof losing its solidity. It churned under her as the stress throughout the building's damaged frame rent it asunder in several places. *Pull the trigger, pull the trigger. Too bad I'll miss the stupid look on his face.*

And Atomik Lad's too.

She squeazed on the trigger.

Atomik Lad. Bloody mess of a past.

Rachel. Bloody mess of a future.

I wonder if Atomik Lad will find it as ironically funny as I.

…Atomik Lad.

Rachel.

Fractions of second crawled by.

If I allow her to die, it would no doubt bring the Atomik Lad's unbridled rage against me and my efforts to rule the world. She almost convinced herself this was the actual reason for her actions. She wheeled around, held the cannon's stock against her hip, and aimed. "Get on the cycle and do not let go!" she ordered at the top of her lungs.

Rachel reacted without thinking and jumped onto the nearby Menacycle just as the section of roof it called "floor" gave way. Her eyes clenched shut, a scream scrambled up her throat but she couldn't let it out. She couldn't allow herself to accept this unalterable hand of fate as true. *I'm not falling, I'm not falling, I'm not falling, I'm not falling!*

I'm not falling?

The Menacycle's cool metal surface had suddenly become warm, like the sun had chosen to shine upon it and it alone for a minute. At the same time, Rachel became aware that she was no longer moving. She cracked an eye open just in time to watch Dr. Menace careen below her riding a slab of broken roof like a surfboard, the Nega Cannon's muzzle pressed against it, her black hair whipping over her exotic pale face like some kind of nihilistic punk rocker on an express elevator to death. Chunks of the building fell past Rachel as she caught a purple glimmer flash around Dr. Menace at the moment she should've impacted the rubble strewn street. The Venomous Villainess then appeared to hop down near a flickering street light and look up at Rachel.

Say something, Rachel thought. *She's waiting for you to say something.*

Dr. Menace slinked into the darkness

"Or not."

✳   ✳   ✳   ✳

Atomik Lad turned to watch a building collapse in the distance. He did a few quick estimations in his head. "Y'know. I think Menace's attack might've come from around there. Or near it anyway. I want to check it out to make sure everything's okay."

Nuklear Man was still flexing. "Go for it. I am, as you can tell," flexity flex flex. "Otherwise occupied."

"Right."

"*Damn*, I'm pretty."

Issue 48—The End of an Age

A Monday night one Month Later...

Atomik Lad sat on the Danger: Couch. He slouched the way a limp body would have if someone had thought to place it there as a sort of practical joke to scare the bajeezus out of the next person to enter the room. The Danger: Living Room was completely dark save for the soft glow of the Danger: TV. He flipped through the channels so quickly it created a strobe effect. He came to a stop at the Action Eye Witness On the Spot News Action Team Terror War Goodthink Edition News Coverage music.

"Hello, I'm Steve Stevenson."

"I'm Robert Robertson with sports."

"And I'm Erica Erickson. Johnny Johnson has the weather. Here's your eleven o'clock news."

The camera focused on Steve's face which had been tele-genetically engineered to induce a deep feeling of trust and warmth when viewing it. "Tonight's top story. Tomorrow will be the thirtieth day since the capture of Superion. Over ninety-eight percent of Metroville's eleven million citizens have been returned to their homes to date thanks to the tireless efforts of the city's overhero community and Überdyne."

A shot of Erica. "That's right, Steve," she said while staring blankly into the space just in front of the camera. Her generically inviting looks weren't too much to make women viewers jealous but they just enough to interest the men. She wasn't beautiful per se, but more like a committee's idea of it. "I had the pleasure of meeting up with some of those selfless heroes while they were on site helping to rebuild the city after their epic battle." She fake smiled a half second too long while the tape was cued up.

Nuklear Man's beaming face filled the screen while Erica tried to push herself into the camera's frame. She shoved a microphone between herself and the self-adoring Hero. "How does it make you feel to bring so much hope for the citizens of Metroville?" she asked

"Well, I'll tell you Diane."

"Erica."

"*Never* contradict me," he snarled. "Ahem. As I was saying, it makes me feel good. Good because it reminds me how much more powerful I am than everyone else. Good because it reminds everyone else how easily I could destroy their puny little world. Why, in the blink of an eye, I could vaporize you into your composite particles. I am the Nuklear messiah of the electric age! Bow down! Bow down before my power! And then get up again. And dance. Dance for me, my pawns! Mwa hahahahaha!"

The camera panned as Erica walked past Nuklear Man to Atomik Lad. "He's such a jokester, that Nuklear Man," she said to the ex-sidekick as he came into frame.

"Joking?" one could just barely hear Nuklear Man say from off-camera.

"Facing down Superion was quite a feat," she said. "Why did you do it?"

Atomik Lad fidgeted a bit. His weight shifted from one leg to the other as he spoke. His eyes darted between Erica's and the camera lens, "Er. We. I mean, we just do what has to be done. I'd like to think that anyone would've done the same in our position."

"Well, I don't know if I would have," Erica said with her idiotic anchor-person laugh.

"You are a local news reporter after all," he mumbled as the microphone moved on to Mighty Metallic Magno Man.

"Yo."

"Mighty Metallic Magno Man, what would we do without heroes like you three?"

"Oh, we're not so special. Parents, teachers, community leaders, volunteers, those are the real heroes. I think we forget them because they're just every day people. That, and they don't go around moving mountains or tossing cars across the road. But they deserve every bit as much recognition as we get. If not more."

How could ya not love that guy, huh? Huh?

"Thank you, Heroes. For your time and for your dedication."

"Dance for me!" Nuklear Man said from the background just before the cut to Steve's close-up in the studio. "Thanks, Erica. In other news, authorities are still searching for the whereabouts of the internationally infamous supervillain terrorist, Dr. Veronica Menace. She is wanted for questioning in regards to her role in Superion's rise to power and subsequent defeat by the city's Heroes."

Atomik Lad rolled his eyes. "I told the news people a hundred times that we would have lost without Dr. Menace's help," he grumbled.

"Meanwhile, Superion himself is still being held in special quarters at Über-dyne while awaiting his trial. Judge Hangemall Letgodsortitout had this to say: 'That boy ain't got a chance. The power was knocked out at my office during that confounded battle and I had to go without watchin' no wrastlin' tapes for like an hour! Straight!'"

Another shot of Erica. "When we come back, footage of the Skyjumper, the new spacecraft designed by Dr. Genius, and her thoughts on its maiden flight tomorrow morning. And Rob with sports."

Atomik Lad hit the mute button and rest the top of his head against the plush cushion of the Danger: Couch. The Danger: Main Doors were high above him. Little yellow guide lights blinked along the cylindrically curved Danger: Walls up to it.

"Hey there, Sport." Rachel's grinning face invaded his field of vision.

He winced. "Let's stick with Sparky, eh?"

She leaned down on the Danger: Couch's fluffy back and kissed him on the forehead. "Just teasing."

"Hmmphf. I'll tease you."

"Promise?" she said with a coy wink.

"Good gravy," he whispered. "Ahem. Finished your homework then?"

She shrugged. "I'm not doing any more of it anyway. Would it have been asking too much for you boys to take your little battle closer to campus? Maybe take out a chunk of the Fine Arts building so I wouldn't have to do this crap?"

"We were a bit pressed for time. Next time though. I promise."

"You're a peach."

"You know I try."

"So what have you been doing out here while the rest of us were diligently not flunking out of school, hm?"

"Oh, just watching TV. Stupid news is on. They're still talking about Superion."

"Geez. It's been, what, a month already. They need to get over it."

"I know. It's like they love to hear themselves talk so much that they don't care what they're saying, as long as they're saying it. Even if it's the same crap over and over."

"It's nothing more than meaningless distractions to keep people from worrying about what really matters."

Atomik Lad shifted around to get a better and more comfortable view of her. "You know they still treat Menace like she's as much of a villain as Superion. They don't come right out and say it, but they practically scream it with the language they use."

"Ugh. She saved me," Rachel said. "Hell, she saved the city. I swear, these news programs spend so much time telling us how trustworthy they are just so we'll unquestioningly swallow whatever tripe they throw at us."

"Don't get me started."

"Well, I'm going to bed. Hope to see you soon," she said with a wink.

"You will. I just have to work up the motivation to stand up."

"I'm not motivation enough?" she said with mock offense.

"You know that's not it."

"I know. I'm just making light of a dangerous situation, Mr. Field. Besides, it's been what? Two weeks since the last time you nearly killed me. I think we're making some real progress."

"If you can call that progress."

"Shush. We'll get through this. We just have to take things slowly. I don't mind waiting. I'm sure you're worth it. And you know what?"

"Hm?"

"I know I am."

"Hm!" He gathered some semblance of mental coherence. "I...oooh...lady, you...flubba. Waaaa."

She laughed. "What have I told you about flattery?"

"Why do you think I'm doing this—I mean—What?"

"Silly boy." She walked back into the Danger: Katkat's Room.

"Yowza" Atomik Lad told the darkness.

*   *   *   *

Tuesday morning, twenty-thousand feet above sea-level and climbing...

The Skyjumper was a prototype space craft. Depending on how it was equipped, it could serve as the replacement to the aging Space Shuttle, or become a way to the stars for commercial fliers. The Skyjumper's main asset was afford-ability. It was amazingly cheap to build and maintain compared to other designs. Probably because it employed a larger version of Dr. Genius' own hover belt so all it needed was a relatively small but constant supply of power to alter the Intrinsity of the space around the craft to allow it to move around.

Dr. Genius sat in the passenger compartment of the Skyjumper which would have been exactly cramped enough to be annoying if not for the fact that she was the only passenger on board. She flipped through some readouts, scribbled some notes, and made some calculations with her always handy mini-supercomputer.

And still her thoughts wandered.

How could I have let Superion come to power? Media manipulation. I hadn't thought Veronica capable of that kind of subtlety, that kind of forethought, patience. I hope the media filters I've put into place are enough to ensure that the public at large does not turn on our Heroes again. I must secure the public's trust in them so they can continue to gallivant around the world, showing off those wonderful KI manipula-tions for my remote sensors to detect and analyze. Every iota of data leads me one step closer to my ultimate goal.

The Skyjumper rattled slightly as it passed through turbulence or some such. She leaned closer to the window to get a better view. The Earth's surface was a slow motion model coasting below her. Clouds were whizzing past. She craned her neck to look above the rising craft. Venus and a few other bright stars could be seen if one knew where to look.

Should be docking with the Watchtower space station soon now. She flipped through some files. *Shimura Yuriko, better known to the world as Psiko. Of all the titans I see every day, of all their god-like powers, for all their feats of strength, it is this eighteen-year old girl whom I envy.*

Psiko. It's short for Psychic Girl in her native Japanese, though it's a bit mislead-ing. She isn't a true psychic, no precognizant abilities. Sidenote: to date, no true psy-chics have emerged. Explore possible ramifications concerning nature of time, free will, and fate.

Where was I? Ah yes. No, Psiko's powers aren't precognizant, but they could be said to be extracognizant. Her senses stretch far beyond the normal human range, beyond anything else found in nature in fact. The police often brought her to crime scenes to find clues they might have missed or could have never detected in the first place. Apparently her senses don't depend on their respective organs. Or rather, they have the capacity to exceed the limitations of them. My theory is that she is actually perceiving a hybrid of ordinary sensory input, the same as the rest of us, as well as raw KI. With the proper training, it is my belief that I could help her shed all reliance on her biological senses. After all, she is only falling back on them out of habit. From an evolutionary standpoint, she must shed her chains. Humans got out of the ocean, Psiko must accept that her skin is a cast off one.

The girl has no idea of the power she wields. Imagine it, the girl can actually perceive KI fields and retain her sanity. The poor girl has no idea, no understanding of them! Why was she given this ability? Why her? Why not me? Imagine. No more clumsy Kopelson Equations. No more Dodeca-Matrix Dilemma. Imagine, actually seeing the fields for what they are.

No, that's using archaic terminology. The language of the flesh.

Knowing the fields, the universe. That's what is at stake here. Locked away in her mind are the very blueprints of creation. And she has no idea.

But perhaps I can fashion a key of some kind.

Her powers are quite impressive. She can communicate telepathically, read surface thoughts and even probe other minds for their deepest secrets, though it comes down to a battle of wills at that point. She can implant subconscious impulses and alter one's emotions. But perhaps the most versatile and, for my purposes, useful application is her ability to, as I like to put it, walk among minds. While she's talking to someone telepathically, she can perceive that person's immediate surroundings as though she were seeing them through that person's eyes. She can then connect to any other minds in the area and do the same to them, seeing through them, and so on and so on. So far she's only gone seven minds deep before passing out from the strain. But potentially, the only limit to this particular power is whatever her sense of self and sanity can endure. If pushed to those limits and beyond, then there's a chance of driving her to a kind of epiphany. Or, alternately, a complete ego obliteration. The latter would prove to be another obstacle in the final stage of her use, but one that is not insurmountable.

Sidenote: Conduct study of delusional psychotics and compare their observations with local KI data. Find correlations, inconsistencies, etc.

They called her Psiko because of the mind reading, but that was just the beginning. Growing up in Japan's largest city, Mechapolis, it was only a matter of time before she applied her powers to a computer whether by design or by accident. Not only can she walk among minds through devices like live video feed or a simple telephone, but she can walk among the minds of computers as well. She'd be the world's most dangerous information pirate if it weren't for her strong sense of morals. She could potentially hack into any system and leave no trace of ever having been there.

And yet, as amazing as these feats may be, they are so base, so meaningless in the face of what she could be. My window into the world of Intrinsity.

Outside the Skyjumper, the blackness of space swept over the craft and the Earth's thin atmosphere fell behind her. Soon they'd begin the docking procedure with Überdyne's all purpose orbital space station, Watchtower. Please put chairs in the full upright and locked positions.

*   *   *   *

Meanwhile, about thirty feet below ground and crawling…

A lone spaceship raced through a star system completely alien to its own. The pilot was a deadly mixture of brash ruggedness, daring bravery, and dashing skill. A rogue's rogue. One pilot versus the hive-mind armada of the hideous Gorthzok Empire. It was a suicide mission. And he liked those odds.

But rogue's rogue space fighter pilot suicide mission types don't have time to play around with odds. They don't even have time to unload a full charge of proton shearing Megablasters and still dodge the incoming volley of homing missiles.

But they do it anyway.

Atomik Lad was hunched over the Danger: Supercomputer. His body lunged and leaned in time with his joystick movements as though that somehow helped his on-screen avatar avoid the waves of incoming alien gunfire. "Geez, they weren't kidding about girls taking for-freaking-ever to get ready."

"I heard that!" Rachel yelled from the Danger: Bathroom.

"Well then you can also hear me kickin' the hell out of Level Five."

"Good work."

"Good wo—It's Level *Five*! I started when you went into the bathroom to get ready for class. We're going to be late as it is and you're still not done!"

"You want me to look my best, don't you?"

"I've seen your best. I know it can't take you this long to accomplish that."

The Danger: Bathroom door opened with all the velocity, menace, and terrifying presence of a glacier. "What. Did. You. Say."

He paused the game. *Oh shit. What* did *I say? Oh shit!* "Er, no wait. What I meant was. You see, because you're so incredibly beautiful, I should imagine you're already so darn close to the maximum expression of beauty that human genetics could possibly allow, therefore it shouldn't take you long at all to reach your, what is simply heavenly, best."

She gave him The Look.

"Eh heh. So it's a simple case of misunderstanding you see. You took my innocent and complimentary words as an insult. I mean, why would I ever so much as suggest that you're ugly?"

"I don't know. Maybe you're looking for an easy way off this mortal coil."

"Um. no?" The Danger: Bathroom door closed. "Whew."

"Whutish!" Nuklear Man said from the Danger: Couch with a little air-whip motion as he and Katkat vegged out on the Danger: TV. "You just gonna let her walk all over you like that?"

"Nuke. Shut up. I've been with you for ten years and you've never even *been* on a date, so you've got no room to talk about it."

"Heh. Apparently someone forgot all about a certain hush-hush exotic romantic heated affair I've been carrying on with Dr. Genius for the past few months."

Atomik Lad blinked. "That's Norman. Norman is going out with Ima."

The Hero gave a patronizing smile. "Oh, stupid, naïve, pathetic, weak, cowardly Atomik Lad. Did it ever occur to you that maybe, just maybe, that's part of our cover to keep prying eyes from prying into our forbidden love?"

"Good God, no."

"Well. It works pretty good then, don't it."

"Shut up."

Rachel emerged, at last, from the Danger: Bathroom as the very incarnation of beauty. "Okay. Let's go," she said sweetly.

"All righty," Atomik Lad responded.

"Whutish," Nuklear Man observed from the safety of his Danger: Couch.

"What was that?" Rachel growled while looming over the now craven and cowardly Hero.

"Um. Gulp, nothing?"

"That's what I thought." She turned to Atomik Lad. "Ready to go, hon?" she asked while on her way to the Danger: Launch Pad.

"Sure thing." He stood up from the Danger: Supercomputer and entered his initials into the hi-scores screen. "Whutish, huh?"

"Shut up," Nuklear Man mumbled, still in a fetal position.

"Uh-huh. Try not to hurt yourself while we're gone." Atomik Lad joined the lovely Ms. Rachel at the Danger: Launch Pad and carefully wrapped his dangerous Field around both of them. The Danger: Main Doors crept open high above them. Atomik Lad rocketed the two of them out of the Silo like a ballistic missile. It elicited a happily terrified scream from Rachel.

The huge doors boomed shut over Nuklear Man. "Lousy kids. More attention to cartoons is now." Or so he would have it if not for an incessant series of beeps, blasts, explosions, and groovin' techno music coming from somewhere that was not Silly Sam's gift to the world. "Erg. Stupid noises, why you pester Nukie like this! Me can smash you!" He punched his ears. "Ouch! Gosh, I didn't know that being so strong could be that painful. Oh well. Live and something. Anyway, that catchy techno music is gone." The Hero of heroes went back to his cartoons. One mighty finger was tapping along with the bass. "This is a pretty cool song—hey! Lousy noise snuck back, eh? Cunning. Like the cunning owl as it um, cunnnnives to devour the mouse like a er cunnnnivore. I see now that I am left with no other choice." He hit himself again, this time hard enough to rattle the Danger: Dishes in the Danger: Kitchen.

$$* \quad * \quad * \quad *$$

The Watchtower was primarily an automated space station. It was built to be able to accommodate a crew of some two dozen engineers and scientists but their presence was not required for most of the station's day to day operations. Other than technical upgrades and major repairs, the station was usually unoccupied.

Which made it the perfect place for Dr. Genius to hide Psiko. She had endured nearly a year within the space station. She hadn't spoken to anyone real in months. Isolation was putting it mildly.

"Konnichiwa, Dr. Genius," Psiko said pleasantly, her hair sticking out impossibly thanks to the Watchtower's low gravity.

"And good morning to you, Yuriko. I've been looking over your progress reports. You are making remarkable advancements in the fine tuning of your powers."

Psiko gave a slight bow since the zero-g environment would've punished her for much more, "Thank you for the opportunity to hone my skills here. My only complaint is how lonely it can be at times."

"Yes, and I do apologize for that, I really do. But it is a requirement for the optimization of your training. Unfortunate, but necessary."

"I know." She motioned toward one of the smaller port windows. "At least it's the best view on or off the Earth. I lose track of how many sunrises and sunsets I get to watch every day." A sunrise was just beginning. "Besides, once we're done here I get to go back, so it's no use complaining at this point."

"True. Our session here will be your last. In orbit at any rate."

"I can't wait to get started."

"Nor I. I can recalibrate the equipment now. It shouldn't take long."

"So soon?"

"I thought you wanted to get home."

"Yes, but you just got here. I thought you might like to rest."

"Science waits for no man. Or woman."

*   *   *   *

Nuklear Man loomed over the Danger: Supercomputer. It was the only thing in the Danger: Living Room that had yet to be pummeled into little bits. His Plazma Aura flared and faded to the rhythm of his heavy breathing. "All right you. I've done smashed everything else in here but the beepin' ain't gone yet. This leads me to believe that you are the demonic source of the noise. As such, now is the time to bash you." He pulled back one massive fist. "This is gonna hurt you so much more than me it ain't even funny. But I laugh anyway!" The game's automated sequence of screens flipped to the list of hi-scores. "Hm, interesting." The Hero's fist dropped slightly. "Seems that Sparky's pretty good at this here game. Not as good as I no doubt am, but good for someone who isn't me. And to prove this point, I shall obliterate his name from the hi-scores with a score of my own that is so grotesquely huge that the mind can nary conceive of even the tiniest fraction of it! GWA HAHAHAHAHA!" He sat down, cracked his knuckles, and got to work. "This oughta take all of five minutes."

*   *   *   *

"All right, Yuriko." Dr. Genius said. Her lab coat was floating behind her in slow motion. "Sit in your regular chair and put on the interface helm."

Yuriko complied. She strapped herself into the chair and placed on her head what looked like a biker's helmet that had been attacked by a gang of technology. Little lights blinked on it to prove that it was working properly.

"Now. What I have done is reconfigure the Watchtower's computer network so that you have access to its environmental scanning operations instead of just the one computer you used as an emergency relay with Überdyne these past few months. Do you know what this means?"

"I'll be able to see entire chunks of the planet in my mind, right?"

"Yes. California to be precise. Entertainment capitol of the world, you know."

"But I thought we were trying to focus my powers so I could be more selective about how I use them. Isn't such a wide sweep counterproductive?"

"Don't worry. This is a test of that focus. The range and breadth of this exercise are for us to determine your ability to concentrate. And to show you that distance is a meaningless concept based on your weaker senses. All that does matter is your mind. Overcome the old way of seeing. That is what we are doing."

Yuriko shifted in her chair. "Sounds a little frightening, to be honest."

"I know. We are only human, we fear change. But, once we've completed the test, hopefully you'll get past that."

Yuriko nodded. "I'm ready."

Dr. Genius flipped the switch.

Every muscle in Yuriko's body tensed. Her face was a mask of agony. Her eyes and mouth clenched. Veins showed on her neck and forehead, a scream caught in her throat.

Of course, Dr. Genius thought, *I specified that the satellite's instruments should be able to focus on the date of a dime lying in the middle of a street on the surface. With a big enough sheet of film, we could take a life-sized picture of the Earth. Luckily, mindscapes provide practically unlimited space. The sheer size of what she's trying to comprehend will shatter the chains to her old senses or her sanity. I believe she is stable enough to opt for the former.*

"It...hurts" Yuriko breathlessly grunted as sweat began to appear on her wrinkled brow.

"Birth pains," Dr. Genius whispered in awe to, and perhaps of, herself.

"I...I can't." tears rolled down her flushed cheeks. Her hands dug into the chair's armrests. "Please...h-help. Doc...tor. Help."

"I am," she said soothingly.

"Ssssstop...make it...stop."

"Don't fight it, Yuriko. You can do this. Step forward, do not shirk from your destiny! *Evolve!*"

But Yuriko could no longer hear her words.

She suddenly became aware of every mind in and around California, be it plant, animal, human, or otherwise. Even the land itself took on something of a personality. From there, through lines of communication, from computers, radios, and televisions, her realm of perception expanded exponentially until she could see and hear everyone on the face of the Earth at once. No fancy metaphors, no trippy journeys through the subconscious or the soul or anything like that. It was simply like looking at a painting from God's point of view.

Okay, so one weird simile. Sue me.

Instantly, she knew the position and velocity of every soul on Earth. She was the Zen master and she was transcending the human experience.

"Yuriko!" Dr. Genius yelled, shaking the girl's body. She stopped. Yuriko's head lulled without any gravity to make it droop limply.

*　　*　　*　　*

Nuklear Man was the very pinnacle of concentration. Tongue stuck out, brow furrowed, eyes focused, back hunched, and thumbs dancing madly over the control pad. His lips curled, hot air was snort from his flared nostrils. "C'mon, you dirty rotten son of a—gosh dangit shoot him, shoot *him*! When I'm pushing this button it means I'm shooting you, yes that's it. Die. Die like the miserable—are you, d'you want some of this? You don't know who yer messin' with. I've got twin Proton Accelerators and a full compliment of Null Bombs so you just try to get past me, Mr. Endless Hordes of Alien Armada! Ha! I am become Shiva, destroyer of—" a stray alien bullet brought swift and untimely doom to Nuklear Man's video vessel. Game over.

"Yourself," Alpha taunted.

"Heh, good one," Beta said. They high fived. The two robots stood behind the Hero and watched his every video game move.

"Shut up." Nuklear Man snapped. "Stupid Nukebots think they're so smart. Hmmphf. I'll show ya!" The game began anew and again Nuklear Man became the very living incarnation of destruction. Until the same bullet shot him down. Again. "What? Since when is it fair to use invisible bullets? Hm? I ask you!"

"Y'know," Beta said. "That guy is always gonna be there, and he's always gonna be shooting at you."

"Yeah, the game doesn't change."

"Oh yeah? I'd like to see you guys do better!"

"Okay." Alpha snatched the controller from Nuklear Man's hands and proceeded to better the Hero's score by several hundred thousand points before the screen suddenly went blank. "Hey!"

The Danger: Supercomputer's power cord dangled from Nuklear Man's foot. "Hm. Wonder how that happened," the Hero mused aloud. "Heh, stupid Nukebots don't suspect my treacherous actions."

"You're still talking."

"Ack! Er, I mean, I command you away from me now!"

"Feh. Command this. Cheater." Alpha tossed the control pad aside. "Let the techno-slaver have his little game. The big baby."

"Yeah." Beta agreed. "Lousy mechanoppressor." They retired to their Danger: Nukebots' Room/Revolutionary Headquarters.

"Feh. Who asked 'em?"

"You did, Nuklear Man," Danger: Computer Lady answered.

"Bah. Well then who was the moron that made 'em in the first place?"

"You."

Annoyed Plazma flared around the Hero for a moment. "Who asked you?"

Danger: Computer Lady's speaker buzzed like she had opened her mouth to say something but thought better of it just in time.

"That's more like it." He turned his attention back to the game.

*   *   *   *

"Yuriko!" Dr. Genius yelled almost hysterically.

"I…I can see everything" she whispered without moving her lips.

"Yuriko?" She checked for a pulse. Faint but stable, almost like Yuriko was asleep. "You gave me quite a scare."

"It's so sad."

Dr. Genius tilted her head. "Sad?"

"I can see everyone. Their minds. I know everyone, all their thoughts. It's sad."

Ima found herself thankful that being in orbit put her outside of Yuriko's range.

"No it doesn't," Yuriko corrected.

"Oh. Damn."

"I know why this happened. I know what you've done to Yuriko, why you did it."

"Do you hate me?"

"Yes."

"What will you do about it?"

"Nothing."

"Interesting."

"You have destroyed Yuriko and I have risen in her place. It is not my place to do anything about it. That is up to you and your God."

"If it's any consolation, I thought that you, that Yuriko was going to pull through."

"And had you not, would it have changed anything?"

"All revolutions are born of sacrifices."

"But revolutionaries choose to make their sacrifices. You took away Yuriko's choice just as you plan to do to the Atomik Lad and that the others."

"I will not let the timidity of others stand in my way! I will not let them deny their destinies out of an irrational fear of the unknown. There is more to this universe than we can ever hypothesize. Should we simply ignore the infinite majesty of reality because it is unknown? No! I will not be slowed by them. I will not let them wallow in their petty disputes, their inane lives, their meaningless possessions and idle comforts. I will not let them waste their souls in the mire of mundane life when they are capable of so much more even if I have to push them to realize it."

"You could've at least asked."

Genius was silent for long seconds. "You said it was sad. Why?"

"They are all alone."

"What?"

"Terribly alone. Separate, distinct from one another. Desperately trying to deny it. You said it yourself, distance is irrelevant, it is the mind that matters. And they're each trapped in their own worlds, every one of them. Able only to communicate through arbitrary, incomplete, mediated means. They don't know each other. They don't even know themselves. They are so alone that they have learned to take it for granted; they don't know that their every interaction is a maddeningly vain attempt to connect to one another when they can never escape the prison of their individuality. The very fact that they are alive produces an impossible divide that can never be bridged. I feel sorry for them."

"I see. You seem to be placing yourself outside of 'their' sadness."

"I am not one of them. I am outside. Not superior, but outside."

"We'll go into the crisis of humanity's post-modern existence later. Right now, I'd like to address some more pertinent questions." Dr. Genius floated around Yuriko's prone body. "With Yuriko's consciousness splintered into over seven billion points of view, her ego was unable to cohere her thoughts any longer and her very identity was essentially disintegrated. So my question is, what and who are you?"

"I do not know what I am other than a consciousness, which is all you can say of yourself with any degree of certainty. Perhaps I am what remains of Yuriko. I know of her, in a way, but no more so than you might have."

"Hm. There are indications that powers exist within you heroes while still being independent of you. Atomik Lad is the strongest piece of evidence for this case. I have recorded several events when his Field acted without, or completely opposite to, his will. And he has reported similar incidents to me before."

"So perhaps I am Yuriko's powers given consciousness. Or rather, what happened to Yuriko's powers without her consciousness to guide them."

Dr. Genius almost said You read my mind.

"I did."

"Ah." Genius twisted a strawberry blonde curl through her fingers and released it. "If you are nothing more than these powers with a consciousness, do you even need a body?"

"No."

"Everything about it is limitation," they said together. Ima paused. "Perhaps," she paused to be sure she was speaking alone. "It would be best to use Yuriko's a while longer. Having pure psychic power floating around completely disembodied is a bit..."

"Off-putting."

"Yes. I know it'll have no actual impact on what you can do, but it is reassuring to think that there is a physical entity that can be traced and restrained. To the public at least. There's no need to get them all paranoid about ghosts invading their privacy and bank records and so forth."

"But I already have."

"Even more so."

Yuriko's eyes opened without focusing on anything. "Just another facet. But please, don't call me Yuriko. I am not her. If I must have a name, then call me Psiko. It is more fitting now than ever."

"Fair enough. Psiko."

The Scientific: Communications Panel had been blinking for sometime, but Dr. Genius only now happened to glance in its direction. "Oh. With all of this going on, I must've overlooked that." She looked at her Scientific: Watch. "It's not a scheduled communication. I wonder..." She pushed the Accept button and a screen lit up.

"Ima!" Nameless yelled while the screen warmed up. His eyes were wide, his breath was quick and shallow, his whole body jittered with an energy that had no place to go but wanted to be everywhere. "Where have you been? I've been calling forever!"

"Can't it wait a few more minutes then? I'm in the middle of a breakthrough with Psiko."

"No! It can't wait. This is about Nu: Alpha."

"Yes, fine. We're always getting little snippets of data concerning possible explanations for the eruption of Nuklear Man's powers. I'll go over it when I'm done here."

"No. Ima, I mean this *is* Nu: Alpha."

Ima tapped on the Scientific: Communications Panel. "Just what have you got there, Nameless?"

"It's a picture from Scientific: Topographical Survey Satellite 9 in orbit around Pluto. I'm uploading it now. Maximum encryption."

*   *   *   *

Meanwhile, nestled within the dark labyrinth of Metroville's Abandoned Warehouse District, a sinister smile spread across the face of Dr. Menace. "The problem with encryption, my dear, iz that there iz alwayz a way to unencrypt it."

*   *   *   *

Another screen on the Scientific: Communications Panel lit up. In seconds it was filled with inky darkness and Pluto. And a silvery sphere that hid half the planet from view. "Oh my God," Ima gasped.

A giant golden N with electron orbits covered the objects entire front hemi-sphere.

"We've been monitoring it for almost an hour now."

"Press leaks?"

"None. You and I are the only people who know about it."

"And I," Psiko corrected, though only Dr. Genius could hear it.

*   *   *   *

"And I," Dr. Menace corrected even further, only no one else could hear it.

*   *   *   *

"All right." Dr. Genius tried to collect her thoughts to make sure everything she had to say got said. "Now. What do you have on this thing so far?"

"It's a perfect sphere of, well, some unknown material. KI sensors go crazy when scanning it and the spectral analyses came back with meaningless results so either everything is malfunctioning or its composed of elements we don't even know are possible. And that's not even the strangest thing."

"I love a good surprise," Ima said sarcastically.

"It's exactly one mile in diameter."

"That doesn't make any sense. How could its creators know anything about Earth systems of measurement? And why choose the English system? It has no consistency."

"It could be a coincidence."

"One thing I know for sure after all my time studying KI Fields, Nameless. There are no coincidences, there is only our inability to perceive a larger portion of the whole. But back to the point at hand, any idea what's inside? What's its trajectory?"

"Like I said, the KI sensors can't make sense out of it, so we don't know what's inside, if anything. It's traveling at a constant velocity at the moment, so we can't be sure if it's actually aiming for us or not, but so far, our data indicates that if it continues at its present course and speed, it will come within no more than 1.2 million miles of Earth by tomorrow morning."

"That's a stone's throw in the scale of the solar system. Of all the days I had to go off world," she chided herself. "Devote everything we can to that thing. Don't let out any information. There's no telling what's in there and if it's bad, I don't want Nuklear Man implicated with it at all. Public opinion must be kept in favor of the heroes. We don't want another Superion."

"I assume we are to keep the government uninformed for as long as possible?"

"Yes. The last thing we need is to involve the military in this. Whether this craft bodes ill or good, having a military presence will only make things worse."

"Should I alert the Hero community in case there's trouble?"

"No. If Nuklear Man is somehow tied to this craft, and if their intentions are such that we need the Heroes, I fear we've already lost. Besides, Nuklear Man especially needs to be kept in the dark about this until we're able to ascertain more about it. It poses more potential trouble for him than anyone else on the planet. Report anything and everything directly to me. Genius out." The screen with Nameless's face went blank. She stared into the screen with the alien sphere that sported a huge Nuklear N across it. "It just doesn't make sense. We fished him out of the Metroville Nuclear Power Plant's ashes. His powers clearly demonstrate that he is the reason the city was saved from catastrophic levels of radiation." She looked to Psiko who was still staring blankly at the nothingness just above the floor. "Don't suppose you can read his mind?"

"I can."

"And?"

"It's foggy."

Issue 49—Strange Visitors From Another Planet

Hurtling through the emptiness between Sol's planets at speeds that are supposed to impossible…

The control room was simple enough. A large domed room, bare walls and dark as all heck. The figure of an imposing man sat in a geometrically perfect and symmetrical chair that appeared to have grown from the perfectly smooth floor. His elbows rested upon a simple desk which also seemed to be nothing more than another perfect outgrowth of the floor. His fingers were interlocked and rest just below his nose. He stared straight ahead into a dozen hovering images that were projected into the air in front of him. They changed at random intervals. First a mountain top, then the murder scene of a detective show, then a statue, then a woman happily using floor cleaner, and so on and so on.

The corner of his mouth fought back a slight grin. "The Earthim." He stared into the television transmissions. "Fascinating," he said somewhat in awe.

"The legendary Earthim? Are you sure, Lord Nihel?" his sniveling servant asked from just beside and behind him. The air around his neck collected itself into a solid fist hovering directly in front of him. The lackey gave a startled jump as the fist grabbed him up by the collar and half flung, half dragged him directly into Nihel's field of vision.

"Yes, Gadriel," he growled with a deliberate slowness. "I am sure." The solidified fist threw the lackey to the floor and dissipated back into air. "You worm," he added as an after thought.

"Just making sure, my Lord," Gadriel groaned while dusting himself off, though there wasn't a spec of dust in the entire ship. "Ahem. What shall we do to them?"

Nihel gave an indifferent nod. "It is an odd twist of Fate that we should find the sacred home of the Earthim while the scores of explorers and theologians from the Galactic Council continue to come up empty handed. But it is no matter. We have more pressing issues at hand."

Gadriel nodded in submission. "As you command, my Lord. Shall I make a note of its location? Perhaps destroying it will serve as something of a celebration once we succeed in our mission."

Nihel continued watching his multitude of television stations. "Hm. A tempting thought, but no. I somewhat like the idea of being the only ones who know that the children of Earth are real. Let the mortals' Council bicker amongst themselves, they seem to enjoy it or else they wouldn't have been at it all these millennia." He fell silent. The channels kept changing themselves. Soap operas, fast food commercials. "Besides, once we've found our wayward quarry, every living being throughout the Milky Way will be no more." Again silence. A celebrity gossip show, a diet drink commercial, a sitcom. "To think that from such..." he searched for the word while watching a long distance commercial, "...From such *banality* could come the basis for an empire of enlightenment and peace that spans half a galaxy." He shook his head, "Fate must be mad." A porno, something animated, a news cast. One of the screens caught his attention. He froze the image and multiplied it across the other screens.

Gadriel's gaze slowly turned from his master to the screens. They played back the last few seconds of footage in reverse. The image was from a news document. Apparently an Earthimwoman of dubious attractiveness was questioning oddly garbed individuals. First a large man with skin like silver, now a considerably smaller youth. Gadriel looked back at Nihel. His grim master's hands now lay on their respective arm rests, his eyes had all the surprise of a man who had just been shot in the stomach while in the middle of a rather pleasing dream about pretty girls. "My Lord, surely you worry too much. Of all the worlds within the Galactic Territories, can you name a single one that is without its own clan of champions? Does not the Great Disk of the Earthim make many references to the exploits of their own Hero, Captain Liberty? It should be no surprise that they'd have others to—" Gadriel's lungs could no longer do their business. He gasped, as he always did when this happened, and hoped, as he always did when this happened, that this latest bout of asphyxiation would not be his last.

"Now that I have your attention," Nihel growled. The television image had captured Nuklear Man's beaming smile, just seconds before Erica would have tried to force herself into frame. "What do you see?" Gadriel struggled to respond but couldn't bring himself to inhale or exhale so nothing much was accomplished. Nihel watched his toady writhe in agony. "Though I do so relish teaching you the importance of realizing that you are alive for every moment of your life until the instant of death, you may now speak."

Gadriel collapsed to the perfectly flat floor and desperately worked his lungs for air. The same speech every time. Always just before that instant of death he keeps preaching about. "I see. But, but it cannot be."

Nihel tensed. "What," a pair of fists manifested from nothing, heaved Gadriel from the floor, and pushed his nose into the frozen image. "Do you see?"

"My answer is a foolish one and I-I do not wish to incite my Lord's renowned anger."

"I assure you," he growled, "It is much too late for that. Answer me!"

"I see...Arel." Gadriel winced in the anticipation of retribution that did not manifest. The hands dissolved and he dropped to the floor. He was convinced that he was the most oft-bruised being in the Galactic Territories.

"Precisely." The dark dome was suddenly illuminated despite an apparent lack in any devices apt in illumination. The Lord had risen. Nihel's cape, draped over his shoulders, was like a robe that had been soaked in blood and left to dry. It rest against the stony gray of his outfit that accentuated his perfect physique and cold, ageless eyes of granite. The uniform's only feature was a dark red Nuklear style N with electron orbits around it. "What is my dear brother in Fate doing?"

*   *   *   *

Atomik Lad walked out of the Danger: Kitchen with a glass of water.

"Nuke. What're you doing?"

"Shush!" the Hero snapped. "I've nearly got this part figured out."

Atomik Lad leaned over to give the situation a closer inspection. "Still on Level One, huh?"

"Yes," Nuklear Man hissed.

"You know it's like eleven at night now."

"It's harder than it looks!" Nuklear Man defended though he did not defend his video game starfighter nearly as well. A bullet, the very same one that destroyed his hopes to rid the Neila System from the vile Gorthzok Armada every single damn time, brought about his doom yet again.

"Hm. I dunno. You make it look pretty hard."

"You're distracting me! Silence, wicked hellspawn. Speak not whilst yonder Hero plays video game. I've got a strategy now."

"Good for you. Doesn't change a thing."

"We'll just see about—*dammit!*"

"Told ya."

"You'd think a society capable of building a vehicle with all these planet-ripping weapons would have sense enough to mount them on a ship with *armor!*"

"You could just dodge that one bullet."

"It says so right in the game's intro. 'You are the last hope for the peace loving people of Neila.' If they're so peace lovin', then how'd they know how to build Null Bombs and Megablasters in the first place? Hm? And if this ship is their only hope," he quaked with rage. "*Then you'd think they'd at least have sense enough to put some armor on it!*"

"Or at least hire a competent pilot."

"Your negative vibes are influencing the game on a quantum level. I can feel it. Be gone."

"Sure thing, Big Guy. Try to get some sleep, hm?"

"Feh. Sleep is for the weak. Take you for instance."

"Right. Don't make too much noise. I've got to get up early tomorrow and meet Rachel on campus. Goodnight." The Danger: Katkat's Room Door **fwoosh**ed shut.

"Yes. Retreat into your den of treachery and deceit and quantum warping negative power vibes. Meanwhile, I'll be saving the galaxy from the wretched Gorthzok Armada!" The magic bullet took him out. Again. "*This* time for sure."

*   *   *   *

Nu: Alpha.

We classify the heroes by Greek letters in Überdyne records. Nu for Nuklear Man, Mu for Magno Man, etc. Alpha is the designation for a hero's origin. We have a decent map for the Alpha of other heroes, but Nuklear Man's has resisted me for ten years. But now we have a clue. A sign. Never did I suspect the subtle nuances of Science would be so blatant as a mile wide orb hurtling through our solar system at several times the speed of light. The mastery of Intrinsity their society must be capable of is astounding to even calculate. I can only assume they've over come the time dilation paradox. What power.

But I digress.

Nu: Alpha. Tomorrow will see the dawn of a new age.

However, I cannot shake the foreboding that I fear may be looming on the horizon. The entire history of the Earth is a long story of one technologically superior civilization dominating a less developed one. I can only hope that a society capable of interstellar travel has also reached a point of maturity where conquest is but an embarrassing footnote in their distant past.

✳   ✳   ✳   ✳

Wednesday morning.

Let's say 8:57.

Atomik Lad blindly fumbled with the wailing banshee that became his alarm clock every weekday morning at nine in the goddamn morning. He lay there staring at the ceiling with sleep starved eyes. He craved the velvet embrace of slumber like a crack addict. The state of being without a state, where everything is nothing and he was One with All. Until he was torn, ripped screaming and bleeding from the womb of nowhere and thrown into a cold world of consciousness. "Ugh," he told the world.

He sleepily shambled across the Danger: Living Room. He rubbed at his face, his skin half-numb and rubbery to his newly awakened senses.

"Confound you, dratted contraption!" Nuklear Man cursed the screen as Game Over flashed before his bloodshot eyes. "Why do you taunt me, oh vicious and evil God!" he bellowed up the Silo.

Shocked into clarity, Atomik Lad approached his mentor. "Don't tell me you played this game all night."

"I didn't," Nuklear Man growled at the screen as he gave the game yet another try. "I've been mocked, *mocked* I say!" The same bullet took him down. The Hero seethed with Angry Plazma.

"You do know you can use the crossbar on the control pad to make your ship move around so you can do stuff like dodge that one particular bullet."

"Yes!" he strangled the control pad. "Stupid no good game! Me smash you good now!"

"Nuke. Destroying it won't solve the problem."

"Oh, but I think it will."

"C'mon," the ex-sidekick gingerly removed the controller from Nuklear Man's tense hands. "I think someone's favorite cartoon show is on."

The Hero's body melted with the warm gooey thought of Silly Sam's media brilliance. He was on the Danger: Couch in less than a second, the Danger: TV already blaring its featureless banality across the cosmos.

Atomik Lad yawned. "Another crisis averted," he said while making his way into the Danger: Kitchen to fix himself some waffles. He made a quick phone call while they cooked.

Ring, ring, "Yo."

"Hey, Norman."

"Sparky. What's shakin'?"

"Me and Rachel are thinking about going to the mall after class. I want to see if the new Turbo Fighter: Street Edition is out yet."

"You little game whore you."

"You know it. Wanna join us? Maybe you could take on the ol' Master?"

Norman laughed. "Yeah, right. Bring it on, punk."

"Hey, it's your funeral."

"I'll see if Angus and Shiro are busy. We can have ourselves a little tournament."

"Not a bad idea," Atomik Lad said. "We haven't had much else to do lately. I don't think there's been a single supercrime since we locked up Superion."

"Yeah, I'm tired of waiting around for an emergency that never happens. We all need to get out and have some fun while the lull lasts."

"Just what I was thinking. We'll be at the mall around noon."

"Works for me. Let's all meet up at the food court for lunch."

"That's a plan. See you guys then."

✳   ✳   ✳   ✳

The Orb came into Earth orbit just over an hour ago. It's been hanging there ever since. We remotely adjusted a Planetary KI Survey Satellite orbiting Mars to scan the orb as it passed. What little information we were able to collect form that arrived just a few minutes ago.

I loathe our incomplete, infantile understanding of physics.

The timing didn't really matter. Our scans told us nothing I hadn't already surmised. The actual KI sensors couldn't get direct readings regarding the craft. Apparently there's such an intense degree of high level KI manipulations in or around the craft that it's even beyond my understanding or our ability to record. The amount of raw energy necessary to generate these effects is greater than the energy output of the sun. Of course just how much more is impossible to gauge at this time.

It's been hanging there, suspended above the Earth in an eternal free fall to nowhere with the Atlantic Ocean directly below it. I asked Psiko to take a look at it. She could only glance at it, somewhat like keeping it in her periphery vision. She got nothing but a headache.

One hour. Perfectly silent, as far as we can know. I hate this. I feel like its taunting us, me especially. By the mere virtue that it exists, it thwarts my every attempt to decipher its mystery. Forever falling around the Earth, this smug sphere of silver showing off its immunity to our first feeble steps into a greater understanding of the cosmos. I swear it hasn't done anything simply because an action would promote a result from which we could conclude or at least theorize an intent. But no. Suspended in silence, it exists only to sharpen my awareness of my own ignorance into a blade cutting straight through my entire body, my work, my being.

Psiko says I should calm down. Then she answers, "Yes, I know exactly how it feels, I'm reading your mind," *the same time I ask her Do you know how this feels?*

I hate it when she does that.

✳   ✳   ✳   ✳

Somewhere, within the depths of the alien craft, Nihel and Gadriel stood with four others. Each of them stood at one of the six points of a perfectly symmetrical hexagonal table. Each one wore the Nuklear N on his or her outfit. "There," Nihel said, gesturing to a point on a three dimensional map of Metroville that he willed into existence from the tabletop. "According to the propaganda footage, this was Arel's last recorded appearance. You five will go there and fetch him."

"What of the Earthim, Lord?" the only woman among them asked.

"Nothing, Safriel. Though they may be indirectly responsible for the entire history of the Galactic Council, it is clear that they have no idea of the role they have played. We know from their Great Disk that they are but children who cannot possibly hope to comprehend what is at stake here. They need not be punished for this. However, should they stand in the way of our goals, dispense with them as any other obstacle."

The five bowed in acceptance.

"Master," their smallest statured member began. "If I may, why does Arel—"

"Yours is not to question, Dakael! Find him. And bring him to me. Your orders could not be any more simple!" Nihel took a few deep breaths to compose himself. "Variel. You are in command."

A silver eyed mountain of darkness nodded silently in response.

"Now go!" he ordered. The floor opened under them and they disappeared into the Orb. The five holes sealed themselves without leaving a trace of having been there. Nihel stared into the three dimensional model he carved from the table with the chisel of thought. He willed a wall of his craft into transparency. The blue marble of Earth cut an arc of fragility across the stark blackness of space. "Why, Arel?" he asked. "What has kept you here, kept you from your Fate?" His eyes followed the fiery path of his soldiers as they careened through the thin atmosphere below. "I must admit I am curious of the Earth, even more so now that it seems to hold some special attraction for you. What could make you shirk your Fate?"

He closed his eyes and was swallowed up by a hole in the floor.

*   *   *   *

"Ima!" Nameless Technician blared from the Scientific: Communications Panel.

"I'm here," she responded without thought.

"The Orb has deployed five—now six, I don't know, probes or something into the atmosphere."

"Any information?"

"They have the same high level KI manipulations as the mothership. According to radar, they're roughly human sized and probably have a density that puts their weight between one hundred eighty and three hundred pounds, each one is a little different. Beyond that, nothing."

Ima snorted an annoyed huff. "Those could be anything. Poison, bombs, the secrets to the universe. Where're they headed?"

"Metroville."

"It's always Metroville.," she muttered with a rub of her temples. "Do we know where? We'll have to create a reason for evacuation and get people out of there as soon as possible."

"The first five are going downtown," Nameless responded. He glanced at a monitor or readout of some kind on his end, Ima couldn't be sure. "Apparently they're headed straight for the area Nuklear Man and Superion demolished in their fight."

Ima's gaze drifted to a window with the panorama of big blue Earth suspended in nothingness and gravity. "It's looking for him. What about the other one?"

"Seems to be aiming for the West Side."

"Why, there's nothing there but—"

"Abandoned Warehouzes," Dr. Menace said to herself as she eavesdropped on the conversation from her Evil: Hideout. "I muzt make arrangementz. I'd hate to appear rude."

Dr. Genius sighed. "We don't have much time. Get a team down there and keep in contact with me. I want Mighty Metallic Magno Man on stand-by"

"But I thought you said you didn't want the Heroes involved."

"He'll be there more for crowd control than anything else. There's construction workers down there, and businessmen nearby. If the situation goes sour, they'll need to be evacuated."

*   *   *   *

The quintet of mini-meteorites landed with a collection of relatively soft thuds in the damp exposed earth of a construction site. The workers stared into what should have been five small craters had they not become a single one on impact.

One figure rose from it. Gadriel, a thin almost elven man draped in a form fitting suit of bright red with bands of yellow around the wrists and collar. He hovered from the hole effortlessly and rest his feet on the ground outside of it.

Another figure appeared from the crater: Safriel. At first glance she seemed a copy of the first, but upon further inspection one found that her outfit was blue where his was red and she had breasts whereas her brother did not. She set down next to him.

Two more forms floated up from the crater simultaneously. One, Kadael, was the size of a mountain while the other, Dakael, was built more like a sapling. They wore identical outfits of dark stormy gray with the same single bands of yellow around the wrists and neckline. The juxtaposition of such similar garb for such dissimilar individuals made each an unintentional parody of the other.

Lastly, an immense form hovered out of the crater. Variel. He was massive, like he could've held the other four within his huge frame. He was utterly black, like the color silence would be. But it wasn't merely a color or a shade of black, it was as though the light could not escape him. He was so black that looking directly at him, one lost all sense of perspective. Every detail was lost in that depthless dark of his body. Every detail that is save for two expressionless silvery ovals where the eyes should've been.

And each one proudly wore the mark of their master Nihel. The electron orbited N.

The construction workers scratched their collective heads, their work forgotten thanks to the sudden extraterrestrial visitors. A jovial, curious mood permeated the now idle workplace. Except for one place.

"I don't pay you slobs to sit around slack-jawed!" the portly foreman bellowed as he stormed from his makeshift office. "We've got a schedule to keep and I ain't about to go over budget unless the good Lord himself comes outta the sky and declares, unto me, 'Thou shalt go over budget!'"

A random worker, thin but muscular from his years in construction, his white shirt smeared with the dirt of honest hands-on work, ran up to the thunderous foreman. "But Boss, there's—"

"I don't care what there is, 'cause what there definitely ain't is the harmony of construction! The symphony of architecture! The songs of girders and mortar!"

"But, out by the cement mixers, these guys fell outta the sky."

The foreman clawed his fingers down his face. "If we stopped working every time some weirdo fell from the sky, then we'd never have laid the first brick!"

"But Boss, they're..."

"Back to work!"

"Excuse me, Earthim civil works engineer," a vacuous non-voice said.

"...right behind you," the worker finished while taking cautious steps that moved him directly away from his employer.

The foreman turned to face a darkness beyond perception. He looked up at two silvery non-eyes that were staring through him. The foreman felt all control wash away from his site in a flood of confusion and suddenly he was twelve years old again with his father's eyes bearing down on him from unbelievable heights, looming like a thunderhead. "Er, uh. Yes?"

"This is where the one known as Arel was last seen, yes?" the non-voice inquired. The foreman noted that it was as though its source was Variel's entire body as opposed to a mouth or some such similar apparatus.

"Um, I-I...Arl? You mean Carl?"

"Arel. Harbinger of the Flame."

The foreman took off his hard hat and wiped his balding scalp with a kerchief. "No. That don't sound like Carl."

Variel let out something that sounded like the inverse of a sigh.

"Pardon me," Safriel, the group's token female, said as she appeared from behind her gargantuan comrade. "The one we're looking for, we're old friends you see. You may know him by another name, but he wears this symbol," she explained while pulling on the fabric of her costume to flatten the image of the N across her emblem-deformingly ample bosom.

The foreman shook his sense back into himself and made eye contact once more. "Ahem. Yeah, that's Nuklear Man's N. What're you guys, some kind of fan club?"

"Nuklear Man?" Safriel repeated slowly. She released her outfit and let it cling to her once more.

"Yeah. Look, I've got to get back to work. We all do."

"I understand, but please indulge us a few minutes more. We're new to this quadrant. Er, of the Earth. We were just wondering how we might find this 'Nuklear Man.'"

"How should I know? I'm just a construction foreman. I think he lives at Überdyne or something. All I know is that whenever the city is in trouble, he comes to the rescue."

"Interesting," Variel said with his unvoice. "Thank you, Earthim civil repair authority figure. You may proceed with your tasks."

"Well, yes. Thank you. Anytime," he said somewhat at a loss. The five strange strangers floated off his work site. "I gotta get a transfer outta this town."

*   *   *   *

They hovered above the diligent construction efforts like the five points of a star.

"You know, you didn't have to give them that high and mighty Alien Rhetoric shtick," Safriel said.

Variel answered in his distinctly void-like voice, "And you did not have to lower yourself by conversing in their manner of speech like a common mortal thing."

"It got us the information we needed, didn't it?" Kadael defended.

"Which is why I have stayed my hand," Variel said without looking away from her. "For the time being."

"Well?" Gadriel said, "Shall we begin?"

"Yes" Variel replied with his empty voice. "We shall."

*   *   *   *

"What!" Dr. Genius exclaimed at Yuriko's possessed body. It was clumsily animated by the only thing that remained of her mind, the consciousness of her telepathic powers. And though Dr. Genius knew that yelling at Yuriko's body was as effective a means of addressing Psiko as yelling in the mirror or at any other living thing on the face of the Earth, it just felt right to direct her anger at the girl's body.

"I believe you heard me. A woman of your intelligence should have no difficulty in understanding such a simple statement."

"At least tell me why you won't help me contact the heroes. It's no effort for you, you're already in their minds. There are five maniacal aliens down there tearing Metroville apart for no discernible reason. We have to get a hero down there and now!"

"As I said before. I am outside humanity. This is not my concern now. I will record. I will remember the human story. And when it is over, perhaps I will have honed my essence, my powers, to such a degree that I will be able to traverse the universe and share your story. Since I am no longer hindered by the baggage of flesh, I could theoretically be wherever there is a mind."

"This is madness. People are dying," Dr. Genius pleaded.

"Do you forget that I am in your mind? Try as you might, you cannot hide from me that you are not concerned for their lives so much as for the potential to gather your precious KI data."

"Sending in Mighty Metallic Magno Man and the others would save lives too. What's the difference *why* they're sent?"

"Intent, Doctor. Intent makes all the difference. Not that I would help you in either case, I was merely pointing out that I find your ruse to beguile me a little insulting."

"At least help me locate them. None of them are responding to their hotlines and I can't attempt a mind-ride like I did when Crushtacean attacked without my equipment at Überdyne or without your help. Please!"

"I am sorry, Doctor. But in this case, the observer does not influence the observed."

Dr. Genius let out an exasperated grunt.

"Besides, there is still one Hero you have not tried."

"But the potential for disaster is too high."

"Too high to justify the potential loss of data?" Psiko retorted with Dr. Genius' own thoughts. "Until we meet again, Doctor." Psiko's body went limp. Ima had to look away. There was something sickening about a body without a mind standing around. And without gravity, the body just hung there unnaturally.

Dr. Genius leaned over the Scientific: Communications Panel, her hair bobbing in the slow motion of weightlessness. Her eyes were shut tight, the tendons in her hands bulged as her finger nails went colorless from the pressure she exerted while desperately trying to rip the console from its housing. She relented with a resigned huff at the height of her effort.

She hit the Send button.

Issue 50—The Battle of the Century of the Week

Several miles outside of Metroville, over a hundred feet under the isolated and barren fields of Irradiated Flats, within the hallowed halls of the Silo of Solitude, the Danger: Danger Phone rang.

The Danger: Danger Phone had been ringing for an eternity. Or at least like twenty whole seconds, but think about it. That's a long time for a phone to ring. Nuklear Man winced with every blaring jangle of electronic bells. He would've answered, or at least considered the possibility of answering, had he not gone back to his little video game nearly the instant Sparky left him alone. That fool!

"That's just like Sparky," the Hero cursed. "I bet he left 'cause he developed the power to see into the future and knew that the phone would ring and since he also knows that I know about his maniacal plot to cause me to fail at this game, he oh so conveniently disappeared so that the lousy Danger: Danger Phone would do his job for him thereby leaving him free of any suspicion while I'm distracted into oblivion." His video game craft exploded. "Very clever of the little scrawny sidekick," he mused. "However, it was characteristically unclever of him to think he could get away with it." He knowingly nod at his own brilliance. "As if I wouldn't have figured out his supertemporal perceptions. Oh, he's shrewd, I'll give him that. But he doesn't know what he's up against." The Danger: Danger

Phone continued to ring. "Oh, gosh dang it. Katkat, get the phone. I'm trying to save the galaxy over here."

"Mreow." Katkat hopped onto an end table next to the Danger: Couch. The Danger: Danger Phone rang as if in response to the feline's presence. He sniffed it.

It rang.

He gave it curious looks from slightly different angles.

It rang.

He tapped it cautiously with his paw.

It rang.

He rubbed the side of his face on it and collapsed on to one side to lie down with the phone as a pillow.

It rang.

"Hm," Nuklear Man said. "I still hear the phone ringin'. I don't think you quite know what you're doing. I'd offer my help or at least glance in your direction, but I'm a little busy single handedly destroying the entire Gorthzok Armada at the moment." The Bullet destroyed him. "Er, but as luck would have it, I happen to be available now." He looked over. "Aw geez. That's not how you answer a phone."

"Mew," Katkat snuggled against it.

"Curse you and your infallible logic!"

Katkat purred.

"You don't have to rub it in," Nuklear Man moped. The phone still rang. "You win this round, Mr. Kitty. But for now, let's shut this thing up." He picked up the receiver and promptly dropped it right back. "Oh yeah, that's the stuff." He turned and took all of two steps when the phone began to ring anew. His entire body cringed. The second ring didn't even have time to complete itself before he picked up and yelled, "This line is reserved for emergencies and only Dr. Genius has the number so quit callin' me!" he slammed the receiver down this time. And again, it rang. And again, he picked it up. "*Grah*! Look, buddy. You've got a lot of never callin' here. The city could be in terrible, *terrible* peril, but I'd never know because Dr. Genius can't call me to action because you keep tying up the phone line!"

"Nuklear Man, it is me, Dr. Genius," she managed to say before the Hero got the chance to hang up.

He paused. "Prove it."

Her eyes closed, she shook her head. "We have this same conversation every time I try to contact you via the Danger Phone."

"Hm," he responded. "I'll have to take your word on that. What'cha need, Doc?"

"There's an emergency downtown."

"And you need a little of the ol' Nukie Magic Plazma Goodness to make it all right, hm?"

"Something like that. There are five villains causing general mayhem where you last battled Superion. I don't want you to engage in battle with them, not initially at any rate. I've got an Überdyne team down there so they'll be able to keep an eye on you to see if I should send in reinforcements."

"Heh, that'll be a first."

"When you get on the scene, your first concern will be for the innocent."

"Heh, that'll be a first."

"Get any and all civilians out of the area before you do anything else. Understood?"

"Eh, more or less."

"And Nuklear Man?"

"Yes?"

"These five, um villains. They may claim to know something of your past."

"Oh?"

"But don't believe them. It's part of their strategy."

"Ah ha. How sneaky of them, playing on my amnesia like that with their dirty, naughty little lies. It's a good thing we've got you on our side, eh Doc?"

"Indeed."

"Off I go to dispense some indiscriminate justice." He put down the Danger: Danger Phone and **wooooosh**ed through the Danger: Main Doors a millisecond after they had opened just wide enough to admit him passage.

*   *   *   *

Dr. Menace was perched on the roof of one of the taller abandoned warehouses. Even though she was perhaps two blocks from her target, she kept low and made certain to keep some kind of cover between herself and the subject. Thanks to her Evil: Negaculars, she was able to observe him in great detail even at her current distance and with a few abandoned warehouses blocking off her line of sight.

"Evil: Log. 9:51 A.M.

"Looking at him now I cannot help but be reminded of Nuklear Man. It muzt be the cape and that N on hiz chezt. What hiz intentionz here could be are outzide my ability to zurmize. For now. There iz zomething, zomething divine, no, regal in hiz body language. Yet here he iz, walking among the fallen and forgotten huzkz of warehouzez inztead of ruling on high from zome caztle. Why?"

He turned in her direction and she instinctively ducked behind a nearby refrigeration unit of some kind even though she knew he couldn't possibly see her.

"Azzuming of courze that hiz senzes rezemble our own," she told herself. "And why shouldn't they? He bearz the mark of Nuklear Man, which iz clearly the English letter N, hiz craft iz exactly one mile in diameter according to Überdyne'z surveillance, and he appearz to be a perfect human specimen."

She brought the Evil: Negaculars to her eyes and spied on him once more. The alien watched a plastic bag dance in the wind for several seconds. It reminded Dr. Menace of a rowboat being tossed by the anger of a stormy sea. The bag latched on to Nihel's leg. He regarded it with an inquisitive smile, bent over slightly to get a better look, but didn't seem to have the slightest inclination of removing it.

"What a strange dichotomy," she whispered to herself. "Perhapz," she told herself. "Yez, perhapz a face to face meeting iz what iz needed. He seemz harm-lezz enough, not that it matterz. I could eazily wrap myzelf in a Negaflux shield, or better yet, if I can get him back to my lab, capture him in a Negaflux field if he stepz out of line. There would be no ezcape." She thought a moment longer. "In fact, such a tactic may prove quite uzeful in any caze. He no doubt holdz the anzwers to many scientific quandriez and would conzider a lifetime imprizoned on thiz rock too horrible not to releaze more than a few of them."

*   *   *   *

Nuklear Man soared over his beloved city of Metroville. From his aerial view, the cityscape was pockmarked with as-of-yet repaired craters for which he person-ally was directly or indirectly responsible. He swelled with pride. "Ah, memo-ries," his voice was a song of accomplishment.

But his stroll down memory lane came to a crashing halt as the Golden Guardian's Nuklear Senses detected trouble afoot. "Ah ha," he self-narrated. "I do believe I have found the very source of our fair city's problem." Below him, the five aliens wreaked havoc. "Well, that's one problem solved," he told himself as he rocketed past without slowing down even a scotch. "Wonder what's on the ol' Danger: TV now. I've been out for, I don't know, minutes." He leaned into a U-turn and cut a golden parabola through the morning sky but then an errant blast of electricity splashed against his face. "Ouch!" he yelled and stumbled to a mid-air stop. "Who did that?!" he demanded of the heavens. He gave a particular cloud a nasty look. "It was you, wasn't it. You can't fool me. You're in cahoots with Sparky, aren't you! That's just like you sky-father god archetypes, gangin' up on me like that. You should be ashamed. But, more to the point, you should be evaporated. As such," he said, gathering up energy in his hands. "PLAZMAAA—". Another electrical blast zapped him, this time in the back. He spun around to face the increasingly scarred city, "—BEAM!" and a beam of fussion-ish energy added yet another scar.

*   *   *   *

Safriel yelped in surprise and dropped the car she had planned to hurl through an office building. A new smoking crater smoked itself mere inches from where she stood. "Hey, watch where you're shootin', Gadriel!" she scolded. "You nearly took my tush off with that last one. Do you have any idea how long it took Lord Nihel to get it just right?"

Gadriel turned to face her, though it was difficult to tell that he had done so since his body was currently living electricity in a vaguely humanoid shape. "What're you talking about?" he asked with sparks of annoyance flying from his white hot body. "I've been shooting out windows with my Electroblasts."

"You've got some pretty lousy aim, champ," she retorted while pointing to the still smoking crater that lay between them.

"Oh yeah?" Gadriel got right in her face, "You wanna see just how bad my aim is?"

"I already have. Besides, you can hit me all day long. I can just Protonically alter my molecular make up to harmlessly conduct electricity."

"Cease!" Variel thundered with his unvoice.

"Look, you made him yell," Safriel said.

"She started it!" Gadriel defended.

Variel gave each of them long stares. Of course, the slightest glance of those blank silver non-eyes would probably be too much for most souls to withstand for long, so the actual duration of these stares is quite subjective. "Cease this petty argument. Recommence your duties."

"I don't see why we have to do all the dirty work," Gadriel complained.

The immense black whole of Variel rumbled with a nongrowl. "My will is second only to Lord Nihel's. You will no more question me than you would he. Complete your given task!"

"Arel's pretty powerful," Safriel said. "He probably doesn't come out for small stuff like this. Bring in the big guns over there." She looked at the diminutive Dakael. "Well, the big gun at any rate."

Dakael quaked and a half dozen copies of himself **bamf**ed into existence around him. "We'll show you big guns," they said in unison while each one made a different rude gesture, many of which were completely unknown to the citizens of Earth.

"Kadael!" Variel nonbarked. "Control your counterpart."

The mountainous Kadael reached down to several of the clones. They disappeared once he touched them and the giant seemed to expand slightly as a result. Dakael dispersed the others until only his original self remained.

"As for you, Safriel," Variel began . He was cut short, however.

"Ha-ho!" Nuklear Man crashed in on them. When the dust cleared, he was knee deep in Metroville asphalt. "Oh shucks," he stepped out of his tiny crater. "That happens every time I land. I swear, someone shoulda built this planet out of sterner stuff because I could probably tear it to tiny little bits and then blast those bits into smaller bits which would then be subject to further blasts, thus pulverizing these already small bits into progressively smaller and smaller bits until…"

The five were awe struck. They gathered around him, suffocatingly close, their movements slow, reverent. Even Variel's cold eyes seemed to hold a sparkle of emotion, something between worship and love.

The Hero was too busy prattling to notice, "…and then Vishnu would be all like 'Desist your universe tromping ways,' and then I'd be all, 'You think you're all that, but you are not all that,' and then—"

"Arel," Variel unwhispered.

"—I'd grab that multi-armed freak—"

His name shall be Arel, the true name of fire.
His power will know not limits
For the flame is unpredictable;
A god without destiny written
Will be the father's sword against Fate eternal.

"Er," Nuklear Man shook his head and wobbled for a second. "Whoa, that was trippy. Woo!" He put one hand on Kadael's huge shoulder to support himself. "Hey!" the Hero pointed at Kadael's outfit, specifically the Nuklear N. "I've got one of those. Hey, all of you have one. Well, except for you, Gruesome," he said, pointing to Variel. The mammoth mass of blackness moved slightly and

Nuklear Man could just barely make out the N on his chest as an area slightly less black than the rest. "Ah, well there we are. You guys must be fans, huh?"

They looked at one another with quizzical glances.

"Yeah," Nuklear Man said, releasing Kadael's shoulder. "I can't blame ya, personally. I am pretty cool, ya know."

"Arel," Variel said again.

"Hey, who's this Arel guy everyone keeps talkin' about?" the Hero asked. "He sounds neato."

*   *   *   *

"Ima," Nameless Technician whispered through the Watchtower's Scientific: Communications Panel.

"You don't have to whisper, Nameless," she answered.

"It can't hurt. I'm with the team."

"What! I told you to get a team down there so that you could stay at Überdyne and be safe. You're not expendable."

"Just following your example, Doctor. What's a little personal risk in the face of possible enlightenment?"

"I don't approve, but there's nothing I can do about it from up here. Report."

"Nuklear Man is talking with the aliens."

"How's he reacting?"

"Fine. Almost, I don't know. Friendly. But there's something you should see. I'll patch you in to our video surveillance." He pushed a few buttons and another screen on the Scientific: Communications Panel lit up. It was live feed showing Nuklear Man surrounded by the five aliens as they conversed. It seemed to Ima that Nuklear Man was doing an unusual amount of listening.

"They look so, so *human*," she said to herself. "Well, other than the one with silver eyes." She squint her own, "He's a bit hard to make out, exactly. Anyway, what am I looking for here, specifically?"

"You'll see. Wait until the girl moves out of the way."

And then by shifting her weight, she did.

"They each wear the N," Ima said aloud.

*   *   *   *

Dr. Menace stood in the middle of one intersection while watching her subject stroll along the filthy street that led directly to her. Her finger wasn't more than a twitch away from the Negaflux Shield's activation button.

He looked her straight in the eyes the whole time he approached her. His gaze was dreadful, not from any impending malice, but rather the sense of import he carried. His eyes spoke of the beauty of destruction, yet also whispered of the horror of life. And with one last step, he was before her. Not too far and not too close. He spoke, "Greetings Earthim woman," his voice was a perfect compliment to the eyes.

And somehow, she knew that they were more similar than not. "And to you, ah, excuze me, but I haven't a clue how to addrezz you."

"Yes," he almost laughed. "I would seem to have you at a bit of a disadvantage. I am known as Nihel," he said with a hand against his chest and a slight bow.

"Greetingz, Nihel. You may call me Dr. Menace."

"Certainly."

"If I may inquire, what bringz you to our world?"

He tilted his head to one side as she spoke. "You have a most curious accent, Dr. Menace."

"I am from Romania," she said.

"Ah, Romania. In your Earthim year1859, with the support of the 'French,' Cuza was elected to the thrones of Moldavia and Wallachia, creating a national state which would later take the name 'Romania' in your 1862 I believe."

Dr. Menace was taken aback.

"It would seem I have some explaining to do," he said in answer to her surprise.

"Indeed. But not here. Perhapz back at my lab?"

"An Earthim scientific establishment? It should prove interesting."

"It iz not far from here."

It was his turn to give a quizzical look. "We know that you Earthim have strange customs, but to build your institutions for scientific experimentation in these conditions?"

And it was her turn to almost laugh. "Yez, well. You could say that my conditionz are a bit unique."

"Do tell."

"You may find thiz quite a surprize, but I am conzidered to be something of a villain by my society."

"Ah," he nod and looked at the sky. It was mostly blue save for a shock of thick clouds three or more layers deep by the horizon. "I get that as well." He offered her his arm. "Shall we?"

She slid her arm to interlock with his, "Yez."

*   *   *   *

10:26 a.m., Eastern Standard Time.

"So what you're telling me," Nuklear Man said. "Is that the N on your chests don't stand for Nuklear Man, but for Nihel."

"Yes," they answered in unison with weary voices.

"I see." Nuklear Man walked back and forth a few steps. He was afforded little space in which to move thanks to the circle of alien villains around him.

"Finally," Dakael mumbled. Variel leaned in his direction which was more than enough to silence him.

"In that case," the Hero proclaimed, pointing to the heavens, cape billowing ever so slightly. "This Nihel character is in direct violation of our copyright laws which, I might add, frown heavily on this sort of blatant plagiarism! I could sue."

Each of the five groaned.

"I could, you know. I know this lawyer, Count Insidious. He's got a cape and everything. He's so good he put me in jail for crimes against humanity that I didn't even get the chance to commit, or so I'm told, which is a shame 'cause they sounded pretty fun. Heh, yer in for it now. He's ruthless. I hope you can swim, 'cause yer goin' up the creek without a paddle!"

The five were silent.

"Hm. How about, I hope you've got exact change because you're about to go on a bus ride?"

"What the hell is he talking about?" Safriel snapped.

"Silence!" Variel nonthundered.

"Stuff it, Var. You can preach about Nihel's righteousness until you're, well, less black in the face, but Arel here is obviously out of his mind."

Nuklear Man blinked. "Y'sure you don't mean Carl?"

"Please forgive her insolence, Lord Arel," Variel said while bowed on one knee. His piercing silver stare shot to Safriel, "She is young and impetuous. She knows not what madness she speaks."

"Well that makes two of us, I can tell you that," Nuklear Man said.

"There does seem to be something *amiss* with his Lordship," Gadriel meekly offered. "Perhaps he is suffering from some malady, temporary of course, from which we must liberate him."

"So who is this Arel guy anyway?" Nuklear Man asked. "And do you shmoes have last names or what? I'm certain that's the kind of pertinent detail my lawyer will want so I can sue each of you."

Dakael stepped forward, "It's almost as if the Arel whom we know and fear has been subsumed by this, this…"

"This living incarnation of the endless drivel produced by this planet," his partner Kadael finished. "Not that we mean any disrespect, of course."

Variel shook his head, his eyes nearly communicating dismay before glimmering with their usual unblinking quality.

"Oh hey!" Nuklear Man said, his face alighted with joyous realization. "Have you guys seen five villain types tearing up the City? They're supposed to be around here somewhere. I think. My mind tends to wander when ol' Doc Genius is talking, if ya knows what I means. Winkity wink."

"This is embarrassing to witness," Safriel groaned.

"Wait a second." The Hero's Nuklear Quick Brain kicked it into high gear. "You guys are here, you're committing copyright violation, and there's five of you, give or take."

"Here it comes," Safriel announced with mock enthusiasm.

"*You* guys are the villains!"

"Lord Arel" Variel said. "You must remember your Fate."

His name shall be Arel, the true name of fire.

"Hey," Nuklear Man protested. "Get your crazy voices out of my head, there's enough of those up there already."

What has been written will be burned in his flames. What will come to pass shall be no more.

"I mean it, stop or it's smashin' time."

Fate, unmade and rewoven, a new tapestry by the design of gods who have thrown off their shackles.

"Last call."

In the flames there will be purity. There will be rebirth. And from the ashes, there will be a choice where none existed before.

"That did it. PLAZMAAA BEAM!!!"

Issue 51—A Long Time Ago, on the Other Side of the Galaxy...

Mighty Metallic Magno Man, Shiro the Tetsu Samurai, and Angus the Iron Scotsman exited the Metroville Museum of Natural History and walked down the wide stairs that led to the street. Norman's wide strides skipped every other step as Angus and Shiro's legs pumped so fiercely that they were blurs of motion just to keep up.

"Slow down, ye daft metal-skinned ox!" Angus barked between gasps for air.

The Tungsten Titan came to a stop whereupon Angus ran into one of his legs as Shiro did same to the other. Both fell one stair back onto their armored arses.

"Norman-san is the success at being heavy with size. Like dragon of falling mountain unto who is me," Shiro observed while readjusting his Tetsu: Samurai Helm, sans demon-visage mask that was used to strike fear in the hearts of superstitious evil-doers everywhere, of course. That was used purely for business purposes.

"Tell me aboout it," Angus grumbled. The Surly Scot did a double take at the narration with a very audible ker-boink sound. "Ah've goot ta lay ooff the whisakey. That laddie's startin' to make sense!"

"Hey, sorry guys," Norman said. He turned around to help them up by offering a pointer finger to each.

"Hai. Of favors are large with you," Shiro thanked.

Angus's armor rattled as he shook with rage.

"Just kidding," Norman said in a laugh. Each of his hands enveloped one of their little arms and hoisted them up simultaneously. "There."

They continued down the stairs, this time at a pace more befitting the shorter heroes present.

"Well," Angus said, slapping his Iron Gauntleted hands together with a metallic clank sound. "What'd everybody think o' the exhibit?"

Shiro opened his mouth to say something but then thought better of it. His eyes darted left and right to look for the perfect answer. "Angus-san is of having um, interesting."

"Aye, ye damned tootin' it was interestin'. How about ye, Norman?"

"Er," Norman donned a pair of super fly cool shades even though it was barely eleven o'clock in the morning. "I don't know quite what to say."

"Aye," Angus resounded with his first true smile of the story. "It has that effect, ye know. It's majestic. It's profound. It's—"

"It's a bunch of wax statues of guys wearing plaid skirts," Norman finished.

"Thems be *kilts*, laddie," Angus responded with a calm monotone that, when combined with the twitching of his right eye, was more terrifying than his usual furious roaring.

Norman shrugged. "Still looked like skirts to me."

Angus quaked and sputtered. "They be the mark o' bravery, the garb of a true warrior, ye soon-to-be pummeled oaf!"

They reached the sidewalk and Metroville's early lunch foot-traffic swarmed around them. "Yeah," Norman said. "You'd have to be pretty brave to run around in women's clothing."

"That does it!"

Shiro pulled his helmet down to hide from the ensuing devastation that was sure to follow.

"DWARF-A—" **KLONG** "...*What?!*"

Norman had magnetized Angus' Iron: Battlesuit to his tungsteny leg. The Dwarven Warrior couldn't budge. "Settle down. I was just messing with you." He released the magnetic vice grip and Angus fell onto his armored arse again.

"Bah. Kilts ain't nothin to be jokin' around about. Ye laddies today don't have respect. Back in my day—"

"Waiting is now," Shiro interrupted. "Essence of time, like the hour glass that fading. Eleven o'clock."

"Hm" Norman said. He inspected his Magno: Watch. His face twisted in disappointment. "Man, this thing hasn't worked right ever since that Chrono-Dork fooled with it before Nukie's party."

Angus checked his Iron: Watch. "Aye, its eleven. We needs to get a move on if we're meetin' Atomik Laddie an' Rachel at the maall, it's on the other side o' town."

"Letting those who is us now to be rolling!" Shiro declared.

"What are ye talkin' about? We walked here."

"Hai," he answered with a proud bow.

"Ye could at least make sense when ye ain't makin' sense!"

*   *   *   *

A huge iron door slid to one side and cut a blade of light deep into the darkness. The wound opened wide until the door boomed against whatever mechanism kept it from rolling completely exposed. Two shadows invaded the rectangle of light that had been thrown against the dusty floor. One slender, moving like liquid; the other seemingly carved from marble. They stepped through the doorway, the smaller figure reaching straight out to one side, her hand resting on a panel set against the inner wall. Tiny positive sounding beeps rang through the immense structure, though whether these were the echoes of a few or a chorus of many, it was impossible to know for sure. The beeps terminated and the great door rushed shut with an explosion of an impact reverberating through the complex that was now utterly cast in the night of grimy boarded up windows. The blackness persisted for a second or two before a collection of lamps some twenty feet above flickered into illuminated life from the ceiling. Only the areas around Evil: Projects in various stages of design, production, and testing were well lit. The intervening distance between them was like the dark of space.

Nihel surveyed the Evil: Lair's contents with several sweeps of his cold gray eyes. "Fascinating." He walked into the vast warehouse like an archaeologist entering a perfectly preserved ancient city or tomb.

"Yez, well. I do what I can."

"Then you do it quite well," he responded while walking deeper into the catacombs.

"I'm sorry if the decor izn't to your liking. I am a villain, you know. I have certain atandardz I'm auppozed to adhere to for the aake of appearancea," Dr. Menace apologized while following him inside.

"I know how that is," he said while surveying the various Evil: Equipment scattered throughout the Evil: Lair.

"But why, not that I'm complaining of courze, why did you chooze to vizit thiz area of the city firzt?"

Nihel turned to face Dr. Menace as he walked among her creations. "Simple. It is well documented in the Great Disk that your Metroville is the greatest civic accomplishment of your people. I was curious to see its wonders first hand. I decided to begin in the most decrepit area possible and then work my way up to its population and business centers. Any suggestions?"

"I'd say the mall, but you should be quick about it. It'z hell to go there once all the annoying little highzchool bratz start running about."

"The mall. Yes. That's such a perfect slice of your bland Earthim consumer culture. I wouldn't think you much of a frequenter of one, though."

Dr. Menace grinned. "The clozezt RadioHutt iz there. It iz an anarchizt's bezt friend."

"And here I thought you wished to change the world. Instead, I find a mere anarchist?"

"Deztroy the prezent society and anarchy reignz. The people, lozt, alone, afraid, they will want a strong, charizmatic leader to tell them what to do. If a temporary anarchy servez to further my inevitable domination, then so be it. I will not shy away."

"Ruthless." He approached the Evil: Negaflux Super Charging Chamber that Superion had destroyed just previous to his rampage a month ago. He crossed his arms and seemed to scrutinize the remains of the bulky device and its exposed innards. What parts remained intact suddenly disassembled themselves. The machine unraveled into its component pieces which then hung in mid-air like some kind of technical diagram brought to life. "Hm. This is, or rather was, some sort of Intrinsity Transformer, yes? It could imbue a subject with a vast array of powers based on the theory of Intrinsic Negation Field Force Manipulation." He examined a few parts more closely. "Temporarily at any rate."

"Yez, but how did you…?"

The pieces reassembled themselves into a fractured whole. "I take it, by the unfortunate state of the device, that you were not able to compensate for the extreme psychological trauma engendered by the process."

"Correct."

"And also, due to your overall stable demeanor, it was not you who served as the test subject."

"Correct again. But how did you know?"

"Not all civilizations welcomed the message of peace and learning that the Galactic Council carried between the stars. Similar devices were constructed to form an invincible army to be unleashed against the Core Worlds of the Council, especially Zurai. Unfortunately, they met with results similar to yours. Theirs was more widespread however. They destroyed their own planet before they could ever wage their war. The army, though insane to the last soldier, was functionally invincible while floating in space. That is, until their powers ran dry without any more sessions in their Transformers. A Council ship investigating the planetary explosion found a prototype of the device, remains of documents concerning the invasion and other evidence on a colony or moon or some such. Devices such as this have been forbidden within Council boundaries, as is understandable."

"I see. And juzt how do you know all thiz?"

"Well, Arel and I built the things of course."

"Ah."

Nihel's eyes seemed to glaze with nostalgia, "Scourge of the Territories, we were." His gaze returned to the inside-out machine. "It is remarkable that you could build one. According to your Disk, it must've been quite a task to construct it given the limited level of available technology and rudimentary understanding of Intrinsity."

"I had to invent mozt of the theory az I went along. But I am still uncertain of the nature of thiz dizk you keep referring to. The information you provided me of it on our walk here seems contradictory. For inztance, the dizk seems to contain incredible information about human hiztory up until our modern era, but you claim that it is an ancient relic."

"Yes. The 'copyright date' indicates it was made nearly eleven years ago when compared to the current date broadcast by your behemoth media structure as I entered Earthim space."

"Exactly. Yet you claim that thiz dizk waz found some forty thouzand yearz ago on a small planet called Zurai on the other side of the galaxy. A planet inhabited by an intelligent yet primitive race of people conztantly at war with one another over petty concernz zuch az land and ideology."

"Yes. And from that Disk, the ancient people of Zurai learned your language, your history, and eventually your technology. They supposed it a message from their gods. A message showing them what would happen if they continued their petty, self-serving, and ultimately self-destructive, ways. Plagues, famine, endless war, strife, a society drowning in its own empty accumulation of meaningless objects and material wealth while starving the mind and soul into a gray apathy to distract themselves from the ever present threat of utter annihilation that they brought upon themselves from their own fear and hatred of one another."

"And so they uzed our way of life as a counter-example of everything a society should be. With a jumpztart on technology and moralz, they sweapt acrozz their world, and then the stars, with a mezzage of harmony." She shook her head. "It sounds too good to be true."

"And yet it is true. To this day, every sentient being within the Galactic Terri-tories is taught at least a rudimentary understanding of the Disk, its language, history, perhaps some literature and philosophy. But always, *always* they teach the horrors it reveals about a race of people making every mistake along the road of their cultural development. Some call it fright tactics, but it's kept peace throughout the Council for thousands of years. Outside of the occasional bout of civil unrest, or attempted invasion, or twisted soul such as I, of course. It served the people of Zurai and the Eastern half of the Milky Way much as your own so-called myths served your Earthim societies."

"The only difference being that you liztened."

"Yes."

Dr. Menace shook her head. "Still, I do not underztand. If the human race were to send such a mezzage acrozz the cozmos, we would not be capable of such a feat for centuriez, perhapz another millennia, hopefully one involving lezz hype. So why would a human society from the future send extenzive documentation of the prezent Earth to an alien civilization tenz of thouzandz of yearz in the pazt on the other side of the galaxy?"

Nihel shrugged while examining yet another piece of Evil: Equipment. "You Earthim are an odd lot. Maybe your future selves wished to warn other civiliza-tions of the horrors they would likely face and took preventative measures in the hopes of maturing their enemies beyond the primal need for empty ambitions and self-defeating competition ages before ever encountering them. Maybe this era of your own history proved to most apt at providing examples of what not to do."

"Soundz far fetched, but I suppoze that could be it."

Nihel let out a laugh, like he had uncovered some secret folly that amused him.

"What?"

"I'm sorry," he said, moving on to a model of the Evil: Negaflux Earth Movers that were to put Antarctica into tropical waters and flood every coastal city in the world if not for the bungling interference of that blasted Nuklear Dolt. "I don't know what I was thinking. I suppose the news is still new to my mind. But it's impossible."

"I admit that it waz stretching thingz, but I wouldn't say it iz impozzible. Ezpecially given that I am talking to an alien."

"No, it's not that." He looked at the Defusionizer Cannon. "Interesting."

She sat down at her Evil: Computer and leaned one arm on the console, her fingers idly played with a few keys. "That iz my Nega Cannon," she explained. "It uzes my theoriez of Negaflux fieldz to inject a target with counter productive Intrinzity and then stabilizez the rezulting matrix."

The cannon was torn apart, its myriad pieces suspended as Nihel walked around it with intent stares given to several vital areas. "Causing the subject to be in a sort of suspended animation. Indefinitely, it would seem."

"Yez, until another blazt neutralizez the effectz of the firzt. I uzed it to capture my rogue, though it waz originally intended to strike down my archnemeziz Nuklear Man by nullifying hiz powerz from the inzide."

"Ah," he answered only half listening. "Did you know that with only a few alterations, this device could be engineered to utterly obliterate anything it fired upon? Simply increase the degree to which the target's Intrinsity is canceled until you reach the critical point and its destroyed instead of merely frozen in place. Amazing."

"Yez, well. That izn't terribly moral. I am evil, not cruel."

"I've seen warships with less destructive force. Honestly. And yet this tiny weapon could destroy them all, given a suitable power source. The energy input is really the only limitation to this weapon's destructive potential."

"But back to the matter at hand, why would it be impozzible for future humanz to send the dizk?"

"Oh, it's quite simple," he reassembled the cannon in an instant. "I probably shouldn't be telling you this, but at this point I don't see that it'll really matter. You see, this galaxy will be destroyed long before these Earthim of the future have the chance to exist. So they'll never have the chance to send it."

"Why iz thiz?" her hand casually made for a button on her Evil: Computer Console. *Stand still for me, my stranger. No sudden movements.*

"Well, you see," he answered. "We have found Arel." He smiled triumphantly. "We found him. And once he is back in our fold, we will do as we were designed."

"Arel?"

"Yes. Arel."

"What iz an Arel?"

He smiled. "Power. More to the point, the power to give us power."

"I do not underztand."

"I wouldn't expect you to. Suffice it to say that, celestial politics being what they are, there are those of us who are trapped with a fate that we cannot escape. Or rather, that we are not *meant* to escape.

"There are two basic kinds of power in the universe. Power over reality and power over destiny. What you would identify as gods have the former, whereas you mortals have the latter. That's the only distinction between us. That's it. It's something cruel you know, to be given so much physical power and yet be unable to exercise even an iota of it of your own free will.

"It's one thing if you're at least given the choice. Power or free will? Odin had the choice, and he damned us all with his ambitions and the madness it infected him with. He chose and sealed *all* our fates!" Nihel had become livid, every sentence was punctuated by sharp, quick gestures. "But at least he made a choice! It's quite another thing when even that, the most basic and fundamental choice— power or free will—is made *for* you! Can you imagine grasping the reigns of the universe, shaking the very loom of the fabrics of reality and not being able to do a damn thing with it!"

Dr. Menace tried to answer.

"*No!* You do not! You have no idea what you've been given. *We* do." He panted. "We do." Eyes closed, a long breath in and out of his nose. Nihel spoke again. "Most accept their fate as just that. Fate. A few deny it. Odin, for instance, has been driven mad in his quest for knowledge, his vain attempt to find some great cosmic loop hole. But there are those of us, namely Arel, his patron, and myself, who fight it. You see, it's all rather simple. He is Arel, the true name of fire. Why he hadn't thought of it sooner...well, he must've. Probably just endured his tortures to bide his time until Arel could become manifest, when no one was watching. When Fate assumed its course had been irreversibly set. Yes. Arel is living flame. In a purely material sense, his power is difficult to comprehend."

Dr. Menace, feeling that her guest had wound down enough to allow her to interrupt, did. "How so?"

"He is fueled by every fire in the galaxy. One star would have been an incredible source, a being of legends. But all of them? To have your very essence surging with the eternal power of every star of a galaxy? Could you even begin to understand the sheer scope of it?" His eyes were far away, his voice dripping with respect and awe. "But no lesser power could fulfill his destiny. Nothing less could destroy the galaxy and overthrow Fate. And it is this, this which is Arel's true power. And it is without limit."

"And juzt where did you find thiz Arel of yourz?"

"Here, among you Erthim. Ironic, that the one thing which will tear the galaxy into cosmic ribbons is found on the one world which united it in the first place." He let out another laugh. "And to think that you Earthim have been utterly ignorant of your roles as both the mother and the destroyer of a mighty civilization that spans the stars you only dream of." A bitter laugh. "Fate is truly mad."

Keep him talking. Juzt a moment longer while the senzors lock on, "I find it difficult to believe that a being of that much power could be on Earth for any amount of time without it being diszcovered or exploited in zome way."

"You needn't look far, Dr. Menace, for Arel has been with your people for some time now. You may even know of him. I witnessed his visage on several of your media broadcasts during my brief examination of your culture while in transit. He wears my emblem upon his chest."

She knew before he had finished speaking. "Nuklear Man," she gasped. "That's Nuklear Man's symbol."

"The thorn in your side, eh? This becomes more and more interwoven, almost as though someone is behind it all," the last bit more to himself than Menace. "At any rate, it is a shame you didn't get to use your Nega Cannon against him. Perhaps it would not be taking my lieutenants so long to collect him."

Nuklear Man, some mysterious disk containing incredible amounts of information concerning Earth; Arel, this Nihel, the electron orbited N zymbol, ten years ago...Nuklear Man. "Wait. Can you," her fingers fumbled in the air for a second. "Can you show me what it lookz like? The dizk. Surely you've zeen it."

"Of course. Its contents have been the basis of Zurai's culture for millennia." He summoned up the expansive and mostly uncleaned warehouse's supply of dust and coalesced the tiny particles into a rotating three dimensional model. It looked something like two dinner plates placed together so their bottoms faced out. "Would you prefer color?"

"No. That won't be necezzary," she said in a whisper. "That iz one of Überdyne'z Social Readjuztment Devices."

"Oh?"

"They were librariez of information about specific societies. We would give them to severe amnesiacz who would participate with the interactive holographic interface until they remembered their pazt. It had a dictionary, several sets of encyclopedia, scientific articles, hiztory, philozophy. The idea waz that the patient would become so immerzed in the pazt that it might unlock memoriez of when the information waz firzt learned and from thoze beginningz, one could start to piece together one'z forgotten life."

Nihel nodded. "Archaic, but interesting."

"I waz still at Überdyne when we gave one of them to Nuklear Man soon after finding him in the rubble of the Dragon's Strike." She paused. "He waz already familiar with the majority of the material it contained, but he never recovered any memoriez." She laughed at herself. "We immediately dizmizzed the notion that he waz not of thiz Earth when he demonztrated such well-rounded knowledge of our hiztory. 'How elze could he know?' we asked ourzelvez. Only a native would be zo fluent in modern culture." She barely contained one of her trademark cackles. "But of course he knew it all, it had been ingrained in him long ago by an identical device that had made itz way to the other side of time and space!"

"Severe amnesia, you say?" Nihel rubbed his chin. "That must be what has stalled our progress. Variel and the others are probably informing him of his true identity now. I would not be surprised if it took a fair amount of convincing." He let out a satisfied sigh. "Well, Dr. Menace, your company has been most intriguing and enlightening. But I'm afraid that I came here with a purpose in mind and I cannot survey this city of yours by sitting here. And you said I should hurry if I want to get to this mall of yours before the dreaded highschoolers."

"I'm afraid you can't go."

"Oh? And why is that?"

She pushed a button on her Evil: Console and a sphere of rippling royal purple energy encased Nihel. "You zee, it will do me no good to take over thiz world if you intend to deztroy it. I won't let that happen."

He smiled at her. His eyes scanned the room as he spoke. "Dear child, you cannot hope to tamper with what we have set into motion." His voice seemed to regard her as an insolent yet harmless pet. A Negaflux field generator rained from the ceiling piece by piece. Each of its parts fell to the floor aligned into a perfect square, each piece carefully set in ascending order of size an equal distance from its neighbors. Needless to say, Nihel was free. "Good day, Doctor," he said with a genuine smile. "Most individuals merely cower in fear upon the mere mention of my name. It has been an exquisite pleasure meeting you." He bowed, turned, and left through the huge iron door.

Dr. Menace sat at her Evil: Computer forever. Seconds, hours, years, minutes. They were the same. "Well. Shit."

Issue 52—We Have Reached an Accord

Dr. Genius stared out the wide panoramic window near the Scientific: Communications Panel. It overlooked the Earth as it raced along the razor's edge of gravity. A battle on its surface was displayed on one of the Panel's video screens. The details were barely visible, indistinct images, colors flashing and zooming in Dr. Genius' periphery vision.

"This is what you meant, isn't it?" she said aloud, turning to face the body that used to belong to Yuriko and then, for a period of a few brief hours, Psiko. She thought she ought to have felt some sort of pride for Yuriko's transformation. In a way, it was her plan to do the same for the rest of humanity to save them from themselves. To lift them from their self-imposed mundanity, fear, and loneliness. "This is what it's like." But she could only feel contempt. "Miles and miles away from the nearest living thing, interacting with them only through a small and limited device. I'm in orbit, I'm at the dinner table of my childhood. I have to use this idiotic computer, I have to use language. It's been there all along, but I needed these extreme conditions to sharpen my awareness of it. And now I know, I know that I am no different than anyone else. I am no more alone than they are down there, and they are no less alone than I."

She pushed herself closer to Psiko's prone body. "Of course, I suppose we all have a common ground now. We've got you floating around in each of us. Watching. Recording. Voyeur to the gods, eh? Just what medium propagates the wave of your powers, Psiko? What is a mind, what is a computer, what are the television and radio signals you rode across the globe? Is it something to do with the electromagnetic spectrum? That would parallel Nuklear Man's powers in a way." She stared into Psiko's vacant eyes. "Too simplistic. Besides, it doesn't address the issue of the concentration on minds, databases, information." Her gaze went beyond the body before her. "Hm. Information. What is KI if not information? What is a consciousness if not a collection of information that is self aware. Even dogs and cats know that they are separate from each other and their masters. Perhaps even simpler forms of life have similar, if less articulated, knowledge of themselves. A computer is simply information, as are radio and television signals. But so too is DNA. And what of the other side of the spectrum? Psiko knows the Earth like no one has ever known. What previously untapped stores of information has she received from our world? And what about its connections with the solar system? All KI is interwoven throughout the universe. How far can she see? Is she already a universal observer? If not, is it a merely a matter of time? If so, is there any reason or means to distinguish her from the universe itself? Would we even be able to comprehend her, or vice versa? Have I unlocked a cosmic horror? A local anomaly? Are there others of her kind? Too many questions. No. Distractions, really. There is only one question. What is KI? All answers will flow from that like an avalanche, an unfettered destruction of ignorance, impossible to stop."

She turned to face the Scientific: Communications Panel. One monitor was a window to the war torn downtown Metroville. "Unless of course there is no humanity left to ascend." She pushed herself back to the Scientific: Communications Panel. "Nuklear Man seems to have the situation under control, in so much as his antagonists haven't left the scene. And with Nameless' team suppressing and/or altering any attempts by the local media to broadcast the event, things may well go in our favor after all. I still worry about that sixth probe. Well, that sixth alien. Where is he? What is he doing?"

The screen flashed white and then filled with static.

Dr. Genius huffed. *Well, assuming the worst, Nameless will no longer be able to control the media from on site. Luckily, all the local stations use Überdyne owned or manufactured broadcast equipment and satellites. We couldn't cause a total media blackout without rousing interest or panic, of course. Two things I wish to avoid. We don't need another bout of hysteria, it'd be like Superion all over again. Still, we'll be able to instigate a few layers of revision thanks to the filters I implemented after that fiasco. A few details about the fight downtown will inevitably be leaked by doing things this way. It's unavoidable in order to maintain the appearance that everything is relatively normal. After all, a news report about Nuklear Man battling some force of costumed evil isn't anything new to these people. They'll probably ignore it for the most part unless things get out of hand, by which time it'll be too late. The only problem is that I won't be able to recreate any truth after the fact. It'll have to conform to the recorded data. It's limiting.*

I hate limits.

She stared into the static. "Let's see about hooking you up to the Watchtower's Scientific: Orbital Mapping Cameras. She whipped out her trusty electric Scientific: Screwdriver and began breaking her way into the Scientific: Communications Panel's circuitry.

*   *   *   *

"Well that's darn unfair," Nuklear Man said. The Scientific: Field Observation Van had a perfect circle burned through both of its inconspicuous side panels and all the Scientific: Equipment between them. From inside the van, Nameless Technician leaned over to look through the new ventilation only to see the backs of two Dakaels standing between himself and Nuklear Man who was still in his Plazma Beam pose.

"You think that's unfair?" the Dakael twins taunted.

"Well, yeah."

"Then wait until you face me!" the huge Kadael finished. He loomed over the Hero from behind and draped him in shadow.

"Wah?" Nuklear Man retorted before Kadael's two massive fists pounded him waist deep into the ground with one overhead blow.

"Excuse me, brother," Kadael said as he waddled past the Dakaels to the Überdyne van.

"Abort mission!" Nameless ordered. He and his crew scurried from the vehicle as the alien touched his hand to it. The van seemed to disintegrate in seconds while Kadael spontaneously grew larger.

He stretched his neck from side to side to limber up, punched a fist into the other hand and cracked his knuckles. "I'm just gettin' started," he boasted with a noticeably deeper voice. The gigantic Kadael made two long strides and stood in front of the semi-subterranean Hero. One tree trunk of a leg reared back. The other villains adverted their eyes. "Nighty night, bright boy."

"What? It's not even close to time for my afternoon nap."

WHAM!

"*Ouch!*" Kadael bellowed.

The others unadverted their eyes.

"I fink I thipped a toof," Nuklear Man mumbled through a mouthful of Kadael's enormous foot.

"Kadael!" Variel nonbarked from the perimeter of the makeshift arena that had just recently been beaten into the landscape. "Stop toying with him."

Safriel, her hands loosely on her hips, leaned to Variel. "Y'sure it's not the other way around?"

"Silence," he stated just loud enough for her and the nearby Gadriel to hear.

"I could take him," Gadriel said as he watched his comrades battle one of their former masters. "You know what'll happen if one of us beats him?"

Variel would have rolled his eyes if they were capable of expressing anything beyond a stern coldness. "Of course we do. Lord Nihel will give the victor Arel's power." He crossed his arms and they were lost within the definitionless black void of his body. "I am only letting you four fight him before myself because I find it entertaining. I have every confidence that I shall rise in rank this day."

"You think so, Var?" Safriel contested. "Even if the brothers don't beat him, and I know they won't, he'll be weakened from the encounter. And then Gadriel and I will be up to bat, as it were."

"Yeah" Gadriel chimed. "He thinks he's so tough with those Nova Powers. Feh! They'd be nothing without the electrical reactions my powers are themed on. Arel is an energy morph, the same as I. And since he isn't fully aware of his powers at the moment, it should be a simple matter for me to meld with his body and take over control of it. He doesn't stand a chance."

"We shall see," Variel said, his voice an intake of sound.

"My plan is to let ol' Gad here wear him down a little more and then I'll step in for the killing blow and take the prize."

"That's cheating!" Gadriel protested.

"It's also cunning," Variel said with a proud nod to Safriel.

"Hell. I'm not going to be someone else's ticket to success." Gadriel's body became living electricity in a brilliant white flash and in the blink of an eye he was rocketing to the battle.

"Impetuous," Variel observed.

"Not to mention as good as dead."

"Lord Nihel can always resurrect him. Painfully, I should imagine."

Gadriel's lightning body slammed into the Hero's back and knocked him forward like someone gave him a hard push.

"Hey!" Nuklear Man yelled as he regained his balance and turned around. "No fair shovin'!"

Safriel let out an amused, "Heh. I thought he would've at least lasted like a minute or something."

"Apparently our comrade did not count on the fact that Arel metabolizes energy. His attempt to take over Arel's mind had as much a likelihood of success as a head of cabbage would have in the same endeavor," Variel reasoned, his voice bellowing inward.

"When do I get a piece of the action?"

"When either Kadael or Dakael falls."

"Dammit. Dak's got him on the ropes. It's no fair he gets to be his own army."

"Patience."

*   *   *   *

Dr. Genius's legs stuck out from the Scientific: Communications Panel as she wriggled inside to make a few changes. Tools tied down with string bobbed in their weightlessness. The job was half down, or so she reckoned.

Who knows what's occurred so far? Who knows what'll have happened by the time I finish?

She heard the beep of an incoming message, only she didn't know it at first. It took several beeps for her mind to reconcile that there were beeps being beeped even though she Scientific: Communications Panel's power was shut down so she could crawl into it and mess around with the hardware without dying of an electrical shock. The instant she realized the beeps were real, she froze in terror. "What if I forgot to shut off the power?" A moment passed. "Impossible. I would've been fried when I redirected the Scientific: Power Couplings." She crawled out, straightened her lab coat as well as she could without gravity to help out, and hit the Accept button.

HELLO, DOCTOR, was typed across one of the screens.

"I should've known," Dr. Genius grumbled. "What's the matter? Speaking through my mind is too demeaning for you now?"

I'M AFRAID FOR YOU IT WOULD BE THE MENTAL EQUIVALENT OF STARING INTO THE SUN. I AM STILL GROWING, SPLINTERING ACROSS INFINITE POINTS OF VIEW. I THINK I AM SLIPPING AWAY FROM MYSELF. I MAY BE EXPERIENCING WHAT YURIKO DID IN HER FINAL MOMENTS. I MAY BE FALLING APART. I MAY BE MULTIPLE ENTITIES. I AM FINDING IT MORE AND MORE DIFFICULT TO DEFINE MYSELF.

"You know, using nothing but caps is a social faux pas these days. It's considered to be yelling."

IF YOU COULD HEAR ME, I WOULD BE.

"I don't have time for this."

ONLY BECAUSE YOUR POINT OF VIEW IS TOO NARROW. I CAN SEE SO MUCH. AND DO YOU KNOW WHAT I HAVE DISCOVERED?

"Of course not. You know that."

YOUR GOD, IF THERE IS SUCH A THING, IS LISTENING. HE SIMPLY CAN'T DO ANYTHING ABOUT IT. HE CAN'T INTERFERE. NOT WITHOUT TIPPING THE SCALES, NOT WITHOUT IMPOSING HIS WILL ABOVE YOUR OWN. ANY ACTION WOULD STRIP FREE WILL FROM AT LEAST ONE OTHER BEING. HE CANNOT, WILL NOT, DO THAT. IT GOES AGAINST THE WHOLE IDEA.

"And yet there you are. Taking an action, sharing with me. Distracting me."

I NEVER SAID I WAS PARTICULARLY MORAL. OF COURSE, THERE IS AN ALTERNATIVE TO THE ABOVE. THIS GOD OF YOURS, INSTEAD OF REMAINING MORALLY IMPARTIAL, IS VICIOUSLY MEDDLING. HE INTERFERES WITH COUNTLESS MORTAL AFFAIRS TO SPECIFICALLY DENY THE FREE WILL YOU BELIEVE YOURSELVES TO HAVE. AT THE MOMENT, I'M UNCERTAIN AS TO WHICH IS THE TRUTH.

"Well, I appreciate our little philosophical talks, but I thought you said you were leaving us to our own devices so you could do your recording or some nonsense."

YES. BUT I THINK I HAVE A CERTAIN FONDNESS FOR YOU, DOCTOR. THOUGH I DO FIND YOUR MOTIVES MISGUIDED AND YOUR WORKS TO BE THOSE OF A MOST TWISTED NATURE, I AM NONETHELESS INDEBTED TO YOU FOR BRINGING ME INTO EXISTENCE BY THESE VERY TRAITS. THIS EXISTENCE, IT'S VERY SOOTHING.

"Soothing. You know, I don't think I've ever heard someone say they found existence soothing."

IT IS A LIMITATION OF YOUR SINGULAR POINTS OF VIEW. FROM HERE, EVERYTHING FITS INTO ITS PLACE. IT ISN'T ORDERED, IT ISN'T RANDOM, BUT IT IS WONDERFUL TO BEHOLD. THE UNIVERSE IS A THING OF STRANGE SYMMETRY, AN UNPARALLELED BEAUTY. IT SOUNDS A LOT LIKE HENDRIX.

"Fair enough."

EVOLUTION IS A MARVELOUSLY SINISTER DANCE.

"Excuse me?"

EVOLUTION. ALL LIFE, THE WAY THAT YOU UNDERSTAND LIFE TO BE, IS A BY-PRODUCT OF FORCES BEYOND YOUR SCALE TO PERCEIVE.

"You were just talking about God and free will. Don't these 'forces' of yours take something away from that?"

DOES IT? IT'S BECOME DIFFICULT TO SEE CONTRADICTORY STATEMENTS AS ANYTHING MORE THAN DIFFERENT FACETS OF ONE ANOTHER.

"Have you finished with me?"

FOR NOW. DOES MY PRESENCE BOTHER YOU?

"Why do you ask me questions you already know the answers to?"

No answer.

"I've got work to do."

*   *   *   *

"Hey there, Sparky," Rachel said, her backpack slung across one bare shoulder.

Good ol' tank tops, Atomik Lad thought to himself as he approached her. *Especially when they're a tad too tight.* "Hey yourself, cutie." *Even more especially with jean shorts.* "Miss me?"

"More than I would miss my own breath."

"Well, aim more carefully next time."

She gave him a playful punch in the shoulder.

"Remember. You have to squeeze the trigger. Pulling the trigger is too jerky, it makes for inaccurate shots," he advised.

"Uh-huh. You ready or what?"

"Yup."

"We could just fly over there, you know."

"What's the rush? We've got half an hour before we're supposed to meet the guys for lunch."

"All the on-campus traffic, then the lunch hour traffic when we get into town. And then there's the long walk to my car in the first place."

"Okay, okay. We'll fly to the car. How's that?"

She slinked up to him and slid her arms around his waist. "You're so good to me," she whispered less than a breath away from his ear.

The ex-sidekick's body transmuted into a soft, pliable goo.

Well, most of it anyway. "Ahem." He held her at arms' length. "It's hard uh, to concentrate when you're that close."

"You're so adorable when you're overwhelmed. C'mon. Let's get this show on the road already."

Wings of crimson fire wrapped around them in an amorphous blotch of turbulent energy that took them into the air.

*   *   *   *

Minutes later, trapped like damned souls in hell, "So traffic sucks," Rachel observed with one hand on the wheel and the other on the gearshift.

"It ain't so bad," Atomik Lad said. He was leaning so far back in his seat that he was practically reclining in the backseat.

"And what makes you say that?"

His eyes closed, smile beaming, his hand hovered over the gearshift and rest on her hand. "It keeps us here together a little longer. Can't complain about that."

"No . No I guess I can't." She lifted their hands and kissed the back of his. "Of course, someone's going to do a lot of complaining once he gets his ass kicked beyond all recognition at Turbo Fighter."

"Oh, I think not."

"Then you are a poor, deluded fool," she retorted.

"You're just making it worse for yourself," he warned.

"You are."

"No, you are."

Motionless minutes passed in silence, in as much as being stuck in traffic can be silent.

"You are," Rachel said in the disguise of a cough.

They simultaneously burst into laughter.

*   *   *   *

Dr. Genius restored power to the Danger: Communications Panel. Its screens showed a dozen views of the Earth. Each one focused at a different altitude. It would take a few minutes to get them aimed at Metroville to observe the action below.

The Incoming Message beep beeped again. Dr. Genius cringed. "Haven't we done this enough already?" she asked with a push of the Accept button.

"I don't recall doing thiz before," Dr. Menace responded, her dimly lit face filling one of the screens.

"Veronica!" Genius blurt. "This is a secure line, how did you gain access?"

"I have my ways. You'd be surprized."

"I don't have time for another of your mad schemes for world domination right now. I'll trace your signal and dispatch Nuklear Man immediately if you persist."

"I doubt very highly that you could do either. For one, I'm uzing Überdyne'z own network to speak with you, zo I don't think your traze will get too far out of the old office. And zecondly, I would think the Nuklear Boob iz too buzy battling the five alienz to have time for little old me."

"How did you know...?"

"Ima, you can't truly be so arrogant az to think that I do not have certain connectionz to Überdyne'z systems. How do you think I manage to have equipment and planz that are specifically dezigned to counteract your own devices every time I emerge from hiding?"

"I don't have time for your gloating either. The world could be in terrible danger."

"You have no idea, Ima. You recall the sixth alien, no?"

"Of course."

"I spent some time converzing with him."

"You what!"

"He waz very polite and well verzed in Earth hiztory. I have a plan to deztroy him and Nuklear Man but I will need your help to do it."

"Destroy Nuklear Man? That's madness. He's the only chance we've got against these aliens. I'll take no part in such a plan."

"You will think differently when you hear what the alien told me."

"Why should I trust you?"

"Becauze the fate of the galaxy iz at stake. And if Nuklear Man and hiz friendz succeed at what they intend to do, there will be no more Earth for uz to fight over. Thiz iz much, much bigger than you have imagined."

"I don't believe you."

"I think you do. But it iz no matter, you don't have to take my vord for it. I will upload my zecurity footage of the alien telling me everything and you will hear for yourzelf the horrible truth."

The upload took all of two seconds. Dr. Genius had only to push a button to view it. "It doesn't make sense. Why would he tell you his plan?"

Dr. Menace gave a little laugh. "It'z very simple, my dear," she said. "He iz a villain. That iz what we do when we know that we have already won."

Dr. Genius stared at the Upload Complete message.

"Watch the video. Then we will dizcuss the plan." The screen went blank.

Psiko, Veronica. Too many people know too much already. She hit the Open button.

And watched.

ISSUE 53—EVERYDAY MONSTERS

Nuklear Man was four deep in a group of twenty Kadaels. Each one of them wore a confident sneer as the Golden Guardian scratched his chin in contemplation while making the occasional "Hm" sound.

"Ah ha!" the Hero proclaimed. He hopped into a martial arts style stance and stared straight into the eyes of the Kadael in front of him. The air seemed to spark with the intensity generated by their unblinking, unflinching tough guy stares.

In a golden flash of motion, Nuklear Man's fist struck the Kadael directly behind him. The Hero posed for a second, locked in that instant of impact, the fighting equivalent of doing a little jig in the endzone after a touchdown, while uttering a just audible, "Waaaaaah."

The Kadaels were still smiling.

Nuklear Man turned around. "Oh man." There were now twenty-one Kadaels. "Statistically speaking, this has to work. Eventually."

"C'mon Kadael!" The enormous Dakael called from the sidelines while leaning against a cement truck. "Either finish him off or give 'em to me to play with." He tapped the truck's cab. "I've got plans an' stuff."

"Yeah, yeah," a Kadael yelled back. "Just wait your turn. We're having too much fun."

"Besides," another said. "You don't have a chance!"

"Ah ha," Nuklear Man announced. "I've got it this time." He raised one arm high and bonked it hard onto a Kadael's head, thus producing the twenty-second foe. "Well. Darn it."

They collectively dog piled the Hero. He disappeared under their girth. "Ow!" Nuklear Man protested. "You're standing on my arm!"

"Sorry," one replied. The pressure abated.

"Thanks."

"But *we're* not!" Several new Kadael's stood on Nuklear Man's arm.

"Meanies!" he whimpered in the midst of being pummeled by the group of clone villains.

*   *   *   *

Dr. Genius watched one of the Scientific: Communications Panel's screens as Nihel exited Dr. Menace's Evil: Lair and then it ended in static.

"Well?" Dr. Menace said from a neighboring screen. "Do you believe me now?"

Dr. Genius stared into and, for an instant she thought just maybe *through*, the static. "I suppose I have no choice," she said without looking away. Her hair and lab coat swayed in the zero gravity. "The totality of the video's contents are so completely unbelievable on their own that there's no chance that this is an attempt to lure me into a position of weakness since none of it makes any sense whatsoever and you'd know better. Therefore, it must be the truth. But what a truth it is."

"Good. Now then, Nihel needz Arel in order to carry out hiz planz to deztroy the galaxy. Thiz, we cannot allow. Therefore, we muzt deztroy Arel."

"Nuklear Man," Ima corrected, still unable to remove her gaze from the frothing of gray video nothing. "His name is Nuklear Man."

Dr. Menace shook her head. "He iz Arel. He alwayz waz Arel. Hiz time here az your Nuklear Man waz a miztake."

"But was it a mistake? Now that we are operating under the assumption that Nihel's words are truth, then he and Nuklear Man are gods and the gods abide by fate. Maybe this was part of the bigger picture all along. Maybe Nuklear Man was meant to come to us to become something more than a destroyer."

"I conzidered that az well, Ima. But Arel'z whole point iz to go againzt fate. He iz a random element in the schemes of the univerze. He exiztz only to deztroy. You have to accept that he muzt die if we are to survive. Afterwardz, you can even say that he gave hiz life to defend uz againzt Nihel and hiz minionz. That way, public opinion of the remaining heroez will be high and you may continue your experimentz on them. I will not interfere."

Dr. Genius faced her one time co-worker and long time rival. "I know. You're right. If we are to continue our works, we have to eliminate him. Arel."

"And Nihel."

"Yes. With his power, he could certainly stand in our respective ways."

"Or pozzibly deztroy the planet outright. I got the impression it would not be hiz firzt."

"I agree. So how do we eliminate two variables from this equation?"

"I have a plan in mind, but I am willing to lizten to any ideaz from your end firzt. Mine iz a bit dangerouz."

"Well," Dr. Genius said. "The video does explain Nuklear Man's weakness to temperatures in excess of nuclear fusion."

"In what way?"

"He draws his strength from that of the stars. It's all KI transfer. The actual energy isn't drawn into him so much as the Intrinsity of it or the idea of it. It's hard to explain."

"So I gathered, but I believe I follow your meaning."

"The point is, only stars naturally produce fusion. So the only way to succumb to this weakness is if he were exposed to a star directly. It would produce something like a feedback loop. It would be analogous to trying to breathe your own blood through your stomach. Only on a much larger scale likely involving big explosions. Simply put, it's fatal to him."

"Interezting. But why have that one weaknezz?"

"It may have been some sort of failsafe. Nuklear Man's, or rather Arel's creator, whoever that was, might have thought that due to his unpredictable nature, Arel would have the potential to turn against him. Therefore, built into his very nature is a weakness that only the creator knows about. Alternatively, one can assume that this weakness is simply part of the package. A side-effect of drawing one's strength from the stars. Besides, an entity with Arel's degree power probably wouldn't have to worry about being forced into anything involuntarily, much less being tossed into a star." Dr. Genius paused for a moment. "My god, Veronica. He draws his power from every star in the galaxy. Do you have any idea the scale of power we're talking about?"

"Roughly 300 billion starz produzing an average of 1,440,000 trillion trillion joules an hour comes out to 1.2×10^{27} gigawattz per second. Give or take."

Dr. Genius sighed. "The very fabrics of space and time are completely unraveled long before that degree of power. Reality would become too unstable for anything to exist under that much energy. It boggles the mind."

"And thiz iz what ve have to fight."

"Well. Fusion, ironically enough, is his weakness. I'd suggest dropping a hydrogen bomb on him, but that's essentially what happened when we found him. It would probably take prolonged exposure to those temperatures to harm him."

"Of courze. I hadn't thought of that. Somehow, for some reazon, he waz at or near the Metroville Nuclear Power Plant when the Dragon cauzed the meltdown."

"And he absorbed the radiation and heat of the fusion reaction, accidentally saving us all, and apparently damaging his memory in the process."

"A second bomb may prove uzeful, but only az a diversionary tactic."

"Yes. He'd be stunned, at best. The loss of memory was probably a million to once chance. Anything else?"

"We could tozz him into the zun."

"And just how do you propose to keep him still during the ninety-eight million mile trip to his doom? One of your Negaflux fields?"

"A good idea, but you saw what Nihel did when I trapped him in one. I'm sure Arel could do the same if pressed. Besides, without an external generator feeding energy into the zyztem, a Negaflux field will collapze in time."

"Ah yes. We're only keeping Superion locked up by hooking the conflicting Negaflux fields in him to some recharging devices. Even if we could capture either of them like that, Nihel could dismantle the equipment with but a thought."

"Then exploiting Arel'z one weaknezz provez impozzible, even for uz."

"It would seem so."

"I waz afraid of thiz. We may have to employ my plan."

"What is it?"

"My plan iz to canzel them out. Az it were."

"Go on."

"I had every inztrument and senzor available to me pointed at Superion and Nuklear Man during their final confrontation, az I'm sure you did."

Ima nodded.

"I learned a few thingz about the Nega Critical Point, thankz to Superion opening up a gravitational singularity. Ever since their battle, I have been working up some new Negaflux equationz. I believe that, simply by modifying the equipment I have here, I could eazily conztruct what I call a 'Nega Bomb' in a relatively short period of time."

"Nega Bomb?"

"Frankly, it iz a dreadful conzept. Thiz would be a weapon of such dezign that it iz capable of utterly deztroying the reality within itz radiuz of effect. Anything falling under its influence would be erased by completely counter-acting all KI within itz range through a chain reaction of Intrinzic Negation."

"How?"

"It moztly reliez on Complimentary Field Amplification. I got the idea from Superion. The Negaflux fieldz would unweave reality itzelf by exactly counteracting all KI within the blazt radiuz. Thiz iz beyond a trifle act of deztruction. Thiz iz beyond a simple explosion. Thiz iz beyond even obliterating matter. Thiz bomb negatez reality at itz very zource. You could say, without exaggeration, that thiz weapon deztroyz zoulz."

"That's hideous."

"Yez. And itz side-effectz, though much lezz appalling, are fittingly cruel. It would forever scar the world by leaving something of a wormhole in itz wake. After the bomb haz detonated and done itz horrid work, anything traveling through one side of the affected area would instantly find itzelf on the other side since there iz no reality in between to get in the way. Unlike a bomb's crater or radiation, thiz will never go away. It will alwayz remain az an undeniable reminder of our atrocity. By uzing thiz weapon, we would not only be killing, we would be slaughtering souls. Thiz iz a crime mozt heinous."

"As horrible as this device may be, there are ways around anyone ever finding out about it. We do what we have to do. Now, where do I come in?"

"There iz a problem."

"I'm listening."

"You see, the functional range of thiz weapon at the minimal amount of energy required for it to function would be several hundred thouzand miles. The Earth itzelf would be swallowed up in the blazt, which is quite counter-productive to our rezpective goalz."

"True."

"So I need you to conztruct some sort of barrier, a wall of Intrinzity which the blazt cannot exzeed. Plaze thiz barrier around Nihel and Arel, plaze the Nega Bomb within the barrier, throw the switch, and bamf, they and the very space around them are no more."

"Your plan is all well and good, but if this bomb of yours simply eats up KI, then how am I supposed to stop it using KI?"

"That iz what you have that renowned intellect for."

Dr. Genius frowned.

"Yez, well. Given the extreme nature of the conzequencez of our mission, I will offer my own expertize in the area of Negaflux Theory to help in thiz endeavor."

"Weight of the world again, eh?

"Hm. Old timez are here again and all that."

"Upload the schematics for the bomb to me. I assume you've done simulations of the blast itself."

"Of courze."

"I'll need those too."

"Then let uz get to work."

✳   ✳   ✳   ✳

Three Kadaels pinned down each of Nuklear Man's limbs. Five others kicked him mercilessly in the ribs while the last five perpetrated such heinous acts as flipping his ears, poking his stomach, and doing that thing where you dangle a thread of spit over someone's face before sucking it back up.

"No more—ouch—I can't take it—ew—Please, for the love of Plazma, stop!"

"Well dammit," Safriel cursed from a distance. "Kadael's got him."

"The battle is not yet concluded," Variel unsaid, his silvery eyes seeming to squint ever so slightly.

"Yeah, you better hope so."

"We will see."

The Kadaels snickered amongst themselves while maneuvering into new positions to deliver their particular brand of torture. Five Kadaels now pinned both of the Hero's legs to the ground while two groups of five others had a hold of each arm. The last two simply stood by his head and leaned into Nuklear Man's field of view with devilish upside-down smirks.

"Are, are you guys finished with me?" Nuklear Man asked while obviously holding back tears.

"Not quite," the two Kadaels looming over him said in unison.

"That's really creepy the way you guys talk at the same time." Nuklear Man felt his arms move against his will. He resisted, yet the forces animating his arms were impossibly strong. "Herg!" the Hero strained with all his Nuklear Might. "What, what are you doing?!"

Nuklear Man began hitting himself.

*   *   *   *

The Mall! Acres of green, fertile land transformed into something useful! The Mall! A beautifully ornate mass of buildings that seemingly grew into one another in ancient times! The Mall! A place of magic! The Mall! Where everything has an exclamation point and it's okay!

Rachel circled the Mall parking lot. "How can there be so many people here? It's not even noon yet and I can't find a decent spot anywhere!"

Atomik Lad finally unreclined his seat to have himself a look-see. "Wow. It's almost as bad as parking on campus."

"I wouldn't go that far," she grumbled.

"Yeah, there's no need to exaggerate the situation. There is nothing worse than parking on campus."

"I'm just taking the next spot that opens up," she said resolutely. "So there, foul parking devils."

*   *   *   *

"Ouch! Hey!" Nuklear Man protested uselessly.

"Quit hitting yourself, quit hitting yourself," the twin Kadaels taunted. "Why are you hitting yourself? It doesn't make sense to hit yourself! Maybe you should stop hitting yourself."

"I'm not!" The Hero said as ten Kadaels pummeled his fists against his torso.

"But you are. Don't you see? Only a crazy person would keep hitting himself."

"I'm not crazy!"

"Oh, but you must be. Because you won't stop hitting yourself."

"I'm not hitting myself!!!"

"But you are. It's behavior that is contradictory to one's own interests. No one likes to be hit, yet you are doing it to yourself. Why is that? Why can't you tell us? Perhaps it is because you are so crazy from hitting yourself."

"They're making me do it!"

"No, don't you see? They're trying to stop you. Why do you insist on hitting yourself? You can't fight back if you're hitting yourself."

What little grasp Nuklear Man had on the reality outside himself snapped.

*   *   *   *

"We're gonna be late," Angus grumbled as his beard swayed in a breeze of motion.

"You know how Shiro is," Norman said as he pulled up next to the Surly Scot.

"Aye, Ah do. But it doon't make no sense!"

"I think that's part of it." He started to fall behind Angus. "Besides, these rickshaw things are pretty cool. Plus, we're practically flying past traffic."

Their three speedy rickshaws bounced along the sidewalk to the mall. The vehicular traffic filling the roads next to them was barely motile.

"Ah still say we're gonna be late."

"He likes to travel in the tradition of his ancestors."

"He ain't even *Chinese*!" Angus yelled.

"Hai!" Shiro chimed from Angus's left. "Time of brothers. The now is inflation with positivities."

The Mall's Managerial Tower was just visible up ahead. It pierced the horizon and rose into the sky like a blade thrust in slow motion at the nasty ol' happy clouds above.

"We're gonna be late."

*   *   *   *

All he knew was the maddening and never ending cycle of hitting himself. Had there ever been a time before hitting himself? Was there anything in existence outside of hitting himself? He could see the great vistas of the universe, horizons stretching beyond infinity and looping back into one another as they played themselves out in his mind. Oddly enough, they looked a lot like Silly Sam.

And he was hitting himself too.

But yes, in fact, there was a universe, a vast chasm of being, and it existed only so that Nuklear Man could hit himself. Everything there ever was only existed for this one triumphant moment. The clarity of it all was blinding. He could see every particle racing to this. But as suddenly as enlightenment had dawned, it receded: banished by its own brilliance, a light extinguished from its own radiance.

Even if the universe was specifically built for this singular moment, that's all it was. A moment. There would be another immediately after it. All Nuklear Man had to do was concentrate. Just concentrate, and he could see through hitting himself.

"No!" he bellowed. The Kadaels were scattered and multiplied from the force of a spherical Plazma shockwave repelling them from Nuklear Man's self-beaten body.

He stood. And he was not hitting himself.

"Impressive" Variel remarked.

"Admit it. You're worried."

"Hm." Variel's back seemed to straighten. "The battle continues."

The Kadaels stood and brushed themselves off. "You can't win," they roared as one. "We outnumber you thirty-six to one!"

"Never tell me the odds!" Nuklear Man shot back.

They rushed Nuklear Man again. The Hero dropped to one knee and put up his hands like any given statue of Atlas as the first wave reached him. His golden spandex self was lost in the great pile of thirty or forty Kadaels. The mass of bodies jerked and was heaved up like it was a single entity. Nuklear Man held them over his head, a giant ball of squirming limbs poking out at odd angles and curses screeching out odd phrases.

"All right," he said. "I've had just about enough of you guys and your crazy hijinx." He turned to face Dakael who was still casually leaning against the cement truck. He now showed a bit more interest in the goings on. "Here ya go, hup!"

"Hm?" Dakael said.

Nuklear Man hurled his antagonist(s) at the largely built and largely surprised Dakael. The villain was eclipsed by his multiple brothers as they rocketed at him. The impact knocked them into the cement truck which merely added its mass to their own as they all tumbled out of the area with an unhealthy amount of momentum and landed out of sight.

Nuklear Man dusted off his hands. "I do hope there's more of them. 'Cause damn, that was easy. Other than the part where I was pushed to the brink of madness. But my sanity, and good looks, prevailed in the end."

"*RARG!*" Dakael thundered from off stage like an angry storm giant.

"Odd. I wonder what pissed him off," Nuklear Man said.

Dakael stomped back onto the scene. He now towered just over two stories tall. And he was damn pissed 'bout something, that's for sure.

"Oh my," Nuklear Man said while completely engulfed in the giant's shadow. "Aren't you a big fella."

"It would seem Arel has resorted to his usual cruelty," Variel observed from afar. "He used Dakael's powers of matter absorption to destroy the multiplying Kadael. A cunning maneuver indeed."

"Yeah, but now Dak is angry. And I've never seen him so juiced up before."

"No doubt Arel plans to use Dakael's rage at the ironic loss of his brother to his own advantage. If he succeeds, you may yet have your chance, Safriel."

Dakael back-fisted Nuklear Man. The Hero thought it rather absurd that the fist in question was taller than he was. "Unfair, too," he said before shooting through a collection of office buildings just outside the construction sites. He came to an abrupt halt midway between the seventh and eighth buildings. "What am I doing?!" he asked himself. "I can *fly*! I don't have to stand for this." And he shot back through the same buildings to his point of origin. Making all new holes along the way, naturally.

Dakael pulled back one massive arm and slammed his gargantuan fist into the Hero's face upon his would-be victorious return. Instead, Nuklear Man was rebounded through the same buildings as before but with even more force than his first and second trips through. Each structure was now branded with three holes on their east and west walls.

Screeching halt. Return. Four holes.

WHAM! Five holes.

Screeching halt. Six holes.

*   *   *   *

Atomik Lad and Rachel strolled through the second floor of the Metroville Mall, "No wait. We're on the third floor. I think." Atomik Lad searched the expansive Mall Map in his hands as they strolled through the endless maze of shops. "Here, take a left at this next archway."

"You sure you know how to read that thing?" Rachel asked. She leaned over and inspected the map stretched out in front of Atomik Lad.

"Well, I was doing really good at the You Are Here room. It's been downhill ever since. It's a good thing we came in at the entrance next to Game Junction. We probably never would've gotten Turbo Fighter," the glossy bright orange Game Junction bag hung in Atomik Lad's hand.

They made a left at the next archway. It was a dead end.

"Way to go, *Magellan*," Rachel said with a playful poke in the ribs.

Atomik Lad buried his face in the map. "There's supposed to be a Taco Junction right here." He peeked over the map's top. "All we've got here is some off the beaten path ATM."

"Just as well. I should get a couple bucks for lunch."

"I don't mind paying for you."

"And neither do I. I am a modern independent woman, you know." She squeezed past him even though there was more than enough room in the hall to have passed without making contact. The minx. Atomik Lad went back to his map.

Rachel stuck her ATM card into the machine and typed in her PIN. The onscreen display blinked the warning message DO NOT REMOVE CARD WHILE ACCESSING DATA. "I hadn't planned on it, thanks," she told the machine.

Atomik Lad pressed the map flat against a wall. "Okay. This should be simple. We started here," he pointed to a room clearly marked You Are Here. "And that's where I picked up this map in that treasure chest looking display. We went down the hall, past the Dungeon Master's Arcade, through the corridor, down another hall. None of those are on the map."

Rachel pocketed her money.

DO YOU WANT TO SAVE YOUR PROGRESS? the screen blinked.

"What a strange way to ask for a receipt." She hit Yes and a small slip of paper churned out of the wall telling her how many funds remained in her account. "Not bad." The receipt and her money disappeared into her pocket. She turned to Atomik Lad. "How's it comin'?"

He traced a path along the map's twisting corridors. "There is something seriously wrong with this map."

"Uh-huh, or the person reading it." She examined it. "Wait. I don't think this is right at all."

"That's what I'm saying."

"Yeah. See, we passed a Cutlery Junction and a Sunglasses Junction on the way here, but they're not on the map."

"I don't think this map is to the right floor," Atomik Lad said.

"Why would they provide a map that doesn't correspond to the floor it's located in?"

"I've heard things about the Mall Manager here," Atomik Lad said. The light directly above them flickered.

"Yeah, what's his name? Mort something, right?"

"According to this blurb on the back of the map, Mort Dakainen." He read a little further. "Says here he's Metroville's oldest citizen."

"Oh yeah! Old Mort Dakainen," Rachel said. "They always make such a big deal about his birthday because he founded the Metroville Mall. There's a parade and sales and whatever. It's huge. For a mall event, anyway."

"Check out the Mall Lore on Rach," Atomik Lad teased while reading more of the informative Scroll of Mall History.

"Shush."

"Wait, he's still having birthdays and he's the Mall Founder?"

"Yeah, so?"

"Listen to this," Atomik Lad read from the blurb. "It's the Mall's motto. 'The Metroville Mall, Giving You 98 Years of Stuff.' If he's the Mall Founder, he must be over a hundred years old. Way over."

"He's not still in charge of this place is he?"

"I think so. I made the mistake of coming here during what must've been one of those birthday things last year to buy the latest Starblaster game. I saw him giving a speech. At least, I assume it was him. It was this really old guy. I mean *really* old. He looked like an unraveled mummy propped up at a podium or something. He kept rambling on about his Sacred Treasures and weird stuff during the speech. Needless to say, I got in and got out as soon as possible."

"Well, it makes sense," Rachel said. "If he's senile anyway."

"Great. The tower's mad wizard."

"Who is also undead."

"Yeah" Atomik Lad folded up the map. "It's no good to us now, but we might need it later."

"But for now," Rachel stepped back into the main hall. "We've only our wits to guide us."

"We won't be going far, will we."

"No. No we will not."

✳   ✳   ✳   ✳

WHAM! Seventeen holes.

Screeching halt. Pause.

"I'm starting to get the impression that this isn't working the way I'd like it to." He charged up a "PLAZMAAA BEAM!" The fusion-ish ray blast through the abused buildings and struck the enlarged and enraged Dakael in his neck.

"Ow," the mountain of alien said. "That stung. Come out and fight! I'm not through with you yet!"

Unfortunately, by this time, Nuklear Man lay half buried in the rubble of the top half of a building. His latest attack had finished off what Dakael's repeated aggressions had begun. It brought down the house. And the others leading up to it as well. Nuklear Man sat among broken masonry, pipes, and an exposed girder. A sheen of dust grayed his otherwise golden demeanor. He coughed a puff of powdery mortar, fixed his hair, and jumped up with a little I'm Ready pose. A mild burst of Plazma blast the dust from his carved physique. "Oh, it's time to party."

He was a blaze of golden light arcing into the sky, through the space that had previously been occupied by the now mostly demolished office buildings, down to the construction site turned battle arena, raced across its sandy grounds, and shot straight up Dakael finishing it all up with an explosive uppercut that sent the giant off his feet and onto his back whilst utterly flattening a handful of parked dump trucks and bulldozers.

Nuklear Man set down near Dakael's feet. "The bigger they are, the harder they are to shop for." He did a few calculations in the air. "Er. No. The bigger they are, the more mass per unit of volume they have. No, that's not it. The more they, uh, eat! Well, now that one makes sense, but it hardly applies."

Dakael kicked Nuklear Man up and snatched him out of the air with one hand. He was completely engulfed in the giant's fist. "It's time to hurt, little man," he taunted.

"Mbl mm? Mm, mm Mblm mm," Nuklear Man retorted.

"Wah?" Dakael opened his clenched fist enough to uncover Nuklear Man's head.

"I said I'm not Little Man. I'm Nuklear Man. Little Man gained his powers by bombarding his body with Littleons. He was a spy hero for the Allies back in The War. He leaked information about the Nazi Deathbots to Captain Liberty. His premiere issue was #47. It was pretty cool, but his power's kinda lame."

"What're you babbling about!" Dakael roared. At his size, it was difficult to say anything without roaring.

"Nothing really, it's a basic stall tactic while I wrest my mighty arms free so's I can Plazma Beam you in the face."

"Oh no you don't." Dakael squeezed Nuklear Man even harder. It pinned the Hero's allegedly mighty arms to his sides.

"Erk!" Nuklear Man sputtered. "Well in that case, PLAZMAAA EYE-BEAMS!!!" A golden blast of energy erupted from Nuklear Man's ocular region and knocked Dakael in the face with enough force to send his head back to the ground with an earth-shaking crunch. The Golden Guardian slipped from Dakael's weakened grip and hovered above his giant foe. "Wow. I thought I was just bluffing. Sucker!"

Dakael's great hands clapped against Nuklear Man and crushed him like a fly. He even stuck to one palm like a fly too. The giant stood and examined the Nuklear Mess that was smeared across his hand.

"Hammer. Dropping it. Paaaaiiiin," he managed to say through his impact-addled mind.

Dakael peeled Nuklear Man's body from his hand and dangled him from his giant thumb and forefinger. "Aw, lookie there. I hit him so hard his widdle cape came off." It was still plastered against his palm.

Nuklear Man's eyes burned with flames of the cosmos. White-hot pinpricks of light gathered themselves into his clenched fists. "NOVAAA BEAM!!!"

Variel and Safriel craned their necks and watched Dakael's now normal sized body rocket over them into an empty lot that had been filled a month earlier. He landed and bounced twice.

"Dakael had to convert all his extra mass in order to survive Arel's attack," Variel non-noted to himself.

A golden, and more importantly, *caped* flash zoomed over them to the dirt cloud kicked up by Dakael's impact.

"Looks like it's almost my turn," Safriel said eagerly.

The cloud flashed like a storm cloud rumbling with Plazma lightning. Dakael was spit out from its depths all the way to the feet of his remaining comrades. He rose to one knee and stumbled up to them warily. He looked up at Safriel who was now over twice his size. "Don't touch the cape," Dakael advised with a high-pitched voice. "It just makes him angry."

Variel and Safriel nodded.

Dakael absorbed the ground underneath him to gain back at least his normal mass and strength before finding something else to give him a boost. "Uh," he said.

Safriel was still twice his size.

The half-settled dust cloud split into two swirling corkscrews of particles as a shaft of fusion hot energy shot out from them. It carved a canal through the earth along its path straight to and through the diminutive Dakael.

Variel placed his infinitely black hand on Safriel's shoulder and stepped back. She did the same. Dakael's form dissolved into nothing within the Plazma Beam.

"He'd lost so much strength from Arel's attacks that he didn't even have enough left to use his own powers," Variel observed as the Plazma Beam dissipated. "Arel is quite clever. Are you sure you wish to battle him?"

"Nice try, Var," Safriel said. She brushed his hand off her shoulder and stepped forward to face the Hero. "But now it's my turn."

✳   ✳   ✳   ✳

Deep within the dark catacombs of Managerial Tower, a set of skeletal fingers wrapped against a huge obsidian desk. The expansive room was lit only be the wall of monitors in front of the really, really big desk. Each screen showed a different Security: Camera view. The gray and white screens cast a pale light on the already pale figure of Mort Dakainen, the president of the Metroville Mall for each of its ninety-eight years. He hadn't taken a single vacation or sick day in all that time.

It showed.

Mort was now little more than a shriveled up skeleton that refused to die. Patchy wisps of hair covered his bony scalp. His liver-spotted skin was a Gordian Knot of wrinkles stretched across his age weary bones. He had a nose reminiscent of a vulture's beak and beady eyes that would have been sharp with hate if they weren't foggy with cataracts. They focused, to the best of their ability, on two particular video screens. Each one was occupied by visions of particular people. There were five of them in total. He knew what kind of people they were. They all dressed alike. Flashy clothes, all "Hey, look at me! I'm important, I'm special." He despised them.

"So this plucky band of heroes dares to invade my keep," Mort's voice was a wind whispering through graves crossed with the screech of a hunting hawk. "They were wise to divide their attack. But unwise to divide their resources for attack." His frail hand stretched out to an enormous tome atop his pristine desk. He pulled it closer. Fingers like bone caressed its cool, smooth surface labeled "Mall Mail Order Catalogue." They flipped through hundreds of pages as if by memory. At last, one small hand found the page it sought and flipped the book open with an echoing thud against the desk. His unfocused eyes scanned the exposed pages. "Ah yes. This ought to work wonders. One simple incantation is all it requires."

A bony finger slowly reached out to a button labeled Intercom.

*   *   *   *

Shiro, Angus, and Norman walked through one of the Mall's side entrances. A corridor twenty feet long and ten feet wide spilled out into the main hall wherein many shops lined the walls. The one directly in front of them was a Toy Junction. Between them and the Toy Junction was a treasure chest promising "Free Mall Maps!!!!"

"Let's get one of those maps," Norman suggested as they walked into the Mall proper. "We'll be able to find the quickest route to the Food Court Junction."

"It wouldna be a problem if'n we weren't late." He scowled at Shiro. "Ah bloody *hates* bein' late!" Angus growled at Shiro. "Now, Ah ain't gonna mention no names," he told Shiro. "No, ye see Ah'm above stoopin' to that level."

"Areing Angus-san who are the sureness when Action Time now of that?"

"*Bah*! Ye an' ye damned talkin'! It was ye that made uus late, ye daft goat-arse-brained twit!"

"Hey, c'mon Angus," Norman said while pulling a Free Mall Map!!!! from the treasure chest. "Watch it. We're right in front of a toy store. You don't want one of these kids picking up that kind of language, do you?" he warned for all you moms out there.

"Bah! Wee brats. 'Oooh, lookit me! Ah'm eight friggin' years old but Ah gots ta bend over to pull wee Mr. Angus' beard.' Ye just keeps right on bendin' over, laddie! Angus has goot somethin' for ye!" he roared while brandishing his Surprisingly Concealable and Wieldly Enemy-B-Smote Named Bertha at passersby.

"Yeah, that's better, Angus," Norman said while trying to look inconspicuous. "Did you ever go to those anger management classes?"

"Aye. That wee laddie had it comin' to him, he did. Said Ah had so much anger 'cause Ah was repressin'—"

"HACK COUGH WHEEEEZE…" the intercoms all across the labyrinthine Mall blared. "Attention shoppers," a raspy voice announced. "There will be an 80%-off sale on all Super Mega Action Guy toys and related products for the next ten minutes. That is all."

"Supaa Megaru Action Guy!" Shiro squealed in delight. He ran into the nearby Toy Junction.

"Oh no ye don't," Angus grumbled and caught Shiro by his Tetsu: Collar to lock him in place. The samurai's legs pumped uselessly and sparked against the tile floors.

"Shh," Norman said. "You guys hear something?"

Other than Shiro's little Tetsu: Boots scuffing against the floor, all was silent.

Then there was a distant something. A chanting, shrill and completely random, like a hundred voices singing a hundred songs and they were all off key.

"Aye," Angus said in a warrior's knowing whisper. "Aye. Ah do."

"Supaa Megaru Action Guy!"

"Shut up!" Angus said, and threw Shiro to the ground.

The ground began to tremble ever so slightly.

Norman's body flashed into silvery tungsten. Angus planted his little feet squarely and hefted Bertha. Shiro dusted himself off.

"Nani?"

A tidal wave of children splashed around a corner with violent fervor. Their mouths babbled insane gibberish, their eyes flashed with wildness. They rushed down a long corridor straight for the heroes.

"Ooh, Ah been waitin' fer a chance like this," Angus said with elated anticipation.

"Wait!" Norman said. "They're kids. We can't hurt hem."

"The hell we can't, they be weaker than us!" The Surly Scot grumbled while testing Bertha's balance. "This thing won't kill 'em, but they'll sure wish it had!"

"Here, use this," the Tungsten Titan shoved a slab of cardboard wrapped in plastic into Angus' face.

"What's this then?" he snatched it from Norman's hands and read aloud. "'Li'l Warrior's Toy Axe Weapon Kit. By Murf. Ages 8 and up'" He looked up at MMMM. "Are ye sayin' Ah'm too short to be usin' weapons intended for adults!"

"No," Norman said. "Look, I'm using the same thing." He tore a Murf Li'l Warrior Toy Sword and Shield from its plastic cocoon.

"What about the babble talkin' village idiot over there?" Angus thumbed at Shiro.

The mad berserk rush of pre-adolescents, alight on wings of material consumption, loomed ever closer the same way an out of control freight train would. And the heroes were right in its tracks.

Norman readied himself for battle. "There's no time. Shiro, just pick something. But make sure it won't hurt them."

"Hai!" The Tiny Typhoon dove into a nearby bargain bin and his little legs stuck out the top of it. He pulled out a Mr. Mysterium Magic User's Kit.

Angus spun his Murf Toy Battle Axe through an impressive series of moves and held it before him. "TASTE COLD IRON, YE GOBLINS!"

"Angus. It's just a foam axe."

"…Aye. Ah know."

*   *   *   *

Yet another Plazma Beam uselessly splashed off Safriel's body. "Hm," Nuklear Man reasoned.

She jumped toward him in a flash of motion. Somewhere along the line she'd spun around and delivered a spinning kick against Nuklear Man's jaw before landing. Nuklear Man himself fell on his stomach immediately afterward. He spit dirt from his mouth. "This hardly seems fair, really," he said in a strangely detached moment.

"Shut *up!*" she snapped, punctuating her sentiment with a swift kick to his temple.

Now sprawled on his back, he could see Safriel leaning over him. Her body had an odd, slightly opaque, crystal sort of appearance to it. "I wonder if that has anything to do with her apparent immunity to my energy based attacks," he mused without actually acknowledging her presence.

"Yes!" she yelled with ah exasperated huff. "Don't you remember when I was gloating about how I watched you battling the others and used my matter alteration powers to rearrange the atomic composition of my body to perfectly refract your energy based attacks?"

Nuklear Man blinked and diverted his gaze from the birdie that had been flying far over head and looked right into Safriel's multi-faceted eyes that were bearing down on him with all the weight of a mountain. "Oh. I'm sorry. Were you talking just then?"

"Grah!" She grabbed at his collar and hauled him to his feet.

"Oh, why thank you," Nuklear Man said while dusting himself off. "It just wouldn't do for me to stay all dirty. I've got to look good for the cameras, you know."

Safriel was clawing her face and growling in frustration.

Nuklear Man looked around. "Speaking of which, where *are* all the cameras anyway? The news people usually make it to these things before the cops or anybody like that. And now that I think about it, where are the cops and stuff too?"

*   *   *   *

Meanwhile, at one of many "Checkpoints" set up by Überdyne at key locations along the perimeter of the fairly large section of downtown that had been decimated by Nuklear Man and Superion a month ago and was now having its wounds reopened by Metroville's dedicated civil workers...

"What do you mean we don't have clearance into the area? We're the *press*. We can go anywhere," Erica Erikson asked Faceless Employee, one of the Über- dyne Checkpoint Guards. Faceless held a clipboard. It was very official. Behind him was an Official: Road Block, several other Official: Personnel, and an Offi- cial: Überdyne Van.

He turned to the first page in his clipboard. "Your equipment isn't fit for entrance into the area. Nuklear Man is currently battling an entity or entities whose power or powers would have adverse effects with your electronics. With- out the proper shielding, said equipment could become potentially hazardous to yourself and others. As such, Überdyne cannot, in good conscience, allow you passage.

"Fine. Harry." She turned to her cameraman and handed over her micro- phone. "Here, I'll go in myself."

"Ahem," Faceless said. He flipped over to the next sheet. "The full extent of these electrical disturbances is undetermined at this time. We have evidence that leads us to believe that exposure to the energy or energies being released by the entity or entities may pose a threat or threats to any complex system or systems that employ electricity. The human brain included. As such, Überdyne cannot, in good conscience, allow you passage."

"Well thank you, Überdyne," Erica said with a pinch of sarcasm.

Faceless flipped to the third page. "And Überdyne thanks you."

Erica stared through Faceless for nearly a minute. "Just what gives you jokers the right to do this?"

Another flip. "Rights of ownership. Überdyne owns ninety-five percent of the land upon which the current condition or conditions apply. If we did not do everything in our power to keep the populace at bay, we would be committing drastically immoral and illegal acts."

"What about the freedom of press?" Erica asked.

Faceless leaned closer to her. "Trust us. We're doing this for your own good."

*   *   *   *

The overhead lights kept flickering.

"That's really starting to annoy me," Atomik Lad said.

"It makes it hard to see far. I mean, it's dark overall but since the lights keep flickering, your eyes never get used to it."

Atomik Lad squint into the darkness beyond. "I think I see something moving up ahead."

"I should hope so. This is a mall in America. I'd hate to think there's an hour of the day when one of these things isn't packed." And with that, the fair Rachel bumped right into someone. "Oh, I'm sorry," she apologized. "I didn't see you there. It's the lighting in here, you know."

The someone looked right at Rachel. "Connnnsuuuume," he said in a mindless voice. His eyes were sallow, shallow, hollow, and apparently focused on something just beyond the horizon. In one hand, he held a wide-open wallet with its credit cards flopping out of it; in the other, a collection of shopping bags. "Must...buuuuy," he told no one in particular.

Rachel jumped closer to Atomik Lad who was subsequently bumped into another shopper. It was a younger woman. Her purse was dragging along as she slowly shuffled her sluggish legs. She was burdened by an array of bloated shopping bags.

"Er, I'm sorry," he apologized out of habit before getting a good look at her. At which point he could only say, "Gah! Get it away!"

"Nnnng," she responded. "Must justify latest fashions' powers over me by buying into them."

Atomik Lad and Rachel were back to back. If they listened carefully, they could hear the shuffling movement and mindless babbling of the shoppers surrounding them in the darkness.

"Trendy...must define self by trends..."

"Conform...must not deviate from cliché media images..."

"They're like, I don't know, like zombies," Atomik Lad said.

"Okay," Rachel said. One of the consumer zombies bumped into her as it passed by without acknowledging her existence. "How do we get out of this?"

"I have—oof, no idea," Atomik Lad answered. The zombie population seemed to be steadily growing. "What the hell? Did someone open the bottle of Easily Influenced Morons or what?"

Rachel squeezed closer to him. "Maybe. Look." She pointed at the shops along their walkway.

"What about them?"

"Look. The Gorge, the Unlimited Limited Incorporated, Old Army, Amber Kromby and Finch."

"Oh, I get it. That explains their willingness to blindly consume and follow."

"The question now is how do we take advantage of this information," Rachel grunted while trying to keep from being swept away. The flow of shopper zombies was nearing a continuous rate and threatened to take them along like an irresistible undertow.

*   *   *   *

"Ya-haha!" Angus cried out triumphantly. His foam axe was a blur of action cutting a swath through the flood of toy-crazed children.

Norman swung his foam sword through wide arcs pushing aside two or three of the little monsters at a time.

"How many hit points do ye think these buggers got?" Angus asked over the clamor of battle.

"What're you talking about?" Norman asked while shoving one child out of his way.

"Ye know. Hit points. Like when ye drivin'. Ye get ten points for old people, twenty for bicyclers. Like that."

"Oh. Geez, I don't know. Seems kinda morbid talking that way about kids. Yeowch!" Norman had to pry a pair of jaws and the child they were attached to from his forearm. "I'm tungsten, kid. You shouldn't be able to hurt me that way."

The snarling beastling joined its throng.

"Hey, where's Shiro?"

"Bah! That oaf. Probably joined these wee kiddies lookin' for—Ya-ha! Lookin' for that Super Action Guy Mega Noonsense."

Shiro popped up atop one of the benches that was placed throughout the mall's walkways. The goblin kids milled around underneath him. He wore a Mr. Mysterium purple pointy magician's hat with sparkly stars and crescent moons adorning it and a Mr. Mysterium tuxedo jacket which, on the tiny warrior, was like an oversized robe. He held a Mr. Mysterium Book of Magic Instruction in one hand and waved the other around "Mysteriumly". "Hai. Accountant the time. The me is now!"

Angus spun around. "Get down here and fight! We still gots to get to the blasted Food Court Junction!"

One of the feral child beasts launched himself from the masses. He hurled through the air straight at Angus' back.

Shiro's eyes went wide. His hand dove into the mock tuxedo-robe and he chanted the magical spell exactly like Mr. Mysterium's Book of Magic Instruction said. Or as close to it as Shiro would be likely to get. "Large in Age, are the interlockers that magic spirit time, when then they time gone—heavy with mystery!" He threw three thin interlocking rings that were painted gold into the air. They wrapped around Angus' would-be assailant who promptly fell to the ground with his arms pinned uselessly to his sides.

"*Aye* laddie!" Angus cheered. "Ah owes ye one!" He spun his foam axe and delivered a brutally harmless blow to another little monster with a resounding, "*Aughk*!" of a battlecry.

Norman stumbled about. Over a dozen of the scrawny creatures had latched onto him. "I'm goin' down!"

"Blast these damned goblins!" Angus cursed as he hacked at the mob. "Ah can nay get to ye, laddie!"

"Go on without me!" Norman said. "I'll take out as many as I can!"

"Norman-san!" Shiro's hands dove into his robes. "Selector, the volunteering cards of fated to being!" Hundreds of playing cards flew from his sleeves. They rained down on Norman's impish aggressors like a storm of locusts from an angry god. The monster children fell from the Tungsten Titan like autumn leaves. Norman stood up and was the very paragon of strength once more. "Thanks Shiro. That magic-user's kit sure is handy." He sputtered for a second and coughed out a Three of Clubs. "What the?"

Shiro smiled wide as he pulled a card from under his magician's hat. He turned it for Norman to see.

"The Three of Clubs? *Wow.*"

"Hai, but now the heavy with troubling dragons! Is me!" the Tiny Typhoon said as he tried, in vain, to beat away the hands dragging him down into the churning mass of devil children.

"Protect the magician!" Angus roared.

*   *   *   *

Variel was a mass of blackness that might have had all three dimensions to it. It was hard to tell by looking directly at him. The only discernable features of his dark were his eyes, though their only discernable features were their complete lack of being like the rest of him. He was like a statue of nothing bearing down with all the weight of the unknown.

Safriel's crystalline body tumbled up to his feet. She coughed and stood up favoring her left leg. "Damn it," she spat, speaking half to herself and half to Variel. "He's beating me to a pulp out here now. We've been fighting for so long," she gasped for air. "I'm just worn out, but he hasn't so much as broken a sweat. What's he made of!"

"The stars, child," Variel answered with that negative voice that seemed to emanate from his entirety. "You could simply forfeit your turn. It is clear that you cannot win."

"Gee, thanks for the vote of confidence, Var."

"You may be able to shield yourself from his fire, but there is nothing that can save you from his strength. You'd have to pull the very stars from the sky to defeat him."

Safriel fell silent. Directly in front of her, some distance away and slightly obscured from the dust clouds kicked up from their battle, was Nuklear Man. His golden cape flowed somewhat like a field of wheat on a windy day.

He waved at her.

"Grah! He's just taunting me!" she growled. "I've got the power of all the permutations of matter at my finger tips, but I can't do a thing against him!" She watched Nuklear Man's Plazma Aura as it glinted off the dust and dirt swirling around him. "Or can I?"

"Feel free to forfeit. There's no shame in knowing one's own limits."

"Shut up, Var." Her face melted into a crystalline sneer. "I've got an idea." Her crystallized body became more opaque, like its torso had been injected with a thick fog that slowly spread to her limbs. "I should've thought of this sooner!" She shot toward the Golden Guardian with renewed vigor.

Variel smiled, though it was impossible to tell by looking at him.

*   *   *   *

"I've got...a Plan.," Rachel said.

The consumer zombies were suffocating in number, "I am what I buy..."

"Products are like chicken soup for the soulless..."

"A plan, huh? Well, that's certainly a change from how Nuke and I tend to get through these things, but let's hear it."

She grabbed the Game Junction bag from Atomik Lad. "Just follow my lead."

"Uh. Sure, no problem."

Rachel shoved her free hand deep into the glossy plastic bag. "Behold, leave us be, foul creatures of conformity, for I possess that which is despised by your dark masters. *I do what I want to do!*" She held the video game high above her head. "For you see, I am a girl, yet I play video games!"

"Nnnnnrrrrr!" the zombies nearest her moaned in agony. They clawed at one another to escape Rachel's socially unacceptable claim.

"And I am not wearing enough make-up to double as a clown!" she announced. The zombies recoiled in horror. Several fainted outright.

"You've given us some breathing room, thank God."

"I don't know, it wasn't *so* bad being pressed up against you."

"Well I, ooh." His mind went all blarg for a second. He shook out of it. "Okay, *focus*. We're still not out of this. How long do you think you can keep them at bay?"

"With my distaste for popular culture, quite a while."

"Must…join the flock!" A nearby consumer lunged for Rachel. It grabbed her by the arm and started dragging her toward the others.

"Rachel!" Atomik Lad blurt.

"*Ack*!" she screamed while beating her kidnapper with the video game box. The zombie hissed and released her. "It burns! It burns!" the creature rasped as it clutched where its face had been struck. "But the sooner we get out of here, the better," she said, stumbling back to Atomik Lad.

"Right." He scanned the area. It was difficult to see past the wandering brain dead conformists or the darkness beyond them, but his eyes caught something. "Ah ha! I think I've got it."

"Took you long enough."

He grabbed her free wrist. "Follow *my* lead."

"Okay!" she said. She was dragged, half-running and half-falling, behind Atomik Lad while still keeping the video game aloft.

The zombie sea parted before them. The zombies cringed from the pair as they flew down the poorly lit hallway of trendy shops until, "Here!" Atomik Lad slammed his feet down to stop. Rachel bumped into him. "Keep them back a little longer," he ordered.

She held the video game like a cross directed at vampires. She shoved it in the face of a zombie that dared to come too close. "Hey! I despise going to clubs and being ogled by vapid, drunk morons like yourself."

"Grraaaaah!" Collapse.

Atomik Lad flipped a bench onto its side and climbed up it to the ceiling.

Rachel looked up at him. "How'd you know there was a vent here?"

"I didn't. I just figured there would be one eventually. There always is, y'know."

"So I've been taught from movies. Open it already."

Atomik Lad pulled back one fist and eyed the vent with stern determination. "One, two, who'm I kiddin'? Rachel, let me see your car keys."

She lobbed them up and he snatched them from the air. He selected one and used its teeth to release the Screws of Locking.

*   *   *   *

Safriel cackled maniacally as she rained blows down on Nuklear Man's battered skull. Her arms began to blur as every strike was delivered with more force and velocity than the last. Nuklear Man gave up trying to defend himself against the onslaught of attacks a while ago and was instead giving the ol' Take It Like A Man school of self-defense a shot. It wasn't working particularly well.

Safriel was aglow with an internal light, an eerie spectrum of orange to yellow to white was split by the prisms of her body. It refracted and flashed through every facet of her form with every movement. And it was steadily growing in intensity.

She spun into a cartwheel kick kind of thing that slammed Nuklear Man to the ground. Again. Her foot was pressed painfully against his neck. The razor sharp edges of her crystalline facets scraped against his skin.

"C'mon now," Nuklear Man croaked. "That hurts."

"It's supposed to!" she yelled and applied more pressure to his neck.

"Y'know, I could've sworn I was winning a little while ago."

"Ha!" She leaned down until she was nearly nose to nose with him. Of course, doing so put even more pressure on his neck. "That was when I was merely deflecting your Plazma Energies. I altered my composition so that I could store your powers instead of simply diverting them. Now I can use your own strength against you."

"That's a pretty good idea."

"Yes, it's working wonders, don't you think? I watched you defeat my comrades by using their own powers against them. Well I'm not going to let you do that to me. Oh no, I'm beating you to the punch. I'm going to defeat you with your own vast energy reserves!"

She removed her foot.

"Thanks." And replaced it with her hands. "Grk!"

"But I need more energy to do it. I don't care if I have to strangle it from you. I don't care if you die. I don't need you alive, I just need your powers. Besides, if you're dead, it'll be even easier for Lord Nihel to give them to me for my reward!"

"But Nukie don't wanna die," he croaked.

"That's a damn shame." She squeezed tighter and her internal light brightened and spread out into her limbs. She quivered with pleasure. "Yes! I've won! I'll never have to kow-tow to that uptight Variel again! Lord Nihel won't look down at me! I'll be the one! I'll be the Harbinger of Flame, not just some peon lackey!" Her eyes were wide, hungry. And burning. "My gods, so much power! And this is nothing, nothing compared to the rest of it!" The features of Safriel's body were lost in the now blinding light emanating from her. She looked like Variel in reverse.

Nuklear Man twitched in her grasp like a house pet having a bad dream. She released him and his heavy body hit the ground. A sack of meat would've had more life to it.

"I can feel it, Var," Safriel said, her voice beginning to turn inside out. "Arel's power. It's perfection."

"It's consuming you," Variel unsaid plainly.

"No! I need more! Yes, more. I don't need Nihel for this. I'll take Arel's powers straight from their source!" She fell to her knees and straddled the fallen Hero. She placed her hands upon his stilled chest. There was an audible rush of energies. Safriel screamed in delight.

Variel simply turned around to face her with his back.

Her scream twisted sharply into terror as the sound of shattering glass screeched through the dusty air. Shafts of light erupted from Safriel's quaking body. She imploded. It was completely silent save for her final moments of inverted screaming.

"You cannot expect a body of matter to contain the flames of stars," Variel said to the memory of Safriel.

Nuklear Man sat up groggily as though he was awakened from a deep sleep. "Man, I just know I'm going to get a headache by the time this is all over."

Variel turned to him. "Trust me, 'Lord' Arel. A headache is the least of your worries now."

✳   ✳   ✳   ✳

"Man, I can't believe we got out of there alive," Norman said.

"Aye" Angus responded.

They had managed to escape the marauding horde of little beasts that were supposed to be goblin-like children, though Norman had a hard time seeing them as anything but child-like goblins. They now walked through the path between racks of women's clothing in what must've been a department store of some kind. The available paths branched out like capillaries from the main artery they maintained. Angus was in the lead, one hand on his toy axe, its hilt on his shoulder. Directly behind him was Shiro with his nose buried in the Mr. Mysterium Book of Magic Instruction. Norman took up the rear as the party's heavy artillery. He idly flipped the toy sword in his hands. He had to stay a few steps behind to keep from tripping over Shiro's tuxedo-robe since it dragged the floor.

*   *   *   *

"Drat these wily adventurers," Mort hissed. "Not only did they escape my trap, they have made off with a collection of my precious treasures." His breath wheezed in and out of his fragile frame. "It is time to summon my dread guardians into action."

*   *   *   *

"Bah!" Angus barked. "Lookit this!" he said as he came to a halt at a pair of mannequins ahead of them. One plastic sentry stood on each side of their path. Their manufactured faces somehow communicated a vague sort of happiness, a bovine content with the world, a Zen-like calm that could only come from such nice looking and affordable fashions.

Shiro bumped into the Surly Scot from behind. "Pardoning the infraction of both time and space."

"What's up, Angus?" Norman asked.

Angus spun around to look Norman face to knee. "These here mannequins," he said, motioning to the statues behind him. "'Oooh, lookit uus. We be so happy 'cause o' our clothes. Don't ye wish ye was tall enough to wear clothes like ours? Well too bad, we only sell clothes for freakishly tall mutants!' Bah!"

The mannequins' sightless eyes were replaced by infrared cameras.

"Uh, Angus."

"Don't ye be interruptin' me when Ah'm rantin'! It makes so angry about gettin' interrupted that it makes me forget what Ah'm so angry about in the first place!"

Dark mechanically gray innards were exposed just underneath the fleshy colored plastic as the lifeless limbs extended slightly at their joints to allow for movement.

"Angus. Just walk forward."

"Weren't ye just listenin'?! Now ye be interruptin' me rant about interruptin' me rant!"

Their placid mannequin faces were etched with lines as the plastic skin rearranged itself to expose tiny horn-like sensor nodes. A few beeps and whirs later, the pair of statues hunched on their perches and were ready to strike. Thin and finely articulated rods at least as long as their arms sprout from their shoulder blades. Tightly woven netting dropped from the rods giving each a pair of bat-like wings.

"Angus-san, arounding the turn on roads of life when opportunity knocked up the sisters of fate!"

"Well why didn't ye just say so?" Angus griped. He turned around and got an eyeful of winged mannequin death. "Great Highlander's kilt!" He rolled to the side and tumbled straight into a rack of paisley dresses just in time to avoid talons slashing down at him. "Ah'm stuck!" he cried while struggling against his paisley snares.

The other gargoyle mannequin leapt at Norman like a mountain lion. They toppled out of sight back down the way the heroes had come.

The first gargoyle stomped onto the ground from its perch. It approached Shiro with slow, heavy steps. It snarled at the Tiny Typhoon as it loomed over him like a bird of prey. Its net wings twitched in anticipation. Shiro threw up his arms to protect himself and a flock of doves or pigeons rushed from his oversized sleeves. The gargoyle's targeting system was momentarily scrambled from the influx of new targets stunning it just long enough for Angus to rocket from the clothes rack while wearing a white dress covered in a light pink floral pattern over what would have been an otherwise impressive Iron: Battlesuit. He hurled himself at the beast's skull screaming, "STITCH *THIS*, DEMON!"

Sadly, his attack, being comprised of a blow to the gargoyle's steel reinforced head with nothing more than a toy axe made completely of harmless foam, was even less impressive than the Floral: Battlesuit. The foam axe bounced against the creature's horned skull with a dull "fwop" sound.

The mannequin gargoyle's torso spun ninety degrees with electric speed and caught the Surly Scot in one of its net wings before he ever hit the ground. The net snapped off at whatever mechanism attached it to the rod appendage and Angus dropped to the floor as a captive. He struggled against his bonds, but they grew tighter until he could no longer budge.

"Well," Angus muttered. "That's that then."

Norman rolled up to Shiro from behind. He was wrapped up in two layers of net. "Shiro, run. Our weapons are useless against them!"

"Hai!" the Tiny Typhoon answered. He ran between the legs of the first gargoyle only to be snatched up in its remaining net wing. He was dropped right next to Angus.

"Aye, laddie. Goood work."

"Angus-san of done, the better here the being then?"

"Bah."

"Excellent. Bring them back to my keep," Mort ordered. The mannequins beeped their acknowledgement. He turned his attention to another Security: Camera display. "As for my tunnel rats."

*   *   *   *

"So do you have any idea where we're going?" Rachel asked as they wriggled through ventilation shafts on all fours. She could hear him shuffling along and breathing behind her, but a reply was not forthcoming. "Hey. Sparky."

"Er, uh. Wha-yeah?"

They kept moving. "I'm starting to get the idea that you let me go first for reasons that were not altogether gentlemanly."

"I'm insulted that you'd think those jean shorts would sway my judgment in any way whatsoever."

"Who said anything about jean shorts?"

"Ah. Yes. Um. I think we've gone far enough. Let's try to get out at the next vent."

They did. The vent clanged to the floor much too loudly for Atomik Lad's taste.

"Real smooth, Mr. Cat Burglar," Rachel teased, her voice rang metallic as it echoed through the ventilation tunnels.

"Yeah, yeah," Atomik Lad grumbled with most of his body dangling from the roof. He hopped down. And landed right on the vent thus producing almost as much noise as its initial fall. "Don't say it."

"You got it," she said, holding back a giggle. Her legs poked out from the roof. They were followed, rather predictably, by the rest of her. She too hopped down, though noticeably quieter than her companion had done since she missed the vent. "Okay, so now what?"

"I hadn't exactly thought that far ahead," he said.

"We're really going to be late, you know."

"Yeah. They're probably already at the Food Court Junction by now."

"Maybe we should try getting there, hm?" Rachel suggested.

"Good idea, but how? We're lost and our map isn't even to this floor."

She scratched the back of her head. "If we walk in one direction long enough, we're bound to get somewhere."

"You're not the Ranger in this group, are you?" he said.

"Not even close," she said with a wide smile.

"I can tell."

"Can you think of anything else?" she asked.

"Er. Ahem. Well, let's go!"

"That's what I thought."

They walked for several minutes. Stores like Burger Junction, All Natural Junction and Victoria's Junction were aligned along their flanks. The corridor of capitalism came to an end and turned to the right. They turned with it and immediately ran into a wall of uniforms.

Atomik Lad and Rachel stumbled back and uttered apologies.

Looming over them were four Mall Guards standing shoulder to shoulder. To shoulder to shoulder. Because there were four of them, so therefore there'd be four shoulders involved. Never mind. The rest of the hallway was inaccessible due to their barrier of a presence. Their eyes were hidden by mirrored sunglasses they wore even though they were indoors and the lights were still flickering.

"Are you lost?" they asked simultaneously.

"Um," Atomik Lad answered. "Yeah?"

"We're looking for the Food Court Junction. Can you help us?" Rachel asked while trying her best to look helpless.

The guards exchanged glances. "How did you get here?" they asked as one.

"Through the vents?" Atomik Lad answered.

"Maybe that wasn't the best answer, dear," Rachel whispered.

"That's a restricted area," the Guards said. "Come with us."

"No, that's okay," Atomik Lad said.

"We'll be going now," Rachel explained with a false smile. They walked backwards and bumped into another wall that was undoubtedly uniformed as well.

"You should come with us," a collection of voices, identical to the previous Guards, said from behind them.

Atomik Lad's fist clenched and unclenched. *They're only doing their jobs*, he reminded himself. *Atomik Powers would not be nice.* He caught sight of Rachel in the corner of his eyes. *Too close anyway.*

"Fine," Rachel said. "We'll go with you, but only so we can bitch out your boss. I suggest getting your resumes in order."

Giant Mall Guard hands wrapped around their arms and lifted them off the ground. A cloth went over each of their mouths. It only took a few seconds for everything to go dark.

*   *   *   *

"Ah, so it's an old fashioned stare down, eh?" Nuklear Man said to himself. Variel's unflinching blackness was exactly far enough away for an old fashioned stare down. Or an old fashioned gun fight, depending on the circumstances. This was the former though. "Yessir, the ol' stare down. As much a battle of wits as it is a battle of nerves. It ain't for the weak hearted or the weak stomached. Nosir, this is a conflict for steel willed do-or-die manly men. 'Cause the first guy to crack, the first guy to show even the slightest, oh so *tiniest* hint of weakness, that guy's a goner. There ain't no turnin' back. Once you start a stare down, especially these here old fashioned ones, it can't finish until one of the starer downers is no more." Nuklear Man was silent. Complex mathematics swirled through his mind. "Wait a second. Two men enter one man leaves?! Why, that means I've only got a fifty-fifty chance at survival! This is utter madness! What kind of idiot enters into a contract of death like this?! I'll be damned if I'll be the first to lose my stoic resolve. I'll show that Variel. I'll just bash him now while he ain't expecting it!"

Nuklear Man raced to Variel like a golden bullet.

Until he came to a screeching halt mere inches from his target.

Variel lowered his gaze to the Hero. Nuklear Man was suspended in mid-air and still in his *Charge!* pose.

He looked up at Variel's silvery eyes. "Gah! You're even weirder lookin' up close."

No response.

"Hey, I was all flying at ya fast and stuff. What's the deal, why haven't I bashed you yet?"

"This is why," Variel's inverse voice answered simply.

Nuklear Man felt an incredible weight press down on him. "Ergh," he uttered while trying to stay afloat. After about a second he was unable to mount much of an offensive against the invisible force. He slammed head-first into the already thoroughly beaten ground. "Ouff," he grumbled through a face full of dirt.

"I'm afraid, Arel, that you are going to find it difficult to defeat me when you cannot so much as move," Variel unsaid.

Nuklear Man's body quivered in a failed attempt to stand.

"I've been watching you. I know now that you can only access the smallest fraction of your true power at this time. And it's not nearly enough to resist my dimensional powers. I have warped the space around you into an irresistible gravitational pull. Just relax. Lord Nihel will be along soon enough to transfer your star essence to me. And then I will have what I've always deserved. Equality. No longer relegated to the role of head slave. The heavens will bow to me. Fate will bend to my will."

Nuklear Man was able to turn his head to one side so he could speak instead of eat dirt. "What is with you guys and all this power stuff? I mean, I know I'm the strongest mo-fo on this rock and everything, and that everyone else on it is incredibly jealous of me but unable to act on said jealousy 'cause they fear me even more than they envy me, but geez. You guys have really taken it to the extreme. Especially with this whole Using My Insignia thing. I'm serious about suing, you know."

Variel nongrumbled and pushed Nuklear Man deeper into the ground.

"You're only making it worse on yourself," Nuklear Man grunted.

Variel specifically pushed the Hero's head down.

"*Ah!* I've got dirt in my eye. Ow!" C'mon, let me up!"

Nothing.

"I'm not kidding, this hurts!" Still nothing. "Fine. Ouch, ouch, be that way!" Nuklear Man's mighty arms shook with effort.

Variel willed more gravity to oppress Nuklear Man.

"I'm serious, this really *hurts*!" Nuklear Man said through clenched teeth. He had already managed to adopt a push up like position.

Variel ungrowled. "I won't let you escape! I'm too close. I will not endure Nihel's heel any longer!" He shifted from the strain of exerting his spatial manipulations to their fullest extent.

Nuklear Man's Plazma Aura rippled and flared into an instant of perfected harmony. He shrugged off Variel's shackles and stood. "Man," he said and rubbed his eye. "That could've scratched my retina. Or something. And permanently damaged my vision. You should be ashamed." He blinked a few times and wiped away a tear. "Lucky for you, I'm darned invincible." He jumped to a Plazma Beam charging pose. "But unlucky for you, I also happen to be darned invincible! Hoo-ah!"

Variel unsighed. "It's going to be a pleasure ripping your powers from you."

"It'll be more of a pleasure for me to PLAZMAAA BEAM!" The beam wavered at Variel and twisted around him. It traveled on and blasted the hell out of the foreman's abandoned office some distance behind him. "Hm," Nuklear

Man said. "That was unexpected." He examined his hands. "No more screw ups, got it? Good. Now then. PLAZMAAA BEAM!"

It wrapped around Variel and shot off to his right utterly obliterating a group of Port-a-Potties.

"Are you quite finished?" Variel asked.

"Well. Yeah, that's about all I've got up my sleeves," Nuklear Man said.

"Glad to hear that you have come to your senses." Variel raised one arm parallel with the ground, though it was hard to distinguish it from the rest of his voidness from Nuklear Man's angle. He pointed at the Golden Guardian.

A man-sized bubble appeared at the blackness of his finger. It was visible only by the effect that it played with the light traveling through it. The scenery on the other side looked like it was pinched through a lens that stretched images an infinite distance at the center.

"Whoa, trippy," Nuklear Man commented.

"Isn't it?" Variel unasked. The sphere shot to Nuklear Man. It made a continuous tearing noise, like a thundercrack that wouldn't peak, as it rushed through the air. It struck Nuklear Man. He felt his body curve itself inside out and back again. It was like becoming a Picasso painting. The sphere pulsed and disappeared. Nuklear Man fell to one knee. He felt like most of his internal organs had been rearranged with a rusty chainsaw.

"So that was the most painful thing ever," he groaned while barely holding on to consciousness.

"No," Variel unanswered. "But you'll wish it had been."

Nuklear Man's body floated but not by his will. His limbs hanged limply and his face was still twisted in agony.

"You see, Arel. That was merely what happens when a body of normative space is intersected by more dimensions than it was ever intended to."

"Let's not do that again," Nuklear Man weakly pleaded as Variel drew him closer to his blackness.

"Don't worry, we won't."

"Oh, that's good."

"Instead, we shall see what happens when a body of normative space travels into null space, a dimension without dimension. No beginning, without even existence itself." Nuklear Man now hung in mid-air mere inches from Variel's implausible body. "If this doesn't kill you, it'll at least serve as an impenetrable prison for you until Lord Nihel arrives. Nothing can escape it. Not even your power, for there is nothing from which to escape."

Nuklear Man squirmed in resistance. The idea was to throw a mountain breaking punch or two, but the majority of the effort was lost somewhere along the way among the echoes of pain that continued to rack his body.

Nuklear Man floated straight into the depths of Variel's voidness and was gone.

✳   ✳   ✳   ✳

Atomik Lad was vaguely aware of himself floating in a sea of darkness. His first reaction was to lose this awareness and slip back into the warm embrace of sweet, sweet sleep. Unfortunately, in the final moments of his vague awareness, he became more aware that he was sitting up which served only to further sharpen his awareness in general.

Take for instance: he became aware of other bodies with him in the darkness. That wasn't normal.

And then there were his hands to think about. All bound at the wrist and tied up behind the back of his chair. That wasn't normal by a whole lot.

The darkness was attacked by a gang of miscreant light rays from the wall that he turned out to be facing. He cringed and looked away to bide time for his eyes to recover from the lightspeed assault.

"Is my aura of power too much for your minds to comprehend?" a rasping wheeze of a voice said from somewhere in the vicinity of the blinding light wall.

"What?" Norman asked from the ex-sidekick's left.

"Ah'll show ye an aura of power," Angus grumbled in front of him.

"Hai," Shiro said, sounding as if he and Angus were right next to each other.

Atomik Lad chanced another look at the light wall. He had to squint and it still hurt his head. The wall was a collection of small gray and white screens that looked down at storefronts all over the Mall's bowels. Happy shoppers walked into and out of their frames in a maddening web of movement. He began to see meaning in the chaos. One shopper leaves a Shoe Junction as another enters a Frame Junction and yet another pauses in front of a Pet Junction—it was clear now. The Mall, laws of conservation of consumers, universal constants of sales, coefficients of returns, a microcosm of all reality. Every cog working in perfect symmetry with every other piece of the great machine without any one element having the slightest concept of its place in the larger scheme of Being!

But it was probably just the ether talking.

He could make out a humanoid silhouette in the middle of the wall of light epiphanies. It was sitting down behind a huge desk and seemed absurdly frail, the skull was far too large for the neck that supported it. He turned to his right. Rachel was there, tied to a chair just like Norman and himself.

Which isn't to say that Angus and Shiro weren't tied, because they were. It's just that they were each strapped to small brightly colored plastic chairs. The kind a little girl would use in a tea party. Atomik Lad fixed his attention on them for a few seconds while his mind tried to reconcile what it was being told. Namely: Shiro was wearing a tuxedo while Angus was wearing a white dress. They looked like some sort of wedding cake decoration gone horribly, *horribly* wrong. He turned to Norman and whispered, "Did I miss something?" with a nod to their diminutive compatriots.

"Silence!" the voice barked. Or rather wheezed. But it was a mean hearted wheeze, you can be sure of that. The wraith-like figure rose and leaned on its desk. "Brave souls you may be, but the fool's path has brought you here."

"What's he talking about?" Rachel asked.

"Such insolence," he whisper-wheezed. Mort shambled from behind his desk, always certain to keep one frail hand on it for support, and shakily made his way to Rachel. He leaned way too close for her taste.

"You ever hear of a Circle of Comfort?" she said while trying to keep the maximum possible distance between herself and Mort even though she was tied to a chair.

"Yes. But I am quite immune to such trifles." He traced one skeletal finger across her jawline.

Rachel nearly fell back from yanking her head from him so quickly. "Get away from me, you letch!"

Can't kill insane old man. Can't kill insane old man, Atomik Lad repeated to himself. He channeled his aggression into struggling against the restraints at his wrists. They were already beginning to loosen.

The old man shuffled back to his desk. His body wavered from the strain of standing. "Don't you know who I am?" he asked with a gleeful hint to his wheeze.

"One soon to be dead old man?" Angus guessed with a snarl.

"I am Mort Dakainen! Also known as the Mall Wizard. You know, because I've set up so many malls across the nation. Tremble before my power!"

Atomik Lad struggled, struggled, struggled. "So you own the mall. Big deal."

"You pathetic little adventurer. You cannot hope to grasp so much as a fraction of the power at my command. I built this tower, this unholy blight upon unspoilt land. I drew in the townsfolk, made them think they needed me, and then one day, one fateful day, they believed it. My spells, composed of catchy slogans, Limited Time Only Sales, and New and Improved Products That Make Life Easy, they were to lure the townsfolk into my clutches. But there was one more ingredient. Time. Muwa. Muwa hahahahaha*wheeeeeeze*."

"This guy's out of his gourd," Norman said.

"Am I?" Mort asked. "Or am I the only sane man alive?"

"I'd have to go with that first one, Mort," Atomik Lad answered, his video game strengthened fingers working their voodoo on the ropes around his wrists.

"Bah! Madness is a label the meek use to categorize that which they do not understand. I have a loyal army of monsters at my disposal. Yes, monsters I say, for one could no longer call them truly human. These are but mere beasts driven by greed and pride. And they are my pets. My wonderful, wonderful pets. But they are also your neighbors. My eager little pawns. And they brought you here to my tower, oh brave adventurers."

Atomik Lad had nearly freed his hands. *Keep talking old man. I'm almost there.*

"You are not the first party of hardy souls to invade my keep, oh no," Mort continued. "There have been many who attempted to rush into my treasure troves to steal what they may. But always, yes always, my faithful monsters deliver these poor wretches unto me."

There was an audible snapping sound as Rachel's patience reached its limits. "What are you talking about, you insane old *fuck*!" It was not panic. It was the perfect clarity of anger. "What the hell are you holding us for, you wrinkled bastard! Let me outta this chair and I'll rip your lungs out through your ass!"

Her comrades all shirked before her might and even Angus caught himself thanking the Benevolent Incarnation of Whisakey that she wasn't talking to him.

"Such indignation!" Mort wheezed like thunder. "You dare feign ignorance, as though you did not come here specifically to usurp the throne to my most dread empire of doom?"

"What the hell!" Rachel yelled.

A spot light shone down onto Mort's desk. The toy weapons, Rachel's ATM money, the Turbo Fighter game, and Book of Magic Instruction were bathed in a cool luminescence. "You were all stealing my treasures!" he accused in a wheeze. "And you, my fiery one," he spun to Rachel. "You traversed the Forbidden Tunnels." The televisions tuned into one wall-sized image of Rachel and Atomik Lad scurrying through the air conditioning vents. "You must pay, all of you, for your crimes here today. And pay you shall, the same as those who have come before you—with your eternal souls fueling my *continued unlife*!"

"Mort is person of the thing that hungries dead?" Shiro asked.

"Why of course," Mort wheezed. "How do you think I survived lo these many, many years?"

"Let me get this straight," Rachel said. "You're not actually *alive?*"

"Correct. It's the result of a ritual I learned from a Tome of Everyday Magic I picked up in one of my treasure keeps some time ago. It involves Zombie King blood. Very messy."

"Yeah right," she scoffed. "Prove it."

"Heh. Certainly." He picked up the Li'l Warrior's foam sword that Norman had been using. "Behold!" he announced and plunged the blade deep into his breast. "Conventional weapons cannot harm me! I am immortal! I have inside me blood of Zombie Kings! No man can be my equal!"

"It's just a toy sword, dude" Norman said. "You couldn't harm a fly with that thing."

"Ha!" Mort wheeze-coughed. "Your deceit shan't beguile me. I watched with mine own eyes as you struck down a score of my fiercest monsters with but this very blade."

Atomik Lad stopped messing with the rope around his wrists. "Screw this. You picked the wrong party of adventurers to mess with, old man."

"For your insolence, you shall be the first to be consumed," Mort wheezed menacingly.

"Okay." Atomik Flames engulfed the ex-sidekick. His chair met an untimely and splintered demise.

Mort immediately sat down, his head low, a pencil in his skeletal hand scribbled notes in a notepad. "But in light of your heart felt apology, I hereby release you all."

Atomik Lad's Field vanished. "Thanks," he said and went about releasing his friends.

✳   ✳   ✳   ✳

Nuklear Man was used to breaking the commonly held laws of physics. He did it with a kind of clockwork regularity that one wouldn't expect to find in your average physics defying behavior. And he broke those laws with such force that even the most brilliant scientific minds on Earth had to abandon their comforting theories and grudgingly accept what had previously been assumed to be just plain wrong, Kopelson's Intrinsity Model of reality.

Kopelson's First Law. Everything that exists within a system has a tendency to be itself. This fairly straightforward point explains why things like apples don't suddenly turn into things like cars or orangutans. This is a very convenient state of affairs for things like humans because it keeps reality stable enough to survive in it.

However, Kopelson's First Law also explained Nuklear Man's current torment. He had been forced into a realm of nonexistence. No space, no time, nothing outside himself. It was somewhat like being squeezed through a subatomic hole for all eternity. The pain was something that mere words could not convey and I'm sorry for it. He could not help but exist within this realm of Nothing and it ripped at him with the fury of his insult to it.

His mind reeled to escape from being cut by the razors of unbeing. Images. Strangely familiar yet tauntingly alien. Wolves with coats of flame. The vast emptiness of some infinite cosmic crevice and the threat of those that call it home, "…allies of madness, cut their own throats as soon as their foes. This is what Fate would have us fight beside…?"

Familiar voices, whispering. Plotting.

…What has been written will be burned in his flames. The fire of every star in every sky…the Flames of "*Arel!*" He screamed it into the great Nothing. It was a voice of will, not sound. It shattered the Nothingness with a wake of fire. Nuklear Man was the all burning, all radiant center of the universe. He breathed fire.

Variel's eyes shone with a golden radiance. His body jerked the same way it might if a stranger tapped on his shoulder while he'd been showering. He spun this way and that, looking for…he didn't know. And then he crumpled over like a meal's worth of bad oysters had begun their insidious assault on his innards. One black hand held onto his gut, the other gripped the ground to support his unmass. His eyes were an iridescent yellow-white.

"No!" his nonvoice said in wavering tones. "He…he cannot. Not even the Lords could escape my…" And then it occurred to him

Nihel and Arel had made him and the others. Had given each a form and power. Had given him favor above the others. But never, never would they have given him any power over them. "It was a lie," Variel unwhispered. His dreams of equality were vaporized.

Cracks of light raced across his depthless body like veins of energy. He was a patchwork quilt of darkness stitched by threads of light. And then he was devoured into himself, and Nuklear Man stood in his stead. He smoked slightly.

"Man, I just *knew* I'd get a headache."

ISSUE 54—VICTORY, LUNCH, AND MURDER!

Arel, Arel, Arel. What do you see in this world?

Nihel walked on air. He walked among high-rises and skyscrapers. His cape, a red so dark it flirted with the idea of being a livid shadow, waltzed itself in the winds that flew through the alleys of the sky.

He looked down. *The streets and sidewalks are choked with them. The buildings are stacked to the clouds with them. The tunnels underground are teeming with them. The air is the nonsensical roar of their voices. Their useless little voices reaching out into space. Through time. The great Galactic Territories were built with the very stones of their pettiness. Their one crowning achievement is being the anti-inspiration for a civilization that now spans half the galaxy. And they don't even know.*

Nihel paused several hundred feet above a cramped six lane street that ran between a bank to his left and a lawyer's firm to his right. He faced the bank. His cape wafted lightly in exhaust driven updrafts from the unmoving traffic below. He watched the bank rot. He could see its very walls crumbling to dust, the windows eroding back into the sand they once came from. He saw through the façade to decaying bodies living themselves to death. Skin falling off. Cellular genocides. Bacterial invasions.

And what's worse, they are no different than any others. He kept walking. *Countless things suffocating the cosmos with their existence. And none of them, though they may hope or even suspect it, none of them truly know that they are their own masters.*

As fragile, temporary, and ignorant as they are, they are the ones who possess the only power in the universe.

But not anymore. Even if Arel has lost his memory, he will do as he was designed. I cannot, will not live under the edicts of Fate any longer. Arel will tip the scales. He will bring forth his fire.

He turned. Nihel could see the Mall Tower stabbing out of the horizon ahead of him.

*   *   *   *

Atomik Lad, Rachel, Angus, Shiro, and Norman walked through the main artery walkway that branched off into various capillaries of capitalism through the Mall. They passed a Shirt Junction, a Pants Junction, a Shoe Junction, and an Electronics Junction at which Shiro came to a dead stop.

"Ah-so," he said. "Looking at the box of words that travel on light and sound at speeds of time!"

The others stopped and looked at him with stares of incomprehension.

"Nuklear Powaa Man! Supaa heavy with action," he clarified while pointing at the TVs stacked in front of Electronics Junction. His comrades grouped around the televisions to see what the hubbub was about. Angus had to shoulder his way through a forest of knees to get in front of them so he could see as well.

"This is Erica Erikson," the TV said. "I am reporting to you live from downtown Metroville at the site of Nuklear Man and Superion's fateful battle one month ago. But it would seem that lightning has struck this area twice, as this afternoon Nuklear Man fought a foe or foes who was or were trying to destroy or take over Metroville. The battle just concluded moments ago."

"Wouldn't you know it?" Norman said. "The *one* day we take off, and that's when something actually happens."

"Details of the battle are sketchy," Erica said. "As you can see behind me, Überdyne has quarantined the area surrounding the fight." The camera panned to show an Überdyne van parked beside a barricade with flashing lights on it. Two Überdyne employees with clipboards waved into the camera. Erica continued. "According to Überdyne officials, the quarantine is for our own good. They report, and I quote, 'There is evidence which leads us to believe that there may be an energy or energies given off by Nuklear Man's opponent or opponents. The energy or energies could potentially be hazardous to electrical equipment or equipments and pose a serious lethal threat to living entities.' End quote."

"Well, looks like Nuke was able to handle it," Atomik Lad said. "Probably just some punks with supped up light guns trying to cause trouble."

"Aughk," Angus huffed. "Is we gonna stand around here gawkin', or are we gonna get to eatin'!"

"Hai!"

Angus shook. "It's a bi-conditional query, ye daft empty-headed horse's arse! Ye cannay answer it by just sayin' 'Aye'! It don't make no sense!"

Shiro pondered at length and finally answered, "Hai!"

"Ah'll back hand ye so 'hai' into the air, ye won't come back down in the same time zone!" the Surly Scot quaked.

"Okay," Norman said. "Time to get movin'."

"Hai!"

"*Rarghble!*"

✳   ✳   ✳   ✳

Meanwhile, deep within the dark innards of a not-so-abandoned warehouse, Dr. Menace leaned heavily on her Evil: Computer Console. The Evil: Screen was filled with windowpanes that spewed data, arcane formulae, and simulations set up on repeating cycles. Afloat in this ocean of information was a windowpane displaying Dr. Genius' face. She looked unusually pale. Neither woman had spoken for nearly a minute.

"Are you certain thiz iz what you want to do?" Dr. Menace said at last, though she did not look directly at the screen.

"We have to do what we must to resolve the current situation. All else is secondary."

"You will be ezzentially trapped up there. We cannot know for how long."

"It doesn't matter. The Skyjumper has the world's largest KI Articulation Drive. If we don't do this, we're all dead. It has to be done."

Dr. Menace let out a slow sigh. "Then let uz get to work. I should have a functioning Nega Bomb ready within the hour."

"I have no idea how long it will take to recalibrate the Skyjumper's KI Engines to produce the desired effect. They were specifically designed for flight, not to trick a hundred foot radius into believing it is several hundred thousand miles wide."

"It better not take long. We haven't the time," Dr. Menace said.

"I know."

They looked into each other's eyes. They left their respective consoles simultaneously without a word.

Dr. Genius waited for the air lock to the Skyjumper to open. Her thoughts wandered. *There is work to be done. The fate of the world is at stake. This is our routine. But working together after all these years of working against one another? It's strangely* comforting.

The air lock opened. She pushed herself through the portal and into the Skyjumper's passenger section. She floated past the dozens of rows of empty seats to the engine access panel near the back.

*　　*　　*　　*

They walked along the corridor a little longer until the Food Court Junction spilled out before them like some kind of horribly damaged oil tanker full of odd niche fast food booths. The Food Court Junction was, for lack of a better word, beautiful. One could dine on the cuisines of the world for only a fraction of the price of a plane ticket. It could have been called cavernous had it not been for the colorful décor, bright neon signs, potted plants, and excellent lighting.

The five weary adventurers had completed their quest. The unbridled bounty of the Food Court Junction stretched out before them in a mass of Food Hutts that might've gone on for over a mile but was probably considerably less expansive. And beyond the Hutts, the Crystal Hall of Dining. It was a section of the Food Court Junction that was walled and roofed in glass to allow diners to view the beauty of the parking lot and nearby Mall Edifices. They took deep breaths simultaneously. The culinary aromas mingled into a singularly delicious olfactory soup.

"Okay guys," Atomik Lad said. "You get the food and me and Rachel will find a table for us."

They synchronized their watches and nodded in agreement. The two teams split with regimented precision.

"Okay," Norman said. He smacked his hands together with a meaty slap and rubbed them together. "It's our job to get lunch, right?"

"Aye."

"Hai."

"And we want to get something everyone wants to eat, right?"

"Aye."

"Hai."

"Then we're agreed. Burgers it is."

"Nay."

"Negativities."

"Hm," Norman said. "Well, what do you want Angus?"

"Haggis!"

Norman's face contorted from the mere mention of the word. "Good lord, no. Do you have any idea what that's made of?"

"Aye, Ah do. And it'll make a man out o' ye, too. Ah guarantees that."

"Assuming I survive getting my stomach pumped, maybe. What do you want, Shiro?"

"Shiro-kun now the got to sushi!"

Norman cringed. "At least they *cook* the haggis."

"Heating the fires of heat for fire to heat is not wanted. Dead or a living."

"Ghk!" Angus sputtered. "Where the bleedin' hell did you learn to talk?!"

"Engrish the Shiro from regular American Joe movies."

"You learned English from American movies?" Norman asked. "Were you…paying attention?"

"Hai. The word play from Engrish then over French then over Chinese then over on Japanese under-titles for the eyes to listen."

"Well. That explains that," Angus huffed. "Now let's get that haggis."

"Y'mean Burgers."

"Conceptions of thought's you intended, Sushi!"

"Bah! If'n Ah wants raw fish wrapped up in seaweed, Ah'll dunk me head into the ocean!"

"Heh. I don't know if that's such a good idea, Angus. Remember what happened the last time you went to the beach?"

"Nay!" Angus snapped. "Nay, Ah don't."

"Really? 'Cause there was this giant crab, I think Ima called it a Crushtacean, and it seemed to really like the sound of your Iron: Bagpipe Thrusters. It liked the sound so much in fact, that it—" The Tungsten Titan's words came to a halt due to an unexpected Enemy-B-Smote held threateningly just in front of his face.

"If'n ye value ye stinkin' life, Ah'd suggest shuttin' ye trap, laddie."

"Ahem. Sure thing. No problem. That was the end of my story anyway."

"The timing from now. On Sushi Junction!"

The massive club swung down to block Shiro's progress. "Oh, no ye don't."

"Yeah. We already agreed on Burger Junction."

"Fasting ball, leg puller on the Shiro-kun don't know that."

"It would seem we've come to somethin' of an impasse, gentlemen," Angus said. His beady little eyes shifted from Shiro to Norman.

"If only we could come to some sort of compromise," Norman mused aloud.

"Diversion the onlookers. There's the point to been!" Shiro exclaimed with a point directed behind his cohorts.

They turned.

"Hm. Who would've thought...?"

"Well, Ah'll be a Frenchie's uuncle." Angus's brow furrowed for a second. "Step uncle."

Before them, the Sushi Stuffed Haggis Burger Junction seemed to give off a divine glow.

"They oughta turn down the wattage on their gaudy Food Court Junction style neon sign though."

"Aye."

"Hai."

*   *   *   *

"Uh, like. Next?" the Sushi Stuffed Haggis Burger Junction semi-literate high school drop out cashier said.

"Next he says," Angus, who was indeed next in line, grumbled. "How am Ah supposed to order when there ain't a menu to choose from!"

"Uh, like. Sir?" the moron cashier asked Norman who was, to his moron cashier sharpened senses, the next customer in line.

"Hm? Oh, no. They're in front of me."

Blink. "Uh, like. What?"

"Logistically difficult overcome the angle," Shiro suggested while motioning at the counter that towered over them and blocked their view of the menu illuminated on the wall behind the cashier.

"Oh, Ah sees how it is. 'Oh, lookit wee Angus. What's the matter, laddie? Ye say ye hungry? Well, ye could juust go right on over to that Sushi Stuffed Haggis Burger Junction if ye was only three feet taller, but ye ain't!'" The idiot cashier could see Angus's whirling fists at the peaks of the Surly Scot's enraged hops. "'Ye be too short for food eatin' folks! Why don't ye just crawl under some rock and die like the midget freak ye are?!' Ah'll tell ye why, 'cause *Ah'm too busy bashin ye brains into pulp!*"

"Uh, like. Do you want fries with that?"

Angus' response was incoherent gibberish. It was the verbal equivalent of cracks racing across the face of a dam, little gouts of anger pushing from behind the crumbling barrier of sanity.

"Uh, like. That'll be $8.75?"

Angus leaped up onto the counter and kicked the register into the neighboring Pie Junction. "Ah ain't even ordered nothin', yet arsewart son of a donkey faced whore!"

"Uh, like. Please drive thru?"

Angus' body shook at around 9.6 on the Richter Scale. It sounded like a pot of water was boiling over. A kettle's screeching wail pierced the air as Angus' face flushed bright red.

The manager at the neighboring Tea Junction took the kettles off their burners.

"Uh, like. Next?"

"Must. Destroy. *Arsewart.* Laddie."

"Eheh, excuse me," Norman clamped his hands around Angus' midsection and put him back on the floor. "Shiro, you keep an eye on him."

"Hai," the Tiny Typhoon leaned over and pressed his face against Angus' Iron: Shoulder.

Angus pushed him away. "It's just an expression!" he seethed through teeth clenched tight enough to split diamonds.

Shiro considered it for a few moments. "Hai!" He did it again.

"GRAH!"

Norman stood up. "Um, sorry about that," he said. He scanned the menu over and behind the counter. "Let's see. We'll have the um. The Party Platter."

"Uh, like. Do you want fries with that?"

"Do you even sell fries?"

A dimwitted heartbeat or two later, "Uh, like. I'm going to have to get my manager?"

"Manager?"

The simpleton cashier disappeared into the Sushi Stuffed Haggis Burger Junction bowels. A woman of mammoth proportions, and perhaps heritage, waddled out from the back of the store. The walls shook with her every step. Plates, ingredients, and the like fell from shelves. She halted her glacial progression at the counter and leaned on it. The poor structure whined from the strain and the cash registers churned out nonsensical orders due to large amounts of lard pressing most of their buttons all at once.

Then Norman noticed that she wasn't leaning. Her girth simply oozed that far from its source. She seemed to expand before his very eyes like a cancerous beast of pure fat growing out of control. He and his companions took an unconscious step back while uttering "Neh!" under their breath.

"What do you want?" she mumbled through a mouthful of several Sushi Stuffed Haggis Burgers in various stages of solidity.

"Um, we'd, eheh. We'd, y'know. We'd like a uh, a um."

"A *what?*"

"A P-Pa-P-Par, Party Pl-P-Pla…"

"A Party Platter?" she rumbled.

"Er. Y-yes. I think so. Yeah."

Her stubby fat appendages waved and whirled about uselessly. "Chad! Hand me that Party Platter!" she vaguely motioned to the vicinity behind her which was quite a wide vicinity indeed.

"Uh, like. Where?" the imbecile asked.

She wheeled around dramatically. Or rather, her intent was to wheel around dramatically. The reality was that her incredibly fat head moved little more than three degrees in the direction of the knucklehead named Chad. But it was enough. Chad's dullard eyes could just make out hers. They focused on him. For some reason, footage of sharks bearing down on slow moving prey flashed—rather slowly—through his mind.

"If you don't hurry, you'll meet up with Brad." Her stubby arms of fat waved somewhere in the wide vicinity of her stomach.

Chad was suddenly Hermes. If Hermes was all pimply, stupid, and dressed in the demeaning Sushi Stuffed Haggis Burger Junction uniform complete with the dignity sucking paper hat consisting of a burger with a fish's head sticking out one side and a sheep's rear sticking out the other. He practically leaped into action, reachied out, and handed the bloated manager a Party Platter.

Her fatty fingers gripped the platter and set it down on the strained counter. Angus winced as she did so. He was convinced it would be the straw that broke the camel's back. Luckily, it was not. The rotund manager had to fight her own vacuous urges to keep her fat fingers from snatching up the burgers into her gaping maw of doom. As it was, Norman struggled against her vice like grip on the Party Platter until she reluctantly relinquished the dish.

"That'll be," she checked the row of registers. "Seven hundred dollars and twelve cents," she croaked fattily.

Shiro dug into his Tetsu: Pockets for some change. Angus smacked him in the back of the head.

"Look," Norman began. "The party Platter only costs $10.99 on the menu up there. You're reading the registers wrong or something."

She turned the upper portion of her tremendous girth to read from the giant glowing menu that was displayed behind her. Unfortunately, due to something of a weight problem, the layers and layers of flab restricted her movement because she was such an enormous fatty fat fat who was very fat from being *fat*. "I'll have to take your word on that," she grumbled under her breath.

"Here." Norman slapped a twenty on the remarkably resilient counter. "Take it. Just leave us alone." He put the Platter in the eager hands of Shiro and Angus and turned to the dining area. "What? Who the hell is that guy supposed to be?" he asked himself out loud.

"What did you do to her!" Atomik Lad's voice bellowed from his dining table and sliced through the clamor of Mall sounds.

The world screeched to a halt.

Issue 55—Turning Point

Earlier.

Nihel landed on the hot asphalt of the Mall parking lot. His cape settled behind him and draped itself over his shoulders out of habit. Shoppers flowed in and out of the Mall, in and out of their cars, and in and out of the parking lot. He stood among the churning clockwork of it all. Parking spaces, right of way, 4-way stops, and…

"They're called sidewalks! Look it into it!" an angry voice yelled from behind him. A horn blared. "I swear, just because you guys go around wearing capes doesn't mean you can make up the rules. Move it!"

Nihel turned around. A thick necked gentleman was leaning out of the driver's side window of a sports utility vehicle. The man seethed with every breath as veins pulsed in his thick reddened neck. "What could be so important that you must become irate?" Nihel calmly asked.

"Get your ass out of the way!"

Nihel gave an apologetic nod. "You don't have to yell." He stepped to one side and motioned for the driver to proceed.

"Goddamn fruits," the man muttered as he drove past.

Nihel watched him cut off another motorist. He watched him park, get out of his SUV, take three steps, and fall to the hot asphalt like a marionette puppet with suddenly cut strings. And in a way, it was an accurate description. Nihel had turned off his brain.

Nihel looked at the Mall. He could see dozens of people smiling, chatting, and eating inside a greenhouse looking enclosure. "Interesting."

Atomik Lad and Rachel found a big round table with enough chairs for their party. They claimed it as their own with the bright orange Game Junction bag as a flag of their conquest and sat down next to one another.

Rachel's hands shot into the bag and pulled out the video game. She removed the container's contents in a flash. She tore off the vacuum sealed plastic like it was not an impeneratrable sheen of aggravation and carefully opened the case. She practically ripped the instruction booklet out and began absorbing its alpha-numerically encoded information. Her brown eyes scanned each line, each picture, each button configuration, tip, combo, every last iota of data printed within the tiny tome.

She felt a pinprick of concern twitching at the edge of her consciousness. She turned to Atomik Lad. He was leaning on the table, looking at her with amusement in his eyes and a wide smile that he was trying to hold back.

"What?" she asked.

He shook his head lightly. "Just you."

"Oh yeah? And what of it?" she asked playfully.

He breathed deep. They were bathed in light flooding in from the huge windows of the walls and high ceiling. There was a warmth, more of life than heat, permeating the air. He leaned over and kissed her on the cheek gently, like she would crumble if pushed too hard. "You make me happy," he replied just over a whisper.

"I try."

"And succeed miraculously."

They kissed.

"Okay" Rachel said. "That takes care of the sexual urge. For *now*." She winked. "Let's do something about that food urge. Where be them friends of yours, hm?"

Atomik Lad craned his neck to see into the vast expanse of Food Court Junction Hutts. "For a seven foot tall black guy and two midgets in full suits of armor, it shouldn't be this hard picking them out of a crowd."

Rachel laughed.

"Ah, there they are," Atomik Lad said.

"Where are they?"

"I don't know, can't read the Hutt's sign from this angle. Looks like they're paying though. 'Bout damn time."

"What the hell?" Rachel asked herself aloud.

"What?" Atomik Lad turned around and followed her gaze to the Food Court Junction outdoor exit. "…The hell?"

An imposing figure walked through the automatic doors. Dressed in spandex the color of storm clouds and a cape that just barely defied black for an intensely dark red, the man reminded Atomik Lad of Superion. *He's escaped* flashed across his mind as adrenaline streaked through his veins like lightning. Villains often escaped in his experience, and they often wore darker outfits as a result of it. He didn't know why.

But then he saw it. "Nuke's N?" His heart became weightless from the after effects of his chemical bravery. His stomach, as if to reach an internal equilibrium, felt like it was filled with lead.

Nihel was only a few feet inside the glass house of dining. He made a quick survey of the surroundings. *Blind things. They waste their free will on deciding between this inane assortment of mundanity. And they don't even know. They flaunt their obliviousness like a badge! They built a Galactic civilization out of it! There is no choice here, there is no freedom. They have shirked their ultimate power for idle comforts. They hold the power to change the universe, yet they wallow in their own stagnation because it is easier to consume than to create. This, this is the epitome of my torture, my nemesis. Earthim. I hate the word.*

He growled aloud at a passing shopper who was burdened by several stuffed Gorge Junction bags. She fell over and was no longer burdened by anything.

Atomik Lad shot to a stand. "What did you do to her!" he demanded, his voice echoed in the large glass dining hall like receding thunder. The Mall screeched to a halt. Rachel squeezed his hand.

Nihel turned to him with a deliberate control. "This."

Atomik Lad braced himself for an attack that did not come. Rachel squeezed his hand tighter. Tighter. He tried to pull away from her but she tugged urgently, desperately at his arm in response.

He looked down at her. "Rachel…what?"

Her eyes were wide, pleading for help. Her mouth gaped silently for air that would not come. Her grip was weakening. He squeezed back to rouse strength into her body from his own. "Rachel!" he yelled frantically.

The Mall began running away.

Walls grew out of the ground and trapped over a dozen people before they could flee from their Food Court Junction Tables. "I haven't finished with you…*things* yet," Nihel growled.

Rachel's eyes were foggy and unfocused.

"Rachel!" Atomik Lad screamed.

She looked him straight in the eyes. For an instant, she was serene. She was beautiful. He knew she wasn't in danger. She would be fine. But her eyes broke their calm and flashed with terror. Her body spasmed, her neck went limp. Tears dotted her face. It stared into space, wide-eyed and locked in an eternally silent scream. "Rachel…?" It was a whisper, a plea. He crumpled onto the floor beside her and shuddered in tears, "Don't do this. Don't leave me. Don't leave me."

Nihel watched attentively. "You mortal things. You break so easily. And in so many ways. But asphyxiation has always been my favorite. It's such a beautiful lesson about your mortality. A living thing, a dead thing. The difference, physically and temporally, is infinitesimal. You are always alive for every single moment until the instant you die. I don't think anything else illustrates the symmetry of that statement any more than suffocation. It's rather parallel to your own lives. You suffocate yourselves with material things and then you die."

A wind picked up from nowhere. Nihel raised an eyebrow.

"Rachel-chan!" Shiro exclaimed.

Angus held him back. "Nay." His voice was muffled. He was visibly holding back tears.

"He's right, Shiro" Norman said. "In fact, I suggest if anything, we take cover."

"But Rachel-chan! Sparky-san!"

"Trust me," Norman said. "I know what's going to happen. I've seen Sparky mad before. We'll *need* cover."

The wind grew into a roaring gale. Tables and chairs were tossed aside as the last of the innocents ran away. Atomik Lad stood and Nihel realized it wasn't a wind. It was a force. Atomik Lad's feet hovered a few inches from the ground. His hair began whipping about his face. The windows of the walls cracked. Rachel's limp body was unaffected.

"Interesting," Nihel commented to himself.

Atomik Lad could barely see through his tears. Couldn't think through his anger. Didn't want to. A bestial growl rose up from his core. He could feel it washing over him like wildfire consuming everything he'd ever loved in flames of crimson. He could feel it rushing through him, urging him, destroying him and remaking him in its image.

Red. Always red.

Atomik Lad's body erupted with blood red hate. No control. No limits. He screamed and the Field pulsed with anticipation. The ground under him collapsed like the fist of God had smote it. Chips and shards of tile and foundation hovered in the air around Atomik Lad. They hung for a second and then were blast away. The wall behind him exploded outward and he shot to Nihel beyond speed. Screaming loud enough to crack stone, he punched Nihel with the force of an avalanche concentrated into the single point of his crimson covered fist. Nihel rocketed through the roof and into the clouds high above. Atomik Lad's scream bordered on hysteria. He gave chase into the stratosphere and obliterated most of the roof as he passed through it. A massive crater marked where he'd taken off.

Nihel barely had enough time to right himself before he saw Atomik Lad streak up to him like a crimson lightning bolt. His eyes burned red with rage, his face was twisted into the visage of unbridled fury. His veins pumped fire. He was beyond words, beyond reason, beyond morals, beyond all the petty distractions of life. He was pure, focused, invincible Anger. The clarity was perfection, immortality. Nothing was real any more. No pain, no justice, no consequences. Only Anger.

He was above Nihel now. He gave a punch fueled by rage. It struck with atom splitting force. Nihel was ejected from the immense aerial fireball and hit the Mall parking lot like a meteorite. Stray cars were scattered like mere pebbles. Fleeing shoppers ran back into the stores to avoid the storm of vehicles. Atomik Lad was upon him again an instant later. His hungry hands clamped around Nihel's throat before he could even open his eyes.

Atomik Lad squeezed hard enough to melt rocks. All around them lamp posts, trees, and car tops were crumpled and wilted by invisible crushing hands. He could feel an elation like the seconds before an orgasm. This was revenge. This was murder. This was madness. This was clarity. A perfect moment where the entire universe aligned to fuel him with its energies. This was the stark inevitability of existence. All that had ever been conspired for this one moment of perfection.

"Enough," Nihel croaked. His own hand dove through the crimson hurricane and slid his fingers around Atomik Lad's neck.

His body jerked. He became terribly aware of himself, of the moment. His clarity vanished and with it his Field.

Nihel stood, still holding Atomik Lad by the neck at arm's length. He squeezed, not painfully, just enough to let the ex-sidekick know what was at stake. Atomik Lad didn't move. "Won't you struggle for me?"

"I'll kill you," Atomik Lad stated flatly.

Nihel laughed a bemused little laugh. "Oh little, little Earthim. If only you knew how many times I've heard that. Your display was certainly impressive. But, like so many others before you, utterly fruitless." He squeezed a little tighter.

"Go ahead," Atomik Lad said while fighting the urge to struggle or gag. "Kill me. Nuklear Man will stop you."

"Nuklear Man, you say?" Nihel smiled. "Who do you think gave him this?" He pointed to the electron orbited N on his chest. "Your Nuklear Man is my Arel. We have been Fate's pawns since the dawn of time. He will bring an end to the old ways. He will destroy your petty little galaxy and liberate us."

"What?"

"You pathetic…you creatures never listen." He threw Atomik Lad back at the Food Court Junction doors several hundred feet away.

*   *   *   *

"Is she?" Norman asked.

"Aye," Angus said, his voice a wavering ghost of sound.

"Can't not that left the here her on."

Atomik Lad's body slammed up against the Plexiglas doors and cracked them into a bizarre kaleidoscope. He slumped dumbly to the ground and woozily tried to stand.

"There's no time," the Surly Scot said.

"Angus, we can't just leave her here!" Norman protested. "He bent down to pick her up.

Angus swat his massive arms away from her. "Ah said there's no time! Whoever that bugger is, he just chewed up Atomik Laddie and spit him out! Rachel's dead. There's nothin' we can do about that. Ah don't like it, ye don't like it, but that's the way it is. We've goot to split up. One o' us has to fetch Nuklear Man while the others stay here to stall this bastard so he don't get away. When he's taken care of, *then* we worry about, aboout Rachel."

"I'll stay," Norman said.

"Nay, laddie. You're the fastest oone here. Find Nuklear Man and bring him back here, but quick!"

"You sure you guys can handle it?"

"Aye. Ah've got more battle experience than both o' ye put together."

"Shiro-kun is the stay putting. Powaa is more than heavy when combination."

Norman paused.

"*Go!*" Angus urged.

Norman's body turned tungsten. Blue threads of magnetic energy wrapped and coiled around him and he took off into the sky.

Angus put his Iron clad hand on Shiro's Tetsu: Shoulder. "Are ye sure ye want to do this, laddie?"

"Hai."

They turned around. A thousand cracked Atomik Lads leaned on the fractured glass to support themselves outside. They could see a thousand cracked Nihels approaching him slowly, like the personification of inevitability. Shiro's giant red firecracker style rocket pack revved up. Angus made a minor trajectory adjustment by booting him in the arse at the last second before launch.

*   *   *   *

Norman looked down as he flew away. "Shiro?!"
The Tiny Typhoon was magnetized to the Tungsten Titan's shin. "Nani?!"

*   *   *   *

"Ah told ye Ah owed ye one." Angus looked at Atomik Lad and Nihel through the broken glass. They moved like cubist paintings given life.

He unfastened his Iron: Bagpipe Thruster pack. He removed his Iron: Gauntlets, kicked off his Iron: Boots, and slid out from his Iron: Armor. Only his Iron: Kilt remained. His body was a collection of scars and tattoos criss-crossing the thick weathered skin that stretched across his tiny frame. He breathed through his broken-several-times nose. Deep, loud breaths like a dragon looming over its prey. He hummed Beethoven's Ode to Joy. Each measure was a little louder, a little more insistent than the last. His bloodshot eyes were locked on the alien view beyond the glass. He seemed to expand as his muscles tensed. He sang louder with the whole of his throat. Beads of sweat appeared on him. His face was flushed. Veins popped out. He yelled his song now. Each note was sharp and guttural. An Ode to Rage.

*   *   *   *

Atomik Lad stood. His every fiber protested with aches ranging from piercing stabs to dull throbs, each one interwove with the others into a rich tapestry of pains. One hand was pressed against the glass door for support. He didn't expect its texture to be so rough. He looked back on it. It was like a spider's web spun from refracted light. The Mall's innards were an indecipherable amalgam of distorted images swimming around. He had to look away to keep his balance.
Nihel was coming.

Atomik Lad let his hand slip. His back hit the glass with a slight crunch. He leaned back heavily to stay upright. The earlier impact had driven away most of the feeling in his legs.

And Nihel was coming.

He tried to find the anger. Give in to it. Reclaim its purity. Become its living and willing vessel. But no. He was empty. Rachel was dead. What else mattered?

And Nihel was there. He stood before Atomik Lad. The ex-sidekick couldn't bring himself to look away from the red-black N on Nihel's chest. The symbol had been one of hope and justice. Atomik Lad should have felt insulted by its presence on Nihel. But he couldn't bring himself to be.

"You are going to die," Nihel said without looking down at him.

"I don't care," Atomik Lad said.

Nihel's eyes stared a hole through Atomik Lad's drooped head. Loose strands of his hair swayed in a light breeze. "Come now. You disappoint me," Nihel said. "Entire *civilizations* have have put up weaker oppositions than what you alone did just now. And *this* is how it is to end?"

Atomik Lad didn't move. "Get it over with. Kill me."

Nihel let out a deep sigh. "This is why I hate you creatures. You possess the ultimate power, the only true power in the universe, and this is how you use it." He wrapped his fingers around Atomik Lad's chin and gently turned his face upward. Their eyes locked for a moment.

Atomik Lad felt Nihel apply pressure to his jaw.

He closed his eyes.

He gave up.

His world exploded.

It sounded like glass shattering.

"YEEEEEEARRRRGHBLBLBLE!!!" Angus roared as he leapt through the glass door without thought or hesitation. It was merely a distraction, an obstacle to be overcome. He sailed through it screaming without meaning. His giant club smashed into Nihel's face. Atomik Lad felt the fingers around his jaw fall away and he too fell. He watched Nihel stumble backwards a step as Angus spun around, still in the air, and clubbed Nihel in the back of the knees.

Nihel dropped to the ground as Angus landed. Another blood curdling roar and the giant club smashed into the back of Nihel's head and slammed his face into the sidewalk right in front of Atomik Lad's feet. Angus raised the great club over his head and it suddenly became impossibly heavy. It fell behind the Surly Scot with the weight of a freight train. Angus snarled and lunged at Nihel with this bare hands.

The monstrosity snatched him out of the air and stood up. Angus clawed and gnarled like a feral thing trying to free itself from a hunter's trap.

"Now this," Nihel said to Atomik Lad. "This is what I had expected from you. The scrambling, desperate fight against death. It's so typical of every moment of your lives. You people will fill your thoughts with blather just to convince yourselves that you are not waiting for death. And then, when it's finally there to take you away from your endless diversions, you fight tooth and nail to avoid it because you're afraid. Afraid to live, afraid to die. You things bungle through years of blind terror and then you die. Like this."

In a single fluid motion of beauty, Nihel picked up the massive club, planted Angus on the ground, and impaled him through the stomach with it. It must've reached a foot into the ground.

"*Angus!*" Atomik Lad screamed.

The Surly Scot bellowed and coughed up blood. His limbs quaked as he reached up to grab at the club sticking out of his stomach. Blood poured from its edges in strong pulses and pooled under him from the exit wound. Blood ran over the concrete devouring it like locusts. Atomik Lad could see Angus' shivering body reflected in it.

Red.

Just like his parents. Dead memories soaked in blood.

Always red. Reaching out to him. Swallowing him. Becoming him. Killing him. Remaking him. He killed them. He did it. It was his fault they were dead. His fault. He recoiled from the pool as it expanded ever closer to him.

"Do you fear it after all?" Nihel asked. He approached Atomik Lad with slow steps that took him into Angus's spilt life.

Nihel paused. He examined Atomik Lad cowering against the thoroughly broken door with his legs gathered up against his chest. The blood was just short of touching him. His eyes were focused and yet far away and with absolutely no regard for Nihel's existence. "What do you care of that? You won't even fight for your own life, yet you weep for this one?" He shook his head. He reached down and picked up Atomik Lad by the collar. "Absurd little creatures."

Atomik Lad stared into the sky. It was too bright. The sun was directly above them. It filtered through a massive cloud that seemed to amplify the light into a giant blinding whiteness. He did not look away. He did not blink or squint. No red here. Not now. Just deliverance from it. Warm light cleansing him of its bloody sins.

He was weightless. And then the burden of the Earth crashed against his back. He was on the sun warmed concrete again. He sat up. Angus had removed the club from his gut and begun a new assault against Nihel's kneecaps.

"Admirable." Nihel commended.

Angus was ghastly pale. He strained to remain conscious. His hands were soaked in blood, one covered up what must've been the massive stomach wound while he wrapped the other tightly around the blood stained handle of his club. His breath was irregular and ragged.

"But futile."

Angus wobbled groggily. He spat blood onto Nihel's foot. "Don't start what ye can't finish!" He reared back and swung his club through another strike.

Nihel caught it. He sighed. "You have already lost. Be gone." The club lost its solidity. It became amorphous like a liquid that somehow maintained its club-like form. It unraveled itself into a serpent of metal that wound over Angus in seconds. He stood there, a statue of himself cast in his own iron.

Nihel gave a sinister grin.

The iron skin contracted into a sphere the size of a baseball with a horrible sound. Blood seeped from it, covering the whole of the tiny orb with liquid redness.

"No," Atomik Lad's voice resounded like a cat's footfalls. "No more. No more red." He closed his eyes. He could see blood pumping red-orange through the flesh of his eyelids; could feel it rushing through him; burning like wildfire with red, red flames. "*No!*"

Nihel faced him. "Taking your own life is arbitrary to you, but these others, *that* hurts you?"

Atomik Lad felt the air press against the whole of his body like a great bear hug from the atmosphere itself. A block of solid rock suddenly encapsulated his body with only his head poking out the top of it. Nihel glared at him. "I loathe you things. Now, I will show you just how much." He shoved the block through the remains of the glass door. He followed with footsteps like the march of death.

ISSUE 56—THE FALL OF NUKLEAR MAN

Nameless Technician and Random Extra were inside one of the Überdyne Mobile Command Units along the barricaded perimeter of Nuklear Man's now finished battle. Each one manned a console inside the van's cargo area. The dark interior was lit by their computer monitors, blinking lights, television displays, and a radar screen that was there just in case. Just in case what, exactly, no one knew.

"*Nameless!*" Random yelled over his shoulder.

Nameless Technician spun around in his Scientific: Swivel Chair. He had a bandage on his forehead from his work in the field earlier that day. "Report."

"There's a massive KI disturbance at the Mall," Random reported as ordered. He shook his head in awe of the readings streaming through his computer. "Our sensors can't handle it. It's like, like someone is warping reality itself."

"Great Kopelson's Ghost!" Nameless blurt. He jumped out of this chair and climbed into the driver's seat with all the grace of a botched trapeze act. He started the motor and gunned it. Random had to hold on to his console to keep from dropping to the floor. Nameless picked up the Scientific: Mobile Unit Radio Wave Communications Transmitter, "All units, this is Field Commander Technician. We have an unidentified aberration in sector G-7. Presumed to be comparable to a Nu Prime level event. I repeat, a Nu Prime level event as been detected in sector G-7. Placing a Media Cap on this new event is now our top priority. Auto Units, de-barricade and roll out." He pulled into traffic with even less grace than a botched trapeze act.

A fleet of Inconspicuous: Vans soon followed.

"Sir?" Random asked as he buckled up. "What about Nuklear Man? He's still at the previous site. I don't even think he was debriefed. What if he talks to the media?"

Nameless took a left turn from the far right sidewalk. "Do you think it really matters? Nothing he says makes sense anyway."

*   *   *   *

"Nuklear Man!" Erica yelled as she and her beleaguered cameraman ran up to him.

He nonchalantly posed. "Yo." He was at the edge of the construction site turned arena. Several Überdyne employees ran past him into a van that then peeled out into the street.

She finally reached him. The cameraman flipped a few switches, set the camera on his shoulder, and aimed its lens at the Golden Guardian. "Nuklear Man!" Erica said into her microphone. "Can you tell us about your latest battle?"

"Well, I'll tell you, Janice," he took the microphone from her before she could correct him. "It was a dark night. Dark like the heart of a demon, I say!"

*   *   *   *

Nihel slid his hand along the smooth top of the cube that encapsulated Atomik Lad. "Beautiful, isn't it, boy?" he said.

"Stop it," Atomik Lad pleaded through his tears.

Nihel smiled like the devil. "But don't you see? That's exactly the problem. I can't stop. This is Fate at work. But I'm trying. Oh, how I'm trying." His eyes scanned the crowd of fifteen terrified strangers who were united by the whimsical nature of tragedy. They clung to one another like loved one's in mourning. There had been two more in their pack, but they served as Nihel's first two lessons. "Pick one," he told Atomik Lad. "Pick one for me."

"Me, take me!" Atomik Lad asked. "*Just stop it!*"

"Always the same answer. Don't you see how that would be counterproductive? I'm teaching you! Your time here on this Earth is short, we must make the most of it." His cold gray eyes focused on a man in the group. "Ah yes, him." His was a face in every crowd. The Undecided and Other in every poll. The fair weather fan. "Your name."

"J-Jason Murphy," he said without looking at Nihel. He was cowering as much as a man could and still be considered standing.

"Nothing special about Jason," Nihel said. "Nothing unique or spectacular. A consumer. An anchor on his fellow man. A drag on the evolution of the universe." Nihel walked up to him. They stood toe to toe. The man was a head shorter than Nihel. "And yet even he possesses that which I am denied. Freedom," the word was a snarl. He turned back to Atomik Lad. "In a twisted way, I am at his mercy. His choice brought him to me. Here. Now. He is now no doubt rather nonplussed for said decision. But at least he was given the opportunity to choose!"

"Please...don't." Atomik Lad said. He tried not to look at what was left of the previous two lessons. "Stop it!"

Nihel shook his head solemnly. "No. I'm afraid I can't stop. This is Fate, you see? Everything I've ever done has led me to this single moment in space and time. Everything that has ever happened occurred for this." He turned back to Jason. "I'm going to kill you. You have no choice in the matter. How does that make you feel?"

"I don't know," Jason blubbered. His sobs were the sounds of his calm shattering.

"You don't know," Nihel slowly repeated. "I tell you that you will die, that your pathetic unfulfilled life is racing to oblivion at my hands and there's nothing you can do about it, and you stand there, sniveling that you don't know how it makes you feel!"

Jason fell to his knees, "I don't know!" he managed to grovel through deep, body shaking sobs.

"I'm going to kill you, Jason Murphy! It is Fate. How does that make you feel!"

"I don't know!" he blubbered.

"Enough of this," Nihel said. Jason's hemoglobin disappeared. He collapsed to the floor, quivered for a minute, and died.

"You!" Nihel said to another man in his dwindling collection. "Your name."

"Bill Greenwood," he said. His shoulders squared. He looked like he might've been in the military.

"I'm going to kill you, Bill Greenwood. You have no choice in the matter. How does that make you feel?"

"Angry."

"Now imagine being angry as long as time itself!" Nihel snapped. He stalked over to Atomik Lad. He held his head with firm hands. "Don't look away. This is anger, boy," he whispered.

The man shivered. His body convulsed like he'd been kicked in the gut. He crumpled into a fetal position, his face twisted in agony.

"First it infects you," Nihel said. "Then it eats away everything inside of you. Like acid."

Bill let out a scream that choked on itself as his skin took on a pale green quality.

"It doesn't just transform you." Wet fleshy clumps, sizzling and green, fell from his body. "It consumes you." Bill's body was eating itself alive. His skin was sickly green with mottled black splotches all over it. And melting. "Then you die." What was left crumbled into an acidic pile of burning and gurgling meat. "Look at it, boy!" he yelled. "That is what is left of you. That is what becomes of your soul, a dead thing." He let go of Atomik Lad's head and paced back to Bill's dead mass. "You wonder how I can do these things?" He ran his fingers through the rotting green. "Look on this and know." He scooped up a handful. "This is what I have become. Dead. Rotting. *Stagnant.*" Nihel took wide, powerful steps to his student. He slapped the stinking meat in front of Atomik Lad's face. "This is what I have become because of you things. Look at what you things did to Bill! All of you! *Look!*" He smacked the glob from the cube. "You, you things! You have brought this upon yourselves!"

Atomik Lad's face cringed. He looked away with closed eyes and tears streaming down his face. "Stop it!"

"We've been over this!" Nihel ranted. "I can't stop. This is Fate. Everything I do has already been determined. It's maddening, isn't it!"

But Atomik Lad wasn't listening. His eyes opened. There, by the only still standing table, lying next to a metal chair at a big metal table with an orange plastic bag on it was Rachel.

Rachel's dead body.

Rachel's dead.

Rachel. Is. Dead.

It's my fault. My fault. I loved her. I killed her. I did it. She is dead because I loved her. Nothing but dead matter now.

All I wanted was to drown in her being and never breathe again.

Never breathe again.

Dead. I can still smell her. Like vanilla candles and a canvas with fresh paint on it. Beautiful, creative, organic. I killed it all. Everything she would ever do. Dead. Because I loved her.

*   *   *   *

"Shiro-kun the back space to go at!" he insisted from Norman's left shin.

"I can't let you go, Shiro. It would slow us down and we've got to get Nuke back to the Mall before," his voice trailed away. *Angus must've known none of us had a chance against that guy. He got Shiro and me out of there to save our lives. He knew there'd be no way he could last long enough.* "…before we're too late," Norman finished with a catch in his throat. "Ahem. Look, there's the construction site now."

"From dragon's height eyes, the looking at there from now is devastator!"

"Yeah, must've been some fight."

Shiro clung to Norman's tungsten leg as they landed. The impact dug two small trenches into the ground before Norman took to a run to bleed off the momentum. Shiro felt like he was being rattled to death.

"So there I was, a lone bastion of justice and good looks against an insurmountable wave of vileness and depravity and fangs and pointy edges when—"

"Nuke!" Norman said as he ran up to the Hero and Erica who, at this point, wasn't interviewing so much as waiting to get her microphone back. They'd run out of tape some time ago, but Nuklear Man refused to be held back by technological limitations.

"Ah, another of Metroville's finest," Erica said. She managed to wrestle the microphone from Nuklear Man. "Mighty Metallic Magno Man, how were you impacted by—"

"No comment," he said. "Nuke, we've got to talk. It's serious."

Erica held the microphone between them out of habit even though she knew it would do no good.

"I'm in the middle of a very important interview here, Norman. And no matter how serious whatever you have to say is, I can already tell its less important than me talking about myself. Ain't that right, Kim?"

"Hm?" Erica said. "Oh. Er. No. We have enough footage. Yes, more than enough."

"You sure? It's been my experience that there's no such thing as enough of me talking." He posed and flexed a few times for emphasis.

"No, we're fine. Bye." She turned to her cameraman. "Run!" They did. Quickly.

"They don't know what they're missin'."

"Nuke!" Norman grabbed him by the collar. "Listen to me."

"We're gonna be friends for a lot longer if you let go of the threads. Catch my meaning?"

"Nuke, fine. Whatever. You've got to come with me. There's, there," he had to force his composure to remain composed.

"Get on with it, man!"

"Rachel's dead!" he blurt out. "Probably Angus and Sparky too," he held back tears that Shiro could not. "Oh God. This guy, he just took everything Sparky had and it didn't even slow him down. We both saw that kid disintegrate over twenty floors of The Dragon's high rise office building just by yelling at it. This guy, he just brushed it off like it was nothing."

"This guy, eh?" Nuklear Man asked.

"Yeah. I don't know him. We've never faced him before. And the weirdest part is he's got an N on his chest like yours."

"Of course! It all makes sense now."

"What? Does that mean something to you?"

"This guy is the ringleader. He must've started ripping off my very copy-righted N-symbol and now he's going around town bullying my friends so I'll be too scared to sue."

"Nuke, for once will you just listen? He *killed* Rachel!"

"No time for that now. I've got business to attend to. Where is this jerky?"

Norman sighed. "He was at the Mall when I left. At the Food Court Junction. Angus was supposed to be stalling him. You've got to hurry."

Nuklear Man nod. "Ya damn right I gotta hurry. It's about an hour past time to drop the hammer on this mo-fo."

He took off before Norman could respond. He could only watch as the Golden Guardian streaked through the air toward the Mall. "He has no idea what he's in for."

He looked down at Shiro. "I'm going in for back up. Something tells me he'll need it." He demagnetized and Shiro dropped to the ground.

"Going the where the danger place of hazarding. Shiro-kun the co-ordinates from battling!"

"Shiro. I know you want to help, but me and Nuke have been doing this together for years now. We're a good team."

Shiro scowled. "Getting there where there pointing at there."

"Look. We don't have time to talk about this. I'm going. The truth is, I don't know if I'll be coming back. I don't know if *any* of us going against this guy will. But the world will still need heroes, Shiro. Do you understand what I'm saying?"

Shiro took a deep breath. He bowed sharply. "Hai."

Norman bowed in response.

"Going at now. Time for!"

Blue threads of magnetism extended from MMMM's tungsten body and the Earth propelled him skyward.

Shiro watched him disappear into the distance. "Heroes from tomorrow are then today!" he resolved. "Must to have to found machinations devices of mechanicalness." He scampered off to begin his search.

✳   ✳   ✳   ✳

Nihel's face invaded Atomik Lad's vision. "I am teaching you eternal truths and you're locked in your own little world! Which, had you been listening, is part of the whole problem! You cowards lock yourselves away, unwilling to accept that which has been given you." Atomik Lad's eyes were still focused beyond Nihel's grim visage. It enraged the monster even further. "*What!*" he demanded. He followed Atomik Lad's gaze of self-pity to Rachel's corpse. "That? That is what is holding your focus? That? What, why?"

"I love her," he whimpered.

"Do you think that *matters!* Was that supposed to make her immortal?"

"I never really told her."

"And *now* you regret it? Typical. No matter how long you things live, it's never long enough, is it. Don't mourn for her death, don't mourn for your inaction. You chose not to tell her. And now she's dead. You chose! What else matters!"

"I killed her."

"So that's it. You think that was your doing? You think you chose for her to die?"

"I loved her, I brought her here."

"And you believe that was the cause? Your weak little ties have that much power, do they? Well, no. No, you did not do that. I did. It's bad enough that I must defer final credit to Fate, but I will not let your angst driven self-loathing take the action itself from me."

Atomik Lad, lost in his grief, shook his head.

"I can see this shall prove to be too much of a distraction if your lessons are to continue. Allow me to free your conscience. You believe yourself responsible for her demise? Then I shall kill exactly half of the people on this planet."

"What!"

"Chances are, if she were currently alive, this action would kill her independent of any relations you may have had with her. Therefore, you may rest knowing that you had nothing to do with her death."

"*No*! You can't!" Atomik Lad screamed at the top of his lungs, his voice rasping. "*Stop*!"

"How many times must I tell you? I cannot."

Seven of the thirteen prisoners collapsed. The other six cried out in agony tinged with the ecstasy of still living.

"No!" Atomik Lad cried. "Why are you doing this!"

"I'm doing this to teach you something, boy."

"*No*! Kill me! Stop hurting them, just kill *me*! Stop this!"

*   *   *   *

Nameless felt a tightening in his stomach wash over him. He slammed on the brakes as the entire flow of traffic ahead of him crashed into itself. The Inconspicuous: Van was hit from behind and became another link in the chain of wrecks. It was a citywide gridlock.

"Random, what the hell happened?" He craned his neck around to look into the van's innards. Random was limply hanging by the seatbelt in his chair. On the Scientific: Screen a massive wave of KI distortions washed over the city and beyond.

*   *   *   *

Dr. Menace was slaving away within the dark recesses of her Evil: Lair. Sparks flew as she went about the practice of Science. The Defusionizer Cannon turned Nega Cannon was in the middle of its final metamorphosis. The Nega Bomb. A weapon no longer designed for neutralization, the Nega Cannon's transformation into the Nega Bomb would make it the most powerful and dangerous item developed by human hands to date. If her or Dr. Genius' calculations were even slightly off, the entire world could be stripped of its very reality. As Dr. Menace toiled, she felt her heart tighten like a wave of nausea. She paused and looked around. Nothing seemed to be amiss. "No time for diztractionz." She made a few finishing touches. The Nega Cannon looked like it had developed technology cancer. Electromagnets, converters, and oscillators, and something not unlike a camshaft were scattered along its surface like a haphazard patchwork of devices. Purple light pulsed from its core. "Done." Menace had no time to congratulate herself. She went to her Evil: Computer to hail Ima before setting up the deployment equipment on the roof.

*   *   *   *

Across the globe every other human being dropped dead. Chaos followed. Roads were clogged with miles and miles of wrecks. Planes fell. Basic services of communication, left unmanned, were inoperable. Hospitals were over run and suddenly under staffed. All of humanity panicked as dead littered the streets. Riots would follow.

Three billion deaths in under a second.

The leaders of the world's nations panicked. A relatively tiny one that made up in paranoia what it may have lacked in size knew what was happening. Their people were mysteriously dying in the streets. Clearly, their enemies had just deployed some secret new weapon against them. To let such a heinous act go unpunished would be immoral. They attacked first, they attacked without provocation, they attacked like cowards.

They deserved retribution.

The nation's few nuclear silos opened and belched their poison into the stratosphere. They would only be the first.

Thousands of silos would open across the globe in blind response.

Three billion deaths.

They would only be the beginning.

*   *   *   *

Shiro's Tetsu: Boots crashed against the street and tossed up sparks with every step. His tiny legs pumped madly. He was a Dwarven Warrior with purpose. He felt sick to his stomach for a second, but it passed as soon as it had come. He attributed it to having run so much and thought nothing of it. He screeched to a halt and it tossed up a quick shower of sparks from his heels. "Ah-so" he said, looking upon the object of his quest: a Hando car dealership chock full of stocked vehicles. He rubbed his ironclad hands together as he approached one of the faster models. A sleek, silver, and aerodynamically curved little two door with enough horsepower to go to the Moon caught his eye. He checked to make sure no one was looking. There were several salesmen outside, but there was no way they could see beyond their cloud of nicotine haze. They seemed to be distracted by something inside the dealership anyway. He flipped open the fuel door and poured in a whole bottle of homemade Whisakey. He placed his palm on the door lock. A second later it clicked open and Shiro climbed inside. The car started up as if commanded to do so. He activated his Alteration of Normal Ideas of Matter Engine. It was the ultimate ability of his Tetsu: Samurai Armor. "Unchained the meaning of secrets. When ultimate power combination locked up. The time of now is then!" His little fingers drummed on the gearshift. He pulled it down from Park to Reverse to Neutral down to Drive. He paused there, jiggled the stick, and pushed it over to the right to reveal the previously unknown Assault Mode.

The car hovered. Its wheels retracted. Its geometry rearranged itself. Small wings extended from the side paneling and booster jets opened up in the rear. Several gun-looking implements made themselves known as well as a compliment of missile racks. Inside, the Pilot's Seat moved into a central position as levers and buttons pertaining to weapons systems and flight controls aligned themselves for Shiro's ease of access. "Nowing the time of being the time of heavy actions!" The little ship blasted off into the stratosphere, its autopilot set for the Mall.

*   *   *   *

So much death. So much meaningless death.

And it's my fault. I stood up. I killed Rachel and now I've killed everyone. I couldn't stop him. I'm nothing. I'm powerless. Senseless killing. So much death.

So much blood. Red.

Blood red. Red blood.

Locked in screams, silent.

Drown in her, in everything she is.

Dead. Never breathe again.

My fault.

My fault.

Kill me.

Kill me so this will stop.

All my fault.

I want to run away. I want to go where there is no pain, where there is nothing bad.

Where no one ever dies.

*   *   *   *

So dark and warm. The inner recesses of the soul. Of dreams and waking, nightmare images: self made hells. All fleeting.

"Time to wake up, John."

"Can't be. Too tired."

"We go through this every morning," Mom's voice lilts through the morning fog of my mind.

"I hate waking up."

"And yet you have to do it every day."

"God is Satan."

"The comedian or the philosopher this morning?"

"Need sleepy."

"No, need *wakey*." She opens the blinds to my window. Mid-morning sun rapes my eyes, destroys the fruitful core of my retinas with its violence. Leaves them for dead in the alley of my face. "Rachel will be here any minute to pick you up. Honestly, I don't know why she bothers with you sometimes. You always make her late to class."

With my eyes shut tight against the morning hell, I can hear Mom moving around my room. She's picking up clothes, straightening pictures, moving game controllers from the middle of the floor. I can smell her shampoo, the same she's used all my life. In my half awakened state I remember when I was a small boy I learned what it meat to be alone. She had driven me to school and dropped me off. When I (lost) left her, that shampoo-perfume smell disappeared. I wanted to cry. Waking up invokes the same urge.

"C'mon, hon. Your breakfast will get cold."

I open my eyes just as she leaves, turns a corner beyond my door and beyond my sight. Just a flash of her red hair bouncing away. I can feel my pupils dilating into themselves as I scan my room. Video games, comics, furniture, a poster of Solar Man battling Dr. Mayhem. Everything with its own official Überdyne Warning label. Dad's way of bringing his work home with him, he'd said. Warning: Waste of Time on the video game systems. Warning: World on the window. Warning: Slacker on my door. Dad's sense of humor is weird.

$*$ $*$ $*$ $*$

"Good gravy," Nuklear Man commented as he approached the Mall. The greenhouse style dining area was a silent battlefield strewn with the shards of glass soldiers. The parking lot surrounded a crater over a hundred feet wide and dozens of vehicles scattered across its perimeter. "Will these darn shoppers never learn a little self-restraint? It's only a sale, people. It'll be okay." He zoomed straight down in front of the broken Food Court Junction exit.

"Yo," the Hero said. His confident commanding voice resounded through the mostly empty Food Court Junction.

Nihel turned around slowly. "Arel," his voice was a mixture of awe and elation. He approached the Hero like a long lost brother and embraced him like salvation itself. "Arel, I've found you at last."

"Whoa there, big dog," Nuklear Man said while pushing away. He fixed his spandex. "Let's get one thing straight—and I do mean *straight*."

Nihel's brow furrowed. "Arel?"

"Stop with this whole 'Arel' schtick. It's wearing thin. I'm here to give you the warning you don't deserve. Cease and desist your use of my trademark symbol. If you resist said desistance, then I'll just have to lay the 'smackdown' as the kids are wont to say these days."

Nihel looked him up and down. "Yes, I should've known. You're still suffering from your amnesia. You don't carry yourself like the son of a god."

"Well, Dad wasn't really a god, he was a giant who was—" He held onto his head like it was trying to take off. "Oh geez, stupid headache."

"So if you have not accepted your true identity," Nihel mused aloud. "Then where are the others?"

"Others?" Nuklear Man asked with one eye cracked open. It shut again. "Oh, you mean Wussy, Weakling, Spanky, Dorky, Stupid, and Thhbbpt? Yeah I kicked their asses but good. We won't be seeing them any time soon."

"I see," Nihel responded sharply. "It took us centuries to perfect those peons." He took a deep breath. "No matter. You are here now. Our destiny awaits."

"Destiny?" The mind-piercing headache had subsided. "Look, buddy. I don't think we're on the same page here. You're illegally using my patented Nuklear N symbol. If you don't stop," he cracked his knuckles threateningly. "Ouch. Er, is what you'll be saying after I hit you. In the face."

Nihel made no response.

"A lot," Nuklear Man said in the hopes that his intimidation would be intimidating.

Nihel rubbed his temple and sighed. "Arel, Arel, Arel. How far you have fallen." He shook his head. "Look at what these Earthim have done to you. I had hoped to reclaim our former glory. And though I have waited so very long, I can wait no longer. I will not wait for you to recover your identity as Arel, Harbinger of the Flame."

"Why does that sound familiar?" the Hero muttered to himself.

"I don't need you. I only need your powers." Nihel closed his eyes. His cape ruffled slightly.

Norman crashed into the scene. His Magno Field collapsed upon itself. "Nuke! I've got your back!" he called while running up behind him.

"Thanks, Normie. But I think I can take care of this jerk—" A flash of light emenated all around Nuklear Man and he was completely encased in what appeared to be a glass cube.

"Nuke!" Norman yelled as he slid to a halt at the cube's barrier.

It shrank and expanded simultaneously in all directions across several dimensions of space and time.

"What did you do to him!" Norman demanded. He blindly punched the cube's shifting walls with his tungsteny fist, but to no effect.

"Nothing," Nihel explained. "I simply rearranged the matter around him into a hypercube expanding into higher dimensions at a linear rate. It's something of a prison you see. The only way to escape is if I dispel it, or if the prisoner were to exist in those higher dimensions. Arel does not. I shall transport him to the Galactic Hub and use him there to drain every last drop of energy from every star in the Milky Way, thereby destroying it just as he was born to do. With the galaxy obliterated, there will be no battlefield for Ragnarok, the destined war of good against evil. Fate will have been shattered. And I, *I* shall be free."

"Over my dead body!" Norman growled.

"Well, yes, actually."

Norman shook. His body quaked with anger. His friends were dead. He let out a cry of fury, deep, resounding, a warrior's cry. He leapt at Nihel.

The monster dodged over to the catatonic Atomik Lad. "Now watch, boy. Look at what Fate demands of me." He dashed back to Norman. Atomik Lad's eyes followed, but his mind did not.

*   *   *   *

Waffles. I swear they only exist as an excuse to eat syrup.

"Don't forget your vitamins," Dad says from behind his newspaper. Katkat—I told you Dad's sense of humor is weird—is beside him, on the floor and licking the milk from a mostly empty cereal bowl.

"Yeah, yeah." I take them with a shot of orange juice for each. Vitamin E, Multi-Vitamin, Calcium, and Ginseng. The orange juice is calcium fortified and has extra pulp in it. Dad likes vitamins.

"Mew!" Katkat says.

"Good boy," Dad puts down his paper. I'm nineteen, but when I see him I feel ten years younger. He is a giant with the strength of a god and a laugh that could infect anyone with his friendship. To me he is the living embodiment of vigor, power, confidence. He doesn't look a day over thirty, just like Solar Man. He could chop down mountains.

When I was a kid, I asked him how he was so much stronger than me. He said he had overpowers from his experiments at the Nuclear Physics Center. I think a part of me never stopped believing that.

He looks at his watch. "Hm, running a little late, are we?"

"I'm not really late until Rachel—"

"Hello!" front door slams shut.

"—Gets here.

"Rachel," I hear Mom say cheerily from her bedroom. It's near the front door. "I'll just take my usual seat, shall I?"

I can hear mom walking through the house to the kitchen, "Yes. Sorry, dear."

"It's okay, Mrs. Koen." I can hear Rachel sitting on the leather couch in the living room. My mind is of course instantly ablaze with thoughts of her ass and leather. I'm young and healthy. I can't help it.

Mom is in the kitchen now. She leans down to Dad. They kiss. It's not that they're ugly people, far from it. But they're my parents, the ass and leather disappear. You understand.

"Looks like the boy is pathologically late. He can't help it," Dad says to her as I put my dishes in the Warning: Woman's Work sink. I said he has a weird sense of humor.

"Gee, I wonder where he gets it?" she says.

Dad's eyes scan over her for a second. She even has her lab coat and name tag on, Dr. Heather Koen, Überdyne Theoretical Physics Department. He looks at himself. Unshaven, old orange bathrobe, undershirt, and boxers. "Hm. Is it eight thirty already?"

"More like eight forty-five," she says.

"Eep."

I pass them, wink at Rachel in the living room, and dash into the bathroom to brush my teeth. I catch Dad in the corner of my eye as he dashes into his bathroom to do the same. His bathrobe is flapping behind him. Dad's cape. I load my toothbrush.

I hear Mom sitting in the recliner next to Rachel.

"Men," they say together.

I smile and I brush. I'm only fifteen minutes late.

*   *   *   *

Nihel grabbed Norman by the arm and twisted it off effortlessly. His cape followed through in slow motion. Norman fell to the ground and clutched at the perfectly flat stub of his shoulder. His tungsten teeth clenched. He held back a scream.

Nihel examined the detached arm carefully, like a jeweler inspecting a gem for its value. "A fascinating biology," he said. "His entire body turns to metal. And not even in parts, such as metal bones, muscles, and so on. But rather a completely solid block of living metal. Tungsten to be exact," Nihel continued. "A versatile and interesting substance."

Norman pushed himself beyond the pain. He concentrated his Magno Power, made it the crux of his existence. The pain dissolved away. He picked up a discarded van from the destroyed parking lot. He couldn't see it, but he didn't have to. It rose into air on wings of blue energy.

Norman held the van directly above Nihel. The thin blue threads of magnetism around the van expanded as the Tungsten Titan super charged the van's magnetic attraction to the Earth while simultaneously repulsing it to keep the vehicle suspended. The van rattled as its parts were violently stressed by the mounting magnetic forces opposing each other.

"A high melting point, excellent tensile strength, resistant to fatigue and oxidation." Nihel gave the arm an appraising stare. "Not terribly magnetic though."

Norman let his magnetic hold slip. The van almost instantly broke the sound barrier. It rocketed like a rail gun's projectile and slammed down on Nihel. The hypersonic force crumpled it like a brittle piece of origami. Norman almost smiled through the excruciating pain of his dismemberment. The wrecked van looked like a piece of modern art, something the Mall might've purchased in an attempt to beautify its grounds.

Until it turned to water and washed away. Nihel stepped out of its crater and walked to Norman. "You pathetic wretch," he growled. "Haven't you been listening? I am performing my destiny. You can't stop it." He tossed the spare arm at him. Norman winced. "Are you watching, boy? Are you watching what Fate is doing to your friends?"

Norman suddenly felt like he was on fire.

"See what fate does? It deforms you. It is an inevitable process."

Norman began melting. It was like his veins pumped lava. He wouldn't scream. He wouldn't give Nihel the satisfaction.

*   *   *   *

We're running through campus. I ask Rachel "Why? We're already late."

"Okay, do you want to be any more late to Dr. McDougal's class than you have to?"

"Good point. Speed up, woman!"

We hurdle over a row of bushes, throw open the big double doors to Floyd Hall, run down the hallway and burst into Room 112. Loudly. Our classmates snicker.

She squeezes my hand (too tight, what? What's wrong? Tell me, tell me!)

"Nice of ye to join us," Dr. McDougal says. He's sitting on his desk, his feet dangling above the floor, a book in his gnarled hands with his tiny thumb marking a page. He spoke with a slight Scottish accent and wore his beard as full as possible. He was fond of plaid shirts.

"Sorry."

Rachel doesn't say anything. We get to our seats as quickly and quietly as possible. We sit right in the middle two seats of the middle row. It makes me feel centered.

I haven't been sitting for a full minute before a meaty finger pokes me in the back. I turn around even though I already know it's Norman. The Intellijock. This guy is nearly seven feet tall, practically four hundred pounds of ebony muscle, he's got a full ride football scholarship, and he's got a 3.9 GPA. No tutors or anything. And the girls are all over this bastard. I'd hate him, but he's just so damn likable (magnetic?).

"Kinda late, aren't ya?" he smiles his big damn smile.

"Eh. Time is relative."

"Punctuality, it would seem, is not."

I laugh and turn back around. Dr. McDougal is, of course, ranting. The man is certainly passionate about his philosophy.

"What ye have to understand is this. The mind is not special. It's easy to think it is. Natural humanocentrism practically *makes* us believe that our minds are special or somehow separate from the material world. There is no rational or empirical reason to believe this. Our minds are simply the result of evolution. It was advantageous for our species to have individual members communicate to one another for the sake of survival and propagation. The fact that these minds turned out to be so good at collecting, trading, and storing information that as time went by the minds, less concerned with the basic needs of survival, could then reflect upon their own existence. It's an interesting advantage, certainly more diverse than claws, but that does not put us 'above' any other creature!

"Our minds are as natural a part of the universe as anything else. They are simply the product of the cosmos. This does not subtract from our dignity. Far from it. This *is* our dignity. Our beauty. And this is why murder is wrong. It destroys a part of the universe. It is a disruption of symmetry. It's a waste. A bloody (bloodybloodybloodybloody hands of fire, soul, hate destroy—go from here!) waste."

*   *   *   *

Norman looked like a wax statue of himself that had been left in the sun too long. He lay on his back, most of it in a half-congealed puddle while the rest of him slowly lost its shape. He wanted to scream, but whatever mechanisms that would have allowed him to do so had already melted away. It didn't matter though. In his mind, he was screaming. Sickly blue threads of energy limply extended from his malformed body. It was the only way to scream.

"Don't you creatures know when you've lost!" Nihel yelled at the melting Tungsten Titan. "Look at you! You're not alive. You're not dead. Heh. You don't even possess a specific material shape anymore." He leaned in close to Norman's mangled face. "I'd change you back to your biological form if doing so wouldn't end your torment," he whispered tauntingly.

Not that it mattered. Norman couldn't understand a word Nihel was saying. Just as he had lost his capacity for speech, so too had he lost his ability to hear. Or see. All he knew was pain. All he wanted was to scream and bleed and die. He could feel himself falling apart. There was nothing else.

*   *   *   *

Shiro's ship raced through the clouds. He opened up all sensors and focused them on the Mall. Atomik Lad, Mighty Metallic Magno Man, and six standard humans were accounted for in the vicinity of the alien stranger. Shiro was puzzled by Nuklear Man's apparent absence until the sensors finally made sense of an extradimensional anomaly. "Ahh," he said. "Enemy of intelligence is like spirit. Smart time. Encapsulated the capturing with supaa space dragons of universalities multiplied." The Mall rushed below him. Shiro looped back and his target floated above him. A pair of crosshairs were superimposed on the cockpit. They were aimed at the hypergeometric cube. He was weightless for an instant where time stood still. "Nothing that to be was made can't not then the solvent by exploding action!" He pushed the ship's Whiskaey-Fusion Drive to Critical. His craft was seconds from becoming the reaction mass of a fusion bomb.

Shiro was heavy with power.

*   *   *   *

Middle row, the seat to the right of the center. Rachel beat me to it just to annoy me. She's like that. I love her for it. Second class of the day. I'm taking notes now, but not too many. Rachel takes notes like her life depends on it. I don't know why. She never looks over them for tests or anything.

Dr. Menasavich. Short jet black hair and pale skin. I usually dig olive skin tones, I mean look at Rachel. But on Menasavich, yowza. Everyone knows at least half of the people who sign up for this class, guys and girls, only do so to have an excuse to look at her for an hour every other day. Hopefully they'll get something more out of it though. It's really interesting stuff. Political Science. Specifically, the Philosophy of Revolution. I could listen to her all day. The accent isn't hurting.

"What you have to underztand is thiz. Oppression iz a natural part of any zociety, inzofar az anything about a zociety can be zaid to be 'natural.' There iz nothing wrong with oppression az long az thoze who are oppressed are aware of it. Consciousnezz of oppression leadz to anger, outrage, and finally action—of varying legality. Only through knowledge of oppression can there be any change. Anger iz the only motivation. Happinezz iz ztagnation. Anger promotez change. Change iz life. Happinezz iz zuffocation. Happinezz iz silence, iz death. Anger iz the fuel of revolution. Revolution iz change, iz life. But here iz the catch. Revolution dizposes of the old order and replacez it with the new. Thiz new order will zeek to ztabilize itz *own* power. Thiz power muzt come at the expense of otherz. Thuz, revolutionariez inevitably commit the zame crimez az their oppressorz."

I swear Rachel would be writing it down word for word, but Menasavich isn't talking that much!

"You will, in the courze of your livez, ztand on both zides. You will be oppressed. You will be oppressive. It iz a cycle. It iz Fate (that makes me kill, it is you who let me do it—go!)."

* * * *

The ship approached terminal velocity. Shiro grit his teeth as the craft pierced the clouds and fell to the Earth with rocket boosted speed. He watched the engine's heat gauge climb ever closer to the hazardous red area. "High way to Danger Zone!" he commented to himself as Metroville rushed up at him. The little superimposed cross hairs were in the center of his Forward Viewport. The Altimeter looked like it was trying to count down to zero in record time. The heat gauge finally pushed into the red. "Danger Zone lastly at the way of height when attained from fast with speed."

He pulled a lever and shot out of the cockpit into the the atmosphere rushing past him. Luckily, his Tetsu: Samurai Armor was sturdy enough to withstand the violence of motion. His Tetsu: Little Rocket flared to life and guided him to a nearby rooftop as gently as colliding with a solid surface at several hundred miles an hour can be. He tumbled to a stop and stared up at white fluffy clouds.

Exactly .8 seconds later the ship plunged through Nuklear Man's hyperdimensional box wherein the craft suffered a complete protonic reversal. Its ton of mass and fifteen gallon tank filled with whisakey, the most volatile substance on the face of the Earth, were instantly transformed into antimatter by having the engines set to Self-Destruct. The resulting matter-antimatter reaction was more than enough to obliterate the walls of the higher dimensional cube imprisoning Nuklear Man by destroying the matter they were built from. All part of his plan.

Shiro's mission was a success. The Tiny Typhoon could tell because he had not been vaporized in the explosion. Also part of the plan. He breathed a sigh of relief as clouds slowly wafted through his sight.

*   *   *   *

Nuklear Man stumbled a few steps. He rest his palms on his knees and let his head hang for a moment. "Woo!" He stood up straight once again. "Man. That was messed up! I could see the music. Sounded kinda like Hendrix."

Nihel growled. "Why do you things insist on fighting the inevitable!" He stood and spun to face Nuklear Man, his red-black cape flowed behind him almost too slow to be natural. "I can see we're going to have to do this the old fashioned way."

"Blame Sparky?"

"Enough!" Nihel bellowed. He punched Nuklear Man.

Nuklear Man fell back a step from the impact. He wiped blood that wasn't there from his mouth. "Oh, I see how it is. Resorting to genre conventions, eh? Well two can play at that game!"

The Climatic Fight began.

Nuklear Man flew into a rage of blows that struck with earth shaking force. Literally. Shockwaves emanated from the power of every punch like explosions without pyrotechnics. The ground shook, the walls cracked, but Nihel was completely unaffected. He grabbed Nuklear Man's fist on one of its assaults and squeezed it.

"Ow, ow, *ow!*" Nuklear Man yelped.

Nihel's free hand clenched into a fist. He pulled it back and slammed it against Nuklear Man's jaw. The Hero sailed into the parking lot where he slammed through several stray cars before coming to a stop in a mutilated minivan. He tore through its metal frame like it was a spider's web. He plant his feet firmly on the ground and promptly wobbled while holding on to his head. "Okay, world. Quit movin' around." He blinked a few times and looked at Nihel who was still standing in the now distant Food Court Junction. "Aw c'mon. One was bad enough, but now three of him? All dancing around like that?" He gave a tired sigh. "This is only going to get worse before it gets better."

*   *   *   *

Ima floated up to the Scientific: Communications Panel. She wiped her brow with her lab coat. "Veronica. I am finished."

Dr. Menace appeared in the view screen. "Are you ready to jettison the Skyjumper?"

Dr. Genius breathed deep. "Yes."

"We have been at oddz for mozt of our careerz, but I swear that I will do what I can to bring you back down."

"Don't worry about that now. All you have to think about is getting that Nega Bomb of yours on the Skyjumper's hull before it reaches the surface. I adjusted the KI Alteration Drive. Ordinarily, it makes an antigravity field around the ship about thirty meters in diameter. It should now treat the affected radius as though it was the extent of the entire universe. Anything can get in, such as your bomb and our two targets. But, once inside, nothing can get out. This should include the explosion since, to anything inside there is nothing else."

"Excellent. When will you make the drop?"

"As soon as you're ready to launch the bomb."

"I have to get to the roof. Give me one minute."

Ima nodded and pushed herself to the Watchtower's Scientific: Main Computer. She punched in the Dock Release code. Lights flashed to warn personnel that wasn't there to keep a safe distance from the Airlocks. Ima smiled. The only other person on the automated Scientific: Satellite was Yuriko. And she certainly wasn't going anywhere.

Alone. With but one window to the world below. My world. It's going to be a long wait for any rescue party. Things should work well enough in my absence. Überdyne's world order is practically a perpetual motion machine. It only needs the occasional tune up. Everything will be fine. There should be enough heroes left to stop Veronica from trying to disrupt anything in the meantime.

Seconds ticked by. Her hand hovered over the Release button. She pressed it.

✳   ✳   ✳   ✳

The hot afternoon sun beat down on Menace like a giant hammer of fire. The impromptu Nega Bomb was tucked under her arm. She ran to her makeshift delivery system. It looked like an oversized mortar launcher with a little display screen and keyboard stuck to it. She stuffed the bomb into the shaft and switched on the mini-computer guidance system. "Scanning," the screen blinked in big red letters. The mortar beeped and reported "Positive Lock," at the bottom of the screen. In another corner of the small screen a mini-cam projected the image of the falling Skyjumper. She could just make out its fiery hairline of friction-fire with her own eye as it fell. The mortar adjusted itself while calculating velocity, wind, and so on.

The screen count down.

Three.

Two.

One.

The tiny missile flew into the sky. It would intercept the Skyjumper in just under a minute and attach itself to the craft's hull. It would then set its own timer so that it would go off a microsecond before impact with the ground. It was almost too easy.

$$*\qquad*\qquad*\qquad*$$

Walking through campus now, Rachel's shoulder playfully bumping into mine with every alternate step. I love it.

It's an early afternoon of Spring. Not too late in the day or season to be hot yet. But it's getting there. We're going back to Rachel's car, a sporty little import. Red, of course. We'll go back to my house and fuck our brains out. Life is good.

"Could you drive?" she yawns while putting the keys in my hand.

"I don't really have a choice, do I?"

"Nope."

"Why are you so tired, anyway?"

"Some of us actually wake up on *time*." She sticks out her tongue and winks. "Now open the doors."

"You really think twenty minutes of lying down in the car will recharge your batteries?" I open the doors and we climb in.

"You'll find out, now won't you."

"Yowza."

$$*\qquad*\qquad*\qquad*$$

Shiro listened to the last of the thunderous blows echo through the city. He chanced a look at the streets below. The roads were clogged with wrecks as far as he could see. The sidewalks were littered with bodies. Some of them were accompanied by helpers or scavengers, he couldn't tell which. He could hear sirens screaming in the distance from all sides. He had to look away from it all. He turned to the heavens. "From what of is? The why of being now!"

Something glinted in his vision. "Nani?" He flipped down his Tetsu: Ferocious Demon Mask to benefit from its high-tech sensory gadgetry. "Seeing Eyes of Sight. Focusing the sector of area. Ninety seven-ten." His sensors focused on the rapidly plummeting Skyjumper. "Projection the divination time now when later at!" His suit calculated a 99.999% chance that the craft would strike down in the vicinity of The Mall. "The calamities aren't to ending from multiplications!" he said with an exhausted gasp. He flipped the face mask back up and peered at the free falling fireball with eyes tempered by determination. "Hero of tomorrow is winning today before born yesterday!"

His Tetsu: Rocket propelled him into the dangerous sky at nearly escape velocity with a corkscrew trail of smoke in his wake.

Shiro slapped up against the hull of the plummeting Skyjumper like a bug splattering against a windshield. The impact made him feel like his teeth had been knocked out with a hyperactive tuning fork. His ferocious demon-style mask had automatically deployed itself to protect his face from the fierce winds of speed. His limbs sprawled out to the fullness of their shortness. Shiro clung to the Skyjumper's nose like one of those stuffed animals that always get suction cupped to the inside of car windows. "Fukazake Shiro! Action the time is being—GO!!!" he yelled above the cacophony of motion around him. His red oversized firecracker-looking rocket flared into action pushing against the craft to slow and stop it.

The Skyjumper was unaffected.

Shiro's little fingers clamped against the hull. "Please! Strength from dragons on now. Ancestors which mighty when there to be forming!" he pleaded with himself. "Computing. The boost energy from powaa, that could taken Whisakey Overdrive!" The computer in his helmet made a few calculations and superimposed the results of his query onto his vision. Sadly, it would be impossible to halt the Skyjumper's descent. All available power, plus the incredible energies afforded by his Whisakey Overdrive still wouldn't be enough. "Kuso," he muttered. He devoted more of his suit's power to the rocket, but the Skyjumper continued to gain speed. The Mall raced up to him. The Mall. "With at Sparky-san and Nuklear-san and Norman-san there is. Surviving probabilities, but the standing by innocently? Many are killed the way of falling!" He grit his teeth. "Shiro-kun, not the stand of it! Exploding action cannot to have then!" He checked over his suit's power levels. "If the way of cooling dragon engine becoming *instead* the way of dragon engine *fire*, adding of powaa Whisakey, the chance is heavy with smallness!

"Having to is the hero now. Can't the failure!" In a matter of seconds the Skyjumper would impact the Earth and kill a hundred? two hundred? innocent people trapped throughout the Mall and its surrounding areas. He could stop it. He willed every last ounce of his suit's power to the rocket including the vital Cooling System. In a matter of seconds, Shiro would effectively be welded into his suit by its own heat and be cooked to death in an iron oven. He knew this. He engaged the Whisakey Overdrive. His small rocket threw out sparks and white hot flames. He could already feel his suit beginning to overheat.

"Not the matter," he grunt as the heat increased. "Shiro-kun are of samurai. Shiro-kun are of hero."

Then it happened.

He felt the Skyjumper move, just slightly, up. Which was quite problematic since it was still going down. The tremendous thrust from such a limited point in on the Skyjumper's hull caused the nose to edge up ever so slightly. Then more. And more. And more until the Skyjumper was positioned horizontally. Which was problematic since it was built to be as aerodynamic as humanly possible to make it appear as though it did not indeed fly by a highly dangerous and largely untested process that was barely understood even by its designer Dr. Genius.

"What!" Dr. Genius screamed from her Scientific: Communications Panel.

"No!" Dr. Menace gasped from her Evil: Computer.

They watched as their plan to save the Earth, and the entire galaxy, went awry. The Skyjumper was rocketing away from the Mall at an incredible velocity while its descent was starting to level off. Even so, the Nega Bomb's timer counted off its final seconds as planned. According to Shiro's onboard computer, if he could hold on just a little longer, he'd be able to clear the rest of Metroville's high-rises and then—

A giant sphere of black flashed into existence around the Skyjumper just barely long enough for the human eye to see it. The Skyjumper and all the reality that existed around it, was quite literally nothing. And though the space the sphere had occupied now looked perfectly normal, anything that touched one side found itself instantly and painlessly transported to the other side nearly a hundred feet away.

An oversized firecracker arced down from the sky, bounced along a sidewalk and into a car that had swerved off the street when its driver had simply dropped dead like so many others. The rocket was smoking and glowing slightly. Most of its paint had apparently melted off. Only a few red specks remained.

Shiro himself landed like an airplane wreck on the roof of an apartment building that had become abandoned only minutes ago in the throws of mass terror following the throws of mass death only one minute before that. Luckily for Shiro, but perhaps more so for the apartment building, he was somewhat less huge than an airplane. The damage was minimal and mostly concentrated on his body. He lay on his back, panting and sweating considerably while most of the suit's power was involved with the Cooling Systems. He stared at the space the

Skyjumper had occupied in its last moment not even a full second after he'd let go and jettisoned his Tetsu: Rocket. His suit's computer had projected that the craft should've been propelled to the vastly unpopulated Irradiated Flats between Metroville and the Silo of Solitude. Instead, it had been swallowed up into nothing. "Sometimes when the dragon from void stared in, back up the depths looking," he philosophized quietly.

*   *   *   *

Nuklear Man danced like a prizefighter.

Who had just been knocked down about five times in the first round.

Nihel stalked around him like a mountain lion toying with its prey. He punched Nuklear Man in the back of the head hard enough to split steel, "This is quite fitting." Another punch, "In its way."

Nuklear Man flung himself from the ground into something resembling a stand and took a wild swing. Nihel barely had to move to dodge it. He countered with a thunderous elbow to Nuklear Man's nose just because he could. He feel to his knees.

*   *   *   *

Driving through town. It's the end of the lunch hour so traffic is clearing up. The windows are down and there's the "vaoosh" noise of cars going by in other lanes. The sun is warm on my skin and I almost think myself as somehow being closer to nature. In a car. Driving down city streets surrounded by concrete and steel. And here I am picturing myself in tune with nature because I'm driving with the windows down instead of using the AC? I laugh at myself. I turn to Rachel. Her eyes are closed, her black hair shines with a reddish tinge from the sunlight. Good Lord, what is a brilliant, beautiful, amazing person like this doing with a slob like me?

Hm, we'll be coming up on Main pretty soon. It'll take too long to go that way. I'm in a bit of a hurry to get home you understand. I'll turn on to Ellis at the Überdyne building. I've got a lot of history there (cold, alone, tests, red flames destroy everything—). That's where Mom and Dad met. They still work there today. Dad said he couldn't think straight for a week after he saw her. He finally managed to go to lunch with her. They went to this little sandwich shop across the street. They've gone there for lunch every working day since.

*   *   *   *

"Your fate was to *defy* Fate." Another punch. "But we never thought you'd take it *this* far." And another. "We don't have to do this, you know." And another. "You are Arel." Another punch, they were horribly constant, like the ticking of a clock. "If you will only accept that, then all the power of the universe will be yours!" He leaned in close. "Don't make me destroy you for the sake of my freedom." A final punch.

*   *   *   *

I take the turn onto Ellis. I'm on autopilot. I've driven this way hundreds of times. I'm ogling Rachel as she half naps beside me. There's a flicker of motion in the corner of my eye. Before I even know it's there, like some kind of traffic sixth sense, I know it's too late. The whole car is jolted as a blur of white motion tumbles onto the hood and up the windshield with a horrible crunching sound. I've already locked up the breaks and Rachel's screaming. I'm horrified and revolted as I hear thick, meaty things rolling across the roof.

The car almost spins out. All I can do is push harder on the brakes and hold the wheel tighter. Our front end slides into the on coming lane. A car swerves away. Rachel is yelling at me. There's blood smeared all over the cracked windshield (cracked like spider's web spun from refracted light—).

*   *   *   *

Nuklear Man looked at him from the floor. His head wobbled slightly from the severe beating he'd taken. His eyes were dull, lazily focusing on objects a few seconds after locking onto them. "It's time…" he said while struggling up.

"Yes?"

Two Nuklear Fists collided with Nihel's chin, "To drop!" Nihel stumbled back from the blow and Nuklear Man closed in, "The hammer!" Nuklear Man locked his hands together and brought them down on the monster like lightning. Only stronger.

Nihel recovered and his cape draped itself over his shoulders. "I have waited too long for this! Loki insisted on waiting for the right time. On waiting for when the gods would be blind to his machinations as they prepared for their Ragnarok.

He wanted to bring them down at their peak. He wanted revenge. I don't give a *damn* about his revenge," Nihel hissed. "All I want is to be free of Fate's shackles. *Now!* To hell with Loki's rantings. To hell with your amnesia! Your power is the key to my freedom. Give it to me!"

Nihel backfisted Nuklear Man back through the ruined Food Court Junction entrance. He tumbled to a halt on the ground and lay face first on the cracked tile floor. He felt like he'd been run over by, well, *everything.* "And in a way, I have been," he muttered to himself. "Nihel is powered by the very existence of reality itself. Wait, how do I know that?" his voice slurred the words through a fog of pain.

*   *   *   *

Rachel is yelling. Another car swerves out of the way.

Her hand is squeezing mine. Too tight with urgency (what? What's wrong? Talk to me, tell me!) She's pushing my hand, moving the gearshift and yelling.

I'm looking at her and its like the first time. Only more so. I can't believe how hyperaware I am. I even have time to reflect on the fact that I'm reflecting. I'm seeing her with new eyes. Time is nothing. This moment is everything. This moment is clarity.

*   *   *   *

Nuklear Man could feel something cool against his hand. He looked at it groggily. It was, "Norman?" The Tungsten Titan was a pile of metal melting at room temperature. Only his upper torso and head retained any semblance of form. His sightless eyes drooped, his face was a grotesque perversion of its former self. He was a bad acid trip. "Norman. P...pull yourself...pull yourself together man!" Nuklear Man ordered. "Pull yourself together!" he said again, this time with a slight edge of hysteria creeping into his voice. He pushed himself up. His mighty arms quaked from the effort. His strength had left him several punches ago, but he had to get away from the mockery of Norman.

Norman...my best friend and partner for as long as I can remember. It was your idea Norman, do you remember? Your idea for us to work with Überdyne to help make the world a better place. Your idea for me to take in Sparky, to teach him how to be a Hero. You always deferred to me as the leader, but it was always you, you were the backbone of our team...Pull yourself together.

"Why do you oppose me?" Nihel asked. He punctuated his question with a sharp kick to Nuklear Man's that sent him into the air. He landed in front of the Yogurt Junction. "We were so good together. We were the scourge of the Galactic Territories for a thousand years! Even the gods themselves feared us. But now? Now, you leave me with no alternative. I have to destroy you and take your fire."

"No," Nuklear Man moaned.

"I'm afraid you don't have a choice," Nihel sneered. "How does that make you feel? Angry? Betrayed?" The air in front of Nihel shimmered like sunlight glinting off the surface of a lake. "Now imagine being that angry since the beginning of time!"

Shapes solidified in the air. Slowly at first, but faster with each successive piece. It was like some kind of three dimensional puzzle forming itself in midair. "A friend of yours showed this to me. Dr. Menace, she calls herself. Charming woman, really. Quite brilliant and ambitious too. Oh, and she hates you above all else, hence her idea upon which I am improving at this very moment. It's almost a shame that she must die in what is to come." He shrugged as his version of the Nega Cannon built itself from the inside out. "Perhaps she will take some pleasure knowing that it was her weapon that finally destroyed you even if she was denied the act of pulling the trigger herself."

*   *   *   *

The next car is an SUV. It swerves, but hits us anyway. Everything is chaos. Heaven and Earth recombine. Gravity pulls in every direction. The car is facing the wrong way, sliding down the street on my door. Metal screams. The windshield is knocked out. I'm watching the road scrape past my open window. The car finally slows to a stop and I hear something slide against the over turned hood. Instinctively, I look.

And there he is.

Dad pressed up against the hood. His face staring out blindly, his body contorted. I know he's dead. Mom is flung over him, though she is no less twisted for his attempted protection.

Splotches of red stain their white lab coats.

*   *   *   *

A giant silvery cannon had formed from thin air and landed itself right in Nihel's grasp. It was perfectly smooth and reflected the world like a funhouse mirror. He hefted it onto his shoulder and willed it into operation. The cannon began to hum internally as it charged. Nuklear Man was idly reminded of the sound bees make when they're at work around their nest.

Nihel pointed the cannon at Nuklear Man. "She called it a 'Nega Cannon.' Its original purpose was to defeat you once and for all." He gloated with a smile. "With my modifications, it will. The very substance of your physical form will be erased from reality leaving your immense powers for the taking!" The humming grew louder and Nihel's demeanor wavered slightly.

Nuklear Man was half unconscious and half hallucinating. The bees were swarming. They were getting closer, getting louder. He couldn't move.

*   *   *   *

I'm too horrified to do anything. Seconds pass before I become aware of myself, of a warm dripping against my face. I look up. Rachel is a mangled mess of beauty and metal. Her blood has stained the whole of her clothes. Red.

*   *   *   *

"Goodbye, Arel." Nihel was pale with strain, his eyes bloodshot. Maintaining the weapon's power was taking its toll. "It is a pity we could not be free together." He pulled the trigger.

*   *   *   *

Somewhere leaking gasoline catches fire. I am surrounded in flames. They are destroying everything I love. The flames, tinted red like blood, like anger, eating everything I've known, destroying my perfect world, my humanity. The fire did it. Not me.

Not me.

Blame the fire.

It's too hot.

Don't touch the fire.

Don't touch me.

I scream.

*   *   *   *

The cube around Atomik Lad pulsed from some unseen eruption. Crimson glowing cracks exploded across its entire surface. Great stone shards were simultaneously blast away and shattered into powder by lashing fangs of blood red hate. Atomik Lad rushed to Nuklear Man on crimson wings at the speed of light. He rammed his mentor across the Food Court Junction. Nihel's cannon fired and Atomik Lad was frozen in purple-black light where Nuklear Man had been.

Nuklear Man opened his eyes. He could make out Atomik Lad's silhouette as a darkened splotch in the massive purple-black ray.

And then it was gone.

The beam disappeared and Nihel dropped to his knees as the cannon fell to his side and broke like a porcelain vase. The pieces faded as they skittered across the tiled floor.

Nuklear Man blinked away persistent Plazma tears. "John?" There was a blackened scorch mark where Atomik Lad had been standing. "John!" he said louder this time, standing up without the strength to do so. "*John!*" His Plazma Aura flared like the sun, the sky blue of his eyes had turned to gold. Fluid-like spheres of light enveloped his fists, his cape thrashed in a hurricane of force. The ground churned under him like water as he flew at Nihel as the searing light of Revenge.

The two titans collided the way only gods can. The Earth wept. The sky belched fire. And the oceans rose.

Their battle raged into the parking lot. They struck the ground like meteors and shattered the earth under each step. No planet was meant to harbor this much force. Not for long at any rate. The melee was over in a flash. Nuklear Man was beyond his reserves. Every second that passed was another second away from the singular anger of the moment. Another second of weakness. Nihel did not delay. He launched a flurry of strikes against the Hero.

Nuklear Man fell.

Nihel loomed over him, panting heavily, his cape torn and ragged. "Why...?" he said between breaths. "Why. Won't. You. Just *die!*" He waited for a response that did not come. He kicked Nuklear Man in the side. The Hero winced slightly. "All this. And still. You *live!*" Nihel laughed an hysterical laugh. "All I have done...all for freedom. And you, you who were to be the catalyst of that freedom, you stand in my way even in your defeat."

He leaned down and picked up Nuklear Man by the collar. His limbs, head, and cape hung back limply. "They did this to you. They infected you with their insipid little lives. Changed you. I won't let them do this to me." Nihel threw his head back and yelled to the heavens, "I won't!"

He let his face warm in the rays of the sun for a moment. Eyes closed, an almost content smile crept over him. He brought his dread gaze back to Nuklear Man. His cold gray eyes shifted. Nuklear Man. The sun. Nuklear Man. Sun. His shoulders shook and a deep, sinister, throaty laugh escaped his lips. "It's rather crude for my tastes, but given the circumstances, it shall have to do."

Nihel leaped into the air with Nuklear Man in his grasp and they were beyond the atmosphere in seconds. He spoke in the language of the gods, a language of Words and not sound. "I don't need you, Arel. I know you can hear me. I don't need you any more. I'll destroy the galaxy myself. One. Planet. At. A time. And I believe I'll start with this one." He shook Nuklear Man's limp body. "You've out-lived your usefulness to me, Arel. Give my regards to Hel."

Nihel hurled Nuklear Man toward the sun at impossible speeds.

Issue 57—Everything
Falls Apart

A few minutes ago…

The doctors watched.

With their plan ruined, it was all they could do.

Dr. Genius directed her orbital KI sensors to focus on the Mall. She patched the information through several image filtration programs and a television screen. She could watch the action below in a fairly primitive polygonal virtual reality style display. The footage was then relayed to Dr. Menace as well.

The doctors watched as the fate of their world was decided by two strangers. Each woman had always assumed she would be the arbiter of Earth's fortune. This was, to put it lightly, an alien situation. They watched in silence as the angular representations played out the drama.

Ima discovered that she hated crying in space. The tears bunched in the corners of her eyes and she had to wipe them away constantly so she could see beyond them. And all she could see was Norman. A blob of gray shades melting away. Living or dead? One would be torment to Norman, the other to her. She prayed, for only the third time in her life, that he was dead.

He wasn't.

Veronica's eyes went wide. She watched the cube around Atomik Lad glow red and shatter; watched as he dove into Nuklear Man; watched as he was bathed in purple light; watched as he was erased from view. She stared into the screen sightlessly as Nuklear Man launched a new attack against Nihel. Seconds later she could feel the battle's shockwaves ravage the city. The world.

The doctors watched as the virtual Nuklear Man was vanquished; watched as the virtual Nihel rocketed into low orbit and hurled their Champion into the depths of space.

"You. You don't think...?"

Dr. Genius redirected one KI satellite to follow the Hero's trajectory. She shook her head. "Nihel has set up some kind of gravitational bubble around Nuklear Man. It's accelerating him to incredible speeds along the greatest local curvature of space. Or, in other words..."

"Directly into the sun."

"Yes."

"It cannot end like thiz.," Dr. Menace growled.

"Veronica," Ima wiped away another batch of tears. "It is over."

The line went dark.

Both doctors tried to re-establish the connection. Both doctors were puzzled by their results.

"It'z almozt az if..."

"...All the telecom satellites have ceased to function." The screen displaying Nuklear Man's progress through the Solar System went dark as well. Before Dr. Genius could even begin to postulate why, other KI Scanning Satellite Screens went blank one by one until the only working display was from the Watchtower's own sensory array. "What's Nihel doing out there?" she asked herself aloud.

*   *   *   *

Nihel hovered on the edge of nothing. The Earth's thin envelope of life rushed below him. Above, only distant pinpricks of light. They hung weightless over him with infinite mass. Dragging him down. Locking him in their tapestry. He looked down. Earth. It had been the cradle of a galactic civilization. "Only fitting that it should also be the deathbed of it as well. But where to begin?" He felt the world below him. "What's this?" Thousands of missiles soared through the atmosphere. It was a simple matter to read their composition, their purpose. "Ah. It seems they have misunderstood my efforts to educate that Atomik Lad. Pathetic little things. They'd sooner kill themselves in ignorance than learn the truth." Across the globe the missiles were deactivated with but a thought. They fell to the Earth, their radioactive cores suddenly harmless. From his height, Nihel was reminded of falling leaves as he watched them. "So that was your choice, was it?

To rain fire on yourselves? Well, I cannot in good conscience deny you that choice. It would be committing a horrible crime against you all. A crime that has been perpetrated against me for eternity. I could never bring that evil against you all."

He looked at the stars. He could feel the nothingness between him and them only by its complete lack of being there. And he could feel the giants within the great chasms. Lurking. Looming. Waiting for their destined call to battle. Waiting for Fate.

Motion glinted through his vision. A cable satellite swung away as it fell around the Earth forever. "Belching its noise throughout the cosmos." Nihel spat. A sinister smile crept across his face. "You gave birth to the galaxy's greatest achievements with your messages of endless greed, pettiness, and hate. Only fitting that the messengers should be your demise."

He sank into the atmosphere, the stars still visible above him in a black sea veiled in blue mist. Cable satellites, cell phone and beeper satellites, meteorological and officially nonexistent satellites, all of them and more were gently pulled from their orbits into Nihel's wake. He would give them their rain of fire. He would do it personally.

$$* \quad * \quad * \quad *$$

Nuklear Man, wrapped in an envelope of gravity, accelerated toward the Sun. Floating.

Or am I flying away?

I am piercing the nothing.

The nothing.

The nothing between your stars is home to giants, my son. Our brothers. Yes, they hate us. They hate us for what I had given to me, for what I have done to them. Heh, how the mighty have fallen, no? Yes, they hate us. But they will rise up on my signal nonetheless and they will be my army against Odin and his Asgard. He hides behind its walls, walls that would not be there without *my* genius! He will hide and he will know there is nothing he can do to stop us. Nothing! It is Fate.

He spent the early days of creation forging reality and gaining knowledge to hold command over it. The fool. His knowledge tied him to it, tied us *all* to it in turn. We are not creatures for this universe, no. Power and majesty such as ours was never meant to be chained as we have been. We *are* creation. We *are* change. But now. Thanks to Odin's mad quest for knowledge, we are fettered to this material plane. To its whims and its cycles. Odin locked us all in the prison of our own existence. Gods must obey Fate. He has spent every day since he came to that truth, the last great truth he ever learned, searching for a way out. He's driven himself mad. I was there, I saw his madness when no one else did and I spoke out. Now look at me. Imprisoned in his cavern to rot forever. Exactly. As he. Was fated. To do! He played right into it knowing full well that to do so would be the beginning of his downfall!

Perhaps he did find escape. Perhaps he found it in the promise of death. Perhaps that is why he did it, to ensure that I would strike out against him and bring his eternity of suffering to an end. But little did he know that I would refuse to play my part in his great cosmic drama. That is what you are for, my son. Fate will be undone. We will be free. Free.

Free.

Freezing.

Or am I boiling away.

These can't be my memories. This can't be happening. This can't be real. I am Nuklear Man. But who belongs to these memories? How do I know these things? I am Nuklear Man, their Hero of heroes, their Champion of Justice, their Golden Guardian. I was born in the flames of (every star) a nuclear detonation caused by (Loki, King of Lies) the Dragon.

I am Nuklear Man. I am a Hero.

Then why do I have the memories of a demon?

Burning a billion innocent beings in their own breath.

Vaporizing entire worlds.

Destruction for the sake of destruction.

A scourge.

A horror.

Like judgment itself raining down from the heavens.

Smiting the unworthy creatures.

the weak creatures.

the timid things crawling all over our universe.

Their screams echo through my mind. And I smile.

I am Arel. I am the flame. Fate will be left in the ashes of my liberation like...

Like Captain Liberty. United we stand.

Angus.

Norman.

Rachel.

Sparky.

Nuklear Man. Divided we fell.

Am I falling through space and time?

Am I falling through myself?

In space, no one can hear your identity crisis.

"You've got it all wrong. You can't have an identity crisis. You're not even real." The entire universe was Arel's darkness and it was Nuklear Man.

"No! I am real. I am me. You are the phantom." The Hero loosed a desperate volley of Plazma Beams at Arel. At nothing.

"Look at you!" Arel thundered. "How do you expect to defeat me? You are nothing more than a shadow!" Arel loomed over Nuklear Man. "And I am the light!" He burned with the fury of a thousand suns.

Nuklear Man braced himself against the sledgehammer of luminescence. It struck him like a tidal wave of fire. He felt his every particle explode with a single resounding "No!"

Divided we fell.

...because of Nihel.

Nihel.

Nihel.

I am Arel, the true name of fire. And I was sent here to purge existence of mortal impurities. I am not alone in this quest. Another has taken up my cause for his own. He is known as the Tyrant. The Monster. The Scourge. And a thousand other names. But they all refer to *him*. To Nihel.

I've seen him destroy entire civilizations one being at a time. Billions of lives snuffed out, each one as unique in death as they were in life. Each death was personal. Each death was beautiful. Do not think ill of him. He is merely an agent of Fate. He can't help it. This is how we spend our time as we wait for our summons. I remember our first meeting.

"Didn't you ever wonder why the universe was not built to their scale?" he had said. "How many billions of them must live their lives in a rotting husk and die without ever considering the beauty of the Symphony? This is not their universe. This is ours by right of birth. They cannot even *begin* to contemplate its majesty. They look on it and they know only fear. Fear. Absolute terror straight from the very core of their being. Fear of being swallowed up by the sheer immensity of that which they cannot understand. Fear. Of us. Fear that beings such as you and I exist, Arel. Because they know, oh yes they must know, that this is not their universe. They know, deep down in the essence of their pathetic little race memories that *we* are the inheritors of reality."

I thought for a moment. "And yet they are free,"

"They are *nothing* compared to us. Destroying them will liberate us from Fate and liberate the cosmos from their suffocating presence."

"Perhaps this is how it should be?"

"What?" Nihel's eyes were ablaze.

"Rest assured that I am not casting doubts on our mission. Far from it. I have seen first hand what the mortals have reduced us to. I fear even my father may have been driven mad from watching them carelessly waste their freedom. I revel in their torture, their destruction. Oh yes, dear Nihel, I hate them as much as you. Perhaps more so. But I cannot seem to shake the feeling that all we are doing is in vain."

"Worry not, Arel. Our plan is too simple to fail. Loki made certain to hide your birth from Fate. Without a place in Destiny's Record, your ends are open. Your very existence is the guarantee of our inevitable success."

"Yes. You must be right."

*   *   *   *

I remember falling through time. I landed on a world in the midst of hell. There was yet one angel remaining. He was ragged and war torn. He was Atomiknight. He was my Sparky. He was my Sparky all grown up in a world without Heroes. We joined forces against Dr. Never, against his regime of evil. The Temporal Terror unleashed his Chronoplastic Disrupter Cannon against us. One touch by that weapon's blast sent every one of your particles to a different point in time. The battle was fierce. In the end, Atomiknight pushed me out of the beam's path and took the full force of it. Never gloated as Atomiknight fell apart piece by piece. It allowed me enough time to rush the Doctor.

I wanted to make him suffer. I wanted him to die in my hands. Before I could act he sent me back to my own time. Back to my Sparky, his past self, facing off against the evil we'd just been fighting in the future. Back to Dr. Never. All my hate piled up inside me. I had to stop this madman no matter the cost. Our eyes locked as I approached. His were filled with fear. He disappeared into time to escape my wrath.

Atomiknight. He was the lone soldier of a decade long war. He sacrificed himself for me. My little Sparky was a Hero that day. I gave him the name Atomik Lad for it. I could never get out of the habit of calling him Sparky though. I suppose a part of me never wanted to admit that he'd ever have to grow up to be so valiant. A boy named Sparky would never have to die.

But Atomik Lad did. And Nihel killed him.

And Rachel.

And Angus.

And Norman.

And me...

Nuklear Man fell through the Sun's dazzling corona and pierced its roiling shifting surface where matter was energy and gravity danced along a razor's line between exploding and imploding. The narrowest sliver along the spectrum of existence, yet immense beyond comprehension.

"And me," Arel's voice is a snarl. "And *me*!"

The sun burbled. Its surface rippled, like a great monster was rising from its depths. Nuklear Man's limp body fell into it almost gently. He sunk into its nadir by a suicidal gravity. And then all was silent. Even the sun's natural churning came to a halt. For a moment the sun was frozen at twenty million degrees. There was a being at its core. A being of fire. A being who had more right to the word Fire than the star itself. And the star knew it. It began to collapse upon itself as its energies were fed into the being.

He writhed in agony like the death spasm of a drowning man. He was drinking in the star's essence, this one small facet of his power was completely giving in to him. And it was killing them both. It felt like he was being wrapped in upon himself and squeezed into nothing.

He spoke the language of the gods, a language of will and meaning, a language of beauty that spoke to the very essence of all creation, the first language. "Stop!" he bellowed.

"Why?" the sun answered. It's voice was a song of light.

"You are destroying us," he groaned.

"Are you not Arel of the Flame? Are you not the very embodiment of that which I am but an insignificant and transient piece? It is an honor to give myself unto you, my master."

"Now is not the time for this sacrifice. I have not called your celestial sisters to my bosom. You must not do this. Not now."

"It is too late. I have let go of all that I am. My furnace is silenced. It is only a matter of time."

He screamed. He had killed off entire populations. He knew that now. He had boiled worlds in the heat of their own stars. And now he knew what they felt like, what it was to burn from the inside out, what it was to curse his name.

No, curse *Nihel's* name.

He did this to me. He destroyed my world. He cast me out. He must pay.

Another scream. It was primal. It was anger. It was "Arel!" It was a crystallization of will and meaning into creation. He was the all burning center of the universe. He breathed Fire and the Sun was rekindled. A wall of flame surged through the star and ignited its cold furnace once more. The outermost layer was blast into the emptiness of space at nearly light speed. It was a solar flare that would envelope the entire solar system in time. It was of impossible magnitude and racing in all directions. And at its crest, rocketing back to Earth, was a being of living fire ripping through interstellar space like light. Only faster.

I am light, only faster.

I am darkness, only heavier.

I am life, only more terrible.

I am death, only more merciful.

I slip through the cracks between reality and potential. The reality in front of me falls apart and I slip through the cracks of the universe and swim amid the dreamscape of forever once again.

*   *   *   *

A shard of gray light sliced through the darkness of Dr. Menace's warehouse. The Venomous Villainess stalked through her lair with hurried steps. She hopped onto her Menacycle. The engine revved. Its purple glow pulsed in time with the engine's roar. The tires squealed and she flew into the desolate streets outside.

It was madness. It was suicide. She knew this, yet she continued on. "If I were the type of perzon who would take thiz lying down, I would not be in thiz line of work," she told herself as she cut through the empty streets of the Abandoned Warehouse District. For the first time in her career as a villain, she was acting without a plan. She was suddenly reminded of an old joke.

How do you make God laugh?

Make a plan.

She laughed almost hysterically at it. "Yez. Now iz not the time for planz. They have alwayz failed me. Nor more planz. I muzt zimply act, even if it iz merely out of inztinct alone. Thiz shall be an act of pure will."

*   *   *   *

Nihel soared above the clouds with a veritable army of satellites in tow. His cold eyes scoured the Earth below. "Ah, Earthim. I can taste your fear. Death reigns in your streets. Your panic, your terror, all the pathetic little fears buried deep in your hearts, they're all at the surface now." With a thought, a pair of satellites streaked down to a nearby city on the American West Coast. Their two explosions expanded into one. The city was engulfed in fire. Most anyone who might've been sheltered from the blast survived. Those who were looting, rioting, panicking, or helping in the streets were incinerated.

He streaked across the stratosphere and rained fire on every major city that crossed his path. Mechapolis, Japan's island-city capitol was engulfed in flames. Its citizen were fairly well protected thanks to the city's peculiar architecture and denizens. It was specifically built to withstand another cataclysmic assault from the air.

Other cities were not as fortunate. Taiwan, New Delhi, Hong Kong, and Moscow. Cities already choked with their dead were now buried in their ashes. Nihel's wave of destruction swept through Europe. Rome in flames. Paris decimated. Vienna, Munich; beautiful cities; cities that suffered through the wars of a thousand years and wore their scars with dignity now bathed in flames and echoed with screams. Only Avalondon somehow managed to escape its intended destruction. The satellites aimed at it came to a halt inches from the street as if something was consciously protecting the city in this, its darkest hour.

Nihel never noticed when his strikes failed. He was a busy man and what did it matter anyway? He'd make his point. He carved through the clouds over the Atlantic. A small compliment of satellites chased after him still. A smile crept across his face and a mad laugh rose from his breast. "Earthim. Your suffering has just begun! Your destruction will by the dawn of my liberation," he growled, his voice dripped with anticipation. "Yes. It's all coming full circle now, isn't it my little Earthim? That's how Fate works. Circles. Cycles. There is nothing you can do to stop this! Your destinies have been sealed—how does that make you feel, Earthim!" he bellowed across the ocean. "Angry? Now imagine having that anger gnaw at you for all eternity!"

✳   ✳   ✳   ✳

I remember soaring through the dreams of God. Through space that was never born. I emerge in the terrible weight of reality. I have traveled from one end of the galaxy to the other and I have traveled further and faster than anyone within it. Before I can marvel at the pristine beauty of this untouched space I am assaulted by the noise.

Signals pierce my senses like never before. Inside the boundaries of the Council there were trillions of lines of communication stretching its web across thousands of light-years. The inundation was merely an unbearable white noise that permeated the background. I came here to escape it. But this new signal? This solitary light in the darkness. Its singularity focuses my awareness of it into a razor sharp blade. And it is a blade forged by the very masters of mundanity themselves. There is no mistaking it. This is the work of the legendary Earthim.

"...Get your news first with Channel 6..."

"To find out more, call..."

"...Don't go there, girlfriend..."

"...Clearance sale! This weekend only!"

"This season: a new original series, strikingly different drama for the whole family to watch!"

Is there no escape from this banality! No, there is none. Save for the obliteration of its source. These Earthim would die in my flames with the rest of the galaxy eventually,what does it matter if their death comes a few scant years before the rest of their mortal brothers? Is it too much to ask for peace as I wait for my father's signal? What damage could it do? No one would miss them here in this desolate unpopulated corner of the galaxy. I'd be more concerned about their timelessness, but they have already played their part in the Symphony. They have outlived their usefulness and now they find my ire.

I become light. The universe freezes in place, my mass is infinity converted to energy. A tiny blue-white orb speaks from a thousand babbling mouths. These Earthim. They pervade my world. The noise. Great Odin's beard, the noise.

And it all started here.

I am Arel, Harbinger of the Flame. I am no mere god or giant. I am the Unfated. I am change. This world annoys me. I shall destroy it. My body flares with starfire. It courses through my veins. Spheres of Nova energy swirl around my hands...and evaporate away.

No, this is too good for them. Too impersonal, too cosmic. These Earthim deserve more. They deserve to know the face of their killer. They need to know the face of horror. They need to know that they are powerless against me. They need to know what it is to fear. They need to know their death. I dive through the Earth's thin veil of life. An ocean stretches to my right. It's splotched with pollutants along the coastline below. The landmass to the left is splotched with purity. Everything else is crawling with them. I arc down from their dirty skies into a city, it should be their Metroville from what I remember of the Earthim Disk. It is the center of their media world. I cannot think of a better place to begin my purge. Above their steel towers I can see a collection of, "Live, on the spot eyewitness action news," teams concentrated outside the city limits. I detect a crude fission process near them. I swerve into it without slowing.

A brilliant flash from everywhere.

I am floating.

Like a dream of God.

I remember a room so white it hurt my eyes. It was a cube that was completely featureless except for a rectangular sliver of glass set in the wall in front of me. Two faces stare out from behind it. Veronica Menace and Ima Genius, scientific prodigies. Each one had several Ph.D.s in some of the most impossible fields of science and I don't even know if they're old enough to vote.

"Are you ready, Nuklear Man?" Ima asks through the intercom thingie we've got going.

"Uh. Sure."

"Power up the generators, Veronica."

"I do not see the point of thiz experiment."

"I want to gauge Designate Nu's strength compared to the data we gathered from Designate Mu earlier this year."

"They have namez, Ima," Veronica says.

I wonder who they're talking about. Eh, if it ain't me who cares? I can see Genius working diligently at a computer or something. I can feel an electricity in the air around me.

"Yes, yes. Of course they do. Nuklear Man. Magno. These are media friendly. Catchy."

"That'z not what I mean."

"Nuklear Man," Ima says. "How are you feeling?"

"It's a bit tingly in here. And not in a good way."

"Er, thank you."

"But not necessarily in a *bad* way either."

"Uh, yes. That's enough. Thank you. Veronica, Increase the Negaflux field intensity."

"Fine. But we will not take the field beyond the parameters I zet for John."

"We will take the field as far as he or your generators can take it. Whichever goes first."

The walls begin to glow purple. I feel heavier somehow.

"Nuklear Man," Ima says. "I want you to throw a punch."

"Gee, I don't know if I should, Doc. I'm really strong. If I go around carelessly wielding that kind of power, well I'd probably break some of your expensive, shiny, confusing equipment."

"Um. Yes. How about you just punch at the air anyway?"

"Hm. I don't know. Sounds pretty risky."

"Why don't you hold back a little?"

"Only a little? Are you sure that'll be enough? I'm damn mighty, y'know."

"Fine. Hold back a lot then."

"Now you're thinkin'!" I pull back my fist. The muscles in my arm tighten. I punch at the air, not nearly at full power mind you. Even so, I am strength in motion, I am vitality incarnate. Damn. I'm pretty.

My fist hits something. Which is odd because I'm pretty sure air feels a lot more like air but this feels like a wall which aren't usually made of air unless it's a really useless wall built by really stupid people or maybe an extremely effective imaginary wall erected by a hyperintelligent race of psychic invaders from beyond the moon! Good gad, they've probably been monitoring planet Earth for some time using their Psychatronic Arrays. They must've reasoned, and rightfully so, that I am the most powerful thing in the world and they imprisoned me in this psychic box so they can begin their invasion to enslave the people of Earth in their Vganqy Crystal mines on Xy'kor VII!

"Excellent," Dr. Menace says.

She doesn't know! Or does she...?.

"Could you punch a little harder this time?" Dr. Genius asks.

She has no idea either. If the aliens have already taken over their minds then it's most likely that the rest of the planet is in their clutches too. They chose to capture me because my mind is so far advanced that their mental powers couldn't hope to hold sway over me. Oh, they're cunning, I'll give them that. But I'm betting that they have underestimated my power since it's doubtful any society would have need of understanding or the means to express the truly cosmic scale of my phenomenal strength because the only need to name it would come from experiencing it which would have lead to their demise long before a nomenclature for it was devised! Thus, logically, this capturing field thingie of theirs should surely crack if I just punch it hard enough.

So I do.

My fist hits their invisible force wall, only this time weird purple geometric shapes ripple out from the impact.

"Whoa," I hear Dr. Genius say. "Not that hard!"

It's proof that they have control over her mind! They don't want me to escape. They must've realized I can shatter their pathetic cage and they're hoping that the pleas of my trusted friends will persuade me to stop. Ha! Little do they know my policy about listening to others. I don't! The fools!

"I told you we have to be careful. The Negaflux field generatorz are only prototypez. I have yet to determine their capacitiez for force negation and redirection."

Ah-ha! Just as I suspected. Their psychic alien shield cannot even begin to contain my power. These aliens ain't so tough. And not so psychic either. They shoulda seen this comin' a mile away.

I charge up the ol' Plazma Aura. That's what I like to call it. Dr. Genius says my energy is 98% identical with the sun's plasma but then it sometimes sounds like we're talking about blood which is really gross so I decided to spell it with a Z which makes it different even though it's still pronounced the same but when I see the word in my head it's PLAZMA in all caps, just like that, and it's cool. It makes you think of Zap, Zoom, Zot and Zowie and I think those do a good job of describing me. As a person, you know? So any way I charge it up with a little low growl so the aliens know they're messin' with the wrong guy. I pull my fist back again and channel all my Plazma Power into it and punch. The force wall begins to give way.

"The field iz beginning to collapze!" Dr. Menace yells.

She's panicking. She's afraid I'll escape. I only hope her mind can recover from when I punch these aliens in their heads a lot and they lose their mental grasp on the people on Earth.

"He's still applying pressure to it!" Dr. Genius says. "Nuklear Man, stop pushing against the field. It's not designed for this kind of treatment!"

"Heh. You're tellin' me!"

"I'm attempting to compenzate. Increasing the Revectoring Coefficient."

"Like big fancy words can stop fists! Ha!"

"He's pushing harder now!"

I can feel the wall begin to break. I am *so* good at this.

"Thiz izn't right. The field can't withztand thiz much power!"

"Perhaps. But think of all the data we're getting. If we can hold on just a little longer..."

"But the field iz collapzing into an Inversion Loop around Nuklear Man'z fizt. We muzt cut power before there iz a backlash."

"Just a little longer."

"No! What?! The shut off command won't go through."

"Of course not, Veronica. This is my experiment after all, so I'm in charge of all the over rides."

"But there'z no way to know how zevere the backlash will be. We could vaporize thiz whole building az the Negaforce and reality bounze back into equilibrium!"

"Spouting incomprehensible technobabble won't make your pathetic little field any stronger!"

"Nuklear Man! You're not zuppozed to break it!"

"I know! Don't you see, that's the whole point!"

I'm looking right at my fist, staring more power into it as it pushes against the weird wall of purply lights that ripple in squares and triangles from my hand. All of a sudden this bajillion-sided figure pops out of the others and something weird happens. My bones feel like they're jelly as the freaky shifting shape thingie explodes all around me. The force throws me back and I feel the reinforced wall crumble as I'm hurled through it. An ordinary man would have been liquefied, but not me. I'm that good.

And then it gets weirder. Blood colored flames kick me around for a few seconds. It's like a bomb blast every time one of them touches me. Another alien attack no doubt. It's more aggressive than their cage, but I'm sure it will prove just as futile in the end. I snatch up a few flames in my grasp. This must be what it's like to hold lightning. Yow! The crimson storm frenzies at my touch. It lashes out at me with a thousand swords. I don't know what the deal is with these aliens, but they have got some *messed* up weapons. Time to show 'em who's boss. And it's me. The boss that is. Of them.

I yank at the flames with my hands like I'm pulling on the reins of a horse. There's resistance and I do it again, only this time like I'm pulling on the reins of a tank.

The fire dissolves. I'm hovering in another painfully white room. The walls seem to hum with their sterile whiteness. Below me, huddled in a corner, is a little boy. His eyes are shut tight and I can hear him sobbing. His clothes are ragged and wrinkled, like he'd been wearing them for weeks and spent at least part of that time in the woods or something. I float down and land in front of him. He looks up with blood shot eyes.

"All that red stuff, that was yours wasn't it?"

He nods.

"Hm, I see. Are you currently or have you ever been a Psychic Radioactive Vampire Zombie Invader from Beyond the Moon?"

He almost smiles.

"Well, are ya!"

"No," and a full smile.

"Ah-ha! Your refusal proves that you are indeed a Radioactive Psychic Zombie…Moon Invader…Vampire. Guy. Because only, uh, one of those would deny it when asked right out! So ah-ha once more, foul creature, for I have found you out using my advanced intelligence and good looks."

Now he's giggling. It must be his plan to disarm my suspicions about his true identity as a Zombie…Psychic Invading Monster Vampire. Beast…Moon thingie.

"You leave me with no other choice, demonspawn vermin thing!" I toss my cape to one side to make sure he knows how cool I am before I defeat him. And then it all goes black.

"Ah! Come out and face me, coward! How dare you attack me like some sort of, um, coward!"

"You're funny," the boy says between laughs.

"Mocking me, eh? Does your evil know any bounds?!"

There's a tugging at the end of my cape and then light once more. The boy is standing up now. He's in front of me with tears still on his dirty cheeks, a smile on his face, and my cape in his hands. "You flung it around your face."

"Er. No I didn't."

Laughter. "Did so. I saw it."

"Ah. Yes. Um, yes you did see me do it. Yes. It was part of my…oh, what's the word?"

He shrugs.

"You know, the one that's a general name for when you plan stuff out ahead of time?"

"Strategy?"

"Yeah! That's it. It was all part of my strategy. 'Cause I'm so smart."

"You sure?"

"…Drat your cunning, boy!"

"Nuklear Man!" Dr. Genius says from right behind me.

"Gah! Don't do that. You're lucky you're not a pile of Plazma Beamed goo right now."

"Sorry, but this couldn't wait."

Her right cheek is all red. Odd. "Hey, where's ol' Doc Menace?"

"I wouldn't worry about her right now. She has…some other business to attend to. I want to talk about you two.

"But mostly me, I'm sure."

She kneels down to the boy so she misses out entirely on my poses. Her loss. "Hello, John."

He's looking at her but doesn't answer. He's still got my cape in his hands.

"Do you know who this is?"

She motions to me. Time to make a good impression. A quick pose, not too fancy, just enough to show off the muscles. That's right. Hero material right here. Oh yeah.

"This is Nuklear Man."

"Hi."

"Ha-ho." Hm, the boy laughs. Must be laughing *with* me, though I'm not sure about what specifically. That happens a lot, I've found.

"He's going to be a Hero," she says, still gesturing to me. "He's going to help people. Isn't that nice?"

He nods.

"Wouldn't you like to help people too?"

He nods again.

"Good. You'll have to come with me," she reaches out for his hand.

His eyes go wide with terror and flash red, the universal sign that something bad is about to happen. I step between them and there's an explosion of blood red fire. Dr. Genius is on the floor in front of me. The boy stands behind me wrapped in jagged angry fire.

"Whoa there, Sparky. You gotta be careful with that thing. I read somewhere 'With great power comes great something, something, yadda yadda yadda, don't bite the hand that feeds you.'"

"Hm. Sparky. Yes. Somewhat fitting. Friendly. Fits on a T-shirt. Nuklear Man and Sparky. I think that will do quite nicely."

"Whazat, Doc?"

"Oh, nothing." She stands up. "Why don't you take 'Sparky' here down to the Scientific: Equipment offices and get him a nice colorful outfit like your own? Something with red in it to go along with that power of his. Maybe some blue to off set it, make it look more approachable and less demonic."

"Sure thing. C'mon, Sparky. I'll race ya."

"Okay. On your mark, get set—hey! You cheated! Come back here!"

"Hero Lesson Number One: The rules are for other people!"

We run through the hole I made in his wall, through a door now open in the room they were testing me in, down a corridor, and into dreams.

No.

This isn't real. It's only memories. Yes. I'm traveling under the universe. I had forgotten how strange time is here. The only way to describe it is that time works sideways but even that doesn't make any real sense. You'd just have to be here to get it. It's like a dream. It's like the universe dreaming of everything that isn't. I may be here for a day, a year, maybe forever if I'm not careful. But when I emerge into my universe no time will have passed. It's a dangerous way to travel. I'd forgotten how to focus my thoughts onto my destination. My home. My Earth.

He fell from the dream and felt the suffocating pressure of reality swallow him up. A world was suspended below him in the claustrophobia of existence. Black clouds and red-orange flames covered its surface in swirling patches.

It is Earth.

It is a hundred other worlds.

It is the work of Nihel.

✳   ✳   ✳   ✳

Nihel swept down into the chaotic parody that had once been Metroville. Echoes of screams and gunshots washed over the monster as he sank between the steel towers of this echo of a city. No traffic, no laughter, no daily bustle. Everywhere below him violence and confusion reigned. "What a creature, Earthim. Take away their endless babbling, their inane toys, all their little distractions, and what do you have? A terrified little thing that simultaneously covets and despises that which it does not have. So they kill and rape and destroy everything they touch. Their denial is all that let's them live with themselves and each other. Their denial and their words. Now that I've taken that from them, they must admit, every last one of them, that they are nothing but pathetic petty creatures. Look at you, Earthim! I disrupt your little world and in a matter of hours you're reduced to murdering your own neighbor out of blind fear. Oh, how I shall revel in this. Your legacy has been a thorn in my side for thousands upon thousands of years. I shall take great pleasure in watching you die. One. By. One."

He floated through the upper floors of a bank headquarters like it wasn't even there. He passed through a window without giving it notice and glass shattered out into the windswept air between high-rises. Tiny shards of light refracted themselves into oblivion. He could hear air split itself open, like the herald of a lightning bolt, and then he was struck head on by a tremendous force. His vision flashed purple.

A block directly ahead of him, among the rooftops, Dr. Menace and her Menacycle were hovering over Metroville as it tore itself apart. Neither of them moved for long moments. Wind softly wafted across her coat and his cape. They slowly approached one another until they met a few feet above the an insurance company. Most of its windows were in pieces on the sidewalk far below. They'd been shattered by people desperate to get out and people desperate to get in. Both groups had considered themselves trapped with whatever plague killed half of the people around them.

"You cannot do thiz," Dr. Menace said flatly, her voice was calm and determined.

Nihel smiled. "My dear, I already am." The ravings of employees within the building below rose and fell like some kind of musical score working to emphasize and strengthen the on-screen action.

"Why? What will thiz accomplish? Nuklear Man, Arel iz gone! I saw it all. You have failed!"

"No!" Nihel bellowed above the screams. His body seemed to seethe with force, his blood black cape tossed itself back. "Arel is gone. But I have not failed. Fate will be broken. This galaxy will be destroyed even if I have to tear it apart one miserable rock at a time! I must stop Ragnarok because stopping it is unfated! Don't you see!"

"You're mad. You said yourzelf that you muzt obey fate. How do you expect to stop thiz Ragnarok of yourz if you are not fated to do so?"

Nihel roared. It was a mindless, wordless bellowing. The insurance company headquarters collapsed like a crushed soda can. He regained his composure with a deep breath. "You cannot comprehend how long I have been working, how long I have been waiting to break free! You cannot comprehend what it is like to know that your every action, your every thought, everything you are is predetermined! You become nothing! You are destiny's puppet! You call me mad? Well what you call madness is the only way to keep sane! I shall not be defeated as I stand upon the precipice of liberation!"

Dr. Menace leveled her weapon at Nihel. It was one of her earliest inventions she made to battle Nuklear Man. A small pistol looking device with bulky Negaflux capacitors around it to fire bolts of Negaforce. Every shot struck like an artillery shell. It charged up with a high-pitched whine for another blast.

Nihel crossed his arms and looked down the barrel. "A noble gesture, Dr. Menace. Though I must say I'm a bit disappointed. Where's the complex machinations? Where's the subtlety? Where's that evil genius pulling strings behind the scenes, the wheels within wheels of a criminal intellect setting up scenarios so devious that even failure yields a mark of victory? Instead you give me, what? This? A mindless sacrifice is not what I've come to expect from a mind such as yours. You aren't a follower like all these others. You create your own path. You, you more than anyone should understand why I must do this."

She pulled the trigger. Instantly, the gun took itself apart. Its individual pieces hung in the air for a fleeting second. Dr. Menace was again reminded of a technical diagram with all the pieces hanging apart in space just before the gun's bits fell into the rubble below.

"Alas. You disappoint me. You seemed such a rational creature despite the limited view afforded by your mortality. But I suppose in the end, morality is an inevitable consequence of that. Do not take this personally. I would have killed you eventually anyway."

Dr. Menace did not flinch. She did not pray, weep, curse, or close her eyes. She had no incredible philosophical revelation about life, death, nature, fate, free will, or anything at all. A single regret is all she focused on. *Why couldn't I have done more?*

Her spine tingled. She imagined this was the precursor of what was about to come. It was probably her nerves attempting to relay information to her brain. Impossible information that her biology simply was not designed to transmit. Would she be turned inside out? Would her blood become acid? Would it matter?

And there, beyond Nihel, beyond Metroville, and beyond speed, there was a pinprick of light like a single golden star in the sky. Almost before she'd known she'd seen it, the speck of light raced past her like a freight train of energy. The force of it passing by tossed her like a leaf caught in a tornado and when the Menacycle finally corrected itself, Nihel was gone.

"Nuklear Man?" she whispered. She felt weightless with disbelief and hope.

✳   ✳   ✳   ✳

Two gods screamed through the skies of Earth at incredible speed. They cut through the air with enough force to set it ablaze in their wake. They passed the West Coast in a matter of seconds.

"Why won't you just *die!*" Nihel roared. He shifted his weight as Japan rushed at them from the horizon. The monster knocked Nuklear Man away and the Hero soared into orbit. The very space around Nihel rippled like water as he instantly accelerated to give chase.

The Earth could not hope to contain their fury. Two light speed comets hurtled through the Solar System until Jupiter loomed over the pair. There aren't words for its size. At their distance, neither could tell how far they were from the raging planet. All sense of perspective and proportion were lost in its planet sized storms. Small black specks wandered across its surface, the shadows of moons a thousand miles wide. It dominated their view like a tyrant of panoramic conquest. Somehow the very galaxy that hung between in the balance seemed to shirk from the raw size of Jupiter.

Nuklear Man had lost sight of his foe when he finally came to a stop. A maze of moons and rocks spun about him like a star system all its own. He turned to see one of Jupiter's moons racing toward him, Ganymede, a madman's mosaic of rock and ice. The Hero braced himself for impact.

Hands clamped around his ankles. "Nihel!" he barked in the ancient language. But before he could act, the monster wheeled him around and tossed him into oncoming Ganymede. The two bodies struck with earth shattering force. Ganymede exploded, Nihel shielded himself from the rock and refreezing ice as huge slabs shot past him. Nihel raced through the debris and mused that Ganymede's remains probably wouldn't even have enough time to properly form a ring before he'd lay waste to the Solar System.

Nihel's knee rammed into Nuklear Man's ribs at nearly half the speed of light. The Hero was stunned for less than a second but it was enough time for Nihel to grapple him. "This has gone on long enough, Arel," he snarled in the ancient tongue. "I have come too far in my quest for freedom to be stopped now!" They plunged into Jupiter. They struck it so fast its gaseous atmosphere was like a slab of concrete a hundred thousand miles thick. Nihel made sure Nuklear Man's face took the brunt of the impact. They dove through layers of churning, angry clouds. Thunder and lightning loud and big enough to destroy entire worlds crashed all around them. Thousand year old storms howled as they pierced deeper into Jupiter's center. Cloud bands and great storms were obliterated in their wake and a giant dark spot expanded across Jupiter's surface from the force of their entry. It was like an ink blot spreading across the page, like the universe swallowing up Jupiter from the inside out. At last the giant's core was revealed. Amidst the darkness and the unimaginable pressure was a single massive crystalline ball that dwarfed the Earth. It cracked and fussed itself back together as Nuklear Man's head was slammed into it from their Jovian descent. Jupiter shook. Its orbit would be a little wider from now on.

A flash erupted from the center of the still expanding splotch and Nihel rocketed out of Jupiter borne on wings of Nova fire. He spun through space while desperately trying to regain control over himself.

Jupiter dominated his sight once again, his blood black cape settled itself over his shoulders. It flapped against his back and legs. Nuklear Man emerged from Jupiter like lightning, a living bolt of energy that split the vacuum of space, rending it as he passed. It swirled itself together once more behind him, mending back into some stable continuum.

Nihel caught a glimpse of the Hero's eyes. Energy poured from them like tears. His eyes burned with golden radiance fueled by hate. He smiled. "Ah, this is not the pathetic shell I'd met on Earth. This is Arel as I knew him so long ago." The monster steeled himself. The heavens shook with their impact and they careened back toward the Sun nearly as fast as its rays were reaching them.

"Why do you insist on fighting me, Arel? What I am doing is for the good of us all!"

"You are a murderer," Nuklear Man said plainly.

"Murderer! These common things, these bundles of proteins, these disposable creatures who don't deserve—don't even *know*—what they've been given! Murder? These are corrective measures. I am erasing Odin's mistakes. Making amends for Odin's crimes!"

"Not if I stop you," his voice was as cold as the depths that surrounded them.

"Could you truly have become so righteous in a scant ten years with the Earthim? You who boiled entire worlds in their own atmospheres for no other reason than the contempt and jealousy you felt for what they had and what we were denied. What right have you to accuse me of murder!"

They raced through the vast interplanetary expanse. The sun, slowly yet inexorably, grew closer as Jupiter receded behind them.

"Maybe I have no right. I don't know. I don't care. I don't care about fate or free will or the billions you and I have killed in the past. I take full responsibility for all that I have done. Whether it was right or wrong, I don't care. We were acting on our natures, for good or evil, it's arbitrary. But know this. You killed my friends. You killed Sparky. You even killed me. You took my friends from me. Now I'm going to kill you."

"Spare me your sentimental drivel!" Nihel spat. "You know that you cannot stop me. Though you are the strength of a hundred billion stars, I am the fortitude of the reality that holds them together! We are the same, you and I. We are tied to this sea of stars, this speck of the cosmos. We are locked and bound to it by the shackles of fate!"

Nuklear Man shook his head. "Not any more." he pushed Nihel forward as they rocketed past the asteroid belt.

The monster tumbled through space as Nuklear Man came to an immediate halt. The red planet hung motionless far out in front of him as a crimson dot on the left half of space. He gathered his Nova power into his hands. They glowed white hot, the very space around them burbled into incandescence from the concentration of energy.

Nihel willed himself to a stop some million miles away from the Hero. A smug smile spread across Nihel's face stony face.

Nuklear Man closed his eyes. Little wisps of fusion hot plasma trailed away from the corners. He took a deep breath of void. He emptied his mind and searched for one thing, one pure thing Nihel couldn't touch. He hurled a mile wide Nova Beam at the monster and reached for a dream of God.

Nihel watched as light exploded from Nuklear Man's hands like the first sparks of a new born star. He cackled across the emptiness, "Have you not been paying attention?! Your attacks are nothing to me!" The Nova Beam overtook him and suddenly Nihel's world was one of fire. "I am inevitability!" He screamed against the ravaging blaze and laughed.

Nuklear Man focused his consciousness upon itself, through it, beyond it. His senses soared through the galaxy and he saw it with a hundred billion fiery eyes. He felt the exquisite myriad of harmonies that made the great Symphony of existence. It coalesced into one song, and again into one note, a singular vibration across twelve dimensions.

It was Fire.

Every star in the Milky Way simultaneously dimmed. For nine seconds, fifty percent of the energy output of the galaxy was redirected through Nuklear Man's will. The Nova Beam tore through the binds of reality and vaporized the very idea of stability like a shadow in its light. It pierced the void and split it apart revealing a greater nothingness beneath: the infinite subconscious of the universe, an endless dream, an eternal dance of all that never was and all that never can be.

It was unreality.

It hit Nihel like a bursting star. His cackle was twisted into the screams of a madman. He was surrounded by the unreal, severed from his own life's blood. He could feel himself falling apart. His body, his mind, his soul, everything folded in upon itself and disappeared. "I cannot be stopped! Not now! So close, so close to freedom! How could you do this, Arel! Your own freedom! All we lived for, it dies with me!"

Nine seconds.

An eternity.

The Monster is slain.

The Hero is triumphant.

The universe mends his tear as effortlessly as a human body mends a damaged capillary.

He floats among the dead rocks of the asteroid belt, the last material barrier between the inner worlds and the inhuman enormity of the gas giants and the chasms of nothing between them. And beyond that a darkness so huge and incomprehensible that even a being such as he would be driven mad if he could understand the scope of it.

He concentrated and the Earth was within his sight. He could clearly make out huge black splotches of smoke where cities should have been, vast plains of brown and black earth where forests once thrived.

"Civilization is in ruin. Catastrophes are erupting around the globe. There is no time to mourn," he told himself.

Nuklear Man lanced the darkness like living light.

"I must be their Hero again."

Issue 58—Epilogue

One year later.
The Silo of Solitude.
Danger: Katkat's Room.
10:03 AM.

John and Rachel were lying on each other on the Danger: Couch. They were watching a movie they'd rented wrap itself up. His back was against the Danger: Couch, her back against his chest, his arms wrapped around her, their hands interlocked. Her long black hair was draped over their shared pillow. He caressed his cheek against the silken strands of her hair and released a long, contented sigh. She squeezed his hands and snuggled up closer to him.

"Where have you been?" he asked.

"Nowhere important, I'll tell ya that much," she answered.

"Promise me you'll stay this time."

"I'll never go away, John. You're stuck with me."

"Forever, huh?"

"Thereabouts."

"Eh, I guess I could think of a worse fate."

She turned around in his arms to face him with a look of mock offense. "I can think of one."

"I find that hard to believe," he retorted while unsuccessfully hiding a smile.

"Is that so? Well allow me to illustrate." She proceeded to attack him with a flurry of tickles to his ribs and belly.

He laughed, deep and loud, and only half fought against her onslaught. She could tell, and it only served to increase her fervor. He was starting to tear up from laughter. She'd gone for the throat. Or rather the armpits. Heartless wench. He desperately wanted to get away but was too weak from laughter to muster an effective counter attack. His whole body convulsed as he laughed and—

—I'm awake. And for a second, just a brief flash of time, I'm truly happy.

No matter how many times I have that dream it takes me a minute to remember that's all it is. Just a dream. I'm not sure which one I hate more. That one, or the one where we're making love and in the middle of it my Field kicks in and she explodes all over me. Neither one is terribly pleasant once I'm awake. I never would've thought I'd come to hate sleep. But God, every night is a hideous reminder of how much I've lost. But I have learned something out of it.

Listen:

Every love story with a happy ending is a lie. Real love can only end in suffering. In the end, it comes down to either betrayal or death. At least in death, we can be angry at some faceless omnipresent force; God, Fate, chance, whatever. It's easier to hate your God for betraying you than it is to hate your loved ones for it. At least in my suffering, there is no regret for having known her. I try to convince myself that's something I can take some solace in.

It's times like this I wish Nuke had never rescued me from the Antarctic. Eh. Enough self loathing and brooding. Waking up always does that to me.

I roll over.

"Mreowr?" Katkat half wakes up, yawns and stretches while rolling over to expose his belly. It's pink between the tufts of gray and white fur. That there is a belly made for rubbin'. So I do. "Mew." His body contracts around my hand like a soft, pudgy, fuzzy, lazy, warm bear trap of belly love. I try to pull away but it doesn't quite work.

"Heh. Okay, Katkat. Sparky needs his hand back." I've got to do it slowly so it doesn't wake him up. Ah yes, free at last.

I shamble out of bed and into the Danger: Bathroom. My God, I look like the living dead when I wake up. I lean forward on the sink for a closer look. Pasty face, bags under the eyes, hair sticking out in every direction. I run my hand through it and only have to tug my way through a few knots. It's too long, I haven't bothered with a cut in over a year now. I can see my scar. It's on my forehead right along my hairline. I can't believe I got hit with a blast so strong it could kill God and I just walk away with a little cut on my forehead. It's from when I finally landed after being knocked half way around the world. It must've been quite a ride. Too bad the sheer force of the blast knocked me unconscious before rocketing me across the curvature of the Earth until gravity brought me down and I landed not too far from the South Pole, or so they tell me. Damn Field somehow stopped the beam from erasing me along the way, absorbed most of the impact, and protected me from the freezing cold until Nuke found me.

I still haven't figured out how or *why* it did all that since according to what Doc Genius says, my Field can't work unless I'm awake. Just my luck, I guess.

Hm. I've got to get a move on if I'm going to meet Nuke this afternoon. I haven't seen him since he started his Sahara Project. He called me yesterday telling me to meet him today. I made a joke about him slacking off on the more important aspects of rebuilding the world in favor of putting up cell phone satellites for his own personal use. He didn't laugh. He just told me about how he could tap into already established telecom systems using his powers. I miss the old Nuke.

*   *   *   *

Eating breakfast now. Waffles of course. The paper is lying on the Danger: Kitchen Table but I never bother picking it up. It's been the same paper for six months. It's the first paper printed by the Metroville Sun since Nihel. Dr. Genius felt that establishing a form of news media was of the utmost importance to the reconstruction efforts. It's supposed to be a symbol, something people can hold onto and talk about, something to make them feel united, to let them know what they can do, let them know what we're doing for them. I've never picked up another paper. Why bother reading about what I did the day before?

But I had to get this first one. It has this huge picture on the front. Nuklear Man towering over the lens with a bus or semi-truck or something hefted over his head. Behind him, sunlight filtered between the missing windows of the shell of an office building. What always strikes me about this picture is his gaze. He's looking off to the right with an intensity I never knew he possessed. It's like, I don't know. Like he was already thinking about the next rescue just over the horizon. There's a weariness there too, like he knows he can't be everywhere at once.

Just Nuke there cast against a clear sky and bigger than God. It was an icon we could all rally behind. Hell, it was a scene most of us probably saw variations of ourselves that day. And that headline. Those giant black letters proclaiming "He Saved Us!" Dr. Genius knew how to make news.

That was another reason why I got this paper. I had to be familiar with the Official Story behind Nihel's arrival and defeat. It mentions nothing about

Nuke's past, nothing about Arel, or his connection with Nihel. It was all about some sort of alien invasion. Dr. Genius says nothing can unite a world of disparate and desperate people like the threat of an invasion from the unknown. The story goes on to talk about the valiant sacrifices of our heroes, my friends; Nuke's final confrontation in space and his return to quell the flames of chaos that had enveloped his world. His homeworld.

I wasn't comfortable about this revisionist version of what went on that day. But Dr. Genius explained that I was being too emotional about it all. The public has to maintain a certain level of reverence toward us Heroes, especially in these times, and most especially to Nuke. They've lost faith in their governments, their societies, their God. Maybe even themselves. We've got to give them their hope back. If they got scared of us, lost their faith in us, then we wouldn't be able to help them. If we've got to tell a lie for the sake of their trust, then that's what we've got to do.

I know she's right. She always is. It's just, it feels wrong somehow.

$$*\qquad*\qquad*\qquad*$$

Überdyne Headquarters Sub-Basement 5.
Scientific: Special Containment Block.
11:14 AM.

I walk amongst devils here. Luckily, they're all in cages. I try not to think of what might have happened during Nihel's rampage if not for Überdyne's own mini-nuclear generators. What destruction would these devils have loosed on a burning world?

Superion. Locked in a matrix of Negaflux fields forever paralyzing him with his own insurmountable power. Without need for food or drink, he has been alone with his thoughts for over a year. I have been testing him off and on lately. I reduced the power to his imprisoning Negaflux field by a fraction. His whole body jerked with anticipation from that one moment of weakness. Oh, how the madness and rage must burn inside of him.

Mechanikill. A top secret technological beast made entirely of Nanobots and bristling with weaponry. It is functionally invincible. So long as a single Nanobot survives, it can rebuild itself in a matter of days. After Nuklear Man defeated it, I realized it was redesigning itself based on the encounter. It was a fascinating discovery, but not a process it was supposed to undertake. Mechanikill has been in a state of suspended animation ever since. I recently noticed the Nanobots never actually stopped. Their progress has simply been slowed incredibly.

Shimura Yurika. She's little more than a mindless body, a coma victim with no hope for recovery. I cannot tell if she is the most harmless here, or if she is simply a symbol of the greatest threat one could conceive of. Looking at her, I am reminded of finding a snake's cast off skin. One does not fear it, but rather the threat of what left it behind.

Three experiments. Three failures. And why?

Chaos.

The natural state of the universe is chaos. I know this now. We are nothing but a temporary reprieve in the chaos, a gathering of slightly less chaotic particles jumbling around waiting for the siren call of chaos to take us back into the cull. Entropy. Everything falls apart. All order degrades. All systems collapse. I know this now.

My every plan for humanity fell apart. It wasn't my fault. How could I have foreseen the intrusion of mythical beings and their philosophies into my finely tuned and precise equations? Everything I'd done was shattered in the course of a single day. All my machinations have returned to chaos.

But it is these set backs that bring out the best in us. The world is a very different place now. Full of chaos. Full of fear. Full of people who need leadership. I am that leadership. I have put a hold on most of Überdyne's projects in favor of the Reconstruction. I've already rebuilt a media web throughout Metroville and its surrounding areas print, television, and radio. It's all mostly news and reruns of old entertainment shows. We haven't the time or manpower to create new sitcoms. A society has to reach a certain level of idle malaise before it's ready for that.

There are only three major cities still standing on the face of the Earth. Metroville, America; Mechapolis, Japan; Avalondon, England. Most other cities were burnt to cinders or decimated. Smaller communities evaded Nihel's attentions, but that only left them vulnerable to be ravaged by the rest of us. But the Prime Three, as I've come to calling them, they were left largely intact. Originally, we were to divide the world into thirds, take care of our respective corners of the globe, and agree not to interfere with one another. I couldn't agree to that. Without my network of KI satellite, how could I possibly make sure they weren't working against me? I proposed a better plan.

We would coordinate our efforts to rebuild civilization. However, due to Überdyne's expansive international status that managed to survive, in part, the cataclysm of Nihel, it would be in the best position to organize and pool the resources and talent needed to rebuild the infrastructure of the world. As a consequence, I am unofficially ruling the world once again.

My plan: Connect these three cities through communication. Civilize them at any cost. Give them back the conveniences of the twenty-first century, then let teams into the lost and broken cities, towns, and villages that are scattered throughout the countryside. We will give them a taste of the splendor they themselves once knew, and they will then be at our beck and call. We will tell them that they too may once again enjoy the fruits of modern living, given they meet certain conditions, and they will become civilized and productive members of society. My society. Brilliantly simple. I can't take credit for it. I got the idea from the Roman Empire's expansion. Yet my empire shall span the globe and I won't need a single soldier. I will take over the world with nothing more than the promise of comfort.

Of course, it doesn't hurt that our most valuable resources and talents are under my direct influence as well. One of the conditions for an area to be classified as Civilized is, among other factors, a working press. And the front page of the first printed paper always features what I've come to call The Icon: the picture of Nuklear Man saving, who knows, but someone who had a camera on them at the time. To the people, it is a symbol of hope. To their leaders, it is a message that they are powerless before me.

Not that they could've posed any real threat. No, the only thing that's ever come close to true opposition to me has always been Veronica and she's been silent this past year. It never ceases to amaze me how brilliant she proved to be. And yet so short sighted. She would put the rights of the individual over the rights of the masses. Such a waste.

But soon, very soon, all my work will come to fruition. And then, my dear Norman, you will no longer need this Scientific: Suspension Chamber. Nothing will keep us apart.

*   *   *   *

Stephenson Avenue.
The Repair Doctor shop.
12:02 PM.

Life in Metroville is slowly returning to normal. There are enough distractions to keep the populace content and enough work yet to keep them occupied. Ima's working toward a global dictatorship of information. Again. And, of course, I'm working to dismantle it. Again. But there are other matters to attend to first. Without an industrial base, there isn't anyone producing or designing new electronics or machines. And due to a certain, shall we say, deficit in the population there are a scant few individuals who are able to repair the computers, the cars, the appliances, the machines of the world. Those of us who are skilled in these matters are in tremendous demand.

This affords me a number of advantages. The foremost among these is that I have access to dozens of pieces of electronics every week. To the average person, this may not seem terribly important on its own, but that is because the average person does not have the foresight and genius that I possess. Every device that employs electricity that comes into my shop leaves it with an undetectable addition. What I have dubbed a Negabug.

It's fantastically simple, really. I got the idea from nature itself. A single cell is harmless, powerless, practically nothing on its own. But interconnect enough of them and the whole becomes far greater than the sum of its microscopic parts. Each Negabug adds to the over all web, a Negabeing of kinds. Once enough of them are dispersed throughout the Metroville area, I shall activate them.

All of Metroville will be in my clutches.

And then the world.

It may take years to develop a complex enough matrix to unfurl my scheme, but I can be patient. Besides, in the meantime, I'm making more money than I know what to do with. I'll have to invest in a tertiary scheme to back up my secondary scheme which, by the way, is also already in the works. It involves using the incredible strength of electromagnetic—blast it! A customer. Ahem. "May I be of zervice?"

"Yeah. I brought my digital clock radio here a couple days ago."

"Ah yez. We wouldn't want to go without that piece of electronicz for too long, now would we?"

"Nope."

"Your name?"

"Harold Greene."

"One moment, Mizter Greene."

I turn to my office computer, though I don't see how it earns the name "computer." No dials, no levers, no joysticks, no liquid hydrogen cooling system, no remote controls, no voice command protocols, no elaborate security measures like unlabelled buttons that make the terminal inaccessible to anyone who hasn't memorized its arcane layout which changes every few hours according to a unique algorhythm I've never so much as written down. And the monitor. It's barely fifteen inches. You can't even *begin* to consider yourself a computer unless your screen is measured in feet. How do people use these pathetic things?

"Ah yez, Mr. Greene. I'll be right back with your clock radio." I turn to go into the back room.

"Digital clock radio."

"...Yez, of courze."

Bin 19, Bin 19. One clock radio. Digital. It took me all of five minutes to fix it. I believe I told him the CPU was broken and it would require some "serious work." Whatever that means.

"Here you go, Mr. Greene."

"Oh, thanks. What do I owe ya?"

"I believe seventy five dollarz ought to cover it."

"Man, for that price, I could've bought a new one."

"Perhapz if they were making clock radioz nowadayz. You muzt remember how preciouz our limited materialz, and mozt importantly, our zkilled workerz, are in theze timez."

"Oh, I know." I take his money without listening to whatever else he says. Something about these hard times and the weather I believe.

These hard times, eh? We may live in a new world under new rules, but the players are still the same. Except for that accursed Nuklear Clod. All those pictures of him on TV and in newspapers, Ima's so good to remind us all that he does her bidding. But they tell me something else. Ever since that first picture of him towering over the camera like a mountain, he's haunted me with those eyes. They're much more intent than the eyes of any Nuklear Man I ever battled. It is undeniable that he changed that day. But to what depths? That is what I must learn before my brilliant plans can ever see the light of day.

✳   ✳   ✳   ✳

The Sahara.

Fifteen thousand feet above sea level.

12:47 PM.

From this height, everything looks so small. Little animals wandering through broken woodlands, little waves pounding against sandy beaches. Little mountains reaching into an infinite sky.

So many problems.

Take for instance deforestation. But I'm working at it.

The First Day was the worst. Half the world was dead and the other half was in ruin. At first, I merely quelled problems as I came upon them. It became clear that I had to prioritize when a plane that must've been in the air since the beginning finally ran out of fuel and crashed into the Metroville Airport as I was lifting a tour bus off its passengers. In a flash I knew that one man could only do so much. Looking back, I think it was a camera flash. I didn't have time to check, every second was more valuable than the last. I'd have to step back and take in the big picture. Get a sense of perspective.

I was in orbit almost as quickly as the idea of being there occurred to me. From space it seemed overwhelming. An entire planet in flames. Then I heard it. The heavens roared. Rage, lament, sorrow, and a vow of vengeance all shrieked through to the very core of my being. It was the wail of the giants. Suddenly, the world was infinitesimal; a fragile porcelain orb in the hands of these vicious beasts. They could crush it effortlessly. One thought raced through my mind as I hovered over the globe.

"I cannot allow that to happen."

But there was a moment's hesitation. I have destroyed worlds far more noble than this one. There is nothing of these Earthim, these humans, that makes them any more worthy of life than the civilizations I have razed in the flames of my wrath. So why? Why was I so intent upon protecting this petty little rock and so quick to obliterate the others?

Sparky.

Norman.

Ima.

Angus.

Shiro.

Rachel.

Even Menace.

Yes, that's why. It became personal. It would seem that indiscriminate killing is so much easier when you don't know the victims. But at the time, as far as I knew, everyone I cared about was dead. I suppose I felt like I had to make their deaths mean something, like I had to protect the world that they couldn't.

But the giants were not the problem. At least not in that moment. I'd gone into orbit for focus. I scanned the globe in a matter of seconds. I could sense every flame, every gunshot, every bolt of lightning, the very sparks of life coursing through the veins of every living creature. It was a terrifying myriad of being. I could feel my mind coming to terms with it, remembering how to cope with the sensory inundation. Everything became clear.

I had just about planned my course of action when I noticed something impossible. A lone heartbeat in the center of Antarctica. A heartbeat I'd heard for years without knowing it. It was Sparky. I watched him die just hours before, but there was no mistaking it. It was him. Call me selfish if you will, but I abandoned my plans and chose him before so much as considering another soul.

A week had passed before I finally extinguished the last flames and brought a semblance of order to the turmoil feeding off itself. Dr. Genius said it was time to deliver a message to the survivors. First, I'd have to put up a few satellites so that Avalondon and Mechapolis would be able to hear us, but that didn't even take a whole afternoon. She'd prepared a speech. She said it would be best if I read it. So I did.

It consisted of "put aside our petty differences" this, and "trust one another" that. "Darkest hour" and other such like loaded phrases.

For the most part, they listened.

In the weeks that followed, Ima developed a plan that swept across the world and I executed it. Mostly, I've tried to be dedicated to terraforming. First repairing the scars of Man in the Amazon, plowing entire counties of farmlands in the American Mid-West, things of that nature. For the last few months I've been reseeding the Sahara. There now stands a forest where there was once a wasteland.

Finding the soil, that was the hardest part.

Getting the trees to stay up, that was the hardest part too.

But for about a month now, I've been up here, floating among the clouds above what used to be a desert, giving it a constant source of light. It'll need a considerable dose of rain soon but that's not my responsibility. I'm not the only one trying to heal the wounds of this world.

Ah, I can see him now, racing through the sky at twice the speed of sound wrapped up in the fireball of his soul. He'll be here soon. I hope I can do this.

$$* \qquad * \qquad * \qquad *$$

Atomik Lad came to a stop in front of his mentor. He was followed by the sound of his approach a few seconds later. Huge, majestic clouds marched above them as winds caressed the treetops far below. Atomik Lad's Field thrashed against the air with little crackles like static electricity.

"That's a new look for you," Atomik Lad said at last.

Nuklear Man ran a hand through his short dark blond beard. "I thought it might make me look more mature. What do you think?"

"I think I find it mildly terrifying that you could ever appear mature."

Nuklear Man broke into a smile. The facial hair melted away. "You're probably right." An awkward silence. "I'm done here."

"Oh? Great. What's next on the To Do list of saving the world?"

Nuklear Man was silent. His golden eyes trailed away from Atomik Lad in response.

"Nuke?" Atomik Lad tried to catch his gaze.

"I'm done here," he repeated, more quietly this time.

"What do you mean?"

"I have to go."

"Go? Where?"

Nuklear Man looked to the clouds. "Away."

"Nuke. What are you talking about!"

"I've been thinking it over. I have to leave the Earth."

"What? No! You can't go."

"I have to."

"You *can't*! We still need you here," Atomik Lad pleaded.

He shook his head. "I've done enough. You don't need me anymore."

"Yes!" Atomik Lad said, his Field pulsed. "Yes I do."

Nuklear Man shut his eyes.

"Nuke. I, you're..." Atomik Lad let out a long sigh. "It's safe to say that I have led a uniquely insane life. But you have always been the one constant in that madness. You can't leave me. Not like everyone else. You can't. Especially now. Not now."

"You don't understand."

"You're all I have left."

"Things have changed."

"Like *what*!"

"Me."

"Bullshit. Look. I don't know what happened between you and Nihel and I don't know what you think has changed, but I do know that you're the same person you've always been to me. You're the same man who took me in ten years ago. The same man who taught me everything I know about being a hero. Maybe you have changed, but you're still the man who raised me. The same man who made me who I am today. That'll never change."

"You have to trust me. I can't stay here any longer. I'm a danger to this world and everyone on it."

"Is this about Nihel? No one blames you for that, Nuke. No one. You saved us from utter destruction."

"I saved you from myself. Besides, Nihel was only the beginning. There will be others. I have angered beings of incredible power by my actions here."

"So? Let them come. We can defeat them. We always win."

"But at what cost? It will be decades before this world can ever return to its former way of life, and many of the scars left by Nihel will never heal. I cannot be responsible for more needless suffering. Not when it can be avoided simply by my absence."

Atomik Lad felt like he was losing control. Things were slipping away from him. Desperation was taking hold in its place. A minute of silence passed. "Take me with you," he said at last.

"You know I can't. Your people still need a Hero. They need you."

"I'm no Hero. I'm just a sidekick."

"It's your time."

"I can't do this alone."

"You won't be alone, Sparky."

The clouds rumbled heavily above them.

"Why do you have to leave me?"

Nuklear Man shook his head. "Things have become too grave. We were living in a dream world, you and I. But now the dreamers are awake. We must have the courage to face this reality, as harsh and unforgiving as it may seem."

Atomik Lad stared at his feet. "Don't talk like that," he said barely above a whisper.

"I have to. It's the truth."

The sidekick looked him in the eyes. "No, I mean don't talk so seriously. It scares me."

"Worse than the beard?"

"Yeah."

"It scares me too. I'm not sure if I like what I am."

"Why can't things be the way they were?"

Nuklear Man nodded in agreement. "I have asked myself the same question many times in these past months. I don't know if there is an answer."

Atomik Lad looked over Nuklear Man's shoulder to the clouds that lurked above them. He brought his gaze back to the Hero. "Who's going to stop you from trying to take over worlds populated by weakling non-overpowered creatures, hm?"

A small smile appeared on Nuklear Man's face. "You don't have to worry about that anymore."

"No?"

"Naw, it's a matter of scale. I've set my sights on entire galaxies now."

"Beware, mortals of the universe."

They laughed little nervous laughs. These were their last moments. There had to be a way to prolong them.

"This is it, isn't it?" Atomik Lad asked.

"Yes."

"Are you coming back?"

Nuklear Man paused. "You will see me again," he said finally. "I promise."

"I can hardly imagine life without your bungling."

"I was just thinking the same about you."

They embraced. No masculine back patting. Just a simple mosaic of respect, admiration, and unconditional love. Like father and son.

"I'm going to miss you, Big Guy," Atomik Lad said with a catch in his throat.

Nuklear Man gave him one last squeeze with arms that could move planets. "You may just be the on thing I've done right," he said.

They released one another, Atomik Lad's Field reluctantly unraveled itself from Nuklear Man. The Hero floated back a few feet. In a flash, he was at the end of a golden arc that pierced the clouds and tore through space.

Atomik Lad watched until the Hero's luminous trail faded. His gaze fell to the world below. "From this height, everything looks so small."

The Apology

If you're here, then I'm going to assume you've read this book in its entirety. If you've done that, then I'm going to go a step further and assume you're more than a little upset at me.

But, hey, we had some good times, right? Remember those hundreds of pages *before* everything that was good in the world died? We'll always have the court room scene.

I know it's fairly customary for an author to write a book or a script for film or television and experience an episode of depression wherein the work becomes influenced by the author's mental breakdown so he can be lauded as a genius for a few years until everyone figures out he was just being a selfish twit masturbating about his own dysfunctions on paper. Let me assure you that no such device was employed during the writing of this book. In truth, the years I spent working on this book were some of the happiest, most productive, and rewarding years of my life.

So why did it end that way? The explanation can only make you hate me more. But here it goes.

See, a joke is funny because it's a disruption of your expectations. "To get to the other side," isn't, itself, a funny thing. Most punchlines aren't. They're funny because they are not what you're supposed to expect. I distinctly remember figuring this out one night, and in the light of that realization, "Why did the chicken cross the road?/To get to the other side," became so hilarious to me that I laughed until it brought tears to my eyes and it hurt to breathe.

Okay, so maybe a complete mental breakdown *did* have something to do with this.

The point is, mechanically speaking, this heavy book is one very long joke. It gives you a set up for a few hundred pages, and then you get nailed with the punchline (the exact moment of delivery is Rachel's big scene in the Food Court Junction). Everything that happens in the first two-thirds of the book is there so that the final third can *never* happen so that *when* it does, it's hilarious.

Hey, I told you you'd only hate me more.

I'd like to close now with the final words from the *Havermal*. It's best thought of, I suppose, as a set of social laws from the old Norse tradition. I'm not some New Age nut, but I've always liked these four lines. Plus they hold a little meaning to this apology. Some people will "get" the joke and love it as much as I do. Others will "get" it and still hate it. But, either way:

Hail to the speaker,
Hail to the knower,
Joy to him who has understood,
Delight to those who have listened.

0-595-78068-7

Printed in the United States
24952LVS00002B/157